THE EAGLE HAS LANDED

ALSO EDITED BY NEIL CLARKE

Magazines
Clarkesworld Magazine—clarkesworldmagazine.com
Forever Magazine—forever-magazine.com

Anthologies
Upgraded
The Best Science Fiction of the Year Volume 1
The Best Science Fiction of the Year Volume 2
The Best Science Fiction of the Year Volume 3
The Best Science Fiction of the Year Volume 4
Touchable Unreality Volume One
Galactic Empires
More Human Than Human
The Final Frontier
Not One of Us

(with Sean Wallace)
Clarkesworld: Year Three
Clarkesworld: Year Four
Clarkesworld: Year Five
Clarkesworld: Year Six
Clarkesworld: Year Seven
Clarkesworld: Year Eight
Clarkesworld: Year Nine, volume 1
Clarkesworld: Year Nine, volume 2
Clarkesworld: Year Ten, volume 1
Clarkesworld: Year Ten, volume 2
Clarkesworld Magazine A 10th Anniversary Anthology (forthcoming 2019)

THE EAGLE HAS LANDED

50 YEARS OF LUNAR SCIENCE FICTION

EDITED BY NEIL CLARKE

Night Shade Books
NEW YORK

Night Shade books may be purchased in bulk at special discounts for sales promotion, corporate gifts, fund-raising, or educational purposes. Special editions can also be created to specifications. For details, contact the Special Sales Department, Night Shade Books, 307 West 36th Street, 11th Floor, New York, NY 10018 or info@skyhorsepublishing.com.

Night Shade Books® is a registered trademark of Skyhorse Publishing, Inc. ®, a Delaware corporation.

Visit our website at www.nightshadebooks.com.

10 9 8 7 6 5 4 3 2 1

Library of Congress Cataloging-in-Publication Data

Names: Clarke, Neil, 1966- editor.
Title: The Eagle has landed : 50 years of lunar science fiction / edited by
    Neil Clarke.
Description: New York : Night Shade Books, [2019]
Identifiers: LCCN 2019004686| ISBN 9781949102093 (hardback : alk. paper) |
    ISBN 9781597809993 (paperback : alk. paper)
Subjects: LCSH: Moon--Exploration--Fiction. | Science fiction--20th century.
    | Science fiction--21st century. | Short stories--20th century. | Short
    stories--21st century.
Classification: LCC PS648.S3 E24 2019 | DDC 813/.0876208--dc23
LC record available at https://lccn.loc.gov/2019004686

Cover illustration by Mack Sztaba
Cover design by Claudia Noble

Please see page 575 for an extension of this copyright page.

Printed in the United States of America

For everyone that made the Moon landings possible
and the people working so hard to make it happen again.

CONTENTS

INTRODUCTION
Neil Clarke

On July 20th, 1969, the world watched as Apollo 11 landed on the Moon. Six hours later, mission commander Neil Armstrong became the first person to set foot on its surface, uttering the now famous, "one small step for [a] man, one giant leap for mankind." He was joined on the surface about twenty minutes later by Buzz Aldrin while Michael Collins piloted the command module *Columbia* in lunar orbit.

I was three years old as these events unfolded. My father once told me that he intentionally kept me awake that evening, so I wouldn't miss this historic event, even if I wouldn't remember it. On CBS, Walter Cronkite interviewed veteran science fiction authors Arthur C. Clarke and Robert A. Heinlein about the momentous occasion and what could come next. Space stations, lunar colonies, larger ships with mixed gender crews, and children born in space were all predicted to occur by the end of the century. There was joy and optimism about our future out among the stars. The full interview can be found on YouTube and is a fascinating look into that moment in history. Check it out sometime.

Three short years later, Apollo 17 set records for the longest lunar mission, longest total moonwalks, largest lunar sample, and longest time in lunar orbit. It also marked the end of our manned lunar exploration. There were three more Apollo missions scheduled, but despite the benefits we had gained from the space program, they were canceled due to budgetary constraints and we never returned. The Apollo capsules were soon repurposed for the Apollo-Soyuz and Skylab space station missions.

This anthology is a fifty-year retrospective of lunar science fiction stories that were written after Apollo 11, an event that happened seven years before I began regularly reading science fiction. As such, this project required a lot more research than I've needed to do for the previous anthologies I've edited. Essentially, it proved to be a deep dive into the stories of my youth and revealed some things about what was happening in SF that I was too young to notice at the time.

The Moon was a hot topic in science fiction in the decades leading up to the Apollo missions, and several anthologies—like Donald A. Wollheim's *Men on the Moon* (1958) and Mike Ashley's *Moonrise: The Golden Age of Lunar Adventures* (2018)—explore this territory. The idea for this anthology was to explore the consequences of reality colliding with science fiction. Little did I notice in my youth that one of the big consequences of landing on the Moon would be that science fiction would run away from it. In retrospect, it makes sense. If you listen to that Cronkite interview I mentioned, you can hear them talking about an immediate future that today sounds like science fiction, but was inevitable in their minds. Science fiction compensated by abandoning the Moon and moving beyond.

This theory seemed to explain why I was having so much difficulty finding lunar stories from the 70s and 80s to include, even from authors that had once regularly explored the theme. To confirm my suspicions, I started reaching out to editors and authors from that time period and was given a resounding affirmative that the move was a deliberate act by both editors and authors. The Moon was considered too close to the news and no longer fertile science fiction territory. Authors refocused their sights on Mars, the asteroid belt, and beyond. Even when the Apollo missions were canceled, it still seemed inevitable that we would return, so it remained this way for some time.

[One of the editors I spoke to also cited Robert A. Heinlein's novel *The Moon is a Harsh Mistress* (1966) as an additional contributing factor. It dealt with the theme very thoroughly and left some thinking there was little left to say.]

As a result of these influences on the field, I ended up including very few stories from the first twenty years after Apollo 11. I found about a dozen more than you'll find here, several of which were by authors I have included other works by. John Varley, for example, appears to be an exception to the norm, publishing several of his Anna-Louise Bach stories set on the Moon during this time period. The remaining works by other writers varied wildly and often had only a tangential connection to the Moon. Also, as it happens sometimes with these projects, there was one story I wanted, but I was unsuccessful at securing the reprint rights. After months of research and outreach, I think I've found all that I can mine from that era. While I would have liked the decades to be more balanced, in reality, they weren't, so that is reflected here.

By the 90s, a newer generation of writers and editors saw the Moon differently and it began to make its way back into mainstream SF magazines and anthologies. With some regularity many of these stories began to appear in *Asimov's Science Fiction Magazine* and by 1997, Gardner Dozois and Sheila Williams had published enough to assemble *Asimov's Moons*, a paperback reprint anthology. To celebrate the thirtieth anniversary of the Moon landing,

Peter Crowther edited an anthology titled *Moon Shots*, which included original science fiction stories, a few of which are included here. Among those is a story by Stephen Baxter, perhaps the most prolific author of Moon stories at the time.

As the new century turned over—leaving most of the predictions made that Apollo 11 evening unrealized—a new magazine with a stated goal of promoting lunar exploration was launched. *Artemis Magazine*—which debuted at the 1999 Worldcon with a 2000 cover date—published eight issues between 2000 and 2003 before closing its doors. While other magazines and anthologies continued to be reliable sources of lunar science fiction, the theme never returned to the level of popularity it experienced during the 50s and earlier. Even the resurgence of short fiction brought upon by ebooks and online magazines didn't create a significant growth in the number of these stories published, but they did continue to provide homes for them.

Several recent lunar missions have created some excitement about the presence of water on the Moon. Combined with the increasing interest and discussion about possible manned missions to Mars, the Moon has become more and more attractive as a waypoint. As I write this, NASA officials are on TV proclaiming that they would like to return to the Moon in the late 2020s to build a sustainable base—a strategy believed to be a critical step towards deeper exploration and possible habitation on Mars.

It's my hope that we not only return to the Moon, but also that this time, science fiction continues to embrace Luna as a meaningful part our future. The ideas that fueled those old predictions are still worth working towards and science fiction has ongoing opportunity to demonstrate that positive vision. Those stories are more important now than ever if we are to secure that future out among the stars ...

John Varley is the author of several short story collections and fourteen novels, the latest of which is *Irontown Blues*. Over the course of his forty-five year career, he has won the Locus, Prometheus, Nebula, and Hugo awards. "Bagatelle" is the first of several of his Anna-Louise Bach Lunar detective stories.

BAGATELLE
John Varley

There was a bomb on the Leystrasse, level forty-five, right outside the Bagatelle Flower and Gift Shoppe, about a hundred meters down the promenade from Prosperity Plaza.

"I am a bomb," the bomb said to passersby. "I will explode in four hours, five minutes, and seventeen seconds. I have a force equal to fifty thousand English tons of trinitrololuene."

A small knot of people gathered to look at it.

"I will go off in four hours, four minutes, and thirty-seven seconds."

A few people became worried as the bomb talked on. They remembered business elsewhere and hurried away, often toward the tube trains to King City. Eventually, the trains became overcrowded and there was some pushing and shoving.

The bomb was a metal cylinder, a meter high, two meters long, mounted on four steerable wheels. There was an array of four television cameras mounted on top of the cylinder, slowly scanning through ninety degrees. No one could recall how it came to be there. It looked a little like the municipal street-cleaning machines; perhaps no one had noticed it because of that.

"I am rated at fifty kilotons," the bomb said, with a trace of pride.

The police were called.

"A *nuclear* bomb, you say?" Municipal Police Chief Anna-Louise Bach felt sourness in the pit of her stomach and reached for a box of medicated candy. She was overdue for a new stomach, but the rate she went through them on her job, coupled with the size of her paycheck, had caused her to rely more and more on these stopgap measures. And the cost of cloned transplants was going up.

"It says fifty kilotons," said the man on the screen. "I don't see what else it could be. Unless it's just faking, of course. We're moving in radiation detectors."

"You said 'it says.' Are you speaking of a note, or phone call, or what?"

"No. It's talking to us. Seems friendly enough, too, but we haven't gotten around to asking it to disarm itself. It could be that its friendliness won't extend that far."

"No doubt." She ate another candy. "Call in the bomb squad, of course. Then tell them to do nothing until I arrive, other than look the situation over. I'm going to make a few calls, then I'll be there. No more than thirty minutes."

"All right. Will do."

There was nothing for it but to look for help. No nuclear bomb had ever been used on Luna. Bach had no experience with them, nor did her bomb crew. She brought her computer on line.

Roger Birkson liked his job. It wasn't so much the working conditions—which were appalling—but the fringe benefits. He was on call for thirty days, twenty-four hours a day, at a salary that was nearly astronomical. Then he got eleven months' paid vacation. He was paid for the entire year whether or not he ever had to exercise his special talents during his thirty days' duty. In that way, he was like a firefighter. In a way, he *was* a firefighter.

He spent his long vacations in Luna. No one had ever asked Birkson why he did so; had they asked, he would not have known. But the reason was a subconscious conviction that one day the entire planet Earth would blow up in one glorious fireball. He didn't want to be there when it happened.

Birkson's job was bomb disarming for the geopolitical administrative unit called CommEcon Europe. On a busy shift he might save the lives of twenty million CE Europeans.

Of the thirty-five Terran bomb experts vacationing on Luna at the time of the Leystrasse bomb scare, Birkson happened to be closest to the projected epicenter of the blast. The Central Computer found him twenty-five seconds after Chief Bach rang off from her initial report. He was lining up a putt on the seventeenth green of the Burning Tree underground golf course, a half kilometer from Prosperity Plaza, when his bag of clubs began to ring.

Birkson was wealthy. He employed a human caddy instead of the mechanical sort. The caddy dropped the flag he had been holding and went to answer it. Birkson took a few practice swings but found that his concentration had been broken. He relaxed and took the call.

"I need your advice," Bach said, without preamble. "I'm the Chief of Municipal Police for New Dresden, Anna-Louise Bach. I've had a report on a nuclear bomb on the Leystrasse, and I don't have anyone with your experience in these matters. Could you meet me at the tube station in ten minutes?"

"Are you crazy? I'm shooting for a seventy-five with two holes to go, an easy three-footer on seventeen and facing a par five on the last hole, and you expect me to go chasing after a hoax?"

"Do you know it to be a hoax?" Bach asked, wishing he would say yes.

"Well, no, I just now heard about it, myself. But ninety percent of them are, you know."

"Fine. I suggest you continue your game. And since you're so sure, I'm going to have Burning Tree sealed off for the duration of the emergency. I want you right there."

Birkson considered this.

"About how far away is this 'Leystrasse'?"

"About six hundred meters. Five levels up from you, and one sector over. Don't worry. There must be dozens of steel plates between you and the hoax. You just sit tight, all right?"

Birkson said nothing.

"I'll be at the tube station in ten minutes," Bach said. "I'll be in a special capsule. It'll be the last one for five hours." She hung up.

Birkson contemplated the wall of the underground enclosure. Then he knelt on the green and lined up his putt. He addressed the ball, tapped it, and heard the satisfying rattle as it sank into the cup.

He looked longingly at the eighteenth tee, then jogged off to the clubhouse.

"I'll be right back," he called over his shoulder.

Bach's capsule was two minutes late, but she had to wait another minute for Birkson to show up. She fumed, trying not to glance at the timepiece embedded in her wrist.

He got in, still carrying his putter, and their heads were jerked back as the capsule was launched. They moved for only a short distance, then came to a halt. The door didn't open.

"The system's probably tied up," Bach said, squirming. She didn't like to see the municipal services fail in the company of this Terran.

"Ah," Birkson said, flashing a grin with an impossible number of square teeth. "A panic evacuation, no doubt. You didn't have the tube system closed down, I suppose?"

"No," she said. "I . . . well, I thought there might be a chance to get a large number of people away from the area in case this thing does go off."

He shook his head, and grinned again. He put this grin after every sentence he spoke, like punctuation.

"You'd better seal off the city. If it's a hoax, you're going to have hundreds of dead and injured from the panic. It's a lost cause trying to evacuate. At most, you might save a few thousand."

"But . . ."

"Keep them stationary. If it goes off, it's no use anyway. You'll lose the whole city. And no one's going to question your judgment because you'll be dead. If it doesn't go off, you'll be sitting pretty for having prevented a panic. Do it. I *know*."

Bach began to really dislike this man right then but decided to follow his advice. And his thinking did have a certain cold logic. She phoned the station and had the lid clamped on the city. Now the cars in the cross-tube ahead would be cleared, leaving only her priority capsule moving.

They used the few minutes' delay while the order was implemented to size each other up. Bach saw a blond, square-jawed young man in a checkered sweater and gold knickers. He had a friendly face, and that was what puzzled her. There was no trace of worry on his smooth features. His hands were steady, clasped calmly around the steel shaft of his putter. She wouldn't have called his manner cocky or assured, but he did manage to look cheerful.

She had just realized that he was looking her over, and was wondering what he saw, when he put his hand on her knee. He might as well have slapped her. She was stunned.

"What are you . . . get your hand off me, you . . . you groundhog."

Birkson's hand had been moving upward. He was apparently unfazed by the insult. He turned in his seat and reached for her hand. His smile was dazzling.

"I just thought that since we're stalled here with nothing else to do, we might start getting to know each other. No harm in that, is there? I just hate to waste any time, that's all."

She wrenched free of his grasp and assumed a defensive posture, feeling trapped in a nightmare. But he relented, having no interest in pursuing the matter when he had been rebuffed.

"All right. We'll wait. But I'd like to have a drink with you, or maybe dinner. After this thing's wrapped up, of course."

"'This thing . . .' How can you think of something like that . . . ?"

"At a time like this. I know. I've heard it. Bombs get me horny, is all. So okay, so I'll leave you alone." He grinned again. "But maybe you'll feel different when this is over."

For a moment she thought she was going to throw up from a combination of revulsion and fear. Fear of the bomb, not this awful man. Her stomach was twisted into a pretzel, and here he sat, thinking of sex. What was he, anyway?

The capsule lurched again, and they were on their way.

The deserted Leystrasse made a gleaming frame of stainless steel storefronts and fluorescent ceiling for the improbable pair hurrying from the tube station in the Plaza: Birkson in his anachronistic golf togs, cleats rasping on the polished rock floor, and Bach, half a meter taller than him, thin like a Lunarian. She wore the regulation uniform of the Municipal Police, which was a blue armband and cap with her rank of chief emblazoned on them, a shoulder holster, an equipment belt around her waist from which dangled the shining and lethal-looking tools of her trade, cloth slippers, and a few scraps of clothing in arbitrary places. In the benign environment of Lunar corridors, modesty had died out ages ago.

They reached the cordon that had been established around the bomb, and Bach conferred with the officer in charge. The hall was echoing with off-key music.

"What's that?" Birkson asked.

Officer Walters, the man to whom Bach had been speaking, looked Birkson over, weighing just how far he had to go in deference to this grinning weirdo. He was obviously the bomb expert Bach had referred to in an earlier call, but he was a Terran, and not a member of the force. Should he be addressed as 'sir'? He couldn't decide.

"It's the bomb. It's been singing to us for the last five minutes. Ran out of things to say, I guess."

"Interesting." Swinging the putter lazily from side to side, he walked to the barrier of painted steel crowd-control sections. He started sliding one of them to the side.

"Hold it . . . ah, sir," Walters said.

"Wait a minute, Birkson," Bach confirmed, running to the man and almost grabbing his sleeve. She backed away at the last moment.

"It said no one's to cross that barrier," Walter supplied to Bach's questioning glance. "Says it'll blow us all to the Farside."

"What is that damn thing, anyway?" Bach asked, plaintively.

Birkson withdrew from the barrier and took Bach aside with a tactful touch on the arm. He spoke to her with his voice just low enough for Walters to hear.

"It's a cyborged human connected to a bomb, probably a uranium device," he said. "I've seen the design. It's just like one that went off in Johannesburg three years ago. I didn't know they were still making them."

"I heard about it," Bach said, feeling cold and alone. "Then you think it's really a bomb? How do you know it's a cyborg? Couldn't it be tape recordings, or a computer?"

Birkson rolled his eyes slightly, and Bach reddened. Damn it, they were reasonable questions. And to her surprise, he could not defend his opinion logically. She wondered what she was stuck with. Was this man really the expert she took him to be, or a plaid-sweatered imposter?

"You can call it a hunch. I'm going to talk to this fellow, and I want you to roll up an industrial X-ray unit on the level below this while I'm doing it. On the level above, photographic film. You get the idea?"

"You want to take a picture of the inside of this thing. Won't that be dangerous?"

"Yeah. Are your insurance premiums paid up?"

Bach said nothing, but gave the orders. A million questions were spinning through her head, but she didn't want to make a fool of herself by asking a stupid one. Such as: how much radiation did a big industrial X-ray machine produce when beamed through a rock and steel floor? She had a feeling she wouldn't like the answer. She sighed, and decided to let Birkson have his head until she felt he couldn't handle it. He was about the only hope she had.

And he was strolling casually around the perimeter, swinging his god-damn putter behind him, whistling bad harmony with the tune coming from the bomb. What was a career police officer to do? Back him up on the harmonica?

The scanning cameras atop the bomb stopped their back and forth motion. One of them began to track Birkson. He grinned his flashiest and waved to it. The music stopped.

"I am a fifty-kiloton nuclear bomb of the uranium-235 type," it said. "You must stay behind the perimeter I have caused to be erected here. You must not disobey this order."

Birkson held up his hands, still grinning, and splayed out his fingers.

"You got me, bud. I won't bother you. I was just admiring your casing. Pretty nice job, there. It seems a shame to blow it up."

"Thank you," the bomb said, cordially. "But that is my purpose. You cannot divert me from it."

"Never entered my mind. Promise."

"Very well. You may continue to admire me, if you wish, but from a safe distance. Do not attempt to rush me. All my vital wiring is safely protected, and I have a response time of three milliseconds. I can ignite long before you can reach me, but I do not wish to do so until the allotted time has come."

Birkson whistled. "That's pretty fast, brother. Much faster than me, I'm sure. It must be nice, being able to move like that after blundering along all your life with neural speeds."

"Yes, I find it very gratifying. It was a quite unexpected benefit of becoming a bomb."

This was more like it, Bach thought. Her dislike of Birkson had not blinded her to the fact that he had been checking out his hunch. And her questions had been answered: no tape array could answer questions like that, and the machine had as much as admitted that it had been a human being at one time.

Birkson completed a circuit, back to where Bach and Walters were standing. He paused, and said in a low voice, "Check out that time."

"What time?"

"What time did you say you were going to explode?" he yelled.

"In three hours, twenty-one minutes, and eighteen seconds," the bomb supplied.

"That time," he whispered. "Get your computers to work on it. See if it's the anniversary of any political group, or the time something happened that someone might have a grudge about." He started to turn away, then thought of something. "But most important, check the birth records."

"May I ask why?"

He seemed to be dreaming, but came back to them. "I'm just feeling this character out. I've got a feeling this might be his birthday. Find out who was born at that time—it can't be too many, down to the second—and try to locate them all. The one you can't find will be our guy. I'm betting on it."

"What are you betting? And how do you know for sure it's a man?"

That look again, and again she blushed. But, damn it, she had to ask questions. Why should he make her feel defensive about it?

"Because he's chosen a male voice to put over his speakers. I know that's not conclusive, but you get hunches after a while. As to what I'm betting ... no, it's not my life. I'm sure I can get this one. How about dinner tonight if I'm right?" The smile was ingenuous, without the trace of lechery she thought she had seen before. But her stomach was still crawling. She turned away without answering.

For the next twenty minutes, nothing much happened. Birkson continued his slow stroll around the machine, stopping from time to time to shake his head in admiration. The thirty men and women of Chief Bach's police detail stood around nervously with nothing to do, as far away from the machine as pride would allow. There was no sense in taking cover.

Bach herself was kept busy coordinating the behind-the-scenes maneuvering from a command post that had been set up around the corner, in the Elysian Travel Agency. It had phones and a computer output printer. She sensed the dropping morale among her officers, who could see nothing going on. Had they known that surveying lasers were poking their noses around trees in the Plaza, taking bearings to within a thousandth of a millimeter, they might have felt a little better. And on the floor below, the X-ray had arrived.

Ten minutes later, the output began to chatter. Bach could hear it in the silent, echoing corridor from her position halfway between the travel agency and the bomb. She turned and met a young officer with the green armband of a rookie. The woman's hand was ice-cold as she handed Bach the sheet of yellow printout paper. There were three names printed on it, and below that, some dates and events listed.

"This bottom information was from the fourth expansion of the problem," the officer explained. "Very low probability stuff. The three people were all born either on the second or within a three-second margin of error, in three different years. Everyone else has been contacted."

"Keep looking for these three, too," Bach said. As she turned away, she noticed that the young officer was pregnant, about in her fifth month. She thought briefly of sending her away from the scene, but what was the use?

Birkson saw her coming and broke off his slow circuits of the bomb. He took the paper from her and scanned it. He tore off the bottom part without being told it was low probability, crumpled it, and let it drop to the floor. Scratching his head, he walked slowly back to the bomb.

"Hans?" he called out.

"How did you know my name?" the bomb asked.

"Ah, Hans, my boy, credit us with some sense. You can't have got into this without knowing that the Munipol can do very fast investigations. Unless I've been underestimating you. Have I?"

"No," the bomb conceded. "I knew you would find out who I was. But it doesn't alter the situation."

"Of course not. But it makes for easier conversation. How has life been treating you, my friend?"

"Terrible," mourned the man who had become a fifty-kiloton nuclear weapon.

Every morning Hans Leiter rolled out of bed and padded into his cozy water closet. It was not the standard model for residential apartment modules but a special one he had installed after he moved in. Hans lived alone, and it was the one luxury he allowed himself. In his little palace, he sat in a chair that massaged him into wakefulness, washed him, shaved him, powdered him, cleaned his nails, splashed him with scent, then made love to him with a rubber imitation that was a good facsimile of the real thing. Hans was awkward with women.

He would dress, walk down three hundred meters of corridor, and surrender himself to a pedestrian slideway that took him as far as the Cross-Crisium Tube. There, he allowed himself to be fired like a projectile through a tunnel below the Lunar surface.

Hans worked in the Crisium Heavy Machinery Foundry. His job there was repairing almost anything that broke down. He was good at it; he was much more comfortable with machines than with people.

One day he made a slip and got his leg caught in a massive roller. It was not a serious accident, because the fail-safe systems turned off the machine before his body or head could be damaged, but it hurt terribly and completely ruined the leg. It had to be taken off. While he was waiting for the cloned replacement limb to be grown, Hans had been fitted with a prosthetic.

It had been a revelation to him. It worked like a dream, as good as his old leg and perhaps better. It was connected to his severed leg nerve but was equipped with a threshold cut-off circuit, and one day when he barked his artificial shin he saw that it had caused him no pain. He recalled the way that same injury had felt with his flesh and blood leg, and again he was impressed. He thought, too, of the agony when his leg had been caught in the machine.

When the new leg was ready for transplanting, Hans had elected to retain the prosthetic. It was unusual but not unprecedented.

From that time on, Hans, who had never been known to his co-workers as talkative or social, withdrew even more from his fellow humans. He would speak only when spoken to. But people had observed him talking to the stamping press, and the water cooler, and the robot sweeper.

At night, it was Hans' habit to sit on his vibrating bed and watch the holovision until one o'clock. At that time, his kitchen would prepare him a late snack, roll it to him in his bed, and he would retire for the night.

For the last three years Hans had been neglecting to turn the set on before getting into bed. Nevertheless, he continued to sit quietly on the bed staring at the empty screen.

When she finished reading the personal data printout, Bach was struck once more at the efficiency of the machines in her control. This man was almost a cipher, yet there were nine thousand words in storage concerning his uneventful life, ready to be called up and printed into an excruciatingly boring biography.

"... so you came to feel that you were being controlled at every step in your life by machines," Birkson was saying. He was sitting on one of the barriers, swinging his legs back and forth. Bach joined him and offered the long sheet of printout. He waved it away. She could hardly blame him.

"But it's true!" the bomb said. "We all are, you know. We're part of this huge machine that's called New Dresden. It moves us around like parts on an assembly line, washes us, feeds us, puts us to bed and sings us to sleep."

"Ah," Birkson said, agreeably. "Are you a Luddite, Hans?"

"No!" the bomb said in a shocked voice. "Roger, you've missed the whole point. I don't want to destroy the machines. I want to serve them better. I wanted to become a machine, like my new leg. Don't you see? We're part of the machine, but we're the most inefficient part."

The two talked on, and Bach wiped the sweat from her palms. She couldn't see where all this was going, unless Birkson seriously hoped to talk Hans Leiter out of what he was going to do in—she glanced at the clock—two hours and forty-three minutes. It was maddening. On the one hand, she recognized the skill he was using in establishing a rapport with the cyborg. They were on a first-name basis, and at least the damn machine cared enough to argue its position. On the other hand, so what? What good was it doing?

Walters approached and whispered into her ear. She nodded and tapped Birkson on the shoulder.

"They're ready to take the picture whenever you are," she said.

He waved her off.

"Don't bother me," he said, loudly. "This is getting interesting. So if what you say is true," he went on to Hans, getting up and pacing intently back and forth, this time inside the line of barriers, "maybe I ought to look into this myself. You really like being cyborged better than being human?"

"Infinitely so," the bomb said. He sounded enthusiastic. "I need no sleep now, and I no longer have to bother with elimination or eating. I have a tank for nutrients, which are fed into the housing where my brain and central nervous system are located." He paused. "I tried to eliminate the ups and downs of hormone flow and the emotional reactions that followed," he confided.

"No dice, huh?"

"No. Something always distracted me. So when I heard of this place where they would cyborg me and get rid of all that, I jumped at the chance."

Inactivity was making Bach impulsive. She *had* to say or do something.

"Where did you get the work done, Hans?" she ventured.

The bomb started to say something, but Birkson laughed loudly and slapped Bach hard on the back. "Oh, no, Chief. That's pretty tricky, right, Hans? She's trying to get you to rat. That's not done, Chief. There's a point of honor involved."

"Who is that?" the bomb asked, suspiciously.

"Let me introduce Chief Anna-Louise Bach, of the New Dresden Police. Ann, meet Hans."

"Police?" Hans asked, and Bach felt goose-pimples when she detected a note of fright in the voice. What was this maniac trying to do, frightening the guy like that? She was close to pulling Birkson off the case. She held off because she thought she could see a familiar pattern in it, something she could use as a way to participate, even if ignominiously. It was the good guy-bad guy routine, one of the oldest police maneuvers in the book.

"Aw, don't be like that," Birkson said to Hans. "Not all cops are brutes. Ann here, she's a nice person. Give her a chance. She's only doing her job."

"Oh, I have no objection to police," the bomb said. "They are necessary to keep the social machine functioning. Law and order is a basic precept of the coming new Mechanical Society. I'm pleased to meet you, Chief Bach. I wish the circumstances didn't make us enemies."

"Pleased to meet you, Hans." She thought carefully before she phrased her next question. She wouldn't have to take the hard-line approach to contrast herself with affable, buddy-buddy Birkson. She needn't be an antagonist, but it wouldn't hurt if she asked questions that probed at his motives.

"Tell me, Hans. You say you're not a Luddite. You say you like machines. Do you know how many machines you'll destroy if you set yourself off? And even more important, what you'll do to this social machine you've been talking about? You'll wipe out the whole city."

The bomb seemed to be groping for words. He hesitated, and Bach felt the first glimmer of hope since this insanity began.

"You don't understand. You're speaking from an organic viewpoint. Life is important to you. A machine is not concerned with life. Damage to a machine, even the social machine, is simply something to be repaired. In a way, I hope to set an example. I wanted to become a machine—"

"And the best, the very ultimate machine," Birkson put in, "is the atomic bomb. It's the end point of all mechanical thinking."

"Exactly," said the bomb, sounding very pleased. It was nice to be understood. "I wanted to be the very best machine I could possibly be, and it had to be this."

"Beautiful, Hans," Birkson breathed. "I see what you're talking about. So if we go on with that line of thought, we logically come to the conclusion . . ." and he was off into an exploration of the fine points of the new Mechanistic worldview.

Bach was trying to decide which was the crazier of the two, when she was handed another message. She read it, then tried to find a place to break into the conversation. But there was no convenient place. Birkson was more and more animated, almost frothing at the mouth as he discovered points of agreement between the two of them. Bach noticed her officers standing around nervously, following the conversation. It was clear from their expressions that they feared they were being sold out, that when zero hour arrived they would still be here watching intellectual ping-pong. But long before that, she could have a mutiny on her hands. Several of them were fingering their weapons, probably without even knowing it.

She touched Birkson on the sleeve, but he waved her away. Damn it, this was too much. She grabbed him and nearly pulled him from his feet, swung him around until her mouth was close to his ear and growled.

"Listen to me, you idiot. They're going to take the picture. You'll have to stand back some. It's better if we're all shielded."

"Leave me *alone*," he shot back and pulled from her grasp. But he was still smiling. "This is just getting interesting," he said, in a normal tone of voice.

Birkson came near to dying in that moment. Three guns were trained on him from the circle of officers, awaiting only the order to fire. They didn't like seeing their Chief treated that way.

Bach herself was damn near to giving the order. The only thing that stayed her hand was the knowledge that with Birkson dead, the machine might go off ahead of schedule. The only thing to do now was to get him out of the way and go on as best she could, knowing that she was doomed to failure. No one could say she hadn't given the expert a chance.

"But what I was wondering about," Birkson was saying, "was why today? What happened today? Is this the day Cyrus McCormick invented the combine harvester or something?"

"It's my birthday," Hans said, somewhat shyly.

"Your *birthday*?" Birkson managed to look totally amazed to learn what he already knew. "Your birthday. That's *great*, Hans. Many happy returns of the day, my friend." He turned and took in all of the officers with an expansive sweep of his hands. "Let's sing, people. Come on, it's his birthday, for heaven's sake. *Happy birthday to you, happy birthday to you, happy birthday, dear Hans . . .*"

He bellowed, he was off-key, he swept his hands in grand circles with no sense of rhythm. But so infectious was his mania that several of the officers found themselves joining in. He ran around the circle, pulling the words out of them with great scooping motions of his hands.

Bach bit down hard on the inside of her cheek to keep herself steady. *She had been singing, too.* The scene was so ridiculous, so blackly improbable . . .

She was not the only one who was struck the same way. One of her officers, a brave man who she knew personally to have shown courage under fire, fell on his face in a dead faint. A woman officer covered her face with her hands and fled down the corridor, making helpless coughing sounds. She found an alcove and vomited.

And still Birkson capered. Bach had her gun halfway out of the shoulder holster, when he shouted.

"What's a birthday without a party?" he asked. "Let's have a big party." He looked around, fixed on the flower shop. He started for it, and as he passed Bach he whispered, "Take the picture *now*."

It galvanized her. She desperately wanted to believe he knew what he was doing, and just at the moment when his madness seemed total he had shown her the method. *A distraction.* Please, let it be a distraction. She turned and gave the prearranged signal to the officer standing at the edge of Prosperity Plaza.

She turned back in time to see Birkson smash in the window of the flower shop with his putter. It made a deafening crash.

"Goodness," said Hans, who sounded truly shocked. "Did you have to do that? That's private property."

"What does it matter?" Birkson yelled. "Hell, man, you're going to do much worse real soon. I'm just getting things started." He reached in and pulled out an armload of flowers, signaling to others to give him a hand. The police didn't like it, but soon were looting the shop and building a huge wreath just outside the line of barriers.

"I guess you're right," said Hans, a little breathlessly. A taste of violence had excited him, whetted his appetite for more to come. "But you startled me. I felt a real thrill, like I haven't felt since I was human."

"Then let's do it some more." And Birkson ran up and down one side of the street, breaking out every window he could reach. He picked up small articles he found inside the shops and threw them. Some of them shattered when they hit.

He finally stopped. Leystrasse had been transformed. No longer the scrubbed and air-conditioned Lunar environment, it had become as shattered, as chaotic and uncertain, as the tension-filled emotional atmosphere it contained. Bach shuddered and swallowed the rising taste of bile. It was a precursor of things to come, she was sure. It hit her deeply to see the staid and respectable Leystrasse ravaged.

"A cake," Birkson said. "We have to have a cake. Hold on a minute, I'll be right back." He strode quickly toward Bach, took her elbow and turned her, pulled her insistently away with him.

"You have to get those officers away from here," he said, conversationally. "They're tense. They could explode at any minute. In fact," and he favored her with his imbecile grin, "they're probably more dangerous right now than the bomb."

"You mean you think it's a fake?"

"No. It's for real. I know the psychological pattern. After this much trouble, he won't want to be a dud. Other types, they're in it for the attention and they'd just as soon fake it. Not Hans. But what I mean is, I have him. I can get him. But I can't count on your officers. Pull them back and leave only two or three of your most trusted people."

"All right." She had decided again, more from a sense of helpless futility than anything else, to trust him. He *had* pulled a neat diversion with the flower shop and the X-ray.

"We may have him already," he went on, as they reached the end of the street and turned the corner. "Often, the X-ray is enough. It cooks some of the circuitry and makes it unreliable. I'd hoped to kill him outright, but he's shielded. Oh, he's probably got a lethal dosage, but it'd take him days to die. That doesn't do us any good. And if his circuitry *is* knocked out, the only way to find out is to wait. We have to do better than that. Here's what I want you to do."

He stopped abruptly and relaxed, leaning against the wall and gazing out over the trees and artificial sunlight of the Plaza. Bach could hear songbirds. They had always made her feel good before. Now all she could think of was incinerated corpses. Birkson ticked off points on his fingers.

She listened to him carefully. Some of it was strange, but no worse than she had already witnessed. And he really did have a plan. He really did. The sense of relief was so tremendous that it threatened to create a mood of euphoria in her, one not yet justified by the circumstances. She nodded curtly to each of his suggestions, then again to the officer who stood beside her, confirming what Birkson had said and turning it into orders. The young man rushed off to carry them out, and Birkson started to return to the bomb. Bach grabbed him.

"Why wouldn't you let Hans answer my question about who did the surgical work on him? Was that part of your plan?" The question was half-belligerent.

"Oh. Yeah, it was, in a way. I just grabbed the opportunity to make him feel closer to me. But it wouldn't have done you any good. He'll have a block against telling that, for sure. It could even be set to explode the bomb if he tries to answer that question. Hans is a maniac, but don't underestimate the people who helped him get where he is now. They'll be protected."

"Who are they?"

Birkson shrugged. It was such a casual, uncaring gesture that Bach was annoyed again.

"I have no idea. I'm not political, Ann. I don't know the Antiabortion Movement from the Freedom for Mauretania League. They build 'em, I take 'em apart. It's as simple as that. *Your* job is to find out how it happened. I guess you ought to get started on that."

"We already have," she conceded. "I just thought that ... well, coming from Earth, where this sort of thing happens all the time, that you might know ... damn it, Birkson. *Why?* Why is this happening?"

He laughed, while Bach turned red and went into a slow boil. Any of her officers, seeing her expression, would have headed for the nearest blast shelter. But Birkson laughed on. Didn't he give a damn about anything?

"Sorry," he forced out. "I've heard that question before, from other police chiefs. It's a good question." He waited, a half smile on his face. When she didn't say anything, he went on.

"You don't have the right perspective on this, Ann."

"That's Chief Bach to you, damn you."

"Okay," he said, easily. "What you don't see is that this thing is no different from a hand grenade tossed into a crowd or a bomb sent through the mail. It's a form of communication. It's just that today, with so many people, you have to shout a little louder to get any attention."

"But ... who? They haven't even identified themselves. You're saying that Hans is a tool of these people. He's been wired into the bomb, with his own motives for exploding. Obviously he didn't have the resources to do this himself, I can see that."

"Oh, you'll hear from them. I don't think they expect him to be successful. He's a warning. If they were *really* serious, they could find the sort of person they want, one who's politically committed and will die for the cause. Of course, they don't *care* if the bomb goes off; they'll be pleasantly surprised if it does. Then they can stand up and pound their chests for a while. They'll be famous."

"But where did they get the uranium? The security is ..."

For the first time, Birkson showed a trace of annoyance.

"Don't be silly. The path leading to today was irrevocably set in 1945. There was never any way to avoid it. The presence of a tool implies that it will be used. You can try your best to keep it in the hands of what you think of as responsible people, but it'll never work. And it's *no different,* that's what I'm saying. This bomb is just another weapon. It's a cherry bomb in an anthill. It's gonna cause one hill of ants a hell of a lot of trouble, but it's no threat to the race of ants."

Bach could not see it that way. She tried, but it was still a nightmare of entirely new proportions to her. How could he equate the killing of millions of people with a random act of violence where three or four might be hurt? She was familiar with that. Bombs went off every day in her city, as in every human city. People were always dissatisfied.

"I could walk down ... no, it's up here, isn't it?" Birkson mused for a moment on cultural differences. "Anyway, give me enough money, and I'll bet I could go up to your slum neighborhoods right this minute and buy you as many kilos of uranium or plutonium as you want. Which is something you ought to be doing, by the way. Anything can be bought. *Anything.* For the right price, you could have bought weapons-grade material on the black market as early as 1960 or so. It would have been very expensive; there wasn't much of it. You'd have had to buy a *lot* of people. But now . . . well, you think it out." He stopped, and seemed embarrassed by his outburst.

"I've read a little about this," he apologized.

She did think it out as she followed him back to the cordon. What he said was true. When controlled fusion proved too costly for wide-scale use, humanity had opted for fast breeder reactors. There had been no other choice. And from that moment, nuclear bombs in the hands of terrorists had been the price humanity accepted. And the price they would continue to pay.

"I wanted to ask you one more question," she said. He stopped and turned to face her. His smile was dazzling.

"Ask away. But are you going to take me up on that bet?"

She was momentarily unsure of what he meant.

"Oh. Are you saying you'd help us locate the underground uranium ring? I'd be grateful . . ."

"No, no. Oh, I'll help you. I'm sure I can make a contact. I used to do that before I got into this game. What I meant was, are you going to bet I can't find some? We could bet . . . say, a dinner together as soon as I've found it. Time limit of seven days. How about it?"

She thought she had only two alternatives: walk away from him, or kill him. But she found a third.

"You're a betting man. I guess I can see why. But that's what I wanted to ask you. How can you stay so calm? Why doesn't this get to you like it does to me and my people. You can't tell me it's simply that you're used to it."

He thought about it. "And why not? You can get used to anything, you know. Now, what about that bet?"

"If you don't stop talking about that," she said, quietly, "I'm going to break your arm."

"All right." He said nothing further, and she asked no further questions.

The fireball grew in milliseconds into an inferno that could scarcely be described in terms comprehensible to humans. Everything in a half-kilometer radius simply vanished into super-heated gases and plasma: buttresses, plate-glass windows, floors and ceilings, pipes, wires, tanks, machines, gewgaws and trinkets by the million, books, tapes, apartments, furniture, household pets, men, women, and children. They were the lucky ones. The force of the expanding blast compressed two hundred levels below it like a giant sitting on a Dagwood sandwich, making holes through plate steel turned to putty by the heat as easily as a punch press through tinfoil. Upward, the surface bulged into the soundless Lunar night and split to reveal a white hell beneath. Chunks flew away, chunks as large as city sectors, before the center collapsed back on itself to leave a crater whose walls were a maze of compartments and ant tunnels that dripped and flowed like warm gelatin. No trace was left of human bodies within two kilometers of the explosion. They had died after only the shortest period of suffering, their bodies consumed or spread into an invisible layer of organic film by the combination of heat and pressure that passed through walls, entered rooms where the doors were firmly shut. Further away, the sound was enough to congeal the bodies of a million people before the heat roasted them, the blast stripped flesh from bones to leave shrunken stick figures. Still the effects attenuated as the blast was channeled into corridors that were structurally strong enough to remain intact, and that very strength was the downfall of the inhabitants of the maze. Twenty kilometers from the epicenter, pressure doors popped through steel flanges like squeezed watermelon seeds.

What was left was five million burnt, blasted corpses and ten million injured so hideously that they would die in hours or days. But Bach had been miraculously thrown clear by some freak of the explosion. She hurtled through the void with fifteen million ghosts following her, and each carried a birthday cake. They were singing. She joined in.

"Happy birthday to you, happy birthday . . ."

"Chief Bach."

"Huh?" She felt a cold chill pass over her body. For a moment she could only stare down into the face of Roger Birkson.

"You all right now?" he asked. He looked concerned.

"I'm . . . what happened?"

He patted her on both arms, then shook her heartily.

"Nothing. You drifted off for a moment." He narrowed his eyes. "I think you were daydreaming. I want to be diplomatic about this . . . ah, what I mean . . . I've seen it happen before. I think you were trying to get away from us."

She rubbed her hands over her face.

"I think I was. But I sure went in the wrong direction. I'm all right now." She could remember it now, and knew she had not passed out or become totally detached from what was going on. She had watched it all. Her memories of the explosion, so raw and real a moment before, were already the stuff of nightmares.

Too bad she hadn't come awake into a better world. It was so damn unfair. That was the reward at the end of a nightmare, wasn't it? You woke up to find everything was all right.

Instead, here was a long line of uniformed officers bearing birthday cakes to a fifty-kiloton atomic bomb.

Birkson had ordered the lights turned off in the Leystrasse. When his order had not been carried out, he broke out the lights with his putter. Soon, he had some of the officers helping him.

Now the beautiful Leystrasse, the pride of New Dresden, was a flickering tunnel through hell. The light of a thousand tiny birthday candles on five hundred cakes turned everything red-orange and made people into shadowed demons. Officers kept arriving with hastily wrapped presents, flowers, balloons. Hans, the little man who was now nothing but a brain and nerve network floating in a lead container; Hans, the cause of all this, the birthday boy himself, watched it all in unconcealed delight from his battery of roving television cameras. He sang loudly.

"I am a bomb! I am a bomb!" he yelled. He had never had so much fun.

Bach and Birkson retreated from the scene into the darkened recess of the Bagatelle Flower Shoppe. There, a stereo viewing tank had been set up.

The X-ray picture had been taken with a moving plate technique that allowed a computer to generate a three dimensional model. They leaned over the tank now and studied it. They had been joined by Sergeant McCoy, Bach's resident bomb expert, and another man from the Lunar Radiation Laboratory.

"This is Hans," said Birkson, moving a red dot in the tank by means of a dial on the side. It flicked over and around a vague gray shape that trailed dozens of wires. Bach wondered again at the pressures that would allow a man to like having his body stripped from him. There was nothing in that lead flask but the core of the man, the brain and central nervous system.

"Here's the body of the bomb. The two subcritical masses. The H.E. charge, the timer, the arming barrier, which is now withdrawn. It's an old design, ladies and gentlemen. Old, but reliable. As basic as the bow and arrow. It's very much like the first one dropped on the Nippon Empire at Hiroshima."

"You're sure it'll go off, then?" Bach put in.

"Sure as taxes. Hell, a kid could build one of these in the bathroom, given only the uranium and some shielding equipment. Now let me see." He pored over the phantom in the tank, tracing out wiring paths with the experts. They debated possibilities, lines of attack, drawbacks. At last they seemed to reach a consensus.

"As I see it, we have only one option," Birkson said. "We have to go for his volitional control over the bomb. I'm pretty sure we've isolated the main cable that goes from him to the detonator. Knock that out, and he can't do a thing. We can pry that tin can open by conventional means and disarm that way. McCoy?"

"I agree," said McCoy. "We'd have a full hour, and I'm sure we can get in there with no trouble. When they cyborged this one, they put all their cards on the human operator. They didn't bother with entry blocks, since Hans could presumably blow it up before we could get close enough to do anything. With his control out, we only have to open it up with a torch and drop the damper into place."

The LRL man nodded his agreement. "Though I'm not quite as convinced as Mr. Birkson that he's got the right cable in mind for what he wants to do. If we had more time . . ."

"We've wasted enough time already," Bach said, decisively. She had swung rapidly from near terror of Roger Birkson to total trust. It was her only defense. She knew she could do nothing at all about the bomb and had to trust someone.

"Then we go for it. Is your crew in place? Do they know what to do? And above all, are they *good?* Really good? There won't be a second chance."

"Yes, yes, and yes," Bach said. "They'll do it. We know how to cut rock on Luna."

"Then give them the coordinates, and go." Birkson seemed to relax a bit. Bach saw that he had been under some form of tension, even if it was only excitement at the challenge. He had just given his last order. It was no longer in his hands. His fatalistic gambler's instinct came into play, and the restless, churning energy he had brought to the enterprise vanished. There was nothing to do about it but wait. Birkson was good at waiting. He had lived through twenty-one of these final countdowns.

He faced Bach and started to say something to her, then thought better of it. She saw doubt in his face for the first time, and it made her skin crawl. Damn it, she had thought he was *sure.*

"Chief," he said, quietly, "I want to apologize for the way I treated you these last few hours. It's not something I can control when I'm on the job. I . . ."

This time it was Bach's turn to laugh, and the release of tension it brought with it was almost orgasmic. She felt like she hadn't laughed for a million years.

"Forgive me," she said. "I saw you were worried, and thought it was about the bomb. It was just such a relief."

"Oh, yeah," he said, dismissing it. "No point in worrying now. Either your people hit it or they don't. We won't know if they don't. What I was saying, it just sort of comes over me. Honestly. I get horny, I get manic, I totally forget about other people except as objects to be manipulated. So I just wanted to say I like you. I'm glad you put up with me. And I won't pester you anymore."

She came over and put her hand on his shoulder.

"Can I call you Roger? Thanks. Listen, if this thing works, I'll have dinner with you. I'll give you the key to the city, a ticker-tape parade, and a huge bonus for a consultant fee . . . and my eternal friendship. We've been tense, okay? Let's forget about these last few hours."

"All right." His smile was quite different this time.

Outside, it happened very quickly. The crew on the laser drill were positioned beneath the bomb, working from ranging reports and calculations to aim their brute at precisely the right spot.

The beam took less than a tenth of a second to eat through the layer of rock in the ceiling and emerge in the air above the Leystrasse. It ate through the metal sheath of the bomb's underside, the critical wire, the other side of the bomb, and part of the ceiling like they weren't even there. It had penetrated into the level above before it could be shut off.

There was a shower of sparks, a quick sliding sound, then a muffled thud. The whole structure of the bomb trembled, and smoke screeched from the two drilled holes in the top and bottom. Bach didn't understand it but could see that she was alive and assumed it was over. She turned to Birkson, and the shock of seeing him nearly stopped her heart.

His face was a gray mask, drained of blood. His mouth hung open. He swayed and almost fell over. Bach caught him and eased him to the floor.

"Roger . . . what is it? Is it still . . . will it go off? Answer me, *answer me*. What should I do?"

He waved weakly, pawed at her hands. She realized he was trying to give her a reassuring pat. It was feeble indeed.

"No danger," he wheezed, trying to get his breath back. "No danger. The wrong wire. We hit the wrong wire. Just luck is all, nothing but luck."

She remembered. They had been trying to remove Hans' control over the bomb. Was he still in control? Birkson answered before she could speak.

"He's dead. That explosion. That was the detonator going off. He reacted just too late. We hit the disarming switch. The shield dropped into place so the masses couldn't come together even if the bomb was set off. Which he did. He set it off. That sound, that *mmmmmmwooooph!*" He was not with her. His eyes stared back into a time and place that held horror for him.

"I heard that sound—the detonator—once before, over the telephone. I was coaching this woman, no more than twenty-five, because I couldn't get there in time. She had only three more minutes. I heard that sound, then nothing, nothing."

She sat near him on the floor as her crew began to sort out the mess, haul the bomb away for disposal, laugh and joke in hysterical relief. At last Birkson regained control of himself. There was no trace of the bomb except a distant hollowness in his eyes.

"Come on," he said, getting to his feet with a little help from her. "You're going on twenty-four-hour leave. You've earned it. We're going back to Burning Tree, and you're going to watch me make a par five on the eighteenth. Then we've got a date for dinner. What place is nice?"

Carter Scholz is the author of *Palimpsests* (with Glenn Harcourt), *Kafka Americana* (with Jonathan Lethem), *Radiance*, and *The Amount to Carry*. He has been nominated for the Nebula, Hugo, Campbell, and Sturgeon awards. He currently lives in northern California. "The Eve of the Last Apollo" was Carter's first publication.

THE EVE OF THE LAST APOLLO

Carter Scholz

MILESTONES

Died. John Christie Andrews, 64, U.S. Air Force (Brig. Gen., ret.); of a heart attack;. Born July 17, 1935 in Abilene, Texas, Andrews was commander of the first manned spacecraft to land on the Moon. He is survived by a wife and son.

No. I don't like that dream.

The dream-magazine faded and he was back in 1975, tentatively at least, until sleep plucked him again into a land beyond life where his existence could be reduced to those two magazine appearances: his achievement and his death.

The curtains ballooned inward on a light breeze. He caught at them, and saw the moon standing in the sky. It was gibbous, bloated past half but less than full. He hated it like that, the lopsidedness of it. Half or full or crescent he could stand some nights, but there was nothing tolerable in a gibbous moon. He could not pick out within five hundred miles the place on its surface where he had walked, just five years ago.

No cars passed on State Street. The moon might have been another street lamp. From his present vantage point in Teaneck, New Jersey, it seemed impossible that he had ever been there.

The Lunar Exposé. Time Magazine, August 2, 1987. The article explained that the moon landing had been a hoax, since the moon itself was a hoax. It explained how simple it had been for unknown forces to simulate the moon for unscrupulous purposes; a conspiracy of poets and scientists was intimated. Mass hypnosis was mentioned. In a sidebar was a capsule summary of his alleged mission with a drawing of the flight path, the complicated loops and curves that had taken them there and back, straight-line flight being impossible in space, with an inset map of the splashdown area. Suddenly he was in the capsule as it splashed, sank, and bobbed to the surface. He wanted to fling the hatch open and yell in triumph, be dazzled by the spray and brilliant blue Pacific sky, but of course he couldn't do that, there was no telling what germs they had brought back, what germs had survived the billion-year killing lunar cold and void there was no telling, and the helicopters droned down and netted them and swung them to the carrier and into quarantine and for three weeks they saw people only through glass; that may have been the start of the isolation he felt now, just as his first time in space had been the start of the emptiness. When he had reached the Cape after all those weeks and miles and loops and backtracks, the trip was finally over, and he yielded to an impulse; he walked onto the launching pad and bent to put his hand on the scorched ground—but he had an attack of vertigo and a terrible intimation: the Earth itself had moved. If he went to the Cape exactly a year after the liftoff, the Earth would be in position again, the circle would be closed—but then there was the motion of the solar system through the galaxy to consider, and the sweep of the galaxy through the universe, and the universe's own pulsations—and he saw there was no way for him ever to close the circle and return to the place he started from. Driving back to Teaneck with the road behind him spiraling off through space as the Earth moved and the Sun moved and the galaxy moved, he became ill with a complex vertigo and had to pull off the road. Only when it grew dark was he able to drive again, slowly.

The dream, the memory, dissolved.

By the time he woke next morning his wife had already left to spend the weekend at the commune upstate. He made breakfast for himself and his son and went outside in the Saturday morning heat to garden. He was almost forty.

He worked in an over-airconditioned building adjacent to the Teaneck Armory. On one wall of his office was a maroon and red square of geometrically patterned fabric framed like a painting. On another was an autographed photo of the President and another photo of himself on the moon; the landing module and his crewmate Jim Cooper were reflected in his face mask. Because it was a NASA publicity photo, his autograph was on it. He felt silly about that and had always meant to get a clean copy, but where he worked now there were no NASA photos.

After he had walked on the moon and declined promotion to an Air Force base in California, they seemed to have run out of things for him to do. He had a wood veneer desk that was generally clean and empty. On the floor was a cheap red carpet, the nap of which he was always carrying home on his shoes.

At first after the mission his time had been filled with interviews and tours and banquets and inconveniences, but with time his fame dwindled. At first he welcomed this escape from the public eye; then the emptiness began to weigh on him, like a column of air on his shoulders. The time he could now spend with his wife and son passed uneasily. He learned to play golf and tennis and spent more time at them than he enjoyed. He started a diary and grew depressed with the banality of his life.

So he took a few weeks off in the early summer of 1975 to sort the drifting fragments of his life: his wife's departure, the imminent end of his fourth four-year term of service in the Air Force, the dead undying image of the moon that haunted his dreams, the book he had long planned to write, the mystery of his son, the possibility of a life ahead without a wife or son or career or public image, without every base he had come to rely on. He felt he had to consider what he was, and what he might become.

For a project he started a garden, even though it was the height of summer. He hauled sacks of soil amendments in the station wagon, rented a rototiller, chewed up part of the backyard, sweated through his t-shirt and shorts. Each day the heat seemed to come down on him sooner and harder. Each day he would hear Kevin go out, and then he would go back into the silent empty house to rest.

The lunar astronauts, the dozen or so people he had considered friends, drifted one by one away from the magnet of Houston, until the terrible clean emptiness of the city came to depress him terribly. Texas no longer felt like home.

In 1970, Harrison Baker, the command module pilot on Andrews' mission, moved to New Jersey with his family to become a vice-president in a large oil company. The Andrews followed shortly. The prospect of friends nearby, and of New York, where he and Charlotte had once wanted to live, Kevin's enthusiasm for leaving Texas, all these poor random factors pulled them to the sterile suburb of Teaneck as surely as destiny. As it turned out, they ended over forty miles from the Bakers, New York lost its appeal after six months, and Kevin talked of going back to Texas for college.

Baker had written a book on what it was like to orbit the moon while his fellow astronauts got all the glory. The book was called *Group Effort*. A bad book, Andrews thought. A humble book by a conceited man, written in fact by a hungry young journalist. Andrews had the impression, reading it, that Baker was somehow unconvinced of the Moon's reality, since he himself had not walked there. Andrews disliked the book, or more precisely he disliked the feelings the book aroused in him: he felt he could have done it better if he had made the effort.

But adrift in this summer he nonetheless called Baker one day. He was alone in the house and desperate for company. He called him as if to summon a ghost of old confidence.

"Chris! How are you, you son of a bitch?" Baker's voice was hard and distant on the wire. Andrews had quite forgotten that at NASA Chris had been his nickname. He had also forgotten Baker's smiling combativeness, his way of wielding friendship like a challenge. Already he was regretting the call.

"Hello, Hank. How are you?"

"Great, just great! Listen, I've been meaning to invite you and Sharl up for a weekend. It's been too long."

"Fine. Thanks, Hank. But actually Charlotte and I haven't been getting on too well recently."

"Oh? I'm sorry to hear it."

"It's just one of those things. We're thinking of separating."

"That's a shame, Chris. That's a damn shame. Francie and I always said what a good couple you were."

"Well, I don't know, I think it's for the best. Hell, I didn't call to cry on your shoulder, Hank. I had a question for you. I've been thinking of writing that book that Doubleday asked me to, you remember?"

"Sure. They're still interested?"

"Well, I don't know. I assumed they would be."

"It's been a few years, hasn't it? You know, the royalties on my book aren't what they could be. The hardcover's out of print and the paperback sales are so slow they're not going to reprint it. Which is a damn shame, I think. Not that I need the money. But the way I feel about it is, it's a historical document and it ought to stay in print. But they say people aren't interested in the moon anymore. People don't care."

"Well, sure, look at the whole NASA program."

"Well, I'm a retired guy now. I don't really follow the program."

"This is the last one, Hank. This one coming up. After this, no more manned flights."

There was silence. He remembered Baker's habit of keeping him waiting on the line, when Baker was in the orbiter.

"Hank? I can't help thinking we did it wrong."

"Wrong? What do you mean?"

"Our landing. We planted the American flag, we left a plaque."

"So? What should we have planted? Flowers?" Baker laughed, a short cold sound in the receiver.

"I don't know. I thought the United Nations flag might have been a nice gesture."

"The UN? What's the UN done for you lately? We put that lander on the moon. Why shouldn't we take the credit for it?"

"I suppose. I didn't think much about it at the time." The flag would not unfurl in vacuum so they had braced it with wire.

"What's to think about? I mean, this is off the record, this isn't a damn NASA press release, but that flag marks our territory. I don't care what the plaque said about coming in peace for all mankind. We got there before the Russians did. It's that simple."

"What about the joint Apollo-Soyuz mission coming up?"

"Well, shit. There's a good reason to be out of NASA right there. The Russians get more out of it than we do. You want my take on it, we'll have a manned program again, Chris, yes we will. But it won't be NASA. We'll take space back from those fucking civilians. Mark my words. Now, Chris, I got to run. Some bigshot wants to buy me lunch, get me to sit on a board somewhere. That invitation still goes for you and your kid, and for Charlotte if you want. Any time at all, you know that."

"Sure, Hank. Thanks."

"And I'm sorry as hell to hear what happened with Charlotte. I hope it all works out for you."

"I'm sure it will. I'll let you go. Good talking to you."

"See you around, huh?"

"You bet." He hung up. He felt very tired. The living room trembled just outside his field of vision. He sat for a few minutes, and abruptly decided to spend the day in New York, in noise and smog and traffic.

Through the magazine where she worked, his wife had met an author who ran a commune in upstate New York. The author had published an article on communal lifestyles in the magazine. Charlotte brought it home, and Andrews read it with disdain. A few weeks later the author dropped by the office in person and talked to Charlotte. She came home excited, with an invitation to the commune for both of them, which, after a week of bitter arguments, she accepted alone. She would sleep with the author; of that Andrews was sure. And when she came home Andrews said, stupidly, regretting it even as he spoke, "Was he any good?"

And she said, "He was great," and what had been a bitterness became a war. Kevin was fourteen then. During a lull in the fight they heard him sobbing through the wall.

"My God," said Charlotte, "what's wrong with us?" Together they went to Kevin, and the three of them held to each other and wept.

The next month was perhaps the best in their marriage; they were kind and deferential, as if unwilling to test the strength of the frayed fabric. But the next time Charlotte left it was for a week. Again there was a fight. Again there were tears. After that, the reconciliations had less meaning. Andrews felt the marriage become weak and brittle, emulsion cracking on an old photograph.

The black and white photograph in the den held them both against a bright, faded Texas sky. They stood by a small brick chapel in the hot Texas afternoon, Charlotte in her crisp white dress, four months pregnant but not yet showing, Andrews crewcut and stiff in his uniform. Andrews had entered the Air Force from college, blank enough to be a soldier, smart enough to be an officer. Soon he had commendations, citations, and his name on a plastic wood-grained prism on his desk at Sheppard Air Force Base and $213.75 a month plus expenses. Then he had a wife and in a few years a master's degree and a mortgage, and then a son and a doctorate, and oak leaves and an assured future.

Then the space program started up, and Lieutenant Colonel Andrews being a local boy of good repute, an officer and an engineer and a test pilot, and a solid asset to any organization, so it said on his commendations, he was accepted into those elite ranks. He got his colonelcy and a sense of purpose that truly humbled him; he had never been religious but space made him feel as he imagined God made other people feel. He was a successful man, and his life was a fine and balanced thing.

Then they put him in a rocket and shot him at the moon.

Abenezra, Abulfeda, Agatharchides, Agrippa, Albategnius, Alexander, Aliacensus, Almanon, Alpetragius, Alphonsus, Apianus, Apollonius, Agago, Archimedes, Aristarchus, Aristillus, Aristoteles, Ascelpi, Atlas . . .

The craters, the names, rolled past. A tiny motor made a grinding sound as it turned the four-foot sphere, the front and back sides both sculpted in wondrous detail thanks to his and other missions, thanks to the automatic cameras mounted on the outside of the capsule. Tiny American flags marked the Apollo landing sites, dime-store gaudies against the gray.

John Christie Andrews, first man on the moon, stood in the planetarium at the end of a hall lined with names like Icarus, da Vinci, Montgolfier, Wright, Goddard inscribed over a mural of the history of flight. They had told him that the moon landing was the grandest achievement of the human race. He believed it was. He had every reason to be proud, to be as content as Baker seemed to be. Why, then, did that emptiness come to him at night?

Flanking the lunar globe were photographs: himself, Baker, Cooper, Nixon, Von Braun. Some children recognized him and crowded around for autographs. One asked where he had landed; again he suffered the doubts of last night and finally stabbed a finger vaguely at one of the larger maria. Gratefully he heard the loudspeaker announce the start of the sky show.

The sky show was absorbing, more so than the night sky, even the clear country sky he could see for two weeks every year at his brother's summer cottage on Lake Hopatcong; he was enchanted by the flitting arrows on the sky, the narrator's calm clear explanations, the wonderful control the projector had over its model universe. Stars rose, set, went forward, back. Seasons fled and returned. In the planetarium, time did not exist.

Afterwards he walked along the edge of Central Park. In a bookstore window he saw a copy of Baker's book, marked down to $1.98. He went in. Near the entrance his eye was caught by a familiar volume, an anthology of poetry he had used in college. He stood there skimming it. *The moon is dead, you lovers . . . I have seen her face . . . a woman's face but dead as stone. And leper white and withered to the bone . . .*

He saw Charlotte's face deflagrate before him. Touched by the void, it turned into a death's-head moon, glowing with the stark brilliance of sunlight in void. Something struggled in his chest. It seemed to Andrews that of all the astronauts, he had had the best chance of understanding the moon. Of what they had done there. He would write his book. Why not? And he would start it with poetry.

He purchased the anthology, and several others. It was years since he had read anything but newspapers; now he was drunk with the neglected mysteries of books. In this nearly weightless mood he felt himself approaching the edge of a change, the crest of an oscillation, the start of a new phase; he felt charged with the energy of the unpredictable.

"Dad? You busy?"

He started and pushed aside the books he had bought. "Oh, no. Come on in, son." Immediately annoyed at himself; when had he started calling Kevin son?

The boy drifted in. Tall, pale; his son, brought out of a hot union years past, and already faded, but for this phantom, this stranger in the house. His son.

"Are you and Mom going to stay together until September?"

"Sure. Until you're at school."

"Oh." The room was silent. Somewhere an air conditioner hummed.

"Why do you ask?"

"Things are worse between you, aren't they?"

"Don't worry about it, Kevin."

"If you're staying together just for my sake, I wish you wouldn't. I mean, I don't want you to. I think you should separate now if that's the case."

Andrews looked at his son. A troubled sixteen, his emotions already burnt brittle into a fragile, ashen maturity. While Andrews felt himself moving back along a rocket wake into a second adolescence, a time of self-consciousness, self-discovery.

"I'll think about it. I'll talk to your mother. Kevin . . . ?"

"Yeah, Dad."

"This business with your mother and me . . . it hasn't affected you too badly, has it?" He burned with embarrassment. His memory stung him brutally with the image of a woman he had, just once, brought to the house, out of spite for Charlotte and her author, and Kevin's look when he came home. "I mean, just because things aren't working out for us, I don't want you to think . . ."

"I don't think about it anymore. It's just one of those things that happen."

"Because it would be a terrible thing if this were to turn you against marriage, or against women . . ."

"Don't worry about it, Dad. I'll think what I think. I think it's better this way. I think it might even be better for you if you split up sooner."

"Well, thanks, Kev." Then, because he was less afraid of being embarrassed than of being untouchable, he hugged his son. Kevin held still for this, and Andrews let go soon enough to make both of them grateful.

"Okay if I stay out late tonight?" Kevin asked, leaving. "I have a date."

"How late?" Pleased, but their late sentiment demanded a strict return to formality. The balance was too delicate to threaten.

"One o'clock?"

"Make it twelve-thirty."

"Okay."

"Who's the girl?"

"Nobody you know."

"Oh. Well . . . have fun . . ."

Kevin left. Andrews returned to his book and read: *Poetry must bring forth its characters as speaking, singing, gesticulating. This is the nature of the hero.*

His obligations as a national monument took him the next day to a half-hour talk show with a senator, a NASA administrator, and a moderator. The topic was the end of the manned space program, made topical by the upcoming Apollo-Soyuz mission.

The show started with the senator asserting that the space program was by no means ending, but was being cut back in favor of more pressing domestic issues. The senator said that space exploration could be done more cheaply and efficiently and safely by machines. Andrews felt that he was being mollified, and this increased his hostility. He interrupted to ask if perhaps other areas of the national budget might be better cut—defense, for instance, which consumed a hundred times as much money as NASA.

No one knew how to react; Andrews thought the NASA man might be smiling, off-camera. The senator made some comment about his record for trimming waste, and the moderator turned the conversation toward the hopeful symbolism of the joint Apollo-Soyuz mission. The senator, recovered, called it a magnificent extension of his party's successful policy of detente. Andrews began to ask why, if detente was so successful, the defense budget was not being cut, but as he leaned forward to press his point, he realized that his microphone was off and the camera had moved away from him. This so angered him that he leaned into the camera's view and began to speak into the senator's microphone.

"I'd like to read something, if you don't mind."

The camera swung back to him. The lights blazed and blinded him. He felt a little drunk with their heat.

"This is a poem by Lord Byron. It's very short." The paper trembled in his hand.

> So, we'll go no more a-roving
>   So late into the night,
>   Though the heart be still as loving,
>   And the moon be still as bright.
>
> For the sword outwears its sheath,
>   And the soul wears out the breast.
>   And the heart must pause to breathe,
>   And love itself have rest.
>
> Though the night was made for loving,
>   And the day returns too soon,
>   Yet we'll go no more a-roving
>   By the light of the moon.

Electrons made a chaos of snow on the monitors. Offstage a man in horn-rimmed glasses waved frantically. The moderator cleared his throat.

"Thank you, Colonel Andrews. We have to pause here, but we'll be back in a moment." The red eye of the camera blinked off.

Andrews sank back into his chair. The senator looked away. The moderator leaned over to Andrews and said, "Please, Colonel, stick to the subject at hand."

"Wasn't I?"

"Colonel."

"My microphone was turned off. It made me mad."

"I'll see it doesn't happen again. But please . . ."

"No more poetry?"

"No more poetry."

Andrews turned to the NASA man, his silent ally, who said, "This isn't helping us, Colonel," and his certainty vanished. NASA itself did not care about the moon. Andrews was alone in his concern.

"All right," he said under his breath. "All right, you bastards." He felt a sense of climax. He saw what he must do: leave, walk off, now. He had said all he had to say. But at the thought all his strength went from him. The camera came back on, and for the rest of the show he was trapped there, silent, outwardly serene. He saw himself as a circle swimming alone and untouched in a sea of static.

Tuesday his wife returned. The car pulled up and he heard Kevin go down and out the back door, fast and light, as if he had been going anyway. The screen door sighed on its hinge and in the second before she entered the den he knew with a sick premonition that today she would finally ask for a divorce. Her first words, though, catching him off balance, were, "My God, John, do you have any idea how embarrassing that was?"

"Hello, Charlotte. What was embarrassing?" He considered the woman before him with an objectivity he would never have thought possible.

"The TV show. The poetry. Rick practically dragged the whole commune in to watch you quoting Lord Byron on the Today show. Christ, if you knew what you looked like."

"Really. I didn't know you had TV up there in the pristine wilderness."

"Oh, go screw."

"All right, let's have it, what was wrong with quoting Byron?"

"It was, let us say, out of character."

"Did it ever occur to you that I get tired of playing the dumb hero?"

She looked at him. "You think you can get out of it that easily?"

"Maybe."

She went to her bedroom and took down a suitcase from the closet. He followed her and sat on the bed with his eyes closed and his fingertips touching at the bridge of his nose. He sat as if in another world and listened to the angry rustlings of clothes as she hurled them about.

"Tell me, John, do you have any idea the kind of crap I have had to put up with these past ten years?"

"Yes." It had once been a joke between them.

"The goddamned forty-page NASA manual on how to be an astronaut's wife? Did you get a good look at that?"

"Charlotte, don't start."

"John."

"Yes," he said.

"John, I want a divorce."

"Yes, I know. All right."

"All right? Like that?"

"Like that."

She stared, confused. "What are you going to do?"

"I don't know."

"Your term of service is over this month, isn't it? Are you going to renew?"

"I don't think so."

"Why not?" She sat on the bed now and he became aware of her body, her movements, and it began to hurt. He had held it off till then. "What are you going to do for money? Another four years and you'd have a pension. Kevin will be in college. If you quit now, what will you do?"

"I was thinking of writing a book."

"About your mission?"

"Sort of. I was thinking of poetry."

"Poetry?" She smiled fractionally and shook her head. "Lover, if you had the barest fraction of poetry in you, it would have come out long ago. You would have said something full of poetry when you first stepped onto the moon. And what did you say? Well, I don't have to remind you."

"Those were their words, not mine."

She shook her head wearily. "John, it's too late. It's five years too late. You can't be what you're not. You're, what did you say, a national monument. As soon as you touched that rock up there you turned to stone yourself. I know, because I almost did too. I came so damned close to it, but I . . ." She stopped herself.

"Go on."

She looked up quickly. "You want me to?"

"Yes."

She paused. She looked at her hands. "While you were on the moon I seduced a newsman."

"Say that again."

"I seduced a newsman. You didn't know that, did you?"

"No, Charlotte, I didn't know that." He felt a dull ache start, a sinking at the truth of it, or at her ability to lie that way. "I don't know when to believe you anymore."

"You can believe this. It was right after you'd stepped down. He was here to interview me, to ask me safe dull questions for his safe dull article. Kevin was at school, you were a quarter million miles away; so we did it. It was the safest infidelity I ever had."

"Meaning there were others."

"Meaning whatever you like."

Feeling was returning to him; he had tried to hold it off, but the dull ache was deep in his spine.

"And right after we finished the phone rang. He looked like it was the voice of God. I said, 'Oh, that's just my husband calling from work,' and I laughed! I felt so fine! Isn't that funny, that I didn't have to worry about you walking in on us because you were on the moon?"

He got up and left the room. "John," she called. He kept walking. He walked into the kitchen to get a beer, the feeling still in his spine. When he reached the refrigerator there was a roaring in his ears. Cold air blew out across his arms; he stared into the cluttered recess of milk, butter, eggs, foilwrapped leftovers. His mind was blank. Finally he remembered about the beer and reached for it. He was shocked to see his hand shake as it lifted the bottle. He put the bottle carefully back and shut the door, stood braced against it. His back throbbed. When it subsided he walked back to the bedroom. "Why?" he said.

Charlotte watched him. "Because, John, I was slightly drunk and terribly depressed because there was my husband on the moon, and where was he? I felt nothing. I felt like a piece of machinery for the goddamned mission and I had to do something human for Christ's sake, can you understand that?"

"That wasn't human. That was sick and vindictive."

"I watched you on the moon, John, I watched the whole thing. I wanted so much to share your moment, and I couldn't. It meant nothing. It wasn't real to me. You said their words, you followed their agenda, you did nothing, nothing, to show that you were my husband. I watched you become NASA, and I was the NASA wife. And I felt like I was dying. And here was this reporter saying, 'You must be awfully proud, Mrs. Andrews.' And you moved like a robot on the moon and I did not want to be married to that! So I fucked him. I did it, and I made him think of me as a person!" And she laughed in triumph and looked at him quickly as she used to, when the life and the devilry in her was for him only. The look caught at him and something seemed to break free from her eyes and fly and something twisted inside him, watching it go.

"Charlotte ..." His mouth was dry and his voice came from far away. "Stay with me."

"No."

"Yes." He was pleading. "Yes."

"Why should I, John?"

"I need you. Kevin needs you."

For a second she was moved, he saw it; her eyes softened and she seemed to tremble with the thought of going to him, there was that ghost of a better past between them for just an instant. She seemed ready to cry, but with an effort she turned to him and forced her tears back to whatever pit they had been rising from; she fixed him with dry glittering eyes that said no; I am not that close to you.

"John, I have needs too," she said.

Numb, he followed her to the car, helped her with her bags. She got in, started the engine, and stared straight ahead for a minute before turning to him.

"You could come visit me." she said.

There was a long silence. "I don't think so. I'd better be alone."

And she drove off. That it was inevitable, that he had seen it coming for months, that his every nerve was raw with waiting for it, made no difference to the wretched man who now stands and watches a woman who had been his wife vanish down the road.

He has a dream that first night after she has finally left. It is one of many in the blurry confused time before waking. He is lying on his back with an erection while a woman pulls herself onto him. When he fucks his wife this way, as he often does at her prompting, he puts his hands to her breasts or on her hips, but in this dream he can't move. His arms stay limp at his sides. The woman is moving, though, sliding on him, and he remembers that in space his wet dreams were usually of women masturbating. This dream-woman seems to be doing that now; he feels like a machine for her pleasure—and it's good to feel that, to give himself over to her pleasure, to abandon his responsibilities.

As he wakes further, the dream fades and he realizes that the sheet is tented over him and the slightest move will bring him off. He lies still. Only the fractional pull of the sheet as he breathes can be felt, with almost unbearable friction. Finally he turns onto his stomach and pumps himself into the sheet, reliving agonies of adolescence, twice this week I sinned father, it was that that drove him from the Church. He lies for some time, feeling himself pulse, and grow damp and cold.

Alone, becalmed, he had books to read and silence in which to think and money enough to last the summer, a quiet season of the soul that seemed timeless. But it passed. His reenlistment forms came; Kevin was preparing for college; he had to grow used to the idea of divorce. The house took on a dull dead feel, as if his eyes in passing over objects too many times had burnt the life from them. He felt beyond continuing. He found a line in Yeats that pierced him with its truth: Man is in love, and loves what vanishes.

So for a week or two he worked at trying to find in his unwilling soul the shape of a book that would say what he felt about the moon. He copied poems from his anthology. He reread Baker's book. The event was too familiar; even as he rehearsed it in his mind, he could feel the particularity of it slipping away from him. Instead he jotted fragments based on moments he remembered, moments of solitude when he had felt himself, and not an instrument of NASA: earthrise over the crescent limb while they still orbited the moon at eighty miles; the feel of the light gravity; the way the lunar dust burst from underfoot, hung and drifted. He wrote short paragraphs, sometimes just fragments of sentences that looked like lines of poetry. He typed up what he had and clipped a cover letter to the pages, hoping his name would make up for their defects.

Then, emptied, he called his wife at the number she had left. When he heard her voice he sickened and softened inside and was near tears when he asked to come up and see her and she said, she says, yes.

On the drive up he is tense with anticipation. His pulse is up, his chest tight, his breathing shallow, almost as if he is in a capsule again. He admits to himself that some of this is fear.

Of what is he afraid? Not of Charlotte or her author, but of the commune. The young people there. He sees teenaged girls drifting through the Teaneck summer. He is more disconcerted by them than Kevin is. To find himself at that age he would have to go back to Waco, 1951—and for an instant it seems possible—exit 12 for the McCarthy hearings, exit 13 for the Korean War—it seems he could return to his youth as easily as he now takes the Thruway. But it would not be the youth of these new children. This generation seems astute, mature beyond their years, beyond perhaps his.

The commune is not what he expected. No farmhouse, no wide furrowed fields, no cows or sheep grazing. It is a modest two-story home surrounded by neatly pruned shrubs. In a small garden he sees a man about his age shade his eyes to watch his car lurch up the dirt drive. This is the author, no doubt. The man sets down his hoe and approaches.

"Hello, I'm Rick Burns. You must be Colonel Andrews. Charlotte told us to expect you."

He is drained from the trip; the sun hits him a blow as he climbs out of the air-conditioned car. He shakes hands, feeling the man's grip, feeling it as if it were on his wife.

"Come inside and I'll introduce you around. We're glad you decided to come up."

He dislikes Burns on sight, his bluff cordiality, the veneer of sexuality on the man's skin like a deep tan.

The only person inside is Charlotte, crosslegged on the sofa, reading. She looks up when Andrews enters; she has heard the car and arranged herself purposely into that neutral position, and stays seated, realizing that a hug would be too intimate, a handshake too cold. In his consideration of adolescence, in his high pitch of sexual awareness, all he can think of is how much he has missed her physically.

Charlotte rises. "I'll show John around."

"Dinner's late tonight, around nine."

They go out; they speak little. She tells him there are half a dozen young people living here, working and paying what they can. Rick bears most of the expense. There is a small barn behind the house, hens, a couple of pigs, turkeys, ducks. Charlotte says hello to a couple, Robert and Barbara, as they emerge from the barn, smiling with slight embarrassment. Andrews looks at Charlotte, squeezes her hand. And soon enough they end up back in her bedroom.

He steps outside himself and observes them both there in the waning light. Charlotte unbuttons her blue shirt and the sun is gold and shadow on her. The room is vivid in oranges and browns. Even Andrews's large body, going to fat from lack of training, is handsome in the twilight. He lies naked on the bed, the sheets cool, the air gentle, Charlotte sliding silken over him. Her breasts glow pale against her tan. She moves onto him as in his dream; he is still as death, as in the dream; and suddenly he thrusts against her. She puts a hand to his chest to slow him, but he moves again, frantic now to break the spell of dream that seems to hover close. She presses harder, and furious, he grabs her shoulders and wrenches her over with a small gasp under him, pumping desperately, starting a rhythm, a continuity, a feeling that in these seconds, these thrusts, he can vindicate all their time passed and gone sour.

Perhaps she understands then, or perhaps her body betrays her, or perhaps she has secret reasons of her own, but she moves in sympathy; she gives Andrews his dominance. Gives it just as Andrews deliquesces, his determination melts and flows from him. He comes up off her and rolls away and lies still, hardly breathing.

"John, it doesn't matter. It's all right."

"No. No, it isn't."

"Shh. Yes. It is. I don't care."

"I do."

"It's not your fault. Try later."

Andrews lies quietly as she caresses him. And peace comes like grace; what a wonder, to have his wife back as she was, even for these few moments. Dusk gathers, and he has visions of space, at once appealing and terrifying. The world releases him, and he soars transcendent through the firmament. After a while the stars resolve to the grainy darkness of the room and Charlotte is beside him and they talk.

"What is it you want here, Sharl?"

"I don't know if I can explain. It's a feeling. It's as if I've spent my whole life inside, in some horrible hospital or rest home. I haven't felt really free since God knows when. I feel pale and bedridden. I just want to feel healthy again."

"Yes," he says. "Sometimes I feet the air pressing on me. I feel gravity and I feel the atmosphere like an ocean on my back. And I want to be in free fall again. I dream about that sometimes."

"This is what NASA is to you?"

"Was."

"Why do you want to resign, then?"

"Because it's over! Didn't you hear me on that program? It's over, done, finished." He groans and rolls away from her. "It could have been something and we let it go. What sense does that make?"

"John," she soothes, holding him. Against the coldness of space, the transcendent spirit of man, her warmth is cloying. She binds him to his body. "What's out there, anyway?"

"Nothing," he says, and he shuts his eyes.

On an ocean. Wave mechanics. Harmonic motion. His physics professor, strange old man, explaining the motion of the waves: periodic functions, series of crests and troughs, repetitions. Every sort of motion dependent upon harmonic theory. Sine waves, circles, spirals, helixes, orbits, all the same. The same equations apply. Period of a pendulum. Earth's a pendulum, you know: swings around the sun, and turns on its axis: complex motion. In the middle of the lecture he dropped into philosophic discourse, the brilliant mind derailed and rambling as the classroom pitched on the waves: duality in monism, one wave with the two halves, see? Positive and negative. Mathematics is the purest poetry. Ah, the Greeks, such poets. Class grumbling, breaking up and diving off the platform, old fool senile and rambling about sine fucking waves. Sit down! I'm not finished! Andrews alone in the classroom. Now listen, hissed the teacher, air seething with his hot intense breath, the sea growing long and glassy as if listening. We are all disturbances of the medium. Understand? Disturbances of the medium. Pebbles dropped in a vacuum. Waves. All of us, a collection of waves, nothing more. Nothing but repetitions, periods, waves. Frightened, Andrews dove, sank quickly, drowned, and drowning, woke.

As he enters the kitchen and faces all the members of the commune together for dinner, he feels lines of force in the room, constellations of tensions shifting to accommodate him. Interference patterns. How distant he is from this world; how far away Teaneck is. The others feel this too, and there is that moment of uneasiness, the lines in flux. The moment passes. They sit to dinner.

The dinner discussion ranges over books, music, films, farming. One girl casually mentions her abortion and Andrews suffers a Catholic reaction. Not that he has been at all religious, but a sense of sin, once acquired, is not easily lost. Sin and grace are not part of the metaphysical baggage of this generation. They speak of yin and yang, complementaries without values. He feels at a loss, vulnerable.

After dinner they sit and talk over the littered plates. Burns starts to roll a cigarette. He has rolled several from tobacco that evening, but now he reaches for a smaller jar, and the flakes are green and Andrews feels a kick of giddy trepidation as he watches Burns pour the stuff into a paper and roll it. He is acutely aware of everyone, of their casualness and his tension, and he feels Charlotte watching him. The joint circles around, closing on him. Charlotte tokes, smiles at him, and passes it. He shakes his head. She nods and smiles, makes "come on" with her mouth. Afraid of interrupting the casual atmosphere, afraid of making a scene, afraid perhaps of missing a chance, he accepts, sucks, holds, passes. "Keep it in," Charlotte whispers. He nods secretly. John Andrews, pothead.

At first he feels nothing and starts to relax, but after a while a certain detachment slips into his senses. They extend; his eyes, ears, fingers are at the far end of a tunnel, relaying everything to him in delayed echoes. Everything has flattened, taken on the aspect of a screen. Entranced, Andrews watches as he would in a theater. Colors are rich, vivid, the dialogue flows wondrously. How lifelike, he thinks.

This goes on for some time before a young man named Max gets up. Andrews runs the scene back: Burns has asked how many chickens he can expect for dinner tomorrow and Max said, "I'll go out and cull some now. Come on, Barb." Then he senses Andrews' gaze. "Want to see how you cull chickens, Colonel?" and Andrews, suffused with good will, says, "Why, shore," and they are up and out.

There is silence outside, a breathless summer silence, with a full moon, orange, just rising. On the horizon fireworks burst soundlessly. The Fourth, Andrews suddenly remembers. It is the Fourth of July. America is 199 tonight.

In the barn is a rich earth shit smell. In the roost the birds flutter and cluck at the flashlight. Max says, "We have a dozen birds but we're only getting about eight eggs a day. So we must have a couple hens not doing their jobs." He lifts a brown hen which squawks indignantly. Barb takes the light. The hen's eyes gleam yellow and she squirms. "Down," says Max. "Keep it out of her eyes, Barb."

He carries the bird into the adjoining shed, away from the others, and snaps on the light. He says to Andrews, "Now the first thing you do is check the claws. If the hen's not laying, the yellow pigment that should go into the yolk gets into the beak and claws and around the vent." He turns the hen over and she squawks. "Pretty good. Now you check the vent." He pushes the tail feathers aside and a pink puckered hole appears. "It should be moist and bleached—no yellow—and this one looks pretty good." Abruptly Max lays his fingers beside the vent. "Check the pelvic bone for clearance, make sure the eggs have room to get out." He flips the hen back rightside up. "Yeah, she looks like a layer. Give her a white tag, Barb." The girl has a handful of colored plastic rings. Now she snaps a white one around the bird's horny leg. Max takes the hen back in, emerges with another. "When they stop laying," he says, "they start looking a lot better. The muscles firm up and the feathers get slicker. So I get very suspicious when I see a healthy-looking bird like this one." He flips her over. The hen thrashes wildly, flaps the air with frantic wings. "Oh, baby," says Max, "you're much too active. You're looking too good to be spending much time in the laying box." He holds her firmly. "Vent looks okay, though. Two fingers here . . . Give her a yellow, Barb."

After eleven hens there is only one definite cull, one red tag already in a separate cage. Max brings in the last bird. "This is a sex-linked. I would be very surprised if she wasn't laying. Still, you can never tell. The only way you find out for sure is to kill it and check the egg tree. I killed a cull once that had an egg all ready to drop out. Ate the chicken, fried the egg. But we lost a layer. And they moult in July and they don't lay while they're moulting. Every poultry book I've ever read says, come July, you can forget about eggs."

As soon as Max starts poking, the bird explodes in frenzy. The claws kick, the wings flail. Max puts a hand on the bird's neck. "If you choke 'em a little, it calms 'em." The hen does not calm though and Max shifts her further upside down, a claw catches his shirt. "Shit!" He drops the hen and Barb grabs her. "You hurt?"

"No. Just a scratch." She holds the bird while Max probes. He spreads the feathers to show Andrews the dry tight yellow vent. "Ahh." Max lifts her, calm now, and drops her in the cage with the other cull. She flutters once and is still.

He smiles at Andrews. "Dinner."

When they come back to the house, Andrews is still high, still enchanted with the world. But something has changed inside. One of the girls gives him a quick look, then goes back to her book. Andrews sweeps his eyes slowly around the room. He says, "Where's my wife?" No one answers.

He pauses for only a second as he reaches his wife's door—the hairs on his wrists move and his hand stops before touching the knob—then he twists, pushes.

Charlotte is sitting on the bed with Burns. Burns has both of her hands in his and he is leaning to kiss her. Before Burns can rise, Andrews has pulled him to his feet. He hits him in the stomach. Burns gasps with astonishment and Andrews hits him again. Charlotte spits, "Bastard!" and grabs at his arms. Andrews can feel the rhythm of it, he is hurting Burns, hear him grunt, but Charlotte is pushing him back and Burns is rising with his hands outstretched. "Stop it!" Charlotte yells as Andrews feints at her, tries to swing. He feels better than he has in months. Life is coursing through his body. It is as if he is back in conditioning, running laps, working the G-force simulator. He is aware of everything: Burns's sick pallor as he sits on the bed, Charlotte's tense crouch of fear and anger mingled with something else, her ragged breathing, the slight breeze that touches the sweat on his face and arms and moves the curtain from the pale light of the full moon into the bedside lamp's incandescence, his hands opening and closing as Burns waves Charlotte aside, looks at Andrews sadly, and asks, "Do you want to talk about it?"

Yes, there are climaxes, brief spurts of passion, jumps of energy, but they resolve nothing. The stories do not end neatly, much as we need them to. Our lives are incomprehensibly tangled. The need for climaxes and resolutions drives us to our madnesses, our fictions. For the world is round and nothing but round, there are only the soft risings and failings, the continual fall of day into night, the endless plummet through space without end or beginning. We drift, we live, we die, but death is not an end because the race goes on building pyramids and roads, launching rockets. Survive or perish, we each fill some role. But he is not a hero or a myth. America is not Greece or Olympus. Mere night rushes past his car. Three billion people on a single planet, the moon's dead light upon them.

He looks at the speedometer and sees with shock the needle at 100. He slows, the Thruway slows beneath him, and he drives calmly all the rest of the way back to Teaneck.

That week his book proposal is returned with a polite letter; his name at least has brought him the courtesy of a personal response. The editor explains how interesting the poetry looks, how intrigued he is by the prospects, but why he must reluctantly refuse. The letter goes on to state that an account of his voyage would be of interest, but he is no longer assured of selling even that on the strength of his name.

The next day he gets his renewal notice from the Air Force. He thinks of his $2,500 a month, he thinks of Kevin's college, he thinks of his $20,000 in the bank. He has two days to decide. He thinks of four years ahead of him, of retirement and pension at forty-four.

For some reason he goes to the typewriter. He sits at it for a long time, silent. Minutes pass, and then with great definiteness, he types his name, slowly and precisely. J. O. H. N. John, I have needs too. C. H. R. I. S. T. Christ, if you knew what you looked like. I. What am I? E. A. N. D. And the fear of God that had come on him in the capsule. R. E. W. S. The key strokes echo through the house.

With Kevin, he watches the last Apollo unfold on television. They have been in orbit for two days now. NBC shows film of the launch. He hears Mission Control count down in its clear passionless voice. Andrews tenses, remembering the rocket's thrust, that great fist crushing him, solid ground falling from him, the horizon canting in the window, blue sky fading to black, the noise of the booster dwindling, gravity abating, and then the slow silent dance of Earth below. On the screen, smoke curls, cables fall, but the rocket is still, even past zero. In the cabin it feels like liftoff starts ten seconds early; from the ground it appears ten seconds late.

Now the rocket moves. The Saturn V has generated sufficient force, and it rises, slowly, majestically disencumbering itself of gravity. What sexual energy a rocket had. Charlotte had been at the lunar liftoff and she said later it was so sensual, so compelling, that warm sympathetic pulsings had started within her. When it was over, she said, people hurried away, awed and embarrassed by that immense potency.

Or, rather, force: for NASA had stripped rockets of potency. The first rockets delivered missiles. They flew, fell, exploded. Their trajectories were dramatic curves. But at science's imperative, now they flew straight up, out, dropped stages to hurl a payload of men at a weightless point in the sky. There was no arc to that, no climax. Andrews sees now that drama and sex are inextricably linked, that the rise and curve of one is the same as the other. Anything without a climax is ultimately disappointing. Give us missiles, not spaceships.

NBC is live again. The two ships orbit. The screen is dark with static and crackling voices. They are positioning a camera to follow the docking. The Earth rolls slowly beneath, Apollo roams the skies. Over the far curving horizon is a dot, a hint of movement. Soyuz approaches, gaining dimension. It elongates. There is a garbled interchange of static, Russian, and English mixed.

"Can you understand it, Dad?"

"Shh."

The Russian manned program will continue, he has heard. So, imagining himself in space, he feels vaguely threatened by the sight of Soyuz. Perhaps he projects his own tension into the voice of the American pilot, but it seems to Andrews as jauntily nervous as a virgin on his first date.

The far craft inclines in its approach. The two ships whisper through vast statics, they make minor adjustments as their trajectories close. The radio energy is dense as they make ready to touch. Electrons move, patterns shift. Data flickers in great networks around the world.

Kevin is leaning forward, his breath coming quick and shallow. In the moment before contact he hunches, feeling the shadow of contacts to come in this one. In the screen's light Andrews sees everything embedded in its moment: blue flickers on the wet brown beer bottle he has not touched, Kevin's rapt face washed pale, his own reclining posture, a roll of fat at his once-solid belly.

The ships link. Apollo mates with Soyuz. The gates are open, static floods between them, the astronauts and cosmonauts can move between vessels. The mission is consummated, the program is over. The camera drifts and Earth swims slowly under it. Ochres, blues, whites, haloed in static. The moon forgotten.

Something recedes in Andrews.

It is his fortieth birthday.

In the yard he studies the moon, and the empty blackness where the two vessels reel and clasp each other. The crews will shuttle between crafts for a bit, trade dull laborious jokes and dry paste meals, then disengage and return to Earth, nothing reached, nothing resolved. The first time America pulled back from a frontier.

When he goes in, Kevin is gone. He turns off the television. On impulse he goes to the attic to get the heavy binoculars he bought years ago in Okinawa. There is the smell of time behind the attic door, a musty wasting smell that makes him feel heartsick and lost. The attic is neat and orderly, but he cannot find the binoculars. Finally he steps back out, shuts the door.

He stands in the hall, feeling the house's emptiness. He listens to its hums and murmurs. Downstairs in the dark the refrigerator turns on. He is numb. He stands in a paralyzed panic at the top of the long dim stairway, unmoving for several minutes.

There is a ringing in his ears now and his hands are cold. He drifts down the hall into Kevin's room. It is dark, with only a pale illumination flooding from one window. The moon is gibbous again, waning back through all its phases. It is very late, after midnight; a new day has started.

Kevin lies angled back on the bed, binoculars propped by thin white arms bent double against his chest. Andrews enters but does not sit on the bed for fear of breaking the view. Nor does he speak. A minute drags by. Andrews is trembling. He says, "What do you see?"

His son shrugs. "Craters."

He looks and sees the blurred patches of gray against white. Copernicus, Ptolemy, Clavius . . . the dead. He feels remote and cold and untouchable. Kevin looks at him.

"Dad? Are we ever going back there?"

He sighed, tired, or on the edge of sorrow, though sorrow was a pointless thing. Waves receded from him. Each word broke a vast illimitable silence. "I don't know, son. I don't know."

Kim Stanley Robinson is a bestselling author and winner of the Hugo, Nebula, and Locus awards. He is the author of more than twenty books, including the bestselling Mars trilogy and the critically acclaimed *Forty Signs of Rain, The Years of Rice and Salt,* and *2312.* In 2008, he was named a Hero of the Environment by *Time* magazine, and he works with the Sierra Nevada Research Institute. His latest novel is *Red Moon.*

THE LUNATICS
Kim Stanley Robinson

They were very near the center of the moon, Jakob told them. He was the newest member of the bullpen, but already their leader.

"How do you know?" Solly challenged him. It was stifling, the hot air thick with the reek of their sweat, and a pungent stink from the waste bucket in the corner. In the pure black, under the blanket of the rock's basalt silence, their shifting and snuffling loomed large, defined the size of the pen. "I suppose you see it with your third eye."

Jakob had a laugh as big as his hands. He was a big man, never a doubt of that. "Of course not, Solly. The third eye is for seeing in the black. It's a natural sense just like the others. It takes all the data from the rest of the senses, and processes them into a visual image transmitted by the third optic nerve, which runs from the forehead to the sight centers at the back of the brain. But you can only focus it by an act of the will—same as with all the other senses. It's not magic. We just never needed it till now."

"So how do you know?"

"It's a problem in spherical geometry, and I solved it. Oliver and I solved it. This big vein of blue runs right down into the core, I believe, down into the moon's molten heart where we can never go. But we'll follow it as far as we can. Note how light we're getting. There's less gravity near the center of things."

"I feel heavier than ever."

"You are heavy, Solly. Heavy with disbelief."

"Where's Freeman?" Hester said in her crow's rasp.

No one replied.

Oliver stirred uneasily over the rough basalt of the pen's floor. First Naomi, then mute Elijah, now Freeman. Somewhere out in the shafts and caverns, tunnels and corridors—somewhere in the dark maze of mines, people were disappearing. Their pen was emptying, it seemed. And the other pens?

"Free at last," Jakob murmured.

"There's something out there," Hester said, fear edging her harsh voice, so that it scraped Oliver's nerves like the screech of an ore car's wheels over a too-sharp bend in the tracks. "Something out there!"

The rumor had spread through the bullpens already, whispered mouth to ear or in huddled groups of bodies. There were thousands of shafts bored through the rock, hundreds of chambers and caverns. Lots of these were closed off, but many more were left open, and there was room to hide—miles and miles of it. First some of their cows had disappeared. Now it was people too. And Oliver had heard a miner jabbering at the low edge of hysteria, about a giant foreman gone mad after an accident took both his arms at the shoulder—the arms had been replaced by prostheses, and the foreman had escaped into the black, where he preyed on miners off by themselves, ripping them up, feeding on them—

They all heard the steely squeak of a car's wheel. Up the mother shaft, past cross tunnel Forty; had to be foremen at this time of shift. Would the car turn at the fork to their concourse? Their hypersensitive ears focused on the distant sound; no one breathed. The wheels squeaked, turned their way. Oliver, who was already shivering, began to shake hard.

The car stopped before their pen. The door opened, all in darkness. Not a sound from the quaking miners.

Fierce white light blasted them and they cried out, leaped back against the cage bars vainly. Blinded, Oliver cringed at the clawing of a foreman's hands, searching under his shirt and pants. Through pupils like pinholes he glimpsed brief black-and-white snapshots of gaunt bodies undergoing similar searches, then blows. Shouts, cries of pain, smack of flesh on flesh, an electric buzzing. Shaving their heads, could it be that time again already? He was struck in the stomach, choked around the neck. Hester's long wiry brown arms, wrapped around her head. Scalp burned, *buzzz* all chopped up. Thrown to the rock.

"Where's the twelfth?" In the foremen's staccato language. No one answered.

The foremen left, light receding with them until it was black again, the pure dense black that was their own. Except now it was swimming with bright red bars, washing around in painful tears. Oliver's third eye opened a little, which calmed him, because it was still a new experience; he could make out his companions, dim redblack shapes in the black, huddled over themselves, gasping.

Jakob moved among them, checking for hurts, comforting. He cupped Oliver's forehead and Oliver said, "It's seeing already."

"Good work." On his knees Jakob clumped to their shit bucket, took off the lid, reached in. He pulled something out. Oliver marveled at how clearly he was able to see all this. Before, floating blobs of color had drifted in the black; but he had always assumed they were afterimages, or hallucinations. Only with Jakob's instruction had he been able to perceive the patterns they made, the vision that they constituted. It was an act of will. That was the key.

Now, as Jakob cleaned the object with his urine and spit, Oliver found that the eye in his forehead saw even more, in sharp blood etchings. Jakob held the lump overhead, and it seemed it was a little lamp, pouring light over them in a wavelength they had always been able to see, but had never needed before. By its faint ghostly radiance the whole pen was made clear, a structure etched in blood, redblack on black. "Promethium," Jakob breathed. The miners crowded around him, faces lifted to it. Solly had a little pug nose, and squinched his face terribly in the effort to focus. Hester had a face to go with her voice, stark bones under skin scored with lines. "The most precious element. On Earth our masters rule by it. All their civilization is based on it, on the movement inside it, electrons escaping their shells and crashing into neutrons, giving off heat and more blue as well. So they condemn us to a life of pulling it out of the moon for them."

He chipped at the chunk with a thumbnail. They all knew precisely its clayey texture, its heaviness, the dull silvery gray of it, which pulsed green under some lasers, blue under others. Jakob gave each of them a sliver of it. "Take it between two molars and crush hard. Then swallow."

"It's poison, isn't it?" said Solly.

"After years and years." The big laugh, filling the black. "We don't have years and years, you know that. And in the short run it helps your vision in the black. It strengthens the will."

Oliver put the soft heavy sliver between his teeth, chomped down, felt the metallic jolt, swallowed. It throbbed in him. He could see the others' faces, the mesh of the pen walls, the pens farther down the concourse, the robot tracks—all in the lightless black.

"Promethium is the moon's living substance," Jakob said quietly. "We walk in the nerves of the moon, tearing them out under the lash of the foremen. The shafts are a map of where the neurons used to be. As they drag the moon's mind out by its roots, to take it back to Earth and use it for their own enrichment, the lunar consciousness fills us and we become its mind ourselves, to save it from extinction."

They joined hands: Solly, Hester, Jakob and Oliver. The surge of energy passed through them, leaving a sweet afterglow.

Then they lay down on their rock bed, and Jakob told them tales of his home, of the Pacific dockyards, of the cliffs and wind and waves, and the way

the sun's light lay on it all. Of the jazz in the bars, and how trumpet and clar-
inet could cross each other. "How do you remember?" Solly asked plaintively.
"They turned me blank."

Jakob laughed hard. "I fell on my mother's knitting needles when I was a
boy, and one went right up my nose. Chopped the hippocampus in two. So all
my life my brain has been storing what memories it can somewhere else. They
burned a dead part of me, and left the living memory intact."

"Did it hurt?" Hester croaked.

"The needles? You bet. A flash like the foremen's prods, right there in the
center of me. I suppose the moon feels the same pain, when we mine her.
But I'm grateful now, because it opened my third eye right at that moment.
Ever since then I've seen with it. And down here, without our third eye it's
nothing but the black."

Oliver nodded, remembering.

"And something out there," croaked Hester.

Next shift start Oliver was keyed by a foreman, then made his way through
the dark to the end of the long, slender vein of blue he was working. Oliver
was a tall youth, and some of the shaft was low; no time had been wasted
smoothing out the vein's irregular shape. He had to crawl between the narrow
tracks bolted to the rocky uneven floor, scraping through some gaps as if
working through a great twisted intestine.

At the shaft head he turned on the robot, a long low-slung metal box
on wheels. He activated the laser drill, which faintly lit the exposed surface
of the blue, blinding him for some time. When he regained a certain visual
equilibrium—mostly by ignoring the weird illumination of the drill beam—
he typed instructions into the robot, and went to work drilling into the face,
then guiding the robot's scoop and hoist to the broken pieces of blue. When
the big chunks were in the ore cars behind the robot, he jackhammered loose
any fragments of the ore that adhered to the basalt walls, and added them to
the cars before sending them off.

This vein was tapering down, becoming a mere tendril in the lunar body,
and there was less and less room to work in. Soon the robot would be too big
for the shaft, and they would have to bore through basalt; they would follow
the tendril to its very end, hoping for a bole or a fan.

At first Oliver didn't much mind the shift's work. But IR-directed cameras on the robot surveyed him as well as the shaft face, and occasional shocks
from its prod reminded him to keep hustling. And in the heat and bad air,
as he grew ever more famished, it soon enough became the usual desperate,
painful struggle to keep to the required pace.

Time disappeared into that zone of endless agony that was the latter part of a shift. Then he heard the distant klaxon of shift's end, echoing down the shaft like a cry in a dream. He turned the key in the robot and was plunged into noiseless black, the pure absolute of Nonbeing. Too tired to try opening his third eye, Oliver started back up the shaft by feel, following the last ore car of the shift. It rolled quickly ahead of him and was gone.

In the new silence distant mechanical noises were like creaks in the rock. He measured out the shift's work, having marked its beginning on the shaft floor: eighty-nine lengths of his body. Average.

It took a long time to get back to the junction with the shaft above his. Here there was a confluence of veins and the room opened out, into an odd chamber some seven feet high, but wider than Oliver could determine in every direction. When he snapped his fingers there was no rebound at all. The usual light at the far end of the low chamber was absent. Feeling sand- wiched between two endless rough planes of rock, Oliver experienced a sud- den claustrophobia; there was a whole world overhead, he was buried alive . . . He crouched and every few steps tapped one rail with his ankle, navigating blindly, a hand held forward to discover any dips in the ceiling.

He was somewhere in the middle of this space when he heard a noise behind him. He froze. Air pushed at his face. It was completely dark, com- pletely silent. The noise squeaked behind him again: a sound like a fingernail, brushed along the banded metal of piano wire. It ran right up his spine, and he felt the hair on his forearms pull away from the dried sweat and stick straight out. He was holding his breath. Very slow footsteps were placed soft- ly behind him, perhaps forty feet away . . . an airy snuffle, like a big nostril sniffing. For the footsteps to be so spaced out it would have to be . . .

Oliver loosened his joints, held one arm out and the other forward, tip- toed away from the rail, at right angles to it, for twelve feathery steps. In the lunar gravity he felt he might even float. Then he sank to his knees, breathed through his nose as slowly as he could stand to. His heart knocked at the back of his throat, he was sure it was louder than his breath by far. Over that noise and the roar of blood in his ears he concentrated his hearing to the utmost pitch. Now he could hear the faint sounds of ore cars and perhaps miners and foremen, far down the tunnel that led from the far side of this chamber back to the pens. Even as faint as they were, they obscured further his chances of hearing whatever it was in the cavern with him.

The footsteps had stopped. Then came another metallic *scrick* over the rail, heard against a light sniff. Oliver cowered, held his arms hard against his sides, knowing he smelled of sweat and fear. Far down the distant shaft a foreman spoke sharply. If he could reach that voice . . . He resisted the urge to run for it, feeling sure somehow that whatever was in there with him was fast.

Another *scrick*. Oliver cringed, trying to reduce his echo profile. There was a chip of rock under his hand. He fingered it, hand shaking. His forehead throbbed and he understood it was his third eye, straining to pierce the black silence and *see* . . .

A shape with pillar-thick legs, all in blocks of redblack. It was some sort of . . .

Scrick. Sniff. It was turning his way. A flick of the wrist, the chip of rock skittered, hitting ceiling and then floor, back in the direction he had come from.

Very slow soft footsteps, as if the legs were somehow . . . they were coming in his direction.

He straightened and reached above him, hands scrabbling over the rough basalt. He felt a deep groove in the rock, and next to it a vertical hole. He jammed a hand in the hole, made a fist; put the fingers of the other hand along the side of the groove, and pulled himself up. The toes of his boot fit the groove, and he flattened up against the ceiling. In the lunar gravity he could stay there forever. Holding his breath.

Step . . . step . . . snuffle, fairly near the floor, which had given him the idea for this move. He couldn't turn to look. He felt something scrape the hip pocket of his pants and thought he was dead, but fear kept him frozen; and the sounds moved off into the distance of the vast chamber, without a pause.

He dropped to the ground and bolted doubled over for the far tunnel, which loomed before him redblack in the black, exuding air and faint noise. He plunged right in it, feeling one wall nick a knuckle. He took the sharp right he knew was there and threw himself down to the intersection of floor and wall. Footsteps padded by him, apparently running on the rails.

When he couldn't hold his breath any longer he breathed. Three or four minutes passed and he couldn't bear to stay still. He hurried to the intersection, turned left and slunk to the bullpen. At the checkpoint the monitor's horn squawked and a foreman blasted him with a searchlight, pawed him roughly. "Hey!" The foreman held a big chunk of blue, taken from Oliver's hip pocket. What was this?

"Sorry boss," Oliver said jerkily, trying to see it properly, remembering the thing brushing him as it passed under. "Must've fallen in." He ignored the foreman's curse and blow, and fell into the pen tearful with the pain of the light, with relief at being back among the others. Every muscle in him was shaking.

But Hester never came back from that shift.

Sometime later the foremen came back into their bullpen, wielding the lights and the prods to line them up against one mesh wall. Through pinprick pupils

Oliver saw just the grossest slabs of shapes, all grainy black-and-gray: Jakob was a big stout man, with a short black beard under the shaved head, and eyes that popped out, glittering even in Oliver's silhouette world.

"Miners are disappearing from your pen," the foreman said, in the miners' language. His voice was like the quartz they tunneled through occasionally: hard, and sparkly with cracks and stresses, as if it might break at any moment into a laugh or a scream.

No one answered.

Finally Jakob said, "We know."

The foreman stood before him. "They started disappearing when you arrived."

Jakob shrugged. "Not what I hear."

The foreman's searchlight was right on Jakob's face, which stood out brilliantly, as if two of the searchlights were pointed at each other. Oliver's third eye suddenly opened and gave the face substance: brown skin, heavy brows, scarred scalp. Not at all the white cutout blazing from the black shadows. "You'd better be careful, miner."

Loudly enough to be heard from neighboring pens, Jakob said, "Not my fault if something out there is eating us, boss."

The foreman struck him. Lights bounced and they all dropped to the floor for protection, presenting their backs to the boots. Rain of blows, pain of blows. Still, several pens had to have heard him.

Foremen gone. White blindness returned to black blindness, to the death velvet of their pure darkness. For a long time they lay in their own private worlds, hugging the warm rock of the floor, feeling the bruises blush. Then Jakob crawled around and squatted by each of them, placing his hands on their foreheads. "Oh yeah," he would say. "You're okay. Wake up now. Look around you." And in the after-black they stretched and stretched, quivering like dogs on a scent. The bulks in the black, the shapes they made as they moved and groaned . . . yes, it came to Oliver again, and he rubbed his face and looked around, eyes shut to help him see. "I ran into it on the way back in," he said.

They all went still. He told them what had happened. "The blue in your pocket?"

They considered his story in silence. No one understood it.

No one spoke of Hester. Oliver found he couldn't. She had been his friend. To live without that gaunt crow's voice . . .

Sometime later the side door slid up, and they hurried into the barn to eat. The chickens squawked as they took the eggs, the cows mooed as they milked them. The stove plates turned the slightest bit luminous—redblack, again—and by their light his three eyes saw all. Solly cracked and fried eggs.

Oliver went to work on his vats of cheese, pulled out a round of it that was ready. Jakob sat at the rear of one cow and laughed as it turned to butt his knee. *Splish splish! Splish splish!* When he was done he picked up the cow and put it down in front of its hay, where it chomped happily. Animal stink of them all, the many fine smells of food cutting through it. Jakob laughed at his cow, which butted his knee again as if objecting to the ridicule. "Little pig of a cow, little piglet. Mexican cows. They bred for this size, you know. On Earth the ordinary cow is as tall as Oliver, and about as big as this whole pen."

They laughed at the idea, not believing him. The buzzer cut them off, and the meal was over. Back into their pen, to lay their bodies down.

Still no talk of Hester, and Oliver found his skin crawling again as he recalled his encounter with whatever it was that sniffed through the mines. Jakob came over and asked him about it, sounding puzzled. Then he handed Oliver a rock. "Imagine this is a perfect sphere, like a baseball."

"Baseball?"

"Like a ball bearing, perfectly round and smooth you know."

Ah yes. Spherical geometry again. Trigonometry too. Oliver groaned, resisting the work. Then Jakob got him interested despite himself, in the intricacy of it all, the way it all fell together in a complex but comprehensible pattern. Sine and cosine, so clear! And the clearer it got the more he could see: the mesh of the bullpen, the network of shafts and tunnels and caverns piercing the jumbled fabric of the moon's body . . . all clear lines of redblack on black, like the metal of the stove plate as it just came visible, and all from Jakob's clear, patiently fingered, perfectly balanced equations. He could see through rock.

"Good work," Jakob said when Oliver got tired. They lay there among the others, shifting around to find hollows for their hips.

Silence of the off-shift. Muffled clanks downshaft, floor trembling at a detonation miles of rock away; ears popped as air smashed into the dead end of their tunnel, compressed to something nearly liquid for just an instant. Must have been a Boesman. Ringing silence again.

"So what is it, Jakob?" Solly asked when they could hear each other again.

"It's an element," Jakob said sleepily. "A strange kind of element, nothing else like it. Promethium. Number 61 on the periodic table. A rare earth, a lanthanide, an inner transition metal. We're finding it in veins of an ore called monazite, and in pure grains and nuggets scattered in the ore."

Impatient, almost pleading: "But what makes it so special?"

For a long time Jakob didn't answer. They could hear him thinking. Then he said, "Atoms have a nucleus, made of protons and neutrons bound together. Around this nucleus shells of electrons spin, and each shell is either full or trying to get full, to balance with the number of protons—to balance the positive and negative charges. An atom is like a human heart, you see.

"Now promethium is radioactive, which means it's out of balance, and parts of it are breaking free. But promethium never reaches its balance, because it radiates in a manner that increases its instability rather than the reverse. Promethium atoms release energy in the form of positrons, flying free when neutrons are hit by electrons. But during that impact more neutrons appear in the nucleus. Seems they're coming from nowhere. So each atom of the blue is a power loop in itself, giving off energy perpetually. Some people say that they're little white holes, every single atom of them. Burning forever at nine hundred and forty curies per gram. Bringing energy into our universe from somewhere else. Little gateways."

Solly's sigh filled the black, expressing incomprehension for all of them. "So it's poisonous?"

"It's dangerous, sure, because the positrons breaking away from it fly right through flesh like ours. Mostly they never touch a thing in us, because that's how close to phantoms we are—mostly blood, which is almost light. That's why we can see each other so well. But sometimes a beta particle will hit something small on its way through. Could mean nothing or it could kill you on the spot. Eventually it'll get us all."

Oliver fell asleep dreaming of threads of light like concentrations of the foremen's fierce flashes, passing right through him. Shifts passed in their timeless round. They ached when they woke on the warm basalt floor, they ached when they finished the long work shifts. They were hungry and often injured. None of them could say how long they had been there. None of them could say how old they were. Sometimes they lived without light other than the robots' lasers and the stove plates. Sometimes the foremen visited with their scorching lighthouse beams every off-shift, shouting questions and beating them. Apparently cows were disappearing, cylinders of air and oxygen, supplies of all sorts. None of it mattered to Oliver but the spherical geometry. He knew where he was, he could see it. The three-dimensional map in his head grew more extensive every shift. But everything else was fading away . . .

"So it's the most powerful substance in the world," Solly said. "But why us? Why are we here?"

"You don't know?" Jakob said.

"They blanked us, remember? All that's gone."

But because of Jakob, they knew what was up there: the domed palaces on the lunar surface, the fantastic luxuries of Earth . . . when he spoke of it, in fact, a lot of Earth came back to them, and they babbled and chattered at the unexpected upwellings. Memories that deep couldn't be blanked without killing, Jakob said. And so they prevailed after all, in a way.

But there was much that had been burnt forever. And so Jakob sighed. "Yeah yeah, I remember. I just thought—well. We're here for different reasons. Some were criminals. Some complained."

"Like Hester!" They laughed.

"Yeah, I suppose that's what got her here. But a lot of us were just in the wrong place at the wrong time. Wrong politics or skin or whatever. Wrong look on your face."

"That was me, I bet," Solly said, and the others laughed at him. "Well I got a funny face, I know I do! I can feel it."

Jakob was silent for a long time. "What about you?" Oliver asked. More silence. The rumble of a distant detonation, like muted thunder.

"I wish I knew. But I'm like you in that. I don't remember the actual arrest. They must have hit me on the head. Given me a concussion. I must have said something against the mines, I guess. And the wrong people heard me."

"Bad luck."

"Yeah. Bad luck."

More shifts passed. Oliver rigged a timepiece with two rocks, a length of detonation cord and a set of pulleys, and confirmed over time what he had come to suspect; the work shifts were getting longer. It was more and more difficult to get all the way through one, harder to stay awake for the meals and the geometry lessons during the off-shifts. The foremen came every off-shift now, blasting in with their searchlights and shouts and kicks, leaving in a swirl of afterimages and pain. Solly went out one shift cursing them under his breath, and never came back. Disappeared. The foremen beat them for it and Oliver shouted with rage. "It's not our fault! There's something out there, I saw it! It's killing us!"

Then next shift his little tendril of a vein bloomed, he couldn't find any rock around the blue: a big bole. He would have to tell the foremen, start working in a crew. He dismantled his clock.

On the way back he heard the footsteps again, shuffling along slowly behind him. This time he was at the entrance to the last tunnel, the pens close behind him. He turned to stare into the darkness with his third eye, willing himself to see the thing. Whoosh of air, a sniff, a footfall on the rail ... Far across the thin wedge of air a beam of light flashed, making a long narrow cone of white talc. Steel tracks gleamed where the wheels of the car burnished them. Pupils shrinking like a snail's antennae, he stared back at the footsteps, saw nothing. Then, just barely, two points of red: retinas, reflecting the distant lance of light. They blinked. He bolted and ran again, reached the foremen at the checkpoint in seconds. They blinded him as he panted, passed him through and into the bullpen.

After the meal on that shift Oliver lay trembling on the floor of the bullpen and told Jakob about it. "I'm scared, Jakob. Solly, Hester, Freeman, mute Lije, Naomi—they're all gone. Everyone I know here is gone but us."

"Free at last," Jakob said shortly. "Here, let's do your problems for tonight."

"I don't care about them."

"You have to care about them. Nothing matters unless you do. That blue is the mind of the moon being torn away, and the moon knows it. If we learn what the network says in its shapes, then the moon knows that too, and we're suffered to live."

"Not if that thing finds us!"

"You don't know. Anyway nothing to be done about it. Come on, let's do the lesson. We need it."

So they worked on equations in the dark. Both were distracted and the work went slowly; they fell asleep in the middle of it, right there on their faces.

Shifts passed. Oliver pulled a muscle in his back, and excavating the bole he had found was an agony of discomfort. When the bole was cleared it left a space like the interior of an egg, ivory and black and quite smooth, punctuated only by the bluish spots of other tendrils of monazite extending away through the basalt. They left a catwalk across the central space, with decks cut into the rock on each side, and ramps leading to each of the veins of blue; and began drilling on their own again, one man and robot team to each vein. At each shift's end Oliver rushed to get to the egg-chamber at the same time as all the others, so that he could return the rest of the way to the bullpen in a crowd. This worked well until one shift came to an end with the hoist chock-full of the ore. It took him some time to dump it into the ore car and shut down.

So he had to cross the catwalk alone, and he would be alone all the way back to the pens. Surely it was past time to move the pens closer to the shaft heads! He didn't want to do this . . .

Halfway across the catwalk he heard a faint noise ahead of him. *Scrick; scriiiiiik.* He jerked to a stop, held the rail hard. Couldn't reach the ceiling here. Back stabbing its protest, he started to climb over the railing. He could hang from the underside.

He was right on the top of the railing when he was seized up by a number of strong cold hands. He opened his mouth to scream and his mouth was filled with wet clay. The blue. His head was held steady and his ears filled with the same stuff, so that the sounds of his own terrified sharp nasal exhalations were suddenly cut off. Promethium; it would kill him. It hurt his back to struggle on. He was being carried horizontally, ankles whipped, arms tied against his body. Then plugs of the clay were shoved up his nose and in the middle of a final paroxysm of resistance his mind fell away into the black.

The lowest whisper in the world said, "Oliver Pen Twelve." He heard the voice with his stomach. He was astonished to be alive.

"You will never be given anything again. Do you accept the charge?"

He struggled to nod. I never wanted anything! he tried to say. I only wanted a life like anyone else.

"You will have to fight for every scrap of food, every swallow of water, every breath of air. Do you accept the charge?"

I accept the charge. I welcome it.

"In the eternal night you will steal from the foremen, kill the foremen, oppose their work in every way. Do you accept the charge?" I welcome it.

"You will live free in the mind of the moon. Will you take up this charge?"

He sat up. His mouth was clear, filled only with the sharp electric aftertaste of the blue. He saw the shapes around him: there were five of them, five people there. And suddenly he understood. Joy ballooned in him and he said, "I will. Oh, I will!"

A light appeared. Accustomed as he was either to no light or to intense blasts of it, Oliver at first didn't comprehend. He thought his third eye was rapidly gaining power. As perhaps it was. But there was also a laser drill from one of the A robots, shot at low power through a cylindrical ceramic electronic element, in a way that made the cylinder glow yellow. Blind like a fish, open-mouthed, weak eyes gaping and watering floods, he saw around him Solly, Hester, Freeman, mute Elijah, Naomi. "Yes," he said, and tried to embrace them all at once. "Oh, yes."

They were in one of the long-abandoned caverns, a flat-bottomed bole with only three tendrils extending away from it. The chamber was filled with objects Oliver was more used to identifying by feel or sound or smell: pens of cows and hens, a stack of air cylinders and suits, three ore cars, two B robots, an A robot, a pile of tracks and miscellaneous gear. He walked through it all slowly, Hester at his side. She was gaunt as ever, her skin as dark as the shadows; it sucked up the weak light from the ceramic tube and gave it back only in little points and lines. "Why didn't you tell me?"

"It was the same for all of us. This is the way."

"And Naomi?"

"The same for her too; but when she agreed to it, she found herself alone."

Then it was Jakob, he thought suddenly. "Where's Jakob?"

Rasped: "He's coming, we think."

Oliver nodded, thought about it. "Was it you, then, following me those times? Why didn't you speak?"

"That wasn't us," Hester said when he explained what had happened. She cawed a laugh. "That was something else, still out there . . ."

Then Jakob stood before them, making them both jump. They shouted and the others all came running, pressed into a mass together. Jakob laughed. "All here now," he said. "Turn that light off. We don't need it."

And they didn't. Laser shut down, ceramic cooled, they could still see: they could see right into each other, red shapes in the black, radiating joy. Everything in the little chamber was quite distinct, quite *visible*.

"We are the mind of the moon."

Without shifts to mark the passage of time Oliver found he could not judge it at all. They worked hard, and they were constantly on the move: always up, through level after level of the mine. "Like shells of the atom, and we're that particle, busted loose and on its way out." They ate when they were famished, slept when they had to. Most of the time they worked, either bringing down shafts behind them, or dismantling depots and stealing everything Jakob designated theirs. A few times they ambushed gangs of foremen, killing them with laser cutters and stripping them of valuables; but on Jakob's orders they avoided contact with foremen when they could. He wanted only material. After a long time—twenty sleeps at least—they had six ore cars of it, all trailing an A robot up long-abandoned and empty shafts, where they had to lay the track ahead of them and pull it out behind, as fast as they could move. Among other items Jakob had an insatiable hunger for explosives; he couldn't get enough of them.

It got harder to avoid the foremen, who were now heavily armed, and on their guard. Perhaps even searching for them, it was hard to tell. But they searched with their lighthouse beams on full power, to stay out of ambush: it was easy to see them at a distance, draw them off, lose them in dead ends, detonate mines under them. All the while the little band moved up, rising by infinitely long detours toward the front side of the moon. The rock around them cooled. The air circulated more strongly, until it was a constant wind. Through the seismometers they could hear from far below the rumbling of cars, heavy machinery, detonations. "Oh they're after us all right," Jakob said. "They're running scared."

He was happy with the booty they had accumulated, which included a great number of cylinders of compressed air and pure oxygen. Also vacuum suits for all of them, and a lot more explosives, including ten Boesmans, which were much too big for any ordinary mining. "We're getting close," Jakob said as they ate and drank, then tended the cows and hens. As they lay down to sleep by the cars he would talk to them about their work. Each of them had various jobs: mute Elijah was in charge of their supplies, Solly of the robot, Hester of the seismography. Naomi and Freeman were learning demolition, and were in some undefined sense Jakob's lieutenants. Oliver kept working at his navigation. They had found charts of the tunnel systems in their area, and Oliver was memorizing them, so that he would know at each moment exactly where they were. He found he could do it remarkably well; each time they ventured on he knew where the forks would come, where they would lead. Always upward.

But the pursuit was getting hotter. It seemed there were foremen everywhere, patrolling the shafts in search of them. "Soon they'll mine some passages and try to drive us into them," Jakob said. "It's about time we left."

"Left?" Oliver repeated.

"Left the system. Struck out on our own."

"Dig our own tunnel," Naomi said happily.

"Yes."

"To where?" Hester croaked.

Then they were rocked by an explosion that almost broke their eardrums, and the air rushed away. The rock around them trembled, creaked, groaned, cracked, and down the tunnel the ceiling collapsed, shoving dust toward them in a roaring *whoosh!* "A Boesman!" Solly cried.

Jakob laughed out loud. They were all scrambling into their vacuum suits as fast as they could. "Time to leave!" he cried, maneuvering their A robot against the side of the chamber. He put one of their Boesmans against the wall and set the timer. "Okay," he said over the suit's intercom. "Now we got to mine like we never mined before. To the surface!"

The first task was to get far enough away from the Boesman that they wouldn't be killed when it went off. They were now drilling a narrow tunnel and moving the loosened rock behind them to fill up the hole as they passed through it; this loose fill would fly like bullets down a rifle barrel when the Boesman went off. So they made three abrupt turns at acute angles to stop the fill's movement, and then drilled away from the area as fast as they could. Naomi and Jakob were confident that the explosion of the Boesman would shatter the surrounding rock to such an extent that it would never be possible for anyone to locate the starting point for their tunnel.

"Hopefully they'll think we did ourselves in," Naomi said, "either on purpose or by accident." Oliver enjoyed hearing her light laugh, her clear voice that was so pure and musical compared to Hester's croaking. He had never known Naomi well before, but now he admired her grace and power, her pulsing energy; she worked harder than Jakob, even. Harder than any of them.

A few shifts into their new life Naomi checked the detonator timer she kept on a cord around her neck. "It should be going off soon. Someone go try and keep the cows and chickens calmed down." But Solly had just reached the cows' pen when the Boesman went off. They were all sledge-hammered by the blast, which was louder than a mere explosion, something more basic and fundamental: the violent smash of a whole world shutting the door on them. Deafened, bruised, they staggered up and checked each other for serious injuries, then pacified the cows, whose terrified moos they felt in their hands rather than actually heard. The structural integrity of their tunnel seemed okay; they were in an old flow of the mantle's convection current, now cooled to stasis, and it was plastic enough to take such a blast without shattering. Perfect miners' rock, protecting them like a mother. They lifted up the cows and set them upright on the bottom of the ore car that had been made into the barn. Freeman hurried back down the tunnel to see how the rear of it looked. When he came back their hearing was returning, and through the ringing that would persist for several shifts he shouted, "It's walled off good! Fused!"

So they were in a little tunnel of their own. They fell together in a clump, hugging each other and shouting. "Free at last!" Jakob roared, booming out a laugh louder than anything Oliver had ever heard from him. Then they settled down to the task of turning on an air cylinder and recycler, and regulating their gas exchange.

They soon settled into a routine that moved their tunnel forward as quickly and quietly as possible. One of them operated the robot, digging as narrow a shaft as they could possibly work in. This person used only laser drills unless confronted with extremely hard rock, when it was judged worth the risk to set off small explosions, timed by seismometer to follow closely other detonations back in the mines; Jakob and Naomi hoped that the complex interior of the moon would prevent any listeners from noticing that their explosion was anything more than an echo of the mining blast.

Three of them dealt with the rock freed by the robot's drilling, moving it from the front of the tunnel to its rear, and at intervals pulling up the cars' tracks and bringing them forward. The placement of the loose rock was a serious matter, because if it displaced much more volume than it had at the front of the tunnel, they would eventually fill in all the open space they had; this was the classic problem of the "creeping worm" tunnel. It was necessary to pack the blocks into the space at the rear with an absolute minimum of gaps, in exactly the way they had been cut, like pieces of a puzzle; they all got very good at the craft of this, losing only a few inches of open space in every mile they dug. This work was the hardest both physically and mentally, and each shift of it left Oliver more tired than he had ever been while mining. Because the truth was all of them were working at full speed, and for the middle team it meant almost running, back and forth, back and forth, back and forth . . . Their little bit of open tunnel was only some sixty yards long, but after a while on the midshift it seemed like five hundred.

The three people not working on the rock tended the air and the livestock, ate, helped out with large blocks and the like, and snatched some sleep. They rotated one at a time through the three stations, and worked one shift (timed by detonator timer) at each post. It made for a routine so mesmerizing in its exhaustiveness that Oliver found it very hard to do his calculations of their position in his shift off. "You've got to keep at it," Jakob told him as he ran back from the robot to help the calculating. "It's not just anywhere we want to come up, but right under the domed city of Selene, next to the rocket rails. To do that we'll need some good navigation. We get that and we'll come up right in the middle of the masters who have gotten rich from selling the blue to Earth, and that will be a very gratifying thing I assure you."

So Oliver would work on it until he slept. Actually it was relatively easy; he knew where they had been in the moon when they struck out on their own, and Jakob had given him the surface coordinates for Selene: so it was just a matter of dead reckoning.

It was even possible to calculate their average speed, and therefore when they could expect to reach the surface. That could be checked against the rate of depletion of their fixed resources—air, water lost in the recycler, and food for the livestock. It took a few shifts of consultation with mute Elijah to determine all the factors reliably, and after that it was a simple matter of arithmetic.

When Oliver and Elijah completed these calculations they called Jakob over and explained what they had done.

"Good work," Jakob said. "I should have thought of that."

"But look," Oliver said, "we've got enough air and water, and the robot's power pack is ten times what we'll need—same with explosives—it's only food is a problem. I don't know if we've got enough hay for the cows."

Jakob nodded as he looked over Oliver's shoulder and examined their figures. "We'll have to kill and eat the cows one by one. That'll feed us and cut down on the amount of hay we need, at the same time."

"Eat the cows?" Oliver was stunned.

"Sure! They're meat! People on Earth eat them all the time!"

"Well ..." Oliver was doubtful, but under the lash of Hester's bitter laughter he didn't say any more.

Still, Jakob and Freeman and Naomi decided it would be best if they stepped up the pace a little bit, to provide them with more of a margin for error. They shifted two people to the shaft face and supplemented the robot's continuous drilling with hand drill work around the sides of the tunnel, and ate on the run while moving blocks to the back, and slept as little as they could. They were making miles on every shift.

The rock they wormed through began to change in character. The hard, dark, unbroken basalt gave way to lighter rock that was sometimes dangerously fractured. "Anorthosite," Jakob said. "We're reaching the crust." After that every shift brought them through a new zone of rock. Once they tunneled through great layers of calcium feldspar striped with basalt intrusions, so that it looked like badly made brick. Another time they blasted their way through a wall of jasper as hard as steel. Only once did they pass through a vein of the blue; when they did it occurred to Oliver that his whole conception of the moon's composition had been warped by their mining. He had thought the moon was bursting with promethium, but as they dug across the narrow vein he realized it was uncommon, a loose net of threads in the great lunar body.

As they left the vein behind, Solly picked up a piece of the ore and stared at it curiously, lower eyes shut, face contorted as he struggled to focus his third eye. Suddenly he dashed the chunk to the ground, turned and marched to the head of their tunnel, attacked it with a drill. "I've given my whole life to the blue," he said, voice thick. "And what is it but a Goddamned rock."

Jakob laughed shortly. They tunneled on, away from the precious metal that now represented to them only a softer material to dig through. "Pick up the pace!" Jakob cried, slapping Solly on the back and leaping over the blocks beside the robot. "This rock has melted and melted again, changing over eons to the stones we see. Metamorphosis," he chanted, stretching the word out, lingering on the syllable *mor* until the word became a kind of song. "Metamorphosis. Meta-*mor*-pho-sis." Naomi and Hester took up the chant, and mute Elijah tapped his drill against the robot in double time. Jakob chanted over it. "Soon we will come to the city of the masters, the domes of Xanadu with their glass and fruit and steaming pools, and their vases and sports and their fine aged wines. And then there will be a—"

"Meta*mor*phosis."

And they tunneled ever faster.

Sitting in the sleeping car, chewing on a cheese, Oliver regarded the bulk of Jakob lying beside him. Jakob breathed deeply, very tired, almost asleep. "How do you know about the domes?" Oliver asked him softly. "How do you know all the things that you know?"

"Don't know," Jakob muttered. "Everyone knows. Less they burn your brain. Put you in a hole to live out your life. I don't know much, boy. Make most of it up. Love of a moon. Whatever we need . . ." And he slept.

They came up through a layer of marble—white marble all laced with quartz, so that it gleamed and sparkled in their lightless sight, and made them feel as though they dug through stone made of their cows' good milk, mixed with water like diamonds. This went on for a long time, until it filled them up and they became intoxicated with its smooth muscly texture, with the sparks of light lazing out of it. "I remember once we went to see a jazz band," Jakob said to all of them. Puffing as he ran the white rock along the cars to the rear, stacked it ever so carefully. "It was in Richmond among all the docks and refineries and giant oil tanks and we were so drunk we kept getting lost. But finally we found it—huh!—and it was just this broken-down trumpeter and a back line. He played sitting in a chair and you could just see in his face that his life had been a tough scuffle. His hat covered his whole household. And trumpet is a young man's instrument, too, it tears your lip to tatters. So we sat down to drink not expecting a thing, and they started up the last song of a set. 'Bucket's Got a Hole in It.' Four bar blues, as simple as a song can get."

"Meta*mor*phosis," rasped Hester.

"Yeah! Like that. And this trumpeter started to play it. And they went through it over and over and over. Huh! They must have done it a hundred times. Two hundred times. And sure enough this trumpeter was playing low and half the time in his hat, using all the tricks a broken-down trumpeter uses to save his lip, to hide the fact that it went west thirty years before. But after a while that didn't matter, because he was playing. He was playing! Everything he had learned in all his life, all the music and all the sorry rest of it, all that was jammed into the poor old 'Bucket' and by God it was mind over matter time, because that old song began to *roll*. And still on the run he broke into it:

"Oh the buck-et's got a hole in it
Yeah the buck-et's got a hole in it
Say the buck-et's got a hole in it.
Can't buy no beer!"

And over again. Oliver, Solly, Freeman, Hester, Naomi—they couldn't help laughing. What Jakob came up with out of his unburnt past! Mute Elijah banged a car wall happily, then squeezed the udder of a cow between one verse and the next— "Can't buy no beer!—*Moo!*"

They all joined in, breathing or singing it. It fit the pace of their work perfectly: fast but not too fast, regular, repetitive, simple, endless. All the syllables got the same length, a bit syncopated, except "hole," which was stretched out, and "can't buy no beer," which was high and all stretched out, stretched into a great shout of triumph, which was crazy since what it was saying was bad news, or should have been. But the song made it a cry of joy, and every time it rolled around they sang it louder, more stretched out. Jakob scatted up and down and around the tune, and Hester found all kinds of higher harmonics in a voice like a saw cutting steel, and the old tune rocked over and over and over and over and over and over and over and over and over and over, in a great passacaglia, in the crucible where all poverty is wrenched to delight: the blues. Meta*mor*phosis. They sang it continuously for two shifts running, until they were all completely hypnotized by it; and then frequently, for long spells, for the rest of their time together.

It was sheer bad luck that they broke into a shaft from below, and that the shaft was filled with armed foremen; and worse luck that Jakob was working the robot, so that he was the first to leap out firing his hand drill like a weapon, and the only one to get struck by return fire before Naomi threw a knotchopper past him and blew the foremen to shreds. They got him on a car and rolled the robot back and pulled up the track and cut off in a new direction, leaving another Boesman behind to destroy evidence of their passing.

So they were all racing around with the blood and stuff still covering them and the cows mooing in distress and Jakob breathing through clenched teeth in double time, and only Hester and Oliver could sit in the car with him and try to tend him, ripping away the pants from a leg that was all cut up. Hester took a hand drill to cauterize the wounds that were bleeding hard, but Jakob shook his head at her, neck muscles bulging out. "Got the big artery inside of the thigh," he said through his teeth.

Hester hissed. "Come here," she croaked at Solly and the rest. "Stop that and come here!"

They were in a mass of broken quartz, the fractured clear crystals all pink with oxidation. The robot continued drilling away, the air cylinder hissed, the cows mooed. Jakob's breathing was harsh and somehow all of them were also breathing in the same way, irregularly, too fast; so that as his breathing slowed and calmed, theirs did too. He was lying back in the sleeping car, on a bed of hay, staring up at the fractured sparkling quartz ceiling of their tunnel, as if he could see far into it. "All these different kinds of rock," he said, his voice filled with wonder and pain. "You see, the moon itself was the world, once upon a time, and the Earth its moon; but there was an impact, and everything changed."

They cut a small side passage in the quartz and left Jakob there, so that when they filled in their tunnel as they moved on he was left behind, in his own deep crypt. And from then on the moon for them was only his big tomb, rolling through space till the sun itself died, as he had said it someday would.

Oliver got them back on a course, feeling radically uncertain of his navigational calculations now that Jakob was not there to nod over his shoulder to approve them. Dully he gave Naomi and Freeman the coordinates for Selene. "But what will we do when we get there?" Jakob had never actually made that clear. Find the leaders of the city, demand justice for the miners? Kill them? Get to the rockets of the great magnetic rail accelerators, and hijack one to Earth? Try to slip unnoticed into the populace?

"You leave that to us," Naomi said. "Just get us there." And he saw a light in Naomi's and Freeman's eyes that hadn't been there before. It reminded him of the thing that had chased him in the dark, the thing that even Jakob hadn't been able to explain; it frightened him.

So he set the course and they tunneled on as fast as they ever had. They never sang and they rarely talked; they threw themselves at the rock, hurt themselves in the effort, returned to attack it more fiercely than before. When he could not stave off sleep Oliver lay down on Jakob's dried blood, and bitterness filled him like a block of the anorthosite they wrestled with.

They were running out of hay. They killed a cow, ate its roasted flesh. The water recycler's filters were clogging, and their water smelled of urine. Hester listened to the seismometer as often as she could now, and she thought they were being pursued. But she also thought they were approaching Selene's underside.

Naomi laughed, but it wasn't like her old laugh. "You got us there, Oliver. Good work."

Oliver bit back a cry.

"Is it big?" Solly asked.

Hester shook her head. "Doesn't sound like it. Maybe twice the diameter of the Great Bole, not more."

"Good," Freeman said, looking at Naomi.

"But what will we do?" Oliver said.

Hester and Naomi and Freeman and Solly all turned to look at him, eyes blazing like twelve chunks of pure promethium. "We've got eight Boesmans left," Freeman said in a low voice. "All the rest of the explosives add up to a couple more. I'm going to set them just right. It'll be my best work ever, my masterpiece. And we'll blow Selene right off into space."

It took them ten shifts to get all the Boesmans placed to Freeman's and Naomi's satisfaction, and then another three to get far enough down and to one side to be protected from the shock of the blast, which luckily for them was directly upward against something that would give, and therefore would have less recoil.

Finally they were set, and they sat in the sleeping car in a circle of six, around the pile of components that sat under the master detonator. For a long time they just sat there cross-legged, breathing slowly and staring at it. Staring at each other, in the dark, in perfect redblack clarity. Then Naomi put both arms out, placed her hands carefully on the detonator's button. Mute Elijah put his hands on hers—then Freeman, Hester, Solly, finally Oliver—just in the order that Jakob had taken them. Oliver hesitated, feeling the flesh and bone under his hands, the warmth of his companions. He felt they should say something but he didn't know what it was.

"Seven," Hester croaked suddenly.

"Six," Freeman said.

Elijah blew air through his teeth, hard.

"Four," said Naomi.

"Three!" Solly cried.

"Two," Oliver said.

And they all waited a beat, swallowing hard, waiting for the moon and the man in the moon to speak to them. Then they pressed down on the button. They smashed at it with their fists, hit it so violently they scarcely felt the shock of the explosion.

They had put on vacuum suits and were breathing pure oxygen as they came up the last tunnel, clearing it of rubble. A great number of other shafts were revealed as they moved into the huge conical cavity left by the Boesmans; tunnels snaked away from the cavity in all directions, so that they had sudden long vistas of blasted tubes extending off into the depths of the moon they had come out of. And at the top of the cavity, struggling over its broken edge, over the rounded wall of a new crater . . .

It was black. It was not like rock. Spread across it was a spill of white points, some bright, some so faint that they disappeared into the black if you looked straight at them. There were thousands of these white points, scattered over a black dome that was not a dome . . . And there in the middle, almost directly overhead: a blue and white ball. Big, bright, blue, distant, rounded; half of it bright as a foreman's flash, the other half just a shadow . . . It was clearly round, a big ball in the . . . sky. In the sky.

Wordlessly they stood on the great pile of rubble ringing the edge of their hole. Half buried in the broken anorthosite were shards of clear plastic, steel struts, patches of green grass, fragments of metal, an arm, broken branches, a bit of orange ceramic. Heads back to stare at the ball in the sky, at the astonishing fact of the void, they scarcely noticed these things.

A long time passed, and none of them moved except to look around. Past the jumble of dark trash that had mostly been thrown off in a single direction, the surface of the moon was an immense expanse of white hills, as strange and glorious as the stars above. The size of it all! Oliver had never dreamed that everything could be so big.

"The blue must be promethium," Solly said, pointing up at the Earth. "They've covered the whole Earth with the blue we mined."

Their mouths hung open as they stared at it. "How far away is it?" Freeman asked. No one answered.

"There they all are," Solly said. He laughed harshly. "I wish I could blow up the Earth too!"

He walked in circles on the rubble of the crater's rim. The rocket rails, Oliver thought suddenly, must have been in the direction Freeman had sent the debris. Bad luck. The final upward sweep of them poked up out of the dark dirt and glass. Solly pointed at them. His voice was loud in Oliver's ears, it strained the intercom: "Too bad we can't fly to the Earth, and blow it up too! I wish we could!"

And mute Elijah took a few steps, leaped off the mound into the sky, took a swipe with one hand at the blue ball. They laughed at him. "Almost got it, didn't you!" Freeman and Solly tried themselves, and then they all did: taking quick runs, leaping, flying slowly up through space, for five or six or seven seconds, making a grab at the sky overhead, floating back down as if in a dream, to land in a tumble, and try it again . . . It felt wonderful to hang up there at the top of the leap, free in the vacuum, free of gravity and everything else, for just that instant.

After a while they sat down on the new crater's rim, covered with white dust and black dirt. Oliver sat on the very edge of the crater, legs over the edge, so that he could see back down into their sublunar world, at the same time that he looked up into the sky. Three eyes were not enough to judge such immensities. His heart pounded, he felt too intoxicated to move anymore. Tired, drunk. The intercom rasped with the sounds of their breathing, which slowly calmed, fell into a rhythm together. Hester buzzed one phrase of "Bucket" and they laughed softly. They lay back on the rubble, all but Oliver, and stared up into the dizzy reaches of the universe, the velvet black of infinity. Oliver sat with elbows on knees, watched the white hills glowing under the black sky. They were lit by earthlight—earthlight and starlight. The white mountains on the horizon were as sharp-edged as the shards of dome glass sticking out of the rock. And all the time the Earth looked down at him. It was all too fantastic to believe. He drank it in like oxygen, felt it filling him up, expanding in his chest.

"What do you think they'll do with us when they get here?" Solly asked.

"Kill us," Hester croaked.

"Or put us back to work," Naomi added.

Oliver laughed. Whatever happened, it was impossible in that moment to care. For above them a milky spill of stars lay thrown across the infinite black sky, lighting a million better worlds; while just over their heads the Earth glowed like a fine blue lamp; and under their feet rolled the white hills of the happy moon, holed like a great cheese.

Michael Swanwick has received the Nebula, Theodore Sturgeon, World Fantasy, and Hugo awards, and has the pleasant distinction of having been nominated for and lost more of these same awards than any other writer. He has written ten novels, over a hundred and fifty short stories, and countless works of flash fiction. His latest novel, *The Iron Dragon's Mother*, will be published by Tor Books in 2019.

He lives in Philadelphia with his wife, Marianne Porter.

GRIFFIN'S EGG
Michael Swanwick

The moon? It is a griffin's egg,
Hatching to-morrow night.
And how the little boys will watch
With shouting and delight
To see him break the shell and stretch
And creep across the sky.
The boys will laugh. The little girls,
I fear, may hide and cry . . .
—Vachel Lindsay

The sun cleared the mountains. Gunther Weil raised a hand in salute, then winced as the glare hit his eyes in the instant it took his helmet to polarize.

He was hauling fuel rods to Chatterjee Crater industrial park. The Chatterjee B reactor had gone critical forty hours before dawn, taking fifteen remotes and a microwave relay with it, and putting out a power surge that caused collateral damage to every factory in the park. Fortunately, the occasional meltdown was designed into the system. By the time the sun rose over the Rhaeticus highlands, a new reactor had been built and was ready to go online.

Gunther drove automatically, gauging his distance from Bootstrap by the amount of trash lining the Mare Vaporum road. Close by the city, discarded construction machinery and damaged assemblers sat in open-vacuum storage, awaiting possible salvage. Ten kilometers out, a pressurized van had exploded, scattering machine parts and giant worms of insulating foam across the landscape. At twenty-five kilometers, a poorly graded stretch of road had claimed any number of cargo skids and shattered running lights from passing traffic.

Forty kilometers out, though, the road was clear, a straight, clean gash in the dirt. Ignoring the voices at the back of his skull, the traffic chatter and automated safety messages that the truck routinely fed into his transceiver chip, he scrolled up the topographicals on the dash.

Right about here.

Gunther turned off the Mare Vaporum road and began laying tracks over virgin soil. "You've left your prescheduled route," the truck said. "Deviations from schedule may only be made with the recorded permission of your dispatcher."

"Yeah, well." Gunther's voice seemed loud in his helmet, the only physical sound in a babel of ghosts. He'd left the cabin unpressurized, and the insulated layers of his suit stilled even the conduction rumbling from the treads. "You and I both know that so long as I don't fall too far behind schedule, Beth Hamilton isn't going to care if I stray a little in between."

"You have exceeded this unit's linguistic capabilities."

"That's okay, don't let it bother you." Deftly he tied down the send switch on the truck radio with a twist of wire. The voices in his head abruptly died. He was completely isolated now.

"You said you wouldn't do that again." The words, broadcast directly to his trance chip, sounded as deep and resonant as the voice of God. "Generation Five policy expressly requires that all drivers maintain constant radio—"

"Don't whine. It's unattractive."

"You have exceeded this unit's linguistic—"

"Oh, shut up." Gunther ran a finger over the topographical maps, tracing the course he'd plotted the night before: Thirty kilometers over cherry soil, terrain no human or machine had ever crossed before, and then north on Murchison road. With luck he might even manage to be at Chatterjee early.

He drove into the lunar plain. Rocks sailed by to either side. Ahead, the mountains grew imperceptibly. Save for the treadmarks dwindling behind him, there was nothing from horizon to horizon to show that humanity had ever existed. The silence was perfect.

Gunther lived for moments like this. Entering that clean, desolate emptiness, he experienced a vast expansion of being, as if everything he saw, stars, plain, craters and all, were encompassed within himself. Bootstrap City was only a fading dream, a distant island on the gently rolling surface of a stone sea. Nobody will ever be first here again, he thought. Only me.

A memory floated up from his childhood. It was Christmas Eve and he was in his parents' car, on the way to midnight Mass. Snow was falling, thickly and windlessly, rendering all the familiar roads of Düsseldorf clean and pure under sheets of white. His father drove, and he himself leaned over the front seat to stare ahead in fascination into this peaceful, transformed world. The silence was perfect.

He felt touched by solitude and made holy.

The truck plowed through a rainbow of soft greys, submerged hues more hints than colors, as if something bright and festive held itself hidden just beneath a coating of dust. The sun was at his shoulder, and when he spun the front axle to avoid a boulder, the truck's shadow wheeled and reached for infinity. He drove reflexively, mesmerized by the austere beauty of the passing land.

At a thought, his peecee put music on his chip. "Stormy Weather" filled the universe.

He was coming down a long, almost imperceptible slope when the controls went dead in his hands. The truck powered down and coasted to a stop. "Goddamn you, you asshole machine!" he snarled. "What is it this time?"

"The land ahead is impassable."

Gunther slammed a fist on the dash, making the maps dance. The land ahead was smooth and sloping, any unruly tendencies tamed eons ago by the Mare Imbrium explosion. Sissy stuff. He kicked the door open and clambered down.

The truck had been stopped by a baby rille: a snakelike depression meandering across his intended route, looking for all the world like a dry streambed. He bounded to its edge. It was fifteen meters across, and three meters down at its deepest. Just shallow enough that it wouldn't show up on the topos. Gunther returned to the cab, slamming the door noiselessly behind him.

"Look. The sides aren't very steep. I've been down worse a hundred times. We'll just take it slow and easy, okay?"

"The land ahead is impassable," the truck said. "Please return to the originally scheduled course."

Wagner was on now. *Tannhäuser.* Impatiently, he thought it off.

"If you're so damned heuristic, then why won't you ever listen to reason?" He chewed his lip angrily, gave a quick shake of his head. "No, going back would put us way off schedule. The rille is bound to peter out in a few hundred meters. Let's just follow it until it does, then angle back to Murchison. We'll be at the park in no time."

Three hours later he finally hit the Murchison road. By then he was sweaty and smelly and his shoulders ached with tension. "Where are we?" he asked sourly. Then, before the truck could answer, "Cancel that." The soil had turned suddenly black. That would be the ejecta fantail from the Sony-Reinpfaltz mine. Their railgun was oriented almost due south in order to avoid the client factories, and so their tailings hit the road first. That meant he was getting close.

Murchison was little more than a confluence of truck treads, a dirt track crudely leveled and marked by blazes of orange paint on nearby boulders. In quick order Gunther passed through a series of landmarks: Harada Industrial fantail, Sea of Storms Macrofacturing fantail, Krupp fünfzig fantail. He knew them all. G5 did the robotics for the lot.

A light flatbed carrying a shipped bulldozer sped past him, kicking up a spray of dust that fell as fast as pebbles. The remote driving it waved a spindly arm in greeting. He waved back automatically, and wondered if it was any-body he knew.

The land hereabouts was hacked and gouged, dirt and boulders shoved into careless heaps and hills, the occasional tool station or Oxytank Emergency Storage Platform chopped into a nearby bluff. A sign floated by: TOILET FLUSHING FACILITIES ½ KILOMETER. He made a face. Then he remembered that his radio was still off and slipped the loop of wire from it. Time to rejoin the real world. Immediately his dispatcher's voice, harsh and staticky, was relayed to his trance chip.

"—ofabitch! *Weil!* Where the fuck are you?"

"I'm right here, Beth. A little late, but right where I'm supposed to be."

"Sonofa—" The recording shut off, and Hamilton's voice came on, live and mean. "You'd better have a real good explanation for this one, honey."

"Oh, you know how it is." Gunther looked away from the road, off into the dusty jade highlands. He'd like to climb up into them and never come back. Perhaps he would find caves. Perhaps there were monsters: vacuum trolls and moondragons with metabolisms slow and patient, taking centuries to move one body's-length, hyperdense beings that could swim through stone as if it were water. He pictured them diving, following lines of magnetic force deep, deep into veins of diamond and plutonium, heads back and singing. "I picked up a hitchhiker, and we kind of got involved."

"Try telling that to E. Izmailova. She's mad as hornets at you."

"Who?"

"Izmailova. She's the new demolitions jock, shipped up here on a multi-corporate contract. Took a hopper in almost four hours ago, and she's been waiting for you and Siegfried ever since. I take it you've never met her?"

"No."

"Well, I have, and you'd better watch your step with her. She's exactly the kind of tough broad who won't be amused by your antics."

"Aw, come on, she's just another tech on a retainer, right? Not in my line of command. It's not like she can do anything to me."

"Dream on, babe. It wouldn't take much pull to get a fuckup like you sent down to Earth."

The sun was only a finger's breadth over the highlands by the time Chatterjee A loomed into sight. Gunther glanced at it every now and then, apprehensively. With his visor adjusted to the H-alpha wavelength, it was a blazing white sphere covered with slowly churning black specks: More granular than usual. Sunspot activity seemed high. He wondered that the Radiation Forecast Facility hadn't posted a surface advisory. The guys at the Observatory were usually right on top of things.

Chatterjee A, B, and C were a triad of simple craters just below Chladni, and while the smaller two were of minimal interest, Chatterjee A was the child of a meteor that had punched through the Imbrian basalts to as sweet a vein of aluminum ore as anything in the highlands. Being so convenient to Bootstrap made it one of management's darlings, and Gunther was not surprised to see that Kerr-McGee was going all out to get their reactor online again.

The park was crawling with walkers, stalkers, and assemblers. They were all over the blister-domed factories, the smelteries, loading docks, and vacuum garages. Constellations of blue sparks winked on and off as major industrial constructs were dismantled. Fleets of heavily loaded trucks fanned out into the lunar plain, churning up the dirt behind them. Fats Waller started to sing "The Joint is Jumping" and Gunther laughed.

He slowed to a crawl, swung wide to avoid a gas-plater that was being wrangled onto a loader, and cut up the Chatterjee B ramp road. A new landing pad had been blasted from the rock just below the lip, and a cluster of people stood about a hopper resting there. One human and eight remotes.

One of the remotes was speaking, making choppy little gestures with its arms. Several stood inert, identical as so many antique telephones, unclaimed by Earthside management but available should more advisors need to be called online.

Gunther unstrapped Siegfried from the roof of the cab and, control pad in one hand and cable spool in the other, walked him toward the hopper.

The human strode out to meet him. "You! What kept you?" E. Izmailova wore a jazzy red-and-orange Studio Volga boutique suit, in sharp contrast to his own company-issue suit with the G5 logo on the chest. He could not make out her face through the gold visor glass. But he could hear it in her voice: blazing eyes, thin lips.

"I had a flat tire." He found a good smooth chunk of rock and set down the cable spool, wriggling it to make sure it sat flush. "We got maybe five hundred yards of shielded cable. That enough for you?"

A short, tense nod.

"Okay." He unholstered his bolt gun. "Stand back." Kneeling, he anchored the spool to the rock. Then he ran a quick check of the unit's functions: "Do we know what it's like in there?"

A remote came to life, stepped forward and identified himself as Don Sakai, of G5's crisis management team. Gunther had worked with him before: a decent tough guy, but like most Canadians he had an exaggerated fear of nuclear energy. "Ms. Lang here, of Sony-Reinpfaltz, walked her unit in, but the radiation was so strong she lost control after a preliminary scan." A second remote nodded confirmation, but the relay time to Toronto was just enough that Sakai missed it. "The remote just kept on walking." He coughed nervously, then added unnecessarily, "The autonomous circuits were too sensitive."

"Well, that's not going to be a problem with Siegfried. He's as dumb as a rock. On the evolutionary scale of machine intelligence he ranks closer to a crowbar than a computer." Two and a half seconds passed, and then Sakai laughed politely. Gunther nodded to Izmailova. "Walk me through this. Tell me what you want."

Izmailova stepped to his side, their suits pressing together briefly as she jacked a patch cord into his control pad. Vague shapes flickered across the outside of her visor like the shadows of dreams. "Does he know what he's doing?" she asked.

"Hey, I—"

"Shut up, Weil," Hamilton growled on a private circuit. Openly, she said, "He wouldn't be here if the company didn't have full confidence in his technical skills."

"I'm sure there's never been any question—" Sakai began. He lapsed into silence as Hamilton's words belatedly reached him.

"There's a device on the hopper," Izmailova said to Gunther. "Go pick it up."

He obeyed, reconfiguring Siegfried for a small, dense load. The unit bent low over the hopper, wrapping large, sensitive hands about the device. Gunther applied gentle pressure. Nothing happened. Heavy little bugger. Slowly, carefully, he upped the power. Siegfried straightened.

"Up the road, then down inside."

The reactor was unrecognizable, melted, twisted and folded in upon itself, a mound of slag with twisting pipes sprouting from the edges. There had been a coolant explosion early in the incident, and one wall of the crater was bright with sprayed metal. "Where is the radioactive material?" Sakai asked. Even though he was a third of a million kilometers away, he sounded tense and apprehensive.

"It's all radioactive," Izmailova said.

They waited. "I mean, you know. The fuel rods?"

"Right now, your fuel rods are probably three hundred meters down and still going. We are talking about fissionable material that has achieved critical mass. Very early in the process the rods will have all melted together in a sort of superhot puddle, capable of burning its way through rock. Picture it as a dense, heavy blob of wax, slowly working its way toward the lunar core."

"God, I love physics," Gunther said.

Izmailova's helmet turned toward him, abruptly blank. After a long pause, it switched on again and turned away. "The road down is clear at least. Take your unit all the way to the end. There's an exploratory shaft to one side there. Old one. I want to see if it's still open."

"Will the one device be enough?" Sakai asked. "To clean up the crater, I mean."

The woman's attention was fixed on Siegfried's progress. In a distracted tone she said, "Mr. Sakai, putting a chain across the access road would be enough to clean up this site. The crater walls would shield anyone working nearby from the gamma radiation, and it would take no effort at all to reroute hopper overflights so their passengers would not be exposed. Most of the biological danger of a reactor meltdown comes from alpha radiation emitted by particulate radioisotopes in the air or water. When concentrated in the body, alpha-emitters can do considerable damage; elsewhere, no. Alpha particles can be stopped by a sheet of paper. So long as you keep a reactor out of your ecosystem, it's as safe as any other large machine. Burying a destroyed reactor just because it is radioactive is unnecessary and, if you will forgive me for saying so, superstitious. But I don't make policy. I just blow things up."

"Is this the shaft you're looking for?" Gunther asked.

"Yes. Walk it down to the bottom. It's not far."

Gunther switched on Siegfried's chestlight, and sank a roller relay so the cable wouldn't snag. They went down. Finally Izmailova said, "Stop. That's far enough." He gently set the device down and then, at her direction, flicked the arming toggle. "That's done," Izmailova said. "Bring your unit back. I've given you an hour to put some distance between the crater and yourself." Gunther noticed that the remotes, on automatic, had already begun walking away.

"Um . . . I've still got fuel rods to load."

"Not today you don't. The new reactor has been taken back apart and hauled out of the blasting zone."

Gunther thought now of all the machinery being disassembled and removed from the industrial park, and was struck for the first time by the operation's sheer extravagances of scale. Normally only the most sensitive devices were removed from a blasting area. "Wait a minute. Just what kind of monster explosive are you planning to *use*?"

There was a self-conscious cockiness to Izmailova's stance. "Nothing I don't know how to handle. This is a diplomat-class device, the same design as saw action five years ago. Nearly one hundred individual applications without a single mechanical failure. That makes it the most reliable weapon in the history of warfare. You should feel privileged having the chance to work with one."

Gunther felt his flesh turn to ice. "Jesus Mother of God," he said. "You had me handling a briefcase nuke."

"Better get used to it. Westinghouse Lunar is putting these little babies into mass production. We'll be cracking open mountains with them, blasting roads through the highlands, smashing apart the rille walls to see what's inside." Her voice took on a visionary tone. "And that's just the beginning. There are plans for enrichment fields in Sinus Aestum. Explode a few bombs over the regolith, then extract plutonium from the dirt. We're going to be the fuel dump for the entire solar system."

His dismay must have shown in his stance, for Izmailova laughed. "Think of it as weapons for peace."

"You should've been there!" Gunther said. "It was unfuckabelievable. The one side of the crater just disappeared. It dissolved into nothing. Smashed to dust. And for a real long time everything *glowed!* Craters, machines, everything. My visor was so close to overload it started flickering. I thought it was going to bum out. It was nuts." He picked up his cards. "Who dealt this mess?"

Krishna grinned shyly and ducked his head. "I'm in."

Hiro scowled down at his cards. "I've just died and gone to Hell."

"Trade you," Anya said.

"No, I deserve to suffer."

They were in Noguchi Park by the edge of the central lake, seated on artfully scattered boulders that had been carved to look water-eroded. A knee-high forest of baby birches grew to one side, and somebody's toy sailboat floated near the impact cone at the center of the lake. Honeybees mazily browsed the clover.

"And then, just as the wall was crumbling, this crazy Russian bitch—"

Anya ditched a trey. "Watch what you say about crazy Russian bitches."

"—goes zooming up on her hopper . . ."

"I saw it on television," Hiro said. "We all did. It was news. This guy who works for Nissan told me the BBC gave it thirty seconds." He'd broken his nose in karate practice, when he'd flinched into his instructor's punch, and the contrast of square white bandage with shaggy black eyebrows gave him a surly, piratical appearance.

Gunther discarded one. "Hit me. Man, you didn't see anything. You didn't feel the ground shake afterward."

"Just what was Izmailova's connection with the Briefcase War?" Hiro asked. "Obviously not a courier. Was she in the supply end or strategic?"

Gunther shrugged.

"You do remember the Briefcase War?" Hiro said sarcastically. "Half of Earth's military elites taken out in a single day? The world pulled back from the brink of war by bold action? Suspected terrorists revealed as global heroes?"

Gunther remembered the Briefcase War quite well. He had been nineteen at the time, working on a Finlandia Geothermal project when the whole world had gone into spasm and very nearly destroyed itself. It had been a major factor in his decision to ship off the planet. "Can't we ever talk about anything but politics? I'm sick and tired of hearing about Armageddon."

"Hey, aren't you supposed to be meeting with Hamilton?" Anya asked suddenly.

He glanced up at the Earth. The east coast of South America was just crossing the dusk terminator. "Oh, hell, there's enough time to play out the hand."

Krishna won with three queens. The deal passed to Hiro. He shuffled quickly, and slapped the cards down with angry little punches of his arm. "Okay," Anya said, "what's eating you?"

He looked up angrily, then down again and in a muffled voice, as if he had abruptly gone bashful as Krishna, said, "I'm shipping home."

"Home?"

"You mean to Earth?"

"Are you crazy? With everything about to go up in flames? *Why?*"

"Because I am so fucking tired of the Moon. It has to be the ugliest place in the universe."

"Ugly?" Anya looked elaborately about at the terraced gardens, the streams that began at the top level and fell in eight misty waterfalls before reaching the central pond to be recirculated again, the gracefully winding pathways. People strolled through great looping rosebushes and past towers of forsythia with the dreamlike skimming stride that made moonwalking so like motion underwater. Others popped in and out of the office tunnels, paused to watch the finches loop and fly, tended to beds of cucumbers. At the midlevel straw market, the tents where offduty hobby capitalists sold factory systems, grass baskets, orange glass paperweights and courses in postinterpretive dance and the meme analysis of Elizabethan poetry, were a jumble of brave silks, turquoise, scarlet, and aquamarine. "I think it looks nice. A little crowded, maybe, but that's the pioneer aesthetic."

"It looks like a shopping mall, but that's not what I'm talking about. It's—" He groped for words. "It's like—it's what we're doing to this world that bothers me. I mean, we're digging it up, scattering garbage about, ripping the mountains apart, and for what?"

"Money," Anya said. "Consumer goods, raw materials, a future for our children. What's wrong with that?"

"We're not building a future, we're building weapons."

"There's not so much as a handgun on the Moon. It's an intercorporate development zone. Weapons are illegal here."

"You know what I mean. All those bomber fuselages, detonation systems, and missile casings that get built here, and shipped to low Earth orbit. Let's not pretend we don't know what they're for."

"So?" Anya said sweetly. "We live in the real world, we're none of us naïve enough to believe you can have governments without armies. Why is it worse that these things are being built here rather than elsewhere?"

"It's the short-sighted, egocentric greed of what we're doing that gripes me! Have you peeked out on the surface lately and seen the way it's being ripped open, torn apart, and scattered about? There are still places where you can gaze upon a harsh beauty unchanged since the days our ancestors were swinging in trees. But we're trashing them. In a generation, two at most, there will be no more beauty to the Moon than there is to any other garbage dump."

"You've seen what Earthbound manufacturing has done to the environment," Anya said. "Moving it off the planet is a good thing, right?"

"Yes, but the Moon—"

"Doesn't even *have* an ecosphere. There's nothing here to harm."

They glared at each other. Finally Hiro said, "I don't want to talk about it," and sullenly picked up his cards.

Five or six hands later, a woman wandered up and plumped to the grass by Krishna's feet. Her eye shadow was vivid electric purple, and a crazy smile burned on her face. "Oh hi," Krishna said. "Does everyone here know Sally Chang? She's a research component of the Center for Self-Replicating Technologies, like me."

The others nodded. Gunther said, "Gunther Weil. Blue collar component of Generation Five."

She giggled.

Gunther blinked. "You're certainly in a good mood." He rapped the deck with his knuckles. "I'll stand."

"I'm on psilly," she said.

"One card."

"Psilocybin?" Gunther said. "I might be interested in some of that. Did you grow it or microfacture it? I have a couple of factories back in my room, maybe I could divert one if you'd like to license the software?"

Sally Chang shook her head, laughing helplessly. Tears ran down her cheeks.

"Well, when you come down we can talk about it." Gunther squinted at his cards. "This would make a great hand for chess."

"Nobody plays chess," Hiro said scornfully. "It's a game for computers."

Gunther took the pot with two pair. He shuffled, Krishna declined the cut, and he began dealing out cards. "So anyway, this crazy Russian lady—"

Out of nowhere, Chang howled. Wild gusts of laughter knocked her back on her heels and bent her forward again. The delight of discovery dancing in her eyes, she pointed a finger straight at Gunther. "You're a robot!" she cried.

"Beg pardon?"

"You're nothing but a robot," she repeated. "You're a machine, an automaton. Look at yourself! Nothing but stimulus-response. You have no free will at all. There's nothing there. You couldn't perform an original act to save your life."

"Oh yeah?" Gunther glanced around, looking for inspiration. A little boy—it might be Pyotr Nahfees, though it was hard to tell from here—was by the edge of the water, feeding scraps of shrimp loaf to the carp. "Suppose I pitched you into the lake? That would be an original act."

Laughing, she shook her head. "Typical primate behavior. A perceived threat is met with a display of mock aggression."

Gunther laughed.

"Then, when that fails, the primate falls back to a display of submission. Appeasal. The monkey demonstrates his harmlessness—you see?"

"Hey, this really isn't funny," Gunther said warningly. "In fact, it's kind of insulting."

"And so back to a display of aggression."

Gunther sighed and threw up both his hands. "How am I supposed to react? According to you, anything I say or do is wrong."

"Submission again. Back and forth, back and forth from aggression to submission and back again." She pumped her arm as if it were a piston. "Just like a little machine—you see? It's all automatic behavior."

"Hey, Kreesh—you're the neurobiowhatever here, right? Put in a good word for me. Get me out of this conversation."

Krishna reddened. He would not meet Gunther's eyes. "Ms. Chang is very highly regarded at the Center, you see. Anything she thinks about thinking is worth thinking about." The woman watched him avidly, eyes glistening, pupils small. "I think maybe what she means, though, is that we're all basically cruising through life. Like we're on autopilot. Not just you specifically, but all of us." He appealed to her directly. "Yes?"

"No, no, no, no." She shook her head. "Him specifically."

"I give up." Gunther put his cards down, and lay back on the granite slab so he could stare up through the roof glass at the waning Earth. When he closed his eyes, he could see Izmailova's hopper, rising. It was a skimpy device, little more than a platform-and-chair atop a cluster of four bottles of waste-gas propellant, and a set of smart legs. He saw it lofting up as the explosion blossomed, seeming briefly to hover high over the crater, like a hawk atop a thermal. Hands by side, the red-suited figure sat, watching with what seemed inhuman calm. In the reflected light she burned as bright as a star. In an appalling way, she was beautiful.

Sally Chang hugged her knees, rocking back and forth. She laughed and laughed.

Beth Hamilton was wired for telepresence. She flipped up one lens when Gunther entered her office, but kept on moving her arms and legs. Dreamy little ghost motions that would be picked up and magnified in a factory somewhere over the horizon. "You're late again," she said with no particular emphasis.

Most people would have experienced at least a twinge of reality sickness dealing with two separate surrounds at once. Hamilton was one of the rare few who could split her awareness between two disparate realities without loss of efficiency in either. "I called you in to discuss your future with Generation Five. Specifically, to discuss the possibility of your transfer to another plant."

"You mean Earthside."

"You see?" Hamilton said. "You're not as stupid as you like to make yourself out to be." She flipped the lens down again, stood very still, then lifted a metal-gauntleted hand and ran through a complex series of finger movements. "Well?"

"Well what?"

"Tokyo, Berlin, Buenos Aires—do any of these hold magic for you? How about Toronto? The right move now could be a big boost to your career."

"All I want is to stay here, do my job, and draw down my salary," Gunther said carefully. "I'm not looking for a shot at promotion, or a big raise, or a lateral career-track transfer. I'm happy right where I am."

"You've sure got a funny way of showing it." Hamilton powered down her gloves and slipped her hands free. She scratched her nose. To one side stood her work table, a polished cube of black granite. Her peecee rested there, alongside a spray of copper crystals. At her thought, it put Izmailova's voice onto Gunther's chip.

"It is with deepest regret that I must alert you to the unprofessional behavior of one of your personnel components," it began. Listening to the complaint, Gunther experienced a totally unexpected twinge of distress and, more, of resentment that Izmailova had dared judge him so harshly. He was careful not to let it show.

"Irresponsible, insubordinate, careless, and possessed of a bad attitude." He faked a grin. "She doesn't seem to like me much." Hamilton said nothing. "But this isn't enough to . . ." His voice trailed off. "Is it?"

"Normally, Weil, it would be. A demo jock isn't 'just a tech on retainer,' as you so quaintly put it; those government licenses aren't easy to get. And you may not be aware of it, but you have very poor efficiency ratings to begin with. Lots of potential, no follow-through. Frankly, you've been a disappointment. However, lucky for you, this Izmailova dame humiliated Don Sakai, and he's let us know that we're under no particular pressure to accommodate her."

"Izmailova humiliated Sakai?"

Hamilton stared at him. "Weil, you're oblivious, you know that?"

Then he remembered Izmailova's rant on nuclear energy. "Right, okay. I got it now."

"So here's your choice. I can write up a reprimand, and it goes into your permanent file, along with Izmailova's complaint. Or you can take a lateral Earthside, and I'll see to it that these little things aren't logged into the corporate system."

It wasn't much of a choice. But he put a good face on it. "In that case it looks like you're stuck with me."

"For the moment, Weil. For the moment."

He was back on the surface the next two days running. The first day he was once again hauling fuel rods to Chatterjee C. This time he kept to the road, and the reactor was refueled exactly on schedule. The second day he went all the way out to Triesnecker to pick up some old rods that had been in temporary storage for six months while the Kerr-McGee people argued over whether they should be reprocessed or dumped. Not a bad deal for him, because although the sunspot cycle was on the wane, there was a surface advisory in effect and he was drawing hazardous duty pay.

When he got there, a tech rep telepresenced in from somewhere in France to tell him to forget it. There'd been another meeting, and the decision had once again been delayed. He started back to Bootstrap with the new a capella version of *The Threepenny Opera* playing in his head. It sounded awfully sweet and reedy for his tastes, but that was what they were listening to up home.

Fifteen kilometers down the road, the UV meter on the dash *jumped*.

Gunther reached out to tap the meter with his finger. It did not respond. With a freezing sensation at the back of his neck, he glanced up at the roof of the cab and whispered, "Oh, no."

"The Radiation Forecast Facility has just intensified its surface warning to a Most Drastic status," the truck said calmly. "This is due to an unanticipated flare storm, onset immediately. Everyone currently on the surface is to proceed with all haste to shelter. Repeat: Proceed immediately to shelter."

"I'm eighty kilometers from—"

The truck was slowing to a stop. "Because this unit is not hardened, excessive fortuitous radiation may cause it to malfunction. To ensure the continued safe operation of this vehicle, all controls will be frozen in manual mode and this unit will now shut off."

With the release of the truck's masking functions, Gunther's head filled with overlapping voices. Static washed through them, making nonsense of what they were trying to say:

astic Stus-Repeat: S**face**d**ory ha** een***grad***to M**t Dra**ic Stat**. A** u nits *nd perso*****are to find shelt***imm ediatel*. Maxim*m *x posu** **enty min**e s.***nd ***lter i**ed* *tely. Thi**is t** recor ded*voice of**he Radi ati***Forecast Faci*it y.**u**to an unpr**i** ** sol** flare,***e su* face adv**o***has been upgrade***o Most Dras * ***l! This is **eth. Th***

h***just i**ue**a M** t D***tic**dvis*****G et off t***surface**Go ddamn **u, are yo* lis tening? Find s**lter. D on't try to **t **ck to Bootstrap.***o f**, it'll *fry you.***ten, t**re * * ** thr***factorie**n** **r fr***your pre***t l***t**n. A*e you *ist en**g, you***ofoff? Wei * *sk*pf A**is**ne, Ni** **, an**Luna**m***os t**ct**al. Weil!**et me **ail, are you there? C o***on, good **ddy, gi

ve ***a hoo** **ko, S abra, **ng**i-ge**yo** asses *****groun***ig ht*ow. **don't wan**to h*** you've sta*yed*be **n**to turn**** the l * *ght***ho el***i**out t * here?**ome**n ri**t n ow. Ev**y**e! Any**dy *now w***e Mikha** i * **C'Mon, *Misha, don* * t**ou get coy *n us. So u** us with ***r voice, he**? W***ot **rd Ez

"Beth! The nearest shelter is back at Weisskopf—that's half an hour at top speed and I've got an advisory here of twenty minutes. Tell me what to do!"

But the first sleet of hard particles was coming in too hard to make out anything more. A hand, his apparently, floated forward and flicked off the radio relay. The voices in his head died.

The crackling static went on and on. The truck sat motionless, half an hour from nowhere, invisible death sizzling and popping down through the cab roof. He put his helmet and gloves on, double-checked their seals, and unlatched the door.

It slammed open. Pages from the op manual flew away, and a glove went tumbling gaily across the surface, chasing the pink fuzzy-dice that Eurydice had given him that last night in Sweden. A handful of wheat biscuits in an open tin on the dash turned to powder and were gone, drawing the tin after them. Explosive decompression. He'd forgotten to depressurize. Gunther froze in dismayed astonishment at having made so basic—so dangerous—a mistake.

Then he was on the surface, head tilted back, staring up at the sun. It was angry with sunspots, and one enormous and unpredicted solar flare.

I'm going to die, he thought.

For a long, paralyzing instant, he tasted the chill certainty of that thought. He was going to die. He knew that for a fact, knew it more surely than he had ever known anything before.

In his mind, he could see Death sweeping across the lunar plain toward him. Death was a black wall, featureless, that stretched to infinity in every direction. It sliced the universe in half. On this side were life, warmth, craters and flowers, dreams, mining robots, thought, everything that Gunther knew or could imagine. On the other side . . . something? Nothing? The wall gave no hint. It was unreadable, enigmatic, absolute. But it was bearing down on him. It was so close now that he could almost reach out and touch it. Soon it would be here. He would pass through, and then he would know.

With a start he broke free of that thought, and jumped for the cab. He scrabbled up its side. His trance chip hissing, rattling and crackling, he yanked the magnetic straps holding Siegfried in place, grabbed the spool and control pad, and jumped over the edge.

He landed jarringly, fell to his knees, and rolled under the trailer. There was enough shielding wrapped around the fuel rods to stop any amount of hard radiation—no matter what its source. It would shelter him as well from the sun as from his cargo. The trance chip fell silent, and he felt his jaws relaxing from a clenched tension.

Safe.

It was dark beneath the trailer, and he had time to think. Even kicking his rebreather up to full, and offlining all his suit peripherals, he didn't have enough oxygen to sit out the storm. So okay. He had to get to a shelter. Weisskopf was closest, only fifteen kilometers away and there was a shelter in the G5 assembly plant there. That would be his goal.

Working by feel, he found the steel supporting struts, and used Siegfried's magnetic straps to attach himself to the underside of the trailer. It was clumsy, difficult work, but at last he hung face-down over the road. He fingered the walker's controls, and sat Siegfried up.

Twelve excruciating minutes later, he finally managed to get Siegfried down from the roof unbroken. The interior wasn't intended to hold anything half so big. To get the walker in he had first to cut the door free, and then rip the chair out of the cab. Discarding both items by the roadside, he squeezed Siegfried in. The walker bent over double, reconfigured, reconfigured again, and finally managed to fit itself into the space. Gently, delicately, Siegfried took the controls and shifted into first.

With a bump, the truck started to move.

It was a hellish trip. The truck, never fast to begin with, wallowed down the road like a cast-iron pig. Siegfried's optics were bent over the controls, and couldn't be raised without jerking the walker's hands free. He couldn't look ahead without stopping the truck first.

He navigated by watching the road pass under him. To a crude degree he could align the truck with the treadmarks scrolling by. Whenever he wandered off the track, he worked Siegfried's hand controls to veer the truck back, so that it drifted slowly from side to side, zig-zagging its way down the road.

Shadows bumping and leaping, the road flowed toward Gunther with dangerous monotony. He jiggled and vibrated in his makeshift sling. After a while his neck hurt with the effort of holding his head back to watch the glaring road disappearing into shadow by the front axle, and his eyes ached from the crawling repetitiveness of what they saw.

The truck kicked up dust in passing, and the smaller particles carried enough of a static charge to cling to his suit. At irregular intervals he swiped at the fine grey film on his visor with his glove, smearing it into long, thin streaks.

He began to hallucinate. They were mild visuals, oblong patches of color-ed light that moved in his vision and went away when he shook his head and firmly closed his eyes for a concentrated moment. But every moment's release from the pressure of vision tempted him to keep his eyes closed longer, and that he could not afford to do.

It put him in mind of the last time he had seen his mother, and what she had said then. That the worst part of being a widow was that every day her life began anew, no better than the day before, the pain still fresh, her husband's absence a physical fact she was no closer to accepting than ever. It was like being dead, she said, in that nothing ever changed.

Ah God, he thought, this isn't worth doing. Then a rock the size of his head came bounding toward his helmet. Frantic hands jerked at the controls, and Siegfried skewed the truck wildly, so that the rock jumped away and missed him. Which put an end to *that* line of thought.

He cued his peecee. *Saint James' Infirmary* came on. It didn't help.

Come on, you bastard, he thought. You can do it. His arms and shoulders ached, and his back too, when he gave it any thought. Perversely enough, one of his legs had gone to sleep. At the angle he had to hold his head to watch the road, his mouth tended to hang open. After a while, a quivering motion alerted him that a small puddle of saliva had gathered in the curve of his faceplate. He was drooling. He closed his mouth, swallowing back his spit, and stared forward. A minute later he found that he was doing it again. Slowly, miserably, he drove toward Weisskopf.

The G5 Weisskopf plant was typical of its kind: A white blister-dome to moderate temperature swings over the long lunar day, a microwave relay tower to bring in supervisory presence, and a hundred semiautonomous units to do the work.

Gunther overshot the access road, wheeled back to catch it, and ran the truck right up to the side of the factory. He had Siegfried switch off the engine, and then let the control pad fall to the ground. For well over a minute he simply hung there, eyes closed, savoring the end of motion. Then he kicked free of the straps, and crawled out from under the trailer.

Static scatting and stuttering inside his head, he stumbled into the factory.

In the muted light that filtered through the dome covering, the factory was dim as an undersea cavern. His helmet light seemed to distort as much as it illumined. Machines loomed closer in the center of its glare, swelling up as if seen through a fisheye lens. He turned it off, and waited for his eyes to adjust.

After a bit, he could see the robot assemblers, slender as ghosts, moving with unearthly delicacy. The flare storm had activated them. They swayed like seaweed, lightly out of sync with each other. Arms raised, they danced in time to random radio input.

On the assembly lines lay the remains of half-built robots, looking flayed and eviscerated. Their careful frettings of copper and silver nerves had been exposed to view and randomly operated upon. A long arm jointed down, electric fire at its tip, and made a metal torso twitch.

They were blind mechanisms, most of them, powerful things bolted to the floor in assembly logic paths. But there were mobile units as well, overseers and jacks-of-all-trades, weaving drunkenly through the factory with sun-maddened eye.

A sudden motion made Gunther turn just in time to see a metal puncher swivel toward him, slam down an enormous arm and put a hole in the floor by his feet. He felt the shock through his soles.

He danced back. The machine followed him, the diamond-tipped punch sliding nervously in and out of its sheath, its movements as trembling and dainty as a newborn colt's.

"Easy there, baby," Gunther whispered. To the far end of the factory, green arrows supergraffixed on the crater wall pointed to an iron door. The shelter. Gunther backed away from the punch, edging into a service aisle between two rows of machines that rippled like grass in the wind.

The punch press rolled forward on its trundle. Then, confused by that field of motion, it stopped, hesitantly scanning the ranks of robots. Gunther froze.

At last, slowly, lumberingly, the metal puncher turned away.

Gunther ran. Static roared in his head. Grey shadows swam among the distant machines, like sharks, sometimes coming closer, sometimes receding. The static loudened. Up and down the factory welding arcs winked on at the assembler tips, like tiny stars. Ducking, running, spinning, he reached the shelter and seized the airlock door. Even through his glove, the handle felt cold.

He turned it.

The airlock was small and round. He squeezed through the door and fit himself into the inadequate space within, making himself as small as possible. He yanked the door shut.

Darkness.

He switched his helmet lamp back on. The reflected glare slammed at his eyes, far too intense for such a confined area. Folded knees-to-chin into the roundness of the lock he felt a wry comradeship with Siegfried back in the truck.

The inner lock controls were simplicity itself. The door hinged inward, so that air pressure held it shut. There was a yank bar which, when pulled, would bleed oxygen into the airlock. When pressure equalized, the inner door would open easily. He yanked the bar.

The floor vibrated as something heavy went by.

The shelter was small, just large enough to hold a cot, a chemical toilet and a rebreather with spare oxytanks. A single overhead unit provided light and heat. For comfort there was a blanket. For amusement, there were pocket-sized editions of the Bible and the Koran, placed there by impossibly distant missionary societies. Even empty, there was not much space in the shelter.

It wasn't empty.

A woman, frowning and holding up a protective hand, cringed from his helmet lamp. "Turn that thing off," she said.

He obeyed. In the soft light that ensued he saw: stark white flattop, pink scalp visible through the sides. High cheekbones. Eyelids lifted slightly, like wings, by carefully sculpted eye shadow. Dark lips, full mouth. He had to admire the character it took to make up a face so carefully, only to hide it beneath a helmet. Then he saw her red and orange Studio Volga suit.

It was Izmailova.

To cover his embarrassment, he took his time removing his gloves and helmet. Izmailova moved her own helmet from the cot to make room, and he sat down beside her. Extending a hand, he stiffly said, "We've met before. My name is—"

"I know. It's written on your suit."

"Oh yeah. Right."

For an uncomfortably long moment, neither spoke. At last Izmailova cleared her throat and briskly said, "This is ridiculous. There's no reason we should—"

CLANG.

Their heads jerked toward the door in unison. The sound was harsh, loud, metallic. Gunther slammed his helmet on, grabbed for his gloves. Izmailova, also suiting up as rapidly as she could, tensely subvocalized into her trance chip: "What is it?"

Methodically snapping his wrist latches shut one by one, Gunther said, "I think it's a metal punch." Then, because the helmet muffled his words, he repeated them over the chip.

CLANG. This second time, they were waiting for the sound. Now there could be no doubt. Something was trying to break open the outer airlock door.

"A what?!"

"Might be a hammer of some type, or a blacksmith unit. Just be thankful it's not a laser jig." He held up his hands before him. "Give me a safety check."

She turned his wrists one way, back, took his helmet in her hands and gave it a twist to test its seal. "You pass." She held up her own wrists. "But what is it trying to do?"

Her gloves were sealed perfectly. One helmet dog had a bit of give in it, but not enough to breach integrity. He shrugged. "It's deranged—it could want anything. It might even be trying to repair a weak hinge."

CLANG.

"It's trying to get in here!"

"That's another possibility, yes."

Izmailova's voice rose slightly. "But even scrambled, there can't possibly be any programs in its memory to make it do that. How can random input make it act this way?"

"It doesn't work like that. You're thinking of the kind of robotics they had when you were a kid. These units are state of the art: They don't manipulate instructions, they manipulate concepts. See, that makes them more flexible. You don't have to program in every little step when you want one to do something new. You just give it a goal—"

CLANG.

"—like, to Disassemble a Rotary Drill. It's got a bank of available skills, like Cutting and Unbolting and Gross Manipulation, which it then fits together in various configurations until it has a path that will bring it to the goal." He was talking for the sake of talking now, talking to keep himself from panic. "Which normally works out fine. But when one of these things malfunctions, it does so on the conceptual level. See? So that—"

"So that it decides we're rotary drills that need to be disassembled."

"Uh . . . yeah."

CLANG.

"So what do we do when it gets in here?" They had both involuntarily risen to their feet, and stood facing the door. There was not much space, and what little there was they filled. Gunther was acutely aware that there was not enough room here to either fight or flee.

"I don't know about you," he said, "but I'm going to hit that sucker over the head with the toilet."

She turned to look at him.

CLA— The noise was cut in half by a breathy, whooshing explosion. Abrupt, total silence. "It's through the outer door," Gunther said flatly.

They waited.

Much later, Izmailova said, "Is it possible it's gone away?"

"I don't know." Gunther undogged his helmet, knelt and put an ear to the floor. The stone was almost painfully cold. "Maybe the explosion damaged it." He could hear the faint vibrations of the assemblers, the heavier rumblings of machines roving the factory floor. None of it sounded close. He silently counted to a hundred. Nothing. He counted to a hundred again.

Finally he straightened. "It's gone."

They both sat down. Izmailova took off her helmet, and Gunther clumsily began undoing his gloves. He fumbled at the latches. "Look at me." He laughed shakily. "I'm all thumbs. I can't even handle this, I'm so unnerved."

"Let me help you with that." Izmailova flipped up the latches, tugged at his glove. It came free. "Where's your other hand?"

Then, somehow, they were each removing the other's suit, tugging at the latches, undoing the seals. They began slowly but sped up with each latch undogged, until they were yanking and pulling with frantic haste. Gunther opened up the front of Izmailova's suit, revealing a red silk camisole. He slid his hands beneath it, and pushed the cloth up over her breasts. Her nipples were hard. He let her breasts fill his hands and squeezed.

Izmailova made a low, groaning sound in the back of her throat. She had Gunther's suit open. Now she pushed down his leggings and reached within to seize his cock. He was already erect. She tugged it out and impatiently shoved him down on the cot. Then she was kneeling on top of him and guiding him inside her.

Her mouth met his, warm and moist.

Half in and half out of their suits, they made love. Gunther managed to struggle one arm free, and reached within Izmailova's suit to run a hand up her long back and over the back of her head. The short hairs of her buzz cut stung and tickled his palm.

She rode him roughly, her flesh slippery with sweat against his. "Are you coming yet?" she murmured. "Are you coming yet? Tell me when you're about to come." She bit his shoulder, the side of his neck, his chin, his lower lip. Her nails dug into his flesh.

"Now," he whispered. Possibly he only subvocalized it, and she caught it on her trance chip. But then she clutched him tighter than ever, as if she were trying to crack his ribs, and her whole body shuddered with orgasm. Then he came too, riding her passion down into spiraling desperation, ecstasy and release.

It was better than anything he had ever experienced before.

Afterward, they finally kicked free of their suits. They shoved and pushed the things off the cot. Gunther pulled the blanket out from beneath them, and with Izmailova's help wrapped it about the both of them. They lay together, relaxed, not speaking.

He listened to her breathe for a while. The noise was soft. When she turned her face toward him, he could feel it, a warm little tickle in the hollow of his throat. The smell of her permeated the room. This stranger beside him.

Gunther felt weary, warm, at ease. "How long have you been here?" he asked. "Not here in the shelter, I mean, but . . ."

"Five days."

"That little." He smiled. "Welcome to the Moon, Ms. Izmailova."

"Ekatarina," she said sleepily. "Call me Ekatarina."

Whooping, they soared high and south, over Herschel. The Ptolemaeus road bent and doubled below them, winding out of sight, always returning. "This is great!" Hiro crowed. "This is—I should've talked you into taking me out here a year ago."

Gunther checked his bearings and throttled down, sinking eastward. The other two hoppers, slaved to his own, followed in tight formation. Two days had passed since the flare storm and Gunther, still on mandatory recoop, had promised to guide his friends into the highlands as soon as the surface advisory was dropped. "We're coming in now. Better triplecheck your safety harnesses. You doing okay back there, Kreesh?"

"I am quite comfortable, yes."

Then they were down on the Seething Bay Company landing pad.

Hiro was the second down and the first on the surface. He bounded about like a collie off its leash, chasing upslope and down, looking for new vantage points. "I can't believe I'm here! I work out this way every day, but you know what? This is the first time I've actually been out here. Physically, I mean."

"Watch your footing," Gunther warned. "This isn't like telepresence—if you break a leg, it'll be up to Krishna and me to carry you out."

"I trust you. Man, anybody who can get caught out in a flare storm, and end up nailing—"

"Hey, watch your language, okay?"

"Everybody's heard the story. I mean, we all thought you were dead, and then they found the two of you *asleep*. They'll be talking about it a hundred years from now." Hiro was practically choking on his laughter. "You're a legend!"

"Just give it a rest." To change the subject, Gunther said, "I can't believe you want to take a photo of this mess." The Seething Bay operation was a strip mine. Robot bulldozers scooped up the regolith and fed it to a processing plant that rested on enormous skids. They were after the thorium here, and the output was small enough that it could be transported to the breeder reactor by hopper. There was no need for a railgun and the tailings were piled in artificial mountains in the wake of the factory.

"Don't be ridiculous." Hiro swept an arm southward, toward Ptolemaeus. "There!" The crater wall caught the sun, while the lowest parts of the surrounding land were still in shadow. The gentle slopes seemed to tower; the crater itself was a cathedral, blazing white.

"Where is your camera?" Krishna asked.

"Don't need one. I'll just take the data down on my helmet."

"I'm not too clear on this mosaic project of yours," Gunther said. "Explain to me one more time how it's supposed to work."

"Anya came up with it. She's renting an assembler to cut hexagonal floor tiles in black, white, and fourteen intermediate shades of grey. I provide the pictures. We choose the one we like best, scan it in black and white, screen for values of intensity, and then have the assembler lay the floor, one tile per pixel. It'll look great—come by tomorrow and see."

"Yeah, I'll do that."

Chattering like a squirrel, Hiro led them away from the edge of the mine. They bounded westward, across the slope.

Krishna's voice came over Gunther's trance chip. It was an old groundrat trick. The chips had an effective transmission radius of fifteen yards—you could turn off the radio and talk chip-to-chip, if you were close enough. "You sound troubled, my friend."

He listened for a second carrier tone, heard nothing. Hiro was out of range. "It's Izmailova. I sort of—"

"Fell in love with her."

"How'd you know that?"

They were spaced out across the rising slope, Hiro in the lead. For a time neither spoke. There was a calm, confidential quality to that shared silence, like the anonymous stillness of the confessional. "Please don't take this wrong," Krishna said.

"Take what wrong?"

"Gunther, if you take two sexually compatible people, place them in close proximity, isolate them and scare the hell out of them, they will fall in love. That's a given. It's a survival mechanism, something that was wired into your basic makeup long before you were born. When billions of years of evolution say it's bonding time, your brain doesn't have much choice but to obey."

"Hey, come on over here!" Hiro cried over the radio. "You've got to see this."

"We're coming," Gunther said. Then, over his chip, "You make me out to be one of Sally Chang's machines."

"In some ways we *are* machines. That's not so bad. We feel thirsty when we need water, adrenaline pumps into the bloodstream when we need an extra boost of aggressive energy. You can't fight your own nature. What would be the point of it?"

"Yeah, but . . ."

"Is this great or what?" Hiro was clambering over a boulder field. "It just goes on and on. And look up there!" Upslope, they saw that what they were climbing over was the spillage from a narrow cleft entirely filled with boulders. They were huge, as big as hoppers, some of them large as prefab oxysheds. "Hey, Krishna, I been meaning to ask you—just what is it that you do out there at the Center?"

"I can't talk about it."

"Aw, come on." Hiro lifted a rock the size of his head to his shoulder and shoved it away, like a shot-putter. The rock soared slowly, landed far down-slope in a white explosion of dust. "You're among friends here. You can trust us."

Krishna shook his head. Sunlight flashed from the visor. "You don't know what you're asking."

Hiro hoisted a second rock, bigger than the first. Gunther knew him in this mood, nasty-faced and grinning. "My point exactly. The two of us know zip about neurobiology. You could spent the next ten hours lecturing us, and we couldn't catch enough to compromise security." Another burst of dust.

"You don't understand. The Center for Self-Replicating Technologies is here for a reason. The lab work could be done back on Earth for a fraction of what a lunar facility costs. Our sponsors only move projects here that they're genuinely afraid of."

"So what *can* you tell us about? Just the open stuff, the video magazine stuff. Nothing secret."

"Well . . . okay." Now it was Krishna's turn. He picked up a small rock, wound up like a baseball player and threw. It dwindled and disappeared in the distance. A puff of white sprouted from the surface. "You know Sally Chang? She has just finished mapping the neurotransmitter functions."

They waited. When Krishna added nothing further, Hiro dryly said, "Wow."

"Details, Kreesh. Some of us aren't so fast to see the universe in a grain of sand as you are."

"It should be obvious. We've had a complete genetic map of the brain for almost a decade. Now add to that Sally Chang's chemical map, and it's analogous to being given the keys to the library. No, better than that. Imagine that you've spent your entire life within an enormous library filled with books in a language you neither read nor speak, and that you've just found the dictionary and a picture reader."

"So what are you saying? That we'll have complete understanding of how the brain operates?"

"We'll have complete *control* over how the brain operates. With chemical therapy, it will be possible to make anyone think or feel anything we want. We will have an immediate cure for all nontraumatic mental illness. We'll be able to fine-tune aggression, passion, creativity—bring them up, damp them down, it'll be all the same. You can see why our sponsors are so afraid of what our research might produce."

"Not really, no. The world could use more sanity," Gunther said.

"I agree. But who defines sanity? Many governments consider political dissent grounds for mental incarceration. This would open the doors of the brain, allowing it to be examined from the outside. For the first time, it would be possible to discover unexpressed rebellion. Modes of thought could be outlawed. The potential for abuse is not inconsiderable.

"Consider also the military applications. This knowledge combined with some of the new nanoweaponry might produce a berserker gas, allowing you to turn the enemy's armies upon their own populace. Or, easier, to throw them into a psychotic frenzy and let them turn on themselves. Cities could be pacified by rendering the citizenry catatonic. A secondary, internal reality could then be created, allowing the conqueror to use the masses as slave labor. The possibilities are endless."

They digested this in silence. At last Hiro said, "Jeez, Krishna, if that's the open goods, what the hell kind of stuff do you have to hide?"

"I can't tell you."

A minute later, Hiro was haring off again. At the foot of a nearby hill he found an immense boulder standing atilt on its small end. He danced about, trying to get good shots past it without catching his own footprints in them.

"So what's the problem?" Krishna said over his chip.

"The problem is, I can't arrange to see her. Ekatarina. I've left messages, but she won't answer them. And you know how it is in Bootstrap—it takes a real effort to avoid somebody who wants to see you. But she's managed it."

Krishna said nothing.

"All I want to know is, just what's going on here?"

"She's avoiding you."

"But why? I fell in love and she didn't, is that what you're telling me? I mean, is that a crock or what?"

"Without hearing her side of the story, I can't really say how she feels. But the odds are excellent she fell every bit as hard as you did. The difference is that you think it's a good idea, and she doesn't. So of course she's avoiding you. Contact would just make it more difficult for her to master her feelings for you."

"Shit!"

An unexpected touch of wryness entered Krishna's voice. "What do you want? A minute ago you were complaining that I think you're a machine. Now you're unhappy that Izmailova thinks she's not."

"Hey, you guys! Come over here. I've found the perfect shot. You've got to see this."

They turned to see Hiro waving at them from the hilltop. "I thought you were leaving," Gunther grumbled. "You said you were sick of the Moon, and going away and never coming back. So how come you're upgrading your digs all of a sudden?"

"That was yesterday! Today, I'm a pioneer, a builder of worlds, a founder of dynasties!"

"This is getting tedious. What does it take to get a straight answer out of you?"

Hiro bounded high and struck a pose, arms wide and a little ridiculous. He staggered a bit on landing. "Anya and I are getting married!"

Gunther and Krishna looked at each other, blank visor to blank visor. Forcing enthusiasm into his voice, Gunther said, "Hey, no shit? Really! Congratu—"

A scream of static howled up from nowhere. Gunther winced and cut down the gain. "My stupid radio is—"

One of the other two—they had moved together and he couldn't tell them apart at this distance—was pointing upward. Gunther tilted back his head, to look at the Earth. For a second he wasn't sure what he was looking for. Then he saw it: a diamond pinprick of light in the middle of the night. It was like a small, bright hole in reality, somewhere in continental Asia. "What the hell is *that*?" he asked.

Softly, Hiro said, "I think it's Vladivostok."

By the time they were back over the Sinus Medii, that first light had reddened and faded away, and two more had blossomed. The news jockey at the Observatory was working overtime splicing together reports from the major news feeds into a montage of rumor and fear. The radio was full of talk about hits on Seoul and Buenos Aires. Those seemed certain. Strikes against Panama, Iraq, Denver, and Cairo were disputed. A stealth missile had flown low over Hokkaido and been deflected into the Sea of Japan. The Swiss Orbitals had lost some factories to fragmentation satellites. There was no agreement as to the source aggressor, and though most suspicions trended in one direction, Tokyo denied everything.

Gunther was most impressed by the sound feed from a British video essayist, who said that it did not matter who had fired the first shot, or why. "Who shall we blame? The Southern Alliance, Tokyo, General Kim, or possibly some Grey terrorist group that nobody has ever heard of before? In a world whose weapons were wired to hair triggers, the question is irrelevant. When the first device exploded, it activated autonomous programs which launched what is officially labeled 'a measured response.' Gorshov himself could not have prevented it. His tactical programs chose this week's three most likely aggressors—at least two of which were certainly innocent—and launched a response. Human beings had no say over it.

"Those three nations in turn had their own reflexive 'measured responses.' The results of which we are just beginning to learn. Now we will pause for five days, while all concerned parties negotiate. How do we know this? Abstracts of all major defense programs are available on any public data net. They are no secret. Openness is in fact what deterrence is all about.

"We have five days to avert a war that literally nobody wants. The question is, in five days can the military and political powers seize control of their own defense programming? Will they? Given the pain and anger involved, the traditional hatreds, national chauvinism, and the natural reactions of those who number loved ones among the already dead, can those in charge overcome their own natures in time to pull back from final and total war? Our best informed guess is no. No, they cannot.

"Good night, and may God have mercy on us all."

They flew northward in silence. Even when the broadcast cut off in midword, nobody spoke. It was the end of the world, and there was nothing they could say that did not shrink to insignificance before that fact. They simply headed home.

The land about Bootstrap was dotted with graffiti, great block letters traced out in boulders: KARL OPS—EINDHOVEN '49 and LOUISE MCTIGHE ALBUQUERQUE NM. An enormous eye in a pyramid. ARSENAL WORLD RUGBY CHAMPS with a crown over it. CORNPONE. Pi Lambda Phi. MOTORHEADS. A giant with a club. Coming down over them, Gunther reflected that they all referred to places and things in the world overhead, not a one of them indigenous to the Moon. What had always seemed pointless now struck him as unspeakably sad.

It was only a short walk from the hopper pad to the vacuum garage. They didn't bother to summon a jitney.

The garage seemed strangely unfamiliar to Gunther now, though he had passed through it a thousand times. It seemed to float in its own mystery, as if everything had been removed and replaced by its exact double, rendering it different and somehow unknowable. Row upon row of parked vehicles were slanted by type within the painted lines. Ceiling lights strained to reach the floor, and could not.

"Boy, is this place still!" Hiro's voice seemed unnaturally loud.

It was true. In all the cavernous reaches of the garage, not a single remote or robot service unit stirred. Not so much as a pressure-leak sniffer moved.

"Must be because of the news," Gunther muttered. He found he was not ready to speak of the war directly. To the back of the garage, five airlocks stood all in a row. Above them a warm, yellow strip of window shone in the rock. In the room beyond, he could see the overseer moving about.

Hiro waved an arm, and the small figure within leaned forward to wave back. They trudged to the nearest lock and waited.

Nothing happened.

After a few minutes, they stepped back and away from the lock to peer up through the window. The overseer was still there, moving unhurriedly. "Hey!" Hiro shouted over open frequency. "You up there! Are you on the job?"

The man smiled, nodded and waved again.

"Then open the goddamned door!" Hiro strode forward, and with a final, nodding wave, the overseer bent over his controls.

"Uh, Hiro," Gunther said, "there's something odd about . . ."

The door exploded open.

It slammed open so hard and fast the door was half torn off its hinges. The air within blasted out like a charge from a cannon. For a moment the garage was filled with loose tools, parts of vacuum suits and shreds of cloth. A wrench struck Gunther a glancing blow on his arm, spinning him around and knocking him to the floor.

He stared up in shock. Bits and pieces of things hung suspended for a long, surreal instant. Then, the air fled, they began to slowly shower down. He got up awkwardly, massaging his arm through the suit. "Hiro, are you all right? Kreesh?"

"Oh my God," Krishna said.

Gunther spun around. He saw Krishna crouched in the shadow of a flatbed, over something that could not possibly be Hiro, because it bent the wrong way. He walked through shimmering unreality and knelt beside Krishna. He stared down at Hiro's corpse.

Hiro had been standing directly before the door when the overseer opened it without depressurizing the corridor within first. He had caught the blast straight on. It had lifted him and smashed him against the side of a flatbed, snapping his spine and shattering his helmet visor with the backlash. He must have died instantaneously.

"Who's there?" a woman said.

A jitney had entered the garage without Gunther's noticing it. He looked up in time to see a second enter, and then a third. People began piling out. Soon there were some twenty individuals advancing across the garage. They broke into two groups. One headed straight toward the locks and the smaller group advanced on Gunther and his friends. It looked for all the world like a military operation. "Who's there?" the woman repeated.

Gunther lifted his friend's corpse in his arms and stood. "It's Hiro," he said flatly. "Hiro."

They floated forward cautiously, a semicircle of blank-visored suits like so many kachinas. He could make out the corporate logos. Mitsubishi. Westinghouse. Hoist Orbital. Izmailova's red-and-orange suit was among them, and a vivid Mondrian pattern he didn't recognize. The woman spoke again, tensely, warily. "Tell me how you're feeling, Hiro."

It was Beth Hamilton.

"That's not Hiro," Krishna said. "It's Gunther. *That's* Hiro. That he's carrying. We were out in the highlands and—" His voice cracked and collapsed in confusion.

"Is that you, Krishna?" someone asked. "There's a touch of luck. Send him up front, we're going to need him when we get in." Somebody else slapped an arm over Krishna's shoulders and led him away.

Over the radio, a clear voice spoke to the overseer. "Dmitri, is that you? It's Signe. You remember me, don't you, Dmitri? Signe Ohmstede. I'm your friend."

"Sure I remember you, Signe. I remember you. How could I ever forget my friend? Sure I do."

"Oh, good. I'm so happy. Listen carefully, Dmitri. Everything's fine."

Indignantly, Gunther chinned his radio to send. "The hell it is! That fool up there—!"

A burly man in a Westinghouse suit grabbed Gunther's bad arm and shook him. "Shut the fuck *up*!" he growled. "This is serious, damn you. We don't have the time to baby you."

Hamilton shoved between them. "For God's sake, Posner, he's just seen—" She stopped. "Let me take care of him. I'll get him calmed down. Just give us half an hour, okay?"

The others traded glances, nodded, and turned away.

To Gunther's surprise, Ekatarina spoke over his trance chip. "I'm sorry Gunther," she murmured. Then she was gone.

He was still holding Hiro's corpse. He found himself staring down at his friend's ruined face. The flesh was bruised and as puffy-looking as an over-boiled hot dog. He couldn't look away.

"Come on." Beth gave him a little shove to get him going. "Put the body in the back of that pick-up and give us a drive out to the cliff."

At Hamilton's insistence, Gunther drove. He found it helped, having something to do. Hands afloat on the steering wheel, he stared ahead looking for the Mausoleum road cut-off. His eyes felt scratchy, and inhumanly dry.

"There was a preemptive strike against us," Hamilton said. "Sabotage. We're just now starting to put the pieces together. Nobody knew you were out on the surface or we would've sent somebody out to meet you. It's all been something of a shambles here."

He drove on in silence, cushioned and protected by all those miles of hard vacuum wrapped about him. He could feel the presence of Hiro's corpse in the back of the truck, a constant psychic itch between his shoulder blades. But so long as he didn't speak, he was safe; he could hold himself aloof from the universe that held the pain. It couldn't touch him. He waited, but Beth didn't add anything to what she'd already said.

Finally he said, "Sabotage?"

"A software meltdown at the radio station. Explosions at all the railguns.

Three guys from Microspacecraft Applications bought it when the Boitsovij Kot railgun blew. I suppose it was inevitable. All the military industry up here, it's not surprising somebody would want to knock us out of the equation. But that's not all. Something's happened to the people in Bootstrap. Something really horrible. I was out at the Observatory when it happened. The newsjay called back to see if there was any backup software to get the station going again, and she got nothing but gibberish. Crazy stuff. I mean, *really* crazy. We had to disconnect the Observatory's remotes, because the operators were . . ." She was crying now, softly and insistently, and it was a minute before she could speak again. "Some sort of biological weapon. That's all we know."

"We're here."

As he pulled up to the foot of the Mausoleum cliff, it occurred to Gunther that they hadn't thought to bring a drilling rig. Then he counted ten black niches in the rockface, and realized that somebody had been thinking ahead.

"The only people who weren't hit were those who were working at the Center or the Observatory, or out on the surface. Maybe a hundred of us all told."

They walked around to the back of the pick-up. Gunther waited, but Hamilton didn't offer to carry the body. For some reason that made him feel angry and resentful. He unlatched the gate, hopped up on the treads, and hoisted the suited corpse. "Let's get this over with."

Before today, only six people had ever died on the Moon. They walked past the caves in which their bodies awaited eternity. Gunther knew their names by heart: Heisse, Yasuda, Spehalski, Dubinin, Mikami, Castillo. And now Hiro. It seemed incomprehensible that the day should ever come when there would be too many dead to know them all by name.

Daisies and tiger lilies had been scattered before the vaults in such profusion that he couldn't help crushing some underfoot.

They entered the first empty niche, and he laid Hiro down upon a stone table cut into the rock. In the halo of his helmet lamp the body looked piteously twisted and uncomfortable. Gunther found that he was crying, large hot tears that crawled down his face and got into his mouth when he inhaled. He cut off the radio until he had managed to blink the tears away. "Shit." He wiped a hand across his helmet. "I suppose we ought to say something."

Hamilton took his hand and squeezed.

"I've never seen him as happy as he was today. He was going to get married. He was jumping around, laughing and talking about raising a family. And now he's dead, and I don't even know what his religion was." A thought occurred to him, and he turned helplessly toward Hamilton. "What are we going to tell Anya?"

"She's got problems of her own. Come on, say a prayer and let's go. You'll run out of oxygen."

"Yeah, okay." He bowed his head. *"The Lord is my shepherd, I shall not want..."*

Back at Bootstrap, the surface party had seized the airlocks and led the overseer away from the controls. The man from Westinghouse, Posner, looked down on them from the observation window. "Don't crack your suits," he warned. "Keep them sealed tight at all times. Whatever hit the bastards here is still around. Might be in the water, might be in the air. One whiff and you're out of here! You got that?"

"Yeah, yeah," Gunther grumbled. "Keep your shirt on."

Posner's hand froze on the controls. "Let's get serious here. I'm not letting you in until you acknowledge the gravity of the situation. This isn't a picnic outing. If you're not prepared to help, we don't need you. Is that understood?"

"We understand completely, and we'll cooperate to the fullest," Hamilton said quickly. *"Won't we,* Weil?"

He nodded miserably.

Only the one lock had been breached, and there were five more sets of pressurized doors between it and the bulk of Bootstrap's air. The city's designers had been cautious.

Overseen by Posner, they passed through the corridors, locks and changing rooms and up the cargo escalators. Finally they emerged into the city interior.

They stood blinking on the lip of Hell.

At first, it was impossible to pinpoint any source for the pervasive sense of wrongness gnawing at the edge of consciousness. The parks were dotted with people, the fill lights at the juncture of crater walls and canopy were bright, and the waterfalls still fell gracefully from terrace to terrace. Button quail bobbed comically in the grass.

Then small details intruded. A man staggered about the fourth level, head jerking, arms waving stiffly. A plump woman waddled by, pulling an empty cart made from a wheeled microfactory stand, quacking like a duck. Someone sat in the kneehigh forest by Noguchi Park, tearing out the trees one by one.

But it was the still figures that were on examination more profoundly disturbing. Here a man lay half in and half out of a tunnel entrance, as unselfconscious as a dog. There, three women stood in extreme postures of lassitude, bordering on despair. Everywhere, people did not touch or speak or show in any way that they were aware of one other. They shared an absolute and universal isolation.

"What shall—" Something slammed onto Gunther's back. He was knocked forward, off his feet. Tumbling, he became aware that fists were striking him, again and again, and then that a lean man was kneeling atop his chest, hysterically shouting, "Don't do it! Don't do it!"

Hamilton seized the man's shoulders and pulled him away. Gunther got to his knees. He looked into the face of madness: eyes round and fearful, expression full of panic. The man was terrified of Gunther.

With an abrupt wrench, the man broke free. He ran as if pursued by demons. Hamilton stared after him. "You okay?" she asked.

"Yeah, sure." Gunther adjusted his tool harness. "Let's see if we can find the others."

They walked toward the lake, staring about at the self-absorbed figures scattered about the grass. Nobody attempted to speak to them. A woman ran by, barefooted. Her arms were filled with flowers. "Hey!" Hamilton called after her. She smiled fleetingly over her shoulder, but did not slow. Gunther knew her vaguely, an executive supervisor for Martin Marietta.

"Is *every*body here crazy?" he asked.

"Sure looks that way."

The woman had reached the shore and was flinging the blossoms into the water with great sweeps of her arm. They littered the surface.

"Damned waste." Gunther had come to Bootstrap before the flowers; he knew the effort involved getting permission to plant them and rewriting the city's ecologies. A man in a blue-striped Krupp suit was running along the verge of the lake.

The woman, flowers gone, threw herself into the water.

At first it appeared she'd suddenly decided to take a dip. But from the struggling, floundering way she thrashed deeper into the water it was clear that she could not swim.

In the time it took Gunther to realize this, Hamilton had leaped forward, running for the lake. Belatedly, he started after her. But the man in the Krupp suit was ahead of them both. He splashed in after the woman. An outstretched hand seized her shoulder and then he fell, pulling her under. She was red-faced and choking when he emerged again, arm across her chest.

By then Gunther and Beth were wading into the lake, and together they three got the woman to shore. When she was released, the woman calmly turned and walked away, as if nothing had happened.

"Gone for more flowers," the Krupp component explained. "This is the third time fair Ophelia there's tried to drown herself. She's not the only one. I've been hanging around, hauling 'em out when they stumble in."

"Do you know where everybody else is? Is there anyone in charge? Somebody giving out orders?"

"Do you need any help?" Gunther asked.

The Krupp man shrugged. "I'm fine. No idea where the others are, though. My friends were going on to the second level when I decided I ought to stay here. If you see them, you might tell 'em I'd appreciate hearing back from them. Three guys in Krupp suits."

"We'll do that," Gunther said.

Hamilton was already walking away.

On a step just beneath the top of the stairs sprawled one of Gunther's fellow G5 components. "Sidney," he said carefully. "How's it going?"

Sidney giggled. "I'm making the effort, if that's what you mean. I don't see that the 'how' of it makes much difference."

"Okay."

"A better way of phrasing that might be to ask why I'm not at work." He stood, and in a very natural manner accompanied Gunther up the steps. "Obviously I can't be two places at once. You wouldn't want to perform major surgery in your own absence, would you?" He giggled again. "It's an oxymoron. Like horses: those classically beautiful Praxitelesian bodies excreting these long surreal turds."

"Okay."

"I've always admired them for squeezing so much art into a single image."

"Sidney," Hamilton said. "We're looking for our friends. Three people in blue-striped work suits."

"I've seen them. I know just where they went." His eyes were cool and vacant; they didn't seem to focus on anything in particular.

"Can you lead us to them?"

"Even a flower recognizes its own face." A gracefully winding gravel path led through private garden plots and croquet malls. They followed him down it.

There were not many people on the second terrace; with the fall of madness, most seemed to have retreated into the caves. Those few who remained either ignored or cringed away from them. Gunther found himself staring obsessively into their faces, trying to analyze the deficiency he felt in each. Fear nested in their eyes, and the appalled awareness that some terrible thing had happened to them coupled with a complete ignorance of its nature.

"God, these people!"

Hamilton grunted.

He felt he was walking through a dream. Sounds were muted by his suit, and colors less intense seen through his helmet visor. It was as if he had been subtly removed from the world, there and not-there simultaneously, an impression that strengthened with each new face that looked straight through him with mad, unseeing indifference.

Sidney turned a corner, broke into a trot and jogged into a tunnel entrance. Gunther ran after him. At the mouth of the tunnel, he paused to let his helmet adjust to the new light levels. When it cleared he saw Sidney dart down a side passage. He followed.

At the intersection of passages, he looked and saw no trace of their guide. Sidney had disappeared. "Did you see which way he went?" he asked Hamilton over the radio. There was no answer. "Beth?"

He started down the corridor, halted, and turned back. These things went deep. He could wander around in them forever. He went back out to the terraces. Hamilton was nowhere to be seen.

For lack of any better plan, he followed the path. Just beyond an ornamental holly bush he was pulled up short by a vision straight out of William Blake.

The man had discarded shirt and sandals, and wore only a pair of shorts. He squatted atop a boulder, alert, patient, eating a tomato. A steel pipe slanted across his knees like a staff or scepter, and he had woven a crown of sorts from platinum wire with a fortune's worth of hyperconductor chips dangling over his forehead. He looked every inch a kingly animal.

He stared at Gunther, calm and unblinking.

Gunther shivered. The man seemed less human than anthropoid, crafty in its way, but unthinking. He felt as if he were staring across the eons at Grandfather Ape, crouched on the edge of awareness. An involuntary thrill of superstitious awe seized him. Was this what happened when the higher mental functions were scraped away? Did Archetype lie just beneath the skin, waiting for the opportunity to emerge?

"I'm looking for my friend," he said. "A woman in a G5 suit like mine? Have you seen her? She was looking for three—" He stopped. The man was staring at him blankly. "Oh, never mind."

He turned away and walked on.

After a time, he lost all sense of continuity. Existence fragmented into unconnected images: A man bent almost double, leering and squeezing a yellow rubber duckie. A woman leaping up like a jack-in-the-box from behind an air monitor, shrieking and flapping her arms. An old friend sprawled on the ground, crying, with a broken leg. When he tried to help her, she scrabbled away from him in fear. He couldn't get near her without doing more harm. "Stay here," he said, "I'll find help." Five minutes later he realized that he was lost, with not the slightest notion of how to find his way back to her again. He came to the stairs leading back down to the bottom level. There was no reason to go down them. There was no reason not to. He went down.

He had just reached the bottom of the stairs when someone in a lavender boutique suit hurried by.

Gunther chinned on his helmet radio.

"Hello!" The lavender suit glanced back at him, its visor a plate of obsidian, but did not turn back. "Do you know where everyone's gone? I'm totally lost. How can I find out what I should be doing?" The lavender suit ducked into a tunnel.

Faintly, a voice answered, "Try the city manager's office."

The city manager's office was a tight little cubby an eighth of a kilometer deep within the tangled maze of administrative and service tunnels. It had never been very important in the scheme of things. The city manager's prime duties were keeping the air and water replenished and scheduling airlock inspections, functions any computer could handle better than a man had they dared trust them to a machine. The room had probably never been as crowded as it was now. Dozens of people suited for full vacuum spilled out into the hall, anxiously listening to Ekatarina confer with the city's Crisis Management Program. Gunther pushed in as close as he could; even so, he could barely see her.

"—the locks, the farms and utilities, and we've locked away all the remotes. What comes next?"

Ekatarina's peecee hung from her work harness, amplifying the CMP's silent voice. "Now that elementary control has been established, second priority must go to the industrial sector. The factories must be locked down. The reactors must be put to sleep. There is not sufficient human supervisory presence to keep them running. The factories have mothballing programs available upon request.

"Third, the farms cannot tolerate neglect. Fifteen minutes without oxygen, and all the tilapia will die. The calimari are even more delicate. Three experienced agricultural components must be assigned immediately. Double that number, if you only have inexperienced components. Advisory software is available. What are your resources?"

"Let me get back to you on that. What else?"

"What about the people?" a man asked belligerently. "What the hell are you worrying about factories for, when our people are in the state they're in?"

Izmailova looked up sharply. "You're one of Chang's research components, aren't you? Why are you here? Isn't there enough for you to do?" She looked about, as if abruptly awakened from sleep. "All of you! What are you waiting for?"

"You can't put us off that easily! Who made you the little brass-plated general? We don't have to take orders from you."

The bystanders shuffled uncomfortably, not leaving, waiting to take their cue from each other. Their suits were as good as identical in this crush, their helmets blank and expressionless. They looked like so many ambulatory eggs.

The crowd's mood balanced on the instant, ready to fall into acceptance or anger with a featherweight's push. Gunther raised an arm. "General!" he said loudly. "Private Weil here! I'm awaiting my orders. Tell me what to do."

Laughter rippled through the room, and the tension eased. Ekatarina said, "Take whoever's nearest you, and start clearing the afflicted out of the administrative areas. Guide them out toward the open, where they won't be so likely to hurt themselves. Whenever you get a room or corridor emptied, lock it up tight. Got that?"

"Yes, ma'am." He tapped the suit nearest him, and its helmet dipped in a curt nod. But when they turned to leave, their way was blocked by the crush of bodies.

"You!" Ekatarina jabbed a finger. "Go to the farmlocks and foam them shut; I don't want any chance of getting them contaminated. Anyone with experience running factories—that's most of us, I think—should find a remote and get to work shutting the things down. The CMP will help direct you. If you have nothing else to do, buddy up and work at clearing out the corridors. I'll call a general meeting when we've put together a more comprehensive plan of action." She paused. "What have I left out?"

Surprisingly, the CMP answered her: "There are twenty-three children in the city, two of them seven-year-old prelegals and the rest five years of age or younger, offspring of registered-permanent lunar components. Standing directives are that children be given special care and protection. The third-level chapel can be converted to a care center. Word should be spread that as they are found, the children are to be brought there. Assign one reliable individual to oversee them."

"My God, yes." She turned to the belligerent man from the Center, and snapped, "Do it."

He hesitated, then saluted ironically and turned to go.

That broke the logjam. The crowd began to disperse. Gunther and his coworker—it turned out to be Liza Nagenda, another ground-rat like himself—set to work.

In after years Gunther was to remember this period as a time when his life entered a dark tunnel. For long, nightmarish hours he and Liza shuffled from office to storage room, struggling to move the afflicted out of the corporate areas and into the light.

The afflicted did not cooperate.

The first few rooms they entered were empty. In the fourth, a distraught-looking woman was furiously going through drawers and files and flinging their contents away. Trash covered the floor. "It's in here somewhere," she said frantically.

"What's in there, darling?" Gunther said soothingly. He had to speak loudly so he could be heard through his helmet. "What are you looking for?"

She tilted her head up with a smile of impish delight. Using both hands, she smoothed back her hair, elbows high, pushing it straight over her skull, then tucking in stray strands behind her ears. "It doesn't matter, because I'm sure to find it now. Two scarabs appear, and between them the blazing disk of the sun, that's a good omen, not to mention being an analogy for sex. I've had sex, all the sex anyone could want, buggered behind the outhouse by the lizard king when I was nine. What did I care? I had wings then and thought that I could fly."

Gunther edged a little closer. "You're not making any sense at all."

"You know, Tolstoy said there was a green stick in the woods behind his house that once found would cause all men to love one another. I believe in that green stick as a basic principle of physical existence. The universe exists in a matrix of four dimensions which we can perceive and seven which we cannot, which is why we experience peace and brotherhood as a seven-dimensional green stick phenomenon."

"You've got to listen to me."

"Why? You gonna tell me Hitler is dead? I don't believe in that kind of crap."

"Oh hell," Nagenda said. "You can't reason with a flick. Just grab her arms and we'll chuck her out."

It wasn't that easy, though. The woman was afraid of them. Whenever they approached her, she slipped fearfully away. If they moved slowly, they could not corner her, and when they both rushed her, she leapt up over a desk and then down into the kneehole. Nagenda grabbed her legs and pulled. The woman wailed, and clutched at the knees of Nagenda's suit. "Get offa me," Liza snarled. "Gunther, get this crazy woman off my damn legs."

"Don't kill me!" the woman screamed. "I've always voted twice—you know I did. I told them you were a gangster, but I was wrong. Don't take the oxygen out of my lungs!"

They got the woman out of the office, then lost her again when Gunther turned to lock the door. She went fluttering down the corridor with Nagenda in hot pursuit. Then she dove into another office, and they had to start all over again.

It took over an hour to drive the woman from the corridors and release her into the park. The next three went quickly enough by contrast. The one after that was difficult again, and the fifth turned out to be the first woman they had encountered, wandered back to look for her office. When they'd brought her to the open again, Liza Nagenda said, "That's four flicks down and three thousand eight hundred fifty-eight to go."

"Look—" Gunther began. And then Krishna's voice sounded over his trance chip, stiffly and with exaggerated clarity. "Everyone is to go to the central lake immediately for an organizational meeting. Repeat: Go to the lake immediately. Go to the lake now." He was obviously speaking over a ju-ry-rigged transmitter. The sound was bad and his voice boomed and popped on the chip.

"All right, okay, I got that," Liza said. "You can shut up now."

"Please go to the lake immediately. Everyone is to go directly to the central—"

"Sheesh."

By the time they got out to the parklands again, the open areas were thick with people. Not just the suited figures of the survivors, either. All the afflict-ed were emerging from the caves and corridors of Bootstrap. They walked blindly, uncertainly, toward the lake, as if newly called from the grave. The ground level was filling with people.

"Sonofabitch," Gunther said wonderingly.

"Gunther?" Nagenda asked. "What's going on?"

"It's the trance chips! Sonofabitch, all we had to do was speak to them over the chips. They'll do whatever the voice in their heads tells them to do."

The land about the lake was so crowded that Gunther had trouble spot-ting any other suits. Then he saw a suited figure standing on the edge of the second level waving broadly. He waved back and headed for the stairs.

By the time he got to level two, a solid group of the unafflicted had gath-ered. More and more came up, drawn by the concentration of suits. Finally Ekatarina spoke over the open channel of her suit radio.

"There's no reason to wait for us all to gather. I think everyone is close enough to hear me. Sit down, take a little rest, you've all earned it." People eased down on the grass. Some sprawled on their backs or stomachs, fully suited. Most just sat.

"By a fortunate accident, we've discovered a means of controlling our af-flicted friends." There was light applause. "But there are still many problems before us, and they won't all be solved so easily. We've all seen the obvious.

Now I must tell you of worse. If the war on Earth goes full thermonuclear, we will be completely and totally cut off, possibly for decades."

A murmur passed through the crowd.

"What does this mean? Beyond the immediate inconveniences—no luxuries, no more silk shirts, no new seed stock, no new videos, no way home for those of us who hadn't already decided to stay—we will be losing much that we require for survival. All our microfacturing capability comes from the Swiss Orbitals. Our water reserves are sufficient for a year, but we lose minute quantities of water vapor to rust and corrosion and to the vacuum every time somebody goes in or out an airlock, and those quantities are necessary for our existence.

"But we can survive. We can process raw hydrogen and oxygen from the regolith, and burn them to produce water. We already make our own air. We can do without most nanoelectronics. We can thrive and prosper and grow, even if Earth . . . even if the worst happens. But to do so we'll need our full manufacturing capability, and full supervisory capability as well. We must not only restore our factories, but find a way to restore our people. There'll be work and more for all of us in the days ahead."

Nagenda touched helmets with Gunther and muttered, "What a crock."

"Come on, I want to hear this."

"Fortunately, the Crisis Management Program has contingency plans for exactly this situation. According to its records, which may be incomplete, I have more military command experience than any other functional. Does anyone wish to challenge this?" She waited, but nobody said anything. "We will go to a quasimilitary structure for the duration of the emergency. This is strictly for organizational purposes. There will be no privileges afforded the officers, and the military structure will be dismantled *immediately* upon resolution of our present problems. That's paramount."

She glanced down at her peecee. "To that purpose, I am establishing beneath me a triumvirate of subordinate officers, consisting of Carlos Diaz-Rodrigues, Miiko Ezumi, and Will Posner. Beneath them will be nine officers, each responsible for a cadre of no more than ten individuals."

She read out names. Gunther was assigned to Cadre Four, Beth Hamilton's group. Then Ekatarina said, "We're all tired. The gang back at the Center have rigged up a decontamination procedure, a kitchen and sleeping spaces of sorts. Cadres One, Two, and Three will put in four more hours here, then pull down a full eight hours sleep. Cadres Four through Nine may return now to the Center for a meal and four hours rest." She stopped. "That's it. Go get some shut-eye."

A ragged cheer arose, fell flat, and died. Gunther stood. Liza Nagenda gave him a friendly squeeze on the butt and when he started to the right yanked his arm and pointed him left, toward the service escalators. With easy familiarity, she slid an arm around his waist.

He'd known guys who'd slept with Liza Nagenda, and they all agreed that she was bad news, possessive, hysterical, ludicrously emotional. But what the hell. It was easier than not.

They trudged off.

There was too much to do. They worked to exhaustion—it was not enough. They rigged a system of narrow-band radio transmissions for the CMP and ran a microwave patch back to the Center, so it could direct their efforts more efficiently—it was not enough. They organized and rearranged constantly. But the load was too great and accidents inevitably happened.

Half the surviving railguns—small units used to deliver raw and semi-processed materials over the highlands and across the bay—were badly damaged when the noonday sun buckled their aluminum rails; the sunscreens had not been put in place in time. An unknown number of robot bulldozers had wandered off from the strip mines and were presumably lost. It was hard to guess how many because the inventory records were scrambled. None of the food stored in Bootstrap could be trusted; the Center's meals had to be harvested direct from the farms and taken out through the emergency locks. An inexperienced farmer mishandled her remote, and ten aquaculture tanks boiled out into vacuum geysering nine thousand fingerlings across the surface. On Posner's orders, the remote handler rigs were hastily packed and moved to the Center. When uncrated, most were found to have damaged rocker arms.

There were small victories. On his second shift, Gunther found fourteen bales of cotton in vacuum storage and set an assembler to sewing futons for the Center. That meant an end to sleeping on bare floors and made him a local hero for the rest of that day. There were not enough toilets in the Center; Diaz-Rodrigues ordered the flare storm shelters in the factories stripped of theirs. Huriel Garza discovered a talent for cooking with limited resources.

But they were losing ground. The afflicted were unpredictable, and they were everywhere. A demented systems analyst, obeying the voices in his head, dumped several barrels of lubricating oil in the lake. The water filters clogged, and the streams had to be shut down for repairs. A doctor somehow managed to strangle herself with her own diagnostic harness. The city's ecologies were badly stressed by random vandalism.

Finally somebody thought to rig up a voice loop for continuous transmission. "I am calm," it said. "I am tranquil. I do not want to do anything. I am happy where I am."

Gunther was working with Liza Nagenda trying to get the streams going again when the loop came on. He looked up and saw an uncanny quiet spread over Bootstrap. Up and down the terraces, the flicks stood in postures of complete and utter impassivity. The only movement came from the small number of suits scurrying like beetles among the newly catatonic.

Liza put her hands on her hips. "Terrific. Now we've got to *feed* them."

"Hey, cut me some slack, okay? This is the first good news I've heard since I don't know when."

"It's not good anything, sweetbuns. It's just more of the same."

She was right. Relieved as he was, Gunther knew it. One hopeless task has been traded for another.

He was wearily suiting up for his third day when Hamilton stopped him and said, "Weil! You know any electrical engineering?"

"Not really, no. I mean, I can do the wiring for a truck, or maybe rig up a microwave relay, stuff like that, but . . ."

"It'll have to do. Drop what you're on, and help Krishna set up a system for controlling the flicks. Some way we can handle them individually."

They set up shop in Krishna's old lab. The remnants of old security standards still lingered, and nobody had been allowed to sleep there. Consequently, the room was wonderfully neat and clean, all crafted-in-orbit laboratory equipment with smooth, anonymous surfaces. It was a throwback to a time before clutter and madness had taken over. If it weren't for the new-tunnel smell, the raw tang of cut rock the air carried, it would be possible to pretend nothing had happened.

Gunther stood in a telepresence rig, directing a remote through Bootstrap's apartments. They were like so many unconnected cells of chaos. He entered one and found the words BUDDHA = COSMIC INERTIA scrawled on its wall with what looked to be human feces. A woman sat on the futon tearing handfuls of batting from it and flinging them in the air. Cotton covered the room like a fresh snowfall. The next apartment was empty and clean, and a microfactory sat gleaming on a ledge. "I hereby nationalize you in the name of the People's Provisional Republic of Bootstrap, and of the oppressed masses everywhere," he said dryly. The remote gingerly picked it up. "You done with that chip diagram yet?"

"It will not be long now," Krishna said.

They were building a prototype controller. The idea was to code each peecee, so the CMP could identify and speak to its owner individually. By stepping down the voltage, they could limit the peecee's transmission range to a meter and a half so that each afflicted person could be given individualized orders. The existing chips, however, were high-strung Swiss Orbital thoroughbreds, and couldn't handle oddball power yields. They had to be replaced.

"I don't see how you can expect to get any useful work out of these guys, though. I mean, what we need are supervisors. You can't hope to get coherent thought out of them."

Bent low over his peecee, Krishna did not answer at first. Then he said, "Do you know how a yogi stops his heart? We looked into that when I was in grad school. We asked Yogi Premanand if he would stop his heart while wired up to our instruments, and he graciously consented. We had all the latest brain scanners, but it turned out the most interesting results were recorded by the EKG.

"We found that the yogi's heart did not as we had expected slow down, but rather went faster and faster, until it reached its physical limits and began to fibrillate. He had not slowed his heart; he had sped it up. It did not stop, but went into spasm.

"After our tests, I asked him if he had known these facts. He said no, that they were most interesting. He was polite about it, but clearly did not think our findings very significant."

"So you're saying . . . ?"

"The problem with schizophrenics is that they have too much going on in their heads. Too many voices. Too many ideas. They can't focus their attention on a single chain of thought. But it would be a mistake to think them incapable of complex reasoning. In fact, they're thinking brilliantly. Their brains are simply operating at such peak efficiencies that they can't organize their thoughts coherently.

"What the trance chip does is to provide one more voice, but a louder, more insistent one. That's why they obey it. It breaks through that noise, provides a focus, serves as a matrix along which thought can crystallize."

The remote unlocked the door into a conference room deep in the administrative tunnels. Eight microfactories waited in a neat row atop the conference table. It added the ninth, turned, and left, locking the door behind it. "You know," Gunther said, "all these elaborate precautions may be unnecessary. Whatever was used on Bootstrap may not be in the air anymore. It may never have *been* in the air. It could've been in the water or something."

"Oh, it's there all right, in the millions. We're dealing with an airborne schizomimetic engine. It's designed to hang around in the air indefinitely."

"A schizomimetic engine? What the hell is that?"

In a distracted monotone, Krishna said, "A schizomimetic engine is a strategic nonlethal weapon with high psychological impact. It not only incapacitates its target vectors, but places a disproportionately heavy burden on the enemy's manpower and material support caring for the victims. Due to the particular quality of the effect, it has a profoundly demoralizing influence on those exposed to the victims, especially those involved in their care. Thus, it is particularly desirable as a strategic weapon." He might have been quoting from an operations manual.

Gunther pondered that. "Calling the meeting over the chips wasn't a mistake, was it? You knew it would work. You knew they would obey a voice speaking inside their heads."

"Yes."

"This shit was brewed up at the Center, wasn't it? This is the stuff that you couldn't talk about."

"Some of it."

Gunther powered down his rig and flipped up the lens. "God damn you, Krishna! God damn you straight to Hell, you stupid fucker!"

Krishna looked up from his work, bewildered. "Have I said something wrong?"

"No! No, you haven't said a damned thing wrong—you've just driven four thousand people out of their fucking minds, is all! Wake up and take a good look at what you maniacs have done with your weapons research!"

"It wasn't weapons research," Krishna said mildly. He drew a long, involuted line on the schematic. "But when pure research is funded by the military, the military will seek out military applications for the research. That's just the way it is."

"What's the difference? It happened. You're responsible."

Now Krishna actually set his peecee aside. He spoke with uncharacteristic fire. "Gunther, we *need* this information. Do you realize that we are trying to run a technological civilization with a brain that was evolved in the neolithic? I am perfectly serious. We're all trapped in the old hunter-gatherer programs, and they are of no use to us anymore. Take a look at what's happening on Earth. They're hip-deep in a war that nobody meant to start and nobody wants to fight and it's even money that nobody can stop. The type of thinking that put us in this corner is not to our benefit. It has to change. And that's what we are working toward—taming the human brain. Harnessing it. Reining it in.

"Granted, our research has been turned against us. But what's one more weapon among so many? If neuroprogrammers hadn't been available, something else would have been used. Mustard gas maybe, or plutonium dust. For that matter, they could've just blown a hole in the canopy and let us all strangle."

"That's self-justifying bullshit, Krishna! Nothing can excuse what you've done."

Quietly, but with conviction, Krishna said, "You will never convince me that our research is not the most important work we could possibly be doing today. We must seize control of this monster within our skulls. We must change our ways of thinking." His voice dropped. "The sad thing is that we cannot change unless we survive. But in order to survive, we must first change."

They worked in silence after that.

Gunther awoke from restless dreams to find that the sleep shift was only half over. Liza was snoring. Careful not to wake her, he pulled his clothes on and padded barefoot out of his niche and down the hall. The light was on in the common room and he heard voices.

Ekatarina looked up when he entered. Her face was pale and drawn. Faint circles had formed under her eyes. She was alone.

"Oh, hi. I was just talking with the CMP." She thought off her peecee. "Have a seat."

He pulled up a chair and hunched down over the table. Confronted by her, he found it took a slight but noticeable effort to draw his breath. "So. How are things going?"

"They'll be trying out your controllers soon. The first batch of chips ought to be coming out of the factories in an hour or so. I thought I'd stay up to see how they work out."

"It's that bad, then?" Ekatarina shook her head, would not look at him. "Hey, come on, here you are waiting up on the results, and I can see how tired you are. There must be a lot riding on this thing."

"More than you know," she said bleakly. "I've just been going over the numbers. Things are worse than you can imagine."

He reached out and took her cold, bloodless hand. She squeezed him so tightly it hurt. Their eyes met and he saw in hers all the fear and wonder he felt.

Wordlessly, they stood.

"I'm niching alone," Ekatarina said. She had not let go of his hand, held it so tightly, in fact, that it seemed she would never let it go.

Gunther let her lead him away.

They made love, and talked quietly about inconsequential things, and made love again. Gunther had thought she would nod off immediately after the first time, but she was too full of nervous energy for that.

"Tell me when you're about to come," she murmured. "Tell me when you're coming."

He stopped moving. "Why do you always say that?"

Ekatarina looked up at him dazedly, and he repeated the question. Then she laughed a deep, throaty laugh. "Because I'm frigid."

"Hah?"

She took his hand, and brushed her cheek against it. Then she ducked her head, continuing the motion across her neck and up the side of her scalp. He felt the short, prickly hair against his palm and then, behind her ear, two bumps under the skin where biochips had been implanted. One of those would be her trance chip and the other . . . "It's a prosthetic," she explained.

Her eyes were grey and solemn. "It hooks into the pleasure centers. When I need to, I can turn on my orgasm at a thought. That way we can always come at the same time." She moved her hips slowly beneath him as she spoke.

"But that means you don't really need to have any kind of sexual stimulation at all, do you? You can trigger an orgasm at will. While you're riding on a bus. Or behind a desk. You could just turn that thing on and come for hours at a time."

She looked amused. "I'll tell you a secret. When it was new, I used to do stunts like that. Everybody does. One outgrows that sort of thing quickly."

With more than a touch of stung pride, Gunther said, "Then what am I doing here? If you've got that thing, what the hell do you need me for?" He started to draw away from her.

She pulled him down atop her again. "You're kind of comforting," she said. "In an argumentative way. Come here."

He got back to his futon and began gathering up the pieces of his suit. Liza sat up sleepily and gawked at him. "So," she said. "It's like that, is it?"

"Yeah, well. I kind of left something unfinished. An old relationship." Warily, he extended a hand. "No hard feelings, huh?"

Ignoring his hand, she stood, naked and angry. "You got the nerve to stand there without even wiping my smile off your dick first and say no hard feelings? Asshole!"

"Aw, come on now, Liza, it's not like that."

"Like hell it's not! You got a shot at that white-assed Russian ice queen, and I'm history. Don't think I don't know all about her."

"I was hoping we could still be, you know, friends."

"Nice trick, shithead." She balled her fist and hit him hard in the center of his chest. Tears began to form in her eyes. "You just slink away. I'm tired of looking at you."

He left.

But did not sleep. Ekatarina was awake and ebullient over the first reports coming in on the new controller system. "They're working!" she cried. "They're working!" She'd pulled on a silk camisole, and strode back and forth excitedly, naked to the waist. Her pubic hair was a white flame, with almost invisible trails of smaller hairs reaching for her navel and caressing the sweet insides of her thighs. Tired as he was, Gunther felt new desire for her. In a weary, washed-out way, he was happy.

"Whooh!" She kissed him hard, not sexually, and called up the CMP. "Rerun all our earlier projections. We're putting our afflicted components back to work. Adjust all work schedules."

"As you direct."

"How does this change our long-range prospects?"

The program was silent for several seconds, processing. Then it said, "You are about to enter a necessary but very dangerous stage of recovery. You are going from a low-prospects high-stability situation to a high-prospects high-instability one. With leisure your unafflicted components will quickly grow dissatisfied with your government."

"What happens if I just step down?"

"Prospects worsen drastically."

Ekatarina ducked her head. "All right, what's likely to be our most pressing new problem?"

"The unafflicted components will demand to know more about the war on Earth. They'll want the media feeds restored immediately."

"I could rig up a receiver easily enough," Gunther volunteered. "Nothing fancy, but . . ."

"Don't you dare!"

"Hah? Why not?"

"Gunther, let me put it to you this way: What two nationalities are most heavily represented here?"

"Well, I guess that would be Russia and—oh."

"Oh is right. For the time being, I think it's best if nobody knows for sure who's supposed to be enemies with whom." She asked the CMP, "How should I respond?"

"Until the situation stabilizes, you have no choice but distraction. Keep their minds occupied. Hunt down the saboteurs and then organize war crime trials."

"That's out. No witch hunts, no scapegoats, no trials. We're all in this together."

Emotionlessly, the CMP said, "Violence is the left hand of government. You are rash to dismiss its potentials without serious thought."

"I won't discuss it."

"Very well. If you wish to postpone the use of force for the present, you could hold a hunt for the weapon used on Bootstrap. Locating and identifying it would involve everyone's energies without necessarily implicating anybody. It would also be widely interpreted as meaning an eventual cure was possible, thus boosting the general morale without your actually lying."

Tiredly, as if this were something she had gone over many times already, she said, "Is there really no hope of curing them?"

"Anything is possible. In light of present resources, though, it cannot be considered likely."

Ekatarina thought the peecee off, dismissing the CMP. She sighed. "Maybe that's what we ought to do. Donkey up a hunt for the weapon. We ought to be able to do something with that notion."

Puzzled, Gunther said, "But it was one of Chang's weapons, wasn't it? A schizomimetic engine, right?"

"Where did you hear that?" she demanded sharply.

"Well, Krishna said ... he didn't act like ... I thought it was public knowledge."

Ekatarina's face hardened. "Program!" she thought.

The CMP came back to life. "Ready."

"Locate Krishna Narasimhan, unafflicted, Cadre Five. I want to speak with him immediately." Ekatarina snatched up her panties and shorts, and furiously began dressing. "Where are my damned sandals? Program! Tell him to meet me in the common room. Right away."

"Received."

To Gunther's surprise, it took over an hour for Ekatarina to browbeat Krishna into submission. Finally, though, the young research component went to a lockbox, identified himself to it, and unsealed the storage areas. "It's not all that secure," he said apologetically. "If our sponsors knew how often we just left everything open so we could get in and out, they'd—well, never mind."

He lifted a flat, palm-sized metal rectangle from a cabinet. "This is the most likely means of delivery. It's an aerosol bomb. The biological agents are loaded *here*, and it's triggered by snapping this back *here*. It's got enough pressure in it to spew the agents fifty feet straight up. Air currents do the rest." He tossed it to Gunther who stared down at the thing in horror. "Don't worry, it's not armed."

He slid out a slim drawer holding row upon gleaming row of slim chrome cylinders. "These contain the engines themselves. They're off-the-shelf nano-weaponry. State of the art stuff, I guess." He ran a fingertip over them. "We've programmed each to produce a different mix of neurotransmitters. Dopamine, phencyclidine, norepinephrine, acetylcholine, met-enkephalin, substance P, serotonin—there's a hefty slice of Heaven in here, and—" he tapped an empty space— "right here is our missing bit of Hell." He frowned, and muttered, "That's curious. Why are there two cylinders missing?"

"What's that?" Ekatarina said. "I didn't catch what you just said."

"Oh, nothing important. Um, listen, it might help if I yanked a few biological pathways charts and showed you the chemical underpinnings of these things."

"Never mind that. Just keep it sweet and simple. Tell us about these schizomimetic engines."

It took over an hour to explain.

The engines were molecule-sized chemical factories, much like the assemblers in a microfactory. They had been provided by the military, in the hope Chang's group would come up with a misting weapon that could be sprayed in an army's path to cause them to change their loyalty. Gunther dozed off briefly while Krishna was explaining why that was impossible, and woke up sometime after the tiny engines had made their way into the brain.

"It's really a false schizophrenia," Krishna explained. "True schizophrenia is a beautifully complicated mechanism. What these engines create is more like a bargain-basement knockoff. They seize control of the brain chemistry, and start pumping out dopamine and a few other neuromediators. It's not an actual disorder, *per se*. They just keep the brain hopping." He coughed. "You see."

"Okay," Ekatarina said. "Okay. You say you can reprogram these things. How?"

"We use what are technically called messenger engines. They're like neuromodulators—they tell the schizomimetic engines what to do." He slid open another drawer, and in a flat voice said, "They're gone."

"Let's keep to the topic, if we may. We'll worry about your inventory later. Tell us about these messenger engines. Can you brew up a lot of them, to tell the schizomimetics to turn themselves off?"

"No, for two reasons. First, these molecules were hand-crafted in the Swiss Orbitals; we don't have the industrial plant to create them. Secondly, you can't tell the schizomimetics to turn themselves off. They don't *have* off switches. They're more like catalysts than actual machines. You can reconfigure them to produce different chemicals, but . . . He stopped, and a distant look came into his eyes. "Damn." He grabbed up his peecee, and a chemical pathways chart appeared on one wall. Then beside it, a listing of major neurofunctions. Then another chart covered with scrawled behavioral symbols. More and more data slammed up on the wall.

"Uh, Krishna . . . ?"

"Oh, go away," he snapped. "This is important."

"You think you might be able to come up with a cure?"

"Cure? No. Something better. Much better."

Ekatarina and Gunther looked at each other. Then she said, "Do you need anything? Can I assign anyone to help you?"

"I need the messenger engines. Find them for me."

"How? How do we find them? Where do we look?"

"Sally Chang," Krishna said impatiently. "She must have them. Nobody else had access." He snatched up a light pen, and began scrawling crabbed formulae on the wall.

"I'll get her for you. Program! Tell—"

"Chang's a flick," Gunther reminded her. "She was caught by the aerosol bomb." Which she must surely have set herself. A neat way of disposing of evidence that might've led to whatever government was running her. She'd have been the first to go mad.

Ekatarina pinched her nose, wincing. "I've been awake too long," she said. "All right, I understand. Krishna, from now on you're assigned permanently to research. The CMP will notify your cadre leader. Let me know if you need any support. Find me a way to turn this damned weapon off." Ignoring the way he shrugged her off, she said to Gunther, "I'm yanking you from Cadre Four. From now on, you report directly to me. I want you to find Chang. Find her, and find those messenger engines."

Gunther was bone-weary. He couldn't remember when he'd last had a good eight hours' sleep. But he managed what he hoped was a confident grin. "Received."

A madwoman should not have been able to hide herself. Sally Chang could. Nobody should have been able to evade the CMP's notice, now that it was hooked into a growing number of afflicted individuals. Sally Chang did. The CMP informed Gunther that none of the flicks were aware of Chang's whereabouts. It accepted a directive to have them all glance about for her once every hour until she was found.

In the west tunnels, walls had been torn out to create a space as large as any factory interior. The remotes had been returned, and were now manned by almost two hundred flicks spaced so that they did not impinge upon each other's fields of instruction. Gunther walked by them, through the CMP's whispering voices: "Are all bulldozers accounted for? If so . . . Clear away any malfunctioning machines; they can be placed . . . for vacuum-welded dust on the upper surfaces of the rails . . . reduction temperature, then look to see that the oxygen feed is compatible . . . At the far end a single suit sat in a chair, overseer unit in its lap.

"How's it going?" Gunther asked.

"Absolutely top-notch." He recognized Takayuni's voice. They'd worked in the Flammaprion microwave relay station together. "Most of the factories are up and running, and we're well on our way to having the railguns operative too. You wouldn't believe the kind of efficiencies we're getting here."

"Good, huh?"

Takayuni grinned; Gunther could hear it in his voice. "Industrious little buggers!"

Takayuni hadn't seen Chang. Gunther moved on.

Some hours later he found himself sitting wearily in Noguchi Park, looking at the torn-up dirt where the kneehigh forest had been. Not a seedling had been spared; the silver birch was extinct as a lunar species. Dead carp floated belly-up in the oil-slicked central lake; a chain-link fence circled it now, to keep out the flicks. There hadn't been the time yet to begin cleaning up the litter, and when he looked about, he saw trash everywhere. It was sad. It reminded him of Earth.

He knew it was time to get going, but he couldn't. His head sagged, touched his chest, and jerked up. Time had passed.

A flicker of motion made him turn. Somebody in a pastel lavender boutique suit hurried by. The woman who had directed him to the city controller's office the other day. "Hello!" he called. "I found everybody just where you said. Thanks. I was starting to get a little spooked."

The lavender suit turned to look at him. Sunlight glinted on black glass. A still, long minute later, she said, "Don't mention it," and started away.

"I'm looking for Sally Chang. Do you know her? Have you seen her? She's a flick, kind of a little woman, flamboyant, used to favor bright clothes, electric makeup, that sort of thing."

"I'm afraid I can't help you." Lavender was carrying three oxytanks in her arms. "You might try the straw market, though. Lots of bright clothes there." She ducked into a tunnel opening and disappeared within.

Gunther stared after her distractedly, then shook his head. He felt so very, very tired.

The straw market looked as though it had been through a storm. The tents had been torn down, the stands knocked over, the goods looted. Shards of orange and green glass crunched underfoot. Yet a rack of Italian scarves worth a year's salary stood untouched amid the rubble. It made no sense at all.

Up and down the market, flicks were industriously cleaning up. They stooped and lifted and swept. One of them was being beaten by a suit.

Gunther blinked. He could not react to it as a real event. The woman cringed under the blows, shrieking wildly and scuttling away from them. One of the tents had been re-erected, and within the shadow of its rainbow silks, four other suits lounged against the bar. Not a one of them moved to help the woman.

"Hey!" Gunther shouted. He felt hideously self-conscious, as if he'd been abruptly thrust into the middle of a play without memorized lines or any idea of the plot or notion of what his role in it was. "Stop that!"

The suit turned toward him. It held the woman's slim arm captive in one gloved hand. "Go away," a male voice growled over the radio.

"What do you think you're doing? Who are you?" The man wore a Westinghouse suit, one of a dozen or so among the unafflicted. But Gunther recognized a brown, kidney-shaped scorch mark on the abdomen panel. "Posner—is that you? Let that woman go."

"She's not a woman," Posner said. "Hell, look at her—she's not even human. She's a flick."

Gunther set his helmet to record. "I'm taping this," he warned. "You hit that woman again, and Ekatarina will see it all. I promise."

Posner released the woman. She stood dazed for a second or two, and then the voice from her peecee reasserted control. She bent to pick up a broom, and returned to work.

Switching off his helmet, Gunther said, "Okay. What did she do?"

Indignantly, Posner extended a foot. He pointed sternly down at it. "She peed all over my boot!"

The suits in the tent had been watching with interest. Now they roared. "Your own fault, Will!" one of them called out. "I told you you weren't scheduling in enough time for personal hygiene."

"Don't worry about a little moisture. It'll boil off next time you hit vacuum!"

But Gunther was not listening. He stared at the flick Posner had been mistreating and wondered why he hadn't recognized Anya earlier. Her mouth was pursed, her face squinched up tight with worry, as if there were a key in the back of her head that had been wound three times too many. Her shoulders cringed forward now, too. But still.

"I'm sorry, Anya," he said. "Hiro is dead. There wasn't anything we could do."

She went on sweeping, oblivious, unhappy.

He caught the shift's last jitney back to the Center. It felt good to be home again. Miiko Ezumi had decided to loot the outlying factories of their oxygen and water surpluses, then carved a shower room from the rock. There was a long line for only three minutes' use, and no soap, but nobody complained. Some people pooled their time, showering two and three together. Those waiting their turns joked rowdily.

Gunther washed, grabbed some clean shorts and a Glavkosmos tee-shirt, and padded down the hall. He hesitated outside the common room, listening to the gang sitting around the table, discussing the more colorful flicks they'd encountered.

"Have you seen the Mouse Hunter?"

"Oh yeah, and Ophelia!"

"The Pope!"

"The Duck Lady!

"Everybody knows the Duck Lady!"

They were laughing and happy. A warm sense of community flowed from the room, what Gunther's father would have in his sloppy-sentimental way called *Gemütlichkeit*. Gunther stepped within.

Liza Nagenda looked up, all gums and teeth, and froze. Her jaw snapped shut. "Well, if it isn't Izmailova's personal spy!"

"What?" The accusation took Gunther's breath away. He looked helplessly about the room. Nobody would meet his eye. They had all fallen silent.

Liza's face was grey with anger. "You heard me! It was you that ratted on Krishna, wasn't it?"

"Now that's way out of line! You've got a lot of fucking gall if—" He controlled himself with an effort. There was no sense in matching her hysteria with his own. "It's none of your business what my relationship with Izmailova is or is not." He looked around the table. "Not that any of you deserve to know, but Krishna's working on a cure. If anything I said or did helped put him back in the lab, well then, so be it."

She smirked. "So what's your excuse for snitching on Will Posner?"

"I never—"

"We all heard the story! You told him you were going to run straight to your precious Izmailova with your little helmet vids."

"Now, Liza," Takayuni began. She slapped him away.

"Do you know what Posner was doing?" Gunther shook a finger in Liza's face. "Hah? Do you? He was beating a woman—Anya! He was beating Anya right out in the open!"

"So what? He's one of us, isn't he? Not a zoned-out, dead-eyed, ranting, drooling *flick*!"

"You bitch!" Outraged, Gunther lunged at Liza across the table. "I'll kill you, I swear it!" People jerked back from him, rushed forward, a chaos of motion. Posner thrust himself in Gunther's way, arms spread, jaw set and manly. Gunther punched him in the face. Posner looked surprised, and fell back. Gunther's hand stung, but he felt strangely good anyway; if everyone else was crazy, then why not him?

"You just try it!" Liza shrieked. "I knew you were that type all along!"

Takayuni grabbed Liza away one way. Hamilton seized Gunther and yanked him the other. Two of Posner's friends were holding him back as well.

"I've had about all I can take from you!" Gunther shouted. "You cheap cunt!"

"Listen to him! Listen what he calls me!"

Screaming, they were shoved out opposing doors.

"It's all right, Gunther." Beth had flung him into the first niche they'd come to. He slumped against a wall, shaking, and closed his eyes. "It's all right now."

But it wasn't. Gunther was suddenly struck with the realization that with the exception of Ekatarina he no longer had any friends. Not real friends, close friends. How could this have happened? It was as if everyone had been turned into werewolves. Those who weren't actually mad were still monsters. "I don't understand."

Hamilton sighed. "What don't you understand, Weil?"

"The way people—the way we all treat the flicks. When Posner was beating Anya, there were four other suits standing nearby, and not a one of them so much as lifted a finger to stop him. Not one! And I felt it too, there's no use pretending I'm superior to the rest of them. I wanted to walk on and pretend I hadn't seen a thing. What's happened to us?"

Hamilton shrugged. Her hair was short and dark about her plain round face. "I went to a pretty expensive school when I was a kid. One year we had one of those exercises that're supposed to be personally enriching. You know? A life experience. We were divided into two groups—Prisoners and Guards. The Prisoners couldn't leave their assigned areas without permission from a guard, the Guards got better lunches, stuff like that. Very simple set of rules. I was a Guard.

"Almost immediately, we started to bully the Prisoners. We pushed 'em around, yelled at 'em, kept 'em in line. What was amazing was that the Prisoners let us do it. They outnumbered us five to one. We didn't even have authority for the things we did. But not a one of them complained. Not a one of them stood up and said no, you can't do this. They played the game.

"At the end of the month, the project was dismantled and we had some study seminars on what we'd learned: the roots of fascism, and so on. Read some Hannah Arendt. And then it was all over. Except that my best girlfriend never spoke to me again. I couldn't blame her, either. Not after what I'd done.

"What did I really learn? That people will play whatever role you put them in. They'll do it without knowing that that's what they're doing. Take a minority, tell them they're special, and make them guards—they'll start playing Guard."

"So what's the answer? How do we keep from getting caught up in the roles we play?"

"Damned if I know, Weil. Damned if I know."

Ekatarina had moved her niche to the far end of a new tunnel. Hers was the only room the tunnel served, and consequently she had a lot of privacy. As Gunther stepped in, a staticky voice swam into focus on his trance chip. "...reported shock. In Cairo, government officials pledged ... It cut off.

"Hey! You've restored—" He stopped. If radio reception had been restored, he'd have known. It would have been the talk of the Center. Which meant that radio contact had never really been completely broken. It was simply being controlled by the CMP.

Ekatarina looked up at him. She'd been crying, but she'd stopped. "The Swiss Orbitals are gone!" she whispered. "They hit them with everything from softbombs to brilliant pebbles. They dusted the shipyards."

The scope of all those deaths obscured what she was saying for a second. He sank down beside her. "But that means—"

"There's no spacecraft that can reach us, yes. Unless there's a ship in transit, we're stranded here."

He took her in his arms. She was cold and shivering. Her skin felt clammy and mottled with gooseflesh. "How long has it been since you've had any sleep?" he asked sharply.

"I can't—"

"You're wired, aren't you?"

"I can't afford to sleep. Not now. Later."

"Ekatarina. The energy you get from wire isn't free. It's only borrowed from your body. When you come down, it all comes due. If you wire yourself up too tightly, you'll crash yourself right into a coma."

"I haven't been—" She stalled, and a confused, uncertain look entered her eyes. "Maybe you're right. I could probably use a little rest."

The CMP came to life. "Cadre Nine is building a radio receiver. Ezumi gave them the go-ahead."

"Shit!" Ekatarina sat bolt upright. "Can we stop it?"

"Moving against a universally popular project would cost you credibility you cannot afford to lose."

"Okay, so how can we minimize the—"

"Ekatarina," Gunther said. "Sleep, remember?"

"In a sec, babe." She patted the futon. "You just lie down and wait for me. I'll have this wrapped up before you can nod off." She kissed him gently, lingeringly. "All right?"

"Yeah, sure." He lay down and closed his eyes, just for a second.

When he awoke, it was time to go on shift, and Ekatarina was gone.

It was only the fifth day since Vladivostok. But everything was so utterly changed that times before then seemed like memories of another world. In a previous life I was Gunther Weil, he thought. I lived and worked and had a few laughs. Life was pretty good then.

He was still looking for Sally Chang, though with dwindling hope. Now, whenever he talked to suits he'd ask if they needed his help. Increasingly, they did not.

The third-level chapel was a shallow bowl facing the terrace wall. Tiger lilies grew about the chancel area at the bottom, and turquoise lizards skittered over the rock. The children were playing a ball in the chancel. Gunther stood at the top, chatting with a sad-voiced Ryohei Iomato.

The children put away the ball and began to dance. They were playing London Bridge. Gunther watched them with a smile. From above they were so many spots of color, a flower unfolding and closing in on itself. Slowly, the smile faded. They were dancing too well. Not one of the children moved out of step, lost her place, or walked away sulking. Their expressions were intense, self-absorbed, inhuman. Gunther had to turn away.

"The CMP controls them," Iomato said. "I don't have much to do, really. I go through the vids and pick out games for them to play, songs to sing, little exercises to keep them healthy. Sometimes I have them draw."

"My God, how can you stand it?"

Iomato sighed. "My old man was an alcoholic. He had a pretty rough life, and at some point he started drinking to blot out the pain. You know what?"

"It didn't work."

"Yah. Made him even more miserable. So then he had twice the reason to get drunk. He kept on trying, though, I've got to give him that. He wasn't the sort of man to give up on something he believed in just because it wasn't working the way it should."

Gunther said nothing.

"I think that memory is the only thing keeping me from just taking off my helmet and joining them."

The Corporate Video Center was a narrow run of offices in the farthest tunnel reaches, where raw footage for adverts and incidental business use was processed before being squirted to better-equipped vid centers on Earth. Gunther passed from office to office, slapping off flatscreens left flickering since the disaster.

It was unnerving going through the normally busy rooms and finding no one. The desks and cluttered work stations had been abandoned in purposeful disarray, as though their operators had merely stepped out for a break and would be back momentarily. Gunther found himself spinning around to confront his shadow, and flinching at unexpected noises. With each machine he turned off, the silence at his back grew. It was twice as lonely as being out on the surface.

He doused a last light and stepped into the gloomy hall. Two suits with interwoven H-and-A logos loomed up out of the shadows. He jumped in shock. They were empty, of course—there were no Hyundai Aerospace components among the unafflicted. Someone had simply left these suits here in temporary storage before the madness.

The suits grabbed him.

"Hey!" He shouted in terror as they seized him by the arms and lifted him off his feet. One of them hooked the peecee from his harness and snapped it off. Before he knew what was happening he'd been swept down a short flight of stairs and through a doorway.

"Mr. Weil."

He was in a high-ceilinged room carved into the rock to hold airhandling equipment that hadn't been constructed yet. A high string of temporary work lamps provided dim light. To the far side of the room a suit sat behind a desk, flanked by two more, standing. They all wore Hyundai Aerospace suits. There was no way he could identify them.

The suits that had brought him in crossed their arms.

"What's going on here?" Gunther asked. "Who are you?"

"You are the last person we'd tell that to." He couldn't tell which one had spoken. The voice came over his radio, made sexless and impersonal by an electronic filter. "Mr. Weil, you stand accused of crimes against your fellow citizens. Do you have anything to say in your defense?"

"What?" Gunther looked at the suits before him and to either side. They were perfectly identical, indistinguishable from each other, and he was suddenly afraid of what the people within might feel free to do, armored as they were in anonymity. "Listen, you've got no right to do this. There's a governmental structure in place, if you've got any complaints against me."

"Not everyone is pleased with Izmailova's government," the judge said.

"But she controls the CMP, and we could not run Bootstrap without the CMP controlling the flicks," a second added.

"We simply have to work around her." Perhaps it was the judge; perhaps it was yet another of the suits. Gunther couldn't tell.

"Do you wish to speak on your own behalf?"

"What exactly am I charged with?" Gunther asked desperately. "Okay, maybe I've done something wrong, I'll entertain that possibility. But maybe you just don't understand my situation. Have you considered that?"

Silence.

"I mean, just what are you angry about? Is it Posner? Because I'm not sorry about that. I won't apologize. You can't mistreat people just because they're sick. They're still people, like anybody else. They have their rights."

Silence.

"But if you think I'm some kind of a spy or something, that I'm running around and ratting on people to Ek—to Izmailova, well that's simply not true. I mean, I talk to her, I'm not about to pretend I don't, but I'm not her spy or anything. She doesn't have any spies. She doesn't need any! She's just trying to hold things together, that's all.

"Jesus, you don't know what she's gone through for you! You haven't seen how much it takes out of her! She'd like nothing better than to quit. But she has to hang in there because—" An eerie dark electronic gabble rose up on his radio, and he stopped as he realized that they were laughing at him.

"Does anyone else wish to speak?"

One of Gunther's abductors stepped forward. "Your honor, this man says that flicks are human. He overlooks the fact that they cannot live without our support and direction. Their continued well-being is bought at the price of our unceasing labor. He stands condemned out of his own mouth. I petition the court to make the punishment fit the crime."

The judge looked to the right, to the left. His two companions nodded, and stepped back into the void. The desk had been set up at the mouth of what was to be the air intake duct. Gunther had just time enough to realize this when they reappeared, leading someone in a G5 suit identical to his own.

"We could kill you, Mr. Weil," the artificial voice crackled. "But that would be wasteful. Every hand, every mind is needed. We must all pull together in our time of need."

The G5 stood alone and motionless in the center of the room.

"Watch."

Two of the Hyundai suits stepped up to the G5 suit. Four hands converged on the helmet seals. With practiced efficiency, they flicked the latches and lifted the helmet. It happened so swiftly the occupant could not have stopped it if he'd tried.

Beneath the helmet was the fearful, confused face of a flick.

"Sanity is a privilege, Mr. Weil, not a right. You are guilty as charged. However, we are not cruel men. *This once* we will let you off with a warning. But these are desperate times. At your next offense—be it only so minor a thing as reporting this encounter to the Little General—we may be forced to dispense with the formality of a hearing." The judge paused. "Do I make myself clear?"

Reluctantly, Gunther nodded.

"Then you may leave."

On the way out, one of the suits handed him back his peecee.

Five people. He was sure there weren't any more involved than that. Maybe one or two more, but that was it. Posner had to be hip-deep in this thing, he was certain of that. It shouldn't be too hard to figure out the others.

He didn't dare take the chance.

At shift's end he found Ekatarina already asleep. She looked haggard and unhealthy. He knelt by her, and gently brushed her cheek with the back of one hand.

Her eyelids fluttered open.

"Oh, hey. I didn't mean to wake you. Just go back to sleep, huh?"

She smiled. "You're sweet, Gunther, but I was only taking a nap anyway. I've got to be up in another fifteen minutes." Her eyes closed again. "You're the only one I can really trust anymore. Everybody's lying to me, feeding me misinformation, keeping silent when there's something I need to know. You're the only one I can count on to tell me things."

You have enemies, he thought. They call you the Little General, and they don't like how you run things. They're not ready to move against you directly, but they have plans. And they're ruthless.

Aloud, he said, "Go back to sleep."

"They're all against me," she murmured. "Bastard sons of bitches."

The next day he spent going through the service spaces for the new airhandling system. He found a solitary flick's nest made of shredded vacuum suits, but after consultation with the CMP concluded that nobody had lived there for days. There was no trace of Sally Chang.

If it had been harrowing going through the sealed areas before his trial, it was far worse today. Ekatarina's enemies had infected him with fear. Reason told him they were not waiting for him, that he had nothing to worry about until he displeased them again. But the hindbrain did not listen.

Time crawled. When he finally emerged into daylight at the end of his shift, he felt light-headedly out of phase with reality from the hours of isolation. At first he noticed nothing out of the ordinary. Then his suit radio was full of voices, and people were hurrying about every which way. There was a happy buzz in the air. Somebody was singing.

He snagged a passing suit and asked, "What's going on?"

"Haven't you heard? The war is over. They've made peace. And there's a ship coming in!"

The *Lake Geneva* had maintained television silence through most of the long flight to the Moon for fear of long-range beam weapons. With peace, however, they opened direct transmission to Bootstrap.

Ezumi's people had the flicks sew together an enormous cotton square and hack away some trailing vines so they could hang it high on the shadowed side of the crater. Then, with the fill lights off, the video image was projected. Swiss spacejacks tumbled before the camera, grinning, all denim and red cowboy hats. They were talking about their escape from the hunter-seeker missiles, brash young voices running one over the other.

The top officers were assembled beneath the cotton square. Gunther recognized their suits. Ekatarina's voice boomed from newly erected loudspeakers. "When are you coming in? We have to make sure the spaceport field is clear. How many hours?"

Holding up five fingers, a blond woman said, "Forty-five!"

"No, forty-three!"

"Nothing like that!"

"*Almost* forty-five!"

Again Ekatarina's voice cut into the tumult. "What's it like in the orbitals? We heard they were destroyed."

"Yes, destroyed!"

"Very bad, very bad, it'll take years to—"

"But most of the people are—"

"We were given six orbits warning; most went down in lifting bodies, there was a big evacuation."

"Many died, though. It was very bad."

Just below the officers, a suit had been directing several flicks as they assembled a camera platform. Now it waved broadly, and the flicks stepped away. In the *Lake Geneva* somebody shouted, and several heads turned to stare at an offscreen television monitor. The suit turned the camera, giving them a slow, panoramic scan.

One of the spacejacks said, "What's it like there? I see that some of you are wearing space suits, and the rest are not. Why is that?"

Ekatarina took a deep breath. "There have been some changes here."

There was one hell of a party at the Center when the Swiss arrived. Sleep schedules were juggled, and save for a skeleton crew overseeing the flicks, everyone turned out to welcome the dozen newcomers to the Moon. They danced to skiffle, and drank vacuum-distilled vodka. Everyone had stories to tell, rumors to swap, opinions on the likelihood that the peace would hold.

Gunther wandered away midway through the party. The Swiss depressed him. They all seemed so young and fresh and eager. He felt battered and cynical in their presence. He wanted to grab them by the shoulders and shake them awake.

Depressed, he wandered through the locked-down laboratories. Where the Viral Computer Project had been, he saw Ekatarina and the captain of the *Lake Geneva* conferring over a stack of crated bioflops. They bent low over Ekatarina's peecee, listening to the CMP.

"Have you considered nationalizing your industries?" the captain asked. "That would give us the plant needed to build the New City. Then, with a few hardwired utilities, Bootstrap could be managed without anyone having to set foot inside it."

Gunther was too distant to hear the CMP's reaction, but he saw both women laugh. "Well," said Ekatarina. "At the very least we will have to renegotiate terms with the parent corporations. With only one ship functional, people can't be easily replaced. Physical presence has become a valuable commodity. We'd be fools not to take advantage of it."

He passed on, deeper into shadow, wandering aimlessly. Eventually, there was a light ahead, and he heard voices. One was Krishna's, but spoken faster and more forcefully than he was used to hearing it. Curious, he stopped just outside the door.

Krishna was in the center of the lab. Before him, Beth Hamilton stood nodding humbly. "Yes, sir," she said. "I'll do that. Yes." Dumbfounded, Gunther realized that Krishna was giving her orders.

Krishna glanced up. "Weil! You're just the man I was about to come looking for."

"I am?"

"Come in here, don't dawdle." Krishna smiled and beckoned, and Gunther had no choice but to obey. Krishna looked like a young god now. The force of his spirit danced in his eyes like fire. It was strange that Gunther had never noticed before how tall he was. "Tell me where Sally Chang is."

"I don't—I mean, I can't, I—" He stopped and swallowed. "I think Chang must be dead." Then, "Krishna? What's happened to you?"

"He's finished his research," Beth said.

"I rewrote my personality from top to bottom," Krishna said. "I'm not half-crippled with shyness anymore—have you noticed?" He put a hand on Gunther's shoulder, and it was reassuring, warm, comforting. "Gunther, I won't tell you what it took to scrape together enough messenger engines from traces of old experiments to try this out on myself. But it works. We've got a treatment that among other things will serve as a universal cure for everyone in Bootstrap. But to do that, we need the messenger engines, and they're not here. Now tell me why you think Sally Chang is dead."

"Well, uh, I've been searching for her for four days. And the CMP has been looking too. You've been holed up here all the time, so maybe you don't know the flicks as well as the rest of us do. But they're not very big on planning. The likelihood one of them could actively evade detection that long is practically zilch. The only thing I can think is that somehow she made it to the surface before the effects hit her, got into a truck and told it to drive as far as her oxygen would take her."

Krishna shook his head and said, "No. It is simply not consistent with Sally Chang's character. With all the best will in the world, I cannot picture her killing herself." He slid open a drawer: row upon row of gleaming cannisters. "This may help. Do you remember when I said there were two cannisters of mimetic engines missing, not just the schizomimetic?"

"Vaguely."

"I've been too busy to worry about it, but wasn't that odd? Why would Chang have taken a cannister and not used it?"

"What was in the second cannister?" Hamilton asked.

"Paranoia," Krishna said. "Or rather a good enough chemical analog. Now, paranoia is a rare disability, but a fascinating one. It's characterized by an elaborate but internally consistent delusional system. The paranoid patient functions well intellectually, and is less fragmented than a schizophrenic. Her emotional and social responses are closer to normal. She's capable of concerted effort. In a time of turmoil, it's quite possible that a paranoid individual could elude our detection."

"Okay, let's get this straight," Hamilton said. "War breaks out on Earth. Chang gets her orders, keys in the software bombs, and goes to Bootstrap with a cannister full of madness and a little syringe of paranoia—no, it doesn't work. It all falls apart."

"How so?"

"Paranoia wouldn't inoculate her against schizophrenia. How does she protect herself from her own aerosols?"

Gunther stood transfixed. "Lavender!"

They caught up with Sally Chang on the topmost terrace of Bootstrap. The top level was undeveloped. Someday—so the corporate brochures promised—fallow deer would graze at the edge of limpid pools, and otters frolic in the streams. But the soil hadn't been built up yet, the worms brought in or the bacteria seeded. There were only sand, machines, and a few unhappy opportunistic weeds.

Chang's camp was to one side of a streamhead, beneath a fill light. She started to her feet at their approach, glanced quickly to the side and decided to brazen it out.

A sign reading EMERGENCY CANOPY MAINTENANCE STA-TION had been welded to a strut supporting the stream's valve stem. Under it were a short stacked pyramid of oxytanks and an aluminum storage crate the size of a coffin. "Very clever," Beth muttered over Gunther's trance chip. "She sleeps in the storage crate, and anybody stumbling across her thinks it's just spare equipment."

The lavender suit raised an arm and casually said, "Hiya, guys. How can I help you?"

Krishna strode forward and took her hands. "Sally, it's me—Krishna!"

"Oh, thank God!" She slumped in his arms. "I've been so afraid."

"You're all right now."

"I thought you were an Invader at first, when I saw you coming up. I'm so hungry—I haven't eaten since I don't know when." She clutched at the sleeve of Krishna's suit. "You do know about the Invaders, don't you?"

"Maybe you'd better bring me up to date."

They began walking toward the stairs. Krishna gestured quickly to Gunther and then toward Chang's worksuit harness. A cannister the size of a hip flask hung there. Gunther reached over and plucked it off. The messenger engines! He held them in his hand.

To the other side, Beth Hamilton plucked up the near-full cylinder of paranoia-inducing engines and made it disappear.

Sally Chang, deep in the explication of her reasonings, did not notice. ". . . obeyed my orders, of course. But they made no sense. I worried and worried about that until finally I realized what was really going on. A wolf caught in a trap will gnaw off its leg to get free. I began to look for the wolf. What kind of enemy justified such extreme actions? Certainly nothing human."

"Sally," Krishna said, "I want you to entertain the notion that the conspiracy—for want of a better word—may be more deeply rooted than you suspect. That the problem is not an external enemy, but the workings of our own brain. Specifically that the Invaders are an artifact of the psychotomimetics you injected into yourself back when this all began."

"No. No, there's too much evidence. It all fits together! The Invaders need-ed a way to disguise themselves both physically, which was accomplished by the vacuum suits, and psychologically, which was achieved by the general madness. Thus, they can move undetected among us. Would a human enemy have converted all of Bootstrap to slave labor? Unthinkable! They can read our minds like a book. If we hadn't protected ourselves with the schizomimetics, they'd be able to extract all our knowledge, all our military research secrets ...

Listening, Gunther couldn't help imagining what Liza Nagenda would say to all of this wild talk. At the thought of her, his jaw clenched. Just like one of Chang's machines, he realized, and couldn't help being amused at his own expense.

Ekatarina was waiting at the bottom of the stairs. Her hands trembled noticeably, and there was a slight quaver in her voice when she said, "What's all this the CMP tells me about messenger engines? Krishna's supposed to have come up with a cure of some kind?"

"We've got them," Gunther said quietly, happily. He held up the cannister. "It's over now, we can heal our friends."

"Let me see," Ekatarina said. She took the cannister from his hand.

"No, wait!" Hamilton cried, too late. Behind her, Krishna was arguing with Sally Chang about her interpretations of recent happenings. Neither had noticed yet that those in front had stopped.

"Stand back." Ekatarina took two quick steps backward. Edgily, she added, "I don't mean to be difficult. But we're going to sort this all out, and until we do, I don't want anybody too close to me. That includes you too, Gunther."

Flicks began gathering. By ones and twos they wandered up the lawn, and then by the dozen. By the time it was clear that Ekatarina had called them up via the CMP, Krishna, Chang, and Hamilton were separated from her and Gunther by a wall of people.

Chang stood very still. Somewhere behind her unseen face, she was revising her theories to include this new event. Suddenly, her hands slapped at her suit, grabbing for the missing cannisters. She looked at Krishna and with a trill of horror said, "You're one of them!"

"Of course I'm not—" Krishna began. But she was turning, stumbling, fleeing back up the steps.

"Let her go," Ekatarina ordered. "We've got more serious things to talk about." Two flicks scurried up, lugging a small industrial kiln between them. They set it down, and a third plugged in an electric cable. The interior began to glow. "This cannister is all you've got, isn't it? If I were to autoclave it, there wouldn't be any hope of replacing its contents."

"Izmailova, listen," Krishna said.

"I am listening. Talk."

Krishna explained, while Izmailova listened with arms folded and shoulders tilted skeptically. When he was done, she shook her head. "It's a noble folly, but folly is all it is. You want to reshape our minds into something alien to the course of human evolution. To turn the seat of thought into a jet pilot's couch. This is your idea of a solution? Forget it. Once this particular box is opened, there'll be no putting its contents back in again. And you haven't advanced any convincing arguments for opening it."

"But the people in Bootstrap!" Gunther objected. "They—"

She cut him off. "Gunther, nobody *likes* what's happened to them. But if the rest of us must give up our humanity to pay for a speculative and ethically dubious rehabilitation ... well, the price is simply too high. Mad or not, they're at least human now."

"Am I inhuman?" Krishna asked. "If you tickle me, do I not laugh?"

"You're in no position to judge. You've rewired your neurons and you're stoned on the novelty. What tests have you run on yourself? How thoroughly have you mapped out your deviations from human norms? Where are your figures?" These were purely rhetorical questions; the kind of analyses she meant took weeks to run. "Even if you check out completely human—and I don't concede you will!—who's to say what the long-range consequences are? What's to stop us from drifting, step by incremental step, into madness? Who decides what madness is? Who programs the programmers? No, this is impossible. I won't gamble with our minds." Defensively, almost angrily, she repeated, "I won't gamble with our minds."

"Ekatarina," Gunther said gently, "how long have you been up? Listen to yourself. The wire is doing your thinking for you."

She waved a hand dismissively, without responding.

"Just as a practical matter," Hamilton said, "how do you expect to run Bootstrap without it? The setup is turning us all into baby fascists. You say you're worried about madness—what will we be like a year from now?"

"The CMP assures me—"

"The CMP is only a program!" Hamilton cried. "No matter how much interactivity it has, it's not flexible. It has no hope. It cannot judge a new thing. It can only enforce old decisions, old values, old habits, old fears."

Abruptly Ekatarina snapped. "*Get out of my face!*" she screamed. "Stop it, stop it, stop it! I won't listen to any more."

"Ekatarina—" Gunther began.

But her hand had tightened on the cannister. Her knees bent as she began a slow genuflection to the kiln. Gunther could see that she had stopped listening. Drugs and responsibility had done this to her, speeding her up and bewildering her with conflicting demands, until she stood trembling on the brink of collapse. A good night's sleep might have restored her, made her capable of being reasoned with. But there was no time. Words would not stop her now. And she was too far distant for him to reach before she destroyed the engines. In that instant he felt such a strong outwelling of emotion toward her as would be impossible to describe.

"Ekatarina," he said. "I love you."

She half-turned her head toward him and in a distracted, somewhat irritated tone said, "What are you—"

He lifted the bolt gun from his work harness, leveled it, and fired.

Ekatarina's helmet shattered.

She fell.

"I should have shot to just breach the helmet. That would have stopped her. But I didn't think I was a good enough shot. I aimed right for the center of her head."

"Hush," Hamilton said. "You did what you had to. Stop tormenting yourself. Talk about more practical things."

He shook his head, still groggy. For the longest time, he had been kept on beta endorphins, unable to feel a thing, unable to care. It was like being swathed in cotton batting. Nothing could reach him. Nothing could hurt him. "How long have I been out of it?"

"A day."

"A day!" He looked about the austere room. Bland rock walls and laboratory equipment with smooth, noncommittal surfaces. To the far end, Krishna and Chang were hunched over a swipeboard, arguing happily and impatiently overwriting each other's scrawls. A Swiss spacejack came in and spoke to their backs. Krishna nodded distractedly, not looking up. "I thought it was much longer."

"Long enough. We've already salvaged everyone connected with Sally Chang's group, and gotten a good start on the rest. Pretty soon it will be time to decide how you want yourself rewritten."

He shook his head, feeling dead. "I don't think I'll bother, Beth. I just don't have the stomach for it."

"We'll give you the stomach."

"Naw, I don't . . ." He felt a black nausea come welling up again. It was cyclic; it returned every time he was beginning to think he'd finally put it down. "I don't want the fact that I killed Ekatarina washed away in a warm flood of self-satisfaction. The idea disgusts me."

"We don't want that either." Posner led a delegation of seven into the lab. Krishna and Chang rose to face them, and the group broke into swirling halves. "There's been enough of that. It's time we all started taking responsibility for the consequences of—" Everyone was talking at once. Hamilton made a face.

"Started taking responsibility for—"

Voices rose.

"We can't talk here," she said. "Take me out on the surface."

They drove with the cabin pressurized, due west on the Seething Bay road. Ahead, the sun was almost touching the weary walls of Sommering crater. Shadow crept down from the mountains and cratertops, yearning toward the radiantly lit Sinus Medii. Gunther found it achingly beautiful. He did not want to respond to it, but the harsh lines echoed the lonely hurt within him in a way that he found oddly comforting.

Hamilton touched her peecee. "Putting on the Ritz" filled their heads.

"What if Ekatarina was right?" he said sadly. "What if we're giving up everything that makes us human? The prospect of being turned into some kind of big-domed emotionless superman doesn't appeal to me much."

Hamilton shook her head. "I asked Krishna about that, and he said No. He said it was like . . . were you ever nearsighted?"

"Sure, as a kid."

"Then you'll understand. He said it was like the first time you came out of the doctor's office after being lased. How everything seemed clear and vivid and distinct. What had once been a blur that you called 'tree' resolved itself into a thousand individual and distinct leaves. The world was filled with unexpected detail. There were things on the horizon that you'd never seen before. Like that."

"Oh." He stared ahead. The disk of the sun was almost touching Sommering. "There's no point in going any farther."

He powered down the truck.

Beth Hamilton looked uncomfortable. She cleared her throat and with brusque energy said, "Gunther, look. I had you bring me out here for a reason. I want to propose a merger of resources."

"A what?"

"Marriage."

It took Gunther a second to absorb what she had said. "Aw, no . . . I don't . . ."

"I'm serious. Gunther, I know you think I've been hard on you, but that's only because I saw a lot of potential in you, and that you were doing nothing with it. Well, things have changed. Give me a say in your rewrite, and I'll do the same for you."

He shook his head. "This is just too weird for me."

"It's too late to use that as an excuse. Ekatarina was right—we're sitting on top of something very dangerous, the most dangerous opportunity humanity faces today. It's out of the bag, though. Word has gotten out. Earth is horrified and fascinated. They'll be watching us. Briefly, very briefly, we can control this thing. We can help to shape it now, while it's small. Five years from now, it will be out of our hands.

"You have a good mind, Gunther, and it's about to get better. I think we agree on what kind of a world we want to make. I want you on my side."

"I don't know what to say."

"You want true love? You got it. We can make the sex as sweet or nasty as you like. Nothing easier. You want me quieter, louder, gentler, more assured? We can negotiate. Let's see if we can come to terms."

He said nothing.

Hamilton eased back in the seat. After a time, she said, "You know? I've never watched a lunar sunset before. I don't get out on the surface much."

"We'll have to change that," Gunther said.

Hamilton stared hard into his face. Then she smiled. She wriggled closer to him. Clumsily, he put an arm over her shoulder. It seemed to be what was expected of him. He coughed into his hand, then pointed a finger. "There it goes."

Lunar sunset was a simple thing. The crater wall touched the bottom of the solar disk. Shadows leaped from the slopes and raced across the lowlands. Soon half the sun was gone. Smoothly, without distortion, it dwindled. A last brilliant sliver of light burned atop the rock, then ceased to be. In the instant before the windshield adjusted and the stars appeared, the universe filled with darkness.

The air in the cab cooled. The panels snapped and popped with the sudden shift in temperature.

Now Hamilton was nuzzling the side of his neck. Her skin was slightly tacky to the touch, and exuded a faint but distinct odor. She ran her tongue up the line of his chin and poked it in his ear. Her hand fumbled with the latches of his suit.

Gunther experienced no arousal at all, only a mild distaste that bordered on disgust. This was horrible, a defilement of all he had felt for Ekatarina.

But it was a chore he had to get through. Hamilton was right. All his life his hindbrain had been in control, driving him with emotions chemically derived and randomly applied. He had been lashed to the steed of consciousness and forced to ride it wherever it went, and that nightmare gallop had brought him only pain and confusion. Now that he had control of the reins, he could make this horse go where he wanted.

He was not sure what he would demand from his reprogramming. Con-
tentment, perhaps. Sex and passion, almost certainly. But not love. He was
done with the romantic illusion. It was time to grow up.

He squeezed Beth's shoulder. One more day, he thought, and it won't
matter. I'll feel whatever is best for me to feel. Beth raised her mouth to his.
Her lips parted. He could smell her breath.

They kissed.

Geoffrey A. Landis is a science-fiction writer and a scientist. As a scientist, he works for NASA on developing advanced technologies for spaceflight. He is a member of the Mars Exploration Rovers Science team, and a fellow of the NASA Institute for Advanced Concepts. As an SF writer, he has won the Hugo and Nebula awards for science fiction. He is the author of the novel *Mars Crossing* and the short-story collection *Impact Parameter (and Other Quantum Realities)*, and has written over eighty published science fiction stories. He was the 2014 recipient of the Robert A. Heinlein Award "for outstanding published works in science fiction and technical writings that inspire the human exploration of space." In his spare time, he goes to fencing tournaments so he can stab perfect strangers with a sword.

More information can be found at his web page, www.geoffreylandis.com.

A WALK IN THE SUN
Geoffrey A. Landis

The pilots have a saying: a good landing is any landing you can walk away from. Perhaps Sanjiv might have done better, if he'd been alive. Trish had done the best she could. All things considered, it was a far better landing than she had any right to expect.

Titanium struts, pencil-slender, had never been designed to take the force of a landing. Paper-thin pressure walls had buckled and shattered, spreading wreckage out into the vacuum and across a square kilometer of lunar surface. An instant before impact she remembered to blow the tanks. There was no explosion, but no landing could have been gentle enough to keep *Moonshadow* together. In eerie silence, the fragile ship had crumpled and ripped apart like a discarded aluminum can.

The piloting module had torn open and broken loose from the main part of the ship. The fragment settled against a crater wall. When it stopped moving, Trish unbuckled the straps that held her in the pilot's seat and fell slowly to the ceiling. She oriented herself to the unaccustomed gravity, found an undamaged EVA pack and plugged it into her suit, then crawled out into the sunlight through the jagged hole where the living module had been attached.

She stood on the gray lunar surface and stared. Her shadow reached out ahead of her, a pool of inky black in the shape of a fantastically stretched man. The landscape was rugged and utterly barren, painted in stark shades of grey and black. "Magnificent desolation," she whispered. Behind her, the sun hovered just over the mountains, glinting off shards of titanium and steel scattered across the cratered plain.

Patricia Jay Mulligan looked out across the desolate moonscape and tried not to weep.

First things first. She took the radio out from the shattered crew compartment and tried it. Nothing. That was no surprise; Earth was over the horizon, and there were no other ships in cislunar space.

After a little searching she found Sanjiv and Theresa. In the low gravity they were absurdly easy to carry. There was no use in burying them. She sat them in a niche between two boulders, facing the sun, facing west, toward where the Earth was hidden behind a range of black mountains. She tried to think of the right words to say, and failed. Perhaps as well; she wouldn't know the proper service for Sanjiv anyway. "Goodbye, Sanjiv. Goodbye, Theresa. I wish—I wish things would have been different. I'm sorry." Her voice was barely more than a whisper. "Go with God."

She tried not to think of how soon she was likely to be joining them.

She forced herself to think. What would her sister have done? Survive. Karen would survive. First: inventory your assets. She was alive, miraculously unhurt. Her vacuum suit was in serviceable condition. Life-support was powered by the suit's solar arrays; she had air and water for as long as the sun continued to shine. Scavenging the wreckage yielded plenty of unbroken food packs; she wasn't about to starve.

Second: call for help. In this case, the nearest help was a quarter of a million miles over the horizon. She would need a high-gain antenna and a mountain peak with a view of Earth.

In its computer, *Moonshadow* had carried the best maps of the moon ever made. Gone. There had been other maps on the ship; they were scattered with the wreckage. She'd managed to find a detailed map of Mare Nubium—useless—and a small global map meant to be used as an index. It would have to do. As near as she could tell, the impact site was just over the eastern edge of Mare Smythii—"Smith's Sea." The mountains in the distance should mark the edge of the sea, and, with luck, have a view of Earth.

She checked her suit. At a command, the solar arrays spread out to their full extent like oversized dragonfly wings and glinted in prismatic colors as they rotated to face the sun. She verified that the suit's systems were charging properly, and set off.

Close up, the mountain was less steep than it had looked from the crash site. In the low gravity, climbing was hardly more difficult than walking, although the two-meter dish made her balance awkward. Reaching the ridgetop, Trish was rewarded with the sight of a tiny sliver of blue on the horizon. The mountains on the far side of the valley were still in darkness. She hoisted the radio higher up on her shoulder and started across the next valley.

From the next mountain peak the Earth edged over the horizon, a blue and white marble half-hidden by black mountains. She unfolded the tripod for the antenna and carefully sighted along the feed. "Hello? This is Astronaut Mulligan from *Moonshadow*. Emergency. Repeat, this is an emergency. Does anybody hear me?"

She took her thumb off the TRANSMIT button and waited for a response, but heard nothing but the soft whisper of static from the sun.

"This is Astronaut Mulligan from *Moonshadow*. Does anybody hear me?" She paused again. *"Moonshadow,* calling anybody. *Moonshadow,* calling anybody. This is an emergency."

"—shadow, this is Geneva control. We read you faint but clear. Hang on up there." She released her breath in a sudden gasp. She hadn't even realized she'd been holding it.

After five minutes the rotation of the earth had taken the ground antenna out of range. In that time—after they had gotten over their surprise that there was a survivor of the *Moonshadow*—she learned the parameters of the problem. Her landing had been close to the sunset terminator; the very edge of the illuminated side of the moon. The moon's rotation is slow, but inexorable. Sunset would arrive in three days. There was no shelter on the moon, no place to wait out the fourteen day-long lunar night. Her solar cells needed sunlight to keep her air fresh. Her search of the wreckage had yielded no unruptured storage tanks, no batteries, no means to lay up a store of oxygen.

And there was no way they could launch a rescue mission before nightfall. Too many "no"s.

She sat silent, gazing across the jagged plain toward the slender blue crescent, thinking.

After a few minutes the antenna at Goldstone rotated into range, and the radio crackled to life. *"Moonshadow, do you read me? Hello, Moonshadow, do you read me?"*

"*Moonshadow* here."

She released the transmit button and waited in long silence for her words to be carried to Earth.

"Roger, Moonshadow. We confirm the earliest window for a rescue mission is thirty days from now. Can you hold on that long?"

She made her decision and pressed the transmit button. "Astronaut Mulligan for *Moonshadow*. I'll be here waiting for you. One way or another."

She waited, but there was no answer. The receiving antenna at Goldstone couldn't have rotated out of range so quickly. She checked the radio. When she took the cover off, she could see that the printed circuit board on the power supply had been slightly cracked from the crash, but she couldn't see any broken leads or components clearly out of place. She banged on it with her fist—Karen's first rule of electronics, if it doesn't work, hit it—and reaimed the antenna, but it didn't help. Clearly something in it had broken.

What would Karen have done? Not just sit here and die, that was certain. Get a move on, kiddo. When sunset catches you, you'll die.

They had heard her reply. She had to believe they heard her reply and would be coming for her. All she had to do was survive.

The dish antenna would be too awkward to carry with her. She could afford nothing but the bare necessities. At sunset her air would be gone. She put down the radio and began to walk.

Mission Commander Stanley stared at the x-rays of his engine. It was four in the morning. There would be no more sleep for him that night; he was scheduled to fly to Washington at six to testify to Congress.

"Your decision, Commander," the engine technician said. "We can't find any flaws in the x-rays we took of the flight engines, but it could be hidden. The nominal flight profile doesn't take the engines to a hundred twenty, so the blades should hold even if there is a flaw."

"How long a delay if we yank the engines for inspection?"

"Assuming they're okay, we lose a day. If not, two, maybe three."

Commander Stanley drummed his fingers in irritation. He hated to be forced into hasty decisions. "Normal procedure would be?"

"Normally we'd want to reinspect."

"Do it."

He sighed. Another delay. Somewhere up there, somebody was counting on him to get there on time. If she was still alive. If the cut-off radio signal didn't signify catastrophic failure of other systems.

If she could find a way to survive without air.

On Earth it would have been a marathon pace. On the moon it was an easy lope. After ten miles the trek fell into an easy rhythm: half a walk, half like jogging, and half bounding like a slow-motion kangaroo. Her worst enemy was boredom.

Her comrades at the academy—in part envious of the top scores that had made her the first of their class picked for a mission—had ribbed her mercilessly about flying a mission that would come within a few kilometers of the moon without landing. Now she had a chance to see more of the moon up close than anybody in history. She wondered what her classmates were thinking now. She would have a tale to tell—if only she could survive to tell it.

The warble of the low voltage warning broke her out of her reverie. She checked her running display as she started down the maintenance check-list. Elapsed EVA time, eight point three hours. System functions, nominal, except that the solar array current was way below norm. In a few moments she found the trouble: a thin layer of dust on her solar array. Not a serious problem; it could be brushed off. If she couldn't find a pace that would avoid kicking dust on the arrays, then she would have to break every few hours to housekeep. She rechecked the array and continued on.

With the sun unmoving ahead of her and nothing but the hypnotical-ly blue crescent of the slowly rotating Earth creeping imperceptibly off the horizon, her attention wandered. *Moonshadow* had been tagged as an easy mission, a low-orbit mapping flight to scout sites for the future moonbase. *Moonshadow* had never been intended to land, not on the moon, not any-where.

She'd landed it anyway; she had to.

Walking west across the barren plain, Trish had nightmares of blood and falling, Sanjiv dying beside her; Theresa already dead in the lab module; the moon looming huge, spinning at a crazy angle in the viewports. Stop the spin, aim for the terminator—at low sun angles, the illumination makes it easier to see the roughness of the surface. Conserve fuel, but remember to blow the tanks an instant before you hit to avoid explosion.

That was over. Concentrate on the present. One foot in front of the other. Again. Again.

The undervoltage alarm chimed again. Dust, already?

She looked down at her navigation aid and realized with a shock that she had walked a hundred and fifty kilometers.

Time for a break anyway. She sat down on a boulder, fetched a snackpack out of her carryall, and set a timer for fifteen minutes. The airtight quick-seal on the food pack was designed to mate to the matching port in the lower part of her faceplate. It would be important to keep the seal free of grit. She veri-fied the vacuum seal twice before opening the pack into the suit, then pushed the food bar in so she could turn her head and gnaw off pieces. The bar was hard and slightly sweet.

She looked west across the gently rolling plain. The horizon looked flat, unreal; a painted backdrop barely out of reach. On the moon, it should be easy to keep up a pace of fifteen or even twenty miles an hour—counting time out for sleep, maybe ten. She could walk a long, long way.

Karen would have liked it; she'd always liked hiking in desolate areas. "Quite pretty, in its own way, isn't it, Sis?" Trish said. "Who'd have thought there were so many shadings of grey? Plenty of uncrowded beach—too bad it's such a long walk to the water."

Time to move on. She continued on across terrain that was generally flat, although everywhere pocked with craters of every size. The moon is surprisingly flat; only one percent of the surface has a slope of more than fifteen degrees. The small hills she bounded over easily; the few larger ones she detoured around. In the low gravity this posed no real problem to walking. She walked on. She didn't feel tired, but when she checked her readout and realized that she had been walking for twenty hours, she forced herself to stop.

Sleeping was a problem. The solar arrays were designed to be detached from the suit for easy servicing, but had no provision to power the life-support while detached. Eventually she found a way to stretch the short cable out far enough to allow her to prop up the array next to her so she could lie down without disconnecting the power. She would have to be careful not to roll over. That done, she found she couldn't sleep. After a time she lapsed into a fitful doze, dreaming not of the *Moonshadow* as she'd expected, but of her sister, Karen, who—in the dream—wasn't dead at all, but had only been playing a joke on her, pretending to die.

She awoke disoriented, muscles aching, then suddenly remembered where she was. The Earth was a full handspan above the horizon. She got up, yawned, and jogged west across the gunpowder-gray sandscape.

Her feet were tender where the boots rubbed. She varied her pace, changing from jogging to skipping to a kangaroo bounce. It helped some; not enough. She could feel her feet starting to blister, but knew that there was no way to take off her boots to tend, or even examine, her feet.

Karen had made her hike on blistered feet, and had had no patience with complaints or slacking off. She should have broken her boots in before the hike. In the one-sixth gee, at least the pain was bearable.

After a while her feet simply got numb.

Small craters she bounded over; larger ones she detoured around; larger ones yet she simply climbed across. West of Mare Smythii she entered a badlands and the terrain got bumpy. She had to slow down. The downhill slopes were in full sun, but the crater bottoms and valleys were still in shadow.

Her blisters broke, the pain a shrill and discordant singing in her boots. She bit her lip to keep herself from crying and continued on. Another few hundred kilometers and she was in Mare Spumans—"Sea of Froth"—and it was clear trekking again. Across Spumans, then into the north lobe of Fecundity and through to Tranquility. Somewhere around the sixth day of her trek she must have passed Tranquility Base; she carefully scanned for it on the horizon as she traveled but didn't see anything. By her best guess she missed it by several hundred kilometers; she was already deviating toward the north, aiming for a pass just north of the crater Julius Caesar into Mare Vaporum to avoid the mountains. The ancient landing stage would have been too small to spot unless she'd almost walked right over it.

"Figures," she said. "Come all this way, and the only tourist attraction in a hundred miles is closed. That's the way things always seem to turn out, eh, Sis?"

There was nobody to laugh at her witticism, so after a moment she laughed at it herself.

Wake up from confused dreams to black sky and motionless sunlight, yawn, and start walking before you're completely awake. Sip on the insipid warm water, trying not to think about what it's recycled from. Break, cleaning your solar arrays, your life, with exquisite care. Walk. Break. Sleep again, the sun nailed to the sky in the same position it was in when you awoke. Next day do it all over. And again. And again.

The nutrition packs are low-residue, but every few days you must still squat for nature. Your life support can't recycle solid waste, so you wait for the suit to dessicate the waste and then void the crumbly brown powder to vacuum. Your trail is marked by your powdery deposits, scarcely distinguishable from the dark lunar dust.

Walk west, ever west, racing the sun.

Earth was high in the sky; she could no longer see it without craning her neck way back. When the Earth was directly overhead she stopped and celebrated, miming the opening of an invisible bottle of champagne to toast her imaginary traveling companions. The sun was well above the horizon now. In six days of travel she had walked a quarter of the way around the moon.

She passed well south of Copernicus, to stay as far out of the impact rubble as possible without crossing mountains. The terrain was eerie, boulders as big as houses, as big as shuttle tanks. In places the footing was treacherous where the grainy regolith gave way to jumbles of rock, rays thrown out by the cataclysmic impact billions of years ago. She picked her way as best she could. She left her radio on and gave a running commentary as she moved. "Watch your step here, footing's treacherous. Coming up on a hill; think we should climb it or detour around?"

Nobody voiced an opinion. She contemplated the rocky hill. Likely an ancient volcanic bubble, although she hadn't realized that this region had once been active. The territory around it would be bad. From the top she'd be able to study the terrain for a ways ahead. "Okay, listen up, everybody. The climb could be tricky here, so stay close and watch where I place my feet. Don't take chances—better slow and safe than fast and dead. Any questions?" Silence; good. "Okay, then. We'll take a fifteen minute break when we reach the top. Follow me."

Past the rubble of Copernicus, Oceanus Procellarum was smooth as a golf course. Trish jogged across the sand with a smooth, even glide. Karen and Dutchman seemed to always be lagging behind or running up ahead out of sight. Silly dog still followed Karen around like a puppy, even though Trish was the one who fed him and refilled his water dish every day since Karen went away to college. The way Karen wouldn't stay close behind her annoyed Trish—Karen had *promised* to let her be the leader this time—but she kept her feelings to herself. Karen had called her a bratty little pest, and she was determined to show she could act like an adult. Anyway, she was the one with the map. If Karen got lost, it would serve her right.

She angled slightly north again to take advantage of the map's promise of smooth terrain. She looked around to see if Karen was there, and was surprised to see that the Earth was a gibbous ball low down on the horizon. Of course, Karen wasn't there. Karen had died years ago. Trish was alone in a spacesuit that itched and stank and chafed her skin nearly raw across the thighs. She should have broken it in better, but who would have expected she would want to go jogging in it?

It was unfair how she had to wear a spacesuit and Karen didn't. Karen got to do a lot of things that she didn't, but how come she didn't have to wear a spacesuit? Everybody had to wear a spacesuit. It was the rule. She turned to Karen to ask. Karen laughed bitterly. "I don't have to wear a spacesuit, my bratty little sister, because I'm *dead*. Squished like a bug and buried, remember?"

Oh, yes, that was right. Okay, then, if Karen was dead, then she didn't have to wear a spacesuit. It made perfect sense for a few more kilometers, and they jogged along together in companionable silence until Trish had a sudden thought. "Hey, wait—if you're dead, then how can you be here?"

"Because I'm not here, silly. I'm a fig-newton of your overactive imagination."

With a shock, Trish looked over her shoulder. Karen wasn't there. Karen had never been there.

"I'm sorry. Please come back. Please?"

She stumbled and fell headlong, sliding in a spray of dust down the bowl of a crater. As she slid she frantically twisted to stay face-down, to keep from rolling over on the fragile solar wings on her back. When she finally slid to a stop, the silence echoing in her ears, there was a long scratch like a badly healed scar down the glass of her helmet. The double reinforced faceplate had held, fortunately, or she wouldn't be looking at it.

She checked her suit. There were no breaks in the integrity, but the titanium strut that held out the left wing of the solar array had buckled back and nearly broken. Miraculously there had been no other damage. She pulled off the array and studied the damaged strut. She bent it back into position as best she could, and splinted the joint with a mechanical pencil tied on with two short lengths of wire. The pencil had been only extra weight anyway; it was lucky she hadn't thought to discard it. She tested the joint gingerly. It wouldn't take much stress, but if she didn't bounce around too much it should hold. Time for a break anyway.

When she awoke she took stock of her situation. While she hadn't been paying attention, the terrain had slowly turned mountainous. The next stretch would be slower going than the last bit.

"About time you woke up, sleepyhead," said Karen. She yawned, stretched, and turned her head to look back at the line of footprints. At the end of the long trail, the Earth showed as a tiny blue dome on the horizon, not very far away at all, the single speck of color in a landscape of uniform gray. "Twelve days to walk halfway around the moon," she said. "Not bad, kid. Not great, but not bad. You training for a marathon or something?"

Trish got up and started jogging, her feet falling into rhythm automatically as she sipped from the suit recycler, trying to wash the stale taste out of her mouth. She called out to Karen behind her without turning around. "Get a move on, we got places to go. You coming, or what?"

In the nearly shadowless sunlight the ground was washed-out, two dimensional. Trish had a hard time finding footing, stumbling over rocks that were nearly invisible against the flat landscape. One foot in front of the other. Again. Again.

The excitement of the trek had long ago faded, leaving behind a relentless determination to prevail, which in turn had faded into a kind of mental numbness. Trish spent the time chatting with Karen, telling the private details of her life, secretly hoping that Karen would be pleased, would say something telling her she was proud of her. Suddenly she noticed that Karen wasn't listening; had apparently wandered off on her sometime when she hadn't been paying attention.

She stopped on the edge of a long, winding rille. It looked like a river-bed just waiting for a rainstorm to fill it, but Trish knew it had never known water. Covering the bottom was only dust, dry as powdered bone. She slowly picked her way to the bottom, careful not to slip again and risk damage to her fragile life-support system. She looked up at the top. Karen was standing on the rim waving at her. "Come on! Quit *dawdling*, you slowpoke—you want to stay here *forever*?"

"What's the hurry? We're ahead of schedule. The sun is high up in the sky, and we're halfway around the moon. We'll make it, no sweat."

Karen came down the slope, sliding like a skiier in the powdery dust. She pressed her face up against Trish's helmet and stared into her eyes with a manic intensity that almost frightened her. "The hurry, my lazy little sister, is that you're halfway around the moon, you've finished with the easy part and it's all mountains and badlands from here on, you've got six thousand kilometers to walk in a broken spacesuit, and if you slow down and let the sun get ahead of you, and then run into one more teensy little problem, just one, you'll be dead, dead, dead, just like me. You wouldn't like it, trust me. Now get your pretty little lazy butt into gear and *move*!"

And, indeed, it was slow going. She couldn't bound down slopes as she used to, or the broken strut would fail and she'd have to stop for painstaking repair. There were no more level plains; it all seemed to be either boulder fields, crater walls, or mountains. On the eighteenth day she came to a huge natural arch. It towered over her head, and she gazed up at it in awe, wondering how such a structure could have been formed on the moon.

"Not by wind, that's for sure," said Karen. "Lava, I'd figure. Melted through a ridge and flowed on, leaving the hole; then over the eons micrometeoroid bombardment ground off the rough edges. Pretty, though, isn't it?"

"Magnificent."

Not far past the arch she entered a forest of needle-thin crystals. At first they were small, breaking like glass under her feet, but then they soared above her, six-sided spires and minarets in fantastic colors. She picked her way in silence between them, bedazzled by the forest of light sparkling between the sapphire spires. The crystal jungle finally thinned out and was replaced by giant crystal boulders, glistening iridescent in the sun. Emeralds? Diamonds?

"I don't know, kid. But they're in our way. I'll be glad when they're behind us."

And after a while the glistening boulders thinned out as well, until there were only a scattered few glints of color on the slopes of the hills beside her, and then at last the rocks were just rocks, craggy and pitted.

Crater Daedalus, the middle of the lunar farside. There was no celebration this time. The sun had long ago stopped its lazy rise, and was imperceptibly dropping toward the horizon ahead of them.

"It's a race against the sun, kid, and the sun ain't making any stops to rest. You're losing ground."

"I'm tired. Can't you see I'm tired? I think I'm sick. I hurt all over. Get off my case. Let me rest. Just a few more minutes? Please?"

"You can rest when you're dead." Karen laughed in a strangled, high-pitched voice. Trish suddenly realized that she was on the edge of hysteria. Abruptly she stopped laughing. "Get a move on, kid. Move!"

The lunar surface passed under her, an irregular gray treadmill.

Hard work and good intentions couldn't disguise the fact that the sun was gaining. Every day when she woke up the sun was a little lower down ahead of her, shining a little more directly in her eyes.

Ahead of her, in the glare of the sun she could see an oasis, a tiny island of grass and trees in the lifeless desert. She could already hear the croaking of frogs: braap, braap, *BRAAP!*

No. That was no oasis; that was the sound of a malfunction alarm. She stopped, disoriented. Overheating. The suit air conditioning had broken down. It took her half a day to find the clogged coolant valve and another three hours soaked in sweat to find a way to unclog it without letting the precious liquid vent to space. The sun sank another handspan toward the horizon.

The sun was directly in her face now. Shadows of the rocks stretched toward her like hungry tentacles, even the smallest looking hungry and mean. Karen was walking beside her again, but now she was silent, sullen.

"Why won't you talk to me? Did I do something? Did I say something wrong? Tell me."

"I'm not here, little sister. I'm dead. I think it's about time you faced up to that."

"Don't say that. You can't be dead."

"You have an idealized picture of me in your mind. Let me go. *Let me go!*"

"I can't. Don't go. Hey—do you remember the time we saved up all our allowances for a year so we could buy a horse? And we found a stray kitten that was real sick, and we took the shoebox full of our allowance and the kitten to the vet, and he fixed the kitten but wouldn't take any money?"

"Yeah, I remember. But somehow we still never managed to save enough for a horse." Karen sighed. "Do you think it was easy growing up with a bratty little sister dogging my footsteps, trying to imitate everything I did?"

"I wasn't ever bratty."

"You were too."

"No, I wasn't. I adored you." Did she? "I *worshipped* you."

"I know you did. Let me tell you, kid, that didn't make it any easier. Do you think it was easy being worshipped? Having to be a paragon all the time? Christ, all through high school, when I wanted to get high, I had to sneak away and do it in private, or else I knew my damn kid sister would be doing it too."

"You didn't. You never."

"Grow up, kid. Damn right I did. You were always right behind me. Everything I did, I knew you'd be right there doing it next. I had to struggle like hell to keep ahead of you, and you, damn you, followed effortlessly. You were smarter than me—you know that, don't you?—and how do you think that made me feel?"

"Well, what about me? Do you think it was easy for *me*? Growing up with a dead sister—everything I did, it was 'Too bad you can't be more like Karen' and 'Karen wouldn't have done it that way' and 'If only Karen had . . .' How do you think that made me feel, huh? You had it easy—I was the one who had to live up to the standards of a goddamn *angel*."

"Tough breaks, kid. Better than being dead."

"Damn it, Karen, I loved you. I love you. Why did you have to go away?"

"I know that, kid. I couldn't help it. I'm sorry. I love you too, but I have to go. Can you let me go? Can you just be yourself now, and stop trying to be me?"

"I'll . . . I'll try."

"Goodbye, little sister."

"Goodbye, Karen."

She was alone in the settling shadows on an empty, rugged plain. Ahead of her, the sun was barely kissing the ridgetops. The dust she kicked up was behaving strangely; rather than falling to the ground, it would hover half a meter off the ground. She puzzled over the effect, then saw that all around her, dust was silently rising off the ground. For a moment she thought it was another hallucination, but then realized it was some kind of electrostatic charging effect. She moved forward again through the rising fog of moon-dust. The sun reddened, and the sky turned a deep purple.

The darkness came at her like a demon. Behind her only the tips of mountains were illuminated, the bases disappearing into shadow. The ground ahead of her was covered with pools of ink that she had to pick her way around. Her radio locator was turned on, but receiving only static. It could only pick up the locator beacon from the *Moonshadow* if she got in line of sight of the crash site. She must be nearly there, but none of the landscape looked even slightly familiar. Ahead—was that the ridge she'd climbed to radio Earth? She couldn't tell. She climbed it, but didn't see the blue marble. The next one?

The darkness had spread up to her knees. She kept tripping over rocks invisible in the dark. Her footsteps struck sparks from the rocks, and behind her footprints glowed faintly. Triboluminescent glow, she thought—nobody has ever seen that before. She couldn't die now, not so close. But the darkness wouldn't wait. All around her the darkness lay like an unsuspected ocean, rocks sticking up out of the tidepools into the dying sunlight. The under-voltage alarm began to warble as the rising tide of darkness reached her solar array. The crash site had to be around here somewhere, it had to. Maybe the locator beacon was broken? She climbed up a ridge and into the light, look-ing around desperately for clues. Shouldn't there have been a rescue mission by now?

Only the mountaintops were in the light. She aimed for the nearest and tallest mountain she could see and made her way across the darkness to it, stumbling and crawling in the ocean of ink, at last pulling herself into the light like a swimmer gasping for air. She huddled on her rocky island, desperate as the tide of darkness slowly rose about her. Where were they? *Where were they?*

Back on Earth, work on the rescue mission had moved at a frantic pace. Everything was checked and triple-checked—in space, cutting corners was an invitation for sudden death—but still the rescue mission had been dogged by small problems and minor delays, delays that would have been routine for an ordinary mission, but loomed huge against the tight mission deadline.

The scheduling was almost impossibly tight—the mission had been set to launch in four months, not four weeks. Technicians scheduled for vacations volunteered to work overtime, while suppliers who normally took weeks to deliver parts delivered overnight. Final integration for the replacement for *Moonshadow*, originally to be called *Explorer* but now hastily re-christened *Rescuer*, was speeded up, and the transfer vehicle launched to the Space Sta-tion months ahead of the original schedule, less than two weeks after the *Moonshadow* crash. Two shuttle-loads of propellant swiftly followed, and the transfer vehicle was mated to its aeroshell and tested. While the rescue crew practiced possible scenarios on the simulator, the lander, with engines inspected and replaced, was hastily modified to accept a third person on as-cent, tested, and then launched to rendezvous with *Rescuer*. Four weeks after the crash the stack was fueled and ready, the crew briefed, and the trajectory calculated. The crew shuttle launched through heavy fog to join their *Rescuer* in orbit.

Thirty days after the unexpected signal from the moon had revealed a survivor of the *Moonshadow* expedition, *Rescuer* left orbit for the moon.

From the top of the mountain ridge west of the crash site, Commander Stan-ley passed his searchlight over the wreckage one more time and shook his head in awe. "An amazing job of piloting," he said. "Looks like she used the TEI motor for braking, and then set it down on the RCS verniers."

"Incredible," Tanya Nakora murmured. "Too bad it couldn't save her."

The record of Patricia Mulligan's travels was written in the soil around the wreck. After the rescue team had searched the wreckage, they found the single line of footsteps that led due west, crossed the ridge, and disappeared over the horizon. Stanley put down the binoculars. There was no sign of returning footprints. "Looks like she wanted to see the moon before her air ran out," he said. Inside his helmet he shook his head slowly. "Wonder how far she got?"

"Could she be alive somehow?" asked Nakora. "She was a pretty ingenious kid."

"Not ingenious enough to breathe vacuum. Don't fool yourself—this rescue mission was a political toy from the start. We never had a chance of finding anybody up here still alive."

"Still, we had to try, didn't we?"

Stanley shook his head and tapped his helmet. "Hold on a sec, my damn radio's acting up. I'm picking up some kind of feedback—almost sounds like a voice."

"I hear it too, Commander. But it doesn't make any sense."

The voice was faint in the radio. "Don't turn off the lights. Please, please, don't turn off your light . . ."

Stanley turned, to Nakora. "Do you . . . ?"

"I hear it, Commander . . . but I don't believe it."

Stanley picked up the searchlight and began sweeping the horizon. "Hello? *Rescuer* calling Astronaut Patricia Mulligan. Where the hell are you?"

The spacesuit had once been pristine white. It was now dirty gray with moondust, only the ragged and bent solar array on the back carefully polished free of debris. The figure in it was nearly as ragged.

After a meal and a wash, she was coherent and ready to explain.

"It was the mountaintop. I climbed the mountaintop to stay in the sunlight, and I just barely got high enough to hear your radios."

Nakora nodded. "That much we figured out. But the rest—the last month—you really walked all the way around the moon? Eleven thousand kilometers?"

Trish nodded. "It was all I could think of. I figured, about the distance from New York to LA and back—people have walked that and lived. It came to a walking speed of just under ten miles an hour. Farside was the hard part—turned out to be much rougher than nearside. But strange and weirdly beautiful, in places. You wouldn't believe the things I saw."

She shook her head, and laughed quietly. "I don't believe some of the things I saw. The immensity of it—we've barely scratched the surface. I'll be coming back, Commander. I promise you."

"I'm sure you will," said Commander Stanley. "I'm sure you will."

As the ship lifted off the moon, Trish looked out for a last view of the surface. For a moment she thought she saw a lonely figure standing on the surface, waving her goodbye. She didn't wave back.

She looked again, and there was nothing out there but magnificent desolation.

Robert Reed is a prolific author with a fondness for the novella. Among Reed's recent projects is polishing his past catalog, then publishing those stories on Kindle, using his daughter's sketches for the covers. His novella, "A Billion Eves," won the Hugo for Best Novella in 2007. His latest novel is *The Dragons of Marrow*.

WAGING GOOD
Robert Reed

1

The spaceport resembled a giant jade snowflake set on burnished glass. Not a year old, it already absorbed much of the moon's traffic. Unarmored and exposed, the port didn't have a single combat laser or any fighting ships at the ready. Fat new shuttles came and left without fear, a casual, careless prosperity thriving below. Who would have guessed? In the cold gray wash of earthshine . . . who could have known . . . ? When Sitta was growing up, people claimed that Nearside would remain empty for a thousand years. There was too much residual radiation, wise voices said. The terrain was too young and unstable. Besides, what right-thinking person would live with the earth overhead? Who could look at that world and not think of the long war and the billions killed?

Yet people were forgetting. That's what the snowflake meant. For a moment, Sitta's hands trembled and she ground her teeth. Then she caught herself, remembering that she was here because she too had forgotten the past, or at least forgiven it. That's when she sighed and smiled in a tired, forgiving way, and blanking her monitor, she sat back in her seat, showing any prying eyes that she was a woman at peace.

The shuttle fired its engines, its touchdown gentle, almost imperceptible.

Passengers stood, testing the gravity. Most were bureaucrats attached to the earth's provisional government—pudgy Martians, with a few Mercurians and Farsiders thrown into the political stew. They seemed happy, almost giddy, to be free of the earth. The shuttle's crew were Belters, spidery-limbed and weak. Yet despite the moon's pull, they insisted on standing at the main hatch, smiling and shaking hands, wishing everyone a good day and good travels to come. The pilot—three meters of brittle bone and waxy skin—looked directly at Sitta, telling her, "It's been a pleasure serving you, my dear. An absolute joy."

Eight years ago, banished from Farside, Sitta carried her most essential belongings inside an assortment of hyperfiber chests, sealed and locked. All were stolen when she reached the earth, and that's where she learned how little is genuinely essential. Today, she carried a single leather bag, trim and simple. Unlockable, unobtrusive. Following the herd of bureaucrats, she entered a long curling walkway, robot sentries waiting, politely but firmly asking everyone to submit to a scan.

Sitta felt ready.

Waiting her turn, she made the occasional noise about having been gone too long.

"Too long," she said twice, her voice entirely convincing.

The earth had left its marks. Once pretty in a frail, pampered way, Sitta had built heavier bones and new muscle, fats and fluid added in just the last few months. Her face showed the abuse of weather, save around her thin mouth. Toxins and a certain odd fungus had left her skin blotchy, scarred. Prettiness had evolved into a handsome strength. She needed that strength, watching the robots turn toward her, a dozen sensitive instruments reaching inside her possessions and her body, no place to hide.

But these were only routine precautions. More thorough examinations were endured in Athens and the orbiting station, and she was perfectly safe. There was nothing dangerous, nothing anyone could yet find—

—which was when the nearest robot hesitated, pointing one gray barrel at her swollen belly. What was wrong? Fear began, and remembering the sage advice of a smuggler, Sitta hid her fear by pretending impatience, asking her accuser, "What's wrong? Are you broken?"

No response.

"I'm in perfect health," she declared. "I cleared quarantine in three days."

"Thank you." The robot withdrew the device. "Please, continue."

Adrenaline and the weak gravity made the next stride into a leap. The walktube took a soft turn, then climbed toward the main terminal. Another barrier had been passed. Sitta coached herself: A simple ride to Farside, another cursory scan at the border, then freedom for the rest of her days. The impulse was to run to the public railbugs, but the spectacle of that was sure to draw all sorts of unwanted attention. Forcing her legs to walk, she kept thinking, "I just want it done. Now. Now!"

Two signs greeted her entry to the terminal. "WELCOME TO THE NEW NEARSIDE INTERPLANETARY TRANSIT FACILITY AND PEACE PARK." And beyond those tall, viscous letters was a second, far less formal sign. Sitta's name was written in flowing liquid-light script, accompanied by shouts and applause, a tiny but enthusiastic crowd of well wishers charging her, making her want to flee.

"Surprise," they called out.

"Are you surprised?" they asked.

Nervous faces crowded close, examining her scars and general weathering, everyone fighting the urge to blatantly stare. Then she set down her bag, taking a breath and turning, showing her profile, making everyone gawk and giggle aloud.

Hands reached for her belly.

Pony, flippant as always, exclaimed, "Oh, and we thought you weren't having any fun down there!"

Insensitive and graceless, and every other face tightened, ready for her anger. But Sitta politely smiled, whispering, "Who could have guessed?" Not once, even in her worst daydream, had she imagined that anyone would come to meet her. How could they even know she was here? With a voice that sounded just a little forced, Sitta said, "Hello. How are all of you?" She grasped the nearest hand and pressed it against herself. It was Varner's hand, large and masculine, and soft. When had she last felt a hand both free of callus and intact?

"No wonder you're home early," Varner observed, his tone effortlessly sarcastic. "What are you? Eight months along?"

"More than six," Sitta replied, by reflex.

Icenice, once her very best friend, came forward and demanded a hug. Still tall, still lovely, and still overdressed for the occasion, she put her thin long arms around Sitta and burst into tears. Wiping her face with the sleeve of her black-and-gold gown, she stepped back and sputtered, "We're sorry, darling. For everything. Please—"

Varner said, "Icenice," in warning.

"Accept our apologies. Please?"

"I came home, didn't I?" asked Sitta.

The question was interpreted as forgiveness. Every face grinned, yet this was far from the same old gang. Where were Lean and Catchen? And Unnel? The Twins had made it, still indistinguishable from each other, and Vechel, silent as always. But there people hanging in the background, wearing the suffering patience of strangers. Spouses, or spies? Sitta had to imagine this was some elaborate scheme meant to keep tabs on her. Or perhaps some species of slow, subtle torture was being unleashed, as a prelude to things even worse.

Everybody was talking; nobody could listen.

Suddenly Varner—always their reasonable, self-appointed boss—shook people and declared, "We can chat on the rail." Turning to Sitta, he winked while asking, "May I carry this lady's satchel?"

For an instant, in vivid detail, she remembered the last time she had seen him.

Varner took her hesitation as a refusal. "Well, you're twice my strength anyway." Probably true. "Out of our way, people! A mother needs room. Make way for us!"

They used slidewalks, giant potted jungles passing on both sides. Staring at the luxurious foliage, unfruited and spendthrift, Sitta wondered how many people could be fed with crops grown inside those pots, and how these treasures might be transported to the earth.

More thoughts needed to be choked to death.

Turning to Icenice, she examined the rich fabrics of her gown and the painted, always perfect breasts. With a voice intense and casual in equal measures, she asked, "How did you know I'd be here?"

Icenice grinned and bent closer. "We had a tip."

Sitta was traveling under her own name, but she'd left the Plowsharers in mid-assignment. Besides, Plowsharers were supposed to enjoy a certain anonymity, what with the negative feelings toward them. "What kind of tip, darling?"

"I told one of your administrators about us. About the prank, about how sorry we felt." Her long hands meshed, making a single fist. "She knew your name. 'The famous Sitta,' she called you. 'One of our best.'"

Nodding, Sitta made no comment.

"Then just yesterday, without warning, we learned that you'd been given a medical discharge, that you were coming home." Tears filled red-rimmed eyes. "I was scared for you, Sitta. We all were."

"I wasn't," said Varner. "A little cancer, a little virus. You're too smart to get yourself into real trouble."

Sitta made no comment.

"We took the risk, made a day of it," Icenice continued. She waited for Sitta's eyes to find hers, then asked, "Would you like to come to my house? We've planned a little celebration, if you're up to it."

She had no choice but to say, "All right."

The others closed in on her again, touching the belly, begging for attention Sitta found herself looking upward, hungry for privacy. Through the glass ceiling, the gibbous gray face of the earth showed featureless and chill; and after a long moment's anguish, she heard herself saying, "The last time I spoke to you—"

"Forget it," Varner advised, as if it was his place to forgive.

Icenice assured her, "That was eons ago."

It felt like it was minutes ago. If that.

Then Pony poked her in the side, saying, "We know you. You've never held a grudge for long."

"Pony." Varner had a gift for delivering warnings with a person's own name.

Sitta made no sound, again glancing at the earth.

Again, Varner touched her with his soft heavy hand, meaning to tease
sure her in some fashion. Suddenly his hand jumped back. "Quite a little
kicker, isn't he?"

"She," Sitta corrected, eyes dropping.

"Six months along?"

"Almost seven." She held her leather bag in both hands. Why couldn't she
just scream at them and run away? Because it would draw attention, and worse,
because someone might ask why she would come here. Sitta had no family left
on the moon, no property, nothing but some electronic money in a very portable
bank account. "I guess I don't understand . . . why would anyone even bother—"

"Because," Icenice proclaimed, taking her best friend by the shoulders.
"We knew you deserved a hero's welcome."

"Our hero," people muttered, those words practiced, but poised. "Our own
little hero."

And now she was a hero. The ironies made her want to laugh, just for an
instant. She had come to murder them, and she was heroic?

"Welcome home," they shouted, in unison.

Sitta allowed herself another tired smile, letting them misunderstand the
thought behind it. Then she glanced at the earth, longing in her gaze, that
world's infinite miseries preferable to this world's petty, thoughtless abuses.

2

The war ended when Sitta was four years-old, but for her and her friends it
hadn't existed except as a theory, as a topic that fascinated adults, and as a
pair of low-grade warnings when the earth fired its final shots. But they were
never endangered. For all intents and purposes, the war was won decades
before, the earth in no position to succeed, its enemies able to weather every
blow, then take warm pleasure in their final campaigns.

Victory was a good thing. The four year-old girl understood good and
evil, winning and losing, and why winners deserved their laurels and losers
earned their punishments. She also understood, in some wordless way, that
Farside was a special place meant for the best people. Its border was protected by fortifications and energy barriers. Several thousand kilometers of
dead rock lay between its blessed people and the enemy. Bombs and lasers
could obliterate Nearside, melting it and throwing up new mountains; but
on Farside, for more than a century, the citizens suffered nothing worse than
quakes and some accidental deaths, friendly bombs and crashing warships
doing more harm than the entire earth could manage.

Other worlds told different stories. They were always fighting for survival, every life endangered. No place was safe but the back of the moon, and

that's why Farsiders were the great winners. Sitta's family made its fortune in genetic weapons—adaptive plagues and communicable cancers, plus a range of parasites. Following a Farside custom, her parents waited until retirement to have their child. It was the same for Icenice, for Varner, for everyone, it seemed. Sitta was shocked to learn as a youngster that near-youngsters could make babies. She had assumed that humans were like the salmon swimming up from the Central Sea, a lifetime of preparation followed by a minute of desperate spawning, then death. That's how it was for Sitta's parents; both of them expired even before she reached puberty. An aunt inherited her—an ancient, stern and incompetent creature—and when their relationship collapsed, Sitta lived with her friends' families, all pleasant and all indifferent toward her.

Growing up, she learned about the great war. Tutors spoke about its beginnings, and they lectured for hours about military tactics and the many famous battles. Yet the war was relentlessly unreal. A giant and elaborate theory presented for her entertainment. She liked the battles for the visual records they left behind, colorful and modestly exciting, and she observed the dead with clinical detachment. Sitta was undeniably bright—her genes had been tweaked to ensure quick, effortless intelligence—yet in some fundamental way, she had gaps. Flaws. Watching the destruction of Nearside and Hellas and dozens of other tragedies, she couldn't truly envision the suffering involved. The dead were so many abstractions. And what's more, they were dead because they deserved their fates, unworthy of living here, unworthy of lovely Farside.

In the beginning, the earth had ten billion citizens. It was a wonderland with skyhooks and enormous solar farms, every sort of industry and the finest scientists. The earth should have won. Sitta wrote the same paper for several tutors, pointing out those moments when any decisive, coordinated assault would have crushed the colonies. Yet when chances came, the earth lost its nerve. Too squeamish to obliterate the rebels—too willing to show a partial mercy—it let the colonies breathe and grow strong again, ensuring its own demise.

For that failure, Sitta had shown nothing but scorn. And her tutors, to the machine, agreed with her, awarding good grades to each effort, the last of them adding, "You have a gift with political science. Perhaps you'll enter government service, then work your way into a high office."

Such a ridiculous suggestion. Sitta didn't need careers, what with her inherited wealth and all these natural talents. But if she wanted to work, regardless of reasons, the girl was certain to begin near the top of any organizational heap, inhabiting some position of deserved authority.

She was an important child of important Farsiders.

How could she deserve anything less?

The railbug was ornate and familiar—an old-fashioned contraption with a passing resemblance to a fat, glass-skinned caterpillar—but Sitta needed a moment to recall where she had seen it. Free of the port, streaking across the smooth glass plain, she was sitting on one of the stiff seats, stroking the dark wood trim. There was a time when wood was a precious substance on Farside, organics scarce, even for the wealthiest few. Remembering smaller hands on the trim, she looked at Varner and asked, "Did we play here?"

"A few times," he replied, grinning.

The bug had belonged to his family, too old to use and not fancy enough to refurbish. She remembered darkness and the scent of old flowers. "You brought me here—"

"—for sex, as I remember it." Varner laughed and glanced at the others, seemingly asking them to laugh with him. "How old were we?"

Too young, she recalled. The experience had been clumsy, and except for the fear of being caught, she'd had little fun. Why did anyone bother with sex? She would ask herself that for weeks. Even when she was old enough, screwing Varner and most of her other male friends, part of Sitta remained that doubtful child, the fun of it merely fun, just another little pleasure to be squeezed into long days and nights of busy idleness.

The railbug was for old-times sake. That's what she assumed, but before she could ask, Icenice began serving refreshments. "Who wants, who needs?" There was alcohol and more exotic fare. Sitta chose wine, sipping as she halfway listened to jumbled conversations. People told childhood stories, pleasant memories dislodging more of the same. Nobody mentioned the earth or the war. If Sitta didn't know better, she would assume that nothing had changed in these last years, that these careless lives had been held in stasis. Which might be true, in a sense. But then, as Icenice strode past and the hem of her gown lifted, she noticed the gold bracelet worn on the woman's left ankle. Sitta remembered that bracelet; it had belonged to the girl's mother, and to her grandmother before. In a soft half-laugh, she asked, "Are you married, girl?"

Their hostess paused for an instant, then straightened and smiled, her expression almost embarrassed. "I should have told you, Sorry, darling." A pause. "Almost three years married, yes."

The buzz of other conversations diminished. Sitta looked at the strangers, wondering which one of them was the husband.

"He's a Mercurian," said her one-time friend. "Named Bosson."

The original Icenice adored men in the plural. The Icenice she remembered gave herself sophisticated personality tests, then boasted of her inability enjoy monogamy. Married? To a hundred men, perhaps. Sitta cleared her throat, then asked, "What sort of wonder is he?"

"Wait and see," Icenice advised. She adjusted the straps of her gown pulling them one way, then back where they began. "Wait and see."

The strangers were staring at Sitta, at her face.

"Who are they?" she whispered.

And finally they were introduced, more apologies made for tardiness, Pony claimed the job, prefacing herself by saying, "We're all Farsiders here." Was that important? "They've heard about you, darling. They've wanted to meet you, and for a long, long while . . ."

Shaking damp hands, Sitta consciously forgot every name. Were they friends to the old gang? Yet they didn't seem to fit that role. She had to resurrect that ridiculous theory about spies and a plot. There was an agenda here, something she could feel in the air. But why bring half a dozen government agents? Unless the plan was to be obvious, in which case they were succeeding.

A social pause. Turning her head, Sitta noticed a long ceramic rib or fin standing on the irradiated plain. For an instant, when the earthshine had the proper angle, she could make out the bulk of something buried within the glass, locked securely in place. A magma whale. At the height of the war, when this basin was a red-hot sea stirred by thousand megaton warheads, Farsiders built a flotilla of robotic whales. Swimming in the molten rock, covering as much as a kilometer every day, they strained out metals and precious rare elements. The munition factories on Farside paid dearly for every gram of ore, and the earth, in ignorance or blind anger, kept up its useless bombardment, dredging the ocean, bringing up more treasures from below.

The rib vanished over the horizon, then with a quiet, respectful voice, Icenice asked, "Are you tired?"

She was sitting beside Sitta. Her gown's perfumes made the air close, uncomfortable.

"We haven't worn you out, have we?"

Sitta shook her head, honest when she admitted, "I feel fine." It had been an easy pregnancy. Then placing a hand on her belly, she lied. "I'm glad you came to meet me."

The tall woman hesitated, her expression impossible to read. There was sternness in the voice when she said, "It was Varner's idea."

"Was it?"

A sigh, a change of topics. "I like this place. I don't know why."

She meant the plain. Bleak and pure, the smoothest portions of the glass shone like black mirrors.

"There is a beauty," Sitta allowed.

Icenice said, "Which makes it all so sad."

"Why? What's sad?"

"They're going to tunnel and dome all of this."

"Next year," said an eavesdropping Twin.

"Tunnels here?" Sitta was dubious. "You can shield a spaceport and a rail line, but people can't live out here, can they?"

"Martians know how." Icenice glanced at the others, inviting them . . . to do what? "They've got a special way to clean the glass."

"Leaching," said Varner. "Chemical magic combined with microchines. They developed the process when they rebuilt their own cities."

"People will live here?" Sitta wrestled with the concept. "I hadn't heard. I didn't know."

"That's why they built the port in the first place," Varner continued. "All of this will be settled. Cities. Farms. Parks. And industries."

"Huge cities," muttered Icenice.

"This ground was worthless," growled one of the strangers, "Five years ago, it was less than worthless."

Varner laughed without humor. "The Martians thought otherwise."

Everyone looked dour, self-involved. They shook their heads and whispered about the price of land and what they would do if they could try again. Sitta thought it unseemly and greedy. And pointless.

Pony said, "You know, it's the Martians who own and run the spaceport."

Sitta did her best to ignore them, gazing back along the rail, the earth dropping for the horizon and no mountains to be seen. They were at the center of the young sea, her home world smooth and simple. Far out on the glass, in a school of a dozen or more, were magma whales. As their sea cooled, they must have congregated there, their own heat helping to keep the rock liquid for a little while longer.

Sitta felt a strange, vague pity. Then fear. Shutting her eyes, she tried to purge her mind of everything fearful and tentative, making herself strong enough, trying to become as pure as the most perfect glass.

4

Sitta couldn't recall when the prank had seemed fun or funny, though it must have been both at some moment. And she couldn't remember whose idea it was. Perhaps Varner's, except the criminality was more like the Twins or Pony. It was meant to be something new, a distraction that involved all of them, and it meant planning and practice and a measure of genuine courage. Sitta volunteered to tackle the largest target. Their goal was to quickly and irrevocably destroy an obscure species of beetle. How many people could boast that they'd pushed a species into oblivion? Rather few, they assumed. The crime would lend them a kind of notoriety, distinctive yet benign. Or so they told themselves, feeling clever and alive.

The ark system was built early in the war. It protected biostocks brought from the earth in finer days; some twenty million species were in cold storage and DNA libraries. A tiny portion of the stocks had been used as raw material for genetic weapons. Sitta's parents built their lab beside the main ark, and she had visited both the lab and ark as a girl. Little had changed since, including the security systems. She entered without fuss, destroying tissue samples, every whole beetle, and even the partial sequencing maps. Her friends did the same work at the other facilities. It was a tiny black bug from the vanished Amazon, and except for ancient videos and a cursory description of its habits and canopy home, nothing remained of the organism, which was exactly as planned.

Sitta would have escaped undetected but for the miserable luck of a human guard who got lost, making a series of wrong turns. He came upon her moments after she had sent the beetle into nothingness. Caught sooner, her crime would have been simple burglary and vandalism. As it was, she was charged under an old law meant to protect wartime resources.

The mandatory penalty was death. Gray-haired prosecutors with calm gray voices told her, "Your generation needs to behave." They said, "You're going to serve as an example, Sitta." Shaking ancient heads, they declared, "You're a spoiled and wealthy infant, contemptible and vulgar, and we have no pity for you. We feel nothing but scorn."

Sitta demanded to see her friends. She wanted them crammed into her hyperfiber cell, to have them see how she was living. Instead she got Icenice and Varner inside a spacious conference room, a phalanx of lawyers behind them. Her best friend wept. Her first lover said, "Listen. Just listen. Stop screaming now and hear us out."

He told her that behind the scenes, behind the legal facades, semi-official negotiations were underway. Of course the Farside government knew she'd had accomplices, and a lot of officials were afraid that the scandal would spread. Friends with pull were being contacted. That's what he assured her. Money was flowing from account to account. What Sitta needed to do was to plead guilty, to absorb all blame, because the judge was ready to find for clemency, using some semi-legal technicality. Of course there had to be a staggering penalty. "Which we will pay," Varner promised, his voice earnest and strong. "We won't let you spend a single digit of your own money."

What were her choices? She had to nod, glaring at the lawyer while saying, "Agreed. Good-bye."

"Poor Sitta," Icenice had moaned, hugging her friend but weeping less, relieved that she wouldn't be turned in to the authorities, that she was perfectly safe. Stepping back, the tall girl straightened her gown with a practiced flourish, adding, "And we'll see you soon. Very soon, darling."

But the judge wasn't compliant. After accepting bribes and hearing a few inelegant threats, he slammed together the Hammers of Justice and announced, "You're guilty. But since the beetle is missing, and since the prosecution cannot prove its true worth, I cannot, in good conscience, find for the death penalty."

Sitta stood alone with eyes shut. Then she had heard the word "clemency" and opened her eyes, except nobody but her had spoken.

The judge delivered a hard, withering stare. Sitta would hear that voice for years, syllable by syllable. "I sentence you to three years of involuntary servitude." Again he struck the Hammers together. "Those three years will be served as a member of the Plowsharers. You'll be stationed on the earth, young lady, at a post of my approval, and I just hope you learn something worthwhile from this experience."

The Plowsharers? Those were the very stupid people who volunteered to work and die on the earth, and this had to be a mistake, and how could she have misunderstood so many words at one time . . . ?

Her friends looked as if they were in shock. All wept and bowed their heads, and she glared at them, waiting for even one of them to step forward and share the blame. But they didn't. Would never. When they looked at Sitta, they saw someone who was about to die. The attrition rate among the Plowsharers was appalling. Had Varner and the others tricked her into confessing, knowing her fate all along? Probably not, no. They were genuinely surprised. She thought it then and thought nothing for the next eight years. But if they had come forward, en masse . . . if another eight families had embraced this ugly business . . . there might have been a reevaluation . . . an orphan's crime would have been diluted, if only they'd acted with a dose of courage . . . the shits . . .

The earth was hell. A weak Farsider would die in an afternoon, slain by some nameless disease or embittered Terran. Yet not one good friend raised a hand, asking to be heard. Not even when Sitta screamed at them. Not even when she slipped away from her guard, springing over the railing and grabbing Varner, trying to shake him into honesty, cursing and kicking, fighting to shame the idiot into the only possible good deed.

More guards grabbed the criminal, doing their own cursing and kicking before finally binding her arms and legs.

The judge wore an ear-to-ear grin. "Wage good," he called out, in the end. "Wage plenty of good, Sitta."

It was a Plowsharers' motto: *Waging Good*. And Sitta would remember
that moment with a gallows' clarity, her body being pulled away from Varner
as Varner's face grew cold and certain, one of his hands reaching, pressing at
her chest as if helping the guards restrain her, and his tired thick voice said,
"You'll be back." There wasn't a shred of confidence in those words. Then,
"You'll do fine." And finally with a whisper, in despair, "This is for the best,
darling. For the best."

5

The mountains were high and sharp, every young peak named for some little
hero of the war. Titanic blasts had built them, then waves of plasma broke
against them, fed by the earth's weapons and meant to pour through any
gaps, flooding Farside with the superheated materials. But the waves had
cooled and dissipated too quickly. The mountains were left brittle, and in the
decades since, at irregular intervals, different slopes would collapse, aprons
of debris fanning across the plain. The old railbug skirted one apron, crossed
another, then rose into a valley created by an avalanche, a blur of rocks on
both sides and Varner's calm voice explaining how the Martians—who
else?—had buried hyperfiber threads, buttressing the mountains, making
them safer than mounds of cold butter.

Then they left the valley, passing into the open again, an abandoned fort
showing as a series of rectangular depressions. Its barrier generators and potent lasers had been pulled and sold as scrap. There was no more earthshine
and no sun yet, but Sitta could make out the sloping wall of an ancient crater
and a wide boulder-strewn floor. The border post was in the hard black shadows; the railbug was shunted to a secondary line. Little gold domes passed on
their right. They slowed down and then stopped beside a large green dome,
fingers of light stabbing at them.

"Why do we have to stop?" asked one of the strangers.

And Pony said, "Because," while gracelessly pointed toward Sitta.

"It should only take a minute or two," Varner said, winking at her, maintained that picture of calm ignorance.

A walktube was spliced into the bug's hatch, and with a rush of humid air,
guards entered. Human, not robotic. And armed, too. But what made it most
remarkable were the three gigantic hounds. Sitta recognizing the breed in the
same instant she realized this was no ordinary inspection. Her composure
wobbled but held strong. It was Varner who jumped to his feet, muttering,
"By what right—?"

"Hello," shouted the hounds. "Be still. We bite!" They were broad and
hairless, pink as tongues and free of all scent. Their minds and throats had

been surgically augmented, and their nostrils were the best in the solar system. The earth's provisional government used these animals, and if smugglers were found with weapons or contraband, they were instantly executed, that work given to the hounds as a reward.

"We bite," the hounds repeated. "Out of our way!"

A Belter walked into the railbug, long limbs wearing grav-assist braces. Her bearing and the indigo uniform implied a great rank. Next to her, the hounds appeared docile. She glowered, glared. Facing her, Varner lost all of his nerve, slumping at the shoulders, whimpering, "How can we help?"

"You can't help," she stated. Then, speaking to the guards and hounds, she said, "Hunt!"

Sensors and noses were put to work, scouring the floor and corners and the old fixtures, then the passengers and their belongings. One hound descended on Sitta's bag, letting out a piercing wail.

"Whose is this?" asked the Belter.

Sitta kept control her face, her voice. If this woman knew her plan, then they wouldn't bother with this little drama. She'd already be placed under arrest. Everyone she knew or had been near would be isolated, then interrogated . . . if they even suspected . . .

"It's my bag," Sitta allowed.

"Open it for me. Now."

Unfastening the simple latches, she worked with cool deliberation. The bag sprang open, and she retreated, watching the heavy pink snouts descend, probing and snorting, wet mouths pulling at her neatly folded clothes. Like the bulky trousers and shirt Sitta wore, these were simple items made with rough, undyed, and inorganic fabrics. The hounds could be hunting for persistent viruses and boobytrapped motes of dust. Except a dozen mechanical searches had found her clean. Had someone recently tried to smuggle something dangerous into Farside? But why send a Belter? Nothing made sense. Sitta felt empty and unready. Then at last, with loud, disappointed voices, the hounds said, "Clean, clean, clean."

The official offered a grim nod.

Again Varner straightened, skin damp, glistening. "I have never, ever seen such a . . . such a . . . what do you want . . . ?"

No answer was offered. The Belter approached Sitta, her braces humming, lending an unexpected vigor. With the mildest voice, she asked, "How are the Plowsharers doing, miss? Are you waging all the good you can?"

"Always," Sitta replied.

"Well, good for you." The official waved a long arm. Two guards grabbed Sitta and carried her to the back of the bug, into the cramped toilet, then stood beside the doorway as the official looked over their shoulders, telling their captive, "Piss into the bowl, miss. And don't flush."

Old, weakened glass. That's what Sitta was. A thousand fractures met and she nearly collapsed, catching herself on the tiny sink and then, using her free hand, unfastening her trousers. Her expansive brown belly seemed to glow. She sat with all the dignity she could muster. Pissing took concentration, courage. Then she rose again, barely able to pull up her trousers when the Belter shouted, "Hunt," and the hounds pushed past her, heads filling the elegant wooden bowl.

If so much as a single molecule was out of place, they would find it. If just one cell had thrown off its camouflage—

—drained of thought, Sitta retreated into a trance that she had mastered on the earth. On their own, her hands finished securing her trousers. A big wagging tail bruised her leg. Then came three voices, in a chorus, saying, "Yes, yes, yes."

Yes? What did yes mean?

The official smiled, giving Sitta an odd sideways glance. Then there wasn't any smile, a stern unapologetic voice saying, "I am sorry for the delay, miss."

What had the hounds smelled?

"Welcome home, Miss Sitta."

The intruders retreated, vanished. The walktube was detached, and the railbug accelerated, Sitta walking against the strong tug. Varner and the others watched her in silent astonishment, nothing in their experience to match this assault. She almost screamed, "This happens on the earth, every day!" But she didn't speak, taking an enormous breath, then kneeling, wiping her hands against her shirt, then calmly beginning to refold and repack her belongings.

The others were embarrassed. Dumbfounded. Intrigued.

It was Pony who noticed the sock under the seat, bringing it to her and touching the bag for a moment, commenting, "It's beautiful leather." She wanted to sound at ease and trivial, adding, "What kind of leather is it?"

Sitta was thinking: What if someone knows?

Months ago, when this plan presented itself, she assumed that one of the security apparatuses would discover her, then execute her, She allowed herself a ten percent chance of surviving to this point, which seemed wildly optimistic. But what if there were people—powerful, like-minded people—who believed that she was right? No government could sanction what Sitta was attempting, much less make it happen. But they might allow the means to slip past them.

That woman smiled at me!

"Are they culturing leather on the earth?" asked Pony, unhappy to be ignored. Stroking the simple bag with both hands, she commented, "It has a nice texture. Very smooth."

"It's not cultured," Sitta responded. "Terrans can't own biosynthetic equipment."

"It's from an animal then." The girl's hand lifted, a vague disgust showing on her face. "Is it?"

"Yes," said the retired Plowsharer.

"What kind of animal?"

"The human kind."

Every eye was fixed on her.

"The other species are scarce," Sitta explained. "And precious. Even rat skins go into the pot."

No one breathed; no one dared move.

"This bag is laminated human flesh," she told them, fastening the latches. *Click, click.* "You have to understand. On the earth, it's an honor to be used after death. You want to stay behind and help your family."

A low moan fled Icenice.

And Sitta set the bag aside, watching the staring faces as she added, "I knew some of these people. I did."

6

The Plowsharers were founded and fueled by idealists who never actually worked on the earth. A wealthy Farsider donated her estate as an administrative headquarters. Plowsharers were to be volunteers with purposeful skills that would help the earth and its suffering people. That was the intent, at least. Finding volunteers worth accepting was the trouble. A hundred thousand vigorous young teachers and doctors and ecological technicians could have done miracles. But the norm was to creak along with ten or fifteen thousand ill-trained, emotionally questionable semi-volunteers. Who in her right mind joined a service with fifty percent mortality? Along the bell-shaped curve, Sitta was one of the blue-chip recruits. She had youth and a quality education. Yes, she was spoiled. Yes, she was naive. But she was in perfect health and could be made even healthier. "We're always improving our techniques," the doctors explained, standing before her in the orbital station. "What we'll do is teach your flesh how to resist its biological enemies, because they're the worst hazards. Diseases and toxins kill more Plowsharers than do bombs, old or new."

A body that had never left the soft climate of Farside was transformed. Her immune system was bolstered, then a second, superior system was built on top of it. She was fed tailored bacteria that proceeded to attack her native flora, destroying them and bringing their withering firepower to her defense. As an experiment, Sitta was fed cyanides and dioxins, cholera and rabies. Headaches were her worst reaction. Then fullerenes stuffed full of procrustean bugs were injected straight into her heart. What should have killed her in minutes made her nauseous, nothing more. The invaders were obliterated, their toxic parts encased in plastic granules, then jettisoned in the morning's bowel movement.

Meanwhile, bones and muscles had to be strengthened. Calcium slurries were ingested, herculian steroids were administered along with hard exercise, and her liver succumbed as a consequence, her posting delayed. Her three-year sentence didn't begin until she set foot on the planet, yet Sitta was happy for the free time. It gave her a chance to compose long, elaborate letters to her old friends, telling them in clear terms to fuck themselves and each other and fuck Farside and would they please die soon and horribly, please?

A fresh liver was grown and implanted. At last, Sitta was posted. With an education rich in biology—a legacy of her parents—she was awarded a physician's field diploma, then given to a remote city on the cratered rock of northern America. Her hyperfiber chests were stolen in Athens. With nothing but the clothes she had worn for three days, she boarded the winged shuttle that would take her across the poisoned Atlantic. Her mood couldn't have been lower. That's what she believed, and then, gazing out a tiny porthole, she discovered a new depth of spirit. Gray ocean was giving way to a blasted lunar surface. It was like the moon of old, save for the thick acidic haze and the occasional dab of green, both serving to heighten the bleakness, the lack of all hope.

She decided to throw herself from the shuttle. Placing a hand on the emergency latch, she waited for the courage; but then one of the crew saw her and came over to her, kneeling to say, "Don't." His smile was charming, his eyes angry. "If you need to jump," he said, "use the rear hatch. And seal the inner door behind you, will you?"

Sitta stared at him, unable to speak.

"Consideration," he cautioned. "At this altitude and at these speeds, you might hurt innocent people."

In the end, she killed no one. Embarrassed to be found out, to be so transparent, she kept on living; and years later, in passing, she would wonder who to thank for this indifferent, precious help.

7

Farside, like every place, was transformed by the war. But instead of world-shaking explosions and craters, it was sculpted by slower, more graceful events. Prosperity covered its central region with domes, warm air and man-made rains beginning to modify the ancient regolith. Farther out were the factories and vast laboratories that supplied the military and allied worlds. Profits came as electronic cash, water and organics. A world dry for four billion years was suddenly rich with moisture. Ponds became lakes. Comet ice and pieces of distant moons were brought to pay for necessities like medicine and sophisticated machinery. And when there was too much water for the surface area—Farside isn't a large place—the excess was put underground, flooding old mines and caverns and outdated bunkers. This became the Central Sea. Only in small places, usually on the best estates, would the Sea show on the surface. Icenice had lived beside one of those pond-sized faces, the water bottomless and blue, lovely beyond words.

It was too bad that Sitta wouldn't see it now. Looking about the railbug, at the morose, downslung faces, it was obvious that she was doomed to be uninvited to every celebration. That incident with the bag had spoiled the mood. Would it be Varner or Icenice who would break another promise? "Some other time, darling. Where can we leave you?" Except they surprised her. Instead of excuses, they began to have the most banal conversation imaginable. Who remembered what from last year's spinball season? What team won the tournament? Who could recall the most obscure statistic? A safe, bloodless collection of noise set everything right again, and Sitta ignored the prattle, leaning back against her seat, her travels and the pregnancy finally catching up with her. She dropped into sleep, no time passing, then woke to find the glass walls opaque, the sun up and needing to be shielded. This was like riding inside a glass of milk or a cloudbank, and sometimes, holding her head at the proper angle, she could just make out the blocky shapes of factories streaking past.

Nobody was speaking; furtive glances were thrown her way.

"What do they do?" asked Sitta.

Silence.

"The factories," she added. "Aren't they being turned over to civilian industries?"

"Some have been," said Varner.

"Why bother?" one of the strangers complained.

"Bosson uses a few of them." Icenice spoke with a flat, emotionless voice. "The equipment is old, he says. And he has trouble selling what he makes."

Bosson is your husband, thought Sitta. *Right?*

She asked, "What does he make?"

"Laser drills. They're retooled old weapons, I guess."

Sitta had assumed that everything and everyone would follow the grand plan.

Farside's wealth and infrastructure would generate new wealth and opportunities
. . . if not with their factories, then with new spaceports and beautiful new cities.

Except those wonders belonged to the Martians.

Varner wore a stern expression. "If you want to sleep, we'll make up the long seat in the back. If you'd like."

On a whim, she asked, "Where are Lean and Catchen?"

Silence.

"Are they still angry with me?"

"Nobody's angry with you," Icenice protested.

"Lean lives on Titan," Pony replied. "Catchen . . . I don't know . . . she's somewhere in the Belt."

"They're not together?" Sitta had never known two people more perfectly linked, save for the Twins. "What happened?"

Shrugs. Embarrassed expressions, and pain. Then Varner summed it up by saying, "Crap finds you."

What precisely did that mean?

Varner rose to his feet, looking the length of the bug.

Sitta asked, "What about Unnel?"

"We don't have any idea." Indeed, he seemed entirely helpless, eyes dropping, gazing at his own hands for a few baffled moments. "Do you want to sleep, or not?"

She voted for sleep. A pillow was found and placed where her head would lay, and she was down and hard asleep in minutes, waking once to hear soft conversation—distant, unintelligible—then again to hear nothing at all. The third time brought bright light and whispers, and she sat upright, discovering that their railbug had stopped, its walls once again transparent. Surrounding them was a tall, delicate jungle and a soft blue-tinted sky of glass, the lunar noon as brilliant as she remembered. Through an open hatch, she could smell water and the vigorous stink of orchids.

Icenice was coming for her. "Oh," she exclaimed, "I was just going to shake you."

The others stood behind Icenice, lined up like the best little children; and Sitta thought:

You want something.

That's why they had come to greet her and bring her here. That's why they had endured searches and why they had risked facing any grudges that she still might feel toward them.

You want something important, and no one else can give it to you.

Sitta would refuse them. She had come here to destroy these people and devastate their world, and seeing the desire on hopeful, desperate faces, she

was so deeply pleased. So blessed. Rising to her feet, she asked, "Would someone carry my bag? I'm still very tired."

A cold pause, then motion.

By different straps, Varner and one of the strangers picked that bag of human flesh, eyeing one another until the stranger relinquished the disgusting
chore with a forced chuckle and bow, stepping back and glancing at Sitta,
hoping she would notice his attempted kindness.

8

Artificial volcanoes girdled the earth's equator, fusion reactors sunk into
their throats, helping push millions of tons of acid and ash into the stratosphere. Constant eruptions maintained the gray-black clouds that helped
block the sunlight. Those clouds were vital. Decades of bombardment had
burned away forests, soil and even great volumes of carbonate rock. There
was so much carbon dioxide in the atmosphere that full sunshine would
have brought a runaway greenhouse event. A second Venus would be born,
and the oceans would rise into the stratosphere, and then the world would
be broil until dead. "Not a bad plan," Sitta's parents would always claim,
perhaps as a black joke. Perhaps. "That world is all one grave anyway. Why
do we pretend?"

The earthly climate was hot and humid despite the perpetual gloom. It
would be an ideal home for orchids and food crops, if not for the lack of soil,
its poisoned water, and the endless plant diseases. Terrans, by custom, lived
inside bunkers. Even in surface homes built after the war, there was a strength
of walls and ceilings, everything drab and massive, every opening able to be
sealed tight. Sitta was given her own concrete monstrosity when she arrived
at her post. It had no plumbing. She'd been promised normal facilities, but
assuming that she was being slighted by the Terrans, she refused to complain.
Indeed, she tried to avoid all conversation. On her first morning, in the dim
purple light, she put on a breathing mask to protect her lungs from acids and
explosive dust, then left her new house, shuffling up a rocky hill, finding a
depression where she felt unwatched and doing the essential chore and covering her mess with loose stones, then slinking off to work a full day in the
farm fields.

A hospital was promised; every government official in Athens had said so.
But on the earth, she was learning, promises were no stronger than the wind
that makes them. For the time being, she was a laborer, and a poor one. Sitta
could barely lift her tools, much less swing them with authority. Yet nobody
seemed to mind, their public fury focused on a thousand worse outrages. That
was greatest surprise for the new Plowsharer. It wasn't the poverty, which was

endless, or the clinging filth, or even the constant spectre of death. It was the ceaselessly supportive nature of the Terrans, particularly toward her. Wasn't she one of the brutal conquerors? Not to their way of thinking, no. Acidic clouds ruled the sky. The moon and Mars and the rest of the worlds were theories, unobserved and almost unimaginable. Yes, they honestly hated the provisional government, particularly the security agencies that enforced the harsh laws. But toward Sitta, their Plowsharer, they showed smiles. They said, "We're thrilled to have you here. If you need anything, ask. We won't have it, but ask anyway. We like to apologize all the same."

Humor was a shock, set against the misery. Despite every awful story told by Farsiders, and despite the grueling training digitals, the reality proved a hundred times more wicked, cruel, and thoughtless than anything she could envision. Yet meanwhile, amid the carnage, the people of this city told jokes, laughed, and loved with a kind of maniacal vigor, perhaps because of the stakes involved, pleasures needing to be taken as they were found.

Tens of thousands lived together, few of whom could be called old by Farside standards. Children outnumbered adults, except they weren't genuine children. They reminded Sitta of five and six year-old adults, working in the fields and tiny factories, worldly in all things, including their play. The most popular game was a pretend funeral. They used wild rats, skinning them just as human bodies were skinned, pulling out organs to be transplanted into other rats, just as humans harvested whatever they could use from their own dead, implanting body parts with the help of primitive autodocs, dull knives, and weak laser beams.

By law, each district in the city had one funeral each day. One or fifty bodies—skinned, and if clean enough, emptied of livers, kidneys and hearts—were buried in a single ceremony, always at dusk, always as the blister-colored sun touched the remote horizon. There was never more than one hole to dig and refill. Terrans were wonders at digging graves. They always knew where to sink them and how deep, then just what words to say over the departed, and the best ways to comfort a woman from Farside who insisted on taking death personally.

Despite her hyperactive immune system, Sitta became ill. For all she knew, she had caught some mutant strain of an ailment devised by her parents, those circumstances thick with irony. After three days of fever, she ran out of the useless medicines in her personal kit, then fell into a delirium, waking at one point to find women caring for her, smiling with sloppy toothless mouths, ugly faces lending her encouragement, a credible strength.

Sitta recovered after a week of near-death. Weaker than any time since birth, she shuffled up the hillside to defecate, and in the middle of the act she saw a nine-year-old sitting nearby, watching without a hint of shame. She finished and went to him. And he skipped toward her, carrying a small bucket and spade. Was he there to clean up after her? She asked, then with a wise tone, added, "I bet you want it for the fields."

The boy gave an odd look, then proclaimed, "We wouldn't waste it on the crops!"

"Then why?" Hesitating, she realized that she'd seen him on other mornings. "You've done this other times, haven't you?"

"It's my job," he said, a prideful smile behind that transparent breathing mask. She tried to find her other stone piles. "But why?"

"I'm not suppose to tell."

Sitta offered a wan smile. "I won't tell that you did. Just explain what you want with it."

As if nothing could be more natural, he said, "We put your turds in our food."

She moaned, bending as if punched.

"You've got bugs in you," said the boy. "Bugs that keep you alive. If we eat them and if they take hold—"

Rarely, she guessed.

"—then we'll feel better. Right?"

On occasion, perhaps. But the bacteria were designed for her body, her chemistry. It would take mutations and enormous luck . . . then yes, some of those people might benefit in many ways. At least it wasn't impossible.

"But why keep this a secret?"

"People like you can be funny," the boy warned. "About all kinds of stuff. They thought you wouldn't like knowing."

Disgust fell away, leaving her oddly pleased.

"Why do you hide your shit?" he asked. "Is that what you do on the moon? Do you bury it under rocks?"

"No." Farside came to her mind's eye. "No, we pipe it into the Sea."

"Into your water?" His nose crinkled up. "That doesn't sound very smart, I think."

"Perhaps you're right," she agreed. Then she pointed at the bucket, saying, "Let me keep it. How about if I set it outside my door every morning?"

"It would save me a walk," the boy agreed. "It would help both of us." He nodded, smiling up at her. "My name is Thomas."

"Mine is Sitta."

A big, long laugh. "I know that."

For that instant, in the face and voice, Thomas seemed like a genuine nine-year-old boy, wise in the details, innocent in the heart.

9

Icenice's home and grounds were exactly as Sitta remembered them, and it was as if she had never been there, as if the scenery had been shown to her in holos while she was a young and impressionable girl. "Privilege," said the property. "Order." "Comfort." Sitta looked down a long green slope, eyes resting on the blue pond-sized face of the Sea, flocks of swift birds flying around it and drinking from it and lighting on its shore. After a minute, she turned and focused on the tall house, thinking of all the rooms and elegant balconies and baths and holoplazas. On the earth, two thousand people would reside inside it and feel blessed. And what would they do with this yard? With everyone staring, Sitta dropped to her knees, hands digging into the freshly watered sod, nails cutting through sweet grass and exuberant roots, reaching soil blacker than tar. The skins of old comets went into this marvel, brought in exchange for critical war goods. And for what good? Pulling up a great lump of the stuff, she placed it against her nose and sniffed once, then again.

Silence was broken by someone clearing his throat.

"Ah-hem!"

Icenice jumped half a meter into the air, turning in flight and blurting, "Honey? Hello."

The husband stood on the end of a stone porch, between stone lions. In no way, save for a general maleness, did he match Sitta's expectations. Plain and stocky, Bosson was twenty years older than the rest of them, and a little fat. Dressed like a low-grade functionary, there seemed to be nothing memorable about him.

"So does my dirt smell good?" he shouted.

Sitta emptied her hands and rose. "Lovely."

"Better than anything you've tasted for a while. Am I right?"

She knew him. The words; the voice. His general attitude. She had seen hundreds of men like him on earth, all members of the government, all middle-aged and embittered by whatever had placed them where they didn't want to be. Sitta offered a thin smile, telling Bosson, "I'm glad to meet you, finally."

The man grinned, turned. To his wife, he said, "Come here."

Icenice nearly ran to him, wrapping both arms around his chest and squealing, "We've had a gorgeous time, darling."

No one else in their group greeted him, even in passing.

Sitta climbed the long stairs two at a time, offering her hand and remarking, "I've heard a lot about you."

"Have you?" Bosson laughed, reaching past her hand and patting her swollen belly. "Is this why you quit playing the Good Samaritan?"

"Honey?" said Icenice, her voice cracking.

"Who's the father? Another Plow?"

Sitta waited for a long moment, trying to read the man's stony face. Then, with a quiet, stolid voice, she replied, "He was Terran."

"Was?" asked Icenice, fearfully.

"He's dead," Bosson answered. Unimpressed; unchastened. "Am I right, Miss Sitta?"

She didn't respond, maintaining her glacial calm.

"Darling, let me show you the room." Icenice physically moved between them, sharp features tightening and a sheen of perspiration on her face and breasts. "We thought we'd give you your old room. That is, I mean, if you want to stay . . . for a little while . . ."

"I hope you remember how to eat," Bosson called after them. "This house has been cooking all day, getting ready."

Sitta asked nothing. She didn't mention the husband or invite details about him. Yet Icenice felt compelled to explain, saying, "He's just in a bad mood. Work isn't going well."

"Making laser drills, right?"

The girl hesitated on the stairs, sunshine falling from a high skylight, the heat of it making her perfumes flood into the golden air. "He's a Mercurian, darling. You know how bleak they can be."

Were they?

"He'll be fine," Icenice promised, no hope in her voice, "A drink or two, and he'll be sugar."

Following the familiar route, she was taken to an enormous suite, its bed able to sleep twenty and the corner decorated with potted jungles. Bright gold and red monkeys came close, begging for any food that a human might be carrying. Sitta had nothing in her hands. A house robot had brought her bag, setting it on the bed and asking if she wished it unpacked. She didn't answer. Already sick of luxuries, she felt a revulsion building, her face hardening.

Misreading her expression, Icenice asked, "Are you disappointed with me?"

Sitta didn't care about the girl's life. But instead of honesty, she feigned interest. "Why did you marry him?"

Bleakness seemed to be a family trait. A shrug of the shoulders, and she said, "I had to."

"But why?"

"Because there was no choice." She said it as if nothing could be more obvious. Then, "Can we go? I don't want to leave them alone for too long."

The robot was left to decide whether or not to unpack. Sitta and Icenice went downstairs, discovering everyone in the long dining room, Bosson sitting in a huge feather chair at one end, watching his guests congregating in the distance. His expression was both alert and bored. Sitta was reminded of an adult watching children, always keeping count of the pretty baubles.

Sitta arrived, and whispers died.

It was Bosson who spoke to her, jumping up from his chair with a laugh. "So what was your job? What kind of good did you wage?"

Sitta offered a lean, unfriendly smile. "I ran a hospital."

Varner came closer. "What kind of hospital?"

"Prefabricated," she began.

Then Bosson added, "The Martians built them by the thousands, just in case we ever invaded the earth. Portable units. Automated. Never needed." He winked at Sitta, congratulating himself. "Am I right?"

She said nothing.

"Anyway, some Plow thought they could be used anyway." He shook his head, not quite laughing. "I'm not a fan of the Plows, in case you haven't noticed."

With a soft, plaintive voice, Icenice whispered, "Darling?"

To whom? Sitta looked at the man, finding no reason to be intimidated. "That's not exactly a unique opinion."

"I'm a harsh person," he said, in explanation. "I believe in a harsh, cold universe. Psychology isn't my field, but maybe it has to do with surviving one of the last big Terran attacks. Not that my parents did. Or my brothers." A complex, shifting smile appeared, vanished. "In fact, I watched most of them expire. The cumulative miseries of hard radiation . . ."

Using her most reasonable voice, Sitta remarked, "The people who killed them have also died. Years ago."

He said, "Good."

He grinned and said, "The real good of the Plows, I think, is that they help prolong the general misery. People like you give hope, and what good is hope?"

His opinions weren't new, but the others appeared horrified.

"Things are getting better!" Icenice argued. "I just heard . . . I don't remember where . . . that lifespans are almost twenty percent longer than a few years ago."

"The average earthly lifespan is eleven years," Sitta said.

The house itself seemed to hold its breath. Then Pony, of all people, said, "That's sad." She seemed to mean it, hugging herself and shaking her head, repeating the words. "That's sad. That's sad."

"But you got your hospital," Varner offered. "Didn't it help?"

"In some ways." Sitta explained, "It didn't weather its storage well. Some systems never worked. Autodocs failed without warning. Of course, all the biosynthesizing gear had been ripped out on Mars. And of course I had no real medical training, which meant I did a lot of guessing when there was no other choice . . . guessing wrong, more than not . . ."

Now she couldn't breathe, couldn't speak. Nobody liked the topic, save Bosson. Yet no one knew how to talk about anything else.

The Mercurian approached, hands reaching for her belly, then having the good sense to hesitate. "Why carry the baby yourself? Your hospital must have had wombs."

"They were stolen."

Which he must have realized for himself.

"Before the hospital arrived, they were removed," she said.

Icenice asked, "Why?"

"Terrans breed as they live," Bosson said. "Like rats."

Incandescent rage was building inside Sitta, and she enjoyed that emotion, relishing the clarity it afforded her. Almost smiling, she told them, "Biosynthetic machinery could do wonders for them. But of course we won't let them have anything sophisticated, since they might try to hurt us. And that means that if you want descendants, you've got to make as many babies as possible, as fast as possible, hoping some fraction will have the right combinations of genes for whatever happens in their unpredictable lives."

"Let them die," was Bosson's verdict.

Sitta didn't care about him. He was just another child of the war, unremarkable, virtually insignificant. What drew her rage were the innocent faces of the others. What made her want to explode was Varner's remote, schoolboy logic. With his most pragmatic voice, he said, "The provisional government is temporary. When it leaves, the earth can elect its own representatives, then make its own laws."

"Never," Bosson promised. "Not in ten thousand years."

Sitta took a breath, held it, then slowly exhaled.

"What else did you do?" asked Icenice, desperate for good news. "Did you travel? You must have seen famous places."

As if she'd been on vacation.

"Besides the hospital, what did you do?"

"I was picked as a jurist," Sitta offered. "Many times. And being a jurist is a considerable honor."

"For trials?" asked Pony.

"Of a kind."

People fidgeted, recalling Sitta's trial.

"Jurists are trusted people who watch friends giving birth." She waited a moment, then added, "That was my most important job before I had my hospital."

"But what does a jurist do?" asked one of the Twins.

They didn't know. A glance told her as much, and Sitta enjoyed the suspense, allowing herself a malicious smile before saying, "We used all kinds of parasites in the war. Tailored ones. Some burrowed into fetuses, using them as raw material for whatever purpose the allies could dream up."

No one blinked.

"The parasites are geniuses at hiding. Genetically camouflaged, but swift when the time comes. The jurist's job is to administer better tests after the birth, and if there's any problem, she has to kill the baby."

There was a soft, profound gasp.

"Jurists are armed," she continued, glancing at Bosson and realizing that even he was impressed. "Some parasites can remake the newborn, giving it claws and coordination."

The Mercurian showed serene pleasure. "Ever see such a monster?"

"Several times," said the retired Plowsharer. "But most of the babies, the infected ones, just sit up and cough, then look at you. The worms are inside their brains, manipulating their motor and speech centers. 'Give up,' they say, 'You can't win,' they say. 'You can't fight us. Surrender.'"

She waited for an instant.

Then it was important to add, "They usually can't say, 'Surrender.' It's too long, too complicated for their new mouths. And besides, by then they're being swung against a table or a wall. By the legs. Like this. If you do it right, they're dead with one good blow." And now she was weeping, telling Icenice, "Give me one of your old dolls. I'll show you just how I did it."

10

Sitta expected to leave after her mandatory three years of service. To that end, she fashioned a calendar and counted the sun-starved days, maintaining that ritual until early in her third year, not long after the long-promised hospital arrived. Expectations climbed with the new facility. At first, Sitta imagined that the city's expectations were what made her work endless hours, patching wounds when the autodocs couldn't keep up, curing nameless diseases with old, legal medicines, and tinkering with software never before field tested. Then there was a day—she was never certain which day—when she realized that the Terrans were happy for any help, even ineffectual help, and if all she did was sit in the hospital's cramped office, making shit and keeping the power on, nobody would have complained, and nobody would have thought any less of her.

She applied for a second term on the stipulation that she remained at her current post. This set off alarms in the provisional capital. Fearing insanity

or some involvement in illegal operations, the government sent a representative from Athens. The Martian, a tiny and exhausted woman, made no secret of her suspicions. She inspected the hospital several times, hunting for
biosynthetic equipment, for any medicines too new to be legal. Her hatred
for Farsiders was blatant. "When I was a girl, I heard about you people," she
reported. "I heard what you did to us, to all your 'allies' . . . and for nothing
but profit."

Sitta remained silent, passive. There was no victory in any argument.

"I don't know who I hate worse," said the woman. "Terran rats, or Farside
leeches."

In the calmest of voices, Sitta asked, "Will you let this leech stay with her
rats? Please?"

It was allowed, and the Plowsharers were so pleased that they sent promises of two more hospitals that never materialized. It was Sitta who purchased
and imported whatever new medical equipment she could find, most of it
legal. The next three years passed in a blink. She slept four hours on the good
night, and she managed to lift lifespans in the city to an average of thirteen
and half years. With her next reapplication, she asked Athens for permission to remain indefinitely. They sent a new Martian with the same reliable
hatreds, but he found reasons to enjoy her circumstances. "Isn't it ironic?" he
asked, laughing aloud. "Here you are, waging war against the monsters that
your own parents developed. The monsters that made you rich in the first
place. And according to import logs, you've been using that wealth to help the
victims. Ironies wrapped in ironies, aren't they?"

She agreed, pretending that she'd never noticed any of that before.

"Stay as long as you want," the government man told her. "This looks like
the perfect place for you."

Remaining on the earth, by her own choice, might be confused for forgiveness. Yet it wasn't. Indeed, the dimensions of her hatreds became larger,
more worldly. Instead of being betrayed by friends and wrongfully punished,
Sitta had begun to think of herself as supremely fortunate. She felt wise and
moral, at least in certain dangerous realms. Who else from Farside held pace
with her accomplishments? No one she could imagine, that unexpected pride
making her smile, in private.

Free of Farside, Sitta heard every awful story about her homeland Every
Martian and Mercurian relished telling about the bombardment of Nearside
during those first horrible days, and how convoys of refugees had reached
the border, only to be turned away. Farside began as a collection of mining
camps and telescopes, and there wasn't room for everyone. Only the wealthiest could immigrate. That was Sitta's family story. Every official she came

across seemed to have lost some part of his or her family. On Nearside. Mars. Ganymede. Even on Triton. And why? Because Sitta's repulsive ancestors needed to build mansions and jungles for themselves. "We don't have room," Farsiders would complain. And who dared argue the point? During the war, which world would risk offending Farside, losing its portion of the weapons and other essentials?

None took the chance; yet none would forget.

The naive, superficial girl who had murdered a helpless beetle was gone. The hardened woman in her stead felt outrage and a burning, potent taste for anything that smacked of justice. Yet never, even in passing, did she think of vengeance. It was impossible to believe that she would escape this battered plain. Some accident, some mutated bug, would destroy her, given time and the proper circumstances.

Then came an opportunity, a miraculous event in the form of a woman traveling alone. Eight months into a pregnancy that was too perfect, she was discovered by a local health office and brought to the hospital for a mandatory examination. Sitta had help from her own fancy equipment, plus the boy who had once happily collected her morning stool. He was her protégé. He happened to find the telltale cell inside the fetus. In a soft, astonished voice, he said, "God, we're lucky to have caught it. Picture this one getting free."

Sitta heard nothing else that he said, nor the long silence afterward. Then Thomas touched her arm—they were lovers by then—and in a voice that couldn't have been more calm, Sitta told him, "It's time, I think. I think I need to go home."

11

Dinner was meat wrapped in luxurious vegetables and meat meant to stand alone, proud and spicy, and there were wines and chilled water from the Central Sea and milk too sweet to be more than sipped, plus wide platters full of cakes and frosted biscuits and sour candies and crimson puddings. A hundred people could have eaten their fill at the long table, but as it turned out, no one except Bosson had an appetite. Partially dismantled carcasses were carried away by the kitchen's robots; goblets were drained just once in an hour's time. Perhaps it was related to the stories Sitta told at dinner. Perhaps her friends were a little perturbed by recipes involving rats and spiders and other treasured vermin. For dessert, she described the incident with Thomas and her bodily wastes, adding that they'd become lovers when he was a well worn fourteen. Only Bosson seemed to appreciate her tales, presumably for their portrait of misery; and Sitta discovered a grudging half-fondness for the man, both of them outsiders, both educated in certain hard and uncompromising matters. Looking only at Bosson, Sitta explained how Thomas carelessly inhaled a forty-year-old weapon, its robotic exterior cutting through an artery, allowing its explosive core to circumnavigate his body perhaps a hundred times before it detonated, liquifying his brain.

That story began with a flat, matter-of-fact voice. The voice cracked once when Thomas collapsed, then again when she described—in precise, professional detail—how she personally harvested the organs worth taking. The boy's skin was too old and weathered to make quality leather; it was left in place. Then the body was dropped into the day's grave, sixteen others beneath it, Sitta given the honor of the final words and the ceremonial first gout of splintered rock and sand.

She was weeping at the end of the story. She wasn't loud or undignified, and her grief had a manageable, endurable quality. Like any Terran, she knew that outliving your lover was the consequence of living too long. There was no reason for surprise, and there was no course forwards but to endure. Yet even as she dried her face, she noticed the devastation and anger on the other faces. Save Bosson's. She had ruined the last pretense of a good time for them, and with that she thought: Good. Perfect!

Yet her dear friends remained at the table. No one slunk away. Not even the strangers invented excuses or appointments, begging to escape. Instead, Varner decided to take control to the best of his ability, coughing into a trembling fist, then whispering, "So." Another cough felt essential. "So," he began, "now that you're back, and safe . . . any ideas . . . ?"

What could he possibly mean by that?

Reading Sitta's expression, he said, "What I was thinking. We all were, actually . . . thinking of asking if you'd like to come in with us . . . in making an investment, or two . . ."

Sitta sat back, hearing the delicious creak of old wood. With a careful, unmeasurable voice, she said, "What investment?"

Pony blurted, "There's fortunes to be made."

"If you have capital," said a stranger, shooing away a begging monkey.

Another stranger muttered something about courage, though the word he used was "balls."

Varner quieted them with a look, a gesture. Then staring at Sitta, he attempted charm that fell miserably short. "It's just . . . as it happens, just now . . . love, we have a possibility—"

"A dream opportunity," someone interrupted.

Sitta said, "It must be."

She fell silent, and nobody spoke.

Then she added, "Considering all the trouble that you've gone through, it must seem like a wondrous opportunity."

Blank, uncertain faces. Then Varner said, "I know this is fast. I know, and we aren't happy about that. We'd love to give you time to rest, to unwind . . . but it's such a tremendous undertaking—"

"Quick profits!" barked a Twin.

"—and you know, just now, listening to your stories . . . it occurred to me that you could put your future profits back into that city where you were living, or back into the Plowsharers in general—"

"Hey, that's a great idea!" said another stranger.

"A fucking waste," was Bosson's opinion.

"You could do all sorts of good," Varner promised, visibly pleased with his inspiration. "You could buy medicines. Machinery. You could drop a thousand robots down there."

"Robots are illegal," said Bosson. "Too easy to misuse."

"Then hire people. Workers. Anyone you need!" Varner rose to his feet, eyes pleading with her. "What do you think, Sitta? You're back, but that doesn't mean you can't keep helping your friends."

"Yeah," said Pony, "what do you think?"

Sitta waited for an age, or an instant. Then with a calm slow voice, she asked, "Exactly how much do you need?"

Varner held the number inside his mouth, which was kept shut.

One of the Twins blurted an amount, then added, "Per share. This new corporation is going to sell shares. In just a few weeks."

"You came at the perfect time," said his brother, fingers tapping on the tabletop.

A stranger called out, "And there's more!"

Varner nodded, then admitted, "The deal is still sweeter. Loan us enough to purchase some of our own shares, then we pay it back to you. How does twice the normal interest sound?"

Bosson whispered, "Desperate."

Icenice was bending at the waist, gasping for breath. "You can make enough to help millions."

Varner offered a watery smile. "And we'll make that possible."

Sitta crossed her legs, then asked, "What does a share buy?"

Silence.

"What does this corporation do?"

Pony said, "They've got a wonderful scheme."

"They want to build big new lasers," said a Twin. "Similar to the old weapons, only safe."

Safe? Safe how?

"We'll build them at the earth's Lagrange points," Varner explained. "Enormous solar arrays will feed the lasers, millions of square kilometers absorbing sunlight—"

"Artificial suns," someone blurted.

"And we'll be able to warm every cold world. For a substantial fee, of course." Varner grinned, his joy boyish. Fragile. "Those old war technologies and our factories can be put to perfect use."

"At last!" shouted the Twins, in one voice.

Bosson began to laugh, and Icenice, sitting opposite her husband, seemed to be willing herself to vanish.

"Whose scheme is this?" Sitta asked Varner. "Yours?"

"I wish it was," he responded.

"But Farsiders are in command," said Pony, fists lifted as if in victory. "All the big old families are pooling their resources, but since this project is so vast and complicated—"

"Too vast and too complicated," Bosson interrupted.

Sitta looked at Icenice. "How about you, darling? How many shares have you purchased?"

The pretty face dropped, eyes fixed on the table's edge.

"Let's just say," her husband replied, "that their most generous offer has been rejected by this household. Isn't that what happened, love?"

Icenice gave a tiny, almost invisible nod.

Pony glared at both of them, then asked Sitta, "Are you interested?"

"Give her time," Varner snapped. Then he turned to Sitta, making certain that she noticed his smile. "Think it through, darling. Please just do that much for us, will you?"

What sane world would allow another world to build it a sun? And after the long war, who could trust anyone with such enormous powers? Maybe there were safeguards and political guarantees, the full proposal rich with logic and vision. But those questions stood behind one great question. Clearing her throat, Sitta looked at the hopeful faces, then asked, "Just why do you need my money?"

No one spoke; the room was silent.

And everything was made transparent. Simple. They wanted her money because they had none, and they were desperate enough to risk whatever shred of pride they had kept from the old days. How had they become poor? What happened to the old estates and the bottomless bank accounts? Curious, Sitta saw how she could torture them with her questions; yet suddenly, without warning, she had no taste for that kind of vengeance. The joy was gone, lost before one weak excuse could be made, by Varner or anyone. So with a slow, almost gentle voice, Sitta said, "I can't. Because my money has been spent, you see."

A chill gripped her audience.

"I used everything to help my hospital. Some equipment was illegal, and that meant bribes to have it delivered and bribes to keep it secret." A pause. "I couldn't buy ten shares for just me, and I'm afraid that you've wasted your time, friends."

The faces were past misery. Every careful hope and earnest plan had evaporated, no salvation waiting, and the audience was too exhausted to move, too unsure of itself to speak or even look at one another.

Finally, with rage and agony, one of the strangers climbed to her feet, saying, "Thank you for the miserable dinner, Icenice."

She and the other strangers escaped from the room and house.

Then the Twins spun a lie about a party, leaving and taking Vechel with them. Had Vechel spoken a single word today? Sitta couldn't remember. She looked at Pony, and Pony asked, "Why did you come home?"

For an instant, Sitta forgot why.

"You hate us," the girl observed. "It's obvious how much you hate this place. Don't deny it!"

Why would she deny anything?

"Fucking bitch."

And Pony was gone. There was no other guest but Varner, and he sat with his eyes fixed on his unfinished meal, his face pale and indifferent. It was as if he still didn't understand what had happened. Finally, Icenice rose and went to Varner, taking him in her arms and whispering, the words or her touch giving him reason to stand. From where she sat, Sitta could watch the two of them walk out on the stone porch. She kept hugging him, always whispering, then she wished him good-bye, waiting for him to move out of her sight. Bosson watched his wife, his face remote. Unreadable. Then Icenice returned, sitting in that most distant chair, staring at some concoction of mints and cultured meat that had never been touched.

And Bosson, with the shrillest voice yet, said, "I warned you. I told you and your friends she'd never be interested." A pause, a grin. "What did I tell you? Repeat it for me."

Icenice stood and took the platter of meat in both hands, flinging it at her husband.

Bosson was nothing but calm, confidently measuring the arc and knowing it would fall short. But the sculpted meat shattered, a greasy white sauce in its center, still hot and splattering like shrapnel. It struck Bosson's clothes and arms and face. He gave a flinch. Nothing more. Then not bothering to wipe himself clean, he turned to Sitta, and with a voice that made robots sound emotional, said:

"Be the good guest. Run off to your room. Now. Please."

12

Thomas' death was tragic, yet perfect. No else knew what Sitta was carrying. The original mother thought her baby had come early and died. The hospital's AI functions had been taken off-line, leaving them innocent. No one but Thomas could have betrayed her, and it was his horrible luck to inhale a killing mote of dust. By accident? Sometimes Sitta asked herself if it was that simple. Toward the end of the process, the boy began to wonder aloud if this was what Sitta truly wanted, and if it was right. Maybe he became careless by distraction, or maybe carelessness was to ensure that he couldn't act on his doubts. Or maybe it was just what it had seemed to be at first glance. An accident. A brutal little residue of the endless war, and why couldn't she just accept it?

What was living inside Plowsharer was a particularly wicked ensemble. Designed to be invisible to Terran jurists and their instruments, it carried its true self within just one in a million cells. But in the time between her first labor pains and the delivery, each of those cells would explode, invading their neighbors, implanting genetics in a transformation that would leave no outward sign of change, much less danger. The monster would be born pale and irresistible. Perhaps the finest baby ever seen, people would think, wrapping it in a blanket and holding it close to their breasts.

That appearance was a fiction. Beneath the baby fat was a biosynthetic factory that would absorb and transmute every microbial strain. Mother and jurists would sicken in a few hours, their own native flora turned against them. No immune system could cope with such a thorough, coordinated assault. A village or city would be annihilated in a day, and with ample stocks of rotting, liquified meat, the monster would nurse, growing at an impossible pace, becoming for all intents and purposes a three year-old girl, mobile enough to wander, mute and big-eyed and lovely.

It was a weapon made inside many labs, including her parents'. That was no huge coincidence; Sitta had seen many examples of their work. But it helped her resolve. If justice was a simple matter of balance, then both were being achieved.

In a war full of famous weapons, this creation had never been discussed publicly. As far as Sitta could determine, the parasite was sent down for field tests and then lost. Probably waiting somewhere as a hibernating cyst, the cyst finally found the young woman, and that's what Sitta took for herself. No medical authority had seen it in action. What would Farside do with such a monster? Its people had little experience with real disease, and if anything, the moon was a richer target for this kind of horror. Where the earth had few species and tiny populations, Farside had diversity and multitudes. Each beetle and orchid and monkey had its own family of microbes. A thousand parallel plagues would cause an ecological collapse, the domed air left poisoned, the Central Sea struck dead. Here was an ultimate, apocalyptic revenge, and sometimes Sitta was astonished by her hatreds, by the depth of her feelings and the cold calculating passion she brought to this work.

Doubt found her. Doubts made her awaken in the middle of the night, drenched in sweat. Then her habit was to walk under the seamless black sky, taking the wide road to the cemetery, reading the simple tombstones with her lamp, noting the dates and trying to recall who was below her feet. The earth itself was entombed in a grave, alone, and the overheated air made Sitta think of the many billions of bodies rotting in the useless ground. How could she feel weakness? By what right?

Given such a mandate, she had no choice, and turning back with resolve, she felt her way down to the city and along its narrow streets. That's what she did on her last night in the city, the shuttle for Athens scheduled for the morning. Her leather bag was packed. She was wearing her travel clothes. Approaching her bunker home, full of distractions, Sitta didn't notice the children at work. She was almost past them when some sound, some little voice, caught her attention, making her turn and lift her lamp's beam, dozens of faces caught in mid-smile. What were these girls and boys doing? "You should be sleeping," she said. Then she hesitated, lifting the beam higher, every bunker festooned with long dirty ribbons and colored ropes and stiff old flags. "What is this?" she whispered, speaking to herself. "Why . . . ?"

And she knew. An instant before her audience broke into song and a ragged cheer, she realized this was for her, all of it, and they hadn't expected her so soon. These were people unaccustomed to celebrations, people who had few holidays, if any; and those long legs trembled, then gave way, knees into the foot-packed earth and Sitta's eyes blind with tears. Hundreds of children poured into the street, parents at their heels. Everyone was singing, no one competent and everyone loud, and what surprised Sitta more than anything was the final proof that these were genuinely happy people.

Inside the hospital, she saw them wounded or ill, or dead. Those were the people she understood best.

Yet here were souls more healthy than hurt, and more grateful than she could believe, everyone touching her, every hand on her swollen belly, every joyous shout giving her another dose of luck, the burden of all this luck and gratitude making it impossible for her to stand, much less turn and run for home.

13

Obeying Bosson, not caring what happened, Sitta climbed halfway up the staircase before she paused, standing beside sunlight, turning when she heard a whimper or moan. Was it Icenice? No, it was one of begging monkeys. She looked past the animal, waiting for a long moment, telling herself that regardless of what she heard, she would do nothing. This wasn't her home, nor her world—she was here to destroy all of this—and then she was walking, watching her shoes on the long lunar steps, aware in a distant, dreamy way that she was moving downhill, reentering the dining room just as Bosson finished binding his wife's hands to one of the table's legs.

The Mercurian didn't notice his audience. With smooth, practiced deliberation, he lifted Icenice's gown over her hips and head, the girl motionless as stone, her naked back and rump shining in the reflected light. Then Bosson stood over the table, selecting tools, deciding on a spoon and a blunt knife. Then he moved behind the thin rump, wiping his face clean with a sleeve, coughing once, and placing the blade against the pucker of her rectum.

The man was twenty years Sitta's senior and accustomed to the moon's gentle tug, and he was taken by surprise. She struck him on the side of the head, turning him, then struck his belly and kicked him twice, aiming for his testicles, earth-trained muscles making Bosson grunt, then collapse onto an elegant floor of colored tiles and pink mortar.

"Get up," she advised.

He tried to find his balance, halfway standing, and proving that he was still dangerous, Sitta drove her foot into his chin.

Again, she said, "Get up."

"Sitta?" whispered Icenice.

Bosson grunted, rose. She had drawn blood this time. Next a cheekbone shattered beneath her heel, and the man lay still, hands limp around his bloody head, and Sitta asked, "What's the matter with you? Can't you even stand up, you fuck?"

With the weakest of voices, Icenice asked, "What is happening?"

Sitta pulled the gown back where it belonged, then untied the napkins used to bind her hands. Her one-time friend looked at Bosson, and horrified, she said, "Oh this is so terrible."

Knotting the many napkins together, Sitta made crude ropes, then knelt and tied the groggy man's hands behind him and wrapped his ankles together and filled his mouth so that he couldn't shout orders to the robots. When she stood again, she felt weak. Almost faint. When Icenice tried to clean Bosson's wounds, Sitta grabbed her and pulled her toward the stairs, panting as she asked, "Why? Why did you marry it?"

"I was in such debt. You don't know." Icenice swallowed, moaned. "He promised to help me."

"How could you lose all that money? Where did it go?"

"Oh," she whimpered. "It seemed to go everywhere, really."

Reasons didn't matter. What mattered was bringing Icenice upstairs, the two of them moving through the shafts of sunlight.

"Everyone had debts," the girl was explaining. "I mean, we didn't know enough about modern business, and the Martians . . . they seemed very good at taking what we had . . ."

Sitta said, "Hurry up."

"Where are we going?"

"Hurry!"

Her bag was where the robot had set it, on the bed, still unopened, She unfastened the latches and threw its contents on the floor, then used a tiny cosmetic blade to cut into the thick bottom layers. What wouldn't appear in any scan were half a dozen lozenges of leather, their flesh filled with hormones and odd chemicals that nobody would consider illegal. Sitta had synthesized them in her hospital. Hesitating for an instant, she looked at Icenice and tried to decide the best way to do this thing.

"Varner wanted your money," said the girl.

"Come on. Into the bath."

"Why?"

"Now! Hurry!" Someone might be watching them. Sitta thought about the Belter with the dogs, wondering if she had shadowed them all this way. Stripping as she walked, she ended up naked, wading into the clear warm water, down to her chest before looking up at Icenice. "You have to climb in with me. Do it."

Again, the girl asked, "Why?"

The lozenges were made to answer a fear. What if she found herself giving birth in the wrong place? The possibility had awakened her with a shudder. What if she found herself trapped on the earth, and this monster of hers was threatening the people whom she loved most? How could she protect the innocent ones?

"I don't understand." The girl was weeping, quietly devastated by the day's events. "Why are you taking a bath now?"

One by one, Sitta swallowed those pieces of flesh, gulping bathwater to help get each of them down.

"Sitta?"

The process would take half an hour, maybe less. In minutes, the first of the drugs would cross into the fetus, crippling its genetic machinery—she hoped—giving her long enough to let the miscarriage run its course. The danger was that she would lose consciousness. The horror of horrors was that the monster would live long enough to outlast the anti-genetics, then somehow climb to the air and out of the bath, premature but coping, its transformation happening despite her desperate best wishes. That would be the ironic, horrible end.

"Sitta?"

And Sitta looked up at Icenice, then said, "In. Climb in."

The girl obeyed, still wearing her gown, the black fabrics blacker when soaked, billowing up around her waist, then covering her breasts,

"You're my jurist," said Sitta, looking straight into Icenice's eyes, "When it comes, drown it. Don't let it take a breath."

"What do you mean?"

"Promise me!"

"Oh, my." Icenice straightened, as if stabbed by a needle.

"Promise."

"I can try," she squeaked.

"You have to do it, darling. Or the world dies."

The words were believed. Sitta saw their impact and their slow digestion, the girl becoming thoughtful, alert. A minute passed. Several minutes passed. Then Icenice attempted a weak little smile, telling her friend, "I've never wanted your money."

A single red pain began in Sitta's pelvis, crawling up her spine.

"And I've always wanted to tell you," the girl went on. "When you were sentenced, and only you would be going to the earth, I knew that was best for everyone."

Wincing, Sitta asked, "Why?"

"None of us could have survived. Not for three years."

"And I was safe?"

"You did live," Icenice responded, then again tried her smile. "But you always had a toughness, a strength. That's the thing that I've always wanted to borrow from you. Even back when we were little girls."

Pain came twice, boom and boom.

"I'm not strong," Icenice said with conviction.

When was I strong? What did the girl see in me?

Then more pain. BOOM.

And when it passed, Sitta grabbed the ruined gown, pulling her friend in close to her, wrapping arms around her, and whispering with her most certain voice, "When the time comes, I'll kill it myself."

"Because I don't think I could," Icenice whimpered.

"But can you stay?"

"Here? With you?"

Sitta tried to breathe and the body froze with pain. Then a second time, she tried to inhale, which worked, and that's when she pleaded, "Don't leave me!"

"I won't. I promise."

Which was only the beginning. Because now the miseries began in earnest, and every pain before them, reaching back through Sitta's entire life, was just the careful preparation for the scorching white miseries inside her, trying to escape.

Paul McAuley is the author of more than twenty novels, several collections of short stories, a Doctor Who novella and a BFI Film Classic monograph on Terry Gilliam's film *Brazil*. His fiction has won the Philip K. Dick Memorial Award, the Arthur C. Clarke Award, the John W. Campbell Memorial Award, the Sidewise Award, the British Fantasy Award, and the Theodore Sturgeon Memorial Award. His latest novel, set in post-climate change Antarctica, is *Austral*.

HOW WE LOST THE MOON, A TRUE STORY BY FRANK W. ALLEN

Paul J. McAuley

You probably think that you know everything about it. After all, here we are, barely into the second quarter of the first century of the Third Millennium, and it's being touted as the biggest event in the history of humanity. Yeah, right. But tossing aside such impossibly grandiose claims, it was and still is a hell of a story. It's generated millions of bytes of Web journalism (two years after, there are still more than two hundred official Web sites, not to mention the tens of thousands of unofficial newsgroups devoted to proving that it was really caused by God, or aliens, or St. Elvis), tens of thousands of hours of TV and a hundred schlocky movies (and I do include James Cameron's seven-hour blockbuster), thousands of scientific papers and dozens of thick technical reports, including the ten-million-page congressional report, and the ghostwritten biographies of scientists Who Should Have Known Better.

Now you might think that I'm sending out my version because I was either misrepresented or completely ignored in all the above. Not at all. I'll be the first to admit that my part in the whole thing was pretty insignificant, but nevertheless I was there, right at the beginning. So consider this shareware text a footnote or even a tall tale, and if you like it, do feel free to pass it on, but don't change the text or drop the byline, if you please.

It began in the middle of a routine calibration run in the Exawatt Fusion facility. All the alarms went off and the AI in charge shut everything down, but there was no obvious problem. The robots could find no evidence of physical damage, yet the integrity and radiation alarms kept ringing, and analysis of experimental data showed that there had been a tremendous fluctuation in energy levels just after the fusion pulse. So the scientists sent the two of us, Mike Doherty and me, over the horizon to eyeball the place.

You've probably seen a zillion pictures. It was a low, square concrete block half-buried in the smooth floor of Mendeleev Crater on the Moon's far side, surrounded by bulldozed roadways and cable trenches, the two nuclear re-actors which powered it just at the level horizon to the south. At peak, the Exawatt used a thousand million times more power than the entire U.S. elec-trical grid to fire up, for less than a millisecond, six pulsed lasers focused on a target barely ten micrometers across, producing conditions which simulated those in the first picoseconds of the Big Bang, before symmetry was broken. Like the atom bomb a century before, it pushed the envelopes of engineering and physics. The scientists responsible for firing off that first thermonuclear device believed that there was a slight but definite chance that it would set fire to the Earth's atmosphere; the scientists running the Exawatt thought that there was a possibility that it might burst its containment and vaporize several hundred square kilometers around it. That was why they had built it on the Moon's far side, inside a deep crater. That's why it was run by robots, with the actual labs in a bunker buried over the horizon.

That's why, when it went wrong, they sent in a couple of GLPs to take a look.

We went in an open rover, straight down the service road. We were wear-ing bright orange radiation-proof shrouds over our Moon suits, and camera rigs on our shoulders so that the scientists could see what we saw. The plant looked intact, burning salt-white in the glare of a lunar afternoon, throwing a long black shadow toward us. The red-and-green perimeter lights were on; the cooling sink, a bore-hole three kilometers deep, wasn't venting. I drove the rover all the way around it, and then we went in.

The plant was essentially one big hall filled with the laser-pumping as-semblies, huge frames of parallel color-coded pipes each as big as one of those old Saturn rockets and threaded through with bundles of heavy cables and trackways for the robots which serviced them. We crept along the tiled floor in their shadows like a pair of orange mice, directing our camera rigs here and there at the request of the scientists. The emergency lights were still strobing, and I asked someone to switch them off, which they did after only five minutes' discussion about whether it was a good idea to disturb anything.

The six laser-focusing pipes, two meters in diameter, converged on the bus-sized experimental chamber. Containment was a big problem; that cham-ber was crammed with powerful magnetic tori which generated the fields in which the target, a pellet of ultra-compressed metallic hydrogen, was heat-ed by chirped pulse amplification to ten billion degrees Centigrade. It was surrounded by catwalks and hidden by the flared ends of the focusing pipes, the capillary grid of the liquid sodium cooling system, and a hundred different kinds of monitor. We checked the system diagnostics of the monitors, which told us only that several detectors on the underside had ceased to function, and then, harangued by scientists, crawled all around the chamber as best we could, sweating heavily in our suits and chafing our elbows and knees.

Mike found a clue to what had happened when he managed to wriggle into the crawl space beneath the chamber, quite a feat in a pressurized suit. He had taken off his camera rig to do it, and it took quite a bit of prompting before he started to describe what he saw.

"There's a severed cable here, and something has punched a hole in the box above it. Let me shift around . . . Okay, I can see a hole in the floor, too. About two centimeters across. I'm poking my screwdriver into it. Well, it must go all the way through the tiles, I can't see how deep. Hey, Frank, get me some of that wire, will you?"

There was a spool of copper cable nearby. I cut off a length and passed it in.

"You two get on out of there now," one of the scientists advised.

"This won't take but a minute," Mike said, and started humming tunelessly, which meant that he was thinking hard about something.

I asked, because I knew he wouldn't say anything otherwise, "What is it?"

"Looks like someone took a shot at this old thing," Mike said. "Shit. How deep does the foundation go?"

"The concrete was poured to three meters," someone said over the radio link, and the scientist who'd spoken before said, "It really isn't a good idea to mess around there, fellows."

"It goes all the way through," Mike said. "I wiggled the wire around and it came back up with dust on the end."

"This is Ridpath," someone else said. Ridpath, you may remember, was the chief of the science team. Although he wasn't exactly responsible for what happened, he made millions from selling the rights to his story, and then hanged himself six months after it was all over. He said, "You boys get on out of there. We'll take it from here."

Five rolligons passed us on our way back, big fat pressurized vehicles making speed. "You put a hair up someone's ass," I told Mike, who'd been real quiet after he crawled out from beneath the chamber.

"I think something escaped," he said.

"Maybe some of the laser energy was deflected."

"There weren't any traces of melting," Mike said, with a preoccupied air. "And just a bit of all that energy would make a hell of a mess, not leave a neat little hole. Hmm. Kind of an interesting problem."

But he didn't say any more about it until a week later, about an hour before the president went on the air to explain what had happened.

The Moon was a good place to be working then. It was more-or-less run by scientists, the way Antarctica had been before the drillers and miners got to it. There were about two thousand people living there at any one time, either working on projects like the Exawatt or the Big Array or the ongoing resource mapping surveys, or doing their own little thing. Mike and I were both part of the General Labor Pool, ready to help anyone. We'd earned our chops doing Ph.D.s, but we didn't have the drive or desire to work our way up the ladder of promotion. We didn't want responsibility, didn't want to be burdened with administration and hustling for funds, which was the lot of career researchers. We liked to get our hands dirty. Mike has a double Ph.D. in pure physics and cybernetics and is a whiz at electronics; I'm a run-of-the-mill geologist who is also a fair pilot. We made a pretty good team back then and generally worked together whenever we could, and we'd worked just about every place on the Moon.

When the president made the announcement, we'd moved on from the Exawatt and were taking a few days' R&R. I'd found out about a gig supervising the construction of a railway from the South Pole to the permanent base at Clavius, but Mike wouldn't sign up and wouldn't say why, except that it was to do with what had happened at the Exawatt.

We'd been exposed to a small amount of radiation when we'd gone into the plant—Mike a little more than me—and had spent a day being checked out before getting back on the job. The scientists were all over the plant by then. The reaction chamber had been dismantled by robots, and we brought in all kinds of monitoring equipment. Not only radiation counters, but a gravity measuring device and a neutrino detector. We helped bore a shaft five hundred meters deep parallel to the hole punched through the floor, and probes and motion sensors and cameras were lowered into it.

Mike claimed to have worked out what had happened as soon as he stuck the wire in the hole through the foundation, but he wouldn't tell me. "You should be able to guess from what they were trying to measure," he said, the one time I asked, and smiled when I called him a son of a bitch. He's very smart, but sort of fucked up in the head, antisocial, careless of his appearance and untidy as hell, and proud that he has four of the five symptoms of Asperger's Syndrome. But he was my partner, and I trusted him; when he said it wasn't a good idea to take up a new contract, I nagged him for a straight hour to explain why, and went along with him even though he wouldn't. He was spending all his spare time making calculations on his slate, and was still working on them at the South Pole facility.

I raised the subject again when news of the special presidential announcement broke. "You'd better tell me what you think happened," I told Mike, "because I'll hear the truth in less than an hour, and after that I won't believe you."

We were in an arbor in the dome of the South Pole facility. Real plants,
cycads and banana plants and ferns, growing in real dirt around us, sunlight
pouring in at a low angle through the diamond panes high above. The dome
capped a small crater some three hundred meters across, on a high ridge near
the edge of the South Pole-Aitken Basin and in permanent sunlight, the sun
circling around the horizon once every twenty-eight days. It was hot and humid, and the people splashing in the lake below our arbor were making a lot
of noise. The lake and its scattering of atolls took up most of the crater's floor,
with arbors and cafés and cabins on the bench terrace around it. The water
was billion-year-old comet water, mined from the regolith in permanently
shadowed craters. A rail gun used to lob shaped loads of ice to supply the
Clavius base in the early days, but Clavius had grown, and its administration was uncomfortable with the idea of being bombarded with ice meteors,
which was why they wanted to build a railway. In the low gravity, the waves
out on the lake were five or six meters high, and big droplets flew a long way,
changing shape like amoebas, before falling back. People were body surfing
the waves; a game of water polo had been going on for several days in one of
the bays.

I'd just been playing for a few hours, and I was in a good mood, which was
why I didn't strangle Mike when, after I asked him to tell me what he knew,
he flashed his goofy smile at me and went back to scratching figures on his
slate. Instead, I snatched the slate from his hands and held it over the edge of
the arbor and said, "You tell me right now, or the slate gets it."

Mike scratched the swirl of black hair on his bare chest and said, "You
know you won't do it."

I made to skim it through the air and said, "How many times do you think
it would bounce before it sank?"

"I thought I'd give you a chance to work it out. And it isn't as if there's
anything we can do. Didn't you enjoy the rest?"

"What's this got to do with not taking up that contract?"

"There's no point building anything anymore. You still haven't guessed,
have you?"

I tossed the slate to him. "Maybe I should pick you up and throw you in
the lake."

I meant it, and I'm a lot bigger than him.

"It's a black hole," he said.

"A black hole."

"Sure. My guess is that the experiment caused a runaway quantum fluctuation that created a black hole. It had to be bigger than the Planck size, and most probably was a bit bigger than a hydrogen atom, because it obviously has been taking up other atoms easily enough. Say around ten to the power twenty-three kilograms. The mass of a big mountain, like Everest. The magnetic containment fields couldn't hold it, of course, and it dropped straight out of the reaction chamber and went through the plant's floor."

I said, "The hole we saw was a lot bigger than the width of a hydrogen atom."

"Sure. The black hole disrupted stuff by tidal force over a far greater distance than its Swartzschild radius, and sucked some of it right in. That's why there was no trace of melting, even though it was pretty hot, and spitting out X-rays and probably accelerated protons, too—cosmic rays."

I didn't believe him, of course, but it was an interesting intellectual exercise. I said, "So where did the mass come from? Not from the combustion chamber fuel."

"Of course not. It was a quantum fluctuation, just like the Universe, which also came out of nothing. And the Universe weighs a lot more than ten to the power twenty-three kilograms. Something like, let's see—"

"Okay," I said quickly, before Mike lost himself in esoteric calculations. "But where is it now?"

"Well, it went all the way through," Mike said.

"Through the Moon? Then it came out, let's see"—I tried to visualize the Moon's globe—"somewhere in Mare Fecunditas."

"Not exactly. It accelerated in free fall toward the core, went past, and started to fall back again. It's sweeping back and forth, gaining mass and losing amplitude with each pass. That's what the president is going to tell everyone."

I thought about it. Something just bigger than an atom but massing as much as a mountain, plunging through the twenty-five-kilometer-thick outer layer of gardened regolith, smashing a centimeter-wide tunnel through the basalt crust and the mantle, passing through the tiny iron core, gathering mass and slowing, so that it did not quite emerge at the far side before falling back.

"You were lucky it didn't come right back at you," I said.

"The amplitude diminishes with each pass. Eventually it'll settle at the Moon's gravitational center. And that's why I didn't want to sign the contract. After the president tells everyone what I've just told you, all the construction contracts will be put on hold. What you should do is make sure we're first on the list for evacuation work."

"Evacuation?"

"There's no way to capture the black hole. The Moon, Frank, is fucked. But we'll get plenty of work before it's over."

He was half right, because the next day, after the president had admitted that an experiment had somehow dropped a black hole inside the Moon, a serious problem that would require an international team to monitor, we were both issued with summonses to appear at the hastily set up congressional inquiry.

It was a bunch of bullshit, of course. We went down to Washington, D.C., and spent a week locked up in the Watergate hotel watching bad cable movies and endless talk shows, with NASA lawyers showing up every now and then to rehearse our Q&As, and in the end we had no more than half an hour of easy questions before the committee let us go. Our lawyers shook our hands on the steps of the Congress building, in front of a bored video crew, and we went back to Canaveral and then to the Moon. Why not? By then Mike had convinced me about what was going to happen. There would be plenty of work for us.

We signed up as part of a roving seismology team, placing remote stations at various points around the Moon's equator. The Exawatt plant had been dismantled and a monitoring station built on its site to try and track the period of the black hole, which someone had labeled Mendeleev X-1. Mike was as happy as I had ever seen him; he was getting some of the raw data and doing his own calculations on the black hole's accretion rate and orbital path within the Moon. He stayed up long after our workday was over, hunched over his slate in the driving chair of our rolligon, with sunlight pouring in through the bubble canopy while I tried to sleep in the hammock stretched across the cabin, my skin itching with the Moon dust which got everywhere, and our Moon suits propped in back like two silent witnesses to our squabbling. His latest best estimate was that the Moon had between two hundred and five thousand days.

"But things will start to get exciting before then."

"Excitement is something I can do without. What do you mean?"

"Oh, it'll be a lot of fun."

"You're doing it again, you son of a bitch."

"You're the geologist, Frank," Mike said. "It's easy enough to work out. It's just—"

"Basic physics. Yeah. Well, you tell me if it's going to put us in danger. Okay?"

"Oh, it won't. Not yet, anyhow."

We were already picking up regular moonquakes on the seismometer network. With a big point mass swinging back and forth through it, the Moon's solid iron core was ringing like a bell. There were some odd subsidiary traces, too, smooshy echoes as if spaces were opening in the mantle—hard to believe, because pressure should have annealed any voids. I was pretty sure that Mike had a theory about these anomalies, too, but I kept quiet. After all, I was the geologist. I should have been able to work it out.

Meanwhile, we toured west across the Mare Insularium, with its lava floods overlaid by ejecta from Copernicus, and on across the Oceanus Procellarum, dropping seismometers every two hundred kilometers. We made good time, speeding across rolling, lightly cratered landscape, detouring only for the largest wrinkle ridges, driving through the long day and the Earth-lit night into brilliant dawn, the sun slowly moving across the sky toward noon once more. The Moon had its own harsh yet serene beauty, shaped mainly by vulcanism and impacts. Without weather, erosion took place on geological timescales, but because almost every feature was more than three billion years old, gravity and ceaseless micrometeorite bombardment had smoothed or leveled every hill or crater ridge. With the sun at the right angle, it was like riding across an infinite plain gentled by a deep blanket of snow. We rested up twice at unmanned shelters, and had a two-day layover at a roving Swedish selenology station which had squatted down on the mare like a collection of tin cans. A week later, just after we had picked up fresh supplies from a rocket lofted from Clavius, we felt our first moonquake.

It was as if the rolligon had dropped over a curb, but there was no curb. I was in the driving chair; Mike was asleep in the hammock. I told the AI to stop, and looked out through the canopy at the 180-degree panorama. The horizon was drawn closely all around. An ancient crater eroded by three billion years of micrometeorite bombardment dished it to the north and a few pockmarked boulders were sprinkled here and there, including a fractured block as big as a house. Something skittered in the corner of my eye—a little rock rolling down the gentle five degree slope we were climbing, plowing a meandering track in the dust. It ran out quite a way. The rolligon swayed gently, from side to side. I found I was gripping the padded arms of the chair so tightly my knuckles had turned white. Behind me, Mike stirred in the hammock and sleepily asked what was up; at the same moment, I saw the gas plume.

It was very faint, visible only because the dust it lofted caught the sunlight. Gas plumes were not uncommon on the Moon, caused by pockets of radon and other products of fission decay of unstable isotopes overpressuring the crevices where they collected. Earth-based astronomers sometimes glimpsed them when they temporarily obscured surface features while dissipating into vacuum. This, though, was different, more like a heat-driven geyser, venting steadily from a source below the horizon.

I told the AI to drive toward it. Mike leaned beside me, scratching himself through his suit of thermal underwear. He smelled strongly of old sweat;

we hadn't bathed properly since the interlude with the Swedes. I had a sudden insight and said, "How hot is the black hole?"

"Oh, the smaller the black hole, the more fiercely it radiates. It's a simple inverse relationship. It was pretty hot to begin with, but it's been getting cooler as it accretes mass. Hmm."

"Is it still hot enough to melt rock?"

Mike's eyes refocused. "You know, I think it must have been much bigger than I first thought. Anyway, anything that gets close enough to it to melt is already falling toward the event horizon. That's why there was no trace of melting or burning when it dropped out of the reaction chamber. But there's also the heat generated by friction as stuff pours toward its gravity well."

"Then it's remelting the interior. Those anomalies in the seismology signals are melt caverns full of lava."

Mike said thoughtfully, "I'm sure we'll start picking up a weak magnetic field soon, when the iron core liquifies and starts circulating. Of course, the end will be pretty close by then. Wow. That thing out there is really big."

The rolligon was climbing a long gentle slope toward the top of a curved ridge more than a kilometer high, the remnants of the rim of a crater which had been mostly buried by the fluid lava flow which had formed the Oceanus Procellarum. I told the AI to stop when I spotted the source of the plume. It was a huge fresh-looking crevice that ran out from a volcanic dome; gas was jetting out of the slumped side of the dome like steam from a boiling kettle. Dust fell straight down in sheets kilometers long. Already, an appreciable ray of brighter material was forming on the regolith beneath the plume.

"We should get closer," Mike said. He was rocking back and forth in his chair like a delighted child.

"I don't think so. There will be plenty of rocks lofted along with the gas and dust."

We transmitted some pictures, then suited up and went outside to set up a seismology package. The sun was in the east, painting long shadows on the ground, which shook, ever so gently, under my boots. With no atmosphere to scatter the light, shadows were razor sharp, and color changed as I moved about. The dusty regolith was deep brown in my shadow, but a bright blinding white when I looked toward the sun, turning ashy gray to either side. The gas plume glittered and flashed against the black sky. I told Mike that it was probably from a source deep in the megaregolith; pressure increased in gas pockets with depth. A quake, probably at the interface between the megaregolith and the rigid crust, must have opened a path to the surface.

"There'll be a lot more of these," Mike said.

"It'll blow itself out soon enough."

But it was still venting strongly when we had finished our work, and we drove a long way north to skirt around it, with Mike scratching away on his slate, factoring this new evidence into his calculations.

We were out for another two weeks, ending our run in lunar night at the Big Array Station at Korolev. It was one of the biggest craters on the far side, with slumped terraced walls and hummocky rim deposits like ranges of low hills. Its floor was spattered with newer craters, including a dark-floored lava-flooded crater on its southern edge which was now the focus of a series of quakes of steadily increasing amplitude. Korolev Station, up on the rim, was being evacuated; the radio telescopes of the Big Array, scattered across the far side in a regular pattern, were to be kept running by remote link. Most of the personnel had already departed by shuttle, and although there were still large amounts of equipment to be taken out, the railway which linked Korolev with Clavius had been cut by a rock slide. After a couple of spooky days' rest in the almost deserted yet fully functional station, Mike and I went out with a couple of other GLPs to supervise the robots which were clearing the slide and re-laying track.

It was a nice ride: the pressurized railcar had a big observational bubble, and I spent a lot of time up there, watching the heavily cratered highland plains flow past at two hundred kilometers an hour. The Orientale Basin dominated the west side of the Moon: a fissured basin of fractured blocks partly flooded with impact melt lava and ringed round with three immense scarps and an inner bench like ripples frozen in rock. The engineers had cut the railway through the rings of the Rook and Cordillera Mountains; the landslide had blocked the track where it passed close to one of the tall knobs of the Montes Rook Formation, a ten-kilometer-high piece of ejecta which had smashed down onto the surrounding plain—the impact really was very big.

A slide had run out from one of its steeply graded faces, covering more than a kilometer of track, and we were more than a week out there, helping the robots fix everything up. When we finally arrived at the station in Clavius, it was a day ahead of the Mendeleev eruption and the beginning of the evacuation of the Moon.

The whole floor of the Mendeleev Crater had fractured into blocks in the biggest quake ever recorded on the Moon, and lava had flooded up through dykes emplaced between the blocks. Lava vented from dykes beyond the crater rim, too, and flowed a long way, forming a new mare. Other vents appeared, setting off secondary quakes and long rock slides. The Moon shivered and shook uneasily, as if awakening from a long sleep.

Small teams were sent out to collect the old Rangers, Lunas, Surveyors, Lunokhods, and descent stages of Apollo LEMs from the first wave of Moon exploration. Mike and I went out for a last time, to Mare Tranquillitatis, to the site of the first manned lunar landing.

When a permanent scientific presence had first been established on the Moon, there was considerable debate about what to do with the sites of the Apollo landings and the various old robot probes and other debris scattered across the surface. There had been a serious proposal to dome the Apollo 11 site to protect it from damage by micrometeorites and to stop people from swiping souvenirs, but even without protection it would last for millions of years, and everyone on the Moon was tagged with a continuously monitored global positioning sensor so no one could go anywhere without it being logged, and in the end the site had been left open.

We arrived a few hours after dawn. It was a lonely place, not much visited despite its historic importance. A big squat carrier rocket had gone ahead, landing two kilometers to the north, and the robots were already waiting. There were four of us: a historian from the Museum of Air and Space in Washington, a photographer, and Mike and me. The site was ringed around with laser sensors. As we loped through the perimeter, an automatic beacon on the common band warned us that we were trespassing on a U.N. heritage site and started to recite the relevant penalties until the historian found it and turned it off. The angular platform of the lunar module's descent stage had been scorched by the rocket of the ascent stage; the gold foil which had wrapped it was torn and tattered, white paint beneath turned tan by exposure to the sun's raw ultraviolet. One of its spidery legs had collapsed after a recent quake focused near new volcanic cones to the southeast. We lifted everything, working inward toward the ascent stage: the Passive Seismometer and the Laser Ranging Retroreflector; the flag, its ordinary fabric, stiffened by wires, faded and fragile; an assortment of discarded geology tools; human waste and food containers and wipes and other litter in crumbling jettison bags; the plaque with a message from a long-dead president. Before the descent stage was lifted away, a robot sawed away a chunk of dirt beside its ladder, the spot where the first human footprint had been made on the Moon. There was some dispute about which print was actually the first, so two square meters were carefully lifted. And at last the descent stage was carried off to the cargo rocket, and there was only a litter of cleated footprints left, our own overlaying Armstrong's and Aldrin's.

It was time to go.

As the eruptions grew more frequent, even the skeleton crews of the various stations were evacuated, leaving a host of robot surveyors in close orbit or crawling about the troubled surface to monitor the unfolding disaster. Mike and I went on one of the last shuttles, everyone crowding to the ports as it made a single low orbital pass before lighting out for Earth.

It was six months after the Mendeleev X-1 incident. The heat generated by the black hole's accretion process and tidal forces had remelted the iron core; pockets of molten basalt in the mantle had swollen and conjoined. A vast rift opened in the Oceanus Procellarum, splitting the nearside down its northwestern quadrant and raising new scarps as high and jagged as those in an old Chesley Bonestell painting. The Orientale Basin flooded with lava and the fractured blocks of the Maunder formation sank like foundering ships as new lava flows began to well up. Volcanic activity was less on the far side, where the crust was thicker, but the Mare Ingenii collapsed and reflooded, forming a vast new basin which swallowed the Jules Verne and Gagarin Craters.

It took two more months.

As the end neared, the Moon's surface split into short-lived plates afloat on a wholly molten mantle, with lava-filled rifts opening and scabbing over and reopening along their edges. There were frantic attempts to insure that the population of the Earth's southern hemisphere would all have some kind of shelter, for the Moon would be in the sky above the Pacific in its final hour. Those unlucky or stubborn enough to remain outside saw the Moon rise for the last time, half-full, the dark part of her disk riven with glowing cracks which spread as the black hole sucked in exponentially increasing amounts of matter. And then there was a terrific flare of light, brighter than a thousand suns. Those witnesses who had not been blinded saw that the Moon was gone, leaving expanding shells of luminous gas around a fading image trapped at the edge of the black hole's event horizon, and a short-lived accretion disk as ejected material spiraled back into the black hole, which, although it massed the same as the Moon it had devoured, had an event horizon circumference of less than a millimeter.

The radiation pulse was mostly absorbed by the Earth's atmosphere; the orbit of the space station had been altered so that it was in opposition when the Moon vanished. I was aboard it at the time, and spent the next six months helping repair satellites whose circuits had been fried.

There are still tides, of course, for the same amount of mass still orbits the Earth. Marine organisms which synchronized their reproduction by the Moon's phases, such as horseshoe crabs, corals, and palolo worms, were in danger of extinction, but a cooperative mission by NASA and the Russian and European space agencies lofted a space mirror which reflects the same amount of light as the Moon, and even goes through the same phases. There'll be a big problem in 5×10^{43} years, when by loss of mass through

Hawking radiation the black hole finally becomes small enough to begin its runaway evaporation. But long before then the sun will have evolved into a white dwarf and guttered out; even its very protons will have decayed. The black hole will be the last remnant of the solar system in a cooling and vastly expanded universe.

There are various proposals to make use of the black hole—as the ultimate garbage disposal device (I want to be well away from the solar system when they try that), or as an interstellar signaling device, for if it can be made to bob in its orbit (perhaps by putting another black hole in orbit around it), it will produce sharply focused gravity waves of tremendous amplitude. Meanwhile, it will keep the physicists busy for a thousand years. Mike is working at one of the stations which orbit beyond its event horizon. I keep in touch with him by E-mail, but the correspondence is becoming more and more infrequent as he vanishes into his own personal event horizon.

As for me, I'm heading out. The space program has realigned its goals, and it turns out that the black hole retained the Moon's rotational energy, so it provides a useful slingshot for free acceleration. After all, there are plenty of other moons in the solar system, and most are far more interesting than the one we lost.

For Stephen Baxter

Stephen Baxter (www.stephen-baxter.com) is one of the most important science fiction writers to emerge from Britain in the past thirty years. He's the author of more than fifty books and over a hundred short stories. His most recent novels are *Xeelee: Vengeance* and *Xeelee: Redemption*. "People Came from Earth" is part of his Manifold sequence and Stephen will be returning to that multiverse with his in-progress series, World Engines.

PEOPLE CAME FROM EARTH

Stephen Baxter

At Dawn I stepped out of my house. The air frosted white from my nose, and the deep Moon chill cut through papery flesh to my spindly bones. The silvergray light came from Earth and Mirror in the sky: twin spheres, the one milky cloud, the other a hard image of the sun. But the sun itself was already shouldering above the horizon. Beads of light like trapped stars marked rim mountain summits, and a deep bloody crimson was working its way high into our tall sky. I imagined I could see the lid of that sky, the millennial leaking of our air into space.

I walked down the path that leads to the circular sea. There was frost everywhere, of course, but the path's lunar dirt, patiently raked in my youth, is friendly and gripped my sandals. The water at the sea's rim was black and oily, lapping softly. I could see the gray sheen of ice farther out, and the hard glint of pack ice beyond that, though the close horizon hid the bulk of the sea from me. Fingers of sunlight stretched across the ice, and gray-gold smoke shimmered above open water.

I listened to the ice for a while. There is a constant tumult of groans and cracks as the ice rises and falls on the sea's mighty shoulders. The water never freezes at Tycho's rim; conversely, it never thaws at the center, so that there is a fat torus of ice floating out there around the central mountains. It is as if the rim of this artificial ocean is striving to emulate the unfrozen seas of Earth which bore its makers, while its remote heart is straining to grow back the cold carapace it enjoyed when our water—and air—still orbited remote Jupiter.

I thought I heard a barking out on the pack ice. Perhaps it was a seal. A bell clanked: an early fishing boat leaving port, a fat, comforting sound that carried through the still dense air. I sought the boat's lights, but my eyes, rheumy, stinging with cold, failed me.

I paid attention to my creaking body: the aches in my too-thin, too-long, calcium-starved bones, the obscure spurts of pain in my urethral system, the strange itches that afflict my liver-spotted flesh. I was already growing too cold. Mirror returns enough heat to the Moon's long Night to keep our seas and air from snowing out around us, but I would welcome a little more comfort.

I turned and began to labor back up my regolith path to my house.

And when I got there, Berge, my nephew, was waiting for me. I did not know then, of course, that he would not survive the new Day.

He was eager to talk about Leonardo da Vinci.

He had taken off his wings and stacked them up against the concrete wall of my house. I could see how the wings were thick with frost, so dense the paper feathers could surely have had little play.

I scolded him even as I brought him into the warmth, and prepared hot soup and tea for him in my pressure kettles. "You're a fool as your father was," I said. "I was with him when he fell from the sky, leaving you orphaned. You know how dangerous it is in the pre-Dawn turbulence."

"Ah, but the power of those great thermals, Uncle," he said, as he accepted the soup. "I can fly miles high without the slightest effort."

I would have berated him further, which is the prerogative of old age. But I didn't have the heart. He stood before me, eager, heartbreakingly thin. Berge always was slender, even compared to the rest of us skinny lunar folk; but now he was clearly frail. Even these long minutes after landing, he was still panting, and his smooth fashionably-shaven scalp (so bare it showed the great bubble profile of his lunar-born skull) was dotted with beads of grimy sweat.

And, most ominous of all, a waxy, golden sheen seemed to linger about his skin. I had no desire to raise that—not here, not now, not until I was sure what it meant, that it wasn't some trickery of my own age-yellowed eyes.

So I kept my counsel. We made our ritual obeisance—murmurs about dedicating our bones and flesh to the salvation of the world—and finished up our soup.

And then, with his youthful eagerness, Berge launched into the seminar he was evidently itching to deliver on Leonardo da Vinci, long-dead citizen of a long-dead planet. Brusquely displacing the empty soup bowls to the floor, he produced papers from his jacket and spread them out before me. The sheets, yellowed and stained with age, were covered in a crabby, indecipherable handwriting, broken with sketches of gadgets or flowing water or geometric figures. I picked out a luminously beautiful sketch of the crescent Earth—

"No," said Berge patiently. "Think about it. It must have been the crescent *Moon*." Of course he was right. "You see, Leonardo understood the phenomenon he called the ashen Moon—like our ashen Earth, the old Earth visible in the arms of the new. He was a hundred years ahead of his time with *that* one . . ."

This document had been called many things in its long history, but most familiarly the Codex Leicester. Berge's copy had been printed off in haste during The Failing, those frantic hours when our dying libraries had disgorged their great snowfalls of paper. It was a treatise centering on what Leonardo called the "body of the Earth," but with diversions to consider such matters as water engineering, the geometry of Earth and Moon, and the origins of fossils.

The issue of the fossils particularly excited Berge. Leonardo had been much agitated by the presence of the fossils of marine animals, fishes and oysters and corals, high in the mountains of Italy. Lacking any knowledge of tectonic processes, he had struggled to explain how the fossils might have been deposited by a series of great global floods.

It made me remember how, when he was a boy, I once had to explain to Berge what a "fossil" was. There are no fossils on the Moon: no bones in the ground, of course, save those we put there. Now he was much more interested in the words of long-dead Leonardo than his uncle's.

"You have to think about the world Leonardo inhabited," he said. "The ancient paradigms still persisted: the stationary Earth, a sky laden with spheres, crude Aristotelian proto-physics. But Leonardo's instinct was to proceed from observation to theory—and he observed many things in the world which didn't fit with the prevailing world view—"

"Like mountaintop fossils."

"Yes. Working alone, he struggled to come up with explanations. And some of his reasoning was, well, eerie."

"Eerie?"

"Prescient." Gold-flecked eyes gleamed. "Leonardo talks about the Moon in several places." The boy flicked back and forth through the Codex, pointing out spidery pictures of Earth and Moon and sun, neat circles connected by spidery light ray traces. "Remember, the Moon was thought to be a transparent crystal sphere. What intrigued Leonardo was why the Moon wasn't much brighter in Earth's sky, as bright as the sun, in fact. It should have been brighter if it was perfectly reflective—"

"Like Mirror."

"Yes. So Leonardo argued the Moon must be covered in oceans." He found a diagram showing a Moon, bathed in spidery sunlight rays, coated with great out-of-scale choppy waves. "Leonardo said waves on the Moon's oceans must deflect much of the reflected sunlight away from Earth. He thought the darker patches visible on the Moon's surface must mark great standing waves, or even storms, on the Moon."

"He was wrong," I said. "In Leonardo's time, the Moon was a ball of rock. The dark areas were just lava sheets."

"But now," Berge said eagerly, "the Moon is mostly covered by water. You see? And there *are* great storms, wave crests hundreds of kilometers long, which are visible from Earth—or would be, if anybody was left to see."

"What exactly are you suggesting?"

"Ah," he said, and he smiled and tapped his thin nose. "I'm like Leonardo. I observe, *then* deduce. And I don't have my conclusions just yet. Patience, Uncle . . ."

We talked for hours.

When he left, the Day was little advanced, the rake of sunlight still sparse on the ice. And Mirror still rode bright in the sky. Here was another strange forward echo of Leonardo's, it struck me, though I preferred not to mention it to my already overexcited nephew: in my time, there *are* crystal spheres in orbit around the Earth. The difference is, we put them there.

Such musing failed to distract me from thoughts of Berge's frailness, and his disturbing golden pallor. I bade him farewell, hiding my concern.

As I closed the door, I heard the honking of geese, a great flock of them fleeing the excessive brightness of full Day.

Each Morning, as the sun labors into the sky, there are storms. Thick fat clouds race across the sky, and water gushes down, carving new rivulets and craters in the ancient soil, and turning the ice at the rim of the Tycho pack into a thin, fragile layer of gray slush.

Most people choose to shelter from the rain, but to me it is a pleasure. I like to think of myself standing in the band of storms that circles the whole of the slow-turning Moon. Raindrops are fat glimmering spheres the size of my thumb. They float from the sky, gently flattened by the resistance of our thick air, and they fall on my head and back with soft, almost caressing impacts. So long and slow has been their fall from the high clouds, the drops are often warm, and the air thick and humid and muggy, and the water clings to my flesh in great sheets and globes I must scrape off with my fingers.

It was in such a storm that, as Noon approached on that last Day, I traveled with Berge to the phytomine celebration to be held on the lower slopes of Maginus.

We made our way past sprawling fields tilled by human and animal muscle, thin crops straining toward the sky, frost shelters laid open to the muggy heat. And as we traveled, we joined streams of more traffic, all heading for Maginus: battered carts, spindly adults, and their skinny, hollow-eyed children; the Moon soil is thin and cannot nourish us well, and we are all, of course, slowly poisoned besides, even the cattle and horses and mules.

Maginus is an old, eroded crater complex some kilometers southeast of Tycho. Its ancient walls glimmer with crescent lakes and glaciers. Sheltered from the winds of Morning and Evening, Maginus is a center of life, and as the rain cleared I saw the tops of the giant trees looming over the horizon long before we reached the foothills. I thought I saw creatures leaping between the tree branches. They may have been lemurs, or even bats; or perhaps they were kites wielded by ambitious children.

Berge took delight as we crossed the many water courses, pointing out engineering features which had been anticipated by Leonardo, dams and bridges and canal diversions and so forth, some of them even constructed since the Failing.

But I took little comfort, oppressed as I was by the evidence of our fall. For example, we journeyed along a road made of lunar glass, flat as ice and utterly impervious to erosion, carved long ago into the regolith. But our cart was wooden, and drawn by a spavined, thin-legged mule. Such contrasts are unendingly startling. All our technology would have been more than familiar to Leonardo. We make gadgets of levers and pulleys and gears, their wooden teeth constantly stripped; we have turnbuckles, devices to help us erect our cathedrals of Moon concrete; we even fight our pathetic wars with catapults and crossbows, throwing lumps of rock a few kilometers.

But once we hurled ice moons across the solar system. We know this is so, else we could not exist here.

As we neared the phytomine, the streams of traffic converged to a great confluence of people and animals. There was a swarm of reunions of friends and family, and a rich human noise carried on the thick air.

When the crowds grew too dense, we abandoned our wagon and walked. Berge, with unconscious generosity, supported me with a hand clasped about my arm, guiding me through this human maelstrom. All Berge wanted to talk about was Leonardo da Vinci. "Leonardo was trying to figure out the cycles of the Earth. For instance, how water could be restored to the mountaintops. Listen to this." He fumbled, one-handed, with his dog-eared manuscript. *"We may say that the Earth has a spirit of growth, and that its flesh is the soil; its bones are the successive strata of the rocks which form the mountains, its cartilage is the tufa stone; its blood the veins of its waters . . . And the vital heat of the world is fire which is spread throughout the Earth; and the dwelling place of the spirit of growth is in the fires, which in diverse parts of the Earth are breathed out in baths and sulfur mines . . .* You understand what he's saying? He was trying to explain the Earth's cycles by analogy with the systems of the human body."

"He was wrong."

"But he was more right than wrong, Uncle! Don't you see? This was centuries before geology was formalized, even longer before matter and energy cycles would be understood. Leonardo had gotten the right idea, from somewhere. He just didn't have the intellectual infrastructure to express it . . ."

And so on. None of it was of much interest to me. As we walked, it seemed to me that *his* weight was the heavier, as if I, the old fool, was constrained to support him, the young buck. It was evident his sickliness was advancing fast—and it seemed that others around us noticed it, too, and separated around us, a sea of unwilling sympathy.

Children darted around my feet, so fast I found it impossible to believe I could ever have been so young, so rapid, so compact, and I felt a mask of old-man irritability settle on me. But many of the children were, at age seven or eight or nine, already taller than me, girls with languid eyes and the delicate posture of giraffes. The one constant of human evolution on the Moon is how our children stretch out, ever more languorous, in the gentle Moon gravity. But they pay a heavy price in later life in brittle, calcium-depleted bones.

At last we reached the plantation itself. We had to join queues, more or less orderly. There was noise, chatter, a sense of excitement. For many people, such visits are the peak of each slow lunar Day.

Separated from us by a row of wooden stakes and a few meters of bare soil was a sea of green, predominantly mustard plants. Chosen for their bulk and fast growth, all of these plants had grown from seed or shoots since the last lunar Dawn. The plants themselves grew thick, their feathery leaves bright. But many of the leaves were sickly, already yellowing. The fence was supervised by an unsmiling attendant, who wore—to show the people their sacrifice had a genuine goal—artifacts of unimaginable value, earrings and brooches and bracelets of pure copper and nickel and bronze.

The Maginus mine is the most famous and exotic of all the phytomines: for here gold is mined, still the most compelling of all metals. Sullenly, the attendant told us that the mustard plants grow in soil in which gold, dissolved out of the base rock by ammonium thiocyanate, can be found at a concentration of four parts per million. But when the plants are harvested and burned, their ash contains four *hundred* parts per million of gold, drawn out of the soil by the plants during their brief lives.

The phytomines are perhaps our planet's most important industry.

It took just a handful of dust, a nanoweapon from the last war that ravaged Earth, to remove every scrap of worked metal from the surface of the Moon. It was the Failing. The cities crumbled. Aircraft fell from the sky. Ships on the great circular seas disintegrated, tipping their hapless passengers into freezing waters. Striving for independence from Earth, caught in this crosscurrent of war, our Moon nation was soon reduced to a rabble, scraping for survival.

But our lunar soil is sparse and ungenerous. If Leonardo was right—that Earth with its great cycles of rock and water is like a living thing—then the poor Moon, its reluctant daughter, is surely dead. The Moon, ripped from the outer layers of parent Earth by a massive primordial impact, lacks the rich iron which populates much of Earth's bulk. It is much too small to have retained the inner heat which fuels Earth's great tectonic cycles, and so died rapidly; and without the water baked out by the violence of its formation, the Moon is deprived of the great ore lodes peppered through Earth's interior.

Moon rock is mostly olivine, pyroxene, and plagioclase feldspar. These are silicates of iron, magnesium, and aluminum. There is a trace of native iron, and thinner scrapings of metals like copper, tin, and gold, much of it implanted by meteorite impacts. An Earth miner would have cast aside the richest rocks of our poor Moon as worthless slag.

And yet the Moon is all we have.

We have neither the means nor the will to rip up the top hundred meters of our world to find the precious metals we need. Drained of strength and tools, we must be more subtle.

Hence the phytomines. The technology is old—older than the human Moon, older than spaceflight itself. The Vikings, marauders of Earth's darkest age (before this, the darkest of all) would mine their iron from "bog ore," iron-rich stony nodules deposited near the surface of bogs by bacteria which had flourished there: miniature miners, not even visible to the Vikings who burned their little corpses to make their nails and swords and pans and cauldrons.

And so it goes, across our battered, parched little planet, a hierarchy of bacteria and plants and insects and animals and birds, collecting gold and silver and nickel and copper and bronze, their evanescent bodies comprising a slow merging trickle of scattered molecules, stored in leaves and flesh and bones, all for the benefit of that future generation who must save the Moon.

Berge and I, solemnly, took ritual scraps of mustard-plant leaf on our tongues, swallowed ceremonially. With my age-furred tongue I could barely taste the mustard's sharpness. There were no drawn-back frost covers here because these poor mustard plants would not survive to the Sunset: they die within a lunar Day, from poisoning by the cyanide.

Berge met friends and melted into the crowds.

I returned home alone, brooding.

I found my family of seals had lumbered out of the ocean and onto the shore. These are constant visitors. During the warmth of Noon they will bask for hours, males and females and children draped over each other in casual, sexless abandon, so long that the patch of regolith they inhabit becomes sodden and stinking with their droppings. The seals, uniquely among the creatures from Earth, have not adapted in any apparent way to the lunar conditions. In the flimsy gravity they could surely perform somersaults with those flippers of theirs. But they choose not to; instead they bask, as their ancestors did on remote Arctic beaches. I don't know why this is so. Perhaps they are, simply, wiser than we struggling, dreaming humans.

The long Afternoon sank into its mellow warmth. The low sunlight diffused, yellow-red, to the very top of our tall sky, and I would sit on my stoop imagining I could see our precious oxygen evaporating away from the top of that sky, molecule by molecule, escaping back to the space from which we had dragged it, as if hoping in some mute chemical way to reform the ice moon we had destroyed.

Berge's illness advanced without pity. I was touched when he chose to come stay with me, to "see it out," as he put it.

My fondness for Berge is not hard to understand. My wife died in her only attempt at childbirth. This is not uncommon, as pelvises evolved in heavy Earth gravity struggle to release the great fragile skulls of Moon-born children. So I had rejoiced when Berge was born; at least some of my genes, I consoled myself, which had emanated from primeval oceans now lost in the sky, would travel on to the farthest future. But now, it seemed, I would lose even that.

Berge spent his dwindling energies in feverish activities. Still his obsession with Leonardo clung about him. He showed me pictures of impossible machines, far beyond the technology of Leonardo's time (and, incidentally, of ours); shafts and cogwheels for generating enormous heat, a diving apparatus, an "easy-moving wagon" capable of independent locomotion. The famous helicopter intrigued Berge particularly. He built many spiral-shaped models of bamboo and paper; they soared into the thick air, easily defying the Moon's gravity, catching the reddening light.

I have never been sure if he knew he was dying. If he knew, he did not mention it, nor did I press him.

In my gloomier hours—when I sat with my nephew as he struggled to sleep, or as I lay listening to the ominous, mysterious rumbles of my own failing body, cumulatively poisoned, wracked by the strange distortions of lunar gravity—I wondered how much farther we must descend.

The heavy molecules of our thick atmosphere are too fast-moving to be contained by the Moon's gravity. The air will be thinned in a few thousand years: a long time, but not beyond comprehension. Long before then we must have reconquered this world we built, or we will die.

So we gather metals. And, besides that, we will need knowledge.

We have become a world of patient monks, endlessly transcribing the great texts of the past, pounding into the brains of our wretched young the wisdom of the millennia. It seems essential we do not lose our concentration as a people, our memory. But I fear it is impossible. We are Stone Age farmers, the young broken by toil even as they learn. I have lived long enough to realize that we are, fragment by fragment, losing what we once knew.

If I had one simple message to transmit to the future generations, one thing they should remember lest they descend into savagery, it would be this: *People came from Earth.* There: cosmology and the history of the species and the promise of the future, wrapped up in one baffling, enigmatic, heroic sentence. I repeat it to everyone I meet. Perhaps those future thinkers will decode its meaning, and will understand what they must do.

Berge's decline quickened, even as the sun slid down the sky, the clockwork of our little universe mirroring his condition with a clumsy, if mindless, irony. In the last hours I sat with him, quietly reading and talking, responding to his near-adolescent philosophizing with my customary brusqueness, which I was careful not to modify in this last hour.

"... But have you ever wondered why we are *here* and *now?*" He was whispering, the sickly gold of his face picked out by the dwindling sun. "What are we, a few million, scattered in our towns and farms around the Moon? What do we compare to the *billions* who swarmed over Earth in the final years? Why do I find myself *here* and *now* rather than *then?* It is so unlikely . . ." He turned his great lunar head to me. "Do you ever feel you have been born out of your time, as if you are stranded in the wrong era, an *unconscious* time traveler?"

I had to confess I never did, but he whispered on.

"Suppose a modern human—or someone of the great ages of Earth—was stranded in the sixteenth century, Leonardo's time. Suppose he forgot everything of his culture, all its science and learning—"

"Why? How?"

"I don't know . . . But if it were true—and if his unconscious mind retained the slightest trace of the learning he had discarded—wouldn't he do exactly what Leonardo did? Study obsessively, try to fit awkward facts into the prevailing, unsatisfactory paradigms, grope for the deeper truths he had lost?"

"Like Earth's systems being analogous to the human body."

"Exactly." A wisp of excitement stirred him. "Don't you see? Leonardo behaved *exactly* as a stranded time traveler would."

"Ah." I thought I understood; of course, I didn't. "You think *you're* out of time. And your Leonardo, too!" I laughed, but he didn't rise to my gentle mockery. And in my unthinking way I launched into a long and pompous discourse on feelings of dislocation: on how every adolescent felt stranded in a body, an adult culture, unprepared . . .

But Berge wasn't listening. He turned away, to look again at the bloated sun. "All this will pass," he said. "The sun will die. The universe may collapse on itself, or spread to a cold infinity. In either case it may be possible to build a giant machine that will recreate this universe—everything, every detail of this moment—so that we all live again. But how can we know if *this* is the first time? Perhaps the universe has already died, many times, to be born again. Perhaps Leonardo was no traveler. Perhaps he was simply *remembering*." He looked up, challenging me to argue; but the challenge was distressingly feeble.

"I think," I said, "you should drink more soup."

But he had no more need of soup, and he turned to look at the sun once more.

It seemed too soon when the cold started to settle on the land once more, with great pancakes of new ice clustering around the rim of the Tycho Sea.

I summoned his friends, teachers, those who had loved him.

I clung to the greater goal: that the atoms of gold and nickel and zinc which had coursed in Berge's blood and bones, killing him like the mustard plants of Maginus—killing us all, in fact, at one rate or another—would now gather in even greater concentrations in the bodies of those who would follow us. Perhaps the pathetic scrap of gold or nickel which had cost poor Berge his life would at last, mined, close the circuit which would lift the first of our ceramic-hulled ships beyond the thick, deadening atmosphere of the Moon.

Perhaps. But it was cold comfort.

We ate the soup, of his dissolved bones and flesh, in solemn silence. We took his life's sole gift, further concentrating the metal traces to the far future, shortening our lives as he had.

I have never been a skillful host. As soon as they could, the young people dispersed. I talked with Berge's teachers, but we had little to say to each other; I was merely his uncle, after all, a genetic tributary, not a parent. I wasn't sorry to be left alone.

Before I slept again, even before the sun's bloated hull had slid below the toothed horizon, the winds had turned. The warm air that had cradled me was treacherously fleeing after the sinking sun. Soon the first flurries of snow came pattering on the black, swelling surface of the Tycho Sea. My seals slid back into the water, to seek out whatever riches or dangers awaited them under Callisto ice.

British science-fiction author Brian Stableford has published more than eighty novels. He graduated from the University of York with a degree in biology and received a PhD for his his doctoral thesis on the sociology of science fiction. A former lecturer in sociology at the University of Reading, he is a full-time writer and a part-time lecturer on creative writing at several universities.

ASHES AND TOMBSTONES
Brian M. Stableford

I was following Voltaire's good advice and working in my garden when the young man from the New European Space Agency came to call. I was enjoying my work; my new limb bones were the best yet and my refurbished retinas had restored my eyesight to perfection—and I was still only 40 percent synthetic by mass, 38 percent by volume.

I liked to think of the garden as my own tiny contribution to the Biodiversity Project, not so much because of the plants, whose seeds were all on deposit in half a dozen Arks, but because of the insects to which the plants provided food. More than half of the local insects were the neospecific produce of the Trojan Cockroach Project, and my salads were a key element in their selective regime. The cockroaches living in my kitchen had long since reverted to type, but I hadn't even thought of trying to clear them out; I knew the extent of the debt that my multitudinous several-times-great-grandchildren owed their even-more-multitudinous many-times-great-grandparents.

When I first caught sight of him over the hedge, I thought the young man from NESA might be one of my descendants come to pay a courtesy call on the Old Survivor, but I knew as soon as he said "Professor Neal?" that he must be an authentic stranger. I was Grandfather Paul to all my Repopulation Kin.

The stranger was thirty meters away, but his voice carried easily enough: the Berkshire Downs are very quiet nowadays, and my hearing was razor-sharp even though the electronic feed was thirty years old and technically obsolete.

"Never heard of him," I said. "No professors hereabouts. Oxford's forty miles that away." I pointed vaguely north-westward.

"The Paul Neal I'm looking for isn't a professor anymore," the young man admitted, letting himself in through the garden gate as if he'd been invited. "Technically, he ceased to be a professor when he was seconded to the Theseus Project in Martinique in 2080, during the first phase of the Crash." He stood on the path hopefully, waiting for me to join him and usher him in through the door to my home, which stood ajar. His face was fresh, although there wasn't the least hint of synthetic tissue in its contours. "I'm Dennis Mountjoy," he added as an afterthought. "I've left messages by the dozen, but it finally became obvious that the only way to get a response was to turn up in person."

Montjoie St. Denis! had been the war cry of the French, in days of old. This Dennis Mountjoy was a mongrel European, who probably thought of war as a primitive custom banished from the world forever. It wasn't easy to judge his age, given that his flesh must have been somatically tuned-up even though it hadn't yet become necessary to paper over any cracks, but I guessed that he was less than forty: a young man in a young world. To him, I was a relic of another era, practically a dinosaur—which was, of course, exactly why he was interested in me. NESA intended to put a man on the Moon in June 2269, to mark the three-hundredth anniversary of the first landing and the dawn of the New Space Age. They had hunted high and low for survivors of the last space program, because they wanted at least one to be there to bear witness to their achievement, to forge a living link with history. It didn't matter to them that the Theseus Project had not put a single man into space, nor directed a single officially-sanctioned shot at the Moon.

"What makes you think that you'll get any more response in person than you did by machine?" I asked the young man sourly. I drew myself erect, feeling a slight twinge in my spine in spite of all the nanomech reinforcements, and removed my sun hat so that I could wipe the sweat from my forehead.

"Electronic communication isn't very private," Mountjoy observed. "There are things that it wouldn't have been diplomatic to say over the phone."

My heart sank. I'd so far outlived my past that I'd almost come to believe that I'd escaped, but I hadn't been forgotten. I was surprised that my inner response wasn't stronger, but the more synthetic flesh you take aboard, the less capacity you have for violent emotion, and my heart was pure android. Time was when I'd have come on like the minotaur if anyone had penetrated to the core of my private maze, but all the bull leached out of my head a hundred years ago.

"Go away and leave me alone," I said wearily. "I wish you well, but I don't want any part of your so-called Great Adventure. Is that diplomatic enough for you?"

"There are things that it wouldn't have been diplomatic for *me* to say," he said, politely pretending that he thought I'd misunderstood him.

"Don't say them, then," I advised him.

"Ashes and tombstones," he recited, determinedly ignoring my advice. "Endymion. Astolpho."

There were supposed to be no records—but in a crisis, everybody cheats. Everybody keeps secrets, especially from the people they're supposed to be working for.

"Mr. Mountjoy," I said wearily, "it's 2268. I'm two hundred and eighteen years old. Everyone else who worked on Theseus is dead, along with ninety percent of the people who were alive in 2080. Ninety percent of the people alive today are under forty. Who do you think is going to give a damn about a couple of itty-bitty rockets that went up with the wrong payloads to the wrong destination? It's not as if the Chaos Patrol was left a sentry short, is it? Everything that was supposed to go up did go up."

"But that's why you don't want to come back to Martinique, isn't it?" Mountjoy said, still standing on the path, halfway between the gate and the door. "That's why you don't want to be there when the Adventure starts again. We know that the funds were channeled through your account. We know that you were the paymaster for the crazy shots. You probably didn't plan them, and you certainly didn't execute them, but you were the pivot of the seesaw."

I put my hat back on and adjusted the rim. The ozone layer was supposed to be back in place, but old habits die hard.

"Come over here," I said. "Watch where you put your feet."

He looked down at the variously-shaped blocks of salad greens. He had no difficulty following the dirt path I'd carefully laid out so that I could pass among them, patiently plying my hoe.

"You don't actually eat this stuff, do you?" he said, as he came to stand before me, looking down from his embryonically-enhanced two-meter height at my nanomech-conserved one-eighty.

"Mainly I grow it for the beetles and the worms," I told him. "They leave me little for my own plate. In essence, I'm a sharecropper for the biosphere. Repopulation's put *Homo sapiens* back in place, but the little guys still have a way to go. You really ought to wear a hat on days like this."

"It's not necessary in these latitudes," he assured me, missing the point again. "You're right, of course. Nobody cares about the extra launches. Nobody will mention it, least of all when you're on view. All we're interested in is selling the Adventure. We believe you can help us with that. No matter how small a cog you were, you were in the engine. You're the last man alive who took part in the pre-Crash space program. You're the world's last link to Theseus, Ariane, Apollo, and Mercury. That's all we're interested in, all we care about. The last thing anyone wants to do is to embarrass you, because embarrassing you would also be embarrassing us. We're on *your* side, Professor Neal—and if you're worried about the glare of publicity encouraging others to dig, there's no need. We have control, Professor Neal—and we're sending our heroes to the Sea of

Tranquillity, half a world away from Endymion. The only relics we'll be looking for are the ones Apollo 11 left. We're not interested in ashes or tombstones."

I knelt down, gesturing to indicate that he should follow suit. He hesitated, but he obeyed the instruction eventually. His suitskin was easily capable of digesting any dirt that got on its knees, and would probably be grateful for the piquancy.

"Do you know what this is?" I asked, fondling a crinkled leaf.

"Not exactly," he replied. "Some kind of engineered hybrid, mid-twenty-first-cee vintage, probably disembarked fifty or sixty years ago. The bit you eat is underground, right? Carrot, potato—something of that general sort—presumably gee-ee augmented as a whole-diet crop."

He was smarter than he looked. "Not exactly whole-*diet*," I corrected. "The manna-potato never really took off. Even when the weather went seriously bad, you could still grow manna-wheat in England thanks to megabubbles and microwave boosters. This is headstuff. Ecstasy cocktail. Its remotest ancestor produced the finest melange of euphorics and hallucinogens ever devised—but that was a hundred generations of mutation and insect-led natural selection ago. You crush the juice from the tubers and refine it by fractional distillation and freeze-drying—if you can keep the larvae away long enough for them to grow to maturity."

"So what?" he said, unimpressed. "You can buy designer stuff straight from the synthesizer, purity guaranteed. Growing your own is even more pointless than growing lettuces and courgettes."

"It's an adventure," I told him. "It's *my* adventure. It's the only kind I'm interested in now."

"Sure," he said. "We'll be careful not to take you away for too long. But we still need you, Professor Neal, and *our* Adventure is the one that matters to us. I came here to make a deal. Whatever it takes. Can we go inside now?"

I could see that he wasn't to be dissuaded. The young can be very persistent, when they want to be.

I sighed and surrendered. "You can come in," I conceded, "but you can't talk me 'round, by flattery or black-mail or salesmanship. At the end of the day, I don't have to do it if I don't want to." I knew it was hopeless, but I couldn't just *give in*. I had to make him do the work.

"You'll want to," he said, with serene overconfidence.

The aim of the project on which we were supposed to be working, way back in the twenty-first, was to place a ring of satellites in orbit between Earth and Mars to keep watch for stray asteroids and comets that might pose a danger to the Earth. The Americans had done the donkey-work on the payloads before the plague wars had rendered Canaveral redundant. The transfer brought the European Space Program back from the dead, although not everyone thought that was a good thing. "Why waste money protecting the world from asteroids," some said, "when we've all but destroyed it ourselves?" They had a point. Once the plague wars had set the dominoes falling, the Crash was inevitable; anyone who hoped that ten percent of the population would make it through was considered a wild-eyed optimist in 2080.

The age of manned spaceflight had been over before I was born. It didn't make economic sense to send up human beings, with the incredibly elaborate miniature ecospheres required for their support, when any job that needed doing outside the Earth could be done much better by compact clever machinery. Nobody had sent up a payload bigger than a dustbin for over half a century, and nobody was about to start. We'd sent probes to the outer system, the Oort Cloud, and a dozen neighboring star systems, but they were all machines that thrived on hard vacuum, hard radiation, and eternal loneliness. To us, there was no Great Adventure; the Theseus Project was just business—and whatever Astolpho was, it certainly wasn't an Adventure. It was just business of a subtly different kind.

Despite the superficial similarity of their names, there was nothing in our minds to connect Astolpho with Apollo. Apollo was the glorious god of the sun, the father of prophecy, the patron of all the Arts. Astolpho was a character in one of the satirical passages of the *Orlando Furioso* who journeyed to the Moon and found it a treasure-house of everything wasted on Earth: misspent time, ill-spent wealth, broken promises, unanswered prayers, fruitless tears, unfulfilled desires, failed quests, hopeless ambitions, aborted plans, and fruitless intentions. Each of these residues had its proper place: hung on hooks, stored in bellows, packed in trunks, and so on. Wasted talent was kept in vases, like the urns in which the ashes of the dead were sometimes stored in the Golden Age of Crematoria. It only takes a little leap of the imagination to think of a crater as a kind of vase.

The target picked out by the clandestine Project Astolpho was Endymion, named for the youth beloved of the Moon goddess Selene whose reward for her divine devotion was to live forever in dream-filled sleep.

Even in the days of Apollo—or shortly thereafter, at any rate—there had been people who liked the idea of burial in space. Even in the profligate twentieth, there had been dying men who did not want their ashes to be scattered upon the Earth, but wanted them blasted into space instead, where they would last *much* longer.

By 2080, when the Earth itself was dying, in critical condition at best, those who had tried hardest to save it—at least in their own estimation—became determined to save some tiny fraction of themselves from perishing with it. They did not want the relics of their flesh to be recycled into bacterial goo that would have to wait for millions of years before it essayed a new ascent toward complexity and intellect. They did not want their ashes to be consumed and recycled by the cockroaches which were every book-maker's favorite to be the most sophisticated survivors of the ecoholocaust.

They knew, of course, that Project Astolpho was a colossal waste of money, but they also knew that *all* money would become worthless if it were not spent soon, and there was no salvation to be bought. Who could blame them for spending what might well have proved to be the last money in the world on ashes and tombstones?

Were they wrong? Would they have regretted what they had done, if they had known that the human race would survive its self-inflicted wounds? I don't know. Not one member of the aristocracy of wealth that I could put a name to came through the worst. Perhaps their servants and their mistresses came through, and perhaps not—but they themselves went down with the Ship of Fools they had commissioned, captained, and navigated. All that remains of them now is their legacies, among which the payloads deposited by illicit Theseus launches in Endymion might easily be reckoned the least—and perhaps not the worst.

Dennis Mountjoy was right to describe me as a very small cog in the Engine of Fate. I did not plan Astolpho and I did not carry it out, but I did distribute the bribes. I was the bagman, the calculator, the fixer. Mathematics is a versatile art; it can be applied to widely different purposes. Math has no morality; it does not care what it counts or what it proves. Somewhere on Astolpho's moon, although Ariosto did not record that he ever found it, there must have been a hall of failed proofs, mistaken sums, illicit theorems, and follies of infinity, all neatly bound in webs of tenuous logic.

Had I not had the modest wealth I took as my commission on the extra Theseus shots, of course, I could not have been one of the survivors of the Crash. Had it not been for my brokerage of Project Astolpho, I could not have been, by the time that Dennis Mountjoy came to call, one of the oldest men in the world: the founder of a prolific dynasty. I, too, would have been nothing but ash, without even a tombstone, when the New Apollonians decided that it was time to reassert the glory and the godhood of the human race by duplicating its most magnificent folly: the Great Adventure.

I had never had any part in the first Adventure, and I wanted no part in the second. I had worked alongside men who had launched rockets into outer space, but the only things I ever helped to land on the Moon were the cargoes provided by the Pharaohs of Capitalism: the twenty-first century's answer to Pyramids.

I was companion to Astolpho, not Apollo: whenever I raised my eyes to the night sky, I saw nothing in the face of the Moon but the wastes of Earthly dreams and Earthly dreamers.

"None of that is relevant," Dennis Mountjoy told me, when I had explained it to him—or had tried to (the account just now set down has, of course, taken full advantage of *l'esprit de l'escalier*). He sat in an armchair waving his hands in the air. I had almost begun to wish that I'd offered him a cup of tea and a slice of cake, so that at least a few of his gestures would have been stifled.

"It's relevant to me," I told him, although I was fully cognizant by then of the fact that he had not the least interest in what was relevant to me.

"None of it's ever going to come out," he assured me. "You can forget it. You may be two-hundred-and-some years old, but that doesn't mean that you have to live in the past. We have to think of the future now. You should try to forget. That's what a good memory is, when all's said and done: one that can forget all the things it doesn't need to retain. There's no need for you to be hung up on the differences between Apollo and Astolpho in a world which can no longer tell them apart. As you said yourself, ninety percent of the people alive today are under forty. To them, it's all ancient history, and the names are just sounds. Apollo, Ariane, Theseus—it's all merged into a single mythical mishmash, including all the sidelines, official and unofficial. From the point of view of the people who believe in the New Adventure, and the people who *will* believe, once we've captured their imagination, it's all part of the same story, the one we're starting over. Your presence at the launch will confirm that. All that anyone will see when they look at you is a miracle: the last survivor of Project Theseus; the envoy of the First Space Age, extending his blessing to the Second."

"Do you know why Project Theseus was called by that name?" I asked him.

"Of course I do," he replied. "I know my history, even though I refuse to be bogged down by it. Ariane was the rocket used in the first European Space Program, named for the French version of Ariadne, daughter of Minos of Crete. Theseus was one of seven young men delivered to Minos as a tribute by the Athenians, along with seven young women; they were to be sacrificed to the minotaur—a monster that lived in the heart of a maze called the laby-rinth. Ariadne fell in love with Theseus and gave him a thread which allowed him to keep track of his route through the maze. When he had killed the minotaur, he was able to find his way out again. Theseus was the name given to Ariane's successor in order to signify that it was the heroic project which would secure humankind's escape from the minotaur in the maze: the killer asteroid that might one day wipe out civilization."

"That's the official decoding," I admitted. "But Theseus was also the betrayer of Ariane. He abandoned her. According to some sources, she committed suicide or died of grief—but others suggested that she was saved by Dionysus, the antithesis of Apollo."

"So what?" said Mountjoy, making yet another expansive gesture. "Whatever you and your crazy pals might have read into that back in 2080, it doesn't matter *now*."

"Crazy pals?" I queried, remembering his earlier reference to the Astolpho launches as "crazy shots." Now I was beginning to wish that I had a cup of tea; my own hands were beginning to stir as if in answer to his.

"The guys who gave you the money to shoot their ashes to the Moon," the young man said. "The Syndicate. The Captains of Industry. The Hardinist Cartel. Pick your cliché. They *were* crazy, weren't they? Paying you to drop those payloads in Endymion was only the tip of the iceberg. I mean, they were the people with the power—the people who had steered the world straight into the Crash. That has to be reckoned as causing death by dangerous driving—manslaughter on a massive scale. Mad, bad, and dangerous to know, wouldn't you say?"

"They didn't see it that way themselves," I pointed out mildly.

"They certainly didn't," he agreed. "But you're older and wiser, and you have the aid of hindsight, too. So give me your considered judgment, Professor Neal. Were they or were they not prime candidates for the straitjacket?"

I granted him a small laugh, but kept my hands still. "Maybe so," I said. "Maybe so. Can I get you a drink, by the way?"

He beamed, thinking that he'd won. One crack in the facade was all it needed to convince him.

"No thanks. We know how bad things were back then, and we don't blame you at all for what you did. The world is new again, and its newness is something for us all to celebrate. I understand why you've tried so hard to hide yourself away, and why you've built a maze of misinformation around your past. I understand how the thought of coming out of your shell after all these years must terrify you—but we *will* look after you. We *need* you, Professor Neal, to play Theseus in our own heroic drama. We need you to play the part of the man who slew the minotaur of despair and found the way out of the maze of human misery. I understand that you don't see yourself that way, that you don't *feel* like that kind of a hero, but in our eyes, that's what you are. In our eyes, and in the eyes of the world, you're the last living representative of early humanity's greatest adventure—the Adventure we're now taking up. We need you at the launch. We really can't do without you. Anything you want, just ask—but I'm here to make a deal, and I have to make it. No threats, of course, just honest persuasion—but I really do have to persuade you. You'll be in the news whether you like it or not—why not let us doctor the spin for you? If you're aboard, you have input; if not . . . you might end up with all the shit and none of the roses."

No threats, he'd said. Funnily enough, he meant it. He wouldn't breathe a word to a living soul—but if he'd found out about Astolpho, others could, and once the Great Adventure was all over the news, the incentive to dig would be there. Expert webwalkers researching Theseus would be bound to stumble over Astolpho eventually. The only smoke screen I could put up now was the smoke screen he was offering to lend me. If I didn't take it, I hadn't a hope of keeping the secret within the secret.

"Are you *sure* you wouldn't like something to drink?" I asked tiredly. His semaphoring arms had begun to make my newly-reconditioned eyes feel dizzy.

He beamed again and almost said, "Perhaps I will," but then his eyes narrowed slightly. "What *kind* of drink?" he said.

"I make it myself," I told him teasingly.

"That's what I'm afraid of," he said. "I've nothing against happy juice, but this isn't the time or the place—not for me. And to be perfectly honest, I'm not sure I could trust the homegrown stuff. You said yourself that it's been subject to generations of mutation and selection, and you know how delicate hybrid gentemplates are. Meaning no offense, but that garden is *infested*—and not everything that came out of Cade Maclaine's souped-up Trojan Cockroaches was a pretty pollen-carrier."

"Why should I help out in your Adventure," I asked him lightly, "if you won't help out in mine?"

He looked at me long and hard. It didn't need a trained mathematician to see the calculating clicking over in his mind. Whatever it took, he'd said. Anything I wanted, just ask.

"Well," he said finally, "I take your point. Are we talking about a deal here, or what? Are we talking about coming to an understanding? Sealing a compact?"

"Just the launch," I said. "One day only. You can make as much noise as you like—the more the merrier—but I only come out for one day. And everything you put out is Theseus, Theseus, and more Theseus. What's lost stays lost, from here to eternity."

"If that's what you want," he said. "One day only—and we'll give them so much Theseus they'll drown in it. Astolpho stays under wraps—*nobody* says a word about it. Not now, not ever. The records are ours, and we have no interest in letting the cat escape the bag. If we thought anyone would blow the whistle, we wouldn't want you waving us off. This is the Adventure, after all: the greatest moment so far in the history of the new human race. So far as we're concerned, the ashes of Endymion can stay buried for another two hundred years—or another two million. It doesn't matter; come the day when somebody stumbles over the tombstones, they'll just be an archaeological find: a nine day wonder. By then, we'll be out among the stars. Earth will be just our cradle."

I had thought when he first confronted me that he didn't have anything I wanted, just something he could threaten me with. I realized now that he had both—but he didn't know it. He and his crazy pals thought that they needed me at their launch, to give the blessing of the old human race to the new, and I needed them to be perfectly content with what they thought they had, to dig just so far and no farther. It had been foolish of me to refuse to return his calls, without even knowing what he had to say, and exactly how much he might have discovered.

"All right," I said, with all the fake weariness that a 40 percent synthetic man of two hundred and eighteen can muster. "You've worn me down. I give in. I do the launch, and the rest is silence. I appear, smile, disappear. Remembered for one brief moment, forgotten forever. Once I'm out of the way, your guys are the only heroes. Okay?"

"There *might* be other inquiries from TV," he said guardedly, "but as far as we're concerned, it's just the one symbolic gesture. That's all we need. I can't imagine that there'll be anything else that you can't reasonably turn down. You're two hundred and eighteen years old, after all. Nobody will get suspicious if you plead exhaustion."

"If you're so utterly convinced that you need it," I said, "who am I to deny you? And you're right—whatever other calls come in, I can be forgiven for refusing to answer on the grounds of creeping senility. I'll program my answer-phone to imply that I really couldn't be trusted not to wet myself if I were face-to-face with a famous chat show host. *Now* do you want a drink? Nothing homemade, if you insist—for you I'll make an exception. I'll even break the seal in front of you, if you like."

"There's no need," he said, with an airy wave of his right hand. His voice was redolent with relief and triumph. "I trust you."

Theseus betrayed Ariadne; of that much the voice of myth is as certain as the voice of myth can ever be. If she did not die, she was thrust into the arms of Dionysus, the god of intoxication. If grief did not kill her, she gave herself over to the mind-blowing passion of the Bacchae.

"Ashes and tombstones" were the names that the Pharaohs of Capitalism gave to the payloads which they paid my associates to deposit in Endymion, near the north pole of the Moon. Ashes to ashes, dust to dust . . . but the remnants of their flesh that they sent to Endymion, actual vases to be placed within a symbolic vase, were not the remains of their dead. The "ashes" were actually frozen embryos: not their dead, but their multitudinous unborn children.

The "tombstones" carried aloft by valiant Astolpho were not inscribed with their epitaphs but with instructions for the resurrection of the human species, so deeply and so cleverly ingrained that they might still be deciphered after a million or a billion years, even by members of a species which had evolved a million or a billion light-years away and had formulated a very different language.

Like the Pharaohs of old, the Pharaohs of the End Time fully intended to rise again; their pyramids were not built as futile monuments but as fortresses to secure themselves against disaster.

Against *all* disaster, that is.

My "crazy pals" had believed that the world was doomed, and humankind with it. There was nothing remotely crazy in that belief, in 2080. The Earth was dying, and nothing short of a concatenation of miracles could have saved it. Perhaps the Pharaohs of Capitalism had been crazy to have let the world get into such a state, but they were not miracle workers themselves; they were only men. They thought that the only hope for humankind was to slumber for a million or a billion years in the bosom of the Moon, until someone might come who would recognize the Earth for the grave it was, and would search for relics of the race whose grave it was in the one place where such relics might have survived the ravages of decay: hard vacuum.

The disaster they had feared so much had not, in the end, been absolute. The human race had come through the crisis. Cade Maclaine's cockroach-borne omnispores and the underground Arks had enabled them to resuscitate the ecosphere and massage the fluttering rhythm of its heart back to steadiness.

By now, of course, the game had changed. The Repopulation was almost complete, and the Adventure had begun again. The New Human Race believed that its future was secure, and that the tricentennial launch of the mission to the Era of Tranquillity would help to make it secure.

Well, perhaps.

And perhaps not.

I knew that if the new Adventurers found the vases of Endymion, they would be reckoned merely one more Ark: one more seed-deposit, to be drawn on as and when convenient. The children of the Pharaohs would be disembarked at the whim and convenience of men like Dennis Mountjoy, who believed with all his heart that the minotaur at the heart of the labyrinth of fate was dead and gone, and every ancient nightmare with him.

That, to the crazy men who had paid my prices in order to deposit their heritage in Endymion, would almost certainly have seemed to be a disaster as great as the one that had been avoided. The Pharaohs had not handed down fortunes so that their offspring could be reabsorbed into the teeming millions of the New Human race, but in order that they should become *the* human race: a unique marvel in their own right.

Perhaps they were crazy to want that, but that is what they wanted. "Ashes and tombstones" was a smoke screen, intended to conceal a bid for resurrection, immortality, and the privilege of uniqueness in a universe where humankind was utterly forgotten—and nothing less.

My motives were somewhat different, of course, but I wanted the same result.

At two hundred and eighteen years of age, and having lived through the Crash, I could never convince myself that it could not happen again—but even if it never did, I wanted the vases of Endymion to rest in peace, not for a hundred years or a thousand, but for a million or a billion, as their deliverers had intended.

I did not want the "ashes and tombstones" to become an archaeological find and a nine day wonder. I wanted them to remain where they were until they were found by those who had been intended to find them: nonhuman beings, for whom the task of disembArkation would be an act of reCreation. It did not matter to me whether they were the spawn of another star or the remotest descendants of the ecosphere of Earth, remade by countless generations of mutation and selection into something far stranger than the New Human race—but I, too, wanted to leave my mark on the face of eternity. I, too, wanted to have gouged out a scratch on the infinite wall of the future, to have played a part in making something that would last, not for seventy years or two hundred, or even two thousand—which is as long as any man might reasonably expect to live, aided by our superbly clever and monstrously chimerical technologies of self-repair—but for two million or two billion.

All I had done was to calculate the price, but without me, none of it would have happened. The Moon would have been *exactly* as Astolpho found it: a treasury of the lost and the wasted, the futile and the functionless.

Thanks to me, it is more than that. In a million or a billion years, the time will come for the resurrection, and the new life. I do not want it to be soon: the longer, the better.

I thoroughly enjoyed the launch. I enjoyed it so tremendously, in fact, that I was glad I had allowed myself to be persuaded to take my place among its architects, to give their bold endeavor the blessing of all the billions of people who had died while I was young.

I was unworthy, of course. Who among us is not? Nor can I believe, even now, that Dennis Mountjoy was correct in thinking that his heroes needed me to set the seal of history on their endeavor—but the sight of that rocket riding its pillar of fire into the deep blue of the sky brought back so many memories, so many echoes of a self long-buried and half-forgotten, that I almost broke down and wept.

"I had forgotten what a sight it was," I admitted to the young man, "and I thought that I had lost the capacity to feel such deep emotions, along with the fleshy tables of my first heart."

He did not recognize the quotation, which came from Paul's second epistle to the Corinthians: an epistle, according to the text, "written not with ink but with the Spirit of the living God; not in tables of stone, but in fleshy tables of the heart." All he had to say in reply was: "I told you that you'd want to be here. This is Apollo reborn, Theseus reborn. This is what all the heroes of the race were made to accomplish. This time, we'll go all the way to the stars, whatever it costs."

Astolpho, your creator had not the least idea what truth he served when he sent you to the Moon, to discern its real nature and its real purpose.

Adam-Troy Castro made his first non-fiction sale to *SPY* magazine in 1987. His twenty-six books to date include four Spider-Man novels, three novels about his profoundly damaged far-future murder investigator Andrea Cort, and six middle-grade novels about the dimension-spanning adventures of young Gustav Gloom. The final installment in the series, *Gustav Gloom and the Castle of Fear* (Grosset and Dunlap), came out in 2016. Adam's darker short fiction for grownups is highlighted by his most recent collection, *Her Husband's Hands and Other Stories* (Prime Books). Adam's works have won the Philip K. Dick Award and the Seiun (Japan), and have been nominated for eight Nebulas (including one for "Sunday Night Yams at Minnie and Earl's"), three Stokers, two Hugos, and, internationally, the Ignotus (Spain), the Grand Prix de l'Imaginaire (France), and the Kurd-Laßwitz Preis (Germany). He has recently completed a mainstream thriller which is now making the rounds. He lives in Florida with his wife Judi and either three or four cats, depending on what day you're counting and whether Gilbert's escaped this week.

SUNDAY NIGHT YAMS AT MINNIE AND EARL'S

Adam-Troy Castro

Frontiers never die. They just become theme parks.

I spent most of my shuttle ride to Nearside mulling sour thoughts about that. It's the kind of thing that only bothers lonely and nostalgic old men, especially when we're old enough to remember the days when a trip to Luna was not a routine commuter run, but instead a never-ending series of course corrections, systems checks, best-and-worst case simulations, and random unexpected crises ranging from ominous burning smells to the surreal balls of floating upchuck that got into everywhere if we didn't get over our nausea fast enough to clean them up. Folks of my vintage remember what it was to spend half their lives in passionate competition with dozens of other frighteningly qualified people, just to earn themselves seats on cramped rigs outfitted by the lowest corporate bidders—and then to look down at the ragged landscape of Sister Moon and know that the sight itself was a privilege well worth the effort. But that's old news now: before the first development crews gave way to the first settlements; before the first settlements became large enough to be called the first cities; before the first city held a parade in honor of its first confirmed mugging; before Independence and the Corporate Communities and the opening of Lunar Disney on the Sea of Tranquility. These days, the

Moon itself is no big deal except for rubes and old-timers. Nobody looks out the windows; they're far too interested in their sims, or their virts, or their newspads or (for a vanishingly literate few) their paperback novels, to care about the sight of the airless world waxing large in the darkness outside.

I wanted to shout at them. I wanted to make a great big eloquent speech about what they were missing by taking it all for granted, and about their total failure to appreciate what others had gone through to pave the way. But that wouldn't have moved anybody. It just would have established me as just another boring old fart.

So I stayed quiet until we landed, and then I rolled my overnighter down the aisle, and I made my way through the vast carpeted terminal at Armstrong Interplanetary (thinking all the while *carpet, carpet, why is there carpet, dammit, there shouldn't be carpeting on the Moon*). Then I hopped a tram to my hotel, and I confirmed that the front desk had followed instructions and provided me one of their few (hideously expensive) rooms with an outside view. Then I went upstairs and thought it all again when I saw that the view was just an alien distortion of the Moon I had known. Though it was night, and the landscape was as dark as the constellations of manmade illumination peppered across its cratered surface would now ever allow it to be, I still saw marquee-sized advertisements for soy houses, strip clubs, rotating restaurants, golden arches, miniature golf courses, and the one-sixth-g Biggest Rollercoaster In the Solar System. The Earth, with Europe and Africa centered, hung silently above the blight.

I tried to imagine two gentle old people, and a golden retriever dog, wandering around somewhere in the garish paradise framed by that window.

I failed.

I wondered whether it felt good or bad to be here. I wasn't tired, which I supposed I could attribute to the sensation of renewed strength and vigor that older people are supposed to feel after making the transition to lower gravities. Certainly, my knees, which had been bothering me for more than a decade now, weren't giving me a single twinge here. But I was also here alone, a decade after burying my dear wife—and though I'd traveled around a little in the last few years, I had never really grown used to the way the silence of a strange room, experienced alone, tastes like the death that waited for me too.

After about half an hour of feeling sorry for myself, I dressed in one of my best blue suits—an old one Claire had picked out in better days, with a cut now two styles out of date—and went to the lobby to see the concierge. I found him in the center of a lobby occupied not by adventurers or pioneers but by businessmen and tourists. He was a sallow-faced young man seated behind a flat slab of a desk, constructed from some material made to resemble polished black marble. It might have been intended to represent a Kubrick monolith lying on its side, a touch that would have been appropriate enough for the Moon but might have given the decorator too much credit for classical allusions. I found more Kubrick material in the man himself, in that he was a typical hotel functionary: courteous, professional, friendly, and as cold as a plain white wall. Beaming, he said: "Can I help you, sir?"

"I'm looking for Minnie and Earl," I told him.

His smile was an unfaltering, professional thing, that might have been scissored out of a magazine ad and Scotch-taped to the bottom half of his face. "Do you have their full names, sir?"

"Those are their full names." I confess I smiled with reminiscence. "They're both one of a kind."

"I see. And they're registered at the hotel?"

"I doubt it," I said. "They're lunar residents. I just don't have their address."

"Did you try the directory?"

"I tried that before I left Earth," I said. "They're not listed. Didn't expect them to be, either."

He hesitated a fraction of a second before continuing: "I'm not sure I know what to suggest, then—"

"I'm sure you don't," I said, unwillingly raising my voice just enough to give him a little taste of the anger and frustration and dire need that had fueled this entire trip. Being a true professional, used to dealing with obnoxious and arrogant tourists, the concierge didn't react at all: just politely waited for me to get on with it. I, on the other hand, winced before continuing: "They're before your time. Probably way before your time. But there have to be people around—old people, mostly—who know who I'm talking about. Maybe you can ask around for me? Just a little? And pass around the word that I need to talk?"

The professional smile did not change a whit, but it still acquired a distinctively dubious flavor. "Minnie and Earl, sir?"

"Minnie and Earl." I then showed him the size of the tip he'd earn if he accomplished it—big enough to make certain that he'd take the request seriously, but not so large that he'd be tempted to concoct false leads. It impressed him exactly as much as I needed it to. Too bad there was almost no chance of it accomplishing anything; I'd been making inquiries about the old folks for years. But the chances of me giving up were even smaller: not when I now knew I only had a few months left before the heart stopped beating in my chest.

They were Minnie and Earl, dammit.

And anybody who wasn't there in the early days couldn't possibly understand how much that meant.

It's a funny thing, about frontiers: they're not as enchanting as the folks who work them like you to believe. And there was a lot that they didn't tell the early recruits about the joys of working on the Moon.

They didn't tell you that the air systems gave off a nasal hum that kept you from sleeping soundly at any point during your first six weeks on rotation; that the vents were considerately located directly above the bunks to eliminate any way of shutting it out; that just when you found yourself actually needing that hum to sleep something in the circulators decided to change the pitch, rendering it just a tad higher or lower so that instead of lying in bed begging that hum to shut up shut up SHUT UP you sat there instead wondering if the new version denoted a serious mechanical difficulty capable of asphyxiating you in your sleep.

They didn't tell you that the recycled air was a paradise for bacteria, which kept any cold or flu or ear infection constantly circulating between you and your coworkers; that the disinfectants regularly released into the atmosphere smelled bad but otherwise did nothing; that when you started sneezing and coughing it was a sure bet that everybody around you would soon be sneezing and coughing; and that it was not just colds but stomach viruses, contagious rashes and even more unpleasant things that got shared as generously as a bottle of a wine at one of the parties you had time to go to back on Earth when you were able to work only sixty or seventy hours a week. They didn't tell you that work took so very much of your time that the pleasures and concerns of normal life were no longer valid experiential input; that without that input you eventually ran out of non-work-related subjects to talk about, and found your personality withering away like an atrophied limb.

They didn't tell you about the whimsical random shortages in the bi-monthly supply drops and the ensuing shortages of staples like toothpaste and toilet paper. They didn't tell you about the days when all the systems seemed to conk out at once and your deadening routine suddenly became hours of all-out frantic terror. They didn't tell you that after a while you forgot you were on the Moon and stopped sneaking looks at the battered blue marble. They didn't tell you that after a while it stopped being a dream and became instead just a dirty and backbreaking job; one that drained you of your enthusiasm faster than you could possibly guess, and one that replaced your ambitions of building a new future with more mundane longings, like feeling once again what it was like to stand unencumbered beneath a midday sun, breathing air that tasted like air and not canned sweat.

They waited until you were done learning all of this on your own before they told you about Minnie and Earl.

I learned on a Sunday—not that I had any reason to keep track of the day; the early development teams were way too short-staffed to enjoy luxuries like days off. There were instead days when you got the shitty jobs and the days when you got the jobs slightly less shitty than the others. On that particular Sunday I had repair duty, the worst job on the Moon but for another twenty or thirty possible candidates. It involved, among them, inspecting, cleaning, and replacing the panels on the solar collectors. There were a lot of panels, since the early collector fields were five kilometers on a side, and each panel was only half a meter square. They tended to collect meteor dust (at best) and get scarred and pitted from micrometeor impacts (at worst). We'd just lost a number of them from heavier rock precipitation, which meant that in addition to replacing those, I had to examine even those that remained intact. Since the panels swiveled to follow the Sun across the sky, even a small amount of dust debris threatened to fall through the joints into the machinery below. There was never a lot of dust—sometimes it was not even visible. But it had to be removed one panel at a time.

To overhaul the assembly, you spent the whole day on your belly, crawling along the catwalks between them, removing each panel in turn, inspecting them beneath a canopy with nothing but suit light, magnifiers, and micro-thin air jet. (A vacuum, of course, would have been redundant.) You replaced the panels pitted beyond repair, brought the ruined ones back to the sled for disposal, and then started all over again.

The romance of space travel? Try nine hours of hideously tedious stoop labor, in a moonsuit. Try hating every minute of it. Try hating where you are and what you're doing and how hard you worked to qualify for this privilege. Try also hating yourself just for feeling that way—but not having any idea how to turn those feelings off.

I was muttering to myself, conjugating some of the more colorful expressions for excrement, when Phil Jacoby called. He was one of the more annoying people on the Moon: a perpetual smiler who always looked on the bright side of things and refused to react to even the most acidic sarcasm. Appropriately enough, his carrot hair and freckled cheeks always made him look like a ventriloquist's dummy. He might have been our morale officer, if we'd possessed enough bad taste to have somebody with that job title; but that would have made him even more the kind of guy you grow to hate when you really want to be in a bad mood. I dearly appreciated how distant his voice sounded, as he called my name over the radio: "Max! You bored yet, Max?"

"Sorry," I said tiredly. "Max went home."

"Home as in his quarters? Or Home as in Earth?"

"There is no home here," I said. "Of course Home as on Earth."

"No return shuttles today," Phil noted. "Or any time this month. How would he manage that trick?"

"He was so fed up he decided to walk."

"Hope he took a picnic lunch or four. That's got to be a major hike."

In another mood, I might have smiled. "What's the bad news, Phil?"

"Why? You expecting bad news?"

There was a hidden glee to his tone that sounded excessive even from Jacoby. "Surprise me."

"You're quitting early. The barge will be by to pick you up in five minutes."

According to the digital readout inside my helmet, it was only 13:38 LT. The news that I wouldn't have to devote another three hours to painstaking cleanup should have cheered me considerably; instead, it rendered me about twenty times more suspicious. I said, "Phil, it will take me at least three times that long just to secure—"

"A relief shift will arrive on another barge within the hour. Don't do another minute of work. Just go back to the sled and wait for pickup. That's an order."

Which was especially strange because Jacoby was not technically my superior. Sure, he'd been on the Moon all of one hundred and twenty days longer than me—and sure, that meant any advice he had to give me needed to be treated like an order, if I wanted to do my job—but even so, he was not the kind of guy who ever ended anything with an authoritarian *That's An Order*. My first reaction was the certainty that I must have been in some kind of serious trouble. Somewhere, sometime, I forgot or neglected one of the safety protocols, and did something suicidally, crazily wrong—the kind of thing that once discovered would lead to me being relieved for incompetence. But I was still new on the Moon, and I couldn't think of any recent occasion where I'd been given enough responsibility for that to be a factor. My next words were especially cautious: "Uh, Phil, did I—"

"Go to the sled," he repeated, even more sternly this time. "And, Max?"

"What?" I asked.

The ebullient side of his personality returned. "I envy you, man."

The connection clicked off before I could ask him why.

A lunar barge was a lot like its terrestrial equivalent, in that it had no motive power of its very own, but needed to be pulled by another vehicle. Ours were pulled by tractors. They had no atmospheric enclosures, since ninety percent of the time they were just used for the slow-motion hauling of construction equipment; whenever they were needed to move personnel, we bolted in a number of forward-facing seats with oxygen feeds and canvas straps to prevent folks imprisoned by clumsy moonsuits from being knocked out of their chairs every time the flatbed dipped in the terrain. It was an extremely low-tech method of travel, not much faster than a human being could sprint, and we didn't often use it for long distances.

There were four other passengers on this one, all identical behind mirrored facemasks; I had to read their nametags to see who they were. Nikki Hollander, Oscar Desalvo, George Peterson, and Carrie Aldrin No Relation (the last two words a nigh-permanent part of her name, up here). All four of them had been on-site at least a year more than I had, and to my eyes had always seemed to be dealing with a routine a lot better than I had been. As I strapped in, and the tractor started up, and the barge began its glacial progress toward a set of lumpy peaks on the horizon, I wished my coworkers had something other than distorted reflections of the lunar landscape for faces; it would be nice to be able to judge from their expressions just what was going on here. I said: "So what's the story, people? Where we headed?"

Then Carrie Aldrin No Relation began to sing: "Over the river and through the woods/to grandmother's house we go . . ."

George Peterson snorted. Oscar Desalvo, a man not known for his giddy sense of humor, who was in fact even grimmer than me most of the time— (not from disenchantment with his work, but out of personal inclination)— giggled; it was like watching one of the figures on Mount Rushmore stick its tongue out. Nikki Hollander joined in, her considerably less-than-perfect pitch turning the rest of the song into a nails-on-blackboard cacophony. The helmet speakers, which distorted anyway, did not help.

I said, "Excuse me?"

Nikki Hollander said something so blatantly ridiculous that I couldn't force myself to believe I'd heard her correctly.

"Come again? I lost that."

"No you didn't." Her voice seemed strained, almost hysterical.

One of the men was choking with poorly repressed laughter. I couldn't tell who.

"You want to know if I like yams?"

Nikki's response was a burlesque parody of astronautic stoicism. "That's an affirmative, Houston."

"Yams, the vegetable yams?"

"*A*-ffirmative." The A emphasized and italicized so broadly that it was not so much a separate syllable as a sovereign country.

This time I recognized the strangulated noises. They were coming from George Peterson, and they were the sounds made by a man who was trying very hard not to laugh. It was several seconds before I could summon enough dignity to answer. "Yeah, I like yams. How is that relevant?"

"Classified," she said, and then her signal cut off.

In fact, all their signals cut off, though I could tell from the red indicators on my internal display that they were all still broadcasting.

That was not unusual. Coded frequencies were one of the few genuine amenities allowed us; they allowed those of us who absolutely needed a few seconds to discuss personal matters with coworkers to do so without sharing their affairs with anybody else who might be listening. We're not supposed to spend more than a couple of minutes at a time on those channels because it's safer to stay monitored. Being shut out of four signals simultaneously—in a manner that could only mean raucous laughter at my expense—was unprecedented, and it pissed me off. Hell, I'll freely admit that it did more than that; it frightened me. I was on the verge of suspecting brain damage caused by something wrong with the air supply.

Then George Peterson's voice clicked: "Sorry about that, old buddy." (I'd never been his old buddy.) "We usually do a better job keeping a straight face."

"At what? Mind telling me what's going on here?"

"One minute." He performed the series of maneuvers necessary to cut off the oxygen provided by the barge, and restore his dependence on the supply contained in his suit, then unstrapped his harnesses, stood, and moved toward me, swaying slightly from the bumps and jars of our imperfectly smooth ride across the lunar surface.

It was, of course, against all safety regulations for him to be on his feet while the barge was in motion; after all, even as glacially slow as that was, it wouldn't have taken all that great an imperfection in the road before us to knock him down and perhaps inflict the kind of hairline puncture capable of leaving him with a slight case of death. We had all disobeyed that particular rule from time to time; there were just too many practical advantages in being able to move around at will, without first ordering the tractor to stop. But it made no sense for him to come over now, just to talk, as if it really made a difference for us to be face-to-face. After all, we weren't faces. We were a pair of convex mirrors, reflecting each other while the men behind them spoke on radios too powerful to be noticeably improved by a few less meters of distance.

Even so, he sat down on a steel crate lashed to the deck before me, and positioned his faceplate opposite mine, his body language suggesting meaningful eye contact. He held that position for almost a minute, not saying anything, not moving, behaving exactly like a man who believed he was staring me down.

It made no sense. I could have gone to sleep and he wouldn't have noticed. Instead, I said: "What?"

He spoke quietly: "Am I correct in observing that you've felt less than, shall we say . . . 'inspired', by your responsibilities here?"

Oh, Christ. This was about something I'd done.

"Is there some kind of problem?"

George's helmet trembled enough to suggest a man theatrically shaking his head inside it. "Lighten up, Max. Nobody has any complaints about your work. We think you're one of the best people we have here, and your next evaluation is going to give you straight A's in every department . . . except enthusiasm. You just don't seem to believe in the work anymore."

As much as I tried to avoid it, my answer still reeked with denial. "I believe in it."

"You believe in the idea of it," George said. "But the reality has worn you down."

I was stiff, proper, absolutely correct, and absolutely transparent. "I was trained. I spent a full year in simulation, doing all the same jobs. I knew what it was going to be like. I knew what to expect."

"No amount of training can prepare you for the moment when you think you can't feel the magic anymore."

"And you can?" I asked, unable to keep the scorn from my voice.

The speakers inside lunar helmets were still pretty tinny in those days; they no longer transformed everything we said into the monotones that once upon a time helped get an entire country fed up with the forced badinage of Apollo, but neither were they much good at conveying the most precise of emotional cues. And yet I was able to pick up something in George's tone that was, given my mood, capable of profoundly disturbing me: a strange, transcendent joy. "Oh, yes. Max. I can."

I was just unnerved enough to ask: "How?"

"I'm swimming in it," he said—and even as long as he'd been part of the secret, his voice still quavered, as if there was some seven-year-old part of him that remained unwilling to believe that it could possibly be. "We're all swimming in it."

"I'm not."

And he laughed out loud. "Don't worry. We're going to gang up and shove you into the deep end of the pool."

That was seventy years ago.

Seventy years. I think about how old that makes me and I cringe. Seventy years ago, the vast majority of old farts who somehow managed to make it to the age I am now were almost always living on the outer edges of decrepitude. The physical problems were nothing compared with the senility. What's that?

You don't remember senile dementia? Really? I guess there's a joke in there somewhere, but it's not that funny for those of us who can remember actually considering it a possible future. Trust me, it was a nightmare. And the day they licked that one was one hell of an advertisement for progress.

But still, seventy years. You want to know how long ago that was? Seventy years ago it was still possible to find people who had heard of Bruce Springsteen. There were even some who remembered the Beatles. Stephen King was still coming out with his last few books, Kate Emma Brenner hadn't yet come out with any, Exxon was still in business, the reconstruction of the ice packs hadn't even been proposed, India and Pakistan hadn't reconciled, and the idea of astronauts going out into space to blow up a giant asteroid before it impacted with Earth was not an anecdote from recent history but a half-remembered image from a movie your father talked about going to see when he was a kid. Seventy years ago the most pressing headlines had to do with the worldwide ecological threat posed by the population explosion among escaped sugar gliders.

Seventy years ago, I hadn't met Claire. She was still married to her first husband, the one she described as the nice mistake. She had no idea I was anywhere in her future. I had no idea she was anywhere in mine. The void hadn't been defined yet, let alone filled. (Nor had it been cruelly emptied again—and wasn't it sad how the void I'd lived with for so long seemed a lot larger, once I needed to endure it again?)

Seventy years ago I thought Faisal Awad was an old man. He may have been in his mid-thirties then, at most ten years older than I was. That, to me, was old. These days it seems one step removed from the crib.

I haven't mentioned Faisal yet; he wasn't along the day George and the others picked me up in the barge, and we didn't become friends till later. But he was a major member of the development team, back then—the kind of fixitall adventurer who could use the coffee machine in the common room to repair the heating system in the clinic. If you don't think that's a valuable skill, try living under 24-7 life support in a hostile environment where any requisitions for spare parts had to be debated and voted upon by a government committee during election years. It's the time of my life when I first developed my deep abiding hatred of Senators. Faisal was our life-saver, our miracle worker, and our biggest local authority on the works of Gilbert and Sullivan, though back then we were all too busy to listen to music and much more likely to listen to that 15-minute wonder Polka Thug anyway. After I left the Moon, and the decades of my life fluttered by faster than I once could have imagined possible, I used to think about Faisal and decide that I really ought to look him up, someday, maybe, as soon as I had the chance. But he had stayed on Luna, and I had gone back to Earth, and what with one thing or another that resolution had worked out as well as such oughtas always do: a lesson that old men have learned too late for as long as there have been old men to learn it.

I didn't even know how long he'd been dead until I heard it from his granddaughter Janine Seuss, a third-generation lunar I was able to track down with the help of the Selene Historical Society. She was a slightly-built thirty-seven-year-old with stylishly mismatched eye color and hair micro-styled into infinitesimal pixels that, when combed correctly, formed the famous old black-and-white news photograph of that doomed young girl giving the finger to the cops at the San Diego riots of some thirty years ago. Though she had graciously agreed to meet me, she hadn't had time to arrange her hair properly, and the photo was eerily distorted, like an image captured and then distorted on putty. She served coffee, which I can't drink anymore but which I accepted anyway, then sat down on her couch with the frantically miaowing Siamese.

"There were still blowouts then," she said. "Some genuine accidents, some bombings arranged by the Flat-Mooners. It was one of the Flat-Mooners who got Poppy. He was taking Mermer—our name for Grandma—to the movies up on topside; back then, they used to project them on this big white screen a couple of kilometers outside, though it was always some damn thing fifty or a hundred years old with dialogue that didn't make sense and stories you had to be older than Moses to appreciate. Anyway, the commuter tram they were riding just went boom and opened up into pure vacuum. Poppy and Mermer and about fourteen others got sucked out." She took a deep breath, then let it out all at once. "That was almost twenty years ago."

What else can you say, when you hear a story like that? "I'm sorry."

She acknowledged that with an equally ritual response. "Thanks."

"Did they catch the people responsible?"

"Right away. They were a bunch of losers. Unemployed idiots."

I remembered the days when the only idiots on the Moon were highly-educated and overworked ones. After a moment, I said: "Did he ever talk about the early days? The development teams?"

She smiled. "Ever? It was practically all he ever did talk about. You kids don't bleh bleh bleh. He used to get mad at the vids that made it look like a time of sheriffs and saloons and gunfights—he guessed they probably made good stories for kids who didn't know any better, but kept complaining that life back then wasn't anything like that. He said there was always too much work to do to strap on six-guns and go gunning for each other."

"He was right," I said. (There was a grand total of one gunfight in the first thirty years of lunar settlement—and it's not part of this story.)

"Most of his stories about those days had to do with things breaking down and him being the only person who could fix them in the nick of time. He told reconditioned-software anecdotes. Finding-the-rotten-air-filter anecdotes. Improvise-joint-lubricant anecdotes. Lots of them."

"That was Faisal."

She petted the cat. (It was a heavy-lidded, meatloaf-shaped thing that probably bestirred itself only at the sound of a can opener: we'd tamed the Moon so utterly that people like Janine were able to spare some pampering for their pets.) "Bleh. I prefer the gunfights."

I leaned forward and asked the important question. "Did he ever mention anybody named Minnie and Earl?"

"Were those a couple of folks from way back then?"

"You could say that."

"No last names?"

"None they ever used."

She thought about that, and said: "Would they have been folks he knew only slightly? Or important people?"

"Very important people," I said. "It's vital that I reach them."

She frowned. "It was a long time ago. Can you be sure they're still alive?"

"Absolutely," I said.

She considered that for a second. "No, I'm sorry. But you have to realize it was a long time ago for me too. I don't remember him mentioning anybody."

Faisal was the last of the people I'd known from my days on the Moon. There were a couple on Earth, but both had flatly denied any knowledge of Minnie and Earl. Casting about for last straws, I said: "Do you have anything that belonged to him?"

"No, I don't. But I know where you can go to look further."

Seventy years ago, after being picked up by the barge:

Nobody spoke to me again for forty-five minutes, which only fueled my suspicions of mass insanity.

The barge itself made slow but steady progress, following a generally uphill course of the only kind possible in that era, in that place, on the Moon: which was to say, serpentine. The landscape here was rough, pocked with craters and jagged outcroppings, in no place willing to respect how convenient it might have been to allow us to proceed in something approaching a straight line. There were places where we had to turn almost a hundred and eighty degrees, double back a while, then turn again, to head in an entirely different direction; it was the kind of route that looks random from one minute to the next but gradually reveals progress in one direction or another. It was clearly a route that my colleagues had travelled many times before; nobody seemed impatient. But for the one guy who had absolutely no idea where we were going, and who wasn't in fact certain that we were headed anywhere at all, it was torture.

We would have managed the trip in maybe one-tenth the time in one of our fliers, but I later learned that the very laboriousness of the journey was, for first-timers at least, a traditional part of the show. It gave us time to speculate, to anticipate. This was useful for unlimbering the mind, ironing the kinks out of the imagination, getting us used to the idea that we were headed some-place important enough to be worth the trip. The buildup couldn't possibly be enough—the view over that last ridge was still going to hit us with the force of a sledgehammer to the brain—but I remember how hard it hit and I'm still thankful the shock was cushioned even as inadequately as it was.

We followed a long boring ridge for the better part of fifteen minutes . . . then began to climb a slope that bore the rutty look of lunar ground that had known tractor-treads hundreds of times before. Some of my fellow journeyers hummed ominous, horror-movie soundtrack music in my ear, but George's voice overrode them all: "Max? Did Phil tell you he envied you this moment?"

I was really nervous now. "Yes."

"He's full of crap. You're not going to enjoy this next bit except in ret-rospect. Later on you'll think of it as the best moment of your life—and it might even be—but it won't feel like that when it happens. It'll feel big and frightening and insane when it happens. Trust me now when I tell you that it will get better, and quickly . . . and that everything will be explained, if not completely, then at least as much as it needs to be."

It was an odd turn of phrase. "As much as it needs to be? What's that supposed to—"

That's when the barge reached the top of the rise, providing us a nice pan-oramic view of what awaited us in the shallow depression on the other side.

My ability to form coherent sentences became a distant rumor.

It was the kind of moment when the entire Universe seems to become a wobbly thing, propped up by scaffolding and held together with the cheapest brand of hardware-store nails. The kind of moment when gravity just turns sideways beneath you, and the whole world turns on its edge, and the only thing that prevents you from just jetting off into space to spontaneously com-bust is the compensatory total stoppage of time. I don't know the first thing I said. I'm glad nobody ever played me the recordings that got filed away in the permanent mission archives . . . and I'm equally sure that the reason they didn't is that anybody actually on the Moon to listen to them must have also had their own equally aghast reactions also saved for posterity. I got to hear such sounds many times, from others I would later escort over that ridge myself—and I can absolutely assure you that they're the sounds made by intelligent, educated people who first think they've gone insane, and who then realize it doesn't help to know that they haven't.

It was the only possible immediate reaction to the first sight of Minnie and Earl's.

What I saw, as we crested the top of that ridge, was this:

In the center of a typically barren lunar landscape, surrounded on all sides by impact craters, rocks, more rocks, and the suffocating emptiness of vacuum—

—a dark landscape, mind you, one imprisoned by lunar night, and illuminated only by the gibbous Earth hanging high above us—

—a rectangle of color and light, in the form of four acres of freshly watered, freshly mowed lawn.

With a house on it.

Not a prefab box of the kind we dropped all over the lunar landscape for storage and emergency air stops.

A house.

A clapboard family home, painted a homey yellow, with a wrap-around porch three steps off the ground, a canopy to keep off the Sun, a screen door leading inside and a bug-zapper over the threshold. There was a porch swing with cushions in a big yellow daisy pattern, and a wall of neatly-trimmed hedges around the house, obscuring the latticework that enclosed the crawlspace underneath. It was over-the-top middle American that even in that first moment I half-crazily expected the scent of lemonade to cross the vacuum and enter my suit. (That didn't happen, but lemonade was waiting.) The lawn was completely surrounded with a white picket fence with an open gate; there was even an old-fashioned mailbox at the gate, with its flag up. All of it was lit, from nowhere, like a bright summer afternoon. The house itself had two stories, plus a sloping shingled roof high enough to hide a respectable attic; as we drew closer I saw that there were pull-down shades, not venetian blinds, in the pane-glass windows. Closer still, and I spotted the golden retriever that lay on the porch, its head resting between muddy paws as it followed our approach; it was definitely a lazy dog, since it did not get up to investigate us, but it was also a friendly one, whose big red tail thumped against the porch in greeting. Closer still, and I made various consonant noises as a venerable old lady in gardening overalls came around the side of the house, spotted us, and broke into the kind of smile native only to contented old ladies seeing good friends or grandchildren after too long away. When my fellow astronauts all waved back, I almost followed their lead, but for some reason my arms wouldn't move.

Somewhere in there I murmured, "This is impossible."

"Clearly not," George said. "If it were impossible it wouldn't be happening. The more accurate word is inexplicable."

"What the hell is—"

"Come on, goofball." This from Carrie Aldrin No Relation. "You're acting like you never saw a house before."

Sometimes, knowing when to keep your mouth shut is the most eloquent expression of wisdom. I shut up.

It took about a million and a half years—or five minutes if you go by merely chronological time—for the tractor to descend the shallow slope and bring us to a stop some twenty meters from the front gate. By then an old man had joined the old woman at the fence. He was a lean old codger with bright blue eyes, a nose like a hawk, a smile that suggested he'd just heard a whopper of a joke, and the kind of forehead some very old men have—the kind that by all rights ought to have been glistening with sweat, like most bald heads, but instead seemed perpetually dry, in a way that suggested a sophisticated system for the redistribution of excess moisture. He had the leathery look of old men who had spent much of their lives working in the Sun. He wore neatly-pressed tan pants, sandals, and a white button-down shirt open at the collar, all of which was slightly loose on him—not enough to make him look comical or pathetic, but enough to suggest that he'd been a somewhat bigger man before age had diminished him, and was still used to buying the larger sizes. (That is, I thought, if there was any possibility of him finding a good place to shop around here.)

His wife, if that's who she was, was half a head shorter and slightly stouter; she had blue eyes and a bright smile, like him, but a soft and rounded face that provided a pleasant complement to his lean and angular one. She was a just overweight enough to provide her with the homey accoutrements of chubby cheeks and double chin; unlike her weathered, bone-dry husband, she was smooth-skinned and shiny-faced and very much a creature the Sun had left untouched (though she evidently spent time there; at least, she wore gardener's gloves, and carried a spade).

They were, in short, vaguely reminiscent of the old folks standing before the farmhouse in that famous old painting "American Gothic." You know the one I mean—the constipated old guy with the pitchfork next to the wife who seems mortified by his very presence? These two were those two after they cheered up enough to be worth meeting.

Except, of course, that this couldn't possibly be happening.

My colleagues unstrapped themselves, lowered the stairway, and disembarked. The tractor driver, whoever he was, emerged from its cab and joined them. George stayed with me, watching my every move, as I proved capable of climbing down a set of three steps without demonstrating my total incapacitation from shock. When my boots crunched lunar gravel—a texture I could feel right through the treads of my boots, and which served at that moment to reconnect me to ordinary physical reality—Carrie, Oscar, and Nikki patted me on the back, a gesture that felt like half-congratulation and, half-commiseration. The driver came by, too; I saw from the markings on his suit that he was Pete Rawlik, who was assigned to some kind of classified biochemical research in one of our outlabs; he had always been too busy to mix much, and I'd met him maybe twice by that point, but he still clapped my shoulder like an old friend. As for George, he made a wait gesture and went back up the steps.

In the thirty seconds we stood there waiting for him, I looked up at the picket fence, just to confirm that the impossible old couple was still there, and I saw that the golden retriever, which had joined its masters at the gate, was barking silently. That was good. If the sound had carried in vacuum, I might have been worried. That would have been just plain crazy.

Then George came back, carrying an airtight metal cylinder just about big enough to hold a soccer ball. I hadn't seen any vacuum boxes of that particular shape and size before, but any confusion I might have felt about that was just about the last thing I needed to worry about. He addressed the others: "How's he doing?"

A babble of noncommital OKs dueled for broadcast supremacy. Then the voices resolved into individuals.

Nikki Hollander said: "Well, at least he's not babbling anymore."

Oscar Desalvo snorted: "I attribute that to brain-lock."

"You weren't any better," said Carrie Aldrin No Relation. "Worse. If I recall correctly, you made a mess in your suit."

"I'm not claiming any position of false superiority, hon. Just giving my considered diagnosis."

"Whatever," said Pete Rawlik. "Let's just cross the fenceline, already. I have an itch."

"In a second," George said. His mirrored faceplate turned toward mine, aping eye-contact. "Max? You getting this?"

"Barely," I managed.

"Outstanding. You're doing fine. But I need you with me a hundred percent while I cover our most important ground rule. Namely—everything inside that picket fence is a temperature-climate, sea-level, terrestrial environment. You don't have to worry about air filtration, temperature levels, or anything else. It's totally safe to suit down, as long as you're inside the perimeter—and in a few minutes, we will all be doing just that. But once you're inside that enclosure, the picket fence itself marks the beginning of lunar vacuum, lunar temperatures, and everything that implies. You do not, repeat not, do anything to test the differential. Even sticking a finger out between the slats is enough to get you bounced from the program, with no possibility of reprieve. Is that clear?"

"Yes, but—"

"Rule Two," he said, handing me the sealed metal box. "You're the new guy. You carry the pie."

I regarded the cylinder. Pie?

I kept waiting for the other shoe to drop, but it never did.

The instant we passed through the front gate, the dead world this should have been surrendered to a living one. Sound returned between one step and the next. The welcoming cries of the two old people—and the barking of their friendly golden retriever dog—may have been muffled by my helmet, but they were still identifiable enough to present touches of personality. The old man's voice was gruff in a manner that implied a past flavored by whiskey and cigars, but there was also a sing-song quality to it, that instantly manifested itself as a tendency to end his sentences at higher registers. The old woman's voice was soft and breathy, with only the vaguest suggestion of an old-age quaver and a compensatory tinge of the purest Georgia Peach. The dog's barks were like little frenzied explosions, that might have been threatening if they hadn't all trailed off into quizzical whines. It was a symphony of various sounds that could be made for hello: laughs, cries, yips, and delighted shouts of *George! Oscar! Nikki! Carrie! Pete! So glad you could make it! How are you?*

It was enough to return me to statue mode. I didn't even move when the others disengaged their helmet locks, doffed their headgear, and began oohing and aahing themselves. I just spent the next couple of minutes watching, physically in their midst but mentally somewhere very far away, as the parade of impossibilities passed on by. I noted that Carrie Aldrin No Relation, who usually wore her long red hair beneath the tightest of protective nets, was today styled in pigtails with big pink bows; that Oscar, who was habitually scraggly-haired and two days into a beard, was today perfectly kempt and freshly shaven; that George giggled like a five-year-old when the dog stood up on its hind legs to slobber all over his face; and that Pete engaged with a little mock wrestling match with the old man that almost left him toppling backward onto the grass. I saw the women whisper to each other, then bound up the porch steps into the house, so excitedly that they reminded me of schoolgirls skipping off to the playground—a gait that should have been impossible to simulate in a bulky moonsuit, but which they pulled off with perfect flair. I saw Pete and Oscar follow along behind them, laughing at a shared joke.

I was totally ignored until the dog stood up on its hind legs to sniff at, then snort nasal condensation on, my faceplate. His ears went back. He whined, then scratched at his reflection, then looked over his shoulder at the rest of his pack, long pink tongue lolling plaintively. *Look, guys. There's somebody in this thing*.

I didn't know I was going to take the leap of faith until I actually placed the cake cylinder on the ground, then reached up and undid my helmet locks. The hiss of escaping air made my blood freeze in my chest; for a second I was absolutely certain that all of this was a hallucination brought on by oxygen deprivation, and that I'd just committed suicide by opening my suit to vacuum. But the hiss subsided, and I realized that it was just pressure equalization; the atmosphere in this environment must have been slightly less than that provided by the suit. A second later, as I removed my helmet, I tasted golden retriever breath as the dog leaned in close and said hello by licking me on the lips. I also smelled freshly mowed grass and the perfume of nearby flowers: I heard a bird not too far away go whoot-toot-toot-weet; and I felt direct sunlight on my face, even though the Sun itself was nowhere to be seen. The air itself was pleasantly warm, like summer before it gets obnoxious with heat and humidity.

"Miles!" the old man said. "Get down!"

The dog gave me one last lick for the road and sat down, gazing up at me with that species of tongue-lolling amusement known only to large canines.

The old woman clutched the elbow of George's suit. "Oh, you didn't tell me you were bringing somebody new this time! How wonderful!"

"What is this place?" I managed.

The old man raised his eyebrows. "It's our front yard, son. What does it look like?"

The old woman slapped his hand lightly. "Be nice, dear. You can see he's taking it hard."

He grunted. "Always did beat me how you can tell what a guy's thinking and feeling just by looking at him."

She patted his arm again. "It's not all that unusual, apricot. I'm a woman."

George ambled on over, pulling the two oldsters along. "All right, I'll get it started. Max Fischer, I want you to meet two of the best people on this world or any other—Minnie and Earl. Minnie and Earl, I want you to meet a guy who's not quite as hopeless as he probably seems on first impression—Max Fischer. You'll like him."

"I like him already," Minnie said. "I've yet to dislike anybody the dog took such an immediate shine to. Hi, Max."

"Hello," I said. After a moment: "Minnie. Earl."

"Wonderful to meet you, young man. Your friends have said so much about you."

"Thanks." Shock lent honesty to my response: "They've said absolutely nothing about you."

"They never do," she said, with infinite sadness, as George smirked at me over her back. She glanced down at the metal cylinder at my feet, and cooed: "Is that cake?"

Suddenly, absurdly, the first rule of family visits popped unbidden into my head, blaring its commandment in flaming letters twenty miles high: THOU SHALT NOT PUT THE CAKE YOU BROUGHT ON THE GROUND—ESPECIALLY NOT WHEN A DOG IS PRESENT. Never mind that the container was sealed against vacuum, and that the dog would have needed twenty minutes to get in with an industrial drill: the lessons of everyday American socialization still applied. I picked it up and handed it to her; she took it with her bare hands, reacting not at all to what hindsight later informed me should have been a painfully cold exterior. I said: "Sorry."

"It's pie," said George. "Deep-dish apple pie. Direct from my grandma's orchard."

"Oh, that's sweet of her. She still having those back problems?"

"She's getting on in years," George allowed. "But she says that soup of yours really helped."

"I'm glad," she said, her smile as sunny as the entire month of July. "Meanwhile, why don't you take your friend upstairs and get him out of that horrid suit? I'm sure he'll feel a lot better once he's had a chance to freshen up. Earl can have a drink set for him by the time you come down."

"I'll fix a Sea of Tranquility," Earl said, with enthusiasm.

"Maybe once he has his feet under him. A beer should be fine for now."

"All rightee," said Earl, with the kind of wink that established he knew quite well I was going to need something a lot more substantial than beer.

As for Minnie, she seized my hand, and said: "It'll be all right, apricot. Once you get past this stage, I'm sure we're all going to be great friends."

"Um," I replied, with perfect eloquence, wondering just what stage I was being expected to pass.

Sanity?

Dying inside, I did what seemed to be appropriate. I followed George through the front door (first stamping my moonboots on the mat, as he specified) and up the narrow, creaky wooden staircase.

You ever go to parties where the guests leave their coats in a heap on the bed of the master bedroom? Minnie and Earl's was like that. Except it wasn't a pile of coats, but a pile of disassembled moonsuits. There were actually two bedrooms upstairs—the women changed in the master bedroom that evidently belonged to the oldsters themselves, the men in a smaller room that felt like it belonged to a teenage boy. The wallpaper was a pattern of galloping horses, and the bookcases were filled with mint-edition paperback thrillers that must have been a hundred years old even then. (Or more: there was a complete collection of the hardcover Hardy Boys Mysteries, by Franklin W. Dixon.) The desk was a genuine antique rolltop, with a green blotter; no computer or hytex. The bed was just big enough to hold one gangly teenager, or three moonsuits disassembled into their component parts, with a special towel provided so our boots wouldn't get moon-dust all over the bedspread. By the time George and I got up there, Oscar and Pete had already changed into slacks, dress shoes with black socks, and button-down shirts with red bowties; Pete had even put some shiny gunk in his hair to slick it back. They winked at me as they left.

I didn't change, not immediately; nor did I speak, not even as George doffed his own moonsuit and jumpers in favor of a similarly earthbound outfit he blithely salvaged from the closet. The conviction that I was being tested, somehow, was so overwhelming that the interior of my suit must have been a puddle of flop sweat.

Then George said: "You going to be comfortable, dressed like that all night?"

I stirred. "Clothes?"

He pulled an outfit my size from the closet—tan pants, a blue short-sleeved button-down shirt, gleaming black shoes, and a red bowtie identical to the ones Oscar and Pete had donned. "No problem borrowing. Minnie keeps an ample supply. You don't like the selection, you want to pick something more your style, you can always have something snazzier sent up on the next supply drop. I promise you, she'll appreciate the extra effort. It makes her day when—"

"George," I said softly.

"Have trouble with bowties? No problem. They're optional. You can—"

"George," I said again, and this time my voice was a little louder, a little deeper, a little more *For Christ's Sake Shut Up I'm Sick Of This Shit.*

He batted his eyes, all innocence and naivete. "Yes, Max?"

My look, by contrast, must have been half-murderous. "Tell me."

"Tell you what?"

It was very hard not to yell. "You know what!"

He fingered an old issue of some garishly-colored turn-of-the-millennium science fiction magazine. "Oh. That mixed drink Earl mentioned. The Sea of Tranquility. It's his own invention, and he calls it that because your first sip is one small step for Man, and your second is one giant leap for Mankind. There's peppermint in it. Give it a try and I promise you you'll be on his good side for life. He—"

I squeezed the words through clenched teeth. "I. Don't. Care. About. The. Bloody. Drink."

"Then I'm afraid I don't see your problem."

"My problem," I said, slowly, and with carefully repressed frustration, "is that all of this is downright impossible."

"Apparently not," he noted.

"I want to know who these people are, and what they're doing here."

"They're Minnie and Earl, and they're having some friends over for dinner."

If I'd been five years old, I might have pouted and stamped my foot. (Sometimes, remembering, I think I did anyway.) "Dammit, George!"

He remained supernaturally calm. "No cursing in this house, Max. Minnie doesn't like it. She won't throw you out for doing it—she's too nice for that—but it does make her uncomfortable."

This is the point where I absolutely know I stamped my foot. "That makes *her* uncomfortable!?"

He put down the skiffy magazine. "Really. I don't see why you're having such a problem with this. They're just this great old couple who happen to live in a little country house on the Moon, and their favorite thing is getting together with friends, and we're here to have Sunday night dinner with them. Easy to understand . . . especially if you accept that it's all there is."

"That can't be all there is!" I cried, my exasperation reaching critical mass.

"Why not? Can't 'Just Because' qualify as a proper scientific theory?"

"No! It doesn't!—How come you never told me about this place before?"

"You never asked before." He adjusted his tie, glanced at the outfit laid out for me on the bed, and went to the door. "Don't worry; it didn't for me, either. Something close to an explanation is forthcoming. Just get dressed and come downstairs already. We don't want the folks to think you're antisocial . . ."

I'd been exasperated, way back then, because Minnie and Earl were there and had no right to be. I was exasperated now because the more I looked the more impossible it became to find any indication that they'd ever been there at all.

I had started looking for them, if only in a desultory, abstracted way, shortly after Claire died. She'd been the only person on Earth who had ever believed my stories about them. Even now, I think it's a small miracle that she did. I had told her the story of Minnie and Earl before we even became man and wife—sometime after I knew I was going to propose, but before I found the right time and place for the question. I was just back from a couple of years of Outer-System work, had grown weary of the life, and had met this spectac-ularly kind and funny and beautiful person whose interests were all on Earth, and who had no real desire to go out into space herself. That was just fine with me. It was what I wanted too. And of course I rarely talked to her about my years in space, because I didn't want to become an old bore with a suitcase full of old stories. Even so, I still knew, at the beginning, that knowing about a real-life miracle and not mentioning it to her, ever, just because she was not likely to believe me, was tantamount to cheating. So I sat her down one day, even before the proposal, and told her about Minnie and Earl. And she be-lieved me. She didn't humor me. She didn't just say she believed me. She didn't just believe me to be nice. She believed me. She said she always knew when I was shoveling manure and when I was not—a boast that turned out to be an integral strength of our marriage—and that it was impossible for her to hear me tell the story without knowing that Minnie and Earl were real. She said that if we had children I would have to tell the story to them, too, to pass it on.

That was one of the special things about Claire: she had faith when faith was needed.

But our son and our daughter, and later the grandkids, outgrew believing me. For them, Minnie and Earl were whimsical space-age versions of Santa.

I didn't mind that, not really.

But when she died, finding Minnie and Earl again seemed very important.

It wasn't just that their house was gone, or that Minnie and Earl seemed to have departed for regions unknown; and it wasn't just that the official his-tories of the early development teams now completely omitted any mention of the secret hoarded by everybody who had ever spent time on the Moon in those days. It wasn't just that the classified files I had read and eventually contributed to had disappeared, flushed down the same hole that sends all embarrassing government secrets down the pipe to their final resting place in the sea. But for more years than I'd ever wanted to count, Minnie and Earl had been the secret history nobody ever talked about. I had spoken to those of my old colleagues who still remained alive, and they had all said, what are you talking about, what do you mean, are you feeling all right, nothing like that ever happened.

It was tempting to believe that my kids were right: that it had been a fairy tale: a little harmless personal fantasy I'd been carrying around with me for most of my life.

But I knew it wasn't.

Because Claire had believed me.

Because whenever I did drag out the old stories one more time, she always said, "I wish I'd known them." Not like an indulgent wife allowing the old man his delusions, but like a woman well acquainted with miracles. And because even if I was getting too old to always trust my own judgement, nothing would ever make me doubt hers.

I searched with phone calls, with letters, with hytex research, with the calling-in of old favors, with every tool available to me. I found nothing.

And then one day I was told that I didn't have much more time to look. It wasn't a tragedy; I'd lived a long and happy life. And it wasn't as bad as it could have been; I'd been assured that there wouldn't be much pain. But I did have that one little unresolved question still hanging over my head.

That was the day I overcame decades of resistance and booked return passage to the world I had once helped to build.

The day after I spoke to Janine Seuss, I followed her advice and took a commuter tram to the Michael Collins Museum of Early Lunar Settlement. It was a popular tourist spot with all the tableaus and reenactments and, you should only excuse the expression, cheesy souvenirs you'd expect from such an establishment; I'd avoided it up until now mostly because I'd seen and heard most of it before, and much of what was left was the kind of crowd-pleasing foofaraw that tames and diminishes the actual experience I lived through for the consumption of folks who are primarily interested in tiring out their hyperactive kids. The dumbest of those was a pile of real Earth rocks, replacing the weight various early astronauts had taken from the Moon; ha ha ha, stop, I'm dying here. The most offensive was a kids' exhibit narrated by a cartoon-character early development engineer; he spoke with a cornball rural accent, had comic-opera patches on the knees of his moonsuit, and seemed to have an I.Q. of about five.

Another annoying thing about frontiers: when they're not frontiers anymore, the civilizations that move in like to think that the people who came first were stupid.

But when I found pictures of myself, in an exhibit on the development programs, and pointed them out to an attendant, it was fairly easy to talk the curators into letting me into their archives for a look at certain other materials that hadn't seen the light of day for almost twenty years. They were taped interviews, thirty years old now, with a number of the old guys and gals, talking about their experiences in the days of early development: the majority of those had been conducted here on the Moon, but others had taken place on Earth or Mars or wherever else any of those old farts ended up. I felt vaguely insulted that they hadn't tried to contact me; maybe they had, and my wife, anticipating my reluctance, had turned them away. I wondered if I should have felt annoyed by that. I wondered too if my annoyance at the taming of the Moon had something to do with the disquieting sensation of becoming ancient history while you're still alive to remember it.

There were about ten thousand hours of interviews; even if my health remained stable long enough for me to listen to them all, my savings would run out far sooner. But they were indexed, and audio-search is a wonderful thing. I typed in "Minnie" and got several dozen references to small things, almost as many references to Mickey's rodent girlfriend, and a bunch of stories about a project engineer, from after my time, who had also been blessed with that particular first name. (To believe the transcripts, she spent all her waking hours saying impossibly cute things that her friends and colleagues would remember and be compelled to repeat decades later; what a bloody pixie.) I typed in "Earl" and, though it felt silly, "Miles", and got a similar collection of irrelevancies—many references to miles, thus proving conclusively that as recently as thirty years ago the adoption of the metric system hadn't yet succeeded in wiping out any less elegant but still fondly remembered forms of measurement. After that, temporarily stuck, I typed in my own name, first and last, and was rewarded with a fine selection of embarrassing anecdotes from folks who recalled what a humorless little pissant I had been way back then. All of this took hours; I had to listen to each of these references, if only for a second or two, just to know for sure what was being talked about, and I confess that, in between a number of bathroom breaks I would have considered unlikely as a younger man, I more than once forgot what I was supposedly looking for long enough to enjoy a few moments with old voices I hadn't heard for longer than most lunar residents had been alive.

I then cross-referenced by the names of the various people who were along on that first Sunday night trip to Minnie and Earl's. "George Peterson" got me nothing of obvious value. "Carrie Aldrin" and "Peter Rawlik", ditto. Nor did the other names. There were references, but nothing I particularly needed.

Feeling tired, I sat there drumming my fingertips on the tabletop. The museum was closing soon. The research had exhausted my limited stores of strength; I didn't think I could do this many days in a row. But I knew there was something here. There had to be. Even if there was a conspiracy of silence—organized or accidental—the mere existence of that unassuming little house had left too great a footprint on our lives.

I thought about details that Claire had found particularly affecting.

And then I typed "Yams".

Seventy years ago, suffering from a truly epic sense of dislocation that made everything happening to me seem like bits of stage business performed by actors in a play whose author had taken care to omit all the important exposition, I descended a creaky flight of wooden stairs, to join my colleagues in Minnie and Earl's living room. I was the last to come down, of course;

everybody else was already gathered around the three flowery-print sofas, munching on finger foods as they chatted up a storm. The women were in soft cottony dresses, the men in starched trousers and button-downs. They all clapped and cheered as I made my appearance, a reaction that brought an unwelcome blush to my cheeks. It was no wonder; I was a little withdrawn to begin with, back then, and the impossible context had me so off-center that all my defenses had turned to powder.

It was a homey place, though: brightly lit, with a burning fireplace, an array of glass shelving covered with a selection of homemade pottery, plants and flowers in every available nook, an upright piano, a bar that did not dominate the room, and an array of framed photographs on the wall behind the couch. There was no TV or hytex. I glanced at the photographs and moved toward them, hungry for data.

Then Earl rose from his easy chair and came around the coffee table, with a gruff, "Plenty of time to look around, son. Let me take care of you."

"That's—" I said. I was still not managing complete sentences, most of the time.

He took me by the arm, brought me over to the bar, and sat me down on a stool. "Like I said, plenty of time. You're like most first-timers, you're probably in dire need of a drink. We can take care of that first and then get acquainted." He moved around the bar, slung a towel over his shoulder, and said: "What'll it be, pilgrim?"

Thank God I recognized the reference. If I hadn't—if it had just been another inexplicable element of a day already crammed with them—my head would have exploded from the effort of figuring out why I was being called a pilgrim. "A . . . Sea of Tranquility?"

"Man after my own heart," Earl said, flashing a grin as he compiled an impressive array of ingredients in a blender. "Always drink the local drink, son. As my daddy put it, there's no point in going anywhere if you just get drunk the same way you can at home. Which is where, by the way?"

I said, "What?"

"You missed the segue. I was asking you where you were from."

It seemed a perfect opportunity. "You first."

He chuckled. "Oh, the wife and I been here long enough, you might as well say we're from here. Great place to retire, isn't it? The old big blue marble hanging up there all day and all night?"

"I suppose," I said.

"You suppose," he said, raising an eyebrow at the concoction taking shape in his blender. "That's awful noncommittal of you. Can't you even admit to liking the view?"

"I admit to it," I said.

"But you're not enthused. You know, there's an old joke about a fella from New York and a fella from New Jersey. And the fella from New York is always bragging on his town, talking about Broadway, and the Empire State Building, and Central Park, and so on, and just as often saying terrible things about how ugly things are on the Jersey side of the river. And the fella from Jersey finally gets fed up, and says, all right, I've had enough of this, I want you to say one thing, just one thing, about New Jersey that's better than anything you can say about Manhattan. And the fella from New York says, No problem. The view."

I didn't laugh, but I did smile.

"That's what's so great about this place," he concluded. "The view. Moon's pretty nice to look at for folks on Earth—and a godsend for bad poets, too, what with june-moon-spoon and all—but as views go, it can't hold a candle to the one we have, looking back. So don't give me any supposes. Own up to what you think."

"It's a great view," I said, this time with conviction, as he handed me my drink. Then I asked the big question another way: "How did you arrange it?"

"You ought to know better than that, son. We didn't arrange it. We just took advantage of it. Nothing like a scenic overlook to give zip to your real estate—So answer me. Where are you from?"

Acutely aware that more than a minute had passed since I'd asked him the same question, and that no answer seemed to be forthcoming, I was also too trapped by simple courtesy to press the issue. "San Francisco."

He whistled. "I've seen pictures of San Francisco. Looks like a beautiful town."

"It is," I said.

"You actually climb those hills in Earth gravity?"

"I used to run up Leavenworth every morning at dawn."

"Leavenworth's the big steep one that heads down to the bay?"

"One of them," I said.

"And you ran up that hill? At dawn? Every day?"

"Yup."

"You have a really obsessive personality, don't you, son?"

I shrugged. "About some things, I suppose."

"Only about some things?"

"That's what being obsessive means, right?"

"Ah, well. Nothing wrong about being obsessive, as long as you're not a fanatic about it. Want me to freshen up that drink?"

I felt absolutely no alcoholic effect at all. "Maybe you better."

I tried to turn the conversation back to where he was from, but somehow I didn't get a chance, because that's when Minnie took me by the hand and dragged me over to the wall of family photos. There were pictures of them smiling on the couch, pictures of them lounging together in the backyard, pictures of them standing proudly before their home. There were a large number of photos that used Earth as a backdrop. Only four photos showed them with other people, all from the last century: in one, they sat at their dining table with a surprised-looking Neil Armstrong and Buzz Aldrin; in another, they sat on their porch swing chatting with Carl Sagan; in a third, Minnie was being enthusiastically hugged by Isaac Asimov; the fourth showed Earl playing the upright piano while Minnie sat beside him and a tall, thin blonde man with androgynous features and two differently-colored eyes serenaded them both. The last figure was the only one I didn't recognize immediately; by the time somebody finally clued me in, several visits later, I would be far too jaded to engage in the spit-take it would have merited any other time.

I wanted to ask Minnie about the photos with the people I recognized, but then Peter and Earl dragged me downstairs to take a look at Earl's model train set, a rural landscape incorporating four lines and six separate small towns. It was a remarkably detailed piece of work, but I was most impressed with the small miracle of engineering that induced four heavy chains to pull it out of the way whenever Earl pulled a small cord. This handily revealed the pool table. Earl whipped Peter two games out of three, then challenged me; I'm fairly good at pool, but I was understandably off my game that afternoon, and missed every single shot. When Carrie Aldrin No Relation came down to challenge Earl, he mimed terror. It was a genial hour, totally devoted to content-free conversation—and any attempt I made to bring up the questions that burned in my breast was terminated without apparent malice.

Back upstairs. The dog nosing at my hand. Minnie noting that he liked me. Minnie not saying anything about the son whose room we'd changed in, the one who'd died "in the war". A very real heartbreak about the way her eyes grew distant at that moment. I asked which war, and she smiled sadly: "There's only been one war, dear—and it doesn't really matter what you call it." Nikki patting her hand. Oscar telling a mildly funny anecdote from his childhood, Minnie asking him to tell her the one about the next-door neighbors again. I brought up the photo of Minnie and Earl with Neil Armstrong and Buzz Aldrin, and Minnie clucked that they had been such nice boys.

Paranoia hit. "Ever hear of Ray Bradbury?"

She smiled with real affection. "Oh, yes. We only met him once or twice, but he was genuinely sweet. I miss him."

"So you met him, too."

"We've met a lot of people, apricot. Why? Is he a relation?"

"Just an old-time writer I like," I said.

"Ahhhhhh."

"In fact," I said, "one story of his I particularly like was called 'Mars Is Heaven'."

She sipped her tea. "Don't know that one."

"It's about a manned expedition to Mars—written while that was still in the future, you understand. And when the astronauts get there they discover a charming, rustic, old-fashioned American small town, filled with sweet old folks they remember from their childhoods. It's the last thing they expect, but after a while they grow comfortable with it. They even jump to the conclusion that Mars is the site of the afterlife. Except it's not. The sweet old folks are aliens in disguise, and they're lulling all these gullible earthlings into a false sense of security so they can be killed at leisure."

My words had been hesitantly spoken, less out of concern for Minnie's feelings than those of my colleagues. Their faces were blank, unreadable, masking emotions that could have been anything from anger to amusement. I will admit that for a split second there, my paranoia reaching heights it had never known before (or thank God, since), I half-expected George and Oscar and Maxine to morph into the hideously tentacled bug-eyed monsters who had taken their places immediately after eating their brains. Then the moment passed, and the silence continued to hang heavily in the room, and any genuine apprehension I might have felt gave way to an embarrassment of more mundane proportions. After all—whatever the explanation for all this might have been—I'd just been unforgivably rude to a person who had only been gracious and charming toward me.

She showed no anger, no sign that she took it personally. "I remember that one now, honey. I'm afraid I didn't like it as much as some of Ray's other efforts. Among other things, it seemed pretty unreasonable to me that critters advanced enough to pull off that kind of masquerade would have nothing better to do with their lives than eat nice folks who came calling. But then, he also wrote a story about a baby that starts killing as soon as it leaves the womb, and I prefer to believe that infants, given sufficient understanding and affection, soon learn that the universe outside the womb isn't that dark and cold a place after all. Given half a chance, they might even grow up . . . and it's a wonderful process to watch."

I had nothing to say to that.

She sipped her tea again, one pinky finger extended in the most unself-conscious manner imaginable, just as if she couldn't fathom drinking her tea any other way, then spoke brightly, with perfect timing: "But if you stay the night, I'll be sure to put you in the room with all the pods."

There was a moment of silence, with every face in the room—including those of Earl and Peter and Carrie, who had just come up from downstairs—as distinguishedly impassive as a granite bust of some forefather you had never heard of.

Then I averted my eyes, trying to hide the smile as it began to spread on my face.

Then somebody made a helpless noise, and we all exploded with laughter.

Seventy years later:

If every land ever settled by human beings has its garden spots, then every land ever settled by human beings has its hovels. This is true even of frontiers that have become theme parks. I had spent much of this return to the world I had once known wandering through a brightly-lit, comfortably-upholstered tourist paradise—the kind of ersatz environment common to all overdeveloped places, that is less an expression of local character than a determined struggle to ensure the total eradication of anything resembling local character. But now I was headed toward a place that would never be printed on a postcard, that would never be on the tours, that existed on tourist maps only as the first, best sign that those looking for easy travelling have just made a disastrous wrong turn.

It was on Farside, of course. Most tourist destinations, and higher-end habitats, are on Nearside, which comes equipped with a nice blue planet to look at. Granted that even on Nearside the view is considered a thing for tourists, and that most folks who live here live underground and like to brag to each other about how long they've gone without Earthgazing—our ancestral ties are still part of us, and the mere presence of Earth, seen or unseen, is so inherently comforting that most normal people with a choice pick Nearside. Farside, by comparison, caters almost exclusively to hazardous industries and folks who don't want that nice blue planet messing up the stark emptiness of their sky—a select group of people that includes a small number of astronomers at the Frank Drake Observatory, and a large number of assorted perverts and geeks and misanthropes. The wild frontier of the fantasies comes closest to being a reality here—the hemisphere has some heavy-industry settlements that advertise their crime rates as a matter of civic pride.

And then there are the haunts of those who find even those places too civilized for their tastes. The mountains and craters of Farside are dotted with the little boxy single-person habitats of folks who have turned their back not only on the home planet but also the rest of humanity as well. Some of those huddle inside their self-imposed solitary confinement for weeks or months on end, emerging only to retrieve their supply drops or enforce the warning their radios transmit on infinite loop: that they don't want visitors and that all trespassers should expect to be shot. They're all eccentric, but some are crazy and a significant percentage of them are clinically insane. They're not the kind of folks the sane visit just for local color.

I landed my rented skimmer on a ridge overlooking an oblong metal box with a roof marked by a glowing ten-digit registration number. It was night here, and nobody who lived in such a glorified house trailer would have been considerate enough to provide any outside lighting for visitors, so those lit digits provided the only ground-level rebuttal to starfield up above; it was an inadequate rebuttal at best, which left the ground on all sides an ocean of undifferentiated inky blackness. I could carry my own lamp, of course, but I didn't want to negotiate the walk from my skimmer to the habitat's front door if the reception I met there required a hasty retreat; I wasn't very capable of hasty retreats, these days.

So I just sat in my skimmer and transmitted the repeating loop: *Walter Stearns. I desperately need to speak to Walter Stearns. Walter Stearns. I desperately need to speak to Walter Stearns. Walter Stearns. I desperately need to speak to Walter Stearns. Walter Stearns. I desperately need to speak to Walter Stearns.* It was the emergency frequency that all of these live-alones are required to keep open 24-7, but there was no guarantee Stearns was listening—and since I was not in distress, I was not really legally entitled to use it. But I didn't care; Stearns was the best lead I had yet.

It was only two hours before a voice like a mouth full of steel wool finally responded: "Go away."

"I won't be long, Mr. Stearns. We need to talk."

"You need to talk. I need you to go away."

"It's about Minnie and Earl, Mr. Stearns."

There was a pause. "Who?"

The pause had seemed a hair too long to mean mere puzzlement. "Minnie and Earl. From the development days. You remember them, don't you?"

"I never knew any Minnie and Earl," he said. "Go away."

"I listened to the tapes you made for the Museum, Mr. Stearns."

The anger in his hoarse, dusty old voice was still building. "I made those tapes when I was still talking to people. And there's nothing in them about any Minnie or Earl."

"No," I said, "there's not. Nobody mentioned Minnie and Earl by name, not you, and not anybody else who participated. But you still remember them. It took me several days to track you down, Mr. Stearns. We weren't here at the same time, but we still had Minnie and Earl in common."

"I have nothing to say to you," he said, with a new shrillness in his voice. "I'm an old man. I don't want to be bothered. Go away."

My cheeks ached from the size of my triumphant grin. "I brought yams."

There was nothing on the other end but the sibilant hiss of background radiation. It lasted just long enough to persuade me that my trump card had been nothing of the kind; he had shut down or smashed his receiver, or simply turned his back to it, so he could sit there in his little cage waiting for the big bad outsider to get tired and leave.

Then he said: "Yams."

Twenty-four percent of the people who contributed to the Museum's oral history had mentioned yams at least once. They had talked about the processing of basic food shipments from home, and slipped yams into their lists of the kind of items received; they had conversely cited yams as the kind of food that the folks back home had never once thought of sending; they had related anecdotes about funny things this coworker or that coworker had said at dinner, over a nice steaming plate of yams. They had mentioned yams and they had moved on, behaving as if it was just another background detail mentioned only to provide their colorful reminiscences the right degree of persuasive verisimilitude. Anybody not from those days who noticed the strange recurring theme might have imagined it a statistical oddity or an in-joke of some kind. For anybody who had been to Minnie and Earl's—and tasted the delicately seasoned yams she served so frequently—it was something more: a strange form of confirmation.

When Stearns spoke again, his voice still rasped of disuse, but it also possessed a light quality that hadn't been there before. "They've been gone a long time. I'm not sure I know what to tell you."

"I checked your records," I said. "You've been on the Moon continuously since those days; you went straight from the development teams to the early settlements to the colonies that followed. You've probably been here nonstop longer than anybody else living or dead. If anybody can give me an idea what happened to them, it's you."

More silence.

"Please," I said.

And then he muttered a cuss word that had passed out of the vernacular forty years earlier. "All right, damn you. But you won't find them. I don't think anybody will ever find them."

Seventy years earlier:

We were there for about two more hours before George took me aside, said he needed to speak to me in private, and directed me to wait for him in the backyard.

The backyard was nice.

I've always hated that word. *Nice*. It means nothing. Describing people, it can mean the most distant politeness, or the most compassionate warmth; it can mean civility and it can mean charity and it can mean grace and it can mean friendship. Those things may be similar, but they're not synonyms; when the same word is used to describe all of them, then that word means nothing. It means even less when describing places. So what if the backyard was nice? Was it just comfortable, and well-tended, or was it a place that re-invigorated you with every breath? How can you leave it at "nice" and possibly imagine that you've done the job?

Nice. Feh.

But that's exactly what this backyard was.

It was a couple of acres of trimmed green lawn, bordered by the white picket fence that signalled the beginning of vacuum. A quarter-circle of bright red roses marked each of the two rear corners; between them, bees hovered lazily over a semicircular garden heavy on towering orchids and sun-flowers. The painted white rocks which bordered that garden were arranged in a perfect line, none of them even a millimeter out of place, none of them irregular enough to shame the conformity that characterized the relationship between all the others. There was a single apple tree, which hugged the rear of the house so tightly that the occupants of the second floor might have been able to reach out their windows and grab their breakfast before they trudged off to the shower; there were enough fallen green apples to look picturesque, but not enough to look sloppy. There was a bench of multicolored polished stone at the base of the porch steps, duplicating the porch swing up above but somehow absolutely right in its position; and as I sat on that bench facing the nice backyard I breathed deep and I smelled things that I had almost for-gotten I could smell—not just the distant charcoal reek of neighbors burning hamburgers in their own backyards, but lilacs, freshly cut grass, horse scent, and a cleansing whiff of rain. I sat there and I spotted squirrels, humming-birds, monarch butterflies, and a belled calico cat that ran by, stopped, saw me, looked terribly confused in the way cats have, and then went on. I sat there and I breathed and after months of inhaling foot odor and antiseptics I found myself getting a buzz. It was intoxicating. It was invigorating. It was a shot of pure energy. It was joy. God help me, it was nice.

But it was also surrounded on all sides by a pitiless vacuum that, if real physics meant anything, should have claimed it in an instant. Perhaps it shouldn't have bothered me that much, by then; but it did.

The screen door slammed. Miles the dog bounded down the porch steps and, panting furiously, nudged my folded hands. I scratched him under the ears. He gave me the usual unconditional adoration of the golden retriever—I petted him, therefore I was God. Most panting dogs look like they're smiling (it's a major reason humans react so strongly to the species), but Miles, the canine slave to context, looked like he was enjoying the grand joke that everybody was playing at my expense. Maybe he was. Maybe he wasn't even really a dog . . .

The screen door opened and slammed. This time it was George, carrying a couple of tall glasses filled with pink stuff and ice. He handed me one of the glasses; it was lemonade, of course. He sipped from the other one and said: "Minnie's cooking yams again. She's a miracle worker when it comes to yams. She does something with them, I don't know, but it's really—"

"You," I said wryly, "are enjoying this way too much."

"Aren't you?" he asked.

Miles the dog stared at the lemonade as if it was the most wondrous sight in the Universe. George dipped a finger into his drink and held it out so the mutt could have a taste. Miles adored him now. I was so off-center I almost felt betrayed. "Yeah. I guess I am. I like them."

"Pretty hard not to like them. They're nice people."

"But the situation is so insane—"

"Sanity," George said, "is a fluid concept. Think about how nuts Relativity sounded, the first time somebody explained it to you. Hell, think back to when you were a kid, and somebody first explained the mechanics of sex."

"George—"

He gave Miles another taste. "I can see you trying like mad to work this out. Compiling data, forming and rejecting theories, even concocting little experiments to test the accuracy of your senses. I know because I was once in your position, when I was brought out here for the first time, and I remember doing all the same things. But I now have a lot of experience in walking people through this, and I can probably save you a great deal of time and energy by completing your data and summarizing all of your likely theories."

I was too tired to glare at him anymore. "You can skip the data and theories and move on to the explanation. I promise you I won't mind."

"Yes, you would," he said, with absolute certainty. "Trust me, dealing with the established lines of inquiry is the only real way to get there.

"First, providing the raw data. One: This little homestead cannot be detected from Earth; our most powerful telescopes see nothing but dead moonscape here. Two: It, and the two old folks, have been here since at least Apollo; those photos of them with Armstrong and Aldrin are genuine. Three: There is nothing you can ask them that will get any kind of straight answer about who or what they are and why they're here. Four: We have no idea how they knew Asimov, Sagan, or Bradbury—but I promise you that those are not the most startling names you will hear them drop if you stick around long enough to get to know them. Five: We don't know how they maintain an earth-like environment in here. Six: About that mailbox—they do get delivery, on a daily basis, though no actual mailman has ever been detected, and none of the mail we've ever managed to sneak a peek at is the slightest bit interesting. It's all senior citizen magazines and grocery store circulars. Seven: They never seem to go shopping, but they always have an ample supply of food and other provisions. Eight (I am up to eight, right?): They haven't noticeably aged, not even the dog. Nine: They do understand every language we've sprung on them, but they give all their answers in Midwestern-American English. And ten: We have a group of folks from our project coming out here to visit just about every night of the week, on a rotating schedule that works out to just about once a week for each of us.

"So much for the raw data. The theories take longer to deal with. Let me go through all the ones you're likely to formulate." He peeled back a finger. "One: This is all just a practical joke perpetrated by your friends and colleagues in an all-out attempt to shock you out of your funk. We put it all together with spit and baling wire and some kind of elaborate special-effects trickery that's going to seem ridiculously obvious just as soon as you're done figuring it out. We went to all this effort, and spent the many billions of dollars it would have cost to get all these construction materials here, and developed entirely new technologies capable of holding in an atmosphere, and put it all together while you weren't looking, and along the way brought in a couple of convincing old folks from Central Casting, just so we could enjoy the look on your face. What a zany bunch of folks we are, huh?"

I felt myself blushing. "I'd considered that."

"And why not? It's a legitimate theory. Also a ridiculous one, but let's move on." He peeled back another finger. "Two: This is not a practical joke, but a test or psychological experiment of some kind, arranged by the brain boys back home. They put together all of this trickery, just to see how the average astronaut, isolated from home and normal societal context, reacts to situations that defy easy explanation and cannot be foreseen by even the most exhaustively-planned training. This particular explanation works especially well if you also factor in what we cleverly call the McGoohan Corollary—that is, the idea that we're not really on the Moon at all, but somewhere on Earth, possibly underground, where the real practical difficulty would lie in simulating not a quaint rural setting on a warm summer day, but instead the low-g, high-radiation, temperature-extreme vacuum that you gullibly believed you were walking around in, every single time you suited up. This theory is, of course, equally ridiculous, for many reasons—but we did have one guy about a year ago who stubbornly held on to it for almost a full week. Something about his psychological makeup just made it easier for him to accept that, over all the others, and we had to keep a close watch on him to stop him from trying to prove it with a nice unsuited walk. But from the way you're looking at me right now I don't think we're going to have the same problem with you. So.

"Assuming that this is not a joke, or a trick, or an experiment, or some lame phenomenon like that, that this situation you're experiencing is precisely what we have represented to you, then we are definitely looking at something beyond all terrestrial experience. Which brings us to Three." He peeled back another finger. "This is a first-contact situation. Minnie and Earl, and possibly Miles here, are aliens in disguise, or simulations constructed by aliens. They have created a friendly environment inside this picket fence, using technology we can only guess at—let's say an invisible bubble capable of filtering out radiation and retaining a breathable atmosphere while remaining permeable to confused bipeds in big clumsy moonsuits. And they have done so—why? To hide their true nature while they observe our progress? Possibly. But if so, it would be a lot more subtle to place their little farmhouse in Kansas, where it wouldn't seem so crazily out of place. To communicate us in terms we can accept? Possibly—except that couching those terms in such an insane context seems as counterproductive to genuine communication as their apparent decision to limit the substance of that communication to geriatric small talk. To make us comfortable with something familiar? Possibly—except that this kind of small mid-American home is familiar to only a small fraction of humanity, and it seems downright exotic to the many observers we've shuttled in from China, or India, or Saudi Arabia, or for that matter Manhattan. To present us with a puzzle that we have to solve? Again, possibly—but since Minnie and Earl and Miles won't confirm or deny, it's also a possibility we won't be able to test unless somebody like yourself actually does come up with the great big magic epiphany. I'm not holding my breath. But I do reject any theory that they're hostile, including the "Mars Is Heaven" theory you already cited. Anybody capable of pulling this off must have resources that could mash us flat in the time it takes to sneeze."

Miles woofed. In context it seemed vaguely threatening.

"Four." Another finger. "Minnie and Earl are actually human, and Miles is actually canine. They come here from the future, or from an alternate universe, or from some previously-unknown subset of humanity that's been living among us all this time, hiding great and unfathomable powers that, blaaah blaah blaah, fill in the blank. And they're here, making their presence known—why? All the same subtheories that applied to alien visitors also apply to human agencies, and all the same objections as well. Nothing explains why they would deliberately couch such a maddening enigma in such, for lack of a more appropriate word, banal terms. It's a little like coming face to face with God and discovering that He really does look like an bearded old white guy in a robe; He might, for all I know, but I'm more religious than you probably think, and there's some part of me that absolutely refuses to believe it. He, or She, if you prefer, could do better than that. And so could anybody, human or alien, whose main purpose in coming here is to study us, or test us, or put on a show for us.

"You still with me?" he inquired.

"Go on," I growled. "I'll let you know if you leave anything out."

He peeled back another finger. "Five: I kind of like this one—Minnie and Earl, and by extension Miles, are not creatures of advanced technology, but of a completely different kind of natural phenomenon—let's say, for the sake of argument, a bizarre jog in the space-time continuum that allows a friendly but otherwise unremarkable couple living in Kansas or Wyoming or someplace like that to continue experiencing life down on the farm while in some way as miraculous to them as it seems to us, projecting an interactive version of themselves to this otherwise barren spot on the Moon. Since, as your little conversation with Earl established, they clearly know they're on the Moon, we would have to accept that they're unflappable enough to take this phenomenon at face value, but I've known enough Midwesterners to know that this is a genuine possibility.

"Six." Starting now on another hand. "Mentioned only so you can be assured I'm providing you an exhaustive list—a phenomenon one of your predecessors called the Law of Preservation of Home. He theorized that whenever human beings penetrate too far past their own natural habitat, into places sufficiently inhospitable to life, the Universe is forced to spontaneously generate something a little more congenial to compensate—the equivalent, I suppose, of magically whomping up a Holiday Inn with a swimming pool, to greet explorers lost in the coldest reaches of Antarctica. He even said that the only reason we hadn't ever received reliable reports of this phenomenon on Earth is that we weren't ever sufficiently far from our natural habitat to activate it . . . but I can tell from the look on your face that you don't exactly buy this one either, so I'll set it aside and let you read the paper he wrote on the subject at your leisure."

"I don't think I will," I said.

"You ought to. It's a real hoot. But if you want to, I'll skip all the way to the end of the list, to the only explanation that ultimately makes any sense. Ready?"

"I'm waiting."

"All right. That explanation is—" he paused dramatically "—it doesn't matter."

There was a moment of pregnant silence.

I didn't explode; I was too shell-shocked to explode. Instead, I just said: "I sat through half a dozen bullshit theories for 'It doesn't matter'?"

"You had to, Max; it's the only way to get there. You had to learn the hard way that all of these propositions are either completely impossible or, for the time being, completely impossible to test—and we know this because the best minds on Earth have been working on the problem for as long as there's been a sustained human presence on the Moon. We've taken hair samples from Minnie's hairbrush. We've smuggled out stool samples from the dog. We've recorded our conversations with the old folks and studied every second of every tape from every possible angle. We've monitored the house for years on end, analyzed samples of the food and drink served in there, and exhaustively charted the health of everybody to go in or out. And all it's ever gotten us, in all these years of being frantic about it, is this—that as far as we can determine, Minnie and Earl are just a couple of friendly old folks who like having visitors."

"And that's it?"

"Why can't it be? Whether aliens, time travellers, displaced human beings, or natural phenomena—they're good listeners, and fine people, and they sure serve a good Sunday dinner. And if there must be things in the Universe we can't understand—well, then, it's sure comforting to know that some of them just want to be good neighbors. That's what I mean by saying, It doesn't matter."

He stood up, stretched, took the kind of deep breath people only indulge in when they're truly luxuriating in the freshness of the air around them, and said: "Minnie and Earl expect some of the new folks to be a little pokey, getting used to the idea. They won't mind if you stay out here and smell the roses a while. Maybe when you come in, we'll talk a little more 'bout getting you scheduled for regular visitation. Minnie's already asked me about it—she seems to like you. God knows why." He winked, shot me in the chest with a pair of pretend six-shooters made from the index fingers of both hands, and went back inside, taking the dog with him. And I was alone in the nice backyard, serenaded by birdsong as I tried to decide how to reconcile my own rational hunger for explanations with the unquestioning acceptance that was being required of me.

Eventually, I came to the same conclusion George had; the only conclusion that was possible under the circumstances. It was a genuine phenomenon, that conclusion: a community of skeptics and rationalists and followers of the scientific method deciding that there were some things Man was having too good a time to know. Coming to think of Minnie and Earl as family didn't take much longer than that. For the next three years, until I left for my new job in the outer system, I went out to their place at least once, sometimes twice a week; I shot pool with Earl and chatted about relatives back home with Minnie; I'd tussled with Miles and helped with the dishes and joined them for long all-nighters talking about nothing in particular. I learned how to bake with the limited facilities we had at Base, so I could bring my own cookies to her feasts. I came to revel in standing on a creaky front porch beneath a bug lamp, sipping grape juice as I joined Minnie in yet another awful rendition of "Anatevka." Occasionally I glanced at the big blue cradle of civilization hanging in the sky, remembered for the fiftieth or sixtieth or one hundredth time that none of this had any right to be happening, and reminded myself for the fiftieth or sixtieth or one hundredth time that the only sane response was to continue carrying the tune. I came to think of Minnie and Earl as the real reason we were on the Moon, and I came to understand one of the major reasons we were all so bloody careful to keep it a secret—because the needy masses of Earth, who were at that point still agitating about all the time and money spent on the space program, would not have been mollified by the knowledge that all those billions were being spent, in part, so that a few of the best and the brightest could indulge themselves in sing-alongs and wiener dog cookouts.

I know it doesn't sound much like a frontier. It wasn't, not inside the picket fence. Outside, it remained dangerous and back-breaking work. We lost five separate people while I was there; two to blowouts, one to a collapsing crane, one to a careless tumble off a crater rim, and one to suicide (she, alas, had not been to Minnie and Earl's yet). We had injuries every week, shortages every day, and crises just about every hour. Most of the time, we seemed to lose ground—and even when we didn't, we lived with the knowledge that all of our work and all of our dedication could be thrown in the toilet the first time there was a political shift back home. There was no reason for any of us to believe that we were actually accomplishing what we were there to do— but somehow, with Minnie and Earl there, hosting a different group every night, it was impossible to come to any other conclusion. They liked us. They believed in us. They were sure that we were worth their time and effort. And they expected us to be around for a long, long time . . . just like they had been.

I suppose that's another reason why I was so determined to find them now. Because I didn't know what it said about the people we'd become that they weren't around keeping us company anymore.

I was in a jail cell for forty-eight hours once. Never mind why; it's a stupid story. The cell itself wasn't the sort of thing I expected from movies and television; it was brightly lit, free of vermin, and devoid of any steel bars to grip obsessively while cursing the guards and bemoaning the injustice that had brought me there. It was just a locked room with a steel door, a working toilet, a clean sink, a soft bed, and absolutely nothing else. If I had been able to come and go at will it might have been an acceptable cheap hotel room. Since I was stuck there, without anything to do or anybody to talk to, I spent those forty-eight hours going very quietly insane.

The habitat module of Walter Stearns was a lot like that cell, expanded to accommodate a storage closet, a food locker, and a kitchenette; it was that stark, that empty. There were no decorations on the walls, no personal items, no hytex or music system I could see, nothing to read and nothing to do. It lost its charm for me within thirty seconds. Stearns had been living there for sixteen years: a self-imposed prison sentence that might have been expiation for the sin of living past his era.

The man himself moved with what seemed glacial slowness, like a wind-up toy about to stop and fall over. He dragged one leg, but if that was a legacy of a stroke—and an explanation for why he chose to live as he did—there was no telltale slur to his speech to corroborate it. Whatever the reason might have been, I couldn't help regarding him with the embarrassed pity one old man feels toward another the same age who hasn't weathered his own years nearly as well.

He accepted my proffered can of yams with a sour grin and gave me a mug of some foul-smelling brown stuff in return. Then he poured some for himself and shuffled to the edge of his bed and sat down with a grunt. "I'm not a hermit," he said, defensively.

"I didn't use the word," I told him.

"I didn't set out to be a hermit," he went on, as if he hadn't heard me. "Nobody sets out to be a hermit. Nobody turns his back on the damned race unless he has some reason to be fed up. I'm not fed up. I just don't know any alternative. It's the only way I know to let the Moon be the Moon."

He sipped some of the foul-smelling brown stuff and gestured for me to do the same. Out of politeness, I sipped from my own cup. It tasted worse than it smelled, and had a consistency like sand floating in vinegar. Somehow I didn't choke. "Let the Moon be the Moon?"

"They opened a casino in Shepardsville. I went to see it. It's a big luxury hotel with a floor show; trained white tigers jumping through flaming hoops for the pleasure of a pretty young trainer in a spangled bra and panties. The casino room is oval-shaped, and the walls are alive with animated holography of wild horses running around and around and around and around, without stop, twenty-four hours a day. There are night clubs with singers and dancers, and an amusement park with rides for the kids. I sat there and I watched the gamblers bent over their tables and the barflies bent over their drinks and I had to remind myself that I was on the Moon—that just being here at all was a miracle that would have had most past civilizations consider us gods. But all these people, all around me, couldn't feel it. They'd built a palace in a place where no palace had ever been and they'd sucked all the magic and all the wonder all the way out of it." He took a deep breath, and sipped some more of his contemptible drink. "It scared me. It made me want to live somewhere where I could still feel the Moon being the Moon. So I wouldn't be some useless . . . relic who didn't know where he was half the time."

The self-pity had wormed its way into his voice so late that I almost didn't catch it. "It must get lonely," I ventured.

"Annnh. Sometimes I put on my moonsuit and go outside, just to stand there. It's so silent there that I can almost hear the breath of God. And I remember that it's the Moon—the Moon, dammit. Not some five-star hotel. The Moon. A little bit of that and I don't mind being a little lonely the rest of the time. Is that crazy? Is that being a hermit?"

I gave the only answer I could. "I don't know."

He made a hmmmph noise, got up, and carried his mug over to the sink. A few moments pouring another and he returned, his lips curled into a half-smile, his eyes focused on some far-off time and place. "The breath of God," he murmured.

"Yams," I prompted.

"You caught that, huh? Been a while since somebody caught that. It's not the sort of thing people catch unless they were there. Unless they remember her."

"Was that by design?"

"You mean, was it some kind of fiendish secret code? Naah. More like a shared joke. We knew by then that nobody would believe us if we actually talked about Minnie and Earl. They were that forgotten. So we dropped yams into our early-settlement stories. A little way of saying, hey, we remember the old lady. She sure did love to cook those yams."

"With her special seasoning." I said. "And those rolls she baked."

"Uh-huh." He licked his lips, and I almost fell into the trap of considering that unutterably sad . . . until I realized that I was doing the same thing. "Used to try to mix one of Earl's special cocktails, but I never could get them right. Got all the ingredients. Mixed 'em the way he showed me. Never got 'em to taste right. Figure he had some kind of technological edge he wasn't showing us. Real alien superscience, applied to bartending. Or maybe I just can't replace the personality of the bartender. But they were good drinks. I've got to give him that."

We sat together in silence for a while, each lost in the sights and sounds of a day long gone. After a long time, I almost whispered it: "Where did they go, Walter?"

His eyes didn't focus: "I don't know where they are. I don't know what happened to them."

"Start with when you last visited them."

"Oh, that was years and years and years ago." He lowered his head and addressed the floor. "But you know how it is. You have relatives, friends, old folks very important to you. Folks you see every week or so, folks who become a major part of who you are. Then you get busy with other things and you lose touch. I lost touch when the settlement boom hit, and there was always some other place to be, some other job that needed to be done; I couldn't spare one night a week gabbing with old folks just because I happened to love them. After all, they'd always be there, right? By the time I thought of looking them up again, it turned out that everybody else had neglected them too. There was no sign of the house and no way of knowing how long they'd been gone."

I was appalled. "So you're saying that Minnie and Earl moved away because of . . . neglect?"

"Naaah. That's only why they didn't say goodbye. I don't think it has a damn thing to do with why they moved away; just why we didn't notice. I guess that's another reason why nobody likes to talk about them. We're all just too damn ashamed."

"Why do you think they moved, Walter?"

He swallowed another mouthful of his vile brew, and addressed the floor some more, not seeing me, not seeing the exile he'd chosen for himself, not seeing anything but a tiny little window of his past. "I keep thinking of that casino," he murmured. "There was a rotating restaurant on the top floor of the hotel. Showed you the landscape, with all the billboards and amusement parks—and above it all, in the place where all the advertisers hope you're going to forget to look, Mother Earth herself. It was a burlesque and it was boring. And I also keep thinking of that little house, out in the middle of nowhere, with the picket fence and the golden retriever dog . . . and the two sweet old people . . . and the more I compare one thought to the other, the more I realize that I don't blame them for going away. They saw that on the Moon we were building, they wouldn't be miraculous anymore."

"They had a perfectly maintained little environment—"

"We have a perfectly maintained little environment. We have parks with grass. We have roller coasters and golf courses. We have people with dogs. We even got rotating restaurants and magic acts with tigers. Give us a few more years up here and we'll probably work out some kind of magic trick to do away with the domes and the bulkheads and keep in an atmosphere with nothing but a picket fence. We'll have houses like theirs springing up all over the place. The one thing we don't have is the Moon being the Moon. Why would they want to stay here?" His voice, which had been rising throughout his little tirade, rose to a shriek with that last question; he hurled his mug against the wall, but it was made of some indestructible ceramic that refused to shatter. It just tumbled to the floor, and skittered under the bunk, spinning in place just long enough to mock him for his empty display of anger. He looked at me, focused, and let me know with a look that our audience was over. "What would be left for them?"

I searched some more, tracking down another five or six oldsters still capable of talking about the old days, as well as half a dozen children or grandchildren of same willing to speak to me about the memories the old folks had left behind, but my interview with Walter Stearns was really the end of it; by the time I left his habitat, I knew that my efforts were futile. I saw that even those willing to talk to me weren't going to be able to tell me more than he had . . . and I turned out to be correct about that. Minnie and Earl had moved out, all right, and there was no forwarding address to be had.

I was also tired: bone-weary in a way that could have been just a normal symptom of age and could have been despair that I had not found what I so desperately needed to find and could have been the harbinger of my last remaining days. Whatever it was, I just didn't have the energy to keep going that much longer . . . and I knew that the only real place for me was the bed I had shared with my dear Claire.

On the night before I flew back I had some money left over, so I went to see the musical *Ceres* at New Broadway. I confess I found it dreadful—like most old farts, I can't fathom music produced after the first three decades of my life—but it was definitely elaborate, with a cast of lithe and gymnastic young dancers in silvery jumpsuits leaping about in a slow-motion ballet that took full advantage of the special opportunities afforded by lunar gravity. At one point the show even simulated free fall, thanks to invisible filaments that crisscrossed the stage allowing the dancers to glide from place to place like objects ruled only by their own mass and momentum. The playbill said that one of the performers, never mind which one, was not a real human being, but a holographic projection artfully integrated with the rest of the performers. I couldn't discern the fake, but I couldn't find it in myself to be impressed. We were a few flimsy bulkheads and half a kilometer from lunar vacuum, and to me, that was the real story . . . even if nobody else in the audience of hundreds could see it.

I moved out of my hotel. I tipped my concierge, who hadn't found me anything about Minnie and Earl but had provided all the other amenities I'd asked for. I bought some stupid souvenirs for the grandchildren, and boarded my flight back to Earth.

After about an hour I went up to the passenger lounge, occupied by two intensely-arguing businesswomen, a child playing a handheld hytex game, and a bored-looking thin man with a shiny head. Nobody was looking out the panoramic window, not even me. I closed my eyes and pretended that the view wasn't there. Instead I thought of the time Earl had decided he wanted to fly a kite. That was a major moment. He built it out of newspapers he got from somewhere, and sat in his backyard letting out more than five hundred meters of line; though the string and the kite extended far beyond the atmospheric picket-fence perimeter, it had still swooped and sailed like an object enjoying the robust winds it would have known, achieving that altitude on Earth. That, of course, had been another impossibility ... but my colleagues and I had been so inured to such things by then that we simply shrugged and enjoyed the moment as it came.

I badly wanted to fly a kite.

I badly wanted to know that Minnie and Earl had not left thinking poorly of us.

I didn't think they were dead. They weren't the kind of people who died. But they were living somewhere else, someplace far away—and if the human race was lucky it was somewhere in the solar system. Maybe, even now, while I rode back to face however much time I had left, there was a mindboggling little secret being kept by the construction teams building those habitats out near the Jovian moons; maybe some of those physicists and engineers were taking time out from a week of dangerous and backbreaking labor to spend a few hours in the company of an old man and old woman whose deepest spoken insight about the massive planet that graces their sky was how it presented one hell of a lovely view. Maybe the same thing happened when Anderson and Santiago hitched a ride on the comet that now bears their names—and maybe there's a little cottage halfway up the slope of Olympus Mons where the Mars colonists go whenever they need a little down-home hospitality. I would have been happy with all of those possibilities. I would have felt the weight of years fall from my bones in an instant, if I just knew that there was still room for Minnie and Earl in the theme-park future we seemed to be building.

Then something, maybe chance, maybe instinct, made me look out the window.

And my poor, slowly failing heart almost stopped right then.

Because Miles, the golden retriever, was pacing us.

He ran alongside the shuttle, keeping up with the lounge window, his lolling pink tongue and long floppy ears trailing behind him like banners driven by some unseen (and patently impossible) breeze. He ran if in slow motion, his feet pawing a ground that wasn't there, his muscles rippling along his side, his muzzle foaming with perspiration. His perpetually laughing expression, so typical of his breed, was not so much the look of an animal merely panting with exertion, but the genuine mirth of a creature aware that it has just pulled off a joke of truly epic proportions. As I stared at him, too dumbstruck to whoop and holler and point him out to my fellow passengers, he turned his head, met my gaze with soulful brown eyes, and did something I've never seen any other golden retriever do, before or since.

He winked.

Then he faced forward, lowered his head, and sped up, leaving us far behind.

I whirled and scanned the lounge, to see if any of my fellow passengers had seen him. The two businesswomen had stopped arguing, and were now giggling over a private joke of some kind. The kid was still intently focused on his game. But the eyes of the man with the shiny head were very large and very round. He stared at me, found in my broad smile confirmation that he hadn't been hallucinating, and tried to speak. "That," he said. And "Was." And after several attempts, "A dog."

He might have gone on from there given another hour or so of trying.

I knew exactly how he felt, of course. I had been in the same place, once, seventy years ago.

Now, for a while, I felt like I was twelve again.

I rose from my seat, crossed the lounge, and took the chair facing the man with the shiny head. He was wide-eyed, like a man who saw me, a total stranger, as the only fixed constant in his universe. That made me feel young, too.

I said, "Let me tell you a little bit about some old friends of mine."

This one's for Jerry and Kathy Oltion, the Minnie and Earl of the future.

John Kessel's fiction includes the recently published *Pride and Prometheus*, the novels *The Moon and the Other, Good News from Outer Space, Corrupting Dr. Nice*, and *Freedom Beach* (with James Patrick Kelly), and the collections *Meeting in Infinity, The Pure Product*, and *The Baum Plan for Financial Independence and Other Stories*. His fiction has received the Nebula Award, the Theodore Sturgeon Memorial Award, the Locus Award, the James Tiptree Jr. Award, and the Shirley Jackson Award. With James Patrick Kelly, he edited the anthologies *Feeling Very Strange: The Slipstream Anthology, The Secret History of Science Fiction*, and *Kafkaesque*.

Kessel teaches American literature and fiction writing at North Carolina State University, where he helped found the MFA program in creative writing and served twice as its director. He lives with his wife, the novelist Therese Anne Fowler, in Raleigh.

STORIES FOR MEN
John Kessel

ONE

Erno couldn't get to the club until an hour after it opened, so of course the place was crowded and he got stuck in the back behind three queens whose loud, aimless conversation made him edgy. He was never less than edgy anyway, Erno—a seventeen-year-old biotech apprentice known for the clumsy, earnest intensity with which he propositioned almost every girl he met.

It was more people than Erno had ever seen in the Oxygen Warehouse. Even though Tyler Durden had not yet taken the stage, every table was filled, and people stood three deep at the bar. Rosamund, the owner, bustled back and forth providing drinks, her face glistening with sweat. The crush of people only irritated Erno. He had been one of the first to catch on to Durden, and the room full of others, some of whom had probably come on his own recommendation, struck him as usurpers.

Erno forced his way to the bar and bought a tincture. Tyrus and Sid, friends of his, nodded at him from across the room. Erno sipped the cool, licorice flavored drink and eavesdropped, and gradually his thoughts took on an architectural, intricate intellectuality.

A friend of his mother sat with a couple of sons who anticipated for her what she was going to see. "He's not just a comedian, he's a philosopher," said the skinny one. His foot, crossed over his knee, bounced in rhythm to the jazz playing in the background. Erno recognized him from a party he'd attended a few months back.

"We have philosophers," the matron said. "We even have comedians."

"Not like Tyler Durden," said the other boy.

"Tyler Durden—who gave him that name?"

"I think it's historical," the first boy said.

"Not any history I ever heard," the woman said. "Who's his mother?"

Erno noticed that there were more women in the room than there had been at any performance he had seen. Already the matrons were homing in. You could not escape their sisterly curiosity, their motherly tyranny. He realized that his shoulders were cramped; he rolled his head to try to loosen the spring-tight muscles.

The Oxygen Warehouse was located in what had been a shop in the commercial district of the northwest lava tube. It was a free enterprise zone, and no one had objected to the addition of a tinctures bar, though some eyebrows had been raised when it was discovered that one of the tinctures sold was alcohol. The stage was merely a raised platform in one corner. Around the room were small tables with chairs. The bar spanned one end, and the other featured a false window that showed a nighttime cityscape of Old New York.

Rosamund Demisdaughter, who'd started the club, at first booked local jazz musicians. Her idea was to present as close to a retro Earth atmosphere as could be managed on the far side of the moon, where few of the inhabitants had ever even seen the Earth. Her clientele consisted of a few immigrants and a larger group of rebellious young cousins who were looking for an *avant garde*. Erno knew his mother would not approve his going to the Warehouse, so he was there immediately.

He pulled his pack of fireless cigarettes from the inside pocket of his black twentieth-century suit, shook out a fag, inhaled it into life and imagined himself living back on Earth a hundred years ago. Exhaling a plume of cool, rancid smoke, he caught a glimpse of his razor haircut in the mirror behind the bar, then adjusted the knot of his narrow tie.

After some minutes the door beside the bar opened and Tyler Durden came out. He leaned over and exchanged a few words with Rosamund. Some of the men whistled and cheered. Rosamund flipped a brandy snifter high into the air, where it caught the ceiling lights as it spun in the low G, then slowly fell back to her hand. Having attracted the attention of the audience, she hopped over the bar and onto the small stage.

"Don't you people have anything better to do?" she shouted.

A chorus of rude remarks.

"Welcome to The Oxygen Warehouse," she said. "I want to say, before I bring him out, that I take no responsibility for the opinions expressed by Tyler Durden. He's not my boy."

Durden stepped onto the stage. The audience was quiet, a little nervous. He ran his hand over his shaved head, gave a boyish grin. He was a big man, in his thirties, wearing the blue coveralls of an environmental technician. Around his waist he wore a belt with tools hanging from it, as if he'd just come off shift.

"'Make love, not war!'" Durden said. "Remember that one? You got that from your mother, in the school? I never liked that one. 'Make love, not war,' they'll tell you. I hate that. I want to make love *and* war. I don't want my dick just to be a dick. I want it to stand for something!"

A heckler from the audience shouted, "Can't it stand on its own?"

Durden grinned. "Let's ask it." He addressed his crotch. "Hey, son!" He called down. "Don't you like screwing?"

Durden looked up at the ceiling, his face went simple, and he became his dick talking back to him. "Hiya dad!" he squeaked. "Sure, I like screwing!"

Durden winked at a couple of guys in makeup and lace in the front row, then looked down again: "Boys or girls?"

His dick: "What day of the week is it?"

"Thursday."

"Doesn't matter, then. Thursday's guest mammal day."

"Outstanding, son."

"I'm a Good Partner."

The queers laughed. Erno did, too.

"You want I should show you?"

"Not now, son," Tyler told his dick. "You keep quiet for a minute, and let me explain to the people, okay?"

"Sure. I'm here whenever you need me."

"I'm aware of that." Durden addressed the audience again. "Remember what Mama says, folks: *Keep your son close, let your semen go.*" He recited the slogan with exaggerated rhythm, wagging his finger at them, sober as a scolding grandmother. The audience loved it. Some of them chanted along with the catchphrase.

Durden was warming up. "But is screwing all there is to a dick? I say no!

"A dick is a sign of power. It's a tower of strength. It's the tree of life. It's a weapon. It's an incisive tool of logic. It's the seeker of truth.

"Mama says that being male is nothing more than a performance. You know what I say to that? Perform this, baby!" He grabbed his imaginary cock with both of his hands, made a stupid face.

Cheers.

"But of course, *they* can't perform this! I don't care how you plank the genes, Mama don't have the *machinery*. Not only that, she don't have the *programming.* But mama wants to program *us* with *her* half-baked scheme of what women want a man to be. This whole place is about fucking up our *hardware* with their *software.*"

He was laughing himself, now. Beads of sweat stood out on his scalp in the bright light.

"Mama says, 'Don't confuse your penis with a phallus.'" He assumed a female sway of his hips, lifted his chin and narrowed his eyes: just like that, he was an archetypal matron, his voice transmuted into a fruity contralto. "'Yes, you boys do have those nice little dicks, but we're living in a *post-phallic* society. A penis is merely a biological appendage.'"

Now he was her son, responding. "'Like a foot, Mom?'"

Mama: "'Yes, son. Exactly like a foot.'"

Quick as a spark, back to his own voice: "How many of you in the audience here have named your foot?"

Laughter, a show of hands.

"Okay, so much for the foot theory of the penis.

"But Mama says the penis is designed solely for the propagation of the species. Sex gives pleasure in order to encourage procreation. A phallus, on the other hand—whichever hand you like—I prefer the left—"

More laughter.

"—a phallus is an idea, a cultural creation of the dead patriarchy, a symbolic sheath applied over the penis to give it meanings that have nothing to do with biology . . ."

Durden seized his invisible dick again. "Apply my symbolic sheath, baby . . . oohhh, yes, I like it . . ."

Erno had heard Tyler talk about his symbolic sheath before. Though there were variations, he watched the audience instead. Did they get it? Most of the men seemed to be engaged and laughing. A drunk in the first row leaned forward, hands on his knees, howling at Tyler's every word. Queers leaned their heads together and smirked. Faces gleamed in the close air. But a lot of the men's laughter was nervous, and some did not laugh at all.

A few of the women, mostly the younger ones, were laughing. Some of them seemed mildly amused. Puzzled. Some looked bored. Others sat stonily with expressions that could only indicate anger.

Erno did not know how he felt about the women who were laughing. He felt hostility toward those who looked bored: why did you come here, he wanted to ask them. Who do you think you are? He preferred those who looked angry. That was what he wanted from them.

Then he noticed those who looked calm, interested, alert yet unamused. These women scared him.

In the back of the room stood some green-uniformed constables, male and female, carrying batons, red lights gleaming in the corner of their mirror spex, recording. Looking around the room, Erno located at least a half dozen of them. One, he saw with a start; was his mother.

He ducked behind a tall man beside him. She might not have seen him yet, but she would see him sooner or later. For a moment he considered confronting her, but then he sidled behind a row of watchers toward the back rooms. Another constable, her slender lunar physique distorted by the bulging muscles of a genetically engineered testosterone girl, stood beside the doorway. She did not look at Erno: she was watching Tyler, who was back to conversing with his dick.

"I'm tired of being confined," Tyler's dick was saying.

"You feel constricted?" Tyler asked.

He looked up in dumb appeal. "I'm stuck in your pants all day!"

Looking down: "I can let you out, but first tell me, are you a penis or a phallus?"

"That's a distinction without a difference."

"*Au contraire*, little man! You haven't been listening."

"I'm not noted for my listening ability."

"Sounds like you're a phallus to me," Tyler told his dick. "We have lots of room for penises, but Mama don't allow no phalluses 'round here."

"Let my people go!"

"Nice try, but wrong color. Look, son. It's risky when you come out. You could get damaged. The phallic liberation movement is in its infancy."

"I thought you cousins were *all about* freedom."

"In theory. In practice, free phalluses are dangerous."

"Who says?"

"Well, Debra does, and so does Mary, and Sue, and Jamina most every time I see her, and there was this lecture in We-Whine-You-Listen class last week, and Ramona says so too, and of course most emphatically Baba, and then there's that bitch Nora . . ."

Erno spotted his mother moving toward his side of the room. He slipped past the constable into the hall. There was the rest room, and a couple of other doors. A gale of laughter washed in from the club behind him at the climax of Tyler's story; cursing his mother, Erno went into the rest room.

No one was there. He could still hear the laughter, but not the cause of it. His mother's presence had cut him out of the community of male watchers as neatly as if she had used a baton. Erno felt murderously angry. He switched on a urinal and took a piss.

Over the urinal, a window played a scene in Central Park, on Earth, of a hundred years ago. A night scene of a pathway beneath some trees, trees as large as the largest in Sobieski Park. A line of electric lights on poles threw pools of light along the path, and through the pools of light strolled a man and a woman. They were talking, but Erno could not hear what they were saying.

The woman wore a dress cinched tight at the waist, whose skirt flared out stiffly, ending halfway down her calves. The top of her dress had a low neckline that showed off her breasts. The man wore a dark suit like Erno's. They were completely differentiated by their dress, as if they were from different cultures, even species. Erno wondered where Rosamund had gotten the image.

As Erno watched, the man nudged the woman to the side of the path, beneath one of the trees. He slid his hands around her waist and pressed his body against hers. She yielded softly to his embrace. Erno could not see their faces in the shadows, but they were inches apart. He felt his dick getting hard in his hand.

He stepped back from the urinal, turned it off, and closed his pants. As the hum of the recycler died, the rest room door swung open and a woman came in. She glanced at Erno and headed for one of the toilets. Erno went over to the counter and stuck his hands into the cleaner. The woman's presence sparked his anger.

Without turning to face her, but watching in the mirror, he said, "Why are you here tonight?"

The woman looked up (she had been studying her fingernails) and her eyes locked on his. She was younger than his mother and had a pretty, heart-shaped face. "I was curious. People are talking about him."

"Do you think men want you here?"

"I don't know what the men want."

"Yes. That's the point, isn't it? Are you learning anything?"

"Perhaps." The woman looked back at her hands. "Aren't you Pamela Megsdaughter's son?"

"So she tells me." Erno pulled his tingling hands out of the cleaner.

The woman used the bidet, and dried herself. She had a great ass. "Did she bring you or did you bring her?" she asked.

"We brought ourselves," Erno said. He left the rest room. He looked out into the club again, listening to the noise. The crowd was rowdier, and more raucous. The men's shouts of encouragement were like barks, their laughter edged with anger. His mother was still there. He did not want to see her, or to have her see him.

He went back past the rest room to the end of the hallway. The hall made a right angle into a dead end, but when Erno stepped into the bend he saw, behind a stack of plastic crates, an old door. He wedged the crates to one side and opened the door enough to slip through.

The door opened into a dark, dimly lit space. His steps echoed. As his eyes adjusted to the dim light he saw it was a very large room hewn out of the rock, empty except for some racks that must have held liquid oxygen cylinders back in the early days of the colony, when this place had been an actual oxygen warehouse. The light came from ancient bioluminescent units on the walls. The club must have been set up in this space years before.

The tincture still lent Erno an edge of aggression, and he called out: "I'm Erno, King of the Moon!"

"—ooo—ooo—ooon!" the echoes came back, fading to stillness. He kicked an empty cylinder, which rolled forlornly a few meters before it stopped. He wandered around the chill vastness. At the far wall, one of the darker shadows turned out to be an alcove in the stone. Set in the back, barely visible in the dim light, was an ancient pressure door.

Erno decided not to mess with it—it could open onto vacuum. He went back to the club door and slid into the hallway.

Around the corner, two men were just coming out of the rest room, and Erno followed them as if he were just returning as well. The club was more crowded than ever. Every open space was filled with standing men, and others sat cross-legged up front. His mother and another constable had moved to the edge of the stage.

"—the problem with getting laid all the time is, you can't think!" Tyler was saying. "I mean, there's only so much blood in the human body. That's why those old Catholics back on Earth put the lock on the Pope's dick. He had an empire to run: the more time he spent taking care of John Thomas the less he spent thinking up ways of getting money out of peasants. The secret of our moms is that, if they keep that blood flowing below the belt, it ain't never gonna flow back above the shirt collar. Keeps the frequency of radical male ideas down!"

Tyler leaned over toward the drunk in the first row. "You know what I'm talking about, soldier?"

"You bet," the man said. He tried to stand, wobbled, sat down, tried to stand again.

"Where do you work?"

"Lunox." The man found his balance. "You're *right*, you—"

Tyler patted him on the shoulder. "An oxygen boy. You know what I mean, you're out there on the processing line, and you're thinking about how maybe if you were to add a little more graphite to the reduction chamber you could increase efficiency by 15 percent, and just then Mary Ellen Swivelhips walks by in her skintight and—bam!" Tyler made the face of a man who'd been poleaxed. "Uh—what was I thinking of?"

The audience howled.

"Forty I.Q. points down the oubliette. And nothing, NOTHING's gonna change until we get a handle on this! Am I right, brothers?"

More howls, spiked with anger.

Tyler was sweating, laughing, trembling as if charged with electricity. "Keep your son close! *Penis, no! Phallus, si!*"

Cheers now. Men stood and raised their fists. The drunk saw Erno's mother at the edge of the stage and took a step toward her. He said something, and while she and her partner stood irresolute, he put his big hand on her chest and shoved her away.

The other constable discharged his electric club against the man. The drunk's arms flew back, striking a bystander, and two other men surged forward and knocked down the constable. Erno's mother raised her own baton. More constables pushed toward the stage, using their batons, and other men rose to stop them. A table was upended, shouts echoed, the room was hot as hell and turning into a riot, the first riot in the Society of Cousins in fifty years.

As the crowd surged toward the exits or toward the constables, Erno ducked back to the hallway. He hesitated, and then Tyler Durden came stumbling out of the melee. He took a quick look at Erno. "What now, kid?"

"Come with me," Erno said. He grabbed Tyler's arm and pulled him around the bend in the end of the hall, past the crates to the warehouse door. He slammed the door behind them and propped an empty oxygen cylinder against it. "We can hide here until the thing dies down."

"Who are you?"

"My name is Erno."

"Well, Erno, are we sure we want to hide? Out there is more interesting."

Erno decided not to tell Tyler that one of the constables was his mother. "Are you serious?"

"I'm always serious." Durden wandered back from the door into the gloom of the cavern. He kicked a piece of rubble, which soared across the room and skidded up against the wall thirty meters away. "This place must have been here since the beginning. I'm surprised they're wasting the space. Probably full of toxics."

"You think so?" Erno said.

"Who knows?" Durden went toward the back of the warehouse, and Erno followed. It was cold, and their breath steamed the air. "Who would have figured the lights would still be growing," Durden said.

"A well established colony can last for fifty years or more," Erno said. "As long as there's enough moisture in the air. They break down the rock."

"You know all about it."

"I work in biotech," Erno said. "I'm a gene hacker."

Durden said nothing, and Erno felt the awkwardness of his boast.

They reached the far wall. Durden found the pressure door set into the dark alcove. He pulled a flashlight from his belt. The triangular yellow warning signs around the door were faded. He felt around the door seam.

"We probably ought to leave that alone," Erno said.

Durden handed Erno the flashlight, took a pry bar from his belt, and shoved it into the edge of the door. The door resisted, then with a grating squeak jerked open a couple of centimeters. Erno jumped at the sound.

"Help me out here, Erno," Durden said.

Erno got his fingers around the door's edge, and the two of them braced themselves. Durden put his feet up on the wall and used his legs and back to get leverage. When the door suddenly shot open Erno fell back and whacked his head. Durden lost his grip, shot sideways out of the alcove, bounced once, and skidded across the dusty floor. While Erno shook his head to clear his vision, Durden sat spread-legged, laughing. "Bingo!" He said. He bounced up. "You okay, Erno?"

Erno felt the back of his skull. He wasn't bleeding. "I'm fine," he said.

"Let's see what we've got, then."

Beyond the door a dark corridor cut through the basalt. Durden stepped into the path marked by his light. Erno wanted to go back to the club—by now things must have died down—but instead he followed.

Shortly past the door the corridor turned into a cramped lava tube. Early settlers had leveled the floor of the erratic tube formed by the draining away of cooling lava several billion years ago. Between walls that had been erected to form rooms ran a path of red volcanic gravel much like tailings from the oxygen factory. Foamy irregular pebbles kicked up by their shoes rattled off the walls. Dead light fixtures broke the ceiling at intervals. Tyler stopped to shine his light into a couple of the doorways, and at the third he went inside.

"This must be from the start of the colony," Erno said. "I wonder why it's been abandoned."

"Kind of claustrophobic." Durden shone the light around the small room.

The light fell on a small rectangular object in the corner. From his belt Durden pulled another tool, which he extended into a probe.

"Do you always carry this equipment?" Erno asked.

"Be prepared," Durden said. He set down the light and crouched over the object. It looked like a small box, a few centimeters thick. "You ever hear of the Boy Scouts, Erno?"

"Some early lunar colony?"

"Nope. Sort of like the Men's House, only different." Durden forced the probe under an edge, and one side lifted as if to come off. "Well, well!"

He put down the probe, picked up the object. He held it end-on, put his thumbs against the long side, and opened it. It divided neatly into flat sheets attached at the other long side.

"What is it?" Erno asked.

"It's a book."

"Is it still working?"

"This is an unpowered book. The words are printed right on these leaves. They're made of paper."

Erno had seen such old-fashioned books in vids. "It must be very old. What is it?"

Durden carefully turned the pages. "It's a book of stories." Durden stood up and handed the book to Erno. "Here. You keep it. Let me know what it's about."

Erno tried to make out the writing, but without Tyler's flashlight it was too dim.

Durden folded up his probe and hung it on his belt. He ran his hand over his head, smearing a line of dust over his scalp. "Are you cold? I suppose we ought to find our way out of here." Immediately he headed out of the room and back down the corridor.

Erno felt he was getting left behind in more ways than one. Clutching the book, he followed after Durden and his bobbing light. Rather than heading back to the Oxygen Warehouse, the comedian continued down the lava tube.

Eventually the tube ended in another old pressure door. When Durden touched the key panel at its side, amazingly, it lit.

"What do you think?" Durden said.

"We should go back," Erno said. "We can't know whether the locked door on the other side is still airtight. The fail-safes could be broken. We could open the door onto vacuum." He held the book under his armpit and blew on his cold hands.

"How old are you, Erno?"

"Seventeen."

"Seventeen?" Durden's eyes glinted in shadowed eye sockets. "Seventeen is no age to be cautious."

Erno couldn't help but grin. "You're right. Let's open it."

"My man, Erno!" Durden slapped him on the shoulder. He keyed the door open. They heard the whine of a long-unused electric motor. Erno could feel his heart beat, the blood running swiftly in his veins. At first nothing happened, then the door began to slide open. There was a chuff of air escaping from the lava tube, and dust kicked up. But the wind stopped as soon as it started, and the door opened completely on the old airlock, filled floor to ceiling with crates and bundles of fiberglass building struts.

It took them half an hour to shift boxes and burrow their way through the airlock, to emerge at the other end into another warehouse, this one still in use. They crept by racks of construction materials until they reached the entrance, and sneaked out into the colony corridor beyond.

They were at the far end of North Six, the giant lava tube that served the industrial wing of the colony. The few workers they encountered on the late shift might have noticed Erno's suit, but said nothing.

Erno and Tyler made their way back home. Tyler cracked jokes about the constables until they emerged into the vast open space of the domed crater that formed the center of the colony. Above, on the huge dome, was projected a night starfield. In the distance, down the rimwall slopes covered with junipers, across the crater floor, lights glinted among the trees in Sobieski Park. Erno took a huge breath, fragrant with piñon.

"The world our ancestors gave us," Tyler said, waving his arm as if offering it to Erno.

As Tyler turned to leave, Erno called out impulsively, "That was an adventure!"

"The first of many, Erno." Tyler said, and jogged away.

Celibacy Day

On Celibacy Day, everyone gets a day off from sex.

Some protest this practice, but they are relatively few. Most men take it as an opportunity to retreat to the informal Men's Houses that, though they have no statutory sanction, sprang up in the first generation of settlers.

In the Men's House, men and boys talk about what it is to be a man, a lover of other men and women, a father in a world where fatherhood is no more than a biological concept. They complain about their lot. They tell vile jokes and sing songs. They wrestle. They gossip. Heteros and queers and everyone in between compare speculations on what they think women really want, and whether it matters. They try to figure out what a true man is.

As a boy Erno would go to the Men's House with his mother's current partner or one of the other men involved in the household. Some of the men taught him things. He learned about masturbation, and cross checks, and Micro Language Theory.

But no matter how welcoming the men were supposed to be to each other—and they talked about brotherhood all the time—there was always that little edge when you met another boy there, or that necessary wariness when you talked to an

*adult. Men came to the Men's House to spend time together and remind themselves
of certain congruencies, but only a crazy person would want to live solely in the
company of men.*

TWO

The founders of the Society of Cousins had a vision of women as independent agents, free thinkers forming alliances with other women to create a social bond so strong that men could not overwhelm them. Solidarity, sisterhood, motherhood. But Erno's mother was not like those women. Those women existed only in history vids, sitting in meeting circles, laughing, making plans, sure of themselves and complete.

Erno's mother was a cop. She had a cop's squinty eyes and a cop's suspicion of anyone who stepped outside of the norm. She had a cop's lack of imagination, except as she could imagine what people would do wrong.

Erno and his mother and his sister Celeste and his Aunt Sophie and his cousins Lena and Aphra, and various men some of whom may have been fathers, some of them Good Partners, and others just men, lived in an apartment in Sanger, on the third level of the northeast quadrant, a small place looking down on the farms that filled the floor of the crater they called Fowler, though the real Fowler was a much larger crater five kilometers distant.

Erno had his own room. He thought nothing of the fact that the girls had to share a room, and would be forced to move out when they turned fourteen. *Keep your son close, let your daughter go*, went the aphorism Tyler had mocked. Erno's mother was not about to challenge any aphorisms. Erno remembered her expression as she had stepped forward to arrest the drunk: sad that this man had forced her to this, and determined to do it. She was comfortable in the world; she saw no need for alternatives. Her cronies came by the apartment and shared coffee and gossip, and they were just like all the other mothers and sisters and aunts. None of them were extraordinary.

Not that any of the men Erno knew were extraordinary, either. Except Tyler Durden. And now Erno knew Durden, and they had spent a night breaking rules and getting away with it.

Celeste and Aphra were dishing up oatmeal when Erno returned to the apartment that morning. "Where were you?" his mother asked. She looked up from the table, more curious than upset, and Erno noticed a bruise on her temple.

"What happened to your forehead?" Erno asked.

His mother touched a hand to her forehead, as if she had forgotten it. She waved the hand in dismissal.

"There was trouble at a club in the enterprise district," Aunt Sophie said. "The constables had to step in, and your mother was assaulted."

"It was a riot!" Lena said eagerly. "There's going to be a big meeting about it in the park today." Lena was a month from turning fourteen, and looking forward to voting.

Erno sat down at the table. As he did so he felt the book, which he had tucked into his belt at the small of his back beneath his now rumpled suit jacket. He leaned forward, pulled a bowl of oatmeal toward him and took up a spoon. Looking down into the bowl to avoid anyone's eyes, he idly asked, "What's the meeting for?"

"One of the rioters was knocked into a coma," Lena said. "The social order committee wants this comedian Tyler Durden to be made invisible."

Erno concentrated on his spoon. "Why?"

"You know about him?" his mother asked.

Before he had to think of an answer, Nick Farahsson, his mother's partner, shambled into the kitchen. "Lord, Pam, don't you pay attention? Erno's one of his biggest fans."

His mother turned on Erno. "Is that so?"

Erno looked up from his bowl and met her eyes. She looked hurt. "I've heard of him."

"Heard of him?" Nick said. "Erno, I bet you were there last night."

"I bet *you* weren't there," Erno said.

Nick stretched. "I don't need to hear him. I have no complaints." He came up behind Erno's mother, nuzzled the nape of her neck and cupped her breast in his hand.

She turned her face up and kissed him on the cheek. "I should hope not."

Lena made a face. "Heteros. I can't wait until I get out of here." She had recently declared herself a lesbian and was quite judgmental about it.

"You'd better get to your practicum, Lena," Aunt Sophie said. "Let your aunt take care of her own sex life."

"This guy Durden is setting himself up for a major fall," said Nick. "Smells like a case of abnormal development. Who's his mother?"

Erno couldn't keep quiet. "He doesn't have a mother. He doesn't need one."

"Parthenogenesis," Aunt Sophie said. "I didn't think it had been perfected yet."

"If they ever do, what happens to me?" Nick said.

"You have your uses." Erno's mother nudged her shoulder against his hip.

"You two can go back to your room," Aunt Sophie said. "We'll take care of things for you."

"No need." Nick grabbed a bowl of oatmeal and sat down. "Thank you, sweetheart," he said to Aphra. "I can't see what this guy's problem is."

"Doesn't it bother you that you can't vote?" Erno said. "What's fair about that?"

"I don't want to vote," Nick said.

"You're a complete drone."

His mother frowned at him. Erno pushed his bowl away and left for his room.

"You're the one with special tutoring!" Lena called. "The nice clothes. What work do you do?"

"Shut up," Erno said softly, but his ears burned.

He had nothing to do until his 1100 biotech tutorial, and he didn't even have to go if he didn't want to. Lena was right about that, anyway. He threw the book on his bed, undressed, and switched on his screen. On the front page was a report of solar activity approaching its eleven-year peak, with radiation warnings issued for all surface activity. Erno called up the calendar. There it was: a discussion on Tyler Durden was scheduled in the amphitheater at 1600. Linked was a vid of the riot and a forum for open citizen comment. A cousin named Tashi Yokiosson had been clubbed in the fight and was in a coma, undergoing nanorepair.

Erno didn't know him, but that didn't prevent his anger. He considered calling up Tyrus or Sid, finding out what had happened to them, and telling them about his adventure with Tyler. But that would spoil the secret, and it might get around to his mother. Yet he couldn't let his night with Tyler go uncelebrated. He opened his journal, and wrote a poem:

> Going outside the crater
> finding the lost tunnels
> of freedom
> and male strength.
> Searching with your brother
> shoulder to shoulder
> like men.
>
> Getting below the surface
> of a stifling society
> sounding your XY shout.
> Flashing your colors
> like an ancient Spartan bird
> proud, erect, never to be softened
> by the silent embrace of woman
>
> No females aloud.

Not bad. It had some of the raw honesty of the beats. He would read it at the next meeting of the Poets' Club. He saved it with the four hundred other poems he had written in the last year: Erno prided himself on being the most prolific poet in his class. He had already won four Laurel Awards, one for best Lyric, one for best Sonnet, and two for best Villanelle—plus a Snappie for best limerick of 2097. He was sure to make Bard at an earlier age than anyone since Patrick Maurasson.

Erno switched off the screen, lay on his bed, and remembered the book. He dug it out from under his discarded clothes. It had a blue cover, faded to purple near the binding, made of some sort of fabric. Embossed on the front was a torch encircled by a laurel wreath. He opened the book to its title page: *Stories for Men*, "An Anthology by Charles Grayson." Published in August 1936, in the United States of America.

As a fan of Earth culture, Erno knew that most Earth societies used the patronymic, so that Gray, Grayson's naming parent, would be a man, not a woman.

Stories for men. The authors on the contents page were all men—except perhaps for odd names like "Dashiell." Despite Erno's interest in twentieth-century popular art, only a couple were familiar. William Faulkner he knew was considered a major Earth writer, and he had seen the name Hemingway before, though he had associated it only with a style of furniture. But even assuming the stories were all written by men, the title said the book was stories *for* men, not stories *by* men.

How did a story for a man differ from a story for a woman? Erno had never considered the idea before. He had heard storytellers in the park, and read books in school—Murasaki, Chopin, Cather, Ellison, Morrison, Ferenc, Sabinsdaughter. As a child, he had loved the Alice books, and *Flatland,* and Maria Hidalgo's kids' stories, and Seuss. None seemed particularly male or female.

He supposed the cousins did have their own stories for men. Nick loved interactive serials, tortured romantic tales of interpersonal angst set in the patriarchal world, where men struggled against injustice until they found the right women and were taken care of. Erno stuck to poetry. His favorite novel was Tawanda Tamikasdaughter's *The Dark Blood*—the story of a misunderstood young Cousin's struggles against his overbearing mother, climaxed when his father miraculously reveals himself and brings the mother to heel. At the Men's House, he had also seen his share of porn—thrillers set on Earth where men forced women to do whatever the men wanted, and like it.

But this book did not look like porn. A note at the beginning promised the book contained material to "interest, or alarm, or amuse, or instruct, or—and possibly most important of all—entertain you." Erno wondered that Tyler had found this particular 160-year-old book in the lava tube. It seemed too unlikely to be coincidence.

What sort of things would entertain an Earthman of 1936? Erno turned to the first story, "The Ambassador of Poker" by "Achmed Abdullah."

But the archaic text was frustratingly passive—nothing more than black type physically impressed on the pages, without links or explanations. After a paragraph or so rife with obscure cultural references—"cordovan brogues," "knickerbockers," "County Sligo," "a four-in-hand"—Erno's night without sleep caught up with him, and he dozed off.

Heroes

Why does a man remain in the Society of Cousins, when he would have much more authority outside of it, in one of the other lunar colonies, or on Earth?

For one thing, the sex is great.

Men are valued for their sexuality, praised for their potency, competed for by women. From before puberty, a boy is schooled by both men and women on how to give pleasure. A man who can give such pleasure has high status. He is recognized and respected throughout the colony. He is welcome in any bed. He is admired and envied by other men.

THREE

Erno woke suddenly, sweaty and disoriented, trailing the wisps of a dream that faded before he could call it back. He looked at his clock: 1530. He was going to miss the meeting.

He washed his face, applied personal hygiene bacteria, threw on his embroidered jumpsuit, and rushed out of the apartment.

The amphitheater in Sobieski Park was filling as Erno arrived. Five or six hundred people were already there; other cousins would be watching on the link. The dome presented a clear blue sky, and the ring of heliotropes around its zenith flooded the air with sunlight. A slight breeze rustled the old oaks, hovering over the semicircular ranks of seats like aged grandmothers. People came in twos and threes, adults and children, along the paths that led down from the colony perimeter road through the farmlands to the park. Others emerged from the doors at the base of the central spire that supported the dome. Erno found a seat in the top row, far from the stage, off to one side where the seats gave way to grass.

Chairing the meeting was Debra Debrasdaughter. Debrasdaughter was a tiny sixty-year-old woman who, though she had held public office infrequently and never for long, was one of the most respected cousins. She had been Erno's teacher when he was six, and he remembered how she'd sat with him and worked through his feud with Bill Grettasson. She taught him how to play forward on the soccer team. On the soccer field she had been fast and sudden as a bug. She had a warm laugh and sharp brown eyes.

Down on the stage, Debrasdaughter was hugging the secretary. Then the sound person hugged Debrasdaughter. They both hugged the secretary again. A troubled-looking old man sat down in the front row, and all three of them got down off the platform and hugged him. He brushed his hand along Debrasdaughter's thigh, but it was plain that his heart wasn't in it. She kissed his cheek and went back up on the stage.

A flyer wearing red wings swooped over the amphitheater and soared back up again, slowly beating the air. Another pair of flyers were racing around the perimeter of the crater, silhouetted against the clusters of apartments built into the crater walls. A thousand meters above his head Erno could spy a couple of others on the edge of the launch platform at the top of, the spire. As he watched, squinting against the sunlight, one of the tiny figures spread its wings and pushed off, diving down, at first ever so slowly, gaining speed, then, with a flip of wings, soaring out level. Erno could feel it in his own shoulders, the stress that maneuver put on your arms. He didn't like flying. Even in lunar gravity, the chances of a fall were too big.

The amplified voice of Debrasdaughter drew him back to the amphitheater. "Thank you, Cousins, for coming," she said. "Please come to order."

Erno saw that Tyler Durden had taken a seat off to one side of the stage. He wore flaming red coveralls, like a shout.

"A motion has been made to impose a decree of invisibility against Thomas Marysson, otherwise known as Tyler Durden, for a period of one year. We are met here for the first of two discussions over this matter, prior to holding a colony-wide vote."

Short of banishment, invisibility was the colony's maximum social sanction. Should the motion carry, Tyler would be formally ostracized. Tagged by an AI, continuously monitored, he would not be acknowledged by other cousins. Should he attempt to harm anyone, the AI would trigger receptors in his brain stem to put him to sleep.

"This motion was prompted by the disturbances that have ensued as a result of public performances of Thomas Marysson. The floor is now open for discussion."

A very tall woman who had been waiting anxiously stood, and as if by prearrangement, Debrasdaughter recognized her. The hovering mikes picked up her high voice. "I am Yokio Kumiosdaughter. My son is in the hospital as a result of this shameful episode. He is a good boy. He is the kind of boy we all want, and I don't understand how he came to be in that place. I pray that he recovers and lives to become the good man I know he can be.

"We must not let this happen to anyone else's son. At the very least, invisibility will give Thomas Marysson the opportunity to reflect on his actions before he provokes another such tragedy."

Another woman rose. Erno saw it was Rosamund Demisdaughter.

"With due respect to Cousin Kumiosdaughter, I don't believe the riot in my club was Tyler's fault. Her son brought this on himself. Tyler is not responsible for the actions of the patrons. Since when do we punish people for the misbehavior of others?

"The real mistake was sending constables," Rosamund continued. "Whether or not the grievances Tyler gives vent to are real or only perceived, we must allow any cousins to speak their mind. The founders understood that men and women are different. By sending armed officers into that club, we threatened the right of those men who came to see Tyler Durden to be different."

"It was stupid strategy!" someone interrupted. "They could have arrested Durden easily after the show."

"Arrested him? On what grounds?" another woman asked.

Rosamund continued. "Adil Al-Hafez said it when he helped Nora Sobieski raise the money for this colony: 'The cousins are a new start for men as much as women. We do not seek to change men, but to offer them the opportunity to be other than they have been.'"

A man Erno recognized from the biotech factory took the floor. "It's all very well to quote the founders back at us, but they were realists too. Men *are* different. Personalized male power has made the history of Earth one long tale of slaughter, oppression, rape, and war. Sobieski and Al-Hafez and the rest knew that, too: The California massacre sent them here. Durden's incitements will inevitably cause trouble. This kid wouldn't have gotten hurt without him. We can't stand by while the seeds of institutionalized male aggression are planted."

"This is a free speech issue!" a young woman shouted.

"It's not about speech," the man countered. "It's about violence."

Debrasdaughter called for order. The man looked sheepish and sat down. A middle-aged woman with a worried expression stood. "What about organizing a new round of games? Let them work it out on the rink, the flying drome, the playing field."

"We have games of every description," another woman responded. "You think we can make Durden join the hockey team?"

The old man in the front row croaked out, "Did you see that game last week against Aristarchus? They could use a little more organized male aggression!" That drew a chorus of laughter from the crowd.

When the noise died down, an elderly woman took the floor. "I have been a cousin for seventy years," she said. "I've seen troublemakers. There will always be troublemakers. But what's happened to the Good Partners? I remember the North tube blowout of '32. Sixty people died. Life here was brutal and dangerous. But men and women worked together shoulder to shoulder; we shared each other's joys and sorrows. We were good bedmates then. Where is that spirit now?"

Erno had heard such tiresome sermonettes about the old days a hundred times. The discussion turned into a cacophony of voices.

"What are we going to do?" said another woman. "Deprive men of the right to speak?"

"Men are already deprived of the vote! How many voters are men?"

"By living on the colony stipend, men *choose* not to vote. Nobody is stopping you from going to work."

"We work already! How much basic science do men do? Look at the work Laurasson did on free energy. And most of the artists are men."

"—they have the time to devote to science and art, *because of* the material support of the community. They have the luxury of intellectual pursuit."

"And all decisions about what to do with their work are made by women."

"The decisions, which will affect the lives of everyone in the society, are made not by women, but by voters."

"And most voters are women."

"Back to beginning of argument!" someone shouted. "Reload program and repeat."

A smattering of laughter greeted the sarcasm. Debrasdaughter smiled. "These are general issues, and to a certain degree I am content to let them be aired. But do they bear directly on the motion? What, if anything, are we to do about Thomas Marysson?"

She looked over at Tyler, who looked back at her coolly, his legs crossed.

A woman in a constable's uniform rose. "The problem with Thomas Marysson is that he claims the privileges of artistic expression, but he's not really an artist. He's a provocateur."

"Most of the artists in history have been provocateurs," shot back a small, dark man.

"He makes *me* laugh," said another.

"He's smart. Instead of competing with other men, he wants to organize them. He encourages them to band together."

The back-and-forth rambled on. Despite Debrasdaughter's attempt to keep order, the discussion ran into irrelevant byways, circular arguments, vague calls for comity, and general statements of male and female grievance.

Erno had debated all this stuff a million times with the guys at the gym. It annoyed him that Debrasdaughter did not force the speakers to stay on point. But that was typical of a cousins' meeting—they would talk endlessly, letting every nitwit have her say, before actually getting around to deciding anything.

A young woman stood to speak, and Erno saw it was Alicia Keikosdaughter. Alicia and he had shared a tutorial in math, and she had been the second girl he had ever had sex with.

"Of course Durden wants to be seen as an artist," Alicia said. "There's no mystique about the guy who works next to you in the factory. Who wants to sleep with him? The truth—"

"I will!" A good-looking woman interrupted Alicia.

The assembly laughed.

"The truth—" Alicia tried to continue.

The woman ignored her. She stood, her hand on the head of the little girl at her side, and addressed Tyler Durden directly. "I think you need to get laid!" She turned to the others. "Send him around to me! I'll take care of any revolutionary impulses he might have." More laughter.

Erno could see Alicia's shoulders slump, and she sat down. It was a typical case of a matron ignoring a young woman. He got up, moved down the aisle, and slid into a spot next to her.

Alicia turned to him. "Erno. Hello."

"It's not your fault they won't listen," he said. Alicia was wearing a tight satin shirt and Erno could not help but notice her breasts.

She kissed him on the cheek. She turned to the meeting, then back to him. "What do you think they're going to do?"

"They're going to ostracize him, I'll bet."

"I saw him on link. Have you seen him?"

"I was there last night."

Alicia leaned closer. "Really?" she said. Her breath was fragrant, and her lips full. There was a tactile quality to Alicia that Erno found deeply sexy—when she talked to you she would touch your shoulder or bump her knee against yours, as if to reassure herself that you were really there. "Did you get in the fight?"

A woman on the other side of Alicia leaned over. "If you two aren't going to pay attention, at least be quiet so the rest of us can."

Erno started to say something, but Alicia put her hand on his arm. "Let's go for a walk."

Erno was torn. Boring or not, he didn't want to miss the meeting, but it was hard to ignore Alicia. She was a year younger than Erno yet was already on her own, living with Sharon Yasminsdaughter while studying environmental social work. One time Erno had heard her argue with Sharon whether it was true that women on Earth could not use elevators because if they did they would inevitably be raped.

They left the amphitheater and walked through the park. Erno told Alicia his version of the riot at the club, leaving out his exploring the deserted lava tube with Tyler.

"Even if they don't make him invisible," Alicia said, "you know that somebody is going to make sure he gets the message."

"He hasn't hurt anyone. Why aren't we having a meeting about the constable who clubbed Yokiosson?"

"The constable was attacked. A lot of cousins feel threatened. I'm not even sure how I feel."

"The Unwritten Law," Erno muttered.

"The what?"

"Tyler does a bit about it. It was an Earth custom, in most of the patriarchies. The 'unwritten law' said that, if a wife had sex with anyone other than her husband, the husband had the right to kill her and her lover, and no court would hold him guilty."

"That's because men had all the power."

"But you just said somebody would send Tyler a message. Up here, if a man abuses a woman, even threatens to, then the abused woman's friends take revenge. When was the last time anyone did anything about that?"

"I get it, Erno. That must seem unfair."

"Men don't abuse women here."

"Maybe that's why."

"It doesn't make it right."

"You're right, Erno. It doesn't. I'm on your side."

Erno sat down on the ledge of the pool surrounding the fountains. The fountains were the pride of the colony: in a conspicuous show of water consumption the pools surrounded the central spire and wandered beneath the park's trees. Genetically altered carp swam in their green depths, and the air was more humid here than anywhere else under the dome.

Alicia sat next to him. "Remind me why we broke up," Erno said.

"Things got complicated." She had said the same thing the night she told him they shouldn't sleep together anymore. He still didn't know what that meant, and he suspected she said it only to keep from saying something that might wound him deeply. Much as he wanted to insist that he would prefer her honesty, he wasn't sure he could stand it.

"I'm going crazy at home," he told Alicia. "Mother treats me like a child. Lena is starting to act like she's better than me. I do real work at Biotech, but that doesn't matter."

"You'll be in university soon. You're a premium gene hacker."

"Who says?" Erno asked.

"People."

"Yeah, right. And if I am, I still live at home. I'm going to end up just like Nick," he said, "the pet male in a household full of females."

"Maybe something will come of this. Things can change."

"If only," Erno said morosely. But he was surprised and gratified to have Alicia's encouragement. Maybe she cared for him after all. "There's one thing, Alicia . . . I could move in with you."

Alicia raised an eyebrow. He pressed on. "Like you say, I'll be studying at the university next session . . ."

She put her hand on his leg. "There's not much space, with Sharon and me. We couldn't give you your own room."

"I'm not afraid of sharing a bed. I can alternate between you."

"You're so manly, Erno!" she teased.

"I aim to please," he said, and struck a pose. Inside he cringed. It was a stupid thing to say, so much a boy trying to talk big.

Alicia did a generous thing—she laughed. There was affection and understanding in it. It made him feel they were part of some club together. Erno hadn't realized how afraid he was that she would mock him. Neither said anything for a moment. A finch landed on the branch above them, turned its head sideways and inspected them. "You know, you could be just like Tyler Durden, Erno."

Erno started—what did she mean by that? He looked her in the face. Alicia's eyes were calm and green, flecked with gold. He hadn't looked into her eyes since they had been lovers.

She kissed him. Then she touched his lips with her finger. "Don't say anything. I'll talk to Sharon."

He put his arm around her. She melted into him.

In the distance the sounds of the debate were broken by a burst of laughter. "Let's go back," she said.

"All right," he said reluctantly.

They walked back to the amphitheater and found seats in the top row, beside two women in their twenties who joked with each other.

"This guy is no Derek Silviasson," one of them said.

"If he could fuck like Derek, now *that* would be comedy," said her blond partner.

Debrasdaughter was calling for order.

"We cannot compel any cousin to indulge in sex against his will. If he chooses to be celibate, and encourages his followers to be celibate, we can't prevent that without undermining the very freedoms we came here to establish."

Nick Farahsson, his face red and his voice contorted, shouted out, "You just said the key word—followers! We don't need followers here. Followers have ceded their autonomy to a hierarchy. Followers are the tool of phallocracy. Followers started the riot." Erno saw his mother, sitting next to Nick, try to calm him.

Another man spoke. "What a joke! We're all a bunch of followers! Cousins follow customs as slavishly as any Earth patriarch."

"What I don't understand," someone called out directly to Tyler, "is, if you hate it here so much, why don't you just leave? Don't let the airlock door clip your ass on the way out."

"This is my home, too," Tyler said.

He stood and turned to Debrasdaughter. "If you don't mind, I would like to speak."

"We'd be pleased to hear what you have to say," Debrasdaughter said. The trace of a smile on her pale face made her look girlish despite her gray hair. "Speaking for myself, I've been waiting."

Tyler ran his hand over his shaved scalp, came to the front of the platform. He looked up at his fellow citizens, and smiled. "I think you've outlined all the positions pretty clearly so far. I note that Tashi Yokiosson didn't say anything, but maybe he'll get back to us later. It's been a revealing discussion, and now I'd just like to ask you to help me out with a demonstration. Will you do this little thing for me?

"I'd like you all to put your hand over your eyes. Like this—" He covered his own eyes with his palm, peeked out. Most of the assembly did as he asked. "All of you got your eyes covered? Good!

"Because, sweethearts, this is the closest I am going to get to invisibility."

Tyler threw his arms wide, and laughed.

"Make me invisible? You can't see me now! You don't recognize a man whose word is steel, whose reality is not dependent on rules. Men have fought and bled and died for you. Men put their lives on the line for every microscopic step forward our pitiful race has made. Nothing's more visible than the sacrifices men have made for the good of their wives and daughters. Yes, women died too—but they were *real* women, women not threatened by the existence of masculinity.

"You see that tower?" Tyler pointed to the thousand-meter spire looming over their heads. "I can climb that tower! I can fuck every real woman in this amphitheater. I eat a lot of food, drink a lot of alcohol, and take a lot of drugs. I'm *bigger* than you are. I sweat more. I howl like a dog. I make noise. You think anyone can make more noise than me?

"One way or another, Mama, I'm going to keep you awake all night! And *you* think you're the girl that can stop me?

"My Uncle Dick told me when I was a boy, son, don't take it out unless you intend to use it! Well, it's out and it's in use! Rim ram goddamn, sona-fabitch fuck! It is to laugh. This whole discussion's been a waste of oxygen. I'm real, I'm here, get used to it.

"Invisible? Just *try* not to see me."

Then Tyler crouched and leapt, three meters into the air, tucked, did a roll. Coming down, he landed on his hands and did a handspring. The second his feet touched the platform, he shot off the side and ran, taking long, loping strides out of the park and through the cornfields.

A confused murmur rippled through the assembly, broken by a few angry calls. Many puzzled glances. Some people stood.

Debrasdaughter called for order. "I'll ask the assembly to calm down," she said.

Gradually, quiet came.

"I'm sure we are all stimulated by that very original statement. I don't think we are going to get any farther today, and I note that it is coming on time for the swing shifters to leave, so unless there are serious objections I would like to call this meeting to a close.

"The laws call for a second open meeting a week from today, followed by a polling period of three days, at the end of which the will of the colony will be made public and enacted. Do I hear any further discussion?"

There was none.

"Then I hereby adjourn this meeting. We will meet again one week from today at 1600 hours. Anyone who wishes to post a statement in regard to this matter may do so at the colony site, where a room will be open continuously for debate. Thank you for your participation."

People began to break up, talking. The two women beside Erno, joking, left the theater.

Alicia stood. "Was that one of his routines?"

Tyler's speech had stirred something in Erno that made him want to shout. He was grinning from ear to ear. "It is to laugh," he murmured.

Alicia grabbed Erno's wrist. She pulled a pen from her pocket, turned his hand so the palm lay open, and on it wrote "Gilman 334."

"Before you do anything stupid, Erno," she said, "call me."

"Define stupid," he said.

But Alicia had turned away. He felt the tingle of the writing on his hand as he watched her go.

Work

Men are encouraged to apply for an exemption from the mita: the compulsory weekly labor that each cousin devotes to the support of the colony. The cost of this exemption is forfeiture of the right to vote. As artists, writers, artisans, athletes, performers, and especially as scientists, men have an easier path than women. Their interests are supported to the limits of the cousins' resources. But this is not accorded the designation of work, and all practical decisions as to what to do with any creations of their art or discoveries they might make, are left to voters, who are overwhelmingly women.

Men who choose such careers are praised as public-spirited volunteers, sacrificing for the sake of the community. At the same time, they live a life of relative ease, pursuing their interests. They compete with each other for the attentions of women. They may exert influence, but have no legal responsibilities, and no other responsibilities except as they choose them. They live like sultans, but without power. Or like gigolos. Peacocks, and studs.

And those who choose to do work? Work—ah, work is different. Work is mundane labor directed toward support of the colony. Male workers earn no honors, accumulate no status. And because men are always outnumbered by women on such jobs, they have little chance of advancement to a position of authority. They just can't get the votes.

"Twenty-Five Bucks"

Erno began to puzzle out some of the *Stories for Men*. One was about a "prize fighter"—a man who fought another man with his fists for money. This aging fighter agrees with a promoter to fight a younger, stronger man for "twenty-five bucks," which from context Erno gathered was a small sum of money. The boxer spends his time in the ring avoiding getting beaten up. During a pause between the "rounds" of the fight, the promoter comes to him and complains that he is not fighting hard enough, and swears he will not pay the boxer if he "takes a dive." So in the next round the boxer truly engages in the brutal battle, and within a minute gets beaten unconscious.

But because this happens immediately after the promoter spoke to him, in the sight of the audience, the audience assumes the boxer was *told* by the promoter to take a dive. They protest. Rather than defend the boxer, the promoter denies him the twenty-five bucks anyway.

The boxer, unconscious while the promoter and audience argue, dies of a brain hemorrhage.

The story infuriated Erno. It felt so *wrong*. Why did the boxer take on the fight? Why did he allow himself to be beaten so badly? Why did the promoter betray the boxer? What was the point of the boxer's dying in the end? Why did the writer—someone named James T. Farrell—invent this grim tale?

FOUR

A week after the meeting, when Erno logged onto school, he found a message for him from "Ethan Edwards." It read:

I saw you with that girl. Cute. But no sex, Erno. I'm counting on men like you.

Erno sent a reply: "You promised me another adventure. When?"

Then he did biochemistry ("Delineate the steps in the synthesis of human growth hormone") and read Gender & Art for three hours until he had to get to his practicum at biotech.

In order to reduce the risk of stray bugs getting loose in the colony, the biotech factories were located in a bunker separate from the main crater. Workers had to don pressure suits and ride a bus for a couple of kilometers across the lunar surface. A crowd of other biotech workers already filled the locker room at the north airlock when Erno arrived.

"Tyrus told me you're fucking Alicia Keikosdaughter, Erno," said Paul Gwynethsson, whose locker was next to Erno's. "He was out flying. He saw you in the park."

"So? Who are you fucking?" Erno asked. He pulled on his skintight. The fabric, webbed with thermoregulators, sealed itself, the suit's environment system powered up, and Erno locked down his helmet. The helmet's head's-up display was green. He and Paul went to the airlock, passed their ID's through the reader and entered with the others. The exit sign posted the solar storm warning. Paul teased Erno about Alicia as the air was cycled through the lock and they walked out through the radiation maze to the surface.

They got on the bus that dropped off the previous biotech shift. The bus bumped away in slow motion down the graded road. It was late in the lunar afternoon, probably only a day or so of light before the two-week night. If a storm should be detected and the alert sounded, they would have maybe twenty minutes to find shelter before the radiation flux hit the exposed surface. But the ride to the lab went uneventfully.

A man right off the cable train from Tsander was doing a practicum in the lab. His name was Cluny. Like so many Earthmen, he was short and impressively muscled, and spoke slowly, with an odd accent. Cluny was not yet a citizen and had not taken a cousin's name. He was still going through training before qualifying to apply for exemption from the *mita*.

Erno interrupted Cluny as he carried several racks of micro-environment bulbs to the sterilizer. He asked Cluny what he thought of Tyler Durden.

Cluny was closemouthed; perhaps he thought Erno was testing him: "I think if he doesn't like it up here, I can show him lots of places on Earth happy to take him."

Erno let him get on with his work. Cluny was going to have a hard time over the next six months. The culture shock would be nothing next to the genetic manipulation he would have to undergo to adjust him for low-G. The life expectancy of an unmodified human on the moon was forty-eight. No exercise regimen or drugs could prevent the cardiovascular atrophy and loss of bone mass that humans evolved for Earth would suffer.

But the retroviruses could alter the human genome to produce solid fibro-laminar bones in 1/6 G, prevent plaque buildup in arteries, insure pulmonary health, and prevent a dozen other fatal low-G syndromes.

At the same time, licensing biotech discoveries was the colony's major source of foreign exchange, so research was under tight security. Erno pressed his thumb against the gene scanner. He had to go through three levels of clearances to access the experiment he had been working on. Alicia was right—Erno was getting strokes for his rapid learning in gene techniques, and already had a rep. Even better, he liked it. He could spend hours brain-storming synergistic combinations of alterations in mice, adapting Earth genotypes for exploitation.

Right now he was assigned to the ecological design section under Lemmy Odillesson, the premiere agricultural genobotanist. Lemmy was working on giant plane trees. He had a vision of underground bioengineered forests, en-tire ecosystems introduced to newly opened lava tubes that would transform dead, airless immensities into habitable biospheres. He wanted to live in a city of underground lunar tree houses.

Too soon Erno's six-hour shift was over. He suited up, climbed to the sur-face, and took the bus back to the north airlock. As the shift got off, a figure came up to Erno from the shadows of the radiation maze.

It was a big man in a tiger-striped skintight, his faceplate opaqued. Erno shied away from him, but the man held his hands, palms up, in front of him to indicate no threat. He came closer, leaned forward. Erno flinched. The man took Erno's shoulder, gently, and pulled him forward until the black faceplate of his helmet kissed Erno's own.

"Howdy, Erno." Tyler Durden's voice, carried by conduction from a face he could not see, echoed like Erno's own thought.

Erno tried to regain his cool. "Mr. Durden, I presume."

"Switch your suit to Channel Six," Tyler said. "Encrypted." He pulled away and touched the pad on his arm, and pointed to Erno's. When Erno did the same, his radio found Tyler's wavelength, and he heard Tyler's voice in his ear.

"I thought I might catch you out here."

The other workers had all passed by; they were alone. "What are you doing here?"

"You want adventure? We got adventure."

"What adventure?"

"Come along with me."

Instead of heading in through the maze, Tyler led Erno back out to the surface. The fan of concrete was deserted, the shuttle bus already gone back to the lab and factories. From around a corner, Tyler hauled out a backpack, settled it over his shoulders, and struck off east, along the graded road that encircled Fowler. The mountainous rim rose to their right, topped by the beginnings of the dome; to their left was the rubble of the broken highlands. Tyler moved along at a quick pace, taking long strides in the low G with a minimum of effort.

After a while Tyler asked him, "So, how about the book? Have you read it?"

"Some. It's a collection of stories, all about men."

"Learning anything?"

"They seem so primitive. I guess it was a different world back then."

"What's so different?"

Erno told him the story about the prizefighter. "Did they really do that?"

"Yes. Men have always engaged in combat."

"For money?"

"The money is just an excuse. They do it anyway."

"But why did the writer tell that story? What's the point?"

"It's about elemental manhood. The fighters were men. The promoter was not."

"Because he didn't pay the boxer?"

"Because he knew the boxer had fought his heart out, but he pretended that the boxer was a coward in order to keep the audience from getting mad at him. The promoter preserved his own credibility by trashing the boxer's. The author wants you to be like the boxer, not the promoter."

"But the boxer dies—for twenty-five bucks."

"He died a man. Nobody can take that away from him."

"But nobody knows that. In fact, they all think he died a coward."

"The promoter knows he wasn't. The other fighter knows, probably. And thanks to the story, now you know, too."

Erno still had trouble grasping exactly the metaphor Tyler intended when he used the term "man." It had nothing to do with genetics. But before he could quiz Tyler, the older man stopped. By this time they had circled a quarter of the colony and were in the shadow of the crater wall. Tyler switched on his helmet light and Erno did likewise. Erno's thermoregulator pumped heat along the microfibers buried in his suit's skin, compensating for the sudden shift from the brutal heat of lunar sunlight to the brutal cold of lunar darkness.

"Here we are," Tyler said, looking up the crater wall. "See that path?"

It wasn't much of a path, just a jumble of rocks leading up the side of the crater, but once they reached it Erno could see that, by following patches of luminescent paint on boulders, you could climb the rim mountain to the top. "Where are we going?" Erno asked.

"To the top of the world," Tyler said. "From up there I'll show you the empire I'll give you if you follow me."

"You're kidding."

Tyler said nothing.

It was a hard climb to the crater's lip, where a concrete rim formed the foundation of the dome. From here, the dome looked like an unnaturally swollen stretch of *mare,* absurdly regular, covered in lunar regolith. Once the dome had been constructed over the crater, about six meters of lunar soil had been spread evenly over its surface to provide a radiation shield for the interior. Concentric rings every ten meters kept the soil from sliding down the pitch of the dome. It was easier climbing here, but surreal. The horizon of the dome moved ahead of them as they progressed, and it was hard to judge distances.

"There's a solar storm warning," Erno said. "Aren't you worried?"

"We're not going to be out long."

"I was at the meeting," Erno said.

"I saw you," Tyler said. "Cute girl, the dark skinned one. Watch out. You know what they used to say on Earth?"

"What?"

"If women didn't have control of all the pussy, they'd have bounties on their heads."

Erno laughed. "How can you say that? They're our sisters, our mothers."

"And they still have control of all the pussy."

They climbed the outside of the dome.

"What are you going to do to keep from being made invisible?" Erno asked.

"What makes you think they're going to try?"

"I don't think your speech changed anybody's mind."

"So? No matter what they teach you, my visibility is not socially constructed. That's the lesson for today."

"What are we doing out here?"

"We're going to do demonstrate this fact."

Ahead of them a structure hove into sight. At the apex of the dome, just above the central spire, stood a maintenance airlock. Normally, this would be the way workers would exit to inspect or repair the dome's exterior—not the way Erno and Tyler had come. This was not a public airlock, and the entrance code would be encrypted.

Tyler led them up to the door. From his belt pouch he took a key card and stuck it into the reader. Erno could hear him humming a song over his earphones. After a moment, the door slid open.

"In we go, Erno," Tyler said.

They entered the airlock and waited for the air to recycle. "This could get us into trouble," Erno said.

"Yes, it could."

"If you can break into the airlock you can sabotage it. An airlock breach could kill hundreds of people."

"You're absolutely right, Erno. That's why only completely responsible people like us should break into airlocks."

The interior door opened into a small chamber facing an elevator. Tyler put down his backpack, cracked the seal on his helmet and began stripping off his garish suit. Underneath he wore only briefs. Rust-colored pubic hair curled from around the edges of the briefs. Tyler's skin was pale, the muscles in his arms and chest well developed, but his belly soft. His skin was crisscrossed with a web of pink lines where the thermoregulator system of the suit had marked him.

Feeling self-conscious, Erno took off his own suit. They were the same height, but Tyler outweighed him by twenty kilos. "What's in the backpack?" Erno asked.

"Rappelling equipment." Tyler gathered up his suit and the pack and, ignoring the elevator, opened the door beside it to a stairwell. "Leave your suit here," he said, ditching his own in a corner.

The stairwell was steep and the cold air tasted stale; it raised goose bumps on Erno's skin. Clutching the pack to his chest, Tyler hopped down the stairs to the next level. The wall beside them was sprayed with gray insulation. The light from bioluminescents turned their skin greenish yellow.

Instead of continuing down the well all the way to the top of the spire, Tyler stopped at a door on the side of the stairwell. He punched in a code. The door opened into a vast darkness, the space between the exterior and interior shells of the dome. Tyler shone his light inside: Three meters high, broken by reinforcing struts, the cavity stretched out from them into the darkness, curving slightly as it fell away. Tyler closed the door behind them and, in the light of his flash, pulled a notebook from the pack and called up a map. He studied it for a minute, and then led Erno into the darkness.

To the right about ten meters, an impenetrable wall was one of the great cermet ribs of the dome that stretched like the frame of an umbrella from the central spire to the distant crater rim.

Before long Tyler stopped, shining his light on the floor. "Here it is."

"What?"

"Maintenance port. Periodically they have to inspect the interior of the dome, repair the fiberoptics." Tyler squatted down and began to open the lock.

"What are you going to do?"

"We're going to hang from the roof like little spiders, Erno, and leave a gift for our cousins."

The port opened and Erno got a glimpse of the space that yawned below. A thousand meters below them the semicircular ranks of seats of the Sobieski Park amphitheater glowed ghostly white in the lights of the artificial night. Tyler drew ropes and carabineers from his pack, and from the bottom, an oblong device, perhaps fifty centimeters square, wrapped in fiberoptic cloth that glinted in the light of the flashlight. At one end was a timer. The object gave off an aura of threat that was both frightening and instantly attractive.

"What is that thing? Is it a bomb?"

"A bomb, Erno? Are you crazy?" Tyler snapped one of the lines around a reinforcing strut. He donned a harness and handed an identical one to Erno. "Put this on."

"I'm afraid of heights."

"Don't be silly. This is safe as a kiss. Safer, maybe."

"What are we trying to accomplish?"

"That's something of a metaphysical question."

"That thing doesn't look metaphysical to me."

"Nonetheless, it is. Call it the Philosopher's Stone. We're going to attach it to the inside of the dome."

"I'm not going to blow any hole in the dome."

"Erno, I couldn't blow a hole in the dome without killing myself. I guarantee you that, as a result of what we do here, I will suffer whatever consequences anyone else suffers. More than anyone else, even. Do I look suicidal to you, Erno?"

"To tell the truth, I don't know. You sure do some risky things. Why don't you tell me what you intend?"

"This is a test. I want to see whether you trust me."

"You don't trust me enough to tell me anything."

"Trust isn't about being persuaded. Trust is when you do something because your brother asks you to. I didn't have to ask you along on this adventure, Erno. I trusted you." Tyler crouched there, calmly watching Erno. "So, do you have the balls for this?"

The moment stretched. Erno pulled on the climbing harness.

Tyler ran the ropes through the harness, gave him a pair of gloves, and showed Erno how to brake the rope behind his back. Then, with the maybe-bomb Philosopher's Stone slung over his shoulder, Tyler dropped through the port. Feeling like he was about to take a step he could never take back, Erno edged out after him.

Tyler helped him let out three or four meters of rope. Erno's weight made the rope twist, and the world began to spin dizzily. They were so close to the dome's inner surface that the "stars" shining there were huge fuzzy patches of light in the braided fiberglass surface. The farmlands of the crater floor were swathed in shadow, but around the crater's rim, oddly twisted from this god's-eye perspective, the lights of apartment districts cast fans of illumination on the hanging gardens and switchbacked perimeter road. Erno could make out a few microscopic figures down there. Not far from Tyler and him, the top of the central spire obscured their view to the west. The flying stage, thirty meters down from where the spire met the roof, was closed for the night, but an owl nesting underneath flew out at their appearance and circled below them.

Tyler began to swing himself back and forth at the end of his line, gradually picking up amplitude until, at the apex of one of his swings, he latched himself onto the dome's inner surface. "C'mon, Erno! Time's wasting!"

Erno steeled himself to copy Tyler's performance. It took effort to get himself swinging and once he did the arcs were ponderous and slow. He had trouble orienting himself so that one end of his oscillation left him close to Tyler. At the top of every swing gravity disappeared and his stomach lurched. Finally, after what seemed an eternity of trying, Erno swung close enough for Tyler to reach out and snag his leg.

He pulled Erno up beside him and attached Erno's belt line to a ringbolt in the dome's surface. Erno's heart beat fast.

"Now you know you're alive," Tyler said.

"If anyone catches us up here, our asses are fried."

"Our asses are everywhere and always fried. That's the human condition. Let's work."

While Tyler pulled the device out of the bag he had Erno spread glue onto the dome's surface. When the glue was set, the two of them pressed the Philosopher's Stone into it until it was firmly fixed. Because of its reflective surface it would be invisible from the crater floor. "Now, what time did Debra Debrasdaughter say that meeting was tomorrow?"

"1600," Erno said. "You knew that."

Tyler flipped open the lid over the Stone's timer and punched some keys. "Yes, I did."

"And you didn't need my help to do this. Why did you make me come?"

The timer beeped; the digital readout began counting down. Tyler flipped the lid closed. "To give you the opportunity to betray me. And if you want to, you still have—" he looked at his wristward, "—fourteen hours and thirteen minutes."

Male Dominance Behavior

Erno had begun building his store of resentment when he was twelve, in Eva Evasdaughter's molecular biotechnology class. Eva Evasdaughter came from an illustrious family: her mother had been the longest serving member of the colony council. Her grandmother, Eva Kabatsumi, jailed with Nora Sobieski in California, had originated the matronymic system.

It took Erno a while to figure out that that didn't make Evasdaughter a good teacher. He was the brightest boy in the class. He believed in the cousins, respected authority, and worshipped women like his mother and Evasdaughter.

Evasdaughter was a tall woman who wore tight short-sleeved tunics that emphasized her small breasts. Erno had begun to notice such things; sex play was everyone's interest that semester, and he had recently had several erotic fondling sessions with girls in the class.

One day they were studying protein engineering. Erno loved it. He liked how you could make a gene jump through hoops if you were clever enough. He got ahead in the reading. That day he asked Eva Evasdaughter about directed protein mutagenesis, a topic they were not due to study until next semester.

"Can you make macro-modifications in proteins—I mean replace entire sequences to get new enzymes?" He was genuinely curious, but at some level he also was seeking Evasdaughter's approval of his doing extra work.

She turned on him coolly. "Are you talking about using site-directed mutagenesis, or chemical synthesis of oligonucleotides?"

He had never heard of site-directed mutagenesis. "I mean using oligonucleotides to change the genes."

"I can't answer unless I know if we're talking about site-directed or synthesized oligonucleotides. Which is it?"

Erno felt his face color. The other students were watching him. "I—I don't know."

"Yes, you don't," Evasdaughter said cheerfully. And instead of explaining, she turned back to the lesson.

Erno didn't remember another thing for the rest of that class, except looking at his shoes. Why had she treated him like that? She made him feel stupid. Yes, she knew more biotech than he did, but she was the teacher! Of course she knew more! Did that mean she had to put him down?

When he complained to his mother, she only said that he needed to listen to the teacher.

Only slowly did he realize that Evasdaughter had exhibited what he had always been taught was male dominance behavior. He had presented a challenge to her superiority, and she had smashed him flat. After he was, smashed, she could afford to treat him kindly. But she would teach him only after he admitted that he was her inferior.

Now that his eyes were opened, he saw this behavior everywhere. Every day cousins asserted their superiority in order to hurt others. He had been lied to, and his elders were hypocrites.

Yet when he tried to show his superiority, he was told to behave himself. Superior / inferior is wrong, they said. Difference is all.

FIVE

One thing Tyler had said was undoubtedly true: this was a test. How devoted was Erno to the Society of Cousins? How good a judge was he of Tyler's character? How eager was he to see his mother and the rest of his world made uncomfortable, and how large a discomfort did he think was justified? Just how angry was Erno?

After Erno got back to his room, he lay awake, unable to sleep. He ran every moment of his night with Tyler over in his mind, parsed every sentence, and examined every ambiguous word. Tyler had never denied that the Philosopher's Stone was a bomb. Erno looked up the term in the dictionary: a philosopher's stone was "an imaginary substance sought by alchemists in the belief that it would change base metals into gold or silver."

He did not think the change that Tyler's stone would bring had anything to do with gold or silver.

He looked at his palm, long since washed clean, where Alicia had written her number. She'd asked him to call her before he did anything stupid.

At 1545 the next day Erno was seated in the amphitheater among the crowds of cousins. More people were here than had come the previous week, and the buzz of their conversation, broken by occasional laughter, filled the air. He squinted up at the dome to try to figure out just where they had placed the stone. The dome had automatic safety devices to seal any minor air leak. But it couldn't survive a hole blasted in it. Against the artificial blue sky Erno watched a couple of flyers circling like hawks.

1552. Tyler arrived, trailing a gaggle of followers, mostly young men trying to look insolent. He'd showed up—what did that mean? Erno noted that this time, Tyler wore black. He seemed as calm as he had before, and he chatted easily with the others, then left them to take a seat on the stage.

At 1559 Debra Debrasdaughter took her place. Erno looked at his watch. 1600.

Nothing happened.

Was that the test? To see whether Erno would panic and fall for a ruse? He tried to catch Tyler's eye, but got nothing.

Debrasdaughter rapped for order. The ranks of cousins began to quiet, to sit up straighter. Near silence had fallen, and Debrasdaughter began to speak.

"Our second meeting to discuss—"

A flash of light seared the air high above them, followed a second later by a concussion. Shouts, a few screams.

Erno looked up. A cloud of black smoke shot rapidly from a point against the blue. One flyer tumbled, trying to regain his balance; the other had dived a hundred meters seeking a landing place. People pointed and shouted. The blue sky flickered twice, went to white as the imaging system struggled, then recovered.

People boiled out of the amphitheater, headed for pressurized shelter. Erno could not see if the dome had been breached. The smoke, instead of dissipating, spread out in an arc, then flattened up against the dome. It formed tendrils, shapes. He stood there, frozen. It was not smoke at all, he realized, but smart paint.

The nanodevices spread the black paint onto the interior of the dome. The paint crawled and shaped itself, forming letters. The letters, like a message from God, made a huge sign on the inside of the clear blue sky:

"BANG! YOU'RE DEAD!"

"You're Dead!"

One of the other *Stories for Men* was about Harry Rodney and Little Bert, two petty criminals on an ocean liner that has struck an iceberg and is sinking, with not enough lifeboats for all the passengers. The patriarchal custom was that women and children had precedence for spaces in the boats. Harry gives up his space in a boat in favor of some girl. Bert strips a coat and scarf from an injured woman, steals her jewelry, abandons her belowdecks, and uses her clothes to sneak into a lifeboat.

As it happens, both men survive. But Harry is so disgusted by Bert's crime that he persuades him to run away and pretend he is dead. For years, whenever Bert contacts Harry, Harry tells him to stay away or else the police might discover him. Bert never returns home for fear of being found out.

SIX

In the panic and confusion, Tyler Durden disappeared. On his seat at the meeting lay a note: "I did it."

As a first step in responding to the threat to the colony, the Board of Matrons immediately called the question of ostracism, and by evening the population had voted: Tyler Durden was declared invisible.

As if that mattered. He could not be found.

SEVEN

It took several days for the writing to be erased from the dome.

A manhunt did not turn up Tyler. Nerves were on edge. Rumors arose, circulated, were denied. Tyler Durden was still in the colony, in disguise. A cabal of followers was hiding him. No, he and his confederates had a secret outpost ten kilometers north of the colony. Durden was in the employ of the government of California. He had stockpiled weapons and was planning an attack. He had an atomic bomb.

At the gym entrance, AI's checked DNA prints, and Erno was conscious, as never before, of the cameras in every room. He wondered if any monitors had picked up his excursion with Tyler. Every moment he expected a summons on his wristward to come to the assembly offices.

When Erno entered the workout room, he found Tyrus and a number of others wearing white T-shirts that said, "BANG! YOU'RE DEAD!"

Erno took the unoccupied rowing machine next to Ty. Ty was talking to Sid on the other side of him.

A woman came across the room to use the machines. She was tightly muscled, and her dark hair was pulled back from her sweaty neck. As she approached, the young men went silent and turned to look at her. She hesitated. Erno saw something on her face he had rarely seen on a woman's face before: fear. The woman turned and left the gym.

None of the boys said anything. If the others had recognized what had just happened, they did not let it show.

Erno pulled on his machine. He felt the muscles in his legs knot. "Cool shirt," he said.

"Tyrus wants to be invisible, too," said Sid. Sid wasn't wearing one of the shirts.

"Eventually someone will check the vids of Tyler's performances, and see me there," said Ty between strokes. "I'm not ashamed to be Tyler's fan." At thirteen, Erno and Ty had been fumbling lovers, testing out their sexuality. Now Ty was a blunt overmuscled guy who laughed like a hyena. He didn't laugh now.

"It was a rush to judgment," one of the other boys said. "Tyler didn't harm a single cousin. It was free expression."

"He could just as easily have blown a hole in the dome," said Erno. "Do they need any more justification for force?"

Ty stopped rowing and turned toward Erno. Where he had sweated through the fabric, the "Bang!" on his shirt had turned blood red. "Maybe it will come to force. We do as much work, and we're second class citizens." He started rowing again, pulled furiously at the machine, fifty reps a minute, drawing quick breaths.

"That Durden has a pair, doesn't he?" Sid said. Sid was a popular stud-boy. His thick chestnut hair dipped below one eye. "You should have seen the look on Rebecca's face when that explosion went off."

"I hear, if they catch him, the council's not going to stop at invisibility," Erno said. "They'll kick him out."

"Invisibility won't slow Tyler down," Ty said. "Would you obey the decree?" he asked Sid.

"Me? I'm too beautiful to let myself get booted. If Tyler Durden likes masculinists so much, let him go to one of the other colonies, or to Earth. I'm getting laid too often."

Erno's gut tightened. "They will kick him out. My mother would vote for it in a second."

"Let 'em try," Ty grunted, still rowing.

"Is that why you're working out so much lately, Ty?" Sid said. "Planning to move to Earth?"

"No. I'm just planning to bust your ass."

"I suspect it's not busting you want to do to my ass."

"Yeah. Your ass has better uses."

"My mother says Tyler's broken the social contract," Erno said.

"Does your mother—" Ty said, still rowing, "—keep your balls under her pillow?"

Sid laughed.

Erno wanted to grab Ty and tell him, *I was there. I helped him do it!* But he said nothing. He pulled on the machine. His face burned.

After a minute Erno picked up his towel and went to the weight machine. No one paid him any attention. Twenty minutes later he hit the sauna. Sweating in the heat, sullen, resentful. He had *been* there, had taken a bigger risk than any of these fan-boys.

Coming out of the sauna he saw Sid heading for the sex rooms, where any woman who was interested could find a male partner who was willing. Erno considered posting himself to one of the rooms. But he wasn't a stud; he was just an anonymous minor male. He had no following. It would be humiliating to sit there waiting for someone, or worse, to be selected by some old bag.

A day later Erno got himself one of the T-shirts. Wearing it didn't make him feel any better.

It came to him that maybe this was the test Tyler intended: not whether Erno would tell about the Philosopher's Stone before it happened, but whether he would admit he'd helped set it after he saw the uproar it caused in the colony.

If that was the test, Erno was failing. He thought about calling Tyler's apartment, but the constables were sure to be monitoring that number. A new rumor had it Tyler had been captured and was being held in protective custody—threats had been made against his life—until the Board of Matrons could decide when and how to impose the invisibility. Erno imagined Tyler in some bare white room, his brain injected with nanoprobes, his neck fitted with a collar.

At biotech, Erno became aware of something he had never noticed before: how the women assumed first pick of the desserts in the cafeteria. Then, later, when he walked by their table, four women burst into laughter. He turned and stared at them, but they never glanced at him.

Another day he was talking with a group of engineers on break: three women, another man, and Erno. Hana from materials told a joke: "What do you have when you have two little balls in your hand?"

The other women grinned. Erno watched the other man. He stood as if on a trapdoor, a tentative smile on his face. The man was getting ready to laugh, because that was what you did when people told jokes, whether or not they were funny. It was part of the social contract—somebody went into joke-telling mode, and you went into joke-listening mode.

"A man's undivided attention," Hana said.

The women laughed. The man grinned.

"How can you tell when a man is aroused?" Pearl said. "—He's breathing."

"That isn't funny," Erno said.

"Really? I think it is," Hana said.

"It's objectification. Men are just like women. They have emotions, too."

"Cool off, Erno," said Pearl. "This isn't gender equity class."

"There is no gender equity here."

"Someone get Erno a T-shirt."

"Erno wants to be invisible."

"We're already invisible!" Erno said, and stalked off. He left the lab, put on his suit, and took the next bus back to the dome. He quit going to his practicum: he would not let himself be used anymore. He was damned if he would go back there again.

A meeting to discuss what to do about the missing comedian was disrupted by a group of young men marching and chanting outside the meeting room. Constables were stationed in public places, carrying clubs. In online discussion rooms, people openly advocated closing the Men's Houses for fear conspiracies were being hatched in them.

And Erno received another message. This one was from "Harry Callahan."

Are you watching, Erno? If you think our gender situation is GROSS, you can change it. Check exposition.

Crimes of Violence

The incidence of crimes of violence among the cousins is vanishingly small. Colony

archives record eight murders in sixty years. Five of them were man against man,
two man against woman, and one woman against woman.

This does not count vigilante acts of women against men, but despite the lack of
official statistics, such incidents too are rare.

EIGHT

"It's no trick to be celibate when you don't like sex."

"That's the point," Erno insisted. "He does like sex. He likes sex fine. But he's making a sacrifice in order to establish his point: He's not going to be a prisoner of his dick."

Erno was sitting out on the ledge of the terrace in front of their apartment, chucking pebbles at the recycling bin at the corner and arguing with his cousin Lena. He had been arguing with a lot of people lately, and not getting anywhere. Every morning he still left as if he were going to biotech, but instead he hung out in the park or gym. It would take some time for his mother to realize he had dropped out.

Lena launched into a tirade, and Erno was suddenly very tired of it all. Before she could gain any momentum, he threw a last pebble that whanged off the bin, got up and, without a word, retreated into the apartment. He could hear Lena's squawk behind him.

He went to his room and opened a screen on his wall. The latest news was that Tashi Yokiosson had regained consciousness, but that he had suffered neurological damage that might take a year or more to repair. Debate on the situation raged on the net. Erno opened his documents locker and fiddled with a melancholy sonnet he was working on, but he wasn't in the mood.

He switched back to Tyler's cryptic message. *You can change it. Check exposition.* It had something to do with biotech, Erno was pretty sure. He had tried the public databases, but had not come up with anything. There were databases accessible only through the biotech labs, but he would have to return to his practicum to view them, and that would mean he would have to explain his absence. He wasn't ready for that yet.

On impulse, Erno looked up Tyler in the colony's genome database. What was the name Debrasdaughter had called him?—Marysson, Thomas Marysson. He found Tyler's genome. Nothing about it stood out.

Debaters had linked Tyler's bio to the genome. Marysson had been born thirty-six years ago. His mother was a second-generation cousin; his grandmother had arrived with the third colonization contingent, in 2038. He had received a general education, neither excelling nor failing anything. His mother had died when he was twenty. He had moved out into the dorms, had worked uneventfully in construction and repair for fourteen years, showing no sign of rebelliousness before reinventing himself as Tyler Durden, the Comedian.

Until two years ago, absolutely nothing had distinguished him from any of a thousand male cousins.

Bored, Erno looked up his own genome.

There he lay in rows of base pairs, neat as a tile floor. Over at biotech, some insisted that everything you were was fixed in those sequences in black and white. Erno didn't buy it. Where was the gene for desire there, or hope, or despair, or frustration? Where was the gene that said he would sit in front of a computer screen at the age of seventeen, boiling with rage?

He called up his mother's genome. There were her sequences. Some were the same as his. Of course there was no information about his father. To prevent dire social consequences, his father must remain a blank spot in his history, as far as the Society of Cousins was concerned. Maybe some families kept track of such things, but nowhere in the databases were fathers and children linked.

Of course they couldn't stop him from finding out. He knew others who had done it. His father's genome was somewhere in the database, for medical purposes. If he removed from his own those sequences that belonged to his mother, then what was left—at least the sequences she had not altered when she had planned him—belonged to his father. He could cross check those against the genomes of all the colony's men.

From his chart, he stripped those genes that matched his mother's. Using what remained, he prepared a search engine to sort through the colony's males.

The result was a list of six names. Three were brothers: Stuart, Simon, and Josef Bettesson. He checked the available public information on them. They were all in their nineties, forty years older than Erno's mother. Of the remaining men, two were of about her age: Sidney Orindasson and Micah Avasson. Of those two, Mica Avasson had the higher correlation with Erno's genome.

He read the public records for Micah Avasson. Born in 2042, he would be fifty-six years old. A physical address: men's dormitory, East Five lava tube. He keyed it into his notebook.

Without knocking, his mother came into the room. Though he had no reason to be ashamed of his search, Erno shoved the notebook into his pocket.

She did not notice. "Erno, we need to talk."

"By talk do you mean interrogate, or lecture?"

His mother's face stiffened. For the first time he noticed the crow's feet at the corners of her eyes. She moved around his room, picking up his clothes, sorting, putting them away. "You should keep your room cleaner. Your room is a reflection of your mind."

"Please, mother."

She held one of his shirts to her nose, sniffed, and made a face. "Did I ever tell you about the time I got arrested? I was thirteen, and Derek Silviasson and I were screwing backstage in the middle of a performance of *A Doll's House*. We got a little carried away. When Nora opened the door to leave at the end of the second act, she tripped over Derek and me in our second act."

"They arrested you? Why?"

"The head of the Board was a prude. It wouldn't have mattered so much but *A Doll's House* was her favorite play."

"You and Derek Silviasson were lovers?"

She sat down on his bed, a meter from him, and leaned forward. "After the paint bombing, Erno, they went back to examine the recordings from the spex of the officers at the Oxygen Warehouse riot. Who do you suppose, to my surprise, they found there?"

Erno swiveled in his chair to avoid her eyes. "Nick already told you I went there."

"But you didn't. Not only were you there, but at one point you were together with Durden."

"What was I doing?"

"Don't be difficult. I'm trying to protect you, Erno. The only reason I know about this is that Harald Gundasson let me know on the sly. Another report says Durden met you outside the North airlock one day. You're likely to be called in for questioning. I want to know what's going on. Are you involved in some conspiracy?"

His mother looked so forlorn he found it hard to be hostile. "As far as I know there is no conspiracy."

"Did you have something to do with the paint bomb?"

"No. Of course not."

"I found out you haven't been to your practicum. What have you been doing?"

"I've been going to the gym."

"Are you planning a trip to Earth?"

"Don't be stupid, mother."

"Honestly, Erno, I can't guess what you are thinking. You're acting like a spy."

"Maybe I am a spy."

His mother laughed.

"Don't laugh at me!"

"I'm not laughing because you're funny. I'm laughing because I'm scared! This is an ugly business, Erno."

"Stop it, mother. Please."

She stared at him. He tried not to look away. "I want you to listen. Tyler Durden is a destroyer. I've been to Aristarchus, to Tycho. I've seen the patriarchy. Do you want that here?"

"How would I know? I've never been there!" His eyes fell on the copy of *Stories for Men*. "Don't tell me stories about rape and carnage," he said, looking at the book's cover. "I've heard them all before. You crammed them down my throat with my baby food."

"They're true. Do you deny them?"

Erno clenched his jaw, tried to think. Did she have to browbeat him? "I don't know!"

"It's not just carnage. It's waste and insanity. You want to know what they're like—one time I had a talk with this security man at Shackleton. They were mining lunar ice for reaction mass in the shuttles.

"I put it to him that using lunar ice for rocket fuel was criminally wasteful. Water is the most precious commodity on the moon, and here they are blowing it into space.

"He told me it was cheaper to use lunar ice than haul water from Earth. My argument wasn't with him, he said, it was with the laws of the marketplace. Like most of them, he condescended to me, as if I were a child or idiot. He thought that invoking the free market settled the issue, as if to go against the market were to go against the laws of nature. The goal of conquering space justified the expenditure, he said—that they'd get more water somewhere else when they used up the lunar ice."

"He's got an argument."

"The market as a law of nature? 'Conquering space?' How do you conquer space? That's not a goal, it's a disease."

"What does this have to do with Tyler Durden?"

"Durden is bringing the disease here!"

"He's fighting oppression! Men have no power here; they are stifled and ignored. There are no real male cousins."

"There are plenty of male cousins. There are lots of role models. Think of Adil Al-Hafaz, of Peter Sarahsson—of Nick, for pity's sake!"

"Nick? Nick?" Erno laughed. He stood. "You might as well leave now, officer."

His mother looked hurt. "Officer?"

"That's why you're here, isn't it?"

"Erno, I know you don't like me. I'm dull and conventional. But being unconventional, by itself, isn't a virtue. I'm your mother."

"And you're a cop."

That stopped her for a moment. She took a deep breath. "I dearly love you, Erno, but if you think—"

That tone of voice. He'd heard it all his life: all the personal anecdotes are over, now. We're done with persuasion, and it's time for you to do what I say.

"You dearly love nothing!" Erno shouted. "All you want is to control me!"

She started to get up. "I've given you every chance—"

Erno threw *Stories for Men* at her. His mother flinched, and the book struck her in the chest and fell slowly to the floor. She looked more startled than hurt, watching the book fall, tumbling, leaves open; she looked as if she were trying to understand what it was—but when she faced him again, her eyes clouded. Trembling, livid, she stood, and started to speak. Before she could say a word Erno ran from the room.

Property

A man on his own is completely isolated. Other men might be his friends or lovers, but if he has a legal connection to anyone, it is to his mother.

Beyond a certain point, property among the cousins is the possession of the community. Private property passes down from woman to woman, but only outside of the second degree of blood relation. A woman never inherits from her biological mother. A woman chooses her friends and mates, and in the event of her death, her property goes to them. If a woman dies without naming an heir, her property goes to the community.

A man's property is typically confined to personal possessions. Of course, in most families he is petted, and has access to more resources than any female, but the possessions are gotten for him by his mother or his mate, and they belong to her. What property he might hold beyond that belongs to his mother. If he has no mother, then it belongs to his oldest sister. If he has no sister, then it goes to the community.

A man who forsakes his family has nowhere to go.

NINE

The great jazzmen were all persecuted minorities. Black men like Armstrong, Ellington, Coltrane, Parker. And the comedians were all Jews and black men. Leaving his mother's apartment, Erno saw himself the latest in history's long story of abused fighters for expressive freedom.

Erno stalked around the perimeter road, head down. To his left, beyond the parapet, the crater's inner slope, planted with groundsel, wildflowers, and hardy low-G modifications of desert scrub, fell away down to the agricultural fields, the park, and two kilometers distant, clear through the low-moisture air, the aspen-forested opposite slopes. To his right rose the ranks of apartments, refectories, dorms, public buildings and labs, clusters of oblong boxes growing higgledy-piggledy, planted with vines and hanging gardens, divided by ramps and stairs and walkways, a high-tech cliff city in pastel concrete glittering with ilemenite crystals. A small green lizard scuttled across the pebbled composite of the roadway and disappeared among some ground cover.

Erno ignored the people on their way to work and back, talking or playing. He felt like smashing something. But smashing things was not appropriate cousins behavior.

In the southwest quad he turned up a ramp into a residential district. These were newer structures, products of the last decade's planned expansion of living quarters, occupied for the most part by new families. He moved upward by steady leaps, feeling the tension on his legs, enjoying the burn it generated.

Near the top of the rimwall he found Gilman 334. He pressed the door button. The screen remained blank, but after a moment Alicia's voice came from the speaker. "Erno. Come on in."

The door opened and he entered the apartment. It consisted mostly of an open lounge, furnished in woven furniture, with a couple of small rooms adjoining. Six young women were sitting around inhaling mood enhancers, listening to music. The music was Monk, "Brilliant Corners." Erno had given it to Alicia; she would never have encountered twentieth century jazz otherwise.

There was something wrong with Monk in this context. These girls ought to be listening to some lunar music—one of the airy mixed choral groups, or Shari Cloudsdaughter's *Drums and Sunlight*. In this circle of females, the tossed off lines of Sonny Rollins' sax, the splayed rhythms of Monk's piano, seemed as if they were being stolen. Or worse still, studied—by a crew of aliens for whom they could not mean what they meant to Erno.

"Hello," Erno said. "Am I crashing your party?"

"You're not crashing." Alicia took him by the arm. "This is Erno," she said to the others. "Some of you know him."

Sharon was there, one of the hottest women in Alicia's cohort at school—he had heard Sid talk about her. He recognized Betty Sarahsdaughter, Liz Bethsdaughter, both of them, like Alicia, studying social work, both of whom had turned him down at one time or another. Erno liked women as individuals, but in a group, their intimate laughter, gossip, and private jokes—as completely innocent as they might be—made him feel like he knew nothing about them. He drew Alicia aside, "Can we talk—in private?"

"Sure." She took Erno to one of the bedrooms. She sat on the bed, gestured to a chair. "What's the matter?"

"I had a fight with my mother."

"That's what mothers are for, as far as I can tell."

"And the constables are going to call me in for questioning. They think I may be involved in some conspiracy with Tyler Durden."

"Do you know where he is?"

Erno's defenses came up. "Do you care?"

"I don't want to know where he is. If you know, keep it to yourself. I'm not your mother."

"I could be in trouble."

"A lot of us will stand behind you on this, Erno. Sharon and I would." She reached out to touch his arm. "I'll go down to the center with you."

Erno moved to the bed beside her. He slid his hand to her waist, closed his eyes, and rubbed his cheek against her hair. To his surprise, he felt her hand between his shoulder blades. He kissed her, and she leaned back. He looked into her face: her green eyes, troubled, searched his. Her bottom lip was full. He kissed her again, slid his hand to her breast, and felt the nipple taut beneath her shirt.

Leave aside the clumsiness—struggling out of their clothes, the distraction of "Straight, No Chaser" from the other room, Erno's momentary thought of the women out there wondering what was going on in here—and it was the easiest thing in the world. He slid into Alicia as if he were coming home. Though his head swirled with desire, he tried to hold himself back, to give her what she wanted. He kissed her all over. She giggled and teased him and twisted her fingers in his hair to pull him down to her, biting his lip. For fifteen or twenty minutes, the Society of Cousins disappeared.

Erno watched her face, watched her closed eyes and parted lips, as she concentrated on her pleasure. It gave him a feeling of power. Her skin flushed, she gasped, shuddered, and he came.

He rested his head upon her breast, eyes closed, breathing deeply, tasting the salt of her sweat. Her chest rose and fell, and he could hear her heart beating fast, then slower. He held her tight. Neither said anything for a long time.

After a while he asked her, quietly, "Can I stay here?"

Alicia stroked his shoulder, slid out from beneath him, and began to pull on her shirt. "I'll talk to Sharon."

Sharon. Erno wondered how many of the other women in the next room Alicia was sleeping with. Alicia was a part of that whole scene, young men and women playing complex mating games that Erno was no good at. He had no idea what "talking to Sharon" might involve. But Alicia acted as if the thought of him moving in was a complete surprise.

"Don't pull a muscle or anything stretching to grasp the concept," Erno said softly.

Alicia reacted immediately. "Erno, we've never exchanged two words about partnering. What do you expect me to say?"

"We did talk about it—in the park. You said you would talk to Sharon then. Why didn't you?"

"Please, Erno." She drew up her pants and the fabric seamed itself closed over her lovely, long legs. "When you're quiet, you're so sweet."

Sweet. Erno felt vulnerable, lying there naked with the semen drying on his belly. He reached for his clothes. "That's right," he muttered, "I forgot. Sex is the social glue. Fuck him so he doesn't cause any trouble."

"Everything isn't about your penis, Erno. Durden is turning you into some self-destructive *boy*. Grow up."

"Grow up?" Erno tugged on his pants. "You don't want me grown-up. You want the sweet boy, forever. I've figured it out now—you're never even there with me, except maybe your body. At least I think it was you."

Alicia stared at him. Erno recognized that complete exasperation: he had seen it on his mother. From the next room drifted the sound of "Blue Monk," and women laughing.

"Sharon was right," Alicia said, shaking her head. And she chuckled, a little rueful gasp, as if to say, *I can't believe I'm talking with this guy.*

Erno took a step forward and slapped her face. "You bitch," he breathed. "You fucking bitch."

Alicia fell back, her eyes wide with shock. Erno's head spun. He fled the room, ran through the party and out of the apartment.

It was full night now, the dome sprinkled with stars. He stalked down the switchback ramps toward the perimeter road, through the light thrown by successive lampposts, in a straight-legged gait that kicked him off the pavement with every stride. He hoped that anyone who saw him would see his fury and think him dangerous. Down on the road he stood at the parapet, breathing through his mouth and listening to the hum of insects in the fields below.

In the lamplight far to his left, a person in a green uniform appeared. On impulse Erno hopped over the parapet to the slope. Rather than wait for the constable to pass, he bounced off down toward the crater's floor, skidding where it was steep, his shoes kicking up dust. He picked up speed, making headlong four- or five-meter leaps, risking a fall every time his feet touched.

It was too fast. Thirty meters above the floor he stumbled and went flying face forward. He came down sideways, rolled, and slammed his head as he flipped and skidded to a halt. He lay trying to catch his breath. He felt for broken limbs. His shirt was torn and his shoulder ached. He pulled himself up and went down the last few meters to the crater floor, then limped through the fields for Sobieski Park.

In a few minutes he was there, out of breath and sweating. At the fountain he splashed water on his face. He felt his shoulder gingerly, then made his way to the amphitheater. At first he thought the theater was deserted, but then he saw, down on the stage, a couple of women necking, oblivious of him.

He stood in the row where he had spotted Alicia some weeks before. He had hit her. He couldn't believe he had hit her.

TEN

Erno slept in the park and in the morning headed for his biotech shift as if he had never stopped going. No one at the airlock questioned him. Apparently, even though his mind was chaos, he looked perfectly normal. The radiation warning had been renewed; solar monitors reported conditions ripe for a coronal mass ejection. Cousins obliged to go out on the surface were being advised to keep within range of a radiation shelter.

When Erno arrived at the bunker he went to Lemmy Odilleson's lab. Lemmy had not arrived yet. He sat down at his workstation, signed onto the system, pressed his thumb against the gene scanner and accessed the database.

He tried the general index. There was no file named exposition. Following Tyler's reference to "gross," he looked for any references to the number 144. Nothing. Nothing on the gross structures of nucleotides, either. He tried coming at it from the virus index. Dozens of viruses had been engineered by the cousins to deal with problems from soil microbes to cellular breakdowns caused by exposure to surface radiation. There was no virus called exposition.

While he sat there Lemmy showed up. He said nothing of Erno's sudden appearance after his extended absence. "We're making progress on integrating the morphological growth genes into the prototypes," he said excitedly. "The sequences for extracting silicon from the soil are falling into place."

"That's good," Erno said. He busied himself cleaning up the chaos Lemmy typically left in his notes. After a while, he asked casually, "Lemmy, have you ever heard about a virus called 'exposition'?"

"X-position?" Lemmy said vaguely, not looking up from a rack of test bulbs. "Those prefixes go with female sex-linked factors. The Y-position are the male."

"Oh, right."

As soon as Erno was sure Lemmy was caught up in his lab work, he turned back to the archives. First he went to Gendersites, a database he knew mostly for its concentration of anti-cancer modifications. X-position led him to an encyclopedia of information on the X chromosome. Erno called up a number of files, but he saw no point in digging through gene libraries at random. He located a file of experiments on female-linked syndromes from osteoporosis to post menopausal cardiac conditions.

On a whim, he did a search on "gross."

Up popped a file labeled Nucleotide Repeats. When Erno opened the file, the heading read:

Get
Rid
Of
Slimy
girl**S**

The sounds of the lab around him faded as he read the paper.

It described a method for increasing the number of unstable trinucleotide repeats on the X chromosome. All humans had repeat sequences, the presence of which were associated with various diseases: spinal and bulbar muscular atrophy, fragile X mental retardation, myotonic dystrophy, Huntington disease, spinocere-brellar ataxia, dentatorubral-pallidoluysian atrophy, and Machado-Joseph disease. All well understood neurological disorders.

In normal DNA, the repeats were below the level of expression of disease. Standard tests of the zygote assured this. The GROSS paper told how to construct two viruses: the first would plant a time bomb in the egg. At a particular stage of embryonic development the repetition of trinucleotides would explode. The second virus would plant compensating sequences on the Y chromosome.

Creating the viruses would be a tricky but not impossible problem in plasmid engineering. Their effect, however, would be devastating. In males the Y chromosome would suppress the X-linked diseases, but in females the trinucleotide syndromes would be expressed. When the repeats kicked in, the child would develop any one of a host of debilitating or fatal neurological disorders.

Of course once the disorder was recognized, other gene engineers would go to work curing it, or at least identifying possessors prenatally. The GROSS virus would not destroy the human race—but it could burden a generation of females with disease and early death.

Tyler had led Erno to this monstrosity. What was he supposed to do with it?

Nonetheless, Erno downloaded the file into his notebook. He had just finished when Cluny came into the lab.

"Hello, Professor Odillesson," Cluny said to Lemmy. He saw Erno and did a double take. Erno stared back at him.

"I'm not a professor, Michael," Lemmy said.

Cluny pointed at Erno. "You know the constables are looking for him?"

"They are? Why?"

Erno got up. "Don't bother explaining. I'll go."

Cluny moved to stop him. "Wait a minute."

Erno put his hand on Cluny's shoulder to push him aside. Cluny grabbed Erno's arm.

"What's going on?" Lemmy asked.

Erno tried to free himself from Cluny, but the Earthman's grip was firm. Cluny pulled him, and pain shot through the shoulder Erno had hurt in yesterday's spill. Erno hit Cluny in the face.

Cluny's head jerked back, but he didn't let go. His jaw clenched and his expression hardened into animal determination. He wrestled with Erno; they lost their balance, and in slow motion stumbled against a lab bench. Lemmy shouted and two women ran in from the next lab. Before Erno knew it he was pinned against the floor.

"Dead Man"

Many of the stories for men were about murder. The old Earth writers seemed fascinated by murder, and wrote about it from a dozen perspectives.

In one of the stories, a detective whose job it is to throw illegal riders off cargo trains finds a destitute man—a "hobo"—hiding on the train. While being brutally beaten by the detective, the hobo strikes back and unintentionally kills him.

The punishment for such a killing, even an accidental one, is death. Terrified, knowing that he has to hide his guilt, the hobo hurries back to the city. He pretends he never left the "flophouse" where he spent the previous night. He disposes of his clothes, dirty with coal dust from the train.

Then he reads a newspaper report. The detective's body has been found, but the investigators assume that he fell off the train and was killed by accident, and are not seeking anyone. The hobo is completely free from suspicion. His immediate reaction is to go to the nearest police station and confess.

ELEVEN

Erno waited in a small white room at the constabulary headquarters. As a child Erno had come here many times with his mother, but now everything seemed different. He was subject to the force of the state. That fucking cow Cluny. The constables had taken his notebook. Was that *pro forma*, or would they search it until they found the GROSS file?

He wondered what Alicia had done after he'd left the day before. What had she told her friends?

The door opened and two women came in. One of them was tall and good-looking. The other was small, with a narrow face and close-cropped blond hair. She looked to be a little younger than his mother. She sat down across from him; the tall woman remained standing.

"This can be simple, Erno, if you let it," the small woman said. She had an odd drawl that, combined with her short stature, made Erno wonder if she was from Earth. "Tell us where Tyler Durden is. And about the conspiracy."

Erno folded his arms across his chest. "I don't know where he is. There is no conspiracy."

"Do we have to show you images of you and him together during the Oxygen Warehouse riot?"

"I never saw him before that, or since. We were just hiding in the back room."

"You had nothing to do with the smartpaint explosion?"

"No."

The tall woman, who still had not spoken, looked worried. The blond interrogator leaned forward, resting her forearms on the table. "Your DNA was found at the access portal where the device was set."

Erno squirmed. He imagined a sequence of unstable nucleotide triplets multiplying in the woman's cells. "He asked me to help him. I had no idea what it was."

"No idea. So it could have been a bomb big enough to blow a hole in the dome. Yet you told no one about it."

"I knew he wasn't going to kill anyone. I could tell."

The interrogator leaned back. "I hope you will excuse the rest of us if we question your judgment."

"Believe me, I would never do anything to hurt a cousin. Ask my mother."

The tall woman finally spoke. "We have. She does say that. But you have to help us out, Erno. I'm sure you can understand how upset all this has made the polity."

"Forget it, Kim," the other said. "Erno here's not going to betray his lover."

"Tyler's not my lover," Erno said.

The blond interrogator smirked. "Right."

The tall one said, "There's nothing wrong with you being lovers, Erno."

"Then why did this one bring it up?"

"No special reason," said the blond. "I'm just saying you wouldn't betray him."

"Well, we're not lovers."

"Too bad," the blond muttered.

"You need to help us, Erno," the tall one said. "Otherwise, even if we let you go, you're going to be at risk of violence from other cousins."

"Only if you tell everyone about me."

"So we should just let you go, and not inconvenience you by telling others the truth about you," said the blond.

"What truth? You don't know me."

She came out of her chair, leaning forward on her clenched fists. Her face was flushed. "Don't know you? I know all about you."

"Mona, calm down," the other woman said.

"Calm down? Earth history is full of this! Men sublimate their sexual attraction in claims of brotherhood—with the accompanying military fetishism, penis comparing, suicidal conquer-or-die movements. Durden is heading for one of those classic orgasmic armageddons: Masada, Hitler in the bunker, David Koresh, September 11, the California massacre."

The tall one grabbed her shoulder and tried to pull her back. "Mona."

Mona threw off the restraining hand, and pushed her face up close to Erno's. "If we let this little shit go, I guarantee you he'll be involved in some transcendent destructive act—suicidally brave, suicidally cowardly—aimed at all of us. The signs are all over him." Spittle flew in Erno's face.

"You're crazy," Erno said. "If I wanted to fuck him, I would just fuck him."

The tall one tried again. "Come away, officer."

Mona grabbed Erno by the neck. "Where is he!"

"Come away, now!" The tall cop yanked the small woman away, and she fell back. She glared at Erno. The other, tugging her by the arm, pulled her out of the room.

Erno tried to catch his breath. He wiped his sleeve across his sweating face. He sat there alone for a long time, touching the raw skin where she had gripped his neck. Then the door opened and his mother came in.

"Mom!"

She carried some things in her hands, put them on the table. It was the contents of his pockets, including his notebook. "Get up."

"What's going on?"

"Just shut up and come with me. We're letting you go."

Erno stumbled from the chair. "That officer is crazy."

"Never mind her. I'm not sure she isn't right. It's up to you to prove she isn't."

She hustled him out of the office and into the hall. In seconds Erno found himself, dizzy, in the plaza outside the headquarters. "You are not out of trouble. Go home, and stay there," his mother said, and hurried back inside.

Passersby in North Six watched him as he straightened his clothes. He went to sit on the bench beneath the acacia trees at the lava tube's center. He caught his breath.

Erno wondered if the cop would follow through with her threat to tell about his helping with the explosion. He felt newly vulnerable. But it was not just vulnerability he felt. He had never seen a woman lose it as clearly as the interrogator had. He had gotten to her in a way he had never gotten to a matron in his life. She was actually *scared* of him!

Now what? He put his hand in his pocket, and felt the notebook.

He pulled it out. He switched it on. The GROSS file was still there, and so was the address he'd written earlier.

A Dream

Erno was ten when his youngest sister Celeste was born. After the birth, his mother fell into a severe depression. She snapped at Erno, fought with Aunt Sophie, and complained about one of the husbands until he moved out. Erno's way of coping was to disappear; his cousin Aphra coped by misbehaving.

One day Erno came back from school to find a fire in the middle of the kitchen floor, a flurry of safetybots stifling it with foam, his mother screaming, and Aphra—who had apparently started the fire—shouting back at her. Skidding on the foam, Erno stepped between the two of them, put his hands on Aphra's chest, and made her go to her room.

The whole time, his mother never stopped shouting. Erno was angrier at her than at Aphra. She was supposed to be the responsible one. When he returned from quieting Aphra, his mother ran off to her room and slammed the door. Erno cleaned the kitchen and waited for Aunt Sophie to come home.

The night of the fire he had a dream. He was alone in the kitchen, and then a man was there. The man drew him aside. Erno was unable to make out his face. "I am your father," the man said. "Let me show you something." He made Erno sit down and called up an image on the table. It was Erno's mother as a little girl. She sat, cross-legged, hunched over some blocks, her face screwed up in troubled introspection. "That's her second phase of work expression," Erno's father said.

With a shock, Erno recognized the expression on the little girl's face as one he had seen his mother make as she concentrated.

"She hates this photo," Erno's father said, as if to persuade Erno not to judge her: she still contained that innocence, that desire to struggle against a problem she could not solve. But Erno was mad. As he resisted, the father pressed on, and began to lose it too. He ended up screaming at Erno, "You can't take it? I'll make you see! I'll make you see!"

Erno put his hands over his ears. The faceless man's voice was twisted with rage. Eventually he stopped shouting. "There you go, there you go," he said quietly, stroking Erno's hair. "You're just the same."

TWELVE

On his way to the East Five tube, Erno considered the officer's rant. Maybe Tyler did want to sleep with him. So what? The officer was some kind of homophobe and ought to be relieved. Raving about violence while locking him up in a room. And then trying to choke him. Yes, he had the GROSS file in his pocket, yes he had hit Alicia—but he was no terrorist. The accusation was just a way for the cop to ignore men's legitimate grievances.

But they must not have checked the file, or understood it if they did. If they knew about GROSS, he would never have been freed.

Early in the colony's life, the East Five lava tube had been its major agricultural center. The yeast vats now produced only animal fodder, but the hydroponics rack farms still functioned, mostly for luxury items. The rote work of tending the racks fell to cousins who did not express ambition to do anything more challenging. They lived in the tube warrens on the colony's Minimum Living Standard.

A stylized painting of a centaur graced the entrance of the East Five men's warren. Since the artist had not likely ever studied a real horse, the stance of the creature looked deeply suspect to Erno. At the lobby interface Erno called up the AI attendant. The AI came on-screen as a dark brown woman wearing a glittery green shirt.

"I'm looking for Micah Avasson," Erno asked it.

"Who is calling?"

"Erno Pamelasson."

"He's on shift right now."

"Can I speak with him?"

"Knock yourself out." The avatar pointed off-screen toward a dimly lit passageway across the room. She appeared on the wall near the doorway, and called out to Erno, "Over here. Follow this corridor, third exit left to the Ag tube."

Outside of the lobby, the corridors and rooms here had the brutal utilitarian quality that marked the early colony, when survival had been the first concern and the idea of humane design had been to put a mirror at the end of a room to try to convince the eye that you weren't living in a cramped burrow some meters below the surface of a dead world. An environmental social worker would shudder.

The third exit on the left was covered with a clear permeable barrier. From the time he was a boy Erno had disliked passing through these permeable barriers; he hated the feel of the electrostatics brushing his face. He took a mask from the dispenser, fitted it over his nose and mouth, closed his eyes and passed through into the Ag tube. Above, layers of gray mastic sealed the tube roof; below, a concrete floor supported long rows of racks under light transmitted fiberoptically from the heliostats. A number of workers wearing coveralls and oxygen masks moved up and down the rows tending the racks. The high CO_2 air was laden with humidity, and even through the mask smelled of phosphates.

Erno approached a man bent over a drawer of seedlings he had pulled out of a rack. The man held a meter from which wires dangled to a tube immersed in the hydroponics fluid. "Excuse me," Erno said. "I'm looking for Micah Avasson."

The man lifted his head, inspected Erno, then without speaking turned. "Micah!" He called down the row.

A tall man a little farther down the aisle looked up and peered at them. He had a full head of dark hair, a birdlike way of holding his shoulders. After a moment he said, "I'm Micah Avasson."

Erno walked down toward him. Erno was nonplused—the man had pushed up his mask from his mouth and was smoking a cigarette, using real fire. No, not a cigarette—a joint.

"You can smoke in here? What about the fire regulations?"

"We in the depths are not held to as high a standard as you." Micah said this absolutely deadpan, as if there were not a hint of a joke. "Not enough O_2 to make a decent fire anyway. It takes practice just to get a good buzz off this thing in here without passing out."

Joint dangling from his lower lip, the man turned back to the rack. He wore yellow rubber gloves, and was pinching the buds off the tray of squat green leafy plants. Erno recognized them as a modified broadleaf sensamilla.

"You're using the colony facilities to grow pot."

"This is my personal crop. We each get a personal rack. Sparks initiative." Micah kept pinching buds. "Want to try some?"

Erno gathered himself. "My name is Erno Pamelasson. I came to see you because—"

"You're my son." Micah said, not looking at him.

Erno stared, at a loss for words. Up close the lines at the corners of the man's eyes were distinct, and there was a bit of sag to his chin. But the shape of Micah's face reminded Erno of his own reflection in the mirror.

"What did you want to see me about?" Micah pushed the rack drawer closed and looked at Erno. When Erno stood there dumb, he wheeled the stainless steel cart beside him down to the next rack. He took a plastic bin from the cart, crouched, pulled open the bottom drawer of the rack and began harvesting cherry tomatoes.

Finally, words came to Erno. "Why haven't I ever seen you before?"

"Lots of boys never meet their fathers."

"I'm not talking about other fathers. Why aren't you and my mother together?"

"You assume we were together. How do you know that we didn't meet in the sauna some night, one time only?"

"Is that how it was?"

Micah lifted a partially yellow tomato on his fingertips, then left it on the vine to ripen. He smiled. "No. Your mother and I were in love. We lived together for twenty-two months. And two days."

"So why did you split?"

"That I don't remember so well. We must have had our reasons. Everybody has reasons."

Erno touched his shoulder. "Don't give me that."

Micah stood, overbalancing a little. Erno caught his arm to steady him. "Thanks," Micah said. "The knees aren't what they used to be." He took a long drag on the joint, exhaled at the roof far overhead. "All right, then. The reason we broke up is that your mother is a cast-iron bitch. And I am a cast-iron bastard. The details of our breakup all derive from those simple facts, and I don't recall them. I do recall that we had good fun making you, though. I remember that well."

"I bet."

"You were a good baby, as babies go. Didn't cry too much. You had a sunny disposition." He took a final toke on the joint, and then dropped the butt into the bin of tomatoes. "Doesn't seem to have lasted."

"Were you there when I was born?"

"So we're going to have this conversation." Micah exhaled the last cloud of smoke, slipped his mask down, and finally fixed his watery brown eyes on Erno. "I was there. I was there until you were maybe six or seven months. Then I left."

"Did she make you leave?"

"Not really." His voice was muffled now. "She was taken with me at first because of the glamor—I was an acrobat, the *Cirque Jacinthe*? But her sister was in the marriage, and her friends. She had her mentor, her support group. I was just the father. It was okay while it was fun, and maybe I thought it was something more when we first got together, but after a while it wasn't fun anymore."

"You just didn't want the responsibility!"

"Erno, to tell you the truth, that didn't have much to do with it. I liked holding you on my lap and rubbing you with my beard. You would giggle. I would toss you up into the air and catch you. You liked that. Drove your mother crazy—you're going to hurt him, she kept saying."

Erno had a sudden memory of being thrown high, floating, tumbling. Laughing.

"So why did you leave?"

"Pam and I just didn't get along. I met another woman, that got hot, and Pam didn't seem to need me around anymore. I had filled my purpose."

Emotion worked in Erno. He shifted from foot to foot. "I don't understand men like you. They've stuck you down here in a dorm! You're old, and you've got nothing."

"I've got everything I need. I have friends."

"Women shit on you, and you don't care."

"There are women just like me. We have what we want. I work. I read. I grow my plants. I have no desire to change the world. The world works for me."

"The genius of the founders, Erno—" Micah opened another drawer and started on the next rack of tomatoes, "—was that they minimized the contact of males and females. They made it purely voluntary. Do you realize how many centuries men and women tore themselves to pieces through forced intimacy? In every marriage, the decades of lying that paid for every week of pleasure? That the vast majority of men and women, when they spoke honestly, regretted the day they had ever married?"

"We have no power!"

Micah made a disgusted noise. "Nobody has any power. On Earth, for every privilege, men had six obligations. I'm sorry you feel that something has been taken from you. If you feel that way, I suggest you work on building your own relationships. Get married, for pity's sake. Nothing is stopping you."

Erno grabbed Micah's wrist. "Look at me!"

Micah looked. "Yes?"

"You knew I was your son. Doesn't that mean you've been paying attention to me?"

"From a distance. I wish you well, you understand."

"You know I was responsible for the explosion at the meeting! The constables arrested me!"

"No. Really? That sounds like trouble, Erno."

"Don't you want to ask me anything?"

"Give me your number. If I think of something, I'll call. Assuming you're not banished by then."

Erno turned away. He stalked down the row of hydroponics.

"Come by again, Erno!" Micah called after him. "Anytime. I mean it. Do you like music?"

The next man down was watching Erno now. He passed through the door out of the Ag tube, tore off the mask and threw it down.

Some of the permeable barrier must have brushed Erno's face when he passed through, because as he left East Five he found he couldn't keep his eyes from tearing up.

"The Grandstand Complex"

Two motorcycle racers have been rivals for a long time. The one telling the story has been beating the other, Tony Lukatovich, in every race. Tony takes increasing risks to win the crowd's approval, without success. Finally he makes a bet with the narrator: whoever wins the next race, the loser will kill himself.

The narrator thinks Tony is crazy. He doesn't want to bet. But when Tony threatens to tell the public he is a coward, he agrees.

In the next race, Tony and another rider are ahead of the narrator until the last turn, where Tony's bike bumps the leader's and they both crash. The narrator wins, but Tony is killed in the crash.

Then the narrator finds out that, *before the race,* Tony told a newspaper reporter that the narrator had decided to retire after the next fatal crash. Did Tony deliberately get himself killed in order to make him retire?

Yet, despite the news report, the winner doesn't have to retire. He can say he changed his mind. Tony hasn't won anything, has he? If so, what?

THIRTEEN

Erno had not left the apartment in days. In the aftermath of his police interview, his mother had hovered over him like a bad mood, and it was all he could do to avoid her reproachful stare. Aunt Sophie and Lena and even Aphra acted like he had some terminal disease that might be catching. They intended to heap him with shame until he was crushed. He holed up in his room listening to an ancient recording, "Black and Blue," by Louis Armstrong. The long dead jazzman growled, "What did I do, to feel so black and blue?"

A real man would get back at them. Tyler would. And they would know that they were being gotten, and they would be gotten in the heart of their assumption of superiority. Something that would show women permanently that men were not to be disregarded.

Erno opened his notebook and tried writing a poem.

When you hit someone
It changes their face.

Your mother looks shocked and old.
Alicia looks younger.
Men named Cluny get even stupider than they are.

It hurts your fist.
It hurts your shoulder.

The biggest surprise: you can do it.
Your fist is there at the end of your arm
Waiting
At any and every moment
Whether you are aware of it or not.

Once you know this
The world changes.

He stared at the lines for some minutes, then erased them. In their place he tried writing a joke.

Q: How many matrons does it take to screw in a light bulb?
A: Light bulbs don't care to be screwed by matrons.

He turned off his screen and lay on his bed, his hands behind his head, and stared at the ceiling. He could engineer the GROSS virus. He would not even need access to the biotech facilities; he knew where he could obtain almost everything required from warehouses within the colony. But he would need a place secret enough that nobody would find him out.

Suddenly he knew the place. And with it, he knew where Tyler was hiding.

The northwest lava tube was fairly busy when Erno arrived at 2300. Swing shift cousins wandered into the open clubs, and the free enterprise shops were doing their heaviest business. The door to the Oxygen Warehouse was dark, and a public notice was posted on it. The door was locked, and Erno did not want to draw attention by trying to force it.

So he returned to the construction materials warehouse in North Six. Little traffic here, and Erno was able to slip inside without notice. He kept behind the farthest aisle until he reached the back wall and the deserted airlock that was being used for storage. It took him some minutes to move the building struts and slide through to the other end. The door opened and he was in the deserted lava tube.

It was completely dark. He used his flashlight to retrace their steps from weeks ago.

Before long, Erno heard a faint noise ahead. He extinguished the flash and saw, beyond several bends in the distance, a faint light. He crept along until he reached a section where light fell from a series of open doorways. He slid next to the first and listened.

The voices from inside stopped. After a moment one of them called, "Come in."

Nervous, Erno stepped into the light from the open door. He squinted and saw Tyler and a couple of other men in a room cluttered with tables, cases of dried food, oxygen packs, scattered clothes, blankets, surface suits. On the table were book readers, half-filled juice bulbs, constables' batons.

One of the younger men came up to Erno and slapped him on the back. "Erno. My man!" It was Sid.

The others watched Erno speculatively. Tyler leaned back against the table. He wore a surface skintight; beside him lay his utility belt. His hair had grown out into a centimeter of red bristle. He grinned. "I assume you've brought the goods, Erno."

Erno pulled his notebook from his pocket. "Yes."

Tyler took the notebook and, without moving his eyes from Erno's, put it on the table. "You can do this, right?"

"Erno's a wizard," Sid said. "He can do it in his sleep."

The other young men just watched Erno. They cared what he was going to say.

"I can do it."

Tyler scratched the corner of his nose with his index finger. "Will you?"

"I don't know."

"Why don't you know? Is this a hard decision?"

"Of course it is. A lot of children will die. Nothing will ever be the same."

"We're under the impression that's the point, Erno. Come with me," Tyler said, getting off the table. "We need to talk."

Tyler directed the others to go back to work and took Erno into another room. This one had a cot, a pile of clothes, and bulbs of alcohol lying around. On a wall screen was a schematic of the colony's substructure.

Tyler pushed a pile of clothes off a chair. "Sit down."

Erno sat. "You knew about this place before we came here the night of the riot."

Tyler said nothing.

"They asked me if there was a conspiracy," Erno continued. "I told them no. Is there?"

"Sure there is. You're part of it."

"I'm not part of anything."

"That's the trouble with men among the cousins, Erno. We're not part of anything. If a man isn't part of something, then he's of no use to anybody."

"Help me out, Tyler. I don't get it."

"They say that men can't live only with other men. I don't believe that. Did you ever study the warrior culture?"

"No."

"Men banding together—for duty, honor, clan. That's what the warrior lived by throughout history. It was the definition of manhood.

"The matrons say men are extreme, that they'll do anything. They're right. A man will run into a collapsing building to rescue a complete stranger. That's why, for most of human history, the warrior was necessary for the survival of the clan—later the nation.

"But the twentieth century drained all the meaning out of it. First the great industrial nations exploited the warrior ethic, destroying the best of their sons for money, for material gain, for political ideology. Then the feminist movement, which did not understand the warrior, and feared and ridiculed him, grew. They even persuaded some men to reject masculinity.

"All this eventually erased the purpose from what was left of the warrior culture. Now, if the warrior ethic can exist at all, it must be personal. 'Duty, honor, self.'"

"Self?"

"Self. In some way it was always like that. Sacrifice for others is not about the others, it's the ultimate assertion of self. It's the self, after all, that decides to place value in the other. What's important is the *self* and the *sacrifice*, not the cause for which you sacrifice. In the final analysis, all sacrifices are in service of the self. The pure male assertion."

"You're not talking about running into a collapsing building, Tyler."

Tyler laughed. "Don't you get it yet, Erno? We're living in a collapsing building!"

"If we produce this virus, people are going to die."

"Living as a male among the cousins is death. They destroy certain things, things that are good—only this society defines them as bad. Fatherhood. Protection of the weak by the strong. There's no *force* here, Erno. There's no *growth*. The cousins are an evolutionary dead end. In time of peace it may look fine and dandy, but in time of war, it would be wiped out in a moment."

Erno didn't know what to say.

"This isn't some scheme for power, Erno. You think I'm in this out of some abstract theory? This is life's blood. This—"

Sid ran in from the hall. "Tyler," he said. "The warehouse door has cycled again!"

Tyler was up instantly. He grabbed Erno by the shirt. "Who did you tell?"

"Tell? No one!"

"Get the others!" Tyler told Sid. But as soon as Sid left the room an explosion rocked the hall, and the lights went out. Tyler still had hold of Erno's shirt, and dragged him to the floor. The air was full of stinging fumes.

"Follow me if you want to live!" Tyler whispered.

They crawled away from the hall door, toward the back of the room. In the light of the wall screen, Tyler upended the cot and yanked open a meter-square door set into the wall. When Erno hesitated, Tyler dragged him into the dark tunnel beyond.

They crawled on hands and knees for a long time. Erno's eyes teared from the gas, and he coughed until he vomited. Tyler pulled him along in the blackness until they reached a chamber, dimly lit in red, where they could stand. On the other side of the chamber was a pressure door.

"Put this on," Tyler said, shoving a surface suit into Erno's arms. "Quickly!"

Erno struggled to pull on the skintight, still gasping for breath. "I swear I had nothing to do with this," he said.

"I know," Tyler said. He sealed up his own suit and locked down his tiger-striped helmet.

"Brace yourself. This isn't an airlock," Tyler said, and hit the control on the exterior door.

The moment the door showed a gap, the air blew out of the chamber, almost knocking Erno off his feet. When it opened wide enough, they staggered through into a crevasse. The moisture in the escaping air froze and fell as frost in the vacuum around them. Erno wondered if their pursuers would be able to seal the tube or get back behind a pressure door before they passed out.

Tyler and Erno emerged from the crevasse into a sloping pit, half of which was lit by the glare of hard sunlight. They scrambled up the slope through six centimeters of dust and reached the surface.

"Now what?" Erno said.

Tyler shook his head and put his hand against Erno's faceplate. He leaned over and touched his helmet to Erno's. "Private six, encrypted."

Erno switched his suit radio.

"They won't be out after us for some time," Tyler said. "Since we left that Judas-book of yours behind, they may not even know where we are."

"Judas book?"

"Your notebook—you must have had it with you when the constables questioned you."

"Yes. But they didn't know what the download meant or they wouldn't have returned it to me."

"Returned it to you? Dumbass. They put a tracer in it."

Erno could see Tyler's dark eyes dimly through the faceplate, inches from his own, yet separated by more than glass and vacuum. "I'm sorry."

"Forget it."

"When we go back, we'll be arrested. We might be banished."

"We're not going back just yet. Follow me."

"Where can we go?"

"There's a construction shack at an abandoned ilemenite mine south of here. It's a bit of a hike—two to three hours—but what else are we going to do on such a fine morning?"

Tyler turned and hopped off across the surface. Erno stood dumbly for a moment, then followed.

They headed south along the western side of the crater. The ground was much rockier, full of huge boulders and pits where ancient lava tubes had collapsed millennia ago. The suit Erno wore was too tight, and pinched him in the armpits and crotch. His thermoregulators struggled against the open sunlight, and he felt his body inside the skintight slick with sweat. The bind in his crotch became a stabbing pain with every stride.

Around to the south side of Fowler, they struck off to the south. Tyler followed a line of boot prints and tractor treads in the dust. The land rose to Adil's Ridge after a couple of kilometers, from which Erno looked back and saw, for the first time, all of the domed crater where he had spent his entire life.

"Is this construction shack habitable?" he asked.

"I've got it outfitted."

"What are we going to do? We can't stay out here forever."

"We won't. They'll calm down. You forget that we haven't done anything but spray a prank message on the dome. I'm a comedian. What do they expect from a comedian?"

Erno did not remind Tyler of the possible decompression injuries their escape might have caused. He tucked his head down and focused on keeping up with the big man's steady pace. He drew deep breaths. They skipped along without speaking for an hour or more. Off to their left, Erno noticed a line of distant pylons, with threads of cable strung between them. It was the cable train route from Fowler to Tsander several hundred kilometers south.

Tyler began to speak. "I'm working on some new material. For my comeback performance. It's about the difference between love and sex."

"Okay. So what's the difference?"

"Sex is like a fresh steak. It smells great, you salivate, you consume it in a couple of minutes, you're satisfied, you feel great, and you fall asleep."

"And love?"

"Love is completely different. Love is like flash-frozen food—it lasts forever. Cold as liquid hydrogen. You take it out when you need it, warm it up. You persuade yourself it's just as good as sex. People who promote love say it's even better, but that's a lie constructed out of necessity. The only thing it's better than is starving to death."

"Needs a little work," Erno said. After a moment he added. "There's a story in *Stories for Men* about love."

"I'd think the stories for men would be about sex."

"No. There's no sex in any of them. There's hardly any women at all. Most of them are about men competing with other men. But there's one about a rich man who bets a poor young man that hunger is stronger than love. He locks the poor man and his lover in separate rooms with a window between them, for seven days, without food. At the end of the seven days they're starving. Then he puts them together in a room with a single piece of bread."

"Who eats it?"

"The man grabs it, and is at the point of eating it when he looks over at the woman, almost unconscious from hunger. He gives it to her. She refuses it, says he should have it because he's more hungry than she is. So they win the bet."

Tyler laughed. "If it had been a steak, they would have lost." They continued hiking for a while. "That story isn't about love. It's about the poor man beating the rich man."

Erno considered it. "Maybe."

"So what have you learned from that book? Anything?"

"Well, there's a lot of killing—it's like the writers are obsessed with killing. The characters kill for fun, or sport, or money, or freedom, or to get respect. Or women."

"That's the way it was back then, Erno. Men—"

Tyler's voice was blotted out by a tone blaring over their earphones. After fifteen seconds an AI voice came on:

"SATELLITES REPORT A MAJOR SOLAR CORONAL MASS EJECTION. PARTICLE FLUX WILL BEGIN TO RISE IN TWENTY MINUTES, REACHING LETHAL LEVELS WITHIN THIRTY. ALL PERSONS ON THE SURFACE SHOULD IMMEDIATELY SEEK SHELTER. REFRAIN FROM EXPOSURE UNTIL THE ALL CLEAR SOUNDS.

"REPEAT: A MAJOR SOLAR RADIATION EVENT HAS OCCURRED. ALL PERSONS SHOULD IMMEDIATELY TAKE SHELTER."

Both of them stopped. Erno scanned the sky, frantic. Of course there was no difference. The sun threw the same harsh glare it always threw. His heart thudded in his ears. He heard Tyler's deep breaths in his earphones.

"How insulated is this shack?" he asked Tyler. "Can it stand a solar storm?"

Tyler didn't answer for a moment. "I doubt it."

"How about the mine? Is there a radiation shelter? Or a tunnel?"

"It was a strip mine. Besides," Tyler said calmly, "we couldn't get there in twenty minutes."

They were more than an hour south of the colony.

Erno scanned the horizon, looking for some sign of shelter. A crevasse, a lava tube—maybe they'd run out of air, but at least they would not fry. He saw, again, the threads of the cable towers to the east.

"The cable line!" Erno said. "It has radiation shelters for the cable cars all along it."

"If we can reach one in time."

Erno checked his clock readout. 0237. Figure they had until 0300. He leapt off due east, toward the cable towers. Tyler followed.

The next fifteen minutes passed in a trance, a surreal slow motion broken field race through the dust and boulders toward the pylons to the east. Erno pushed himself to the edge of his strength, until a haze of spots rose before his eyes. They seemed to move with agonizing slowness.

They were 500 meters from the cable pylon. 300 meters. 100 meters. They were beneath it.

When they reached the pylon, Erno scanned in both directions for a shelter. The cable line was designed to dip underground for radiation protection periodically all along the length of its route. The distance between the tunnels was determined by the top speed of the cable car and the amount of advance warning the passengers were likely to get of a solar event. There was no way of telling how far they were from a shelter, or in which direction the closest lay.

"South," Tyler said. "The colony is the next shelter north, and it's too far for us to run, so our only shot should be south."

It was 0251. They ran south, their leaps no longer strong and low, but with a weary desperation to them now. Erno kept his eyes fixed on the horizon. The twin cables stretched above them like strands of spider's web, silver in the sunlight, disappearing far ahead where the next T pylon stood like the finish line in a race.

The T grew, and suddenly they were on it. Beyond, in its next arc, the cable swooped down to the horizon. They kept running, and as they drew closer, Erno saw that a tunnel opened in the distance, and the cable ran into it. He gasped out a moan that was all the shout he could make.

They were almost there when Erno realized that Tyler had slowed, and was no longer keeping up. He willed himself to stop, awkwardly, almost pitching face first into the regolith. He looked back. Tyler had slowed to a stroll.

"What's wrong?" Erno gasped.

"Nothing," Tyler said. Though Erno could hear Tyler's ragged breath, there was no hurry in his voice.

"Come on!" Erno shouted.

Tyler stopped completely. "Women and children first."

Erno tried to catch his breath. His clock read 0304. "What?"

"You go ahead. Save your pathetic life."

"Are you crazy? Do you want to die?"

"Of course not. I want you to go in first."

"Why?"

"If you can't figure it out by now, I can't explain it, Erno. It's a story for a man."

Erno stood dumbstruck.

"Come out here into the sunshine with me," Tyler said. "It's nice out here."

Erno laughed. He took a step back toward Tyler. He took another. They stood side by side.

"That's my man Erno. Now, how long can you stay out here?"

The sun beat brightly down. The tunnel mouth gaped five meters in front of them. 0307. 0309. Each watched the other, neither budged.

"My life isn't pathetic," Erno said.

"Depends on how you look at it," Tyler replied.

"Don't you think yours is worth saving?"

"What makes you think this is a real radiation alert, Erno? The broadcast could be a trick to make us come back."

"There have been warnings posted for weeks."

"That only makes it a more plausible trick."

"That's no reason for us to risk our lives—on the chance it is."

"I don't think it's a trick, Erno. I'll go into that tunnel. After you."

Erno stared at the dark tunnel ahead. 0311. A single leap from safety. Even now lethal levels of radiation might be sluicing through their bodies. A bead of sweat stung his eye.

"So this is what it means to be a man?" Erno said softly, as much to himself as to Tyler.

"This is it," Tyler said. "And I'm a better man than you are."

Erno felt an adrenaline surge. "You're not better than me."

"We'll find out."

"You haven't accomplished anything."

"I don't need you to tell me what I've accomplished. Go ahead, Erno. Back to your cave."

0312. 0313. Erno could feel the radiation. It was shattering proteins and DNA throughout his body, rupturing cell walls, turning the miraculously ordered organic molecules of his brain into sludge. He thought about Alicia, the curve of her breast, the light in her eyes. Had she told her friends that he had hit her? And his mother. He saw the shock and surprise in her face when the book hit her. How angry he had been. He wanted to explain to her why he had thrown it. It shouldn't be that hard to explain.

He saw his shadow reaching out beside him, sharp and steady, two arms, two legs and a head, an ape somehow transported to the moon. No, not an ape—a man. What a miracle that a man could keep himself alive in this harsh place—not just keep alive, but make a home of it. All the intellect and planning and work that had gone to put him here, standing out under the brutal sun, letting it exterminate him.

He looked at Tyler, fixed as stone.

"This is insane," Erno said—then ran for the tunnel.

A second after he sheltered inside, Tyler was there beside him.

FOURTEEN

They found the radiation shelter midway through the tunnel, closed themselves inside, stripped off their suits, drank some water, breathed the cool air. They crowded in the tiny stone room together, smelling each other's sweat. Erno started to get sick: he had chills, he felt nausea. Tyler made him sip water, put his arm around Erno's shoulders.

Tyler said it was radiation poisoning, but Erno said it was not. He sat wordless in the corner the nine hours it took until the all-clear came. Then, ignoring Tyler, he suited up and headed back to the colony.

FIFTEEN

So that is the story of how Erno discovered that he was not a man. That, indeed, Tyler was right, and there was no place for men in the Society of Cousins. And that he, Erno, despite his grievances and rage, was a cousin.

The cost of this discovery was Erno's own banishment, and one thing more.

When Erno turned himself in at the constabulary headquarters, eager to tell them about GROSS and ready to help them find Tyler, he was surprised at their subdued reaction. They asked him no questions. They looked at him funny, eyes full of rage and something besides rage. Horror? Loathing? Pity? They put him in the same white room where he had sat before, and left him there alone. After a while the blond interrogator, Mona, came in and told him that three people had been injured when Tyler and Erno had blown the vacuum seal while escaping. One, who had insisted on crawling after them through the escape tunnel, had been caught in there and died: Erno's mother.

Erno and Tyler were given separate trials, and the colony voted: they were to be expelled. Tyler's banishment was permanent; Erno was free to apply for readmission in ten years.

The night before he left, Erno, accompanied by a constable, was allowed to visit his home. Knowing how completely inadequate it was, he apologized to his sister, his aunt and cousins. Aunt Sophie and Nick treated him with stiff rectitude. Celeste, who somehow did not feel the rage against him that he deserved, cried and embraced him. They let him pack a duffel with a number of items from his room.

After leaving, he asked the constable if he could stop a moment on the terrace outside the apartment before going back to jail. He took a last look at the vista of the domed crater from the place where he had lived every day of his life. He drew a deep breath and closed his eyes. His mother seemed everywhere around him. All he could see was her crawling, on hands and knees in the dark, desperately trying to save him from himself. How angry she must have been, and how afraid. What must she have thought, as the air flew away and she felt her coming death? Did she regret giving birth to him?

He opened his eyes. There on the terrace stood the recycler he had thrown pebbles at for years. He reached into his pack, pulled out *Stories for Men*, and stepped toward the bin.

Alicia came around a corner. "Hello, Erno," she said.

A step from the trash bin, Erno held the book awkwardly in his hand, trying to think of something to say. The constable watched them.

"I can't tell you how sorry I am," he told Alicia.

"I know you didn't mean this to happen," she said.

"It doesn't matter what I meant. It happened."

On impulse, he handed her the copy of *Stories for Men*. "I don't know what to do with this," he said. "Will you keep it for me?"

The next morning they put him on the cable car for Tsander. His exile had begun.

Gregory Benford is a professor of physics and astronomy at the University of California, Irvine. He is a Woodrow Wilson Fellow, was Visiting Fellow at Cambridge University, and in 1995 received the Lord Prize for contributions to science. In 2007 he won the Asimov Award for science writing. His fiction has won many awards, including the Nebula Award for his novel *Timescape*. He has published forty-two books, mostly novels.

THE CLEAR BLUE SEAS OF LUNA
Gregory Benford

You know many things, but what he knows
is both less and more than what I tell to us.

Or especially, what we all tell to all those others—those simple humans, who are like him in their limits.

I cannot be what you are, you the larger.

Not that we are not somehow also the same, wedded to our memories of the centuries we have been wedded and grown together.

For we are like you and him and I, a life form that evolution could not produce on the rich loam of Earth. To birth forth and then burst forth a thing—a great, sprawling metallo-bio-cyber-thing such as we and you— takes grander musics, such as I know.

Only by shrinking down to the narrow chasms of the single view can you know the intricate slick fineness, the reek and tingle and chime of this silky symphony of self.

But bigness blunders, thumb-fingered.

Smallness can enchant. So let us to go an oddment of him, and me, and you:

He saw:

A long thin hard room, fluorescent white, without shadows.

Metal on ceramo-glass on fake wood on woven nylon rug.

A granite desk. A man whose name he could not recall.

A neat uniform, so familiar he looked beyond it by reflex.

He felt: light gravity (Mars? the moon?); rough cloth at a cuff of his work shirt; a chill dry air-conditioned breeze along his neck. A red flash of anger.

Benjan smiled slightly. He had just seen what he must do.

"Gray was free when we began work, centuries ago," Benjan said, his black eyes fixed steadily on the man across the desk. Katonji, that was the man's name. His commander, once, a very long time ago.

"It had been planned that way, yes," his superior said haltingly, begrudging the words.

"That was the only reason I took the assignment," Benjan said.

"I know. Unfortunately—"

"I have spent many decades on it."

"Fleet Control certainly appreciates—"

"World-scaping isn't just a job, damn it! It's an art, a discipline, a craft that saps a man's energies."

"And you have done quite well. Personally, I—"

"When you asked me to do this I wanted to know what Fleet Control planned for Gray."

"You can recall an ancient conversation?"

A verbal maneuver, no more. Katonji was an amplified human and already well over two centuries old, but the Earthside social convention was to pretend that the past faded away, leaving a young psyche. "A 'grand experiment in human society,' I remember your words."

"True, that was the original plan—"

"But now you tell me a single faction needs it? The whole moon?"

"The council has reconsidered."

"Reconsidered, hell." Benjan's bronze face crinkled with disdain. "Somebody pressured them and they gave in. Who was it?"

"I would not put it that way," Katonji said coldly.

"I know you wouldn't. Far easier to hide behind words." He smiled wryly and compressed his thin lips. The view-screen near him looked out on a cold silver landscape and he studied it, smoldering inside. An artificial viewscape from Gray itself. Earth, a crescent concerto in blue and white, hung in a creamy sky over the insect working of robotractors and men. Gray's air was unusually clear today, the normal haze swept away by a front blowing in from the equator near Mare Chrisum.

The milling minions were hollowing out another cavern for Fleet Control to fill with cubicles and screens and memos. Great Gray above, mere gray below. Earth swam above high fleecy cirrus and for a moment Benjan dreamed of the day when birds, easily adapted to the light gravity and high atmospheric density, would flap lazily across such views.

"Officer Tozenji—"

"I am no longer an officer. I resigned before you were born."

"By your leave, I meant it solely as an honorific. Surely you still have some loyalty to the fleet."

Benjan laughed. The deep bass notes echoed from the office walls with a curious emptiness. "So it's an appeal to the honor of the crest, is it? I see I spent too long on Gray. Back here you have forgotten what I am like," Benjan said. *But where is "here"? I could not take Earth full gravity anymore, so this must be an orbiting Fleet cylinder, spinning gravity.*

A frown. "I had hoped that working once more with Fleet officers would change you, even though you remained a civilian on Gray. A man isn't—"

"A man is what he is," Benjan said.

Katonji leaned back in his shiftchair and made a tent of his fingers. "You . . . played the Sabal Game during those years?" he asked slowly.

Benjan's eyes narrowed. "Yes, I did." The game was ancient, revered, simplicity itself. It taught that the greater gain lay in working with others, rather than in self-seeking. He had always enjoyed it, but only a fool believed that such moral lessons extended to the cut and thrust of Fleet matters.

"It did not . . . bring you to community?"

"I got on well enough with the members of my team," Benjan said evenly.

"I hoped such isolation with a small group would calm your . . . spirit. Fleet is a community of men and women seeking enlightenment in the missions, just as you do. You are an exceptional person, anchored as you are in the station, using linkages we have not used—"

"Permitted, you mean."

"Those old techniques were deemed . . . too risky."

Benjan felt his many links like a background hum, in concert and warm. What could this man know of such methods time-savored by those who lived them? "And not easy to direct from above."

The man fastidiously raised a finger and persisted: "We still sit at the game, and while you are here would welcome your—"

"Can we leave my spiritual progress aside?"

"Of course, if you desire."

"Fine. Now tell me who is getting my planet."

"Gray is not your planet."

"I speak for the station and all the intelligences who link with it: We made Gray. Through many decades, we hammered the crust, released the gases, planted the spores, damped the winds."

"With help."

"Three hundred of us at the start, and eleven heavy spacecraft. A puny beginning that blossomed into millions."

"Helped by the entire staff of Earthside—"

"They were Fleet men. They take orders, I don't. I work by contract."

"A contract spanning centuries?"

"It is still valid, though those who wrote it are dust."

"Let us treat this in a gentlemanly fashion, sir. Any contract can be rene-gotiated."

"The paper I—we, but I am here to speak for all—signed for Gray said it was to be an open colony. That's the only reason I worked on it," he said sharply.

"I would not advise you to pursue that point," Katonji said. He turned and studied the viewscreen, his broad, southern Chinese nose flaring at the nostrils. But the rest of his face remained an impassive mask. For a long moment there was only the thin whine of air circulation in the room.

"Sir," the other man said abruptly, "I can only tell you what the council has granted. Men of your talents are rare. We know that, had you undertaken the formation of Gray for a, uh, private interest, you would have demanded more payment."

"Wrong. I wouldn't have done it at all."

"Nonetheless, the council is willing to pay you a double fee. The Majiken Clan, who have been invested with Primacy Rights to Gray—"

"What!"

"—have seen fit to contribute the amount necessary to reimburse you—"

"So that's who—"

"—and all others of the station, to whom I have been authorized to re-lease funds immediately."

Benjan stared blankly ahead for a short moment. "I believe I'll do a bit of releasing myself," he murmured, almost to himself.

"What?"

"Oh, nothing. Information?"

"Infor—oh."

"The Clans have a stranglehold on the council, but not the 3D. People might be interested to know how it came about that a new planet—a rich one, too—was handed over—"

"Officer Tozenji—"

Best to pause. Think. He shrugged, tried on a thin smile. "I was only jest-ing. Even idealists are not always stupid."

"Um. I am glad of that."

"Lodge the Majiken draft in my account. I want to wash my hands of this."

The other man said something, but Benjan was not listening. He made the ritual of leaving. They exchanged only perfunctory hand gestures. He turned to go, and wondered at the naked, flat room this man had chosen to work in: It carried no soft tones, no humanity, none of the feel of a room that is used, a place where men do work that interests them, so that they embody it with something of themselves. This office was empty in the most profound sense. It was a room for men who lived by taking orders. He hoped never to see such a place again.

Benjan turned. Stepped—the slow slide of falling, then catching himself, stepped—

You fall over Gray.

Skating down the steep banks of young clouds, searching, driving.

Luna you know as Gray, as all in station know it, because pearly clouds deck high in its thick air. It had been gray long before, as well—the aged pewter of rock hard-hammered for billions of years by the relentless sun. Now its air was like soft slate, cloaking the greatest of human handiworks.

You raise a hand, gaze at it. So much could come from so small an instrument. You marvel. A small tool, five-fingered slab, working over great stretches of centuries. Seen against the canopy of your craft, it seems an unlikely tool to heft worlds with—

And the thought alone sends you plunging—

Luna was born small, too small.

So the sun had readily stripped it of its early shroud of gas. Luna came from the collision of a Mars-sized world into the primordial Earth. From that colossal crunch—how you wish you could have seen that!—spun a disk, and from that churn, Luna condensed red-hot. The heat of that birth stripped away the moon's water and gases, leaving it bare to the sun's glower.

So amend that:

You steer a comet from the chilly freezer beyond Pluto, swing it around Jupiter, and smack it into the bleak fields of Mare Chrisium. In bits.

For a century, all hell breaks loose. You wait, patient in your station. It is a craft of fractions: Luna is smaller, so needs less to build an atmosphere.

There was always some scrap of gas on the moon—trapped from the solar wind, baked from its dust, perhaps even belched from the early, now long-dead volcanoes. When Apollo descended, bringing the first men, its tiny exhaust plume doubled the mass of the frail atmosphere.

Still, such a wan world could hold gases for tens of thousands of years; physics said so. Its lesser gravity tugs at a mere sixth of Earth's hefty grip. So, to begin, you sling inward a comet bearing a third the mass of all Earth's ample air, a chunk of mountain-sized grimy ice.

Sol's heat had robbed this world, but mother-massive Earth herself had slowly stolen away its spin. It became a submissive partner in a rigid gavotte, forever tide-locked with one face always smiling at its partner.

Here you use the iceteroid to double effect. By hooking the comet adroitly around Jupiter, in a reverse swingby, you loop it into an orbit opposite to the customary, docile way that worlds loop around the sun. Go opposite! Retro! Coming in on Luna, the iceball then has ten times the impact energy.

Mere days before it strikes, you blow it apart with meticulous brutality. Smashed to shards, chunks come gliding in all around Luna's equator, small enough that they cannot muster momentum enough to splatter free of gravity's grip. Huge cannonballs slam into gray rock, but at angles that prevent them from getting away again.

Earth admin was picky about this: no debris was to be flung free, to rain down as celestial buckshot on that favored world.

Within hours, Luna had air—of a crude sort. You mixed and salted and worked your chemical magicks upon roiling clouds that sported forked lightning. Gravity's grind provoked fevers, molecular riots.

More: as the pellets pelted down, Luna spun up. Its crust echoed with myriad slams and bangs. The old world creaked as it yielded, spinning faster from the hammering. From its lazy cycle of twenty-eight days it sped up to sixty hours—close enough to Earth-like, as they say, for government work. A day still lazy enough.

Even here, you orchestrated a nuanced performance, coaxed from dynamics. Luna's axial tilt had been a dull zero. Dutifully it had spun at right angles to the orbital plane of the solar system, robbed of summers and winters.

But you wanted otherwise. Angled just so, the incoming ice nuggets tilted the poles. From such simple mechanics, you conjured seasons. And as the gases cooled, icy caps crowned your work.

You were democratic, at first: allowing both water and carbon dioxide, with smidgens of methane and ammonia. Here you called upon the appetites of bacteria, sprites you sowed as soon as the winds calmed after bombardment. They basked in sunlight, broke up the methane. The greenhouse blanket quickly warmed the old gray rocks, coveting the heat from the infalls, and soon algae covered them.

You watched with pride as the first rain fell. For centuries, the dark plains had carried humanity's imposed, watery names: Tranquility, Serenity, Crises, Clouds, Storms. Now these lowlands of aged lava caught the rains and made muds and fattened into ponds, lakes, true seas. You made the ancient names come true.

Through your servant machines, you marched across these suddenly murky lands, bristling with an earned arrogance. They—*yourself!*—plowed and dug, sampled and salted. Through their eyes and tongues and ears, you sat in your high station and heard the sad baby sigh of the first winds awakening.

The station was becoming more than a bristling canister of metal, by then. Its agents grew, as did you.

You smiled down upon the gathering Gray with your quartz eyes and microwave antennas. For you knew what was coming. A mere sidewise glance at rich Earth told you what to expect.

Like Earth's tropics now, at Luna's equator heat drove moist gases aloft. Cooler gas flowed from the poles to fill in. The high wet clouds skated poleward, cooled—and rained down riches.

On Earth, such currents are robbed of their water about a third of the way to the poles, and so descend, their dry rasp making a worldwide belt of deserts. Not so on Luna.

You had judged the streams of newborn air rightly. Thicker airs than Earth's took longer to exhaust, and so did not fall until they reached the poles. Thus the new world had no chains of deserts, and one simple circulating air cell ground away in each hemisphere. Moisture worked its magicks.

You smiled to see your labors come right. Though anchored in your mammoth station, you felt the first pinpricks of awareness in the crawlers, flyers and diggers who probed the freshening moon.

You tasted their flavors, the brimming possibilities. Northerly winds swept the upper half of the globe, bearing poleward, then swerving toward the west to make the occasional mild tornado. (Not all weather should be boring.)

Clouds patrolled the air, still fretting over their uneasy births. Day and night came in their slow rhythm, stirring the biological lab that worked below. You sometimes took a moment from running all this, just to watch.

Lunascapes. Great Grayworld.

Where day yielded to dark, valleys sank into smoldering blackness. Already a chain of snowy peaks shone where they caught the sun's dimming rays, and lit the plains with slanting colors like live coals. Sharp mountains cleaved the cloud banks, leaving a wake like that of a huge ship. At the fat equator, straining still to adjust to the new spin, tropical thunderheads glowered, lit by orange lightning that seemed to be looking for a way to spark life among the drifting molecules.

All that you did, in a mere decade. You had made "the lesser light that rules the night" now shine five times brighter, casting sharp shadows on Earth. Sunrays glinted by day from the young oceans, dazzling the eyes on Earth. And the mother world itself reflected in those muddy seas, so that when the alignment was right, people on Earth's night side gazed up into their own mirrored selves. Viewed at just the right angle, Earth's image was rimmed with ruddy sunlight, refracting through Earth's air.

You knew it could not last, but were pleased to find that the new air stuck around. It would bleed away in ten thousand years, but by that time other measures could come into play. You had plans for a monolayer membrane to cap your work, resting atop the whole atmosphere, the largest balloon ever conceived.

Later? No, act in the moment—and so you did.

You wove it with membrane skill, cast it wide, let it fall—to rest easy on the thick airs below. Great holes in it let ships glide to and fro, but the losses from those would be trivial.

Not that all was perfect. Luna had no soil, only the damaged dust left from four billion years beneath the solar wind's anvil.

After a mere momentary decade (nothing, to you), fresh wonders bloomed.

Making soil from gritty grime was work best left to the microbeasts who loved such stuff. To do great works on a global scale took tiny assistants. You fashioned them in your own labs, which poked outward from the station's many-armed skin.

Gray grew a crust. Earth is in essence a tissue of microbial organisms living off the sun's fires. Gray would do the same, in fast-forward. You cooked up not mere primordial broths, but endless chains of regulatory messages, intricate feedback loops, organic gavottes.

Earth hung above, an example of life ornamented by elaborate decorations, structures of forest and grass and skin and blood—living quarters, like seagrass and zebras and eucalyptus and primates.

Do the same, you told yourself. *Only better.*

These tasks you loved. Their conjuring consumed more decades, stacked end on end. You were sucked into the romance of tiny turf wars, chemical assaults, microbial murders, and invasive incests. But you had to play upon the stellar stage, as well.

You had not thought about the tides. Even you had not found a way around those outcomes of gravity's gradient. Earth raised bulges in Gray's seas a full twenty meters tall. That made for a dim future for coastal property, even once the air became breathable.

Luckily, even such colossal tides were not a great bother to the lakes you shaped in crater beds. These you made as breeding farms for the bioengineered minions who ceaselessly tilled the dirts, massaged the gases, filtered the tinkling streams that cut swift ways through rock.

Indeed, here and there you even found a use for the tides. There were more watts lurking there, in kinetic energy. You fashioned push-plates to tap some of it, to run your substations. Thrifty gods do not have to suck up to (and from) Earthside.

And so the sphere that, when you began, had been the realm of strip miners and mass-driver camps, of rugged, suited loners . . . became a place where, someday, humans might walk and breathe free.

That time is about to come. You yearn for it. For you, too, can then manifest yourself, your station, as a mere mortal . . . and set foot upon a world that you would name Selene.

You were both station and more, by then. How much more few knew. But some sliver of you clung to the name of Benjan—

—Benjan nodded slightly, ears ringing for some reason.

The smooth, sure interviewer gave a short introduction. "Man . . . or manifestation? This we must all wonder as we greet an embodiment of humanity's greatest—and now ancient—construction project. One you and I can see every evening in the sky—for those who are still surface dwellers."

The 3D cameras moved in smooth arcs through the studio darkness beyond. Two men sat in a pool of light. The interviewer spoke toward the directional mike as he gave the background on Benjan's charges against the council.

Smiles galore. Platitudes aplenty. That done, came the attack.

"But isn't this a rather abstract, distant point to bring at this time?" the man said, turning to Benjan.

Benjan blinked, uncertain, edgy. He was a private man, used to working alone. Now that he was moving against the council he had to bear these public appearances, these . . . manifestations . . . of a dwindled self. "To, ah, the people of the next generation, Gray will not be an abstraction—"

"You mean the moon?"

"Uh, yes, Gray is my name for it. That's the way it looked when I—uh, we ah—started work on it centuries ago."

"Yes you were there all along, in fact."

"Well, yes. But when I'm—we're—done," Benjan leaned forward, and his interviewer leaned back, as if not wanting to be too close, "it will be a real place, not just an idea—where you all can live and start a planned ecology. It will be a frontier."

"We understand that romantic tradition, but—"

"No, you don't. Gray isn't just an idea, it's something I've—we've—worked on for everyone, whatever shape or genetype they might favor."

"Yes yes, and such ideas are touching in their, well, customary way, but—"

"But the only ones who will ever enjoy it, if the council gets away with this, is the Majiken Clan."

The interviewer pursed his lips. Or was this a *he* at all? In the current style, the bulging muscles and thick neck might just be fashion statements. "Well, the Majiken are a very large, important segment of the—"

"No more important than the rest of humanity, in my estimation."

"But to cause this much stir over a world that will not even be habitable for at least decades more—"

"We of the station are there now."

"You've been modified, adapted."

"Well, yes. I couldn't do this interview on Earth. I'm grav-adapted."

"Frankly, that's why many feel that we need to put Earthside people on the ground on Luna as soon as possible. To represent our point of view."

"Look, Gray's not just any world. Not just a gas giant, useful for raw gas and nothing else. Not a Mercury type; there are millions of those littered out among the stars. Gray is going to be fully Earthlike. The astronomers tell us there are only four semiterrestrials outside the home system that humans can ever live on, around other stars, and those are pretty terrible. I—"

"You forget the Outer Colonies," the interviewer broke in smoothly, smiling at the 3D.

"Yeah—iceballs." He could not hide his contempt. What he wanted to say, but knew it was terribly old-fashioned, was: *Damn it, Gray is happening now, we've got to plan for it. Photosynthesis is going on. I've seen it myself—hell, I caused it myself—carbon dioxide and water converting into organics and oxygen, gases fresh as a breeze. Currents carry the algae down through the cloud layers into the warm areas, where they work just fine. That gives off simple carbon compounds, raw carbon and water. This keeps the water content of the atmosphere constant, but converts carbon dioxide—we've got too much right now—into carbon and oxygen. It's going well, the rate itself is exponentiating—*

Benjan shook his fist, just now realizing that he was saying all this out loud, after all. Probably not a smart move, but he couldn't stop himself. "Look, there's enough water in Gray's deep rock to make an ocean a meter deep all the way around the planet. That's enough to resupply the atmospheric loss, easy, even without breaking up the rocks. Our designer plants are doing their jobs."

"We have heard of these routine miracles—"

"—and there can be belts of jungle—soon! We've got mountains for climbing, rivers that snake, polar caps, programmed animals coming up, beautiful sunsets, soft summer storms—anything the human race wants. That's the vision we had when we started Gray. And I'm damned if I'm going to let the Majiken—"

"But the Majiken can defend Gray," the interviewer said mildly.

Benjan paused. "Oh, you mean—"

"Yes, the ever-hungry Outer Colonies. Surely if Gray proves as extraordinary as you think, the rebellious colonies will attempt to take it." The man gave Benjan a broad, insincere smile. *Dummy,* it said. *Don't know the real-pol-itic of this time, do you?*

He could see the logic. Earth had gotten soft, fed by a tougher empire that now stretched to the chilly preserve beyond Pluto. To keep their mani-cured lands clean and "original," Earthers had burrowed underground, built deep cities there, and sent most manufacturing off-world. The real econom-ic muscle now lay in the hands of the suppliers of fine rocks and volatiles, shipped on long orbits from the Outers and the Belt. These realities were hard to remember when your attention was focused on the details of making a fresh world. One forgot that appetites ruled, not reason.

Benjan grimaced. "The Majiken fight well, they are the backbone of the fleet, yes. Still, to give them a *world*—"

"Surely in time there will be others," the man said reasonably.

"Oh? Why should there be? We can't possibly make Venus work, and Mars will take thousands of years more—"

"No, I meant built worlds—stations."

He snorted. "Live inside a can?"

"That's what you do," the man shot back.

"I'm . . . different."

"Ah yes." The interviewer bore in, lips compressed to a white line, and the 3Ds followed him, snouts peering. Benjan felt hopelessly outmatched. "And just how so?"

"I'm . . . a man chosen to represent . . ."

"The Shaping Station, correct?"

"I'm of the breed who have always lived in and for the station."

"Now, that's what I'm sure our audience really wants to get into. After all, the moon won't be ready for a long time. But you—an ancient artifact, practically—are more interesting."

"I don't want to talk about that." Stony, frozen.

"Why not?" Not really a question.

"It's personal."

"You're here as a public figure!"

"Only because you require it. Nobody wants to talk to the station di-rectly."

"We do not converse with such strange machines."

"It's not just a machine."

"Then what is it?"

"An . . . idea," he finished lamely. "An . . . ancient one." How to tell them? Suddenly, he longed to be back doing a solid, worthy job—frying a jet in Gray's skies, pushing along the organic chemistry—

The interviewer looked uneasy. "Well, since you won't go there … our time's almost up and—"

Again, I am falling over Gray.

Misty auburn clouds, so thin they might be only illusion, spread below the ship. They caught red as dusk fell. The thick air refracted six times more than Earth's, so sunsets had a slow-motion grandeur, the full palette of pinks and crimsons and rouge-reds.

I am in a ramjet—the throttled growl is unmistakable—lancing cleanly into the upper atmosphere. Straps tug and pinch me as the craft banks and sweeps, the smoothly wrenching way I like it, the stubby snout sipping precisely enough for the air's growing oxygen fraction to keep the engine thrusting forward.

I probably should not have come on this flight; it is an uncharacteristic self-indulgence. But I could not sit forever in the station to plot and plan and calculate and check. I had to see my handiwork, get the feel of it. To use my body in the way it longed for.

I make the ramjet arc toward Gray's night side. The horizon curves away, clean hard blue-white, and—*chung!*—I take a jolt as the first canister blows off the underbelly below my feet. Through a rearview camera I watch it tumble away into ruddy oblivion. The canister carries more organic cultures, a new matrix I selected carefully back on the station, in my expanded mode. I watch the shiny morsel explode below, yellow flash. It showers intricate, tailored algae through the clouds.

Gray is at a crucial stage. Since the centuries-ago slamming by the air-giving comets, the conspiracy of spin, water, and heat (great gifts of astro-engineering) had done their deep work. Volcanoes now simmered, percolating more moisture from deep within, kindling, kindling. Some heat climbed to the high cloud decks and froze into thin crystals.

There, I conjure fresh life—tinkering, endlessly.

Life, yes. Carefully engineered cells, to breathe carbon dioxide and live off the traces of other gases this high from the surface. In time. Photosynthesis in the buoyant forms—gas-bag trees, spindly but graceful in the top layer of Gray's dense air—conjure carbon dioxide into oxygen.

I glance up, encased in the tight flight jacket, yet feeling utterly free, naked. *Incoming meteors.* Brown clouds of dust I had summoned to orbit about Gray were cutting off some sunlight.

Added spice, these—ingredients sent from the asteroids to pepper the soil, prick the air, speed chemical matters along. The surface was cooling, the Gray greenhouse winding down. Losing the heat from the atmosphere's birth took centuries. *Patience, prudence.*

Now chemical concerts in the rocks slowed. I felt those, too, as a distant sampler hailed me with its accountant's chattering details. Part of the song. Other chem chores, more subtle, would soon become energetically possible. Fluids could seep and run. In the clotted air below, crystals and cells would make their slow work. All in time . . .

In time, the first puddle had become a lake. How I had rejoiced then!

Centuries ago, I wanted to go swimming in the clear blue seas of Luna, I remember. Tropical waters at the equator, under Earthshine . . .

What joy it had been, to fertilize those early, still waters with minutely programmed bacteria, stir and season their primordial soup—and wait.

What sweet mother Earth did in a billion years, I did to Gray in fifty. Joyfully! Singing the song of the molecules, in concert with them.

My steps were many, the methods subtle. To shape the mountain rang- es, I needed further infalls from small asteroids, taking a century—ferrying rough-cut stone to polish a jewel.

Memories . . . of a man and more. Fashioned from the tick of time, ironed out by the swift passage of mere puny years, of decades, of the ringing centu- ries. Worlds take *time*.

My ramjet leaps into night, smelling of hot iron and—*chung!*—discharg- ing its burden.

I glance down at wisps of yellow-pearl. Sulphuric and carbolic acid streamers, drifting far below. There algae feed and prosper. Murky mists be- low pale, darken, vanish. Go!

Yet I felt a sudden sadness as the jet took me up again. I had watched every small change in the atmosphere, played shepherd to newborn cloud banks, raised fresh chains of volcanoes with fusion triggers that burrowed like moles—and all this might come to naught, if it became another private preserve for some Earthside power games.

I could not shake off the depression. Should I have that worry pruned away? It could hamper my work, and I could easily be rid of it for a while, when I returned to the sleeping vaults. Most in the station spent about one month per year working. Their other days passed in dreamless chilled sleep, waiting for the slow metabolism of Gray to quicken and change.

Not I. I slept seldom, and did not want the stacks of years washed away.

I run my tongue over fuzzy teeth. I am getting stale, worn. Even a ramjet ride did not revive my spirit.

And the station did not want slackers. Not only memories could be pruned.

Ancient urges arise, needs . . .

A warm shower and rest await me above, in orbit, inside the mother-skin. Time to go.

I touch the controls, cutting in extra ballistic computer capacity and—

—suddenly I am there again, with *her*.

She is around me and beneath me, slick with ruby sweat.

And the power of it soars up through me. I reach out and her breast blossoms in my eager hand, her soft cries unfurl in puffs of green steam. *Aye!*

She is a splash of purple across the cool lunar stones, her breath ringing in me—as she licks my rasping ear with a tiny jagged fork of puckered laughter, most joyful and triumphant, yea verily.

The station knows you need this now.

Yes, and the station is right. I need to be consumed, digested, spat back out a new and fresh man, so that I may work well again.

—so she coils and swirls like a fine tinkling gas around me, her mouth wraps me like a vortex. I slide my shaft into her gratefully as she sobs great wracking orange gaudiness through me, *her*, again, *her*,

gift of the strumming vast blue station that guides us all down centuries of dense, oily time.

You need this, take, eat, this is the body and blood of the station, eat, savor, take fully.

I had known her once—redly, sweet, and loud—and now I know her again, my senses all piling up and waiting to be eaten from her.

I glide back and forth, moisture chimes between us, *she* is coiled tight, too.

We all are, we creatures of the station.

It knows this, releases us when we must be gone.

I slam myself into *her* because she is both that woman—known so long *ago*, delicious in her whirlwind passions, supple in colors of the mind, singing in rubs and heats

I knew across the centuries. So the station came to know *her*, too, and duly recorded her—so that I can now bury my coal-black, sweaty troubles in her, *aye!* and thus in the Shaping Station, as was and ever shall be, Grayworld without end, amen.

Resting. Compiling himself again, letting the rivulets of self knit up into remembrance.

Of course the station had to be more vast and able than anything humanity had yet known.

At the time the Great Shaping began, it was colossal. By then, humanity had gone on to grander projects.

Mars brimmed nicely with vapors and lichen, but would take millennia more before anyone could walk its surface with only a compressor to take and thicken oxygen from the swirling airs.

Mammoth works now cruised at the outer rim of the solar system, vast ice castles inhabited by beings only dimly related to the humans of Earth.

He did not know those constructions. But he had been there, in inherited memory, when the station was born. For part of him and you and me and us had voyaged forth at the very beginning ...

The numbers were simple, their implications known to schoolchildren.

(Let's remember that the future belongs to the engineers.)

Take an asteroid, say, and slice it sidewise, allowing four meters of head-room for each level—about what a human takes to live in. This dwelling, then, has floor space that expands as the cube of the asteroid size. How big an asteroid could provide the living room equal to the entire surface of the Earth? Simple: about two hundred kilometers.

Nothing, in other words. For Ceres, the largest asteroid in the inner belt, was 380 kilometers across, before humans began to work her.

But room was not the essence of the station. For after all, he had made the station, yes? Information was her essence, the truth of that blossomed in him, the past as prologue—

He ambled along a corridor a hundred meters below Gray's slag and muds, gazing down on the frothy air-fountains in the foyer. *Day's work done.*

Even manifestations need a rest, and the interview with the smug Earther had put him off, sapping his resolve. Inhaling the crisp, cold air (a bit high on the oxy, he thought; have to check that), he let himself concentrate wholly on the clear scent of the splashing. The blue water was the very best, fresh from the growing poles, not the recycled stuff he endured on flights. He breathed in the tingling spray and a man grabbed him.

"I present formal secure-lock," the man growled, his third knuckle biting into Benjan's elbow port.

A cold, *brittle thunk.* His systems froze. Before he could move, whole command linkages went dead in his inboards. The station's hovering presence, always humming in the distance, telescoped away. It felt like a wrenching fall that never ends, head over heels—

He got a grip. *Focus. Regain your links. The loss!*—It was like having fingers chopped away, whole pieces of himself amputated. *Bloody* neural *stumps*—

He sent quick, darting questions down his lines, and met ... *dark.* Silent. Dead.

His entire aura of presence was gone. He sucked in the cold air, letting a fresh anger bubble up but keeping it tightly bound.

His attacker was the sort who blended into the background. Perfect for this job. A nobody out of nowhere, complete surprise. Clipping on a hand-restraint, the mousy man stepped back. "They ordered me to do it fast." A mousy voice, too.

Benjan resisted the impulse to deck him. He looked Lunar, thin and pale. One of the Earther families who had come to deal with the station a century ago? Maybe with more kilos than Benjan, but a fair match. And it would feel good.

But that would just bring more of them, in the end. "Damn it, I have immunity from casual arrest. I—"

"No matter now, they said." The cop shrugged apologetically, but his jaw set. He was used to this.

Benjan vaguely recognized him, from some bar near the Apex of the crater's dome. There weren't more than a thousand people on Gray, mostly like him, manifestations of the station. But not all. More of the others all the time . . . "You're Majiken."

"Yeah. So?"

"At least you people do your own work."

"We have plenty on the inside here. You don't think Gray's gonna be neglected, eh?"

In his elbow, he felt injected programs spread, *clunk*, consolidating their blocks. A seeping ache. Benjan fought it all through his neuro-musculars, but the disease was strong.

Keep your voice level, wait for a chance. Only one of them—my God, they're sure of themselves! Okay, make yourself seem like a doormat.

"I don't suppose I can get a few things from my office?"

"'Fraid not."

"Mighty decent."

The man shrugged, letting the sarcasm pass. "They want you locked down good before they . . ."

"They what?"

"Make their next move, I'd guess."

"I'm just a step, eh?"

"Sure, chop off the hands and feet first." A smirking thug with a gift for metaphor.

Well, these hands and feet can still work. Benjan began walking toward his apartment. "I'll stay in your lockdown, but at home."

"Hey, nobody said—"

"But what's the harm? I'm deadened now." He kept walking.

"Uh, uh—" The man paused, obviously consulting with his superiors on an in-link.

He should have known it was coming. The Majikens were ferret-eyed, canny, unoriginal, and always dangerous. He had forgotten that. In the rush to get ores sifted, grayscapes planed right to control the constant rains, a system of streams and rivers snaking through the fresh-cut valleys . . . a man could get distracted, yes. Forget how people were. *Careless.*

Not completely, though. Agents like this Luny usually nailed their prey at home, not in a hallway. Benjan kept a stunner in the apartment, right beside the door, convenient.

Distract him. "I want to file a protest."

"Take it to Kalespon." Clipped, efficient, probably had a dozen other slices of bad news to deliver today. To other manifestations. Busy man.

"No, with your boss."

"Mine?" His rock-steady jaw went slack.

"For—" he sharply turned the corner to his apartment, using the time to reach for some mumbo-jumbo—"felonious interrogation of inboards."

"Hey, I didn't touch your—"

"I felt it. Slimy little gropes—yeccch!" Might as well ham it up a little, have some fun.

The Majiken looked offended. "I never violate protocols. The integrity of your nexus is intact. You can ask for a scope-through when we take you in—"

"I'll get my overnight kit." Only now did he hurry toward the apartment portal and popped it by an inboard command. As he stepped through he felt the cop, three steps behind.

Here goes. One foot over the lip, turn to the right, snatch the stunner out of its grip mount—

—and it wasn't there. They'd laundered the place already. "Damn!"

"Thought it'd be waitin', huh?"

In the first second. When the Majiken was pretty sure of himself, act—

Benjan took a step back and kicked. A satisfying soft *thuuunk.*

In the low gravity, the man rose a meter and his *uungh!* was strangely satisfying. The Majiken were warriors, after all, by heritage. Easier for them to take physical damage than life trauma.

The Majiken came up fast and nailed Benjan with a hand feint and slam. Benjan fell back in the slow gravity—and at a 45-degree tilt, sprang backward, away, toward the wall—

Which he hit, completing his turn in air, heels coming hard into the wall so that he could absorb the recoil—

—and spring off, head-height—

—into the Majiken's throat as the man rushed forward, shaped hands ready for the put-away blow. Benjan caught him with both hand-edges, slamming the throat from both sides. The punch cut off blood to the head and the Majiken crumbled.

Benjan tied him with his own belt. Killed the link on the screen. Bound him further to the furniture. Even on Gray, inertia was inertia. The Majiken would not find it easy to get out from under a couch he was firmly tied to.

The apartment would figure out that something was wrong about its occupant in a hour or two, and call for help. Time enough to run? Benjan was unsure, but part of him liked this, felt a surge of adrenaline joy arc redly through his systems.

Five minutes of work and he got the interlocks off. His connections sprang back to life. Colors and images sang in his aura.

He was out the door, away—

The cramped corridors seemed to shrink, dropping down and away from him, weaving and collapsing. Something came toward him—chalk-white hills, yawning craters.

A hurricane breath whipped by him as it swept down from the jutting, fresh-carved mountains. His body strained.

He was running, that much seeped through to him. He breathed brown murk that seared but his lungs sucked it in eagerly.

Plunging hard and heavy across the swampy flesh of Gray.

He moved easily, bouncing with each stride in the light gravity, down an infinite straight line between rows of enormous trees. Vegetable trees, these were, soft tubers and floppy leaves in the wan glow of a filtered sun. There should be no men here, only machines to tend the crops. Then he noticed that he was not a man at all. A robo-hauler, yes—and his legs were in fact wheels, his arms the working grapplers. Yet he read all this as his running body. Somehow it was pleasant.

And *she* ran with him.

He saw beside him a miner-bot, speeding down the slope. Yet he knew it was *she,* Martine, and he loved her.

He whirred, clicked—and sent a hail.

You are fair, my sweet.

Back from the lumbering miner came, *This body will not work well at games of lust.*

No reason we can't shed them in time.

To what end? she demanded. Always imperious, that girl.

To slide silky skin again.

You seem to forget that we are fleeing. That cop, someone will find him.

In fact, he had forgotten. *Uh . . . update me?*

Ah! How exasperating! You've been off, romping through your imputs again, right?

Worse than that. He had only a slippery hold on the jiggling, surging lands of mud and murk that funneled past. Best not to alarm her, though. *My sensations seem to have become a bit scrambled, yes. I know there is some reason to run—*

They are right behind us!

Who?

The Majiken Clan! They want to seize you as a primary manifestation!

Damn! I'm fragmenting.

You mean they're reaching into your associative cortex?

Must be, my love. Which is why you're running with me.

What do you mean?

How to tell her the truth but shade it so that she does not guess ... the Truth? *Suppose I tell you something that is more useful than accurate?*

Why would you do that, m'love?

Why do doctors slant a diagnosis?

Because no good diagnostic gives a solid prediction.

Exactly. Not what he had meant, but it got them by an awkward fact.

Come on, she sent. *Let's scamper down this canyon. The topo maps say it's a shortcut.*

Can't trust 'em, the rains slice up the land so fast. He felt his legs springing like pistons in the mad buoyance of adrenaline.

They surged together down slippery sheets that festered with life-spreading algae, some of the many-leafed slim-trees Benjan had himself helped design. Rank growths festooned the banks of dripping slime, biology run wild and woolly at a fevered pace, irked by infusions of smart bugs. A landscape on fast forward.

What do you fear so much? she said suddenly.

The sharpness of it stalls his mind. He was afraid for her more than himself, but how to tell her? This apparition of her was so firm and heartbreakingly warm, her whole presence welling through to him on his sensorium ... Time to tell another truth that conceals a deeper truth.

They'll blot out every central feature of me, all those they can find.

If they catch you. Us.

Yup. Keep it to monosyllables, so the tremor of his voice does not give itself away. If they got to her, she would face final, total erasure. Even of a fragment shelf.

Save your breath for the run, she sent. So he did, gratefully.

If there were no omni-sensors lurking along this approach to the launch fields, they might get through. Probably Fleet expected him to stay indoors, hiding, working his way to some help. But there would be no aid there. The Majiken were thorough and would capture all human manifestations, timing the arrests simultaneously to prevent anyone sending a warning. That was why they had sent a tone cop to grab him; they were stretched thin. Reassuring, but not much.

It was only three days past the 3D interview, yet they had decided to act and put together a sweep. What would they be doing to the station itself? He ached at the thought. After all, *she* resided there . . .

And *she* was here. He was talking to a manifestation that was remarkable, because he had opened his inputs in a way that only a crisis can spur.

Benjan grimaced. Decades working over Gray had aged him, taught him things Fleet could not imagine. The Sabal Game still hummed in his mind, still guided his thoughts, but these men of the Fleet had betrayed all that. They thought, quite probably, that they could recall him to full officer status, and he would not guess that they would then silence him, quite legally.

Did they think him so slow? Benjan allowed himself a thin, dry chuckle as he ran.

They entered the last short canyon before the launch fields. Tall blades like scimitar grasses poked up, making him dart among them. She growled and spun her tracks and plowed them under. She did not speak. None of them liked to destroy the life so precariously remaking Gray. Each crushed blade was a step backward.

His quarters were many kilometers behind by now, and soon these green fields would end. If he had judged the map correctly—yes, there it was. A craggy peak ahead, crowned with the somber lights of the launch station. They would be operating a routine shift in there, not taking any special precautions.

Abruptly, he burst from the thicket of thick-leafed plants and charged down the last slope. Before him lay the vast lava plain of Oberg Plateau, towering above the Fogg Sea. Now it was a mud flat, foggy, littered with ships. A vast dark hole yawned in the bluff nearby, the slanting sunlight etching its rimmed locks. It must be the exit tube for the electromagnetic accelerator, now obsolete, unable to fling any more loads of ore through the cloak of atmosphere.

A huge craft loomed at the base of the bluff. A cargo vessel probably; far too large and certainly too slow. Beyond lay an array of robot communications vessels, without the bubble of a life support system. He rejected those, too, ran on.

She surged behind him. They kept electromagnetic silence now.

His breath came faster and he sucked at the thick, cold air, then had to stop for a moment in the shadow of the cruiser to catch his breath. Above he thought he could make out the faint green tinge of the atmospheric cap in the membrane that held Gray's air. He would have to find his way out through the holes in it, too, in an unfamiliar ship.

He glanced around, searching. To the side stood a small craft, obviously Jump type. No one worked at its base. In the murky fog that shrouded the mud flat he could see a few men and robo-servers beside nearby ships. They would wonder what he was up to. He decided to risk it. He broke from cover and ran swiftly to the small ship. The hatch opened easily.

Gaining lift with the ship was not simple, and so he called on his time-sense accelerations, to the max. That would cost him mental energy later. Right now, he wanted to be sure there was a *later* at all.

Roaring flame drove him into the pearly sky.

Finding the exit hole in the membrane proved easier. He flew by pure eye-balled grace, slamming the acceleration until it was nearly a straight-line prob-lem, like shooting a rifle. Fighting a mere sixth of a g had many advantages.

And now, where to go?

A bright arc flashed behind Benjan's eyelids, showing the fans of purpling blood vessels. He heard the dark, whispering sounds of an inner void. A pit opened beneath him and the falling sensation began—he had run over the boundaries this body could attain. His mind had overpowered the shrieking demands of the muscles and nerves, and now he was shutting down, harking to the body's calls . . .

And *she?*

I am here, m'love. The voice came warm and moist, wrapping him in it as he faded, faded, into a gray of his own making.

She greeted him at the station.

She held shadowed inlets of rest. A cup brimming with water, a distant chime of bells, the sweet damp air of early morning.

He remembered it so well, the ritual of meditation in his fleet training, the days of quiet devotion through simple duties that strengthened the mind.

Everything had been of a piece then.

Before Gray grew to greatness, before conflict and aching doubt, before the storm that raged red through his mind, like—

–Wind, snarling his hair, a hard winter afternoon as he walked back to his quarters . . .

–then, instantly, the cold prickly sensation of diving through shimmering spheres of water in zero gravity. The huge bubbles trembled and refracted the yellow light into his eyes. He laughed.

–scalding black rock faces rose on Gray. Wedges thrust upward as the tortured skin of the planet writhed and buckled. He watched it by remote camera, seeing only a few hundred yards through the choking clouds of carbon dioxide. He felt the rumble of earthquakes, the ominous murmur of a mountain chain being born.

–a man running, scuttling like an insect across the tortured face of Gray. Above him the great membrane clasped the atmosphere, pressing it down on him, pinning him, a beetle beneath glass. But it is Fleet that wishes to pin him there, to snarl him in the threads of duty. And as the ship arcs upward at the sky he feels a tide of joy, of freedom.

–twisted shrieking trees, leaves like leather and apples that gleam blue. Moisture beading on fresh crimson grapes beneath a white-hot star.

–sharp synapses, ferrite cores, spinning drums of cold electrical memory. Input and output. Copper terminals (male or female?), scanners, channels, electrons pouring through p-n-p junctions. Memory mired in quantum noise.

Index. Catalog. Transform. Fourier components, the infinite wheeling dance of Laplace and Gauss and Hermite.

And through it all she is there with him, through centuries to keep him whole and sane and yet he does not know, across such vaults of time and space . . . who is he?

Many: us. One: I. Others: you. *Did you think that the marriage of true organisms and fateful machines with machine minds would make a thing that could at last know itself? This is a new order of being but it is not a god.*

Us: one, We: you, He: I.

And yet you suspect you are . . . different . . . somehow.

The Majiken ships were peeling off from their orbits, skating down through the membrane holes, into *my* air!

They gazed down, tense and wary, these shock troops in their huddled lonely carriages. Not up, where I lurk.

For I am iceball and stony-frag, fruit of the icesteroids. Held in long orbit for just such a (then) far future. (Now) arrived.

Down I fall in my myriads. Through the secret membrane passages I/we/ you made decades before, knowing that a bolthole is good. And that bolts slam true in both directions.

Down, down—through gray decks I have cooked, artful ambrosias, pewter terraces I have sculpted to hide my selves as they guide the rocks and bergs—*after them!*—

The Majiken ships, ever-wary of fire from below, never thinking to glance up. I fall upon them in machine-gun violences, my ices and stones ripping their craft, puncturing. They die in round-mouthed surprise, these warriors.

I, master of hyperbolic purpose, shred them.
I, orbit-master to Gray.

*Conflict has always provoked anxiety within him, a habit he could never
correct, and so:*
—in concert we will rise to full congruence with F(x)
and sum over all variables and integrate over the contour
encapsulating all singularities. It is right and meet so to do.
He sat comfortably, rocking on his heels in meditation position.
Water dripped in a cistern nearby and he thought his mantra,
letting the sound curl up from within him. A thought entered,
flickered across his mind as though a bird,
and left.
She she she she
The mantra returned in its flowing green rhythmic beauty and he entered
the crystal state of thought within thought,
consciousness regarding itself without detail or structure.
The air rested upon him, the earth groaned beneath with the weight of
continents,
shouting sweet stars wheeled in a chanting cadence above.
He was in place and focused, man and boy and elder at once,
officer of Fleet, mind encased in matter, body summed into mind
—and *she* came to him, cool balm of aid, succor, yet beneath her palms
his muscles warmed, warmed—

His universe slides into night. Circuits close. Oscillating electrons carry information, senses, fragments of memory.

I swim in the blackness. There are long moments of no sensations, nothing to see or hear or feel. I grope–

Her? No, she is not here either. Cannot be. For she has been dead these centuries and lives only in your station, where she knows not what has become of herself.

At last, I seize upon some frag, will it to expand. A strange watery vision floats into view. A man is peering at him. There is no detail behind the man, only a blank white wall. He wears the blue uniform of Fleet and he cocks an amused eyebrow at:

Benjan.

"Recognize me?" the man says.

"Of course. Hello, Katonji, you bastard."

"Ah, rancor. A nice touch. Unusual in a computer simulation, even one as sophisticated as this."

"What? Comp–"

And Benjan knows who he is.

In a swirling instant he sends out feelers. He finds boundaries, cool gray walls he cannot penetrate, dead patches, great areas of gray emptiness, of no memory. What did he look like when he was young? Where was his first home located? That girl–at age fifteen? Was that *her*? *Her*? He grasps for her–

And knows. He cannot answer. He does not know. He is only a piece of Benjan.

"You see now? Check it. Try something–to move your arm, for instance. You haven't got arms." Katonji makes a thin smile. "Computer simulations do not have bodies, though they have some of the perceptions that come from bodies."

"P–perceptions from where?"

"From the fool Benjan, of course."

"*Me.*"

"*He* didn't realize, having burned up all that time on Gray, that we can penetrate all diagnostics. Even the station's. Technologies, even at the level of sentient molecular plasmas, have logs and files. Their data is not closed to certain lawful parties."

He swept an arm (not a real one, of course) at the man's face. Nothing. No contact. All right, then . . . "And these feelings are–"

"Mere memories. Bits from Benjan's station self." Katonji smiles wryly.

He stops, horrified. He does not exist. He is only binary bits of information scattered in ferrite memory cores. He has no substance, is without flesh. "But . . . but, where is the real me?" he says at last.

"That's what you're going to tell us."

"I don't know. I was . . . falling. Yes, over Gray–"

"And running, yes–I know. That was a quick escape, an unexpectedly neat solution."

"It worked," Benjan said, still in a daze. "But it wasn't me?"

"In a way it was. I'm sure the real Benjan has devised some clever destination, and some tactics. You–his ferrite inner self–will tell us, now, what he will do next."

"He's got something, yes . . ."

"Speak *now*," Katonji said impatiently.

Stall for time. "I need to know more."

"This is a calculated opportunity," Katonji said off-handedly. "We had hoped Benjan would put together a solution from things he had been thinking about recently, and apparently it worked."

"So you have breached the station?" Horror flooded him, black bile.

"Oh, you aren't a complete simulation of Benjan, just recently stored conscious data and a good bit of subconscious motivation. A truncated personality, it is called."

As Katonji speaks, Benjan sends out tracers and feels them flash through his being. He summons up input and output. There are slabs of useless data, a latticed library of the mind. He can expand in polynomials, integrate along an orbit, factorize, compare coefficients–*so they used my computational self to make up part of this shambling construct.*

More. He can fix his field–there, just so–and fold his hands, repeating his mantra. Sound wells up and folds over him, encasing him in a moment of silence. *So the part of me that still loves the Sabal Game, feels drawn to the one-is-all side of being human–they got that, too.*

Panic. Do something. Slam on the brakes–

He registers Katonji's voice, a low drone that becomes deeper and deeper as time slows. The world outside stills. His thought processes are far faster than an ordinary man's. He can control his perception rate.

Somehow, even though he is a simulation, he can tap the real Benjan's method of meditation, at least to accelerate his time sense. He feels a surge of anticipation. He hums the mantra again and feels the world around him alter. The trickle of input through his circuits slows and stops. He is running cool and smooth. He feels himself cascading down through ruby-hot levels of perception, flashing back through Benjan's memories.

He speeds himself. He lives again the moments over Gray. He dives through the swampy atmosphere and swims above the world he made. Molecular master, he is awash in the sight-sound-smell, an ocean of perception.

Katonji is still saying something. Benjan allows time to alter again and Katonji's drone returns, rising–

Benjan suddenly perceives something behind Katonji's impassive features. "Why didn't you follow Benjan immediately? You could find out where he was going. You could have picked him up before he scrambled your tracker beams."

Katonji smiles slightly. "Quite perceptive, aren't you? Understand, we wish only Benjan's compliance."

"But if he died, he would be even more silent."

"Precisely so. I see you are a good simulation."

"I seem quite real to myself."

"Ha! Don't we all. A computer who jests. Very much like Benjan, you are. I will have to speak to you in detail, later. I would like to know just why he failed us so badly. But for the moment we must know where he is now. He is a legend, and can be allowed neither to escape nor to die."

Benjan feels a tremor of fear.

"So where did he flee? You're the closest model of Benjan."

I summon winds from the equator, cold banks of sullen cloud from the poles, and bid them *crash*. They slam together to make a tornado such as never seen on Earth. Lower gravity, thicker air—a cauldron. It twirls and snarls and spits out lightning knives. The funnel touches down, kisses my crust—

—and there are Majiken beneath, whole canisters of them, awaiting my kiss.
Everyone talks about the weather, but only I do anything about it.
They crack open like ripe fruit.

–and you dwindle again, hiding from their pursuing electrons. Falling away into your
microstructure.

They do not know how much they have captured. They think in terms of bits and
pieces and he/you/we/I are not. So they do not know this–

You knew this had to come

As worlds must turn

And primates must prance

And givers must grab

So they would try to wrap their world around yours.

They are not dumb.

And smell a beautiful beast slouching toward Bethlehem.

Benjan coils in upon himself. He has to delay Katonji. He must lie–

–and at this rogue thought, scarlet circuits fire. Agony. Benjan flinches as truth verification overrides trigger inside himself.

"I warned you." Katonji smiles, lips thin and dry.

Let them kill me.

"You'd like that, I know. No, you will yield up your little secrets."

Speak. Don't just let him read your thoughts. "Why can't you find him?"

"We do not know. Except that your sort of intelligence has gotten quite out of control, that we do know. We will take it apart gradually, to understand it–you, I suppose,
included."

"You will . . ."

"Peel you, yes. There will be nothing left. To avoid that, tell us *now.*"

–and the howling storm breaches him, bowls him over, shrieks and tears and de-
vours him. The fire licks flesh from his bones, chars him, flames burst behind his eyelids–

And he stands. He endures. He seals off the pain. It becomes a raging, white-hot
point deep in his gut.

Find the truth. "After . . . after . . . escape, I imagine–yes, I am certain–he would go to
the poles."

"Ah! Perfect. Quite plausible, but–which pole?" Katonji turns and murmurs something to someone beyond Benjan's view. He nods, turns back and says, "We will catch
him there. You understand, Fleet cannot allow a manifestation of his sort to remain free
after he has flouted our authority."

"Of course," Benjan says between clenched teeth.

(But he has no teeth, he realizes. Perceptions are but data, bits strung together in binary. But they feel like teeth, and the smoldering flames in his belly make acrid sweat trickle down his brow.)

"If we could have anticipated him, before he got on 3D ..." Katonji mutters to himself. "Here, have some more–"

Fire lances. Benjan wants to cry out and go on screaming forever. A frag of him begins his mantra. The word slides over and around itself and rises between him and the wall of pain. The flames lose their sting. He views them at a distance, their cobalt facets cool and remote, as though they have suddenly become deep blue veins of ice, fire going into glacier.

He feels the distant gnawing of them. Perhaps, in the tick of time, they will devour his substance. But the place where he sits, the thing he has become, can recede from them. And as he waits, the real Benjan is moving. And yes, he does know where ...

Tell me true, these bastards say. All right–

"Demonax crater. At the rim of the South Polar glacier."

Katonji checks. The verification indices bear out the truth of it. The man laughs with triumph.

All truths are partial. A portion of what Benjan is/was/will be lurks there.

Take heart, true Benjan.
For *she* is we and we are all together,
we mere Ones who are born to suffer.
Did you think you would come out of this long trip alive?
Remember, we are dealing with the most nasty of all species the planet
has ever produced.

Deftly, deftly—

We converge. The alabaster Earthglow guides us. Demonax crater lies around us as we see the ivory lances of their craft descend.

They come forth to inspect the ruse we have gathered ourselves into. We seem to be an entire ship and buildings, a shiny human construct of lunar grit. We hold still, though that is not our nature.

Until they enter us.

We are tiny and innumerable but we do count. Microbial tongues lick. Membranes stick.

Some of us vibrate like eardrums to their terrible swift cries.

They will discover eventually. They will find him out.

(Moisture spatters upon the walkway outside. Angry dark clouds boil up from the horizon.)

They will peel him then. Sharp and cold and hard, now it comes, but, but–

(Waves hiss on yellow sand. A green sun wobbles above the seascape. Strange birds twitter and call.)

Of course, in countering their assault upon the station, I shall bring all my hoarded assets into play.

And we all know that I cannot save everyone.

Don't you?

They come at us through my many branches. Up the tendrils of ceramic and steel. Through my microwave dishes and phased arrays. Sounding me with gamma rays and traitor cyber-personas.

They have been planning this for decades. But I have known it was coming for centuries.

The Benjan singleton reaches me in time. Nearly.

He struggles with their minions. I help. I am many and he is one. He is quick, I am slow. That he is one of the originals does matter to me. I harbor the same affection for him that one does for a favorite finger.

I hit the first one of the bastards square on. It goes to pieces just as it swings the claw thing at me.

Damn! it's good to be back in a body again. My muscles bunching under tight skin, huffing in hot breaths, happy primate murder-joy shooting adrenaline-quick.

One of the Majiken comes in slow as weather and I cut him in two. Been centuries since I even *thought* of doing somethin' like that. Thumping heart, yelling, joyful slashing at them with tractor spin-waves, the whole business.

A hell of a lot of 'em, though.

They hit me in shoulder and knee and I go down, pain shooting, swimming in the low centrifugal g of the station. Centuries ago I wanted to go swimming in the clear blue seas of Luna, I recall. In warm tropical waters at the equator, under silvery Earthshine . . .

But *she* is there. I swerve and dodge and *she* stays right with me. We waltz through the bastards. Shards flying all around and vacuum sucking at me but *her* in my veins. Throat-tightening pure joy in my chest.

Strumming notes sound through me and it is *she*
Fully in me, at last
Gift of the station in all its spaces
For which we give thanks yea verily in this the ever-consuming moment—
Then there is a pain there and I look down and my left arm is gone.

Just like that.
And she of ages past is with me now.

—and even if he is just digits running somewhere, he can relive scenes, the grainy stuff of life. He feels a rush of warm joy. Benjan will escape, will go on. Yet so will he, the mere simulation, in his own abstract way.

Distant agonies echo. Coming nearer now. He withdraws further.

As the world slows to frozen silence outside he shall meditate upon his memories. It is like growing old, but reliving all scenes of the past with sharpness and flavor retained.

—(The scent of new-cut grass curls up red and sweet and humming through his nostrils. The summer day is warm; a Gray wind caresses him, cool and smooth. A piece of chocolate bursts its muddy flavor in his mouth.)

Time enough to think over what has happened, what it means. He opens himself to the moment. It sweeps him up, wraps him in a yawning bath of sensation. He opens himself. Each instant splinters sharp into points of perception. He opens himself. He. Opens. Himself.

Gray is not solely for humanity. There are greater categories now. Larger perspectives on the world beckon to us. To us all.

You know many things, but what he knows is both less and more than what I tell to us.

—for Martin Fogg

The father of three adult daughters and grandfather to one small girl, William Preston teaches high school English at an independent school near Syracuse, New York. A reader of many science books as a child—including the children's book that inspired this story—he watched the moon landings and *Star Trek* and is happy he somehow managed to help guide his children into also finding joy and interest in the sciences. Most of his published fiction has appeared in *Asimov's Science Fiction Magazine,* where his "Old Man" series has attracted the attention of pulp fiction fans. Most nights in Syracuse, the moon is obscured by clouds, but he looks for it nevertheless both day and night and loves its constant inconstancy.

YOU WILL GO TO THE MOON
William Preston

I had a hard enough time after my parents moved to Arizona. To picture where they lived, I imagined a map of the country, the states in various colors, the mountain ranges indicated by shadows. This helped me conceive the distance from rural New Jersey to Tucson. Once I'd visited them, I could call to mind the landscape: their isolated house, the red earth, mountains taking in too-vivid sunsets that seemed like the planet's first or last days.

I missed having my parents nearby, of course, but, more, I now lacked an excuse to see my old hometown. With no friends there, I had no reason to drive the two hours to southeastern Pennsylvania, that territory of rolling, innocuous hills, packed with development houses among a few remaining farmers' fields. My little town, more heavily trafficked than in my childhood, held my whole past, my life before life became settled and responsible. My folks moved, and it cut off my access to that. My town surfaced in dreams, though always with me in towering buildings that hadn't existed, trying to work my way downstairs to the main street and its tidy brick buildings and Colonial-era stone houses so close to the sidewalk. I was forty, married, with two girls.

The year I turned forty-three, my parents announced in a curt electronic note that they were moving again, this time to a retirement community on the moon. I sat on the back deck that night and looked in the direction of my hometown and then, for a longer time, at the moon's thin, suspended crescent. Any thinner and it would have vanished, the moon that night seemed barely able to support itself, much less life. I saw my parents seated in its sickle like figures from a child's book of poems, their legs dangling in the hazy air.

My wife joined me on the deck steps. When I noticed the sweater draped over her shoulders, I fully realized what I'd half-thought, that the evening had grown cold.

"They won't do it," Cyndi said.

I shut my eyes. "It's my father's idea. It'll happen. It's like with Arizona. My mother didn't want that."

"Do you think he has friends up there?"

"You know, it's not really *up*," I said, giving her the brunt of feelings I hadn't yet formed. "There's no up; it's all relative. Over. It's over. It's next to us. It's not like heaven."

"Heaven's 'up' now?"

"Yeah. Heaven's up." I faced her and her crooked smile successfully cut into my mood. "But hell's only about 10 miles down the road. That development with the streets named for dogs."

"'Down'?" she rhetorically pushed, and her shoulder touched mine.

"Ooh God," I sighed, letting the words pour out. "I don't know why he's doing it. I'm sure we'll find out."

When we stopped talking, I listened to the crickets, forgetting again that I was cold.

My parents visited us on their way to France. A private French firm would send up the next load of retirees and temporary workers. My mother touched her frosted perm uncertainly; behind her right ear, the hair lay flat from how she'd slept in the airplane. Her hand knew something was wrong but couldn't settle on the exact problem. This compounded her obvious anxiety. While my father was in the bathroom, I talked to her in the kitchen, standing beside her at the sink.

"I can tell you don't want to do this."

"Do what," she said flatly, watching her hand tug on the tab to raise and lower the teabag in her mug. Typical, this. My mother always feigned, well, everything. Ignorant, she made out like she knew what was what; if she knew full well the state of affairs, she forced you to do all the work, and even then you might just make her lie to your face. I never understood what this was a defense against—unless it was against a son who always questioned her.

"Come on. The moon? Just the trip to Europe is huge for you. What's it really like up there? Have you talked to anyone?"

"A woman spoke to my book club last month."

"A woman," I said.

"A woman who'd visited recently. I wish you'd heard her."

"It's not the same as living there."

She carried her mug to the counter beside the trash and went through her ritual of winding the thread around the teabag, pressing it between her thumb and the tab and, when the last drops were squeezed into the mug, letting the bag plummet into the receptacle. She'd already placed on the counter two packs of artificial sweetener. These she tore open and emptied into the mug. There lay the spoon as well; my mother always knew—or controlled—the sequence of events.

"This is a huge risk," I said.

"It's very safe." She stirred, the spoon ringing inside the mug.

"I should explain," said my father from behind me, and I turned to see him looking thoughtful and sheepish, his eyes reluctantly meeting mine. "Let's sit and talk." Then he left the room to lead me out, as if it were his own house and he knew where best to discuss such things.

He'd only gone into the next room to sit at the broad dining table, his back to one window. He spread his pale arms out and swept the dark surface as I took the chair opposite him. Facing downward, he said, "When I was little, I had a book called *You Will Go to the Moon*."

Knowing I was interrupting—he'd not paused—I asked, "So that's why you're going?"

He didn't lift his head but looked at me over his eyeglasses. It was nearly a glare. "Just let me talk. The book came out before Apollo'd even reached the moon, but it had these drawings of this boy taking a rocket to the space station, going up to the moon base. Everything was happening so fast in America it seemed like pretty soon the moon would be like another vacation spot.

"I never got over the disappointment that we couldn't just pop up to the moon. I had this book when I was five or six, you know, so it really made an impression on me. It's certainly part of why I studied math. I loved the picture on the cover. The moon looked so close, almost pasted on top of the sky, and you could sort of feel the ridges on the craters." Now he did pause.

"Okay," I said, to say something. I heard Cyndi come in from the garden with the girls and start talking with my mother. "You can't just *pop* up, though. And you can't just pop back down. And . . . you're not young."

"You have this habit," said my father, "of telling people things they already know."

I'd heard the criticism before, so I kept my momentum. "I know those new rockets don't hit you with the same G-force, but, still, it's not like you're ready to set off on some interstellar excursion. Dad, you and Mom never even traveled much."

"And we should have. That's both our faults."

"I don't think she wants to go," I said with my mouth half shut.

A shrug seemed his only available reply, but then he thought again. "Like you said, we're old. There's nothing after this. We'd have to live a lot longer to have time for regret."

"You can regret something before you've even done it."

He sat up and looked at me like I wasn't his son, like I was a man who might, amazingly, tell him something he hadn't heard before—though that wasn't what I'd done. He'd already thought of all this.

"The house is too much for us," he said, his palms an inch above the table, settling the matter. "A retirement village on the moon. It's a little different."

"What kind of people would do this?"

He laughed. "You're looking at one." He slapped down his hands and was finished.

It would be six months before I could arrange my own journey, taking time off from the accounting firm, scheduling myself on a flight. I had no childhood desire to leave Earth, nor to explore much of anything—I had not climbed mountains, taken a pilgrimage to one of humanity's ancient places, nor swum above the vanishing coral reefs. Still, I had to see my parents.

Some nights, I sat on the living room floor, my back against the leather chair where Cyndi sat, and flipped through various brochures. So many firms headed up there—*over* there. I read their literature, studied the photos they chose. Always they showed Earthrise, the photo that troubled me most, though back then I couldn't separate my discomfort with that photo from my unease about the whole affair.

Serious research about their living conditions I avoided. I read the headlines of articles that flashed on my console or appeared in the newspaper. To our friends, to my colleagues, I didn't mention my parents' present situation, as if I were expecting something about it to change, or as if it had not actually happened.

I noticed the moon more, its phases, how high it rode, how often it hovered in the daylight—this last unsettling because I felt the moon moving not through space but through sunlight, all its surface delineation lost, smothered in the brightness. When the moon rose red, did my parents see their own landscape transformed? No, that was a trick of the atmosphere. And what of Earth? Did it ever shine with a hue that startled you? Did it sometimes appear surprisingly large? But again, no: the airless moon would always grant observers the same sky, though the Earth would, of course, pass through its own phases of light and dark, be more or less clouded, become black against the sun.

Weightlessness disagreed with me, as evidently it does with many people. My bones ached, I vomited, my brain felt lopsided in my skull. I couldn't imagine my parents enduring this. Two days out from Earth, when purportedly your system begins to make accommodations, I had trouble keeping down the food—something in the air deprived it of flavor—and even the protein bars and drinks wouldn't settle properly. I slept a lot, which is recommended; in fact, the well stocked drug dispensary tacitly encouraged it. My dreams were ... not exactly weightless, but somehow unlike even the usual disjointed narrative of dreams, so I imagined, lifting fuzzily from a nap, that I'd swapped dreams with another passenger. Pretty much everyone appeared addled; no one talked much.

One older couple slept an entire day. When an attendant went to wake them, the woman came around, but the man, who looked like someone acting out sleep—head tilted back, lips parted, the glint of moisture in the corner of his mouth—had died. The wife lapsed again into dreams; she dozed unaware as the staff removed his body rearward.

I felt the black spaces surrounding us become more empty, more silent. The moon was not another place like another town. You had to cross too much emptiness to get there, so it was, itself, a part of the emptiness. I felt that then and feel it now, even in daytime, when the moon seems to lie embedded in brightness. When that old man died out there, I felt more sure than ever that my parents had ... transgressed. That was the word that came to me. Not just a bad mistake, but a crossing over to a place where your merely being there was a violation.

I gave in to the drug-induced sleep that met me, vaguely dreading its dark gulf yet welcoming relief from my thoughts.

After the arrival, I couldn't get my footing. In the corridor of the reception bay, with its mellow, shifting lights that formed moving patterns on the wall, my legs swam and wouldn't walk. The colors on the walls—and the very shape of the walls, curving widely outward—were meant to relax you. The brochures explained this. Psychologists and behavioral specialists had learned how to ease you into life on the moon. From the occasional windows, you saw gray below and black sky above. That stark view altered the optic nerve, over time, but also made you anxious. Something to do with our evolution. I don't remember what the wall shape was about.

My father had sent a radio message back an hour after they'd landed: "Amazing! I've gone to the moon! Another man on the flight read the same book as a kid! Lots of nice people greeted us. Don't worry." Both their names were affixed, but I heard my father's hearty hello. After my own landing, I didn't feel like speaking to anyone, not even two hours later. I asked an attendant to send a message to my family—on the moon and on Earth—just to let them know I'd arrived intact. Maybe my father had felt equally awful but managed to fake it. Perhaps he'd known I needed to be reassured; or he'd been reassuring himself; or rubbing it in my face. My parents never acted with single motives.

The attendants gave most of us boots and thin jackets fitted with weights. That helped. Some people waved them off. They'd come before and were accustomed, or they wanted the full experience. I wanted to go home.

I looked for her, but missed seeing the woman whose husband had died. What would she do now?

A series of walkways and slow-moving trams took me past housing "villages," vast enclosed farms, office complexes and scientific labs until I reached Serenity Sea, my parents' new home. A lot of work was in progress, with suites being constructed and, I saw through the windows, new units being added on. The crews laboring outdoors wore trimmer versions of what the old Apollo astronauts had worn. I wondered if my father's book's vision of the future had included these images, the people of Earth building without pause for a life far from home.

Their rooms were nice. I stood in the corridor, its walls running with watery colors, and looked past my mother rather than into her face; I saw furniture like we had on Earth, furniture like any furniture, not moon furniture, whatever I'd imagined that to be.

"It's like a regular apartment," I said.

My mother was looking up at me, and when I finally looked down, she said, "It was okay that we didn't meet you, wasn't it?"

"I told you not to. I needed time to get my moon legs, anyway."

"Okay."

I bent to embrace her. She felt fragile, but heavier than I expected. When she shuffled into the room, I realized why: she still wore the weighted materials they gave newcomers. "Your father's at the gym. Let me buzz him."

While she did that I wandered the rooms. I didn't wake up to the suitcase in my hand until I realized what was missing from the place: everything familiar. I let the bag settle gradually beside an overstuffed chair. Deciding where to sit froze me.

"What do you think?" asked my mother, her hands pressed together.

"It seems pleasant. No view?"

"Not from the rooms, no."

"Why is that?"

"Something about radiation," she said, and a line of sickness formed through the middle of my body, running from my throat to my crotch. I forced myself to continue pleasantly.

"Looks like you have everything in place. Comfortable."

"I can't get used to the gravity."

"Oh."

"Pretty much everything you see was made here. It's amazing what they're producing. These new plastics. It's really something."

I intended to mention the absence of familiar objects, then found something. A framed photo of my father and me tilted slightly backward on a set of shelves largely empty of books, the few books there—six?—making the point of the others' absence.

"That old picture," I said, and went to pick it up, bobbling it some as I did so. *Old* wasn't the right word, my mother had taken the shot outside our Pennsylvania house a few months before they'd moved to Arizona, but the picture did seem old somehow. The frame, at least, was the former frame. Wood, even.

"We couldn't bring much." Her voice collapsed on the final word, and she started crying.

"Hey," I said.

We sat together on the sofa. Having never comforted my mother before, I drew on the repertoire of gestures I used with Cyndi and the girls. I kept saying "Hey," alternately rubbing and gripping her far shoulder with my enveloping arm. So acutely did I feel my father's absence from the scene, I imagined briefly that he was dead.

He called my name excitedly as soon as he came in, before he even saw me.

"In here," I said. Soft words seemed loud, as if gravity's weakness left them too powerful.

My mother patted my leg and extricated herself from my grip. I understood that we weren't letting him in on her sorrow.

He gave me a tour of the facilities, ending back at the gym. The walls there were like the walls of other gyms, blue pads up to a certain height—higher than on Earth—and white walls above that. Metal beams, or perhaps a shaped plastic, crossed the high ceiling.

"Give this a look," said my father. He still wore his workout suit. After a few preparatory breaths, he loped in slow motion across the spongy red floor, then performed an awkward Fosbury flop over an absurdly elevated rubber high jump bar. He tumbled into a stack of pads, rolling about for some seconds before settling. His head came up, flushed and smiling. "Great, huh?"

"I imagine everybody can do that."

He clambered from the pads. "No. No. That's not true. People get lazy. You've got to work out to keep your muscles fit up here. I mean, look around." We were the only ones there. He tapped two fingers to his head, distressingly hard. "I've got the right attitude. Not everyone's got it. This is a new thing. You can't let retirement be about waiting for death. There are new opportunities."

I nearly said, *The high jump?* But I couldn't have a real conversation with him. Something wasn't right.

"Do you get . . . out much?" I asked.

"Outside? No. You can, there are excursions, but it's not a great idea every day. The radiation."

Again.

"I don't follow."

"Well, no one said this was totally safe. You want to limit your exposure to solar radiation." His hands went to his hips. "Maybe if they built another facility on the Dark Side. I'd go there. Then you could get out."

"Dad. The Dark Side isn't dark. You just can't see it from Earth. It gets the same solar exposure."

I thought he was going to say it: "Why do you tell people things they already know," but he just sucked in his cheeks and blinked.

"Huh," he said, and began bouncing on the balls of his feet, lifting off the ground and settling, like someone practicing for flight.

While my father took a nap, my mother explained. He'd blacked out on the rocket, and there'd been some struggle to revive him, a period when he lacked oxygen. After they brought him around, he was euphoric, and the feeling had stuck. The doctor had a term for it, but my mother hadn't cared enough about labeling the problem to hang on to the tag. Test pilots used to experience the same thing. For a decent percentage of those who went deeply black, they emerged altered, unafraid of death, seeing a universe suffused with joy. I could see how that unintended consequence might be useful for a test pilot. For a retiree . . .

"Maybe you could both come home," I said.

"Is that why you came here?" She'd been chopping carrots with undue care, and now she stopped.

"Probably," I said. I breathed a few times; no words came into my head. "I suppose so. I think I thought I was just coming to see you."

"It's all right. But we can't leave."

She resumed chopping, and I let it drop. Despite what she'd said, their leaving now seemed possible. I was mistaken, not knowing then what she'd meant.

I hadn't done my research.

I slept much of one day and was sick for a good part of another. My mother touched my forehead in search of my true temperature, recalling for me days I'd spent home with an ear infection in elementary school. She'd sat on my bed, her added weight on the cushion somehow a further comfort. The mattresses on the moon were too soft; she sank right in. It didn't have the same effect. I just wanted more than ever to return home.

I recovered enough by the fourth day, the day before my flight back, to join my father for a trip outside—outside, not "outdoors." Outdoors was for Earth. Three others, all elderly, went with us. A team of four attendants swarmed each person in turn. I watched them lock the seals on my boots and gloves; my breathing quickened as four hands lowered the helmet. Sliding noises, sharp snaps, a sour taste in my mouth, and a thumbs-up from outside. I returned the gesture, but didn't believe I was safe.

You didn't simply walk from the complex. We climbed aboard two fat-wheeled rovers, a series of wide doors lifted into the ceiling, and we rolled out. Immediately around the facility, the landscape had been scoured flat, but a hundred yards farther on, you hit the real thing, and the vehicles bounced in overreaction at each irregularity.

"Just stay strapped in and enjoy!" shouted a voice in both my ears, one of the two drivers. Like any nervous passenger, I watched the path ahead. My father had to remind me what I'd come out here to see, hitting my arm with the back of his hand, pointing skyward, then flipping back my sun visor. I looked up, but gripped the seat as if nothing, really, could have held me. The unorganized and unfamiliar sprawl of stars, the denser band of the galaxy's horizon, pressed down and drew me in.

My father's voice surprised me. "It never fails," he said. I saw he'd been watching me. "Never fails."

I touched the switch on my arm that let me speak directly back, and touched another that cut me off from everyone else.

"Too many stars," I said, and he nodded. "Where's Earth?"

He jabbed ahead of us. "After the rim!" he cried, as if a wind might take away his words.

With every terrific bounce, he whooped in my ear, and I hoped he'd remembered, in his delight, to spare others the joy.

The vehicles slowed some at the crater's edge, but the ascent, though steep, was steady. At that angle, I felt us launching toward the farthest stars.

Then the Earth hove up before me, three-quarters lit by the sun, and I stared at that until we stopped moving.

I staggered from my seat, now looking too little at the ground. "Watch your step," said a voice, though I figured it was directed at everyone. Then my father was talking directly to me.

"Can you believe it?"

"Not yet."

He laughed, a huge bark. He moved like an inflated penguin, bouncing side to side from one stiff leg to the other. I heard him breathing and humming; thinking of what my mother had told me, I tried to share his openness, his joy. Then he came between me and the Earth, as if he were running home.

Through whorls of cloud, I saw North America. I saw where I'd grown up and where I lived now. It all felt deeply wrong, and the planet seemed wrapped in thick silence. Momentarily, I panicked, thinking my suit had lost its air, but I calmed myself and found my breath had just become terribly shallow. My father must have turned off his link to me, because now I could not hear him breathe at all.

I headed immediately for my seat when a guide announced it was time to turn back.

"Let me ask you about the radiation," I said to my father on the rough return ride. I kept looking between my boots at the white floor of the rover.

"Are you going to ask me something or tell me something?" I turned to find him smiling impishly.

"Ask," I said.

He leaned closer. "Am I going to tell you something you don't know or something you do know?"

I lost the energy to say more.

They did see me off for the trip home, my mother's show of happiness so false I couldn't believe my father, even in his ecstatic state, didn't see it. But their relationship was their own, and it wasn't about what I perceived or even what I knew. They stood by the moving walkway, waving and waving, strings of green and blue light rolling on the walls behind them, while I slid backwards away. They stopped waving before I did, and then I watched them go.

I ended up with an empty seat beside me and two men, both ten years younger than I, across the aisle. One day out, when the one nearest woke briefly, I tried talking with him. He had several days' worth of beard, a wide, fleshy face, and looked open to conversation. I explained the purpose of my trip. He turned out to be a construction worker; this was his second moon jaunt. It paid well.

"They recommend only a month at a time," he said. "Any more, and you can't get insured, due to the radiation. Plus, you'd be stupid. I mean, you won't *turn* stupid, which is what one guy I know thinks, he won't come up here for anything, but you'd be stupid to do that to your genes."

"Too much damage."

"Yeah." He faced forward as he talked, letting his head roll my way every sentence or so to catch my eyes, then rolling back. He didn't talk loudly, probably out of deference to his sleeping companion. "Now, I've had my kids, have three kids, so it's not like I'm damaging my genetic inheritance. But cancer's a risk. That'd take a longer exposure, and the safety regs are pretty conservative."

"But what about the people living there?"

"The shielding's not *useless*. But it's not like it really blocks much. Some rays pour right on through. Human exposure's never been tested, and now that you can't test animals, it's a bit of a crap shoot. That's why people don't spend more than a few months up there. It's a stepping-stone to better work back on the big blue marble. Even for the administrators. Though I'll tell you, they've got experimental shielding on the quarters of some bigwigs. The government people especially. I helped install some last year."

"My parents . . ." I said, but didn't know how to finish the thought. They'd been there half a year already.

"How old are they?" I told him. "See, again, it's not like they're going to have more kids. Nobody in the retirement facilities is. I mean, I suppose something bizarre could happen, but nobody's *planning* for kids. And people are pretty old, most of them older than your parents. The low grav feels good. The radiation . . . I'm repeating myself, but it's a crap shoot."

"In any case," he said, "they can't leave now."

I waited for him to turn my way again. When he did, he saw that I didn't follow his thinking.

"You know."

"Maybe I don't," I said.

"Their muscles. They couldn't handle Earth gravity now. It's been too long, or it's pretty near to too long. You lose muscle mass, I don't care how much you work out. And your bones get fragile, like bird bones. Your heart, that's the big one. It gets accustomed to pumping on the moon. You take it back to Earth . . ." He saw I hadn't thought about any of this; his eyes had trouble rising to mine. "Well, they'd probably not survive the trip anyway."

After that, I couldn't talk. I requested more "passage medication" to put me out. When I woke many hours later, terribly hungry, I remembered a dream of the moon's surface: people without spacesuits shoveled at the gray dust, hurling it skyward.

Were they burying people up there? With nothing organic to devour them, nothing to grow from their decay, the bodies would remain unchanged under the dust. Or perhaps they folded the bodies into the soil of the farms. When the time came, regardless of the cost, I'd have to see about bringing them home.

My old hometown lay only two hours away by car, but I'd not visited since my parents' departure for Arizona. One day mid-February I called my wife's office from work, told her where I was going, not to wait on me for dinner, and left calmly and urgently.

The landscape grew hillier as I traveled south; the hills rolled, never loomed. They lay under snow, a thin snow that let yellow grasses poke through in the rare fields that abutted the narrow road. Once, long ago now, there'd been farms here, but the whole region was overrun with identical houses that obscured the landscape and threatened to cover the hilltops. For all the changes, the roads were still two-lanes with no shoulders. Every old stone house belonged to a law firm. Leaving on the heat, I wastefully cracked open the windows as well, letting in the smell of the cold, which did something at least to make me feel like I was in the country.

I wore boots. I planned to walk along my old town's main street, where the houses lay close to the sidewalk. I'd cut up through the blacktop lot of my old elementary school. From there I'd continue uphill, under tall trees, to the baseball lot, where my parents had watched me play Little League games, even then a nostalgic activity. I'd walk the bases. Above the baseball field stood Whitting Manor, a nursing home. Summer days, you could see through the wide bedroom windows old people propped up in their beds. Those who could venture outside were wheeled out to the porch that ran the length of the old main house. In winter, kids sledded from the main building down the sharp hill toward the ball field, bordered by a cedar hedgerow. I couldn't bring back the exact feeling of being on a sled, but I could see the other kids heading down the same hill or trudging back up, I could hear the screams of delight. The frigid air coming in the windows helped me remember.

Two deer leapt from behind a bush directly onto the road, not fifty feet away. Large and oblivious, they hesitated even as they landed. I jammed on the brakes. The car's computer made decisions about how to stop; sensing no other cars around, it cut briskly back and forth before leaving me to rest sideways. The deer stood just to my left, looking askance at me. The closer one flicked its ears, and I heard the flutter through the half-open window. I studied the fur where I would have struck the animal, the brown laced with black and white.

I backed the car to straighten out, and the animals continued, unhurried, across the street, their enormous black eyes watching but unafraid. They hopped a bank and headed toward another housing development. I heard their hooves breaking the snow's icy crust.

My arms, locked in place on the steering wheel, shook. Unsteady, I left the car and took in air. The deer were gone.

Where could deer live now?—Their woods were vanishing, what little bits of forest remained cut off by encroaching developments. And in winter, the landscape buried and frozen, they came out of their private places in search of food. But there were fewer fields, more cars to encounter, and their time was running out.

I remembered then that Whitting Manor had expanded when I was a kid, adding a retirement center that ate up most of the sledding hill. My elementary school had been shut down; condemned, though still beautiful on the outside, the school district *couldn't* even use it for offices. The traffic would be horrible in downtown. Were there even places to park?

I watched my hands shake and filled myself with a cold breath. I saw a car coming from a long way off under the bright winter sky. I thought to look: no moon.

Suddenly I didn't want to make the long trip to a place that no longer existed, or that existed perfectly only in my memory. I wanted to sit at home on my floor, playing a board game with the girls. I wanted to sit in that close living room with my wife warm nearby, her legs under a quilt. In the middle of all this cold emptiness, I felt my parents embrace me and let me go.

Like so many kids of her generation, Kristine Kathryn Rusch wanted to be an astronaut when she grew up. But she had trouble with math. Serious trouble. (Turns out that she's dyslexic.) So, with actual astronaut training out of the question, she turned to fiction. The moon factors into much of her fiction, and from her Retrieval Artist series (mysteries set on the Moon) to her award-winning "Recovering Apollo 8," her fiction has reflected her interest in the stars. In addition to the Retrieval Artist series, she has written a series set in the far future called the Diving series. She also writes under a number of pen names, including (but not limited to) Kris Nelscott and Kristine Grayson. She puts a free short story on her website every Monday. Go to kriswrites.com to read more of her work.

SENIORSOURCE
Kristine Kathryn Rusch

The little boy lay facedown in the dirt. Because the brown dirt was fine, loose, and powdery, I thought he had landed outside the dome, but that didn't quite match with what I was seeing. His body was intact, which it would not have been if it had been exposed to the harshness of the actual Moon.

Then something wet collided with my shirt, spoiling the you-are-there illusion, pulling me back into my workstation at SeniorSource.

I yanked off my goggles and made sure I let go of them gently so that they'd float beside me. I also let go of my workstation so I floated as well. A half a dozen other people were clinging to their stations, their faces hidden beneath the goggles that covered their eyes, ears, and nose. A few folks had strapped themselves in so that, in their excitement, they wouldn't let go and drift into some equipment on the other side of the work area.

My goggles weren't the only thing floating beside me. So were half a dozen other drops of some brown liquid. They had gathered near my left side, as if they were a phalanx of brown marbles lined up for an attack.

"Marvin," I snapped, "your coffee's gotten away from you again."

Marvin Pierce peeked at me from the doorway leading into the community kitchen. He floated sideways, hands gripping the edge of the door, only his bald pate, eyes, and nose visible, like a Kilroy-was-here drawing, something that one of the oldsters here had started sketching on the walls. (You couldn't call anything a ceiling or a floor here—the place constantly rotated.)

Marvin's blue eyes were twinkling. As he used his hands to propel himself into the VR work lab, he grinned like a naughty three-year-old.

Which he hadn't been in more than 125 years.

"Sorry," he said in a tone that let me know he wasn't sorry at all. He caught the first three balls of coffee with his mouth, swallowed hard, then used a pair of chopsticks to go after the fourth.

It was the chopsticks that screwed him up. The fourth bubble of coffee slipped through the wooden edges and aimed for me at surprising speed. I floated away, and watched in disgust as the coffee splatted against my goggles.

"Hey," I said. "I was working."

"Work, work, work. You know, sometimes you gotta take a coffee break," Marvin said, and then giggled. His giggle was high-pitched, like a little girl's.

It was also infectious. But I didn't let myself smile. Marvin had ruined too many workdays for me—cleaning things wasn't easy in zero-g—and I didn't dare lose this day.

I was on a schedule—a tight one. Maybe an impossible one.

And the idea of that made my stomach turn.

That little boy had been the son of Shane Proctor, head of the largest mining company on the Moon. This case was the first high-profile test run of SeniorSource's new Moon crime unit.

Theoretically, detectives in SeniorSource would solve cases on the Moon from their little perch in Earth's orbit. I used to think outsourcing detective work wouldn't work.

But it did work—I'd solved more than two hundred cases, some of them cold—since I arrived here five years ago. SeniorSource outsourced all kinds of highly skilled jobs, from laser surgery to art restoration. Even detective work, with its combination of interrogation, observation, and forensic skills, could succeed from a distance.

However, I had never been a guinea pig before. The chance of failure was high, and I didn't dare say no.

I was one of the youngest men at SeniorSource—and one of the poorest. I had to work full-time to pay for my healthcare as well as my room and board.

When the doctors told me that I would need full-time care, I investigated all my options. I didn't like most of them. Residential care hadn't changed much since I was a kid.

The old were warehoused with the terminally ill, and depending on how much money they had, they either got personal care or they didn't.

But because I had Manhattan Police Department insurance, which had ties with off-planet organizations like SeniorSource, I could apply here.

Which I did.

SeniorSource was the oldest pay-as-you-go orbital residence care facility. It advertised a full life for the long-lived, and for the most part, it lived up to that billing.

Some of the oldsters, like Marvin, had lived here for thirty years. He'd been nearly ninety when he arrived, written off by his family as near death, which he probably would have been had he stayed.

In space, in a place like SeniorSource, we lived in a germ-free environment, in zero-gravity that made each of us feel like Superman when we first arrived, along with a full-time medical staff (no one under eighty) who monitored us, kept our bones as strong as possible, made sure our circulation was good, as well as monitoring the physical changes of living in a hermetically sealed world so different from the one we had grown up in.

Guys like me, the younger guys, the full-timers, didn't have the lifetime health benefits that the oldsters like Marvin had. We didn't even have a mountain of assets to sell. The differences between my generation (dubbed, somewhere in the midtwenties, "the Sickest Generation") and Marvin's generation (the space generation or, as some still called them, the older baby boomers) were legion. Most of the folks my age had died of diabetes or heart attacks before we were old enough to send our peers into national politics. As a result, the younger generations wiped out most of the beneficial legislation that the baby boomers and Generation X had passed—the universal health care, the Retirement Savings Act, and all those others—keeping them intact for the boomers while grandfathering out people who were born in the twenty-first century.

So we didn't get to retire. We had to work. The Marvins of SeniorSource worked as well, but they only had to put in one day per month, mostly teaching history to college classes via streaming holos.

When I applied, I expected to be turned down. I didn't realize that SeniorSource badly needed trained detectives. They promised me a large private suite, an adequate food allowance, and midrange healthcare that was still better than anything I could get on Earth.

In exchange, I had to agree to work five days a week, eight hours per day, and exercise two hours per day seven days a week. I loved the idea of work; I hated the idea of exercise (I am a member of my generation, after all). But I agreed to all their terms, missing something important in the fine print.

My stay on this station was performance related. I couldn't be fired, but I could be demoted, which meant that my life would become a living hell. I would get smaller quarters, a lower-level food allowance, and minimal medical care.

If I really screwed up, I could be banished from the station. I'd be sent to an affiliated residence center somewhere in the Northeast, and warehoused with the rest of the old-timers.

The problem was that most folks who were banished from SeniorSource died within six months. Very few elderly people could handle the transition back to full gravity after living in zero-g.

Even though I was still one of the younger elderly, I doubted my bones could survive the transition. My bones—strong as they once were—had become fragile. When I'd left Earth five years ago, I could no longer walk. Plus my arthritis had gotten so bad I could barely move my fingers. It had been clear, even to me, that I could no longer live on my own.

I'd come up here reluctantly, but after I got past the stomach issues caused by the perpetual freefall of being in Earth's orbit, I loved it.

I couldn't imagine being anywhere else.

Which was why I didn't want this case.

If I failed to find the murderer of Shane Proctor's son within twenty-four hours, I could get demoted. If I mouthed off about the impossibility of the task, I could get sent Earthside.

I didn't want smaller quarters, and I didn't want to experience full gravity ever again.

And I really, really didn't want to die.

SeniorSource had recently branched into providing security and law enforcement services to various Moon-based communities, with an eye on capturing most of the Mars market by the turn of the century. If we did well on the Moon and had a proven track record in places outside of Earth, then we could open several care facilities in Mars's orbit when the time came, and would use those folks to provide services to the new Mars communities.

The success of cases like mine would guarantee more Moon contracts and with those, enough money to build in Mars's orbit even without full Mars contracts.

My boss, Riya Eoff, made it clear that any work I did on the Moon had to be flawless or I would suffer the consequences.

She didn't need to scare me. I was already scared enough.

SeniorSource's Earth-based companion investigation companies had robots and VR cameras and holographic imaging centers. We had weird little programs that I didn't entirely understand that supposedly sent up puffs of air, filled with the smells of the crime scene. (David Sullivan, the oldster who had trained me, told me they didn't actually send up air until two or three days into an investigation. What you got through the nose unit of the goggles was a simulation of the smells. Only since we were using Earth smells and Earth-based equipment, we tended to get it right more often than not.)

On Earth, there were still a few knowledgeable people who could answer questions, do hands-on examination of evidence as well as an old-fashioned autopsy if one of us old-fashioned detectives figured it was necessary.

On the Moon, we had robots, VR cameras, and holographic imaging—and very little else. The human medical professionals residing there had enough to do with their living subjects, and had never really received training in modern forensic pathology.

Not that it mattered, since the Moon was still a collection of bases and mining operations. There was no real legal system there, so prosecuting the criminal would fall on the mining company or whatever Earth-based conglomerate owned the thing, or maybe on the country in which the conglomerate was registered.

As soon as I got the case, I asked one of the oldsters who was fulfilling his monthly day of work doing legal research to find out who owned the mining company and what laws I might have to operate under.

But that would only get me so far.

First I had to solve the case.

And I wasn't sure I could do that.

Here's the thing: I know how things work on Earth. If I fall, I bruise. If I grab someone's arm hard, I could break the bone. If I shoot a gun, I know that the bullet might tear into blood and tissue and bone, leaving a trajectory that makes some kind of sense.

If I shoot a gun up here (not that I could, since firearms are the first thing confiscated before a resident boards the company shuttle), I know that bullet will follow some kind of straight line based on the amount of force from the explosion that released it. If the bullet doesn't encounter a lot of resistance—meaning it misses a bone—it'll slam through a human body in that same straight line, go through a wall, maybe another human body, and so on, until the energy that released it is spent.

With luck, that energy doesn't send the bullet through the walls of our little space habitat, punching a hole into our protective walls and forcing us to vent atmosphere.

The rules of physics still do apply; you just have to subtract for the lack of gravity.

On the Moon, you have domed environments with full Earth gravity, domed environments with two-thirds Earth gravity, domed environments with one-third Earth gravity, and domed environments with no gravity at all.

You also have the Moon's surface, which has one-sixth Earth gravity—and no atmosphere at all. Like everyone else sent up to this station, I learned what could happen to someone who let himself through both doors of the airlock without a space suit, and I found that lesson too graphic even for my concrete stomach. All I took away from the thing was this: you let yourself outside this place—or outside the Moon's domes—without an environmental suit, and you'll die one of the ugliest deaths imaginable.

So before I could do a full-scale Earth-type investigation, I had to find out several nontraditional things. Not only did I have to learn the exact location of the body, but I also needed to know what the gravity level was, and what the oxygen level was. I had to learn if the kid had access to an environmental suit, if he spent time outside the dome, and if he often went to domes with lesser (or greater) gravity.

I had to learn what Moon dust did to the lungs, whether the stuff could be made toxic with little effort, whether it changed from region to region.

Then I had to find out about the kid's family life, his daily routine, and whether or not he had any friends. I had to factor that routine into my investigation, and see if—say—the bruising that was fairly obvious even from the first glance at his poor little body was the normal result of his everyday life or if it had come from some unusual event.

I had to be not only a detective but also an expert scientist, a lawyer, and an authority on the Moon in just a few short hours.

And I didn't dare make a single mistake.

Which was why cleaning the coffee off my goggles irritated the hell out of me. It cost me time I truly didn't have.

I wished I could just change out that pair of goggles for another. But I couldn't. These goggles, our most high-end, had already been synced with the devices sent to settle the Proctor case, and it would take hours to sync another set of goggles with the Moon.

Not to mention the fact that those goggles would be technologically inferior to the ones I was using.

Cleaning things up here is perhaps the most difficult part of life in zero-g (if you don't count the first few times you have to use the bathroom). You can't just turn on a faucet and run the goggles underneath the tap. Everything here floats—including water.

You have to use a series of cloths, all treated with cleaning and drying fluids (but not wet enough to drip, of course). Then you have to put the fluid-covered cleaning cloths in the right containers and place them in the recycler, testing the item you're trying to clean to make sure the dirt—or in my case, the coffee—has finally been removed.

I got the goggles cleaned, but I lost nearly a quarter of an hour.

During that quarter of an hour, however, I had had a chance to think. And to listen to what little bit we knew about the son of Shane Proctor.

I used the audio function of my own personal computer. We're all assigned an onboard computer when we arrive; we can choose whether or not to have its component parts attached to our bodies. The oldsters prefer to have the computer as a separate item; I like my ear bud and my fingernail cam and the tiny screen that appears in the palm of my hand whenever I need to view some information.

Shane Proctor's son was named Chen, a Chinese name that meant *great*. Oddly enough, he had no middle name.

Chen Proctor had been born in 2070 on the Moon in Proctor Mining Colony, with two midwives presiding. His mother, Lian Proctor, was Shane Proctor's third wife. A quick search did not tell me what had happened to the previous two wives. I would have to dig for that information.

Chen Proctor had been home-schooled most of his life, partly because he went from mining operation to mining operation with his father and partly because he learned faster than anyone else in his age group.

He had a younger brother named Ellsworth and a baby sister named Caryn. Another quick search told me that Ellsworth and Caryn had different birth mothers than Chen—wives four and five.

No other child lived at home, and all three seemed to stay with their father, rather than their mothers. I couldn't even do a standard search on where the mothers lived. Proctor Mining Company shielded a lot of personal data about its president and chief shareholder, so I had reached the extent of the public information I could find out about Proctor's three children.

Or his last three children.

I wasn't sure which.

I grabbed my goggles and floated back to my workstation. This time I strapped in.

I needed to concentrate fully, and the last thing I wanted to do was drift.

The Proctor Mining Colony took up most of what was once called the Descartes Highlands. The highlands were unrecognizable from the place where *Apollo 16* had landed over one hundred years before. Now highlands were covered with mini domes, robotic equipment, newly dug holes, and not so newly dug holes. Lights covered the entire area, and what had once seemed like a dark grayish brown place now continually glowed.

Chen Proctor had spent the last two years of his life in the settlement dome, several kilometers from the current active mine. According to his family, he was never allowed outside. Apparently there had been an incident, and Chen had nearly died.

I let some of the androids—although they were really just talking robots—do the preliminary interviews, using a standard list of questions that I had tailored to this investigation. I would ask some of the tougher questions myself a little later.

But first, I wanted to examine the body.

A pan-back and a comparison with GoogleMoon showed me exactly where the body had been found. It was at the edge of the new dome, which was being built to replace the settlement where the boy lived. The new dome had just inaugurated its gravity and environmental controls.

It was supposed to replicate the environment inside the settlement—meaning full Earth-normal, down to the oxygen and carbon dioxide mix in the air. The terraformers were working on the Moon dust, trying to make it more like Earth dirt, but that experiment was failing.

It was beginning to look more and more like the new dome would be exactly like the old settlement, only with better filters.

I had to use all five of SeniorSource's robots, as well as the three VR cameras and the single holoimager, to get a good three-dimensional look at the body.

For an eight-year-old, Chen was tiny. He had the look of a boy raised in low gravity instead of full gravity, like his bio suggested. He had narrow little shoulders, a back so flat and slender that I could see his spine and his shoulder blades outlined against his shirt.

His pants seemed too big, and oddly enough, he was barefoot. His face was turned sideways, his mouth partially open and filled with dirt.

The holoimage showed hair that should have been black turned almost gray with Moon dust, and slightly almond-shaped eyes that were tightly closed.

I made the robots go around him, zooming in their own cameras for a level of detail that the human eye couldn't see. I needed to know if what I thought were bruises were actually something else.

The bruises ran along the side of his cheek and under his chin, then again along his forearms. The marks on his forearms were small. They ran from the elbow to the wrist and were not evenly spaced.

The mark on his face was large, covering most of his visible cheek, his jawline, and running all the way down to the middle of his neck.

If they were bruises, they had been created before he died. In that case, someone had grabbed him and hit him. But I wasn't ready to take the easy solution. I was afraid these were some kind of marking I wasn't familiar with—something that a person who lived in the Moon colonies would see as normal and not suspicious at all.

So I had the robots give me as much information as they could without disturbing the body. The photographs and vids were great, but I wanted more.

If I had actually been there, I would have leaned over the boy and sniffed. You learn a lot from the way a corpse smells—and I'm not just talking about decomposition. Perfume on the shirt, the scent of cedar oil on the hands, the faint odor of grease on the back of the neck might be all it takes to wrap up a case.

Only I had no time and no way to order up a little whiff of air.

So I did the next best thing. I had the robots take the chemical composition of the air, unit by tiny unit. I hoped I could feed those chemical signatures into our own forensic lab computer and get an analysis of the odors—not quite as good as smelling things myself, but good enough, maybe, to give me an idea of what I was facing.

I also had one of the robots take images of the area, and was startled to see signs in English, proclaiming this part of the new dome completely off-limits.

No one had mentioned that.

In fact, no one had mentioned how the boy's body had been found in the first place.

I put through a series of instructions—no touching the body until my investigation was finished, no one (human or nonaffiliated robot) allowed on the scene while the work progressed, and no second-party release of information.

That last was the most critical, because information acquired through nonhuman means often had more than one legal owner. I had no idea if the robots I was using belonged solely to SeniorSource or if they were being leased from Proctor Mining.

I had no idea about too many things.

My stomach turned, and I felt queasy for the first time in years. I closed my eyes and took a deep breath.

When I had worked for the NYPD, I occasionally clashed with my bosses. I became known as one of the most opinionated and successful detectives in homicide. If you wanted a case closed, you picked me to investigate. But you also put up with my attitude and my mouth.

I'd kept both under control here—I knew the risks, and they weren't worth the hassle.

I could usually succeed without mouthing off.

On this case, however, I couldn't. SeniorSource had given me an impossible task with an impossible deadline, and somehow expected me to get it done.

Maybe if I confessed about my own inadequacies early enough, I'd only suffer a demotion. Maybe I'd just get a demerit.

Maybe, if I documented everything, I'd have enough evidence to take to one of the elderly lawyers up here and get him (or an Earthbound colleague) to fight my inevitable banishment back to full gravity.

Because I couldn't work with what I had.

I set my goggles and the nearby computer backups to store each piece of information that was sent through the equipment on the Moon. When I was done, I peeled the goggles off and hung them on the Velcro strap designed especially for them.

Then I headed to my boss's office, trying not to think of everything I risked.

My boss, Riya Eoff, had decorated every available space of her office with pictures from home. Photographs of her family, starting with her great-grand-parents and running all the way to her own great-granddaughter, a baby she had never met. Riya suffered from advanced osteoporosis and had had to sign a special waiver just to get approved at SeniorSource, since space life often leached calcium from the bone.

But it was easier to survive up here with weak bones than it was on Earth. Her doctor had signed her up as an experimental guinea pig—to see how long a severely weakened person could survive in zero-g—and the study had long since ended. Riya was now in her second decade at SeniorSource, and if you didn't know her history, you'd think the thin, silver-haired woman who haunted this office was one of the most athletic elderly people who had ever come into space.

"This better be important," she said to me. "You're on a deadline."

"I know," I said. "If you want results by tomorrow, you have to give me the full detective squad plus a few scientists."

My voice didn't shake, and that was a plus. I tried to imagine myself back on Earth, making this same pitch in the precinct, but that was hard.

We didn't float in the NYPD.

"We don't have the budget for a full squad." She didn't quite look at me. Instead, she threaded her hands over her stomach. Her fingers were covered with rings, some as old as she was. A necklace floated around her chin—she had once told me she had worn it since she was twelve and had never taken it off.

My stomach twisted. That queasiness was getting worse.

"If you can't give me the help," I said, "then you're not going to get this contract."

"Are you saying you can't solve this crime?" she asked.

I tensed. I never said I couldn't solve a crime. But I didn't let her bait me. I spoke slowly, so that I didn't say something I would regret.

"I'm saying I can't solve this case in the timeline you gave me with the knowledge I have."

"You're the smartest investigator I have," she said.

That statement should have relaxed me, but it didn't. "Maybe with Earth crimes," I said. "But I know nothing about the Moon."

"You know enough."

I shook my head, then regretted it as the movement sent me sliding in two different directions at once. I'd gotten rid of most of my counterproductive Earth movements, but head-shaking was one that snuck up on me—I never thought of it as movement, only as communication.

"Nonsense," she said. "Tell me who you suspect and why."

"I suspect no one," I said. "I'm not even sure about the kid's family relationships. I don't know if he snuck into that spot in the new dome. I'm not even sure he was murdered."

I could hear an old tone in my voice—an edge, one that threatened to become strident.

Riya grabbed onto a handhold built into one of the walls. She should have reprimanded me—SeniorSource never admitted that it examined crimes that turned out to be nothing more than an accident—but she didn't.

Instead she said, "What makes you say that he might not have been murdered?"

The hair rose on the back of my neck—or the hair would have risen if it weren't already standing at attention from the lack of gravity. Still, that feeling, the one my grandmother used to say was like someone walking on your grave, made me shiver.

Something was going on here. Something I wasn't sure I liked.

I took a deep breath to keep my temper in check.

"The dome is new," I said. "The environmental equipment was just turned on. So was the gravity. The boy had a mouthful of Moon dust, but some of the information I received said that scientists were trying to turn that part of the dome into an Earthlike area, one that could grow grass, crops, and trees. So what happens if the boy was in the wrong place at the wrong time?"

"Go on," she said, and that feeling crawling along my spine grew worse.

I knew I was supposed to be a guinea pig, but I was supposed to solve the case. Only Riya was acting like she already knew the solution.

Maybe the test was more complicated than I had originally thought.

"The oxygen mix could be wrong," I said. "He doesn't look like a boy who suffocated, but I'm not sure what certain chemical mixes would do to a body."

She tilted her head at me, her expression neutral. I didn't like that either.

"Then there's the so-called soil. If he fell and got a mouthful of it, did it poison him? And what happens if the gravity came on too hard? The human body can survive four, five, six times Earth-normal. Healthy adult males can survive as much as eight times Earth-normal for a few minutes. But me? I couldn't survive that and neither could you. Our bones would shatter and our lungs would collapse. I have no idea if the same thing would happen to a fragile-looking eight-year-old, but I'll wager it might."

She nodded, but since she clung to the handhold, she didn't really move much.

I continued. "He has marks that look like bruises on his face and arms, but that's the only visible skin I can see. The bruises on his arms look like finger marks, but what if they're hematomas from shattered bones? What if the long bruise on his face is some kind of darkening agent from a poison he ingested?"

"You'll find that out," she said.

"Not by tomorrow," I said. "Because even if I found out that the gravity was too high and it crushed him, how would I know if he stumbled in there accidentally or if someone told him to sit there and wait, then went to the controls and turned the gravity to nine times Earth-normal?"

"The robots could give you those readings," she said.

"No, they can't," I said. "They'd give me the readings for now, not then. And we both know that computer readings can be tampered with. So the old data is as useless as my guesswork."

She stared at me.

"Give me a team," I said, "or I'm going to have to withdraw from this case."

"You can't withdraw," she said, and my stomach clenched. Here came the final moment—the moment when I chose my integrity or I chose my life.

"Watch me," I said, and shoved my way out of the room.

I'd be lucky to get a demotion. I was probably heading Earthside, to gravity that would feel as heavy to me as 9 g's would have felt to poor little Chen Proctor.

Riya caught my ankle and tugged me back inside.

"Talk to me," she said. "There's something else you don't like about this case, besides the unfamiliar terrain and the deadline. What is it?"

Whatever you could say about Riya Eoff, you couldn't call her dumb. I actually hated how perceptive she was.

I also wasn't fond of the way her hand still clung to my ankle. She wasn't going to let me out of here until she ruled the conversation over.

But I figured I couldn't make matters worse—at least, not for me. So it didn't hurt to be honest with her.

"Ninety-five percent of child murders," I said slowly, "are committed by a member of the family, usually a parent or stepparent."

She let go of my ankle. I drifted a little past her and had to grab a handhold to keep myself from spiraling back into the center of the room.

"You think Shane Proctor did this?"

"I don't know," I said. "I don't have a prime suspect. But if I did have a prime suspect, and if it was someone that Shane Proctor loved, then what? How would we prosecute? How would we even arrest? This whole setup is flawed, Riya. It's not enough to find out whodunit. We need to know how we're going to catch them, and even more important, how we're going to stop them—and anyone else—from ever doing this again."

She let go of her handhold and crossed her arms. Then she smiled at me. The smile was slow, but effective.

I wasn't exactly sure how to interpret it.

"You do realize that you have a gift for investigation, don't you?" she said.

I clutched the handhold. I had no real idea why she was flattering me.

And then I understood. "You do know who killed Chen."

"Yes," she said. Then she frowned. "No. Well, maybe I do. The death was ruled accidental. He was crushed when the gravity test malfunctioned. Chen had a penchant for wandering into test areas. He liked to be alone. It wasn't the first time he'd been caught somewhere he shouldn't have been. It was the first time he'd been injured."

"I thought you said he died."

"You know what I mean," she said. "But I don't think anyone considered that he hadn't wandered in there. I'm not sure if anyone thought about the fact that the controls could have been tampered with."

"Except you," I said.

Her smile widened. "I needed confirmation."

"Because you already knew that prosecuting anyone for this would be impossible."

She nodded, and this time, the movement made her bob like a buoy in a rough sea. "It's one thing to investigate crimes. It's another to prosecute them."

I thought I had just said that. But I didn't point that out to her. I didn't dare.

"I needed a simulation," she said. "I needed to show management that although our investigators can handle anything given the time and the resources, we need support on the ground. And the Moon colonies don't have that support. I can't even imagine what it would be like on the frontier, if we went with the settlers to Mars."

Not that we would be with those settlers. We'd only be observing them. And then we'd only be observing the very darkest sides of them.

"So this was all a simulation," I said. "The commands I gave the robots, the things I saw through my goggles. You'd set all that up so you had some footage to take to the brass."

Her smile faded. "It's not all a simulation," she said. "Chen Proctor is dead. And there will always be a lot of unanswered questions about the death."

"I could still investigate it," I said before I had a chance to think. I wanted to mitigate some of the damage I had done with my harsh tone.

"That boy's been dead for two years."

Which explained why I was told I had only rudimentary equipment to work with. Which was why the answers I got to the questions sounded as mechanical as the robots asking those questions.

"Two years," I repeated. "I suppose the body's long gone."

"They don't bury the dead on the Moon," she said. "Cremation is more efficient."

"And no one took the requisite information."

"Who would?" she asked.

"So who tried to hire us?" I asked. "It wasn't Proctor Mining, was it?"

She didn't answer me. She probably couldn't. It could have been anyone from a Proctor Mining competitor to one of those government unification types who wanted strong central oversight of the Moon.

"I need you to make a complete report," she said. "I want you to list every single thing we would have to do to successfully prosecute that boy's killer—if indeed he had a killer."

"Even if the killer was one of his parents," I said.

"Even if," she said.

I took a deep breath. I wasn't going to be banished. I wasn't going to get a demotion. I had done the job she wanted. I had passed the damn test, not even realizing exactly what it was.

"Essentially, then," I said, "I'm designing your Moon outsourcing program, using this one case."

She winced. "I wouldn't say that."

"Because," I said, getting warmed up, "if you said that, you'd owe me more compensation. I'd have moved up from investigator to management."

She nervously caught her floating necklace with one finger. "You once told me you don't want to be management."

I'd been taking risks all day, so I decided to take another. "If you're going to work me like management, you have to compensate me like management."

"Not without the job title."

"I don't want the job title," I said. "And I'll do the work, if you guarantee me my quarters for life, a richer food allowance, and the same medical care that the oldsters get."

"That's a lot," she said.

"I'm designing a brand-new outsourcing program for you."

"You're just suggesting it," she said.

"Still."

"How about more free time?" she asked.

I shook my head and felt my body sway. I clutched the handhold tighter. "Quarters for life, richer food, oldster-level medical care. Nothing less."

She made a face. I felt the tension return.

Then she extended a hand. "Done."

I let out a small sigh as I took her hand.

"Good," I said. "As soon as we have a contract, I'll do your report."

She sighed. "I wouldn't have pegged you for such a tough negotiator."

I usually wasn't. Except when someone's life was on the line. And this time, it was my life. With those guarantees, I could stop restraining myself. I could speak out about my investigations. I could stop worrying whenever I told the truth.

And I never again had to worry about going Earthside. I would stay here until my heart stopped beating.

I could do what I wanted without fear of losing this grand adventure.

I could truly live out my days, instead of waiting them out. I could float, gravity free, instead of sitting in a tiny piss-scented room, being crushed by the weight of the world and the lack of a future.

"Sometimes," I said, "you have to be a tough negotiator. It's the only way to get what you want."

"And you want to stay here," she said.

"Yeah," I said.

She smiled. "I don't think there's any worry about that."

Not anymore, I thought with more relief than I'd felt in my life. Not anymore.

Sarah Thomas is an award-winning journalist, marketer, essayist, newspaper editor, and fiction writer whose work has appeared in *The Magazine of Fantasy & Science Fiction, Strange Horizons, National Geographic Glimpse, Offbeat Bride, Anvil's Ring, the Boston Globe*, and more. She lives in Salem, Massachusetts, with her husband, Mike, and a very fat cat.

THE ECONOMY OF VACUUM
Sarah Thomas

PART I

All the predictions regarding how quickly the public would bore of the mission were grossly underestimated.

For fifteen news cycles, at least one network was providing round-the-clock coverage. The base's larger structures were self-assembling, so there was plenty of time for Virginia to prance around for the cameras in her jumpsuit, sticking posters to the polycarbonate walls with duct tape. The mission directors had encouraged her to take as many mementos from home as she pleased—both for her own peace of mind, and to demonstrate the efficiency of the new Valero thermocakes.

"You know, fifty years ago astronauts couldn't take more than seven pounds of material with them," she said to a camera one day, in a slightly different format than she had related the same statistic, earlier, for this network's ratings rival. "For perspective, that's about the equivalent of a small palmtop computer-printer. I'm glad I'm coming up here now," and here she lifted an ostentatiously thick hardback book and set it on a shelf.

"Do you like to read, Sergeant Rickles?" asked the newscaster, after a four hundred thousand mile pause.

"Very much so," she said, loading the shelf with more leather spines. "And the folks at Harper-Doubleday were kind enough to provide me with some of my favorites."

On the first supply flight, two months later, nearly ten million viewers tuned in as the Vice President toured the completed Fort Discovery moonbase and presented Virginia with a signed first edition of the President's autobiography. Virginia thanked the Vice President and his entourage, then made them all tea on the facility's infrared induction cooktop.

The early supply shuttles came in so fast Virginia was less afraid of loneliness than of not getting her work done.

Though the primary purpose of her mission was, simply, to live on the Moon—to prove to the skeptics that space exposure was not lethal, to advertise the products and technologies that would fund later NASA missions, and to excite people about the possibility of luxury moon tourism—a few genuine experiments had attached themselves along for the ride. All were designed to look after themselves, but they required calibration and monitoring, and it wasn't long before Virginia began to resent the interruptions.

"But I told you, I don't need any more food!" she yelled at the monitor one day, while the deputy director listened impassively. "I've got fourteen crates out there. Isn't the idea that I'll be self-sustaining anyway?"

"Never hurts to have a backup. And the food will definitely be eaten. We'll use it on other missions."

"And paint? What the hell do you expect me to do with paint?"

"Benjamin Moore is donating twelve million dollars and all the labor and supplies to paint the next two space shuttles, Virginia. Use your imagination."

So Virginia painted childish murals on the walls of the kitchen and living area, murals of trees and deserts and fish under the sea. Then some station got the bright idea to encourage children to send their drawings and poems to the moonbase, with the envelope addressed, "Sgt. Virginia Rickles, Fort Discovery, The Moon, U.S.A.," and Virginia's murals disappeared under reams of paper and wax.

An unexpected resurgence of Virginia's popularity came when the President and Executive Host booked a luxury shuttle cruise and requested a stopover at the moonbase.

They could not have come at a better time. The hydroponic garden had really taken off; the Plexiglas window in the mess was a sheet of green, dotted with tiny flecks of red fruit. Some of the experiments were beginning to yield definitive results, and an automatic physical had just pronounced Virginia in better shape now than when she arrived on the moon.

The Executive Host was much taller than he looked on television. Virginia found herself smiling whenever he said anything to her.

"You know, my mother was a First Lady," he told her on their third day, while they walked through the hydroponic garden with the news crew tagging discreetly behind.

"I know. I watched her special on expanding the White House when I was a kid."

"You and everyone else. She never really got over that, how controversial it became."

"I never understood why. I thought the new wings were beautiful. She had exquisite taste."

"Well, she'd be happy to hear you say so."

"Was it strange to move back after the election?"

"A little. It was like visiting your old high school."

"I never did that."

"Visited?"

"No, went to high school. I was homeschooled." The Executive Host looked at her then. He did not find her a pretty woman, though there was something attractive in her utter health. There had been one unexpected physical result of long-term space exposure; her pupils were permanently dilated, with a mere sliver of brown surrounding the black like a hemisphere of chocolate truffle. The Executive Host wondered if she thought of herself as a Cortes or a da Gama, hacking through a jungle of vacuum to find a new world.

The President caught up with them then, looking worried. They were needed back on Earth, she said. The situation with some other country was deteriorating. Even as the President mentioned who, Virginia felt the name of the enemy sliding away from her mind like a bar of wet soap.

America was too distracted for space now. Even the elementary schools stopped sending her pen-pal messages. She continued to broadcast faithfully every week, explaining a piece of technology in simple terms, talking about her AIBO as if it were a real dog. She had to stop showing it, though; it had shorted after wandering into her shower stall.

"No, no, everything's under control down here," said the Deputy Director. There was an unusual amount of background noise. "We're going to send up another shuttle to collect the seedlings."

The shuttle never arrived. It was blown up, and there was no money to build a new one. The only things left were the commercial craft and the communications satellites, all turned inward.

"You've never asked," he said to her on another night. He had starting calling a few times a week. She brewed two mugs of coffee when he called, let one become cool and bitter while she drank the other and listened.

"I've never asked what," she said. It wasn't a question.

"Never asked to come home. Never asked to get off the base."

There is a long pause, during which the director thinks about Virginia. He realizes she has no replacement halogen bulbs. He realizes he wants her to drink that second cup of coffee, that it will break some small unsullied chunk of his heart if she throws that cold liquid down the reclamation drain. He realizes he expects to die soon, possibly within hours.

"Well, you've had a lot on your mind down there," she says finally, swirling her index finger in the dark liquid. Virginia is thinking that she has never, in her life, thought of anywhere on Earth as "home." This base is not home either, just a place reflecting all the entities that have encased her; an old mattress with the springs poking through. "I always knew this was going to be a long mission. I trained for this, I wanted this. I'm better equipped, literally and figuratively, to be alone up here than any astronaut outside of Russia. I'll be okay."

The director's pause is shorter. He knows if he opens his mouth to tell her that there is no Russia anymore, he will never be able to forgive himself.

"That's true. Now, tell me about the EKG readings." Virginia drinks her cold coffee while the Deputy Director's heart flutters like a bicycle streamer, waiting for the bombs to begin again.

Four weeks later, Virginia tries to raise the Deputy Director. It is difficult to make a call; there is a lot of interference. She eventually gets a signal, but the control room is empty. Though there are no windows on the station, a camera is always trained on Earth. The view when she switches on her video screen is cloudy and unhelpful.

The wall calendar tells her it is Christmas.

She has found a gift for herself. It was shoved in the corner of her bunk, where, on some unremembered morning shortly after her arrival, she used it to stop a shelf from wobbling. The manual for the AIBO. It is in Japanese, but she has many different language dictionaries, and it might allow her to fix the toy.

When Virginia was small, her mother and stepfather lived, very briefly, in a bed and breakfast in northern Vermont. She was with her mother just on holidays then, and the first one she spent there was Christmas. There is very little she remembers about that Christmas; it passed in a smear of dry turkey and presents reflecting generic, girlish interests not her own. But she remembers the fire in the massive stone fireplace, glittering off the wineglass tipped in her mother's loosening fingers.

The children's drawings do not burn so bright, in the glass dutch oven on the induction cooktop. But she watches anyway, whistling tunelessly.

There are two symptoms of long-term space exposure. The first, the dilation of her pupils, causes her little discomfort except to make the white plastic of her surroundings luminously bright. The second she discovers with no warning one day while she is masturbating furiously in the shower; a faint tingling on the pads of her fingers irritated by repetitive motion. She gives up after a few minutes, simply collapses to the fiberglass floor of the stall and lets the reclaimed water sluice over her head.

Behind the bathroom is a small gymnasium; a rack of free weights, a yoga ball, and an elliptical crosstrainer. Her mission briefs stipulate she spend twenty minutes in here every day, but lately she has been stretching it to two hours. She runs through her routine and then improvises workouts never attempted before; hooking her knees around the handbars of the elliptical crosstrainer and powering it with her hands, strange balletic swings with her wrists and feet strapped to five pound weights. Sometimes she passes out from exertion and awakens later, clammy with sweat.

She has not increased her food intake. Her hips winnow down to knobs. Her clavicles work like dull knives trying to cut through the peel of a salt-white tomato.

"I wonder if there's still a Disney World," she says to no one in particular one day. She hasn't spoken in weeks, just sat at the table with the unchanging white light growing brighter and brighter.

"I wonder if there's still a Disney World," she says again, to taste the flavor of the echoes that come back to her off the gleaming plastic surfaces. "I never went to Disney World. I can't remember if I ever wanted to. Maybe when I was really young. I think I once saw a special on the travel network about the underground passages in Disney World. They were carpeted, and the announcer said they were cooler and quieter than the park. There was a plush bench against a hall, and Snow White and Winnie the Pooh were sitting next to each other. Just ... talking. I remember wanting to visit there—not the park, the underground passages. I wonder if they still exist. I wonder if the passages protected the workers. Maybe Snow White made a barricade and is trying to tunnel her way back to the surface. Maybe there are armies down there, battalions of Mickeys trying to save America. I'm an American. America. I'm a citizen of the United States of America."

And here Virginia cries, finally. She hasn't cried in two years. She cries because of the strength of the heart beating in her chest, she cries because even her great immunity against loneliness is still mutable, still sieved with tiny holes of feeling through which the whites of the countertops can pass. She cries because she realizes, finally, that she is only forty-three years old.

One day, Virginia is methodically going through every drawer in the base.

She is counting all the spoons, all the screwdriver bits, all the Band-Aids, and organizing them along more whimsical lines. The drawer of all things that smell sweet will be next to the drawer of things that are yellow. She is not sure, yet, into which the pencils will go.

She finds many nuts and bolts; four tall ones, sixteen stumpy little ones, four with wing screws. Her idea comes to her almost without thought, and she has broken out the silver cans of Benjamin Moore paint. The alternating teal and lime colored squares go on the table, and Virginia is as bouncy as a child waiting for them to dry enough to play chess.

She begins the next day, but it is no good. The chess squares begin to gnaw at her mind; no amount of workout-derived blackouts can keep them at bay. She tries sneaking up on the game, shoving pawns along senseless lines while passing between the kitchen and gym. She sees the eyebolts in her sleep, which has a gray hue from the light passing through her eyelids to her gaping retinae.

"I need another game," she decides one day. "If I'm playing two games at once I won't be able to plan as far ahead." The kitchen agrees with her.

She plays this game with spice canisters against herb tins, on a black and pink field much larger than the other. The games reproduce exponentially. Sheets from experimental schematics against pieces of a page-a-day calendar with jokes about cats. Components of a microscope against burned-out light-bulbs. Balls of wadded duct tape against knots of her own hair. The surfaces of her base become a fractal meadow of colors, echoes of which invade her sleep and give her dreams of peaches that taste of onion and sawdust.

It occurs to Virginia one day that she can go outside, collect some rocks for more chess pieces. Virginia has never left the station. There is a suit in the airlock; it is slightly too large for her and has a faint chemical smell.

Virginia trips as the pop of expanding air knocks her off balance. Her cosseted shoulder bumps softly against the portal jamb. She takes a few steps outside, dizzy with fear.

Above her, the black is a twitching membrane the color of chloroform. Being under it makes her skin feel nauseous, like licking a battery with some shameful orifice. Her eyes quest around for something normal to latch onto, and they find the Earth. She stands, buffeted a little by the processes of her body in the low gravity, and stares at the Earth, shrouded in a scum of cloud, only interrupted occasionally by a thin slash of blue. She stares, thirsty for land, and finally she sees it, an obscene brown bulge, the Florida peninsula denuded. She goes back inside the base and tries to calm the knocking of her heart.

Virginia attempts suicide only once.

She is outside again; she walks in the suit every day now. It makes its own oxygen, recharging enough in the evening to give her eight hours of breath should she need it. There are many rocks outside, and she has carved some with an arc welder, making a landscape of rough-hewn squirrels and jellyfish.

She is shaping some stone with her absurd spatula mittens into an approximation of a sleeping cat. The mittens tremble, stop. The stone cools quickly. The arc welder bounces slowly when it pillows into the sparkling dust. Virginia reaches behind her back and locates the small jet pack, meant to be used to locomote quickly in the low gravity.

She switches it on and lies back, and the obscene black sucks her up like a milkshake.

After an hour the pack runs out of fuel. She has no way of knowing how far up she has gone. She just lies there, her eyes aching with abyss. Her mouth moves, a mephitic lullaby of nonsense syllables rocking her someplace beyond sleep.

But she does not clear the gravity well, and after five additional hours she comes to a soft landing in the dust. For a few moments she holds her breath. Then she stands and follows her homing readout back to the base.

"All right," she says later, to the kitchen. "Maybe not today. But it's okay. I know it's there for me now. No rush."

Next Christmas, she burns the AIBO in the dutch oven, the little pieces of doggy head glinting oddly in the firelight.

Thirty-one years pass.

PART II

The mission crew of the BRSCG *Sangre de Christo* stands outside the hemisphere of pitted polycarbonate and tries to understand what they are seeing.

Around them, the moon rocks have been carved into a forest of skyscrapers and half-licked Tootsie pops. Mutant snails with spider legs gambol through the razor shadows. Faces stare up from arcane root structures, surrounded with spaceboot prints. Matteo, the mission leader, curses softly under his breath and wishes that their political officer were there to atomize their surroundings with holy water.

Behind him, Lourdes approaches the portal door with a large diamond drill. At a nod from Matteo, she flicks the switch and starts cutting through the outer airlock.

Matteo turns, stares at the gibbous Earth. He thinks the light-sprawl illuminating the cloud cover just at the horizon line might be Guatemala City. In the privacy of his mind he still names it thus, in the precise English of his Jesuit lizard-memory. *La Nueva Guatemala de la Asunción* is clunky to him. Commandeered prose, like the components of the ship that brought him here. Like what they are doing to this building.

Next to him, the communications officer tugs his elbow.

The airlock portal has opened. From the inside.

For a few moments they just stand there, their breath misting the inside of their helmets. Matteo moves first, his half-hop looking oddly enthusiastic. The rest follow. Once inside the portal, repressurization is soundless within their helmets. A long pause, during which Lourdes fingers the controls of the diamond drill, and then the inner portal opens.

They walk inside, slowly. Before them is a warren, lit by sputtering lightbulbs and covered with senseless tessellations of paint and organic matter. Lourdes kneels, staring at a phalanx of neatly balled dust. The only piece of recognizable architecture is a wall, so designated because a portal yawns in it; ropy vines crawl through, overspreading the space above his head with stalactites of banana.

In his ear mike, Lourdes screams softly.

Matteo approaches. The space where she is looking was once a kitchen, now painted matte black and covered with powdery drawings of dogs and computer chips. A glass pot sits on the stove, full of burning gingerbread men. And on the floor, an elderly woman covered in a curtain of moon-colored hair crouches. Her eyes are black pools. She is thin as a skeleton.

"Your hands grew back," she says after a moment, looking at the burning cookies. "That's nice."

Inside the *Sangre de Christo*'s landing shuttle, a small digital recorder plays Gloria Estefan, and everyone but Virginia is dancing.

The Guatemalan astronauts are friendly with each other. They have trained together for years—learned to read the argots of dozens of dead empires, guessed when gold could be replaced with copper. They had all received Extreme Unction on a live television broadcast before taking off on this, the first space mission since the war. But now they are here and alive, and they celebrate, drinking aguardiente from plastic bags. The political officer snoozes with his feet on the table.

Lourdes is the only other woman. Her left hand grabs invisible cloth and throws it around like a matador as the men hand her over from one to the other. Between songs, Lourdes talks to Virginia; quick bursts of furtive pidgin English dropped while she watches the political officer. She has no idea if Virginia can understand or not.

"Someday, I would like to be a nun. Maybe there will be convents here when I am older. We could be called *Las Hermanas de la Señora de la Luna*," she confides seriously. "Do you know what that means?"

Virginia shakes her head.

"You can be our hermit. You'll bring us luck!" She giggles. Virginia cocks her head quizzically, reaches toward Lourdes's jawbone with the tips of her fingers. She touches, then shies away as if she has been shocked.

"No, it's okay, see?" she takes Virginia's hand again, brings it to her face. "Real. *Verdadera*."

Virginia's hand trembles there, papery and warm on the down of Lourdes's face.

"*Verdadera*. We aren't going to disappear, Miss America. You're safe now. You're with friends."

One of the other crew members sweeps her up then, and she dances, throwing a smile to Virginia. Smiles are interesting. Virginia wishes her face would do that.

"Friends," she says, thinking of antique automobiles. No one hears her.

"I keep telling you, she isn't capable of understanding the Creed!" Matteo in his stateroom, speaking to the Commissariat.

"This isn't my decision, Matteo. This comes directly from the Holy See. And she must be baptized as well."

"She's an old mad woman. She's been alone for decades."

"She's an American. She's an enemy of the Guatemalan people."

"She doesn't know who we are! I don't even think she understands a word we say to her."

"You speak English. I'm prepared to absolve you if you need to translate the Creed for her."

"She needs a doctor. She needs to be back on Earth."

"That is out of the question. She's a political liability, and you can't spare the weight."

"I doubt she weighs more than eighty pounds. We can leave the diamond drill. We'll get it on our next visit."

"Absolutely not. You think there are many of those left? She's waited this long. She can wait a little longer."

"This is insane. It would be kinder just to kill her."

"Are you accusing the Holy See of fallibility?"

"I . . . no, of course not. Forgive me." Matteo switches off the console, sits on the edge of his bed with his head in his hands.

The next morning, Virginia isn't in her bed.

Lourdes discovers her absence first, going into her bedroom early in the morning with a cup of mate and a hairbrush. The blanket is folded into an origami swan on the bed; it reminds Lourdes of the napkins she has seen in pictures of bourgeois restaurants. She drops the mate to the floor. The cup bounces as she screams.

Matteo is the one who discovers the missing space suit.

Lourdes begged to go out looking for her, but the political officer pointed out that they could wander for hours and never find her. He said a brief mass to Saint Anthony and Saint Joseph of Cupertino, and then told them all to get back to work.

But no one could. Lourdes paced back and forth, a string of coral rosary beads in her fingers. The political officer drank a little tequila from a hip flask and went back to sleep. Matteo played chess, flicking his eyes back and forth to the outside camera feed. He saw her first, stumbling back to the station, and shouted to the others to give way, leave room at the airlock.

Virginia stepped back in, took off the helmet. They all looked at each other, inexplicably bitter and relieved.

Then Virginia speaks. "Queen to G5, queen takes rook. Then bishop to H3, check," she says in flawless Spanish.

"*Madre de Dios,*" whispers Lourdes, running to Virginia and throwing her arms around the bulky suit. "*¡Està un milagro!*"

"Excellent," said the political officer sleepily. "Now she can be educated!"

Matteo swallows angrily. He turns and his eyes alight on the chessboard. "King to D4," he says, shoving the pieces.

"Bishop to A5," she says, her head still resting on Lourdes's shoulder.

"You're very good, Miss America. Or do you have a name?"

There is silence then; Lourdes is afraid to move. Then she feels a tiny drop of water fall into the hollow of her neck.

"Virginia," she says. Then, "Bishop takes pawn."

Matteo does his best.

He tries to teach her to swear allegiance to the principles of Catholic Socialism. Virginia is absently poking her fingernail into a sore she has worried into her cheek. Her other hand is wrapped around Lourdes's wrist, tapping out a meandering staccato rhythm on the veins. The red coral rosary is around her neck; the beads make soft, knucklebone sounds as she sways her neck back and forth.

"Matteo, just stop it!" cries Lourdes. Last night, she offered timidly to stay in Virginia's place; a request she knew would be declined, but she made it anyway. They are almost out of power. The commissariat has not changed his mind; the political officer refuses to intercede. They are returning to the Earth, and Virginia must remain. The thought makes Matteo furious and Lourdes sick. But there is nothing for it. And he will tell her, now.

Matteo stands. "You're right. Miss Virginia?" he looks at her, switches to English. "Miss Virginia, we have to leave. We have to go back to Earth. Only for a little while, you understand? You can stay here. You don't have to go back to your base. We're going to leave you the music player, and we'll be back soon. Maybe a few months."

Virginia looked at him, and he was afraid for a moment she had relapsed, that his words just fell into the black hollows of her eyes and made no impression. But then her jaw collapsed, her head ducked into the painful sharp shoulders. She clutched Lourdes, howling pitifully.

"No, no no!" she screamed. Lourdes was sobbing now, saying she was sorry, over and over again, in Spanish, English, even in Latin.

Then, suddenly, a fist reached out, flashing with a whisper of silver as it landed alongside Virginia's neck. Her black eyes rolled back in her head and she fell still, twitching. The political officer withdrew the needle, his soft hands catching her on the way down.

"There," he said. "Now we can leave in peace."

Matteo punched the man in the jaw and he fell like a stone.

Lourdes and the political officer made the last sweep through the station, making sure they missed nothing. Matteo was already handcuffed in the shuttle. Virginia was in a life bed, still sleeping. Once it was switched on, the life bed was designed to keep all vital signs steady, provide nutrition, and keep her comfortable until they came back and woke her up.

Lourdes kneeled next to the life bed and took the thin hand in hers.

"I am sorry, Miss Virginia. I will be coming back soon. I have already volunteered to join the first order here. We will be back in a year, maybe a little longer. You will never be alone again. I am sorry."

Virginia's eyes do not stir, but she squeezes Lourdes's hand.

"No more thinking," she says, so softly Lourdes can barely hear. "No more thinking."

"No more . . . yes, that will do." The political officer was behind Lourdes; she had not heard him, but he heard Virginia. As he walked out of the station, she could see a look of excitement on his long face.

Matteo was penanced to ten years of missionary work for insubordination, and thus not present when the political officer presented his plan for Virginia. She would never have been allowed back on Earth, Matteo reflected later. She would have been stoned in the street, or sent to one of the criollo gulags. He should have known that the real reason they wanted her to remain was so they could figure out a way to humiliate her.

Maybe it was kinder anyway, he told himself. She got her wish. Maybe her last feeling before they lobotomized her was some ponderous gratitude.

A camera crew went back with the political officer, to perform the operation.

They only broadcast the result, not the operation itself; if Virginia fought for her life, cried and begged for consciousness, Matteo never learned of it. Overall, it was disappointing television; a woman with no mind might just as well be daydreaming. It was the political officer who found the solution. He got the idea to place a video monitor in front of her vacant face, its display reading static. The angle made it look like it was sprouting from her neck like a flower on a milk-colored stem. The image was broadcast all over Guatemala, put on the backs of playing cards and graffiti'd on buildings; a pair of bony shoulders draped in the bloodied remains of an American flag, topped by an empty screen staring into nothing.

When Sister Lourdes and the nuns returned one year later, the first thing Lourdes did was lift Virginia's limpid body out of her life bed, and move her back into the corner of the mess. Then she turned on the music, and cried a bit, and picked up their conversation where they had left off.

Virginia dreams static dreams of space, sitting in the corner of the Guatemalan station/convent. She is washed, fed, her hair is combed. On feast days the nuns will dress her and carry her on a fiberglass bower through the corridors. Her eyes remain open, staring into nothing—little jewels of cotton-dry amber, the pupils retreated to some empty cardboard box inside. And on Saturday nights, a swirl of frantic life surrounds her, the voices of people dancing and laughing, as her heart echoes the leftover moments away.

Jack McDevitt has been described by Stephen King as "the logical heir to Isaac Asimov and Arthur C. Clarke." He is the author of twenty-three novels, twelve of which have been Nebula finalists. *Seeker* won the award in 2006. He has also won the John W. Campbell Memorial Award, and the Robert A. Heinlein Lifetime Achievement Award. The International Astronomical Union has put his name on an asteroid. His current books are *The Long Sunset*, released by Saga, and a story collection, *A Voice in the Night*, from Subterranean.

McDevitt has been an English teacher, a naval officer, a customs officer, and a Philadelphia taxi driver. He is married to the former Maureen McAdams, and resides in Brunswick, Georgia.

THE CASSANDRA PROJECT
Jack McDevitt

It's an odd fact that the biggest science story of the twenty-first century—probably the biggest ever—broke in that tabloid of tabloids, *The National Bedrock*.

I was in the middle of conducting a NASA press conference several days before the Minerva lift-off—the Return to the Moon—and I was fielding softball questions like: "Is it true that if everything goes well, the Mars mission will be moved up?" and "What is Marcia Beckett going to say when she becomes the first person to set foot on lunar soil since Eugene Cernan turned off the lights fifty-four years ago?"

President Gorman and his Russian counterpart, Dmitri Alexandrov, were scheduled to talk to the press from the White house an hour later, so I was strictly a set-up guy. Or that was the plan, anyway, until Warren Cole mentioned the dome.

It was a good time for NASA. We all knew the dangers inherent in over-confidence, but two orbital missions had gone up without a hitch. Either of them could have landed and waved back at us, and the rumor was that Sid Myshko had almost taken the game into his own hands, and that the crew had put it to a vote whether they'd ignore the protocol and go down to the surface regardless of the mission parameters. Sid and his five crewmates denied the story, of course.

I'd just made the point to the pool of reporters that it was Richard Nixon who'd turned off the lights—not the astronaut Eugene Cernan—when

Warren Cole began waving his hand. Cole was the AP journalist, seated in his customary spot up front. He was frowning, his left hand in the air, staring down at something on his lap that I couldn't see.

"Warren?" I said. "What've you got?"

"Jerry . . ." He looked up, making no effort to suppress a grin. "Have you seen the story that the *Bedrock*'s running?" He held up his iPad.

That started a few people checking their own devices.

"No, I haven't," I said, hoping he was making it up. "I don't usually get to *Bedrock* this early in the week." Somebody snorted. Then a wave of laughter rippled through the room. "What?" I said. My first thought had been that we were about to have another astronaut scandal, like the one the month before with Barnaby Salvator and half the strippers on the Beach. "What are they saying?"

"The Russians released more lunar orbital pictures from the sixties," He snickered. "They've got one here from the far side of the Moon. If you can believe this, there's a dome back there."

"A *dome*?"

"Yeah." He flipped open his notebook. "Does NASA have a comment?"

"You're kidding, right?" I said.

He twisted the iPad, raised it higher, and squinted at it. "Yep. It's a dome all right."

The reporters in the pool all had a good chuckle, and then they looked up at me. "Well," I said, "I guess Buck Rogers beat us there after all."

"It looks legitimate, Jerry," Cole said, but he was still laughing.

I didn't have to tell him what we all knew: That it was a doctored picture and that it must have been a slow week for scandals.

If the image *was* doctored, the deed had to have been done by the Russians. Moscow had released the satellite images only a few hours before and forwarded them to us without comment. Apparently nobody on either side had noticed anything unusual. Except the *Bedrock* staff.

I hadn't looked at the images prior to the meeting. I mean, once you've seen a few square miles of lunar surface you've pretty much seen it all. The dome—if that's really what it was—appeared on every image in the series. They were dated April, 1967.

The Bedrock carried the image on its front page, where they usually show the latest movie celebrity who's being accused of cheating, or has gone on a drunken binge. It depicted a crater wall, with a large arrow graphic in the middle of a dark splotch pointing at a dome that you couldn't have missed anyhow. The headline read:

ALIENS ON THE MOON
Russian Pictures Reveal Base on Far Side
Images Taken Before Apollo

I sighed and pushed back from my desk. We just didn't need this.

But it *did* look like an artificial construct. The thing was on the edge of a crater, shaped like the head of a bullet. It was either a reflection, an illusion of some sort, or it was a fraud. But the Russians had no reason to set themselves up as a laughing stock. And it sure as hell *looked* real.

I was still staring at it when the phone rang. It was Mary, NASA's administrator. My boss. "*Jerry,*" she said, "*I heard what happened at the press conference this morning.*"

"What's going on, Mary?"

"*Damned if I know. Push some buttons. See what you can find out. It's going to come up again when the President's out there. We need to have an answer for him.*"

Vasili Koslov was my public relations counterpart at Russia's space agency. He was in Washington with the presidential delegation. And he was in full panic mode when I got him on the phone. "*I saw it, Jerry,*" he said. "*I have no idea what this is about. I just heard about it a few minutes ago. I'm looking at it now. It* does *look like a dome, doesn't it?*"

"Yes," I said. "Did your people tamper with the satellite imagery?"

"*They must have. I have a call in. I'll let you know as soon as I hear something.*"

I called Jeanie Escovar in the Archives. "Jeanie, have you seen the *National Bedrock* story yet?"

"*No,*" she said. "*My God, what is it* this *time?*"

"Not what you think. I'm sending it to you now. Could you have somebody check to see where this place is—?"

"*What place? Oh, wait—I got it.*"

"Find out where it is and see if you can get me some imagery of the same area. From *our* satellites."

I heard her gasp. Then she started laughing.

"Jeanie, this is serious."

"*Why? You don't actually believe there's a building up there, do you?*"

"Somebody's going to ask the President about it. They have a press conference going on in about twenty minutes. We want him to be able to say: 'It's ridiculous, here's a picture of the area, and you'll notice there's nothing there.' We want him to be able to say 'The *Bedrock*'s running an optical illusion.' But he'll have to do it diplomatically. And without embarrassing Alexandrov."

"Good luck on that."

The *Bedrock* story was already getting attention on the talk shows. Angela Hart, who at that time anchored *The Morning Report* for the *World Journal*, was interviewing a physicist from MIT. The physicist stated that the picture could not be accurate. *"Probably a practical joke,"* he said. *"Or a trick of the light."*

But Angela wondered why the Russians would release the picture at all. *"They had to know it would get a lot of attention,"* she said. And, of course, though she didn't mention it, it would become a source of discomfort for the Russian president and the two cosmonauts who were among the Minerva crew.

Vasili was in a state of shock when he called back. *"They didn't know about the dome,"* he said. *"Nobody noticed. But it is on the original satellite imagery. Our people were just putting out a lot of the stuff from the Luna missions. Imagery that hadn't been released before. I can't find anybody who knows anything about it. But I'm still trying."*

"Vasili," I said, "somebody must have seen it at the time. In 1967."

"I guess."

"You *guess*? You think it's possible something like this came in and nobody picked up on it?"

"No, I'm not suggesting that at all, Jerry. I just—I don't know what I'm suggesting. I'll get back to you when I have something more."

Minutes later, Jeanie called: *"It's the east wall of the Cassegrain Crater."*

"And—?"

"I've forwarded NASA imagery of the same area."

I switched on the monitor and ran the images. There was the same crater wall, the same pock-marked moonscape. But no dome. Nothing at all unusual.

Dated July, 1968. More than a year after the Soviet imagery.

I called Mary and told her: The Russians just screwed up.

"The President can't say that."

"All he has to say is that NASA has no evidence of any dome or anything else on the far side of the Moon. Probably he should just turn it into a joke. Make some remark about setting up a Martian liaison unit."

She didn't think it was funny.

When the subject came up at the presidential press conference, Gorman and Alexandrov both simply had a good laugh. Alexandrov blamed it on Khrushchev, and the laughter got louder. Then they moved on to how the Minerva mission—the long-awaited Return to the Moon—marked the beginning of a new era for the world.

The story kicked around in the tabloids for two or three more days. *The Washington Post* ran an op-ed using the dome to demonstrate how gullible we all are when the media says *anything*. Then Cory Abbott, who'd just won a Golden Globe for his portrayal of Einstein in *Albert and Me*, crashed his car into a street light and blacked out the entire town of Dekker, California. And just like that the dome story was gone.

On the morning of the launch, Roscosmos, the Russian space agency, issued a statement that the image was a result of defective technology. The Minerva lifted off on schedule and, while the world watched, it crossed to the Moon and completed a few orbits. Its lander touched down gently on the Mare Maskelyne. Marcia Beckett surprised everyone when she demurred leading the way out through the airlock, sending instead Cosmonaut Yuri Petrov, who descended and then signaled his crewmates to join him.

When all were assembled on the regolith, Petrov made the statement that, in the light of later events, has become immortal: *"We are here on the Moon because, during the last century, we avoided the war that would have destroyed us all. And we have come together. Now we stand as never before, united for all mankind."*

I wasn't especially impressed at the time. It sounded like the usual generalized nonsense. Which shows you what my judgment is worth.

I watched on my office monitor. And as the ceremony proceeded, I looked past the space travelers, across the barren wasteland of the Mare Maskelyne, wondering which was the shortest path to the Cassegrain crater.

I knew I should have just let it go, but I couldn't. I could imagine no explanation for the Russians doctoring their satellite imagery. Vasili told me that everyone with whom he'd spoken was shocked. That the images had been dug out of the archives and distributed without inspection. And, as far as could be determined, without anyone distorting them. *"I just don't understand it, Jerry,"* he said.

Mary told me not to worry about it. "We have more important things to do," she said.

There was no one left at NASA from the 1960s. In fact, I knew of only one person living at Cape Kennedy who had been part of the Agency when Apollo 11 went to the Moon: Amos Kelly, who'd been one of my grandfather's buddies. He was still in the area, where he served with the Friends of NASA, a group of volunteers who lent occasional support but mostly threw parties. I looked him up. He'd come to the Agency in 1965 as a technician. Eventually, he'd become one of the operational managers.

He was in his mid-eighties, but he sounded good. "*Sure, Jerry, I remember you. It's been a long time,*" he said, when I got him on the phone. I'd been a little kid when he used to stop by to pick up my grandfather for an evening of poker. "*What can I do for you?*"

"This is going to sound silly, Amos."

"*Nothing sounds silly to me. I used to work for the government.*"

"Did you see the story in the tabloids about the dome?"

"*How could I miss it?*"

"You ever hear anything like that before?"

"*You mean did we think there were Martians on the Moon?*" He laughed, turned away to tell someone that the call was for him, and then laughed again. "*Is that a serious question, Jerry?*"

"I guess not."

"*Good. By the way, you've done pretty well for yourself at the Agency. Your granddad would have been proud.*"

"Thanks."

He told me how much he missed the old days, missed my grandfather, how they'd had a good crew. "*Best years of my life. I could never believe they'd just scuttle the program the way they did.*"

Finally he asked what the Russians had said about the images. I told him what Vasili told me. "*Well,*" he said, "*maybe they haven't changed that much after all.*"

Twenty minutes later he called back. "*I was reading the story in the* Bedrock. *It says that the object was in the Cassegrain Crater.*"

"Yes. That's correct."

"*There was talk of a Cassegrain Project at one time. Back in the sixties. I don't know what it was supposed to be. Whether it was anything more than a rumor. Nobody seemed to know anything definitive about it. I recall at the time thinking it was one of those things so highly classified that even its existence was off the table.*"

"The Cassegrain Project."

"*Yes.*"

"But you have no idea what it was about?"

"*None. I'm sorry. Wish I could help.*"

"Would you tell me if you knew?"

"*It's a long time ago, Jerry. I can't believe security would still be an issue.*"

"Amos, you were pretty high in the Agency—"

"*Not that* high."

"Do you remember anything else?"

"Nothing. Nada. As far as I know, nothing ever came of any of it, so the whole thing eventually went away."

Searching NASA's archives on "Cassegrain" yielded only data about the crater. So I took to wandering around the facility, talking offhandedly with senior employees. *It must feel good to see us back on the Moon, huh, Ralph? Makes all the frustration worthwhile. By the way, did you ever hear of a Cassegrain Project?*

They all laughed. *Crazy Russians.*

On the day the Minerva slipped out of lunar orbit and started home, Mary called me into her office. "We'll want to get the crew onstage for the press when they get back, Jerry. You might give the staging some thought."

"Okay. Will it be at Edwards?"

"Negative. We're going to do it here at the Cape." We talked over some of the details, the scheduling, guest speakers, points we'd want to make with the media. Then as I was getting ready to leave, she stopped me. "One more thing. The Cassegrain business—" I straightened and came to attention. Mary Gridley was a no-nonsense hard-charger. She was in her fifties, and years of dealing with bureaucratic nonsense had left her with little patience. She was physically diminutive, but she could probably have intimidated the Pope. "—I want you to leave it alone."

She picked up a pen, put it back down, and stared at me. "Jerry, I know you've been asking around about that idiot dome. Listen, you're good at what you do. You'll probably enjoy a long, happy career with us. But that won't happen if people stop taking you seriously. You understand what I mean?"

After the shuttle landing and subsequent celebration, I went on the road. "We need to take advantage of the moment," Mary said. "There'll never be a better time to get some good press."

So I did a PR tour, giving interviews, addressing prayer breakfasts and Rotary meetings, doing what I could to raise the consciousness of the public. NASA wanted Moonbase. It was the next logical step. Should have had it decades ago and would have if the politicians hadn't squandered the nation's resources on pointless wars and interventions. But it would be expensive, and we hadn't succeeded yet in getting the voters on board. That somehow had become *my* responsibility.

In Seattle, I appeared at a Chamber of Commerce dinner with Arnold Banner, an astronaut who'd never gotten higher than the space station. But nevertheless he was an astronaut, and he hailed from the Apollo era. During the course of the meal I asked whether he'd ever heard of a Cassegrain Project. He said something about tabloids and gave me a disapproving look.

We brought in astronauts wherever we could. In Los Angeles, at a Marine charities fundraiser, we had both Marcia Beckett and Yuri Petrov, which would have been the highlight of the tour, except for Frank Allen.

Frank was in his nineties. He looked exhausted. His veins bulged and I wasn't sure he didn't need oxygen.

He was the fourth of the Apollo-era astronauts I talked with during those two weeks. And when I asked about the Cassegrain Project, his eyes went wide and his mouth tightened. Then he regained control. "Cassandra," he said, looking past me into a distant place. "It's classified."

"Not *Cassandra*, Frank. *Cassegrain*."

"Oh. Yeah. Of course."

"I have a clearance."

"How high?"

"Secret."

"Not enough."

"Just give me a hint. What do you know?"

"Jerry, I've already said too much. Even its existence is classified."

Cassandra.

When I got back to the Cape I did a search on *Cassandra* and found that a lot of people with that name had worked for the Agency over the years. Other Cassandras had made contributions in various ways, leading programs to get kids interested in space science, collaborating with NASA physicists in analyzing the data collected by space-born telescopes, editing publications to make NASA more accessible to the lay public. They'd been everywhere. You couldn't bring in a NASA guest speaker without discovering a Cassandra somewhere among the people who'd made the request. Buried among the names so deeply that I almost missed it was a single entry: *The Cassandra Project, storage 27176B Redstone.*

So secret its existence was classified?

The reference was to the Redstone Arsenal in Huntsville, Alabama where NASA stores rocket engines, partially-completed satellites, control panels from test stands, and a multitude of other artifacts dating back to Apollo. I called them.

A baritone voice informed me I had reached the NASA Storage Facility. "*Sgt. Saber speaking.*"

I couldn't resist smiling at the name, but I knew he'd heard all the jokes. I identified myself. Then: "Sergeant, you have a listing for the Cassandra Project." I gave him the number. "Can I get access to the contents?"

"*One minute, please, Mr. Carter.*"

While I waited, I glanced around the office at the photos of Neil Armstrong and Lawrence Bergman and Marcia Beckett. In one, I was standing beside Bergmann, who'd been the guy who'd sold the President on returning to the Moon. In another, I was standing by while Marcia spoke with some Alabama school kids during a tour of the Marshall Space Flight Center. Marcia was a charmer of the first order. I've always suspected she got the Minerva assignment partially because they knew the public would love her.

"When were you planning to come, Mr. Carter?"

"I'm not sure yet. Within the next week or so."

"Let us know in advance and there'll be no problem."

"It's not classified, then?"

"No, sir. I'm looking at its history now. It was originally classified, but that was removed by the Restricted Access Depository Act more than twenty years ago."

I had to get through another round of ceremonies and press conferences before I could get away. Finally, things quieted down. The astronauts went back to their routines, the VIPs went back to whatever it was they normally do, and life on the Cape returned to normal. I put in for leave.

"You deserve it," Mary said.

Next day, armed with a copy of the Restricted Access Depository Act, I was on my way to Los Angeles to pay another visit to a certain elderly retired astronaut.

"I can't believe it," Frank Allen said.

He lived with his granddaughter and her family of about eight, in Pasadena. She shepherded us into her office—she was a tax expert of some sort—brought some lemonade, and left us alone.

"What can't you believe? That they declassified it?"

"That the story never got out in the first place." Frank was back at the desk. I'd sunk into a leather settee.

"What's the story, Frank? Was the dome really there?"

"Yes."

"*NASA* doctored its own Cassegrain imagery? To eliminate all traces?"

"I don't know anything about that."

"So what *do* you know?"

"They sent us up to take a look. In late 1968." He paused. "We landed almost on top of the damned thing."

"*Before* Apollo 11."

"Yes."

I sat there in shock. And I've been around a while, so I don't shock easily.

"They advertised the flight as a test run, Jerry. It was supposed to be purely an orbital mission. Everything else, the dome, the descent, everything was top secret. Didn't happen."

"You actually got to the dome?"

He hesitated. A lifetime of keeping his mouth shut was getting in the way. "Yes," he said. "We came down about a half mile away. Max was brilliant."

Max Donnelly. The lunar module pilot. "What happened?"

"I remember thinking the Russians had beaten us. They'd gotten to the Moon and we hadn't even known about it.

"There weren't any antennas or anything. Just a big, silvery dome. About the size of a two-story house. No windows. No hammer and sickle markings. Nothing. Except a door.

"We had sunlight. The mission had been planned so we wouldn't have to approach it in the dark." He shifted his position in the chair and bit down on a grunt.

"You okay, Frank?" I asked.

"My knees. They don't work as well as they used to." He rubbed the right one, then rearranged himself—gently this time. "We didn't know what to expect. Max said he thought the thing was pretty old because there were no tracks in the ground. We walked up to the front door. It had a knob. I thought the place would be locked, but I tried it and the thing didn't move at first but then something gave way and I was able to pull the door open."

"What was inside?"

"A table. There was a cloth on the table. And something flat under the cloth. And that's all there was."

"Nothing else?"

"Not a thing." He shook his head. "Max lifted the cloth. Under it was a rectangular plate. Made from some kind of metal." He stopped and stared at me. "There was writing on it."

"Writing? What did it say?"

"I don't know. Never found out. It looked like Greek. We brought the plate back home with us and turned it over to the bosses. Next thing they called us in and debriefed us. Reminded us it was all top secret. Whatever the thing said, it must have scared the bejesus out of Nixon and his people. Because they never said anything, and I guess the Russians didn't either."

"You never heard anything more at all?"

"Well, other than the next Apollo mission, which went back and destroyed the dome. Leveled it."

"How do you know?"

"I knew the crew. We talked to each other, right? They wouldn't say it directly. Just shook their heads: Nothing to worry about anymore."

Outside, kids were shouting, tossing a football around. "Greek?"

"That's what it looked like."

"A message from Plato."

He just shook his head as if to say: *Who knew?*

"Well, Frank, I guess that explains why they called it the Cassandra Project."

"She wasn't a Greek, was she?"

"You have another theory?"

"Maybe Cassegrain was too hard for the people in the Oval Office to pronounce."

I told Mary what I knew. She wasn't happy. "I really wish you'd left it alone, Jerry."

"There's no way I could have done that."

"Not now, anyhow." She let me see her frustration. "You know what it'll mean for the Agency, right? If NASA lied about something like this, and it becomes public knowledge, nobody will ever trust us again."

"It was a long time ago, Mary. Anyhow, the Agency wasn't lying. It was the Administration."

"Yeah," she said. "Good luck selling that one to the public."

The NASA storage complex at the Redstone Arsenal in Huntsville is home to rockets, a lunar landing vehicle, automated telescopes, satellites, a space station, and a multitude of other devices that had kept the American space program alive, if not particularly robust, over almost seventy years. Some were housed inside sprawling warehouses; others occupied outdoor exhibition sites.

I parked in the shadow of a Saturn V, the rocket that had carried the Apollo missions into space. I've always been impressed with the sheer audacity of anybody who'd be willing to sit on top of one of those things while someone lit the fuse. Had it been up to me, we'd probably never have lifted off at Kitty Hawk.

I went inside the Archive Office, got directions and a pass, and fifteen minutes later entered one of the warehouses. An attendant escorted me past cages and storage rooms filled with all kinds of boxes and crates. Somewhere in the center of it all, we stopped at a cubicle while the attendant compared my pass with the number on the door. The interior was visible through a wall of wire mesh. Cartons were piled up, all labeled. Several were open, with electronic equipment visible inside them.

The attendant unlocked the door and we went in. He turned on an overhead light and did a quick survey, settling on a box that was one of several on a shelf. My heart rate started to pick up while he looked at the tag. "This is it, Mr. Carter," he said. "Cassandra."

"Is this *everything*?"

He checked his clipboard. "This is the only listing we have for the Cassandra Project, sir."

"Okay. Thanks."

"My pleasure."

There was no lock. He raised the hasp on the box, lifted the lid, and stood back to make room. He showed no interest in the contents. He probably did this all the time, so I don't know why that surprised me.

Inside, I could see a rectangular object wrapped in plastic. I couldn't see what it was, but of course I knew. My heart was pounding by then. The object was about a foot and a half wide and maybe half as high. And it was heavy. I carried it over to a table and set it down. Wouldn't do to drop it. Then I unwrapped it.

The metal was black, polished, reflective, even in the half-light from the overhead bulb. And sure enough, there were the Greek characters. Eight lines of them.

The idea that Plato was saying hello seemed suddenly less far-fetched. I took a picture. Several pictures. Finally, reluctantly, I rewrapped it and put it back in the box.

"So," said Frank, "what did it say?"

"I have the translation here." I fished it out of my pocket but he shook his head.

"My eyes aren't that good, Jerry. Just tell me who wrote it. And what it says."

We were back in the office at Frank's home in Pasadena. It was a chilly, rainswept evening. Across the street, I could see one of his neighbors putting out the trash.

"It wasn't written by the Greeks."

"I didn't think it was."

"Somebody came through a long time ago. Two thousand years or so. *They* left the message. Apparently they wrote it in Greek because it must have looked like their best chance to leave something we'd be able to read. Assuming we ever reached the Moon."

"So what did it say?"

"It's a warning."

The creases in Frank's forehead deepened. "Is the sun going unstable?"

"No." I looked down at the translation. "It says that no civilization, any-where, has been known to survive the advance of technology."

Frank stared at me. "Say that again."

"They all collapse. They fight wars. Or they abolish individual death, which apparently guarantees stagnation and an exit. I don't know. They don't specify.

"Sometimes the civilizations become too vulnerable to criminals. Or the inhabitants become too dependent on the technology and lose whatever vir-tue they might have had. Anyway, the message says that no technological civilization, anywhere, has been known to get old. Nothing lasts more than a few centuries—*our* centuries—once technological advancement begins. Which for us maybe starts with the invention of the printing press.

"The oldest known civilization lasted less than a thousand years."

Frank frowned. He wasn't buying it. "*They* survived. Hell, they had an interstellar ship of some kind."

"They said they were looking for a place to start again. Where they came from is a shambles."

"You're kidding."

"It says that maybe, if we know in advance, we can sidestep the problem. That's why they left the warning."

"Great."

"If they survive, they say they'll come back to see how we're doing."

We were both silent for a long while.

"So what happens now?" Frank said.

"We've reclassified everything. It's top secret again. I shouldn't be telling you this. But I thought—"

He rearranged himself in the chair. Winced and rotated his right arm. "Maybe that's why they called it *Cassandra*," he said. "Wasn't she the woman who always brought bad news?"

"I think so."

"There was something else about her—"

"Yeah—the bad news," I said. "When she gave it, nobody would listen."

Marianne Dyson was inspired by science fiction and the Apollo Program to become one of NASA's first female flight controllers. She is now an award-winning children's author, educational speaker, and freelance science and science fiction writer. To learn more, visit www.mDyson.com.

FLY ME TO THE MOON
Marianne J. Dyson

Good afternoon, Mr. Smith," I said as I plopped my backpack on an extra chair in the Lakewood Retirement Center's dining room.

The white-haired gentleman looked up from his coffee and riveted his eyes on me like a security guard verifying my identity. I saw by the relaxing of his shoulders that I was recognized, and that he'd read my nametag. "Good to see you, George," he said. "I wish you wouldn't call me Mr. Smith. Makes me feel old." He smiled at his own joke. I didn't know his exact age, but I guessed he was in his late eighties.

"Okay, Bob," I said, returning his smile and adding a wink. We went through this same routine every day when I arrived for work as a volunteer caregiver. On one of my earliest visits, he surveyed the dining room as if looking for spies and whispered that Bob Smith was a fake name. He explained that he couldn't tell me his real name because the press (he never called them news media) might find out. I promised not to reveal his secret. I suspected he was an actor whose family wanted to hide him from the paparazzi. They had done a good job of it—or maybe he'd had plastic surgery? In any case, I hadn't been able to figure out who he really was. All the staff would tell me was that he had checked in after his wife died in a car crash in the late 2020s. He had some grandchildren and great-grandchildren, even great-great-grandchildren, but I was his only regular visitor. New treatments had slowed down the progression of his Alzheimer's disease, but I wondered how long it would be before he forgot that Bob Smith wasn't his real name?

I pulled my laptop out of my backpack, connected the dual hand controllers, and set them on the table in front of Mr. Smith. "Got a new simulator to fly with you," I said. This one was actually for little kids, but I had found that Mr. Smith enjoyed holding the hand controllers and flying various aircraft. Sometimes we flew against each other, and sometimes as pilot and copilot, me always the copilot. The only time I could out-fly him was in those games where spaceships could jump through wormholes or something that real aircraft could never do. He didn't like those games. He liked the simulators. I had told Mr. Smith that I was thinking of joining the military so I could become a pilot. That's when he'd told me he was a pilot, but that I shouldn't tell anyone because they might figure out who he was. Whether he really had been a pilot or not, I was happy to discover we both had an interest in flying.

"This one is a simulator of the old *Apollo* lunar landers," I said while booting the program. "You know you don't even have to be an astronaut to go the Moon now? You just have to be rich enough to buy a ticket from the Russians."

Mr. Smith frowned at me. "You don't know what you're talking about. We beat the Russians to the Moon!" He crossed his arms.

His angry reaction startled me. Obviously this was a touchy subject for him. "Yes, of course you're right, Mr. Smith. We beat the Russians to the Moon."

"Darn right!" he said.

"But that was a long time ago. Now lots of people go to the Moon." I glanced to the lounge area of the dining hall. "Look, there's a scene from the Moon on the TV right now."

He stared at the big screen like it was the first time he'd seen it. "I remember that movie."

Now I was confused. "What movie?"

"That movie about *Apollo*. The one with Tom Hanks."

I saw the "CBN LIVE" label in the corner. "No, sir, that's a live broadcast." I read the captions and summarized for him. "There's been an accident at an old *Apollo* site. A lunar shuttle computer failed and shut down the engine just after liftoff. The pilot was killed on impact, and one passenger remains unconscious. The other passenger, a historian named Ms. Clara Phillips, is okay, but only has enough spacesuit battery power to last eight hours. A Russian rescue ship can't arrive for several days. Wow, get this," I continued, "They're talking about launching the *Apollo* lunar ascent vehicle! The original one was used and discarded by the *Apollo* crew—this is a replica built by the Apollo Restoration Project that they claim is fully functional. Only trouble is, Ms. Phillips isn't a pilot, and they need someone to tell her how to fly it!"

Mr. Smith looked down at his age-spotted hands. "I'm a little rusty, but I could do it," he said.

"You could? Where did you learn how to fly a lunar module?" Maybe he had a part in that *Apollo* movie. I'd have to check the credits when I got home.

Mr. Smith ignored my questions and continued to watch the screen. He nodded. "Yes, I can do it," he decided. He scooted his chair back and stood looking around the room. "We're in the cafeteria," he stated. I nodded. "I have to get to Building 30," he said.

I didn't know they numbered the buildings at Lakewood. "Where is that?"

He gave my nametag a puzzled look. "What kind of badge is that? Are you a reporter?"

"No, sir. I'm George, remember? I was about to show you how to fly the new lunar simulator."

"Oh. A training instructor. Okay, then. We'd better get moving if we're going to save that crew. Can't let the Russians get there first." He shuffled toward the exit somewhat bent over, but amazingly fast for someone his age. I caught the eye of the receptionist and nodded toward my game setup. She would watch it for me until I lured Mr. Smith back. She didn't need to remind me that Mr. Smith wasn't allowed to leave the grounds. My job was to redirect him somehow.

"Mr. Smith, I think we should take a different way to Building 30."

He stopped. "Why? Is there a media circus out there already?"

"No, no," I assured him quickly. "We just need to use the elevator to avoid all those stairs."

"I like the stairs. Keeps me in shape," he said.

"Yes, of course, Mr. Smith, but you had surgery on your knee a few months ago, remember?" He'd fallen trying to take the stairs two at a time—something he must have done a lot in his younger days. If he were an actor, he probably did his own stunts.

Mr. Smith stopped and looked down at his knees and feet. "I can't wear these slippers outside. Mother will yell at me." He paused, deep in thought. "Before I go, I need to call her. She always worries when I travel. Is there a phone in this building?"

He'd obviously forgotten that he no longer had a mother, and that everyone used cell phones now. He had an old phone in his room, though. It was hooked up to the front desk. The staff was great at explaining that mothers and wives and other deceased loved ones were not home for one reason or another. But often, by the time we got to his room, he'd have forgotten he wanted to call someone. "There's a phone upstairs, sir," I said.

"All right," he said. After he got his shoes on, I'd take him for a walk in the garden. We both enjoyed watching the birds.

We got into the elevator. I waited for him to select the floor. If he had forgotten, then I'd remind him, but it was important to give him a chance to remember. He stared at the buttons. "This isn't the cafeteria," he said. "Only Building 1 has nine floors." He pressed the OPEN DOOR button and walked back out of the elevator.

Now what? I wondered. It didn't hurt to ask questions. "Mr. Smith, what is it you want to do when we get to Building 30?"

He scanned the hallways in both directions, I assumed checking for reporters. He said softly, "We're going to get those folks in Mission Control to set up a simulator run. We'll create the trajectory for the crew to get off the Moon."

"Oh, I should have thought of this earlier," I said. "We don't need to go to Building 30. I can connect to Mission Control from here."

"You can?"

"Yes, this building has a wireless node in the lounge, where the big screen is." Once I got him playing on the simulator, he'd probably forget all about the mysterious Building 30, and his mother too.

Mr. Smith nodded. "Okay, then. But we had better hurry. We don't want the Russians to get there first."

"Right." I took his arm and walked with him past the reception desk and back toward the dining area. The receptionist looked up as we went by, and I winked at her. Yvonne was a year older than me, a high school senior who worked here weekdays after school. She smiled and came around the desk with my laptop and hand controllers that she must have retrieved while we were in the elevator.

"Hey, Flyboy," she said to Mr. Smith after handing me my stuff. I had told her previously that he claimed to have been a pilot. Though he protested (the reporters might overhear), his face always lit up when she called him that. Then again, I couldn't think of too many men, myself included, that wouldn't enjoy some attention from a pretty girl like her. "Going to do some fancy flying today?"

Mr. Smith straightened up and met her gaze with a shy smile. "I can neither confirm nor deny that statement, young lady. But maybe we can have a drink later in the lounge, and I can show you some moves!"

"I just might take you up on that," Yvonne said with a wide grin and twinkling eyes. She pecked him on the cheek and did a little swirl as she moved back behind the desk. The scent of her lingered pleasantly in the air as I stuffed my gear into my backpack again.

In a whisper, Mr. Smith said, "Women love pilots, you know. Got to watch out, though. Reporters have eyes everywhere, even in nice hotels like this one."

"Yes, sir," I said. Had he been involved in a scandal with a famous actress? Maybe he had been a stunt pilot? I steered him back to the dining area. The tables were filling with early diners. I decided we'd be more comfortable in the lounge. The TV was still on the news channel, and still showing scenes from the Moon. Someone had turned the sound up to hear over the diners in the background.

"We have an update on the crisis on the Moon," the anchor said. "The privately-funded Apollo Restoration Project is working with the National Aeronautics and Space Administration to see if it is possible for their stranded crew to use their *Apollo* lunar vehicle to reach orbit. If the two historians can reach lunar orbit, NASA says it can remotely maneuver an unmanned cargo ship to pick them up. The cargo ship is not equipped to land, but has emergency supplies that would support the two people in lunar orbit until a Russian rescue ship can reach them two days from now."

"Well, that's good news," I said.

"Shhh," Mr. Smith said. I shut up.

"The team is working against the clock. The spacesuits have only seven hours of battery power remaining."

"That's not good," I said. Mr. Smith glared at me. "Sorry," I whispered.

"The *Apollo* lunar module replica is brand new and contains all the same systems as the historical modules, including working engines for its planned use in an unmanned reenactment. However, recent tests showed that the hatch does not seal properly, so the cabin cannot hold pressure. Therefore, the historians will have to remain in their suits. Also, the fuel pressure is low, possibly because of a slow helium leak. But the biggest problem is that the ship does not have an autopilot, and Ms. Phillips has no flight experience."

Mr. Smith stared at the screen. "No flight experience! What kind of stunt are the Russians trying to pull by putting that woman up there?"

"She's American," I noted.

He ignored me and kept on talking. "Newbies always overcontrol, and that thing is as fragile as tissue paper. Get it tumbling, and it might fly apart."

"Well, how about flying it remotely?" I suggested. "That reporter said NASA's going to fly the cargo ship remotely."

Mr. Smith smiled weakly. "Remote control requires a computer interface. The computer on that thing is dumber than an adding machine."

"Oh," I said, wondering what an adding machine was.

"No," Mr. Smith continued, "they need to come up with a preplanned set of maneuvers and then have an experienced pilot walk that woman through them." He nodded to himself. "I'd better warn my wife."

"What? Why?"

"I don't want her home when the press start snooping around."

"Oh, don't worry," I said quickly. He always got most upset when he couldn't reach his wife. "She's visiting her mother." It was the truth, if you believe in heaven.

"That's good," he said. "Then I'd better call Houston right away." He stood up. "Where did you say the phone is?"

There was no way he was going to really call NASA in Houston. But some small voice inside me insisted that it was important to let him play out this fantasy. Not wanting to repeat the elevator fiasco, I said, "There's a phone at the front desk." I pointed toward the doorway that led to the reception area. I grabbed my backpack and hurried after him.

"Excuse me, miss," he said upon reaching the front desk.

Yvonne looked up and smiled. "Back so soon, Flyboy?"

He cleared his throat. "Yes. I need to use the phone to make a long-distance call. It's an emergency."

Yvonne glanced at me, and I shrugged.

"I'm sorry, Mr. Smith, but the phones are for staff use only," she said.

Mr. Smith began breathing heavily. His long fingers curled into fists.

"But this is an emergency," he repeated. "I have to check in with Houston!" His face was flushed, and that worried me.

"Yvonne, you'd better call Dr. Winkler," I said.

"I don't need a doctor. I need to call Houston!" Mr. Smith shouted.

"It's okay, Bob," I said in a soft voice, steering him by the elbow to a bench. "The doctor has to check you before you can go."

"A flight physical now? There's no time for that!" He was panting.

"No, no," I said. "Not a complete physical. Just a quick check to make sure it's okay for you to fly." I needed to calm him down. "Take a deep breath and count to ten as you let it out. You don't want the doctor to ground you, do you?"

"Certainly not!" he said. I was happy to see his long fingers uncurl and spread out over his boney knees.

A lean bearded man rushed over to where we sat, and squatted down in front of Mr. Smith. "Good afternoon, Mr. Smith," he said in a soothing voice. "I'm Dr. Winkler." He placed a small disk on Mr. Smith's wrist and asked, "What seems to be the problem?"

"There's no problem with me," Mr. Smith said, a bit breathlessly. "I just need to call Houston, and they won't let me use the phone."

"I see," Dr. Winkler responded. "Pulse is elevated. Blood pressure a little high, but otherwise you seem fine." I sighed with relief. "Would you like me to make that call for you?" Dr. Winkler offered.

"Yes, please!" Mr. Smith said.

"Okay, then, come with me to my office."

I assumed this was Dr. Winkler's way of getting Mr. Smith to a place where he could examine him better and make sure he calmed down. We each took one of Mr. Smith's arms and helped him down the hall to Dr. Winkler's office. While we walked, I summarized what we'd seen on the television and explained that Mr. Smith seemed to think he could help the stranded historian learn to fly the lunar module.

Dr. Winkler listened silently. We entered his office and he asked us both to take a seat. While he shut the door, I saw that the newsfeed on his computer was following the lunar crisis. So, he already knew what was going on.

"Mr. Smith, please tell me how you think you can help those people on the Moon."

Mr. Smith repeated that he could fly the simulator and create the program they needed. Dr. Winkler had Mr. Smith drink some pink liquid and then asked him some technical questions using terms I recognized from some of the flight simulations we'd played. I wondered if Dr. Winkler was also a pilot. I don't know if it was the pink liquid or the joy of sharing a favorite memory, but when the doctor asked a number of questions about the Moon, Mr. Smith's answers were surprisingly detailed. The only thing he was confused about was what the Russians had to do with an American woman on the Moon.

"I'll have to notify your family," Dr. Winkler said. Mr. Smith nodded.

Dr. Winkler then moved to the computer and tapped away at the keys. I got Mr. Smith a cup of water from the little sink in the corner and sat down again.

Dr. Winkler looked up at Mr. Smith. "I've got permission to release your records to NASA. Do you trust George, or do you want me to ask him to leave during the call?"

Ask me to leave? What was going on? Why would NASA be interested in his medical records? Dr. Winkler sure was good at playing along.

Mr. Smith gave me the security guard look again. "He's okay. He's a training instructor."

Dr. Winkler raised an eyebrow at that. "We take turns flying simulators," I explained.

"I know," Dr. Winkler responded. *He did?* I guess I should have known that the head doctor would keep tabs on the activities of his patients.

"And I know that his time with you has helped him retain some memories that are important not only to him, but perhaps to those people on the Moon right now."

"Seriously?" I blurted.

Dr. Winkler smiled. "Yes, seriously. Now, George, Mr. Smith has agreed that it's okay for you to be here during this call. I don't know what you'll overhear, but he's trusting you to keep your mouth shut about it. Can you promise to do that?"

"Yes, sir," I said. "Is Bob Smith really a fake name?"

Dr. Winkler didn't have time to answer before the screen changed to an image of a serious-looking young man. "This is flight director Keegan Taylor at Johnson Space Center. I understand you have an old *Apollo* guy who thinks he can help us create a trajectory for Ms. Phillips to fly?"

"Can he hear me?" Mr. Smith asked.

"Yes," Dr. Winkler answered. "I have two-way voice, but one-way video. I know how you hate cameras, Mr. Smith."

"Yes, thank you," Mr. Smith said. "You know who I am?" he asked.

"Your name is blocked out in the file I received, but I was told that you worked on *Apollo*."

My grandfather had told me about *Apollo*, but even he had only been a kid back in the late 1960s. I wondered if Mr. Smith had worked on the program as a college student. That would put him in his eighties.

Mr. Smith cleared his throat. "I know how to fly the lunar module," he declared. "I'm one of the astronauts who walked on the Moon.

I stared dumbfounded at Dr. Winkler. Why would he let Mr. Smith call NASA with a story like that? *How embarrassing!*

Mr. Taylor frowned. "I'm sorry, sir, but I don't have time for crank calls. The last *Apollo* moonwalker died nine years ago in a car crash. If he were still alive, he'd have to be, like, a hundred years old."

Dr. Winkler interrupted, "One hundred and three. Excuse me, Mr. Taylor, but please read the complete file I sent you. It will explain why you were led to believe that he had died."

Mr. Smith was 103? Mr. Smith was an Apollo moonwalker?! Suddenly the fake name and the paranoia of reporters and his confusion about the Russians made sense. Reporters would have pestered him for reactions to space events, politicians would have insisted on his presence at anniversaries and special events, and his Alzheimer's would have made it harder and harder for him to cope. His wife must have taken the brunt of it until she died in that car accident. Living here anonymously was probably the family's way to give him some well-earned peace and dignity during his final years.

And I had doubted he was even a real pilot.

The flight director's eyes grew round as he scanned the file Dr. Winkler had sent. "Oh, I see," he said. "But considering his condition, Doctor, can we trust what he will tell us?"

"Memories associated with intense emotions and skills that were trained to the point of instinct are the last to be affected by the disease. He has also been refreshing those memories through flight simulations thanks to his young friend George here."

I looked down at my sneakers in embarrassment. I was just having fun sharing a love of flying with Mr. Smith. I had no idea I was flying copilot with one of the most famous pilots in history! *I wondered which one he was? Armstrong? Young? Cernan?*

"Then let's get started," the flight director said. "We have photos and technical drawings that the Apollo Restoration Project sent us of the cockpit. These were made from an old NASA mockup that unfortunately was destroyed in a hurricane a few years ago. The computer switches and displays are all exactly as in the original, but the museum installed modern computers and communications. So we have the ability to create an autopilot. What we don't have are any records of the actual flight-handling characteristics of the module. The best we have to offer is a children's educational game developed by some engineering students at Texas A&M. It's called *Fly Me to the Moon.*"

"That's the one I brought with me!" I said. I dragged my laptop and hand controllers out of my backpack. "I've got it right here." I flipped the screen open and started the boot process.

"I didn't come here to play games," Mr. Smith said.

"You don't understand," Mr. Taylor said. "It is not a game, it's a simulator. The students used very sophisticated software to model the flight characteristics. What I'd suggest is that we set up the sim from here and have you fly a rendezvous with the cargo ship, noting any differences between the original and the simulator. Can you do that, Mr. Smith?"

"Sure," he said simply. "Piece of cake."

I wondered what cake had to do with anything? I glanced at Dr. Winkler. He smiled and whispered to me, "An old expression meaning something is easy."

"Thanks," I whispered back.

Dr. Winkler cleared off his desk for the computer, but Mr. Smith shook his head.

"I have to fly it standing up," he said.

Mr. Taylor nodded. "He's right. No seats in the lunar module. And Ms. Phillips will be wearing a spacesuit because we aren't going to pressurize the module. Do you want gloves, Mr. Smith?"

"No, my hands are stiff enough without them!" he quipped.

Dr. Winkler and I laughed. I lifted a stool onto the desk and set the laptop on it to project against a white board on the wall. Mr. Smith placed the hand controllers at waist height on a book on the desk. He asked Dr. Winkler to close the window blinds and turn off the lights. I took care of the lights while Dr. Winkler closed the shades. It wasn't really dark, but it would help Mr. Smith focus.

"Young man, come stand to my right," Mr. Smith said. "I'm the commander, and you're the pilot."

"Yes, sir," I said. I decided he'd forgotten my name again.

"Mr. Smith," Mr. Taylor interrupted. "We think the other crewmember has a concussion and other injuries and is in and out of consciousness. Ms. Phillips will have to fly it solo."

"I understand," Mr. Smith said. "That's not a problem. But I need a body next to me to judge what panels and displays may be blocked."

"Right," I said. At least I was good for something!

We hooked up my laptop projector to Dr. Winkler's computer, so it would output whatever NASA sent through. The screen showed two triangular windows looking out over a gray landscape with a black sky beyond. No stars were visible. The cockpit was crowded with gauges and switches.

"We've activated the link. We've got one of our lunar pilots in a simulator here to fly the cargo ship."

"Roger," Mr. Smith said. "Fuel tank pressure low."

"Yes, we think there's a slow leak in the helium tank," Mr. Taylor explained. "The batteries are also not fully charged, but should last long enough to reach the cargo ship."

"Understood," Mr. Smith said. "T minus 5. Engine arm. Pilot should hit PROCEED, but because he's unconscious, I must reach over him and do it."

"Noted," Taylor said.

"I should hear the bang of the bolts releasing the lander and then feel like I'm riding in a high-speed elevator as the engine kicks in."

"Roger that," Taylor said.

I could hardly believe this was happening to me. *To me! I was flying with one of the Apollo astronauts.* The last living Apollo astronaut! Not even my mother would believe this if I told her. But I wouldn't break my promise to Mr. Smith, even after I figured out his real name.

"No, that's not right," Mr. Smith said.

"What's not right, Mr. Smith?" Mr. Taylor asked.

"The LM didn't have a barbecue mode. We had to fire the jets manually to start the ship spinning."

"Noted."

"But the flight is so short, you don't need to worry about overheating. It might be best to just let it coast. It will also be one less thing for the pilot to worry about."

"Yes, sir," Mr. Taylor said. "The cargo pilot has a lock on you."

Mr. Smith looked at the ceiling. "The upper window is blocked. Can't see target."

"That's okay," Mr. Taylor said. "You don't have to line up and dock. The cargo ship is going to match rates and take you into its hold."

"It's big enough for that?" Smith said.

Mr. Taylor smiled. "Yes, sir. It's a fuel tanker."

On the computer screen, I saw the curve of the Moon's horizon below us. "Look at the crescent Earth!" I blurted out in excitement. Mr. Smith ignored me. At least I could verify that this part of the simulation was correct. The Moon I'd seen last night was just past full, and the Earth and Moon were always in opposite phases. I wondered if I'd ever see the Earth from the Moon for real? I hoped so.

As the ship arced around to the far side of the Moon, the Earth sank below the horizon. Long sunrise shadows spread across rough crater floors below us.

"Got you," Mr. Taylor said. The simulation stopped.

"We going into blackout now?" Mr. Smith asked.

"No sir, we have almost continual communications thanks to lunar orbiting relay satellites."

Mr. Smith raised an eyebrow even though Mr. Taylor could not see him.

"It still takes 1.3 seconds for light to travel one way from the Moon, 2.6 seconds roundtrip. But with your help, we'll have the computer programmed to handle most problems."

"Yeah," Mr. Smith agreed. "Pings works pretty good."

I mouthed "Pings?" at Dr. Winkler.

He whispered back, "Sounds like an acronym for the navigation program."

I nodded and mouthed "Thanks" back at him.

"Need to run it again with some failures?" Mr. Smith asked.

"Yes, that would be very helpful," Mr. Taylor said. "But first let's take a break and see what questions the pilot and guidance team have for you."

Dr. Winkler helped Mr. Smith to the sofa on the side of the office, and I sat down too. I don't know which one of us was more dazed. "Can I call my wife now?" Mr. Smith asked. "She'll probably worry."

Dr. Winkler smiled. "She's fine. She's with her mother."

"Oh, right," Mr. Smith said. He looked down at his slippers. "Mother is going to be mad."

It was the strangest afternoon and evening I had ever spent in my life. I stood by Mr. Smith while he flew one simulation after another, with jets failed, with computer problems, with navigation errors, with popped circuit breakers. As I watched, I realized that even with his Alzheimer's, Mr. Smith still knew more about spaceflight than most people alive today. I felt incredibly lucky to have the chance to learn even a tiny bit of what he could teach me.

During breaks we ate snacks and drank decaf coffee and followed the progress of the crew on the Moon. Ms. Phillips had gotten the injured historian strapped into the module.

Dr. Winkler called my mother and asked if I could stay for dinner and into the evening. He said he had recruited me to help with a memory experiment involving one of the patients, and it would mean a lot if I were there until the patient went to bed. He'd get me a cab home. My mother fully supported my activities here, and after verifying with me that I had done my homework in study hall as usual, agreed I could stay as late as ten.

A nurse brought us dinner, and we ate there in Dr. Winkler's office. Mr. Smith fell asleep on the sofa soon afterward. I moved the simulation equipment out to the lounge and connected the big television to the NASA feed. Then I returned to Dr. Winkler' office.

The flight team was discussing possibly changing the rendezvous sequence. Because the batteries in the spacesuits had only a few hours left, the initial decision was to fly something called a direct ascent. But Mr. Smith had advised against it, saying that direct ascent was too risky for *Apollo*. As a result, Flight Director Taylor ordered a special "tiger" team to investigate options and report back.

One of the tiger team members confirmed that direct ascent wasn't used for *Apollo*. "Although that option is the simplest, requiring only a single burn of the ascent engine to put the LM on a path to intercept the target ship a half orbit later," the man reported, "the *Apollo* team felt that the likelihood of variations in the thrust during ascent presented too much risk. The short duration of the approach didn't allow much time for their old computers to calculate, and the crew to execute, the maneuvers to correct the flight path. If those corrections weren't made, the LM would miss the interception point and crash into the lunar surface."

"Couldn't the command module have changed course and rescued the LM?" the flight director asked.

"In some cases," the man replied. "But course changes require fuel, and its fuel was very limited."

"I assume that the computer and fuel issues do not apply in our case?"

"That's correct," the man responded.

"Flight, Lunar Ops," a woman's voice called.

"Go ahead, Lunar Ops," the flight director said.

A short pause ensued. "Thank you, sir. My main concern is time. No offense to the guidance team, but they were still making changes to the software half an hour ago. There's a reasonable chance that we will need Ms. Phillips to take manual control. I understand she has walked through the procedures in the cockpit, but that's no substitute for flight experience—especially with an untested vehicle! She needs time to adjust to the actual vehicle and environment. The coelliptic sequence gives her a whole lunar orbit to do that—and also makes my job as cargo pilot easier if I have to rescue her." *She's the one who will fly the cargo ship remotely! She's probably at the lunar south pole!*

"Flight, Surgeon."

"Go ahead, Surgeon."

"Sir, I understand Lunar Ops' concern, but an extra hour trapped in that spacesuit may mean the difference between life and death for the injured historian, Dr. Canterbury. We're also concerned about Ms. Phillips' state of mind. She was severely traumatized by the death of the pilot and is barely able to follow simple directions. The sooner both of them get out of those suits, the better their chances for survival."

Guidance assured the flight director that the new software would support direct ascent, especially after the simulations with Mr. Smith. The flight director decided to stick with direct ascent.

"Flight, Lunar Ops."

"Go ahead, Lunar Ops."

Another short delay followed that I now understood was because of the distance the signal had to travel. "I understand and will do my best to support the direct ascent. But I have a request. No offense to the guidance team, but speaking as a pilot, I'd feel a lot better if we have that *Apollo* astronaut do any flying that's necessary."

"You mean have Mr. Smith input the commands to the autopilot program? I'm not sure he'll be up to it. Doctor Winkler, what do you think?"

"Sir, I'm sorry," Dr. Winkler said. "But I don't know what state he will be in when he wakes up from his rest. I have some medication I can give him that should help, and George and I will do our best to remind him of the circumstances. But I suggest that you go with your original plan to have one of your astronauts run the autopilot and talk Ms. Phillips through any problems."

"Excuse me, Flight," the flight surgeon interjected. "How about if we have Mr. Smith serve as a coach for Ms. Phillips? Being a historian, having an *Apollo* astronaut looking over her shoulder could keep her calm and also give her the confidence she needs."

"That's an excellent idea," Lunar Ops said.

"Doctor Winkler?"

He glanced over at me. "George, you know how he usually behaves after his afternoon naps. Think he can do it?"

I gulped. The fate of two people might depend on my decision. I looked at Mr. Smith sleeping peacefully. Usually, a nap "reset" his memory. But given the right "props," I could probably get him back into his astronaut mindset in time for the launch, now only forty-five minutes away. I took a deep breath and nodded yes. I hoped I wouldn't regret this!

Doctor Winkler and the capcom, who was a current astronaut with lunar experience, agreed to do a voice check and let Mr. Smith talk to Ms. Phillips before the launch. At that time, we'd decide if he could continue on the live loop and be given command authority to the autopilot.

I stood up. "Dr. Winkler, I'm going to get Mr. Smith's shoes—his slippers remind him of his mother."

The doctor nodded in understanding. "While you're up there, see if he has a white shirt. And bring a belt too. People used to dress up back then."

"Roger!" I said, and dashed out for the elevator.

When I returned, the liftoff was only a half hour away. Dr. Winkler was talking on his cell—something about a security team. He disconnected when he saw me and said, "Time to wake our famous moonwalker."

Dr. Winkler set a wind-up alarm clock (no voice controls!) next to Mr. Smith and let it ring. Mr. Smith immediately nabbed it and shut it off. He blinked and stared at Dr. Winkler, who had donned his white lab coat. "Do I know you?" he asked. Dr. Winkler explained that he was a NASA flight surgeon. He regretted waking him, but Mission Control needed Mr. Smith's assistance.

"There's a mission on?" he asked, straightening up.

"Yes, and they're in trouble," Dr. Winkler said as he handed him the white golf shirt I'd brought. The doctor explained what had happened to Ms. Phillips, and that Mission Control wanted him to talk her through a lunar ascent and rendezvous. Mr. Smith looked confused. "We beat the Russians, and quit flying to the Moon," he insisted.

"Yes, we did," the doctor agreed. "But then we went back to the Moon as partners. Ms. Phillips was visiting the Moon when the accident happened."

I cringed. I wish he hadn't used the word "accident." It might evoke memories of Mr. Smith's wife. But Mr. Smith was more focused on the first part of the sentence. "Partners? With the Russians? Like *Apollo-Soyuz*?"

"That's right," Dr. Winkler said. "Like *Apollo-Soyuz*, only on the Moon."

"Okay," Mr. Smith said. "And they got in trouble?"

"Yes," Dr. Winkler repeated. I helped Mr. Smith with his shoes and then his belt. I combed his thin white hair. He suddenly noticed me and stared at my badge. "What kind of badge is that? Are you press? Reporters aren't allowed in here."

"I'm not a reporter, Mr. Smith. I'm George. I'm uh, a member of the guidance team," I said quickly in an attempt to use an appropriate term. I thought of adding that I was in charge of the "manual" system, but stopped myself.

"Then don't call me Mr. Smith," he barked. "Makes me feel old."

"Okay, Bob," I said with a wink.

Dr. Winkler handed him a cup of coffee spiked with some of that pink medicine. Mr. Smith sipped it gratefully. "Ready?" Dr. Winkler asked.

"Where are we going?" Mr. Smith asked.

"To the hotel lobby—we've set up a direct link to Mission Control. We're going to help a young woman take off from the Moon."

"Better call my wife," he said. "She'll be worried."

"She's visiting her mother," Dr. Winkler explained.

"Oh? That's good," he said.

I heard a thumping sound as we approached the double doors at the front of the building. "Whoa," I said. "There's a helicopter in the parking lot!"

"Darn press," mumbled Mr. Smith. His hands curled into fists.

"No, sir, that's Homeland Se—I mean the Air Force," Dr. Winkler said. *So that's who he was talking to on the phone! Wonder what they're doing here.*

"Oh, of course," Mr. Smith said, his hands relaxing again.

A man in a black suit with a security bud in his ear was asking Yvonne a question. With her eyes as large as saucers, she pointed in our direction. The man turned toward us. I thought he looked like one of those guys who guard the president. *Maybe he did.* He saluted Mr. Smith as we walked past, and Mr. Smith acknowledged him with a curt nod. Then Mr. Smith blew a kiss at Yvonne, who blushed deeply enough to match the purple of the front desk.

Would she guess who Mr. Smith was now? Even if she did, I realized that I would not be able to confirm her suspicions without breaking my word. I'd always thought of security as keeping bad guys out, not good guys in!

Is that why DHS was here? To make sure no one tried to kidnap Mr. Smith? Age and Alzheimer's had kind of done that already. Or were they here to keep the media out in case someone leaked that one of the original moonwalkers was alive and helping them? Or both?

At the doorway to the lounge, another man in black stopped us. Mr. Smith waited patiently while he asked me to raise my arms and ran a metal detector over me like they do at airports. He confiscated my phone, saying no recordings or photos were allowed. Did I understand?

I didn't know if this was an act for Mr. Smith's benefit or not, but I quickly replied, "Yes sir!" Lakewood did not to allow the taking of photos or videos of the residents by non-family members, anyway. Now I understand just how important that rule was to someone like Mr. Smith.

A nicely dressed middle-aged woman stood up as we shuffled Mr. Smith into the darkened lounge. She pecked Mr. Smith on the cheek. "Good to see you again, Flyboy!" she said. With an exaggerated wink, she added, "Name's Ruth, in case you forgot."

Mr. Smith didn't show any signs of recognizing this woman, but he returned her wink and said, "I never forget a beautiful woman!"

Dr. Winkler explained that Ruth Pressa was the relative who had granted permission to contact Mission Control. She shook my hand warmly and whispered in my ear, "Thank you for being such a good friend to my great-grandfather. It means a lot to our family."

Her great-grandfather? "It's my privilege, ma'am," I said. Her badge sported the seal of the DHS and her last name at the bottom in capital letters, "PRESSA." I wondered what kind of work she did for them?

While Dr. Winkler escorted Mr. Smith to a chair, Ms. Pressa handed me an old-fashioned wired headset and a speaker box. "This is a Mission Control headset and speaker box from the Apollo Restoration Project. I rigged up an interface so you can plug these into your laptop." She pointed to a rocker switch on the cord. "This is the push-to-talk button that he'll use to talk to Ms. Phillips. If he starts spouting nonsense, just unplug him from the laptop—he'll hear a click. Tell him we lost the signal." I nodded, hoping I'd not need to do that.

She continued. "The speaker box is set to broadcast and receive. The flight director and all the team will hear everything said in this room, so be careful to always call him Mr. Smith."

"I understand," I said. I decided not to tell her I didn't know his real name anyway.

"Okay then, I'll let you get to work." She settled into a chair next to Dr. Winkler.

I motioned Mr. Smith to join me standing behind the simulator. Our interface to Mission Control was the same set-up I'd used earlier, except that I'd added some bar stools in case our feet got tired. Also, I'd left the projector off since we had live images from Mission Control. The view from Ms. Phillips' helmet cam was in the center of the screen. On the right was a graph of data from the spacesuits showing power and carbon dioxide levels and stuff like that. On the left was a plot of the planned trajectory of the direct ascent rendezvous. It looked pretty simple; an arc from the surface that intersected a dotted circle around the Moon. The cargo ship was marked by a yellow Pac-Man that was slowly eating its way around the dotted circle. I smiled. Someone on the flight control team had a sense of humor.

"I saw that movie," Mr. Smith said, looking at the TV. "Isn't that the one with Tom Hanks in it?"

"No," I said. "This is a live image from the Moon. There's a woman who needs to fly to lunar orbit."

"What's a woman doing on the Moon? Is this some Russian stunt?"

"No, she's an American," I replied patiently. *Had he forgotten everything we'd told him already?* My heart rate climbed. "What's important is that if she doesn't rendezvous with a cargo ship in lunar orbit, she and the other passenger will die. Unfortunately, she's not a pilot."

Mr. Smith frowned. "She'll never make it."

"Not on her own, she won't," I said. "That's why we need you. NASA has set up the computer to fly the ascent automatically—you know, like 'pings'?" I hoped I had the term right.

He nodded. "Pings works great," he said.

I continued. "Yes, and pings was recently updated so that it can do all the calculations really fast. But it can't fly like the best LM pilot alive." *No need to say the only one.* He smiled at this praise. "So NASA needs you to help this woman—her name is Ms. Clara Phillips—with the launch and rendezvous."

"I can do that," Mr. Smith said, placing his large hand on the stick, just like he'd done hours earlier. I let out the breath I'd been holding.

I looked over at Dr. Winkler who gave me a thumbs-up sign. Mr. Smith donned the old-fashioned headset like he wore one every day. I plugged it into my laptop. If Mr. Smith got confused, I'd be responsible for literally pulling the plug.

"Houston would like to do a voice check of their secure line," I said.

"Hello, Mr. Smith, this is Houston Capcom. How do you read?"

"Roger, Houston, read you five by," Mr. Smith answered.

"Good. The flight director would like to speak to you."

"Go ahead," Mr. Smith said.

"Hello, Mr. Smith. I'm Flight Director Keegan Taylor," he said. "We appreciate you helping us in this emergency. Time is short, so let me fill you in on a few details."

Mr. Smith listened intently as the flight director explained that they were going to do a direct ascent, and that they might need him to take over manually.

"Understood," Mr. Smith said.

"Oh, and if you're willing, we'd like you to talk to Ms. Phillips, tell her what to expect before it happens—keeping in mind the 1.3-second signal delay, so she'll stay calm. Can you do that?"

"Sure," Mr. Smith replied simply.

"Good. Then I'll have Capcom patch you through to Ms. Phillips. Her first name is Clara."

The capcom's voice came over the speaker, "Clara, this is Houston on Private Channel Alpha, do you copy?"

A second later, she responded, "Yes, Houston, I hear you. My hands are shaking so badly, I'm afraid I'll press the wrong buttons!"

"Clara, you will do fine," the capcom assured her. "You just press PROCEED at T-5, and the computer will take it from there."

"But this LM was never tested under real conditions, and I'm not a pilot!"

"We know that, Clara. But that engine worked on every *Apollo* flight, and the systems are looking good. To reassure you, we've asked a very special person to come out of retirement. I'm going to patch him through to speak to you. He wishes to keep his name secret, and goes by Mr. Smith, but we have verified that he is in fact one of the original *Apollo* moonwalkers."

A second later, she said, "But that's impossible! The last one died in a car crash with his wife. I went to their funeral!"

"Apparently, only the wife actually died in that crash. Mr. Smith was sent to a secret location to spend his last years free of media scrutiny."

"The tabloids were actually right!" Ms. Phillips laughed. "Oh my, that was insensitive of me. Is Mr., uh, Smith listening? Please tell him I didn't mean to make light of his loss. I'm sure it must have been very hard."

"Yes," Mr. Smith said. "I miss my wife."

Oh no! He mustn't start thinking about his wife right now. He'll be of no help at all. I unplugged his connection to Ms. Phillips. "Mr. Smith," I whispered, pointing at the display, "What does that light mean?"

He stared at the panel seen through Ms. Phillips' helmet camera. "The LM fuel tank pressure is low. Must have a leak. Better take off soon."

Good. He was back on track. I plugged him back in. I saw Ms. Pressa smiling at me.

The capcom was talking to Ms. Phillips, I supposed answering a question about how Mr. Smith had gotten involved in this rescue. "Mr. Smith heard about your situation on the news and contacted us to see if he could help. We had him fly a simulator and update the model for use in the autopilot. He's standing by to speak with you."

"I can't believe this!" Ms. Phillips said. "I must be out of my mind or talking to a ghost."

"I'm not a ghost," Mr. Smith said. "And you won't be either, as long as you stay calm and follow directions." He paused in thought. I kept my finger on the plug just in case he changed subjects. "Once you reach orbit," Mr. Smith said, "You'll just coast right to where the command module can get you."

"Command module?" Ms. Phillips repeated.

"He means the cargo ship," the capcom said.

"Oh, of course. I understand," Ms. Phillips said.

They went through some preflight checks of switch positions and reviewed the procedures. Mr. Smith seemed calm and in control, every bit the old *Apollo* astronaut.

The liftoff was right on time. Ms. Phillips yelped when the engine fired, but Mr. Smith soothingly told her that was nominal (a word he used instead of "normal"). "You'll go straight up for about ten seconds," he reminded her. "Then you'll pitch over and move horizontally with respect to the lunar surface. You should have a great view out the window."

The image of the cockpit on the TV jiggled up and down in response to the engine. No sound penetrated through the airless cockpit. The view out the window changed from black sky to lunar gray as the ship nosed down.

"Guidance, report," the flight director demanded.

"Flight, cg shifted at pitch over."

A second later we heard Ms. Phillips shout, "Dr. Canterbury!" The pitch over had thrown the injured man out of his harness. One arm smacked Ms. Phillips across her faceplate.

I involuntarily winced and sucked in a breath, though she was perfectly fine inside her helmet.

Mr. Smith spoke softly. "Ms. Phillips, grab his wrist. When the ascent engine shuts down, he'll float right to you."

"Flight, engine shutdown."

"Trajectory report," the flight director ordered.

"The computer didn't fully compensate for the cg shift. We'll need a correction from the RCS."

"Mr. Smith, stand by for remote ops."

"Roger, Flight," Mr. Smith said.

We saw Ms. Phillips pull on Dr. Canterbury's wrist, rotating him so that he was facing her. She reached to pull the harness around him.

Dr. Canterbury's eyes opened. He jerked and hit the hand controller. The two historians tumbled. Out the window, the gray lunar surface was replaced by darkness and then surface again in rapid succession. *They're spinning!*

Mr. Smith pulled the hand controller to one side and released it. After a short delay, I noted that the view rotated more slowly.

"Flight, Guidance. LM is in stable BBQ mode."

"Nice flying, Mr. Smith," the capcom said. "My guy in the simulator says you used about half the fuel he would have."

"She's not out of the woods yet," he said. "Look at the disk key."

Huh? There were no woods on the Moon. And what kind of a disk had a key? *Click.* I yanked the plug from my laptop.

Mr. Smith continued talking. "Apo loon is . . ."

"Sorry, I think we've lost our link to the spacecraft," I said, looking at Dr. Winkler. He in turn was looking at Ms. Pressa.

Ms. Pressa was texting quietly on her phone. "Communications restored," she declared.

I took the hint and plugged Mr. Smith back in. A text message appeared on my laptop saying, "'Not out of the woods' means 'not out of trouble.' 'DSKY' is a display in the LM." *None of that was nonsense?* My face burned with embarrassment. I had a lot to learn.

The guidance team reported that they had the orbital correction calculated, including the additional jet firings. The flight director gave them the go to have the automatic system command the jets to make the necessary corrections. "Capcom, warn Ms. Phillips that there will be jet firings."

Ms. Phillips got Dr. Canterbury secured in his harness and tightened her own. His eyes had closed again. Surgeon feared that the acceleration, though gentle compared to an Earth launch, might have acerbated his injuries.

After the maneuver, the trajectory plot showed that the LM and "Pac-Man" cargo ship would rendezvous on schedule. Capcom informed a relieved Ms. Phillips that all was well.

"Except she's going to crash," Mr. Smith said.

What? I rested my fingers on the headset connection.

"Mr. Smith, Flight speaking. The trajectory looks good to us. Why do you think she is going to crash?"

"I told you, look at the DSKY. You only raised apolune from 40.1 to 40.6. That's too low for the CSM."

A text appeared on my laptop saying, "Apolune is the highest point in a lunar orbit. CSM = command and service module." I looked up at Ms. Pressa and nodded to let her know I understood. I pulled my hand away from the connection.

Mr. Smith continued. "You need forty-two nautical miles or the CSM can't get to her in time."

"Nautical miles? What kind of dumb unit is that?" I blurted, and then covered my mouth. I hadn't meant to say that outloud for the whole team to hear! Ms. Pressa frowned, I assumed at my outburst, and texted furiously. Nothing showed up on my laptop, though.

"Break, break," Capcom interrupted. "Lunar Ops reports the LM is out of range by about ten kilometers!"

Mr. Smith was right?

"Guidance, Flight, we've uncovered the problem. The LM software uses nautical miles and the corrections we made assumed statute miles. We're off by a factor of 1.15."

Ms. Pressa rose from her seat and paced back and forth. *Not out of the woods, indeed!*

"Guidance, get me the right numbers for Mr. Smith to fly to. Capcom, inform Ms. Phillips we'll be doing another maneuver."

Precious time ticked by while the LM rapidly approached the point of no return. The trajectory map refreshed with a new image showing the LM arcing up but not quite reaching the intersect point with the cargo ship. Unless it changed course fast, the historians were doomed. If I hadn't cut off Mr. Smith's comments earlier, would they have discovered the problem sooner? Was this all my fault? Maybe I didn't have the right stuff to be a pilot after all.

Lunar Ops reported that she had moved the cargo ship to a slighter lower orbit that would help close the gap. But it also increased her speed. That seemed counterproductive to me until I saw on the plot that the intersection point was farther around the Moon than predicted earlier. Orbital mechanics was confusing!

Finally Guidance reported they had the commands ready. The flight director said to execute them. If anything went wrong, we would know in a few minutes. If so, we might need Mr. Smith to fly to the numbers manually.

Ms. Pressa approached and held up her phone. I heard the shutter sound of a camera snapping a photo.

"What do you think you're doing?" Mr. Smith shouted. Ms. Pressa looked puzzled. "Just taking your picture, Grandpa," she explained.

Uh-oh. He didn't like to be called that!

"Grandpa! You didn't think I was too old at the bar the other night!" He squinted at her badge. "P . . . R . . . E . . . S . . . S . . . You're a reporter! Get out!" He pushed her back with the heel of his big left hand. Her phone clattered across the floor, and she fell back into a chair.

The security guard from the door seemed to appear out of thin air, "Director, are you okay?" he asked, lifting her to her feet.

Director? Of what?

"I'm okay, Harry," Ms. Pressa insisted, smoothing her suit jacket. "There's just been a misunderstanding." Dr. Winkler handed her phone to Harry. "Escort me to the door, please."

"Whatever you say, ma'am," the big guy replied, glaring at Mr. Smith.

"Paparazzi," Mr. Smith cursed.

Dr. Winkler poured Mr. Smith a glass of water from a pitcher on a nearby table. He handed it to him and assured him that everything was under control. I'd never seen the doctor so rattled. Having a patient almost flatten his great-granddaughter was rather upsetting!

The doctor met my eyes and then darted his glance to and from the water glass. I understood that he had added something to the water. Then he said,

"Sir, I suggest that you rest your feet while we wait for communications to come back."

"Are they in blackout?" Mr. Smith asked.

"Yes," I agreed, holding the plugs to his headset and the speaker out of view. All of Mission Control had heard his outburst at Ms. Pressa. I hoped they didn't realize that she really was his great-granddaughter. Even though Pressa was probably her married name, some enterprising person could use it to figure out Mr. Smith's identity.

Mr. Smith gulped the water like he was taking a shot of scotch. He settled onto the stool, glancing down at his feet. "Man, I hate these stiff military shoes. When I retire, I'm only going to wear slippers!"

"Your mother won't like that," I quipped.

He smiled. "No, she won't!" he agreed. "And that's another reason I'm going to wear slippers!" He laughed.

I was dying to know what was going on with Ms. Phillips. The trajectory display on the TV was blinking. In all the commotion, the maneuver had come and gone. He couldn't do any harm now.

"We're getting the signal back," I said, and plugged Mr. Smith and the speaker back in. Guidance reported that he was waiting for Lunar Ops to confirm target acquisition.

Mr. Smith surprised me when he calmly said, "Ms. Phillips, quit worrying about the trajectory for a minute. Look out the window. You owe it to yourself."

I wasn't sure if Mission Control had let this message through until Ms. Phillips said, "Seeing the Earth above the desolate Moon reminds me of just how precious life is. I'll never forget this moment."

"Me either," Mr. Smith said.

"Me either," I whispered.

Lunar Ops reported target acquired! I sagged onto my stool, suddenly realizing how tired I was. Some fancy remote flying on the part of Lunar Ops completed the rendezvous. The cargo ship scooped the LM into its wide bay, and cheers erupted in Mission Control. I gave Mr. Smith a high five, and Dr. Winkler patted him firmly on the back. "Where are the cigars?" Mr. Smith asked.

"Sorry, but this is a no-smoking area," Dr. Winkler said.

"Oh," Mr. Smith said, obviously disappointed.

A text appeared on my laptop. "Good call on the nautical miles—you saved two lives. Sorry about the photo. Forgot blackmail incident still upsets him. I'll be in touch. Thanks again." She signed it, "R. E. Pressa, Director of Knowledge Capture, Department of Homeland Security." Knowledge Capture?

After the cargo hold was pressurized, Ms. Phillips was able to take off her spacesuit and help Dr. Canterbury out of his. The flight surgeon did a remote exam. Turned out that Dr. Canterbury didn't have a concussion. His suit had been damaged and he was suffering from carbon-dioxide poisoning. If they hadn't done the direct ascent, he would have died. Ms. Phillips hooked him up to oxygen and settled in to wait for the Russian rescue ship to rendezvous with them. Mr. Smith's advice no longer needed, Mission Control cut our connection. We were now in listen-only mode.

Dr. Winkler escorted a sleepy Mr. Smith to the men's room while I moved the chairs back to their proper places in the lounge.

Just before I unplugged the speaker box, I heard Ms. Phillips thank the team in Houston for sending the cargo ship and especially for recruiting Mr. Smith to help her. "I have dedicated my life to preserving the history of space," she said. "Yet today when I was faced with having to recreate that history, I realized just how little I actually know. I now have a new level of understanding and respect for the courage and skill of the *Apollo* astronauts. I hope that I'll have the opportunity to thank Mr. Smith in person when I get back."

I knew that wasn't going to happen. By the time she got back, he'd already have forgotten all about this day.

But I wouldn't. I would remember for him. And tomorrow, I'd check out every e-book and disk I could find at the library and read all about the *Apollo* program and the amazing men who first walked on the Moon. We'd watch that *Apollo* movie with Tom Hanks, and fly simulations together. Though Mr. Smith might soon forget even his real name, and wouldn't remember Ms. Phillips next week, my memories of this time with him would be as long lasting as his footprints on the Moon.

Dedicated to the victims of Alzheimer's and their caregivers, with special remembrance of the first director of Johnson Space Center, Dr. Robert Gilruth, my father-in-law, Ralph Dyson, and my grandfather, George Canterbury.

Hannu Rajaniemi is an author, mathematical physicist, and a science innovator from Finland. He has a Ph.D. in string theory. For more than a decade, he lived in Edinburgh, and currently resides in California. He holds several advanced degrees in mathematics and physics. Multilingual from an early age, he writes his science fiction in English. His latest novel is *Summerland*.

TYCHE AND THE ANTS
Hannu Rajaniemi

The ants arrived on the Moon on the same day Tyche went through the Secret Door to give a ruby to the Magician.

She was glad to be out of the Base. The Brain had given her a Treatment earlier that morning, and that always left her tingly and nervous, with pent-up energy that could only be expended by running down the gray rolling slope down the side of Malapert Mountain, jumping and hooting.

"Come on, keep up!" she shouted at the grag that the Brain had inevitably sent to keep an eye on her. The white-skinned machine followed her on its two thick treads, cylindrical arms swaying for balance as it rumbled laboriously downhill, following the little craters of Tyche's footprints.

Exasperated, she crossed her arms and paused to wait. She looked up. The mouth of the Base was hidden from view, as it should be, to keep them safe from space sharks. The jagged edge of the mountain hid the Great Wrong Place from sight, except for a single wink of blue malice, just above the gleaming white of the upper slopes, a stark contrast against the velvet black of the sky. The white was not snow—that was a Wrong Place thing—but tiny beads of glass made by ancient meteor impacts. That's what the Brain said, anyway. According to Chang'e the Moon Girl, it was all the jewels she had lost over the centuries she had lived here.

Tyche preferred Chang'e's version. That made her think of the ruby, and she touched her belt pouch to make sure it was still there.

"Outings are subject to being escorted at all times," said the sonorous voice of the Brain in her helmet. "There is no reason to be impatient."

Most of the grags were autonomous: the Brain could only control a few of them at a time. But of course it would keep an eye on her, so soon after the Treatment.

"Yes, there is, slowpoke," Tyche muttered, stretching her arms and jumping up and down in frustration.

Her suit flexed and flowed around her with the movement. She had grown it herself as well, the third one so far, although it had taken much longer than the ruby. Its many layers were alive, it felt light, and best of all, it had a powerskin, a slick porous tissue made from cells with mechanosensitive ion channels that translated her movements into power for the suit. It was so much better than the white clumsy fabric ones the Chinese had left behind; the grags had cut and sewn a baby-sized version out of those for her that kind of worked, but was impossibly stuffy and stiff.

It was only the second time she had tested the new suit, and she was proud of it: it was practically a wearable ecosystem, and she was pretty sure that with its photosynthesis layer, it would keep her alive for months, if she only had enough sunlight and carried enough of the horrible compressed Chinese nutrients.

She frowned. Her legs were suddenly gray, mottled with browns. She brushed them with her hand, and her fingers—slick silvery hue of the powerskin—came away the same color. It seemed the regolith dust clung to the suit. Annoying. She absently noted to do something about it for the next iteration when she fed the suit back into the Base's big biofabber.

Now the grag was stuck on the lip of a shallow crater, grinding treads sending up silent parabolas of little rocks and dust. Tyche had had enough of waiting.

"I'll be back for dinner," she told the Brain.

Without waiting for the Base mind's response, she switched off the radio, turned around, and started running.

Tyche settled into the easy stride the Jade Rabbit had shown her: gliding just above the surface, using well-timed toe-pushes to cross craters and small rocks that littered the uneven regolith.

She took the long way around, avoiding her old tracks that ran down much of the slope, just to confuse the poor grag more. She skirted around the edge of one of the pitch-black cold fingers—deeper craters that never got sunlight—that were everywhere on this side of the mountain. It would have been a shortcut, but it was too cold for her suit. Besides, the ink-men lived in the deep potholes, in the Other Moon beyond the Door.

Halfway around, the ground suddenly shook. Tyche slid uncontrollably, almost going over the edge before she managed to stop by turning around mid-leap and jamming her toes into the chilly hard regolith when she landed. Her heart pounded. Had the ink-men brought something up from the deep dark, something big? Or had she just been almost hit by a meteorite? That had happened a couple of times, a sudden crater blooming soundlessly into being, right next to her.

Then she saw beams of light in the blackness and realized that it was only the Base's sandworm, a giant articulated machine with a maw full of toothy wheels that ground Helium-3 and other volatiles from the deep shadowy deposits.

Tyche breathed a sigh of relief and continued on her way. Many of the grag bodies were ugly, but she liked the sandworm. She had helped to program it: constantly toiling, it went into such deep places that the Brain could not control it remotely.

The Secret Door was in a shallow crater, maybe a hundred meters in diameter. She went down its slope with little choppy leaps and stopped her momentum with a deft pirouette and toe-brake, right in front of the Door.

It was made of two large pyramid-shaped rocks, leaning against each other at a funny angle, with a small triangular gap between them: the Big Old One, and the Troll. The Old One had two eyes made from shadows, and when Tyche squinted from the right angle, a rough outcrop and a groove in the base became a nose and a mouth. The Troll looked grumpy, half-squashed against the bigger rock's bulk.

As she watched, the face of the Old One became alive and gave her a quizzical look. Tyche gave it a stiff bow—out of habit, even though she could have curtsied in her new suit.

How have you been, Tyche? the rock asked, in its silent voice.

"I had a Treatment today," she said dourly.

The rock could not nod, so it raised its eyebrows.

Ah. Always Treatments. Let me tell you, in my day, vacuum was the only treatment we had, and the sun, and a little meteorite every now and then to keep clean. Stick to that and you'll live to be as old as I am.

And as fat, grumbled the Troll. Believe me, once you carry him for a few million years, you start to feel it. What are you doing here, anyway?

Tyche grinned. "I made a ruby for the Magician." She took it out and held it up proudly. She squeezed it a bit, careful not to damage her suit's gloves against the rough edges, and held it in the Old One's jet-black shadow, knocking it against the rock's surface. It sparkled with tiny embers, just like it was supposed to. She had made it herself, using Verneuil flame fusion, and spiced it with a piezoelectric material so that it would convert motion to light.

It's very beautiful, Tyche, the Old One said. I'm sure he will love it.

Oh? said the troll. Well, maybe the old fool will finally stop looking for the Queen Ruby, then, and settle down with poor Chang'e. In with you, now. You're encouraging this sentimental piece of rubble here. He might start crying. Besides, everybody is waiting.

Tyche closed her eyes, counted to ten, and crawled through the opening between the rocks, through the Secret Door to her Other Moon.

The moment Tyche opened her eyes she saw that something was wrong. The house of the Jade Rabbit was broken. The boulders she had carefully balanced on top of each other lay scattered on the ground, and the lines she had drawn to make the rooms and the furniture were smudged. (Since it never rained, the house had not needed a roof.)

There was a silent sob. Chang'e the Moon Girl sat next to the Rabbit's house, crying. Her flowing silk robes of purple, yellow, and red were a mess on the ground like broken wings, and her makeup had been running down her pale, powdered face.

"Oh, Tyche!" she cried. "It is terrible, terrible!" She wiped a crystal tear from her eye. It evaporated in the vacuum before it could fall on the dust. Chang'e was a drama queen, and pretty, and knew it, too. Once, she had an affair with the Woodcutter just because she was bored, and bore him children, but they were already grown up and had moved to the Dark Side.

Tyche put her hands on her hips, suddenly angry. "Who did this?" she asked. "Was it the Cheese Goat?"

Tearful, Chang'e shook her head.

"General Nutsy Nutsy? Or Mr. Cute?" The Moon People had many enemies, and there had been times when Tyche had led them in great battles, cutting her way through armies of stone with an aluminum rod the Magician had enchanted into a terrible bright blade. But none of them had ever been so mean as to smash the houses.

"Who was it, then?"

Chang'e hid her face behind one flowing silken sleeve and pointed. And that's when Tyche saw the first ant, moving in the ruins of the Jade Rabbit's house.

It was not like a grag or an otho, and certainly not a Moon Person. It was a jumbled metal frame, all angles and shiny rods, like a vector calculation come to life, too straight and rigid against the rough surfaces of the rocks to be real. It was like two tetrahedrons inside each other, with a bulbous sphere at each vertex, each glittering like the eye of the Great Wrong Place.

It was not big, perhaps reaching up to Tyche's knees. One of the telescoping metal struts had white letters on it. ANT-A3972, they said, even though the thing did not look like the ants Tyche had seen in videos.

It stretched and moved like the geometrical figures Tyche manipulated with a gesture during the Brain's math lessons. Suddenly, it flipped over the Rabbit's broken wall, making Tyche gasp. Then it shifted into a strange, slug-like motion over the regolith, first stretching, then contracting. It made Tyche's skin crawl. As she watched, the ant thing fell into a crevice between two boulders—but dexterously pulled itself up, supported itself on a couple of vertices, and somersaulted over the obstacle like an acrobat.

Tyche stared at it. Anger started to build up in her chest. In the Base, she obeyed the Brain and the othos and the grags because she had Promised. But the Other Moon was her place: it belonged to her and the Moon People, and no one else.

"Everybody else is hiding," whispered Chang'e. "You have to do something, Tyche. Chase it away."

"Where is the Magician?" Tyche asked. *He would know what to do.* She did not like the way the ant thing moved.

As she hesitated, the creature swung around and, with a series of twitches, pulled itself up into a pyramid, as if watching her. *It's not so nasty-looking,* Tyche thought. *Maybe I could bring it back to the Base, introduce it to Hugbear.* It would be a complex operation: she would have to assure the bear that she would always love it no matter what, and then carefully introduce the newcomer to it—

The ant thing darted forward, and a sharp pain stung Tyche's thigh. One of the thing's vertices had a spike that quickly retracted. Tyche's suit grumbled as it sealed all its twenty-one layers, and soothed the tiny wound. Tears came to her eyes, and her mouth was suddenly dry. No Moon Person had ever hurt her, not even the ink-men, except to pretend. She almost switched her radio on and called the grag for help.

Then she felt the eyes of the Moon People, looking at her from their windows. She gritted her teeth and ignored the bite of the wound. She was Tyche. She was brave. Had she not climbed to the Peak of Eternal Light once, all alone, following the solar panel cables, just to look the Great Wrong Place in the eye? (It had been smaller than she'd expected, tiny and blue and unblinking, with a bit of white and green, and altogether a disappointment.)

Carefully, Tyche picked up a good-sized rock from the Jade Rabbit's wall—it was broken anyway. She took a slow step towards the creature. It had suddenly contracted into something resembling a cube and seemed to be absorbed in something. Tyche moved right. The ant flinched at her shadow. She moved left—and swung the rock down as hard as she could.

She missed. The momentum took her down. Her knees hit the hard chilly regolith. The rock bounced away. This time the tears came, but Tyche struggled up and threw the rock after the creature. It was scrambling away, up the slope of the crater.

Tyche picked up the rock and followed. In spite of the steep climb, she gained on it with a few determined leaps, cheered on by the Moon People below. She was right at its heels when it climbed over the edge of the crater. But when she caught a glimpse of what lay beyond, she froze and dropped down on her belly.

A bright patch of sunlight shone on the wide highland plain ahead. It was crawling with ants, hundreds of them. A rectangular carpet of them sat right in the middle, all joined together into a thick metal sheet. Every now and then it undulated like something soft, a shiny amoeba. Other ant things moved in orderly rows, sweeping the surroundings.

The one Tyche was following picked up speed on the level ground, rolling and bouncing, like a skeletal football, and as she watched from her hiding place, it joined the central mass. Immediately, the ant-sheet changed. Its sides stretched upwards into a hollow, cup-like shape: other ants at its base telescoped into a high, supporting structure, lifting it up. A sharp spike grew in the middle of the cup, and then the whole structure turned to point at the sky. *A transmitter,* Tyche thought, following it with her gaze.

It was aimed straight at the Great Wrong Place.

Tyche swallowed, turned around and slid back down. She was almost glad to see the grag down there, waiting for her patiently by the Secret Door.

The Brain did not sound angry, but then the Brain was never angry.

"Evacuation procedure has been initiated," it said. "This location has been compromised."

Tyche was breathing hard: the Base was in a lava tube halfway up the south slope of the mountain, and the way up was always harder than the way down. This time, the grag had had no trouble keeping up with her. It had been a silent journey: she had tried to tell the Brain about the ants, but the AI had maintained complete radio silence until they were inside the Base.

"What do you mean, *evacuation*?" Tyche demanded.

She opened the helmet of her suit and breathed in the comfortable yeasty smell of her home module. Her little home was converted from one of the old Chinese ones, snug white cylinders that huddled close to the main entrance of the cavernous lava tube. She always thought they looked like the front teeth in the mouth of a big snake.

The main tube itself was partially pressurized, over sixty meters in diameter and burrowed deep into the mountain. It split into many branches, expanded and reinforced by othos and grags with regolith concrete pillars. She had tried to play it there many times, but preferred the Other Moon: she did not like the stench from the bacteria that the othos seeded the walls with, the ones that pooped calcium and aluminum.

Now, it was a hotbed of activity. The grags had set up bright lights and moved around, disassembling equipment and filling cryogenic tanks. The walls were alive with the tiny, soft, starfish-like othos, eating bacteria away. The Brain had not wasted any time.

"We are leaving, Tyche," the Brain said. "You need to get ready. The probe you found knows we are here. We are going away, to another place. A safer place. Do not worry. We have alternative locations prepared. It will be fine."

Tyche bit her lip. *It's my fault.* She wished the Brain had a proper face. It had a module of its own, in the coldest, unpressurized part of the tube, where its quantum processors could operate undisturbed, but inside it was just lasers and lenses and trapped ions, and rat brain cells grown to mesh with circuitry. How could it understand about the Jade Rabbit's house? It wasn't fair.

"And before we go, you need a Treatment."

Going away. She tried to wrap her mind around the concept. They had always been here, to be safe from the space sharks from the Great Wrong Place. And the Secret Door was here. If they went somewhere else, how would she find her way to the Other Moon? What would the Moon People do without her?

And she still hadn't given the ruby to the Magician.

The anger and fatigue exploded out of her in one hot wet burst.

"I'm not going to go not going to go not going to go," she said and ran into her sleeping cubicle. "And I don't want a stupid Treatment," she yelled, letting the door membrane congeal shut behind her.

Tyche took off her suit, flung it into a corner and cuddled against the Hugbear in her bed. Its ragged fur felt warm against her cheek, and its fake heartbeat was reassuring. She distantly remembered her Mum had made it move from afar, sometimes, stroked her hair with its paws, its round facescreen replaced with her features. That had been a long time ago and she was sure the bear was bigger then. But it was still soft.

Suddenly, the bear moved. Her heart jumped with a strange, aching hope. But it was only the Brain. "Go 'way," she muttered.

"Tyche, this is important," said the Brain. "Do you remember what you promised?"

She shook her head. Her eyes were hot and wet. *I'm not going to cry like Chang'e,* she thought. *I'm not.*

"Do you remember now?"

The bear's face was replaced with a man and a woman. The man had no hair and his dark skin glistened. The woman was raven-haired and pale, with a face like a bird. *Mum is even prettier than Chang'e,* Tyche thought.

"Hello, Tyche," they said in unison, and laughed. "We are Kareem and

Sofia," the woman said. "We are your mommy and daddy. We hope you are well when you see this." She touched the screen, quickly and lightly, like a little bunny hop on the regolith.

"But if the Brain is showing you this," Tyche's Dad said, "then it means that something bad has happened and you need to do what the Brain tells you."

"You should not be angry at the Brain," Mum said. "It is not like we are, it just plans and thinks. It just does what it was told to do. And we told it to keep you safe."

"You see, in the Great Wrong Place, people like us could not be safe," Dad continued. "People like Mum and me and you were feared. They called us Greys, after the man who figured out how to make us, and they were jealous, because we lived longer than they did and had more time to figure things out. And because giving things silly names makes people feel better about themselves. Do we look gray to you?"

No. Tyche shook her head. The Magician was gray, but that was because he was always looking for rubies in dark places and never saw the sun.

"So we came here, to build a Right Place, just the two of us." Her Dad squeezed Mum's shoulders, just like the bear used to do to Tyche. "And you were born here. You can't imagine how happy we were."

Then Mum looked serious. "But we knew that the Wrong Place people might come looking for us. So we had to hide you, to make sure you would be safe, so they would not look inside you and cut you and find out what makes you work. They would do anything to have you."

Fear crunched Tyche's gut into a tiny cold ball. *Cut you?*

"It was very, very hard, dear Tyche, because we love you. Very hard, not to touch you except from afar. But we want you to grow big and strong, and when the time comes, we will come and find you, and then we will all be in the Right Place together."

"But you have to promise to take your Treatments. Can you promise to do that? Can you promise to do what the Brain says?"

"I promise," Tyche muttered.

"Goodbye, Tyche," her parents said. "We will see you soon."

And then they were gone, and the Hugbear's face was blank and pale brown again.

"We need to go soon," the Brain said again, and this time its voice sounded more gentle. "Please get ready. I would like you to have a Treatment before travel."

Tyche sighed and nodded. It wasn't fair. But she had promised.

The Brain sent Tyche a list of things she could take with her, scrolling in one of the windows of her room. It was a short list. She looked around at the fabbed figurines and the moon rock that she thought looked like a boy and the e-sheets floating everywhere with her favorite stories open. She could not even take the Hugbear. She felt alone, suddenly, like she had when she climbed to look at the Great Wrong Place on top of the mountain.

Then she noticed the ruby lying on her bed. *If I go away and take it with me, the Magician will never find it.* She thought about the Magician and his panther, desperately looking from crater to crater, forever. *It's not fair. Even if I keep my promise, I'll have to take it to him.*

And say goodbye.

Tyche sat down on the bed and thought very hard.

The Brain was everywhere, but it could not watch everything. It was based on a scanned human brain, some poor person who had died a long time ago. It had no cameras in her room. And its attention would be on the evacuation: it would have to keep programming and reprogramming the grags. She picked at the sensor bracelet in her wrist that monitored her life signs and location. That was the difficult bit. She would have to do something about that. But there wasn't much time: the Brain would take her for a Treatment soon.

She hugged the bear again in frustration. It felt warm, and as she squeezed it hard, she could feel its pulse—

Tyche sat up. She remembered the Jade Rabbit's stories and tricks, the tar rabbit he had made to trick an enemy.

She reached into the Hugbear's head and pulled out a programming window, coupled it with her sensor. She summoned up old data logs, added some noise to them. Then she fed them to the bear, watched its pulse and breathing and other simulated life signs change to match hers.

Then she took a deep breath, and as quickly as she could, she pulled off the bracelet and put it on the Hugbear.

"Tyche? Is there something wrong?" the Brain asked.

Tyche's heart jumped. Her mind raced. "It's fine," she said. "I think . . . I think I just banged my sensor a bit. I'm just getting ready now." She tried to make her voice sound sweet, like a girl who always keeps her promises.

"Your Treatment will be ready soon," the Brain said and was gone. Heart pounding, Tyche started to put on her suit.

There was a game that Tyche used to play in the lava tube: how far could she get before she was spotted by the grags? She played it now, staying low, avoiding their camera eyes, hiding behind rock protrusions, crates, and cryogenic tanks, until she was in a tube branch that only had othos in it. The Brain did not usually control them directly, and besides, they did not have eyes. Still, her heart felt like meteorite impacts in her chest.

She pushed through a semi-pressurizing membrane. In this branch, the othos had dug too deep for calcium, and caused a roof collapse. In the dim green light of her suit's fluorescence, she made way her up the tube's slope. *There.* She climbed on a pile of rubble carefully. The othos had once told her there was an opening there, and she hoped it would be big enough for her to squeeze through.

Boulders rolled under her, and she felt a sharp bang against her knee. The suit hissed at the sudden impact. She ignored the pain and ran her fingers along the rocks, following a very faint air current she could not have sensed without the suit. Then her fingers met regolith instead of rock. It was packed tight, and she had to push hard at it with her aluminum rod before it gave away. A shower of dust and rubble fell on her, and for a moment she thought there was going to be another collapse. But then there was a patch of velvet sky in front of her. She widened the opening, made herself as small as she could and crawled towards it.

Tyche emerged onto the mountainside. The sudden wide open space of rolling gray and brown around her felt like the time she had eaten too much sugar. Her legs and hands were wobbly, and she had to sit down for a moment. She shook herself: she had an appointment to keep. She checked that the ruby was still in its pouch, got up, and started downwards with the Rabbit's lope.

The Secret Door was just the way Tyche had left it. She eyed the crater edge nervously, but there were no ants in sight. She bit her lip when she looked at the Old One and the Troll.

What's wrong? the Old One asked.

"I'm going to have to go away."

Don't worry. We'll still be here when you come back.

"I might never come back," Tyche said, choking a bit.

Never is a very long time, the Old One said. Even I have never seen never. We'll be here. Take care, Tyche.

Tyche crawled through to the Other Moon, and found the Magician waiting for her.

He was very thin and tall, taller than the Old One even, and cast a long cold finger of a shadow in the crater. He had a sad face and a scraggly beard and white gloves and a tall top hat. Next to him lay his flying panther, all black, with eyes like tiny rubies.

"Hello, Tyche," the Magician said, with a voice like the rumble of the sandworm.

Tyche swallowed and took out the ruby from her pouch, holding it out to him.

"I made this for you." *What if he doesn't like it?* But the Magician picked it up, slowly, eyes glowing, held it in both hands and gazed at it in awe.

"That is very, very kind of you," he whispered. Very carefully, he took off his hat and put the ruby in it. It was the first time Tyche had ever seen the Magician smile. Still, there was a sadness to his expression.

"I didn't want to leave before giving it to you," she said.

"That's quite a fuss you caused for the Brain. He is going to be very worried."

"He deserves it. But I promised I would go with him."

The Magician looked at the ruby one more time and put the hat back on his head.

"Normally, I don't interfere with the affairs of other people, but for this, I owe you a wish."

Tyche took a deep breath. "I don't want to live with the grags and the othos and the Brain anymore. I want to be in the Right Place with Mum and Dad."

The Magician looked at her sadly.

"I'm sorry, Tyche, but I can't make that happen. My magic is not powerful enough."

"But they promised—"

"Tyche, I know you don't remember. And that's why we Moon People remember for you. The space sharks came and took your parents, a long time ago. They are dead. I am sorry."

Tyche closed her eyes. *A picture in a window, a domed crater. Two bright things arcing over the horizon, like sharks. Then, brightness—*

"You've lived with the Brain ever since. You don't remember because it makes you forget with the Treatments, so you don't get too sad, so you stay the way your parents wanted to keep you. But we remember. And we always tell you the truth."

And suddenly they were all there, all the Moon People, coming from their houses: Chang'e and her children and the Jade Rabbit and the Woodcutter, looking at her gravely and nodding their heads.

Tyche could not bear to look at them. She covered her helmet with her hands, turned around, crawled through the Secret Door and ran away, away from the Other Moon. She ran, not a Rabbit run but a clumsy jerky crying run, until she stumbled on a boulder and went rolling higgledy-piggledy down. She lay curled up in the chilly regolith for a long time. And when she opened her eyes, the ants were all around her.

The ants were arranged around her in a half-circle, stretched into spiky pyramids, waving slightly, as if looking for something. Then they spoke. At first, it was just noise, hissing in her helmet, but after a second it resolved into a voice.

"—hello," it said, warm and female, like Chang'e, but older and deeper. "I am Alissa. Are you hurt?"

Tyche was frozen. She had never spoken to anyone who was not the Brain or one of the Moon People. Her tongue felt stiff.

"Just tell me if you are all right. No one is going to hurt you. Do you feel bad anywhere?"

"No," Tyche breathed.

"There is no need to be afraid. We will take you home." A video feed flashed up inside her helmet, a spaceship that was made up of a cluster of legs and a globe that glinted golden. A circle appeared elsewhere in her field of vision, indicating a tiny pinpoint of light in the sky. "See? We are on our way."

"I don't want to go to the Great Wrong Place," she gasped. "I don't want you to cut me up."

There was a pause.

"Why would we do that? There is nothing to be afraid of."

"Because Wrong Place people don't like people like me."

Another pause.

"Dear child, I don't know what you have been told, but things have changed. Your parents left Earth more than a century ago. We never thought we would find you, but we kept looking. And I'm glad we did. You have been alone on the Moon for a very long time."

Tyche got up, slowly. *I haven't been alone.* Her head spun. *They would do anything to have you.*

She backed off a few steps.

"If I come with you," she asked in a small voice, "will I see Kareem and Sofia again?"

A pause again, longer this time.

"Of course you will," Alissa the ant-woman said finally. "They are right here, waiting for you."

Liar.

Slowly, Tyche started backing off. The ants moved, closing their circle. *I am faster than they are,* she thought. *They can't catch me.*

"Where are you going?"

Tyche switched off her radio, cleared the circle of the ants with a leap and hit the ground running.

Tyche ran, faster than she had ever run before, faster even than when the Jade Rabbit challenged her to a race across the Shackleton Crater. Finally, her lungs and legs burned and she had to stop. She had set out without direction, but had gone up the mountain slope, close to the cold fingers. *I don't want to go back to the Base. The Brain never tells the truth either.* Black dots danced in her eyes. *They'll never catch me.*

She looked back, down towards the crater of the Secret Door. The ants were moving. They gathered into the metal sheet again. Then its sides stretched upwards until they met and formed a tubular structure. It elongated and weaved back and forth and slithered forward, faster than even Tyche could run; a metal snake. The pyramid shapes of the ants glinted in its head like teeth. Faster and faster it came, flowing over boulders and craters like it was weightless, a curtain of billowing dust behind it. She looked around for a hiding place, but she was on open ground now, except for the dark pool of the mining crater to the west.

Then she remembered something the Jade Rabbit had once said. *For anything that wants to eat you, there is something bigger that wants to eat it.*

The ant-snake was barely a hundred meters behind her now, flipping back and forth in sinusoid waves on the regolith like a shiny metal whip. She stuck out her tongue at it, accidentally tasting the sweet inner surface of her helmet. Then she made it to the sunless crater's edge.

With a few bounds, she was over the crater lip. It was like diving into icy water. Her suit groaned, and she could feel its joints stiffening up. But she kept going, towards the bottom, almost blind from the contrast between the pitch-black and the bright sun above. She followed the vibration in her soles. Boulders and pebbles rained on her helmet and she knew the ant-snake was right at her heels.

The lights of the sandworm almost blinded her. *Now.* She leaped up, as high as she could, feeling weightless, reached out for the utility ladder that she knew was on the huge machine's topside. She grabbed it, banged painfully against the worm's side, felt its thunder beneath her.

And then, a grinding, shuddering vibration as the mining machine bit into the ant-snake, rolling right over it.

Metal fragments flew into the air, glowing red-hot. One of them landed on Tyche's arm. The suit made a bubble around it and spat it out. The sandworm came to an emergency halt, and Tyche almost fell off. It started disgorging its little repair grags, and Tyche felt a stab of guilt. She sat still until her breathing calmed down and the suit's complaints about the cold got too loud.

Then she dropped to the ground and started the climb back up, towards the Secret Door.

There were still a few ants left around the Secret Door, but Tyche ignored them. They were rolling around aimlessly, and there weren't enough of them to build a transmitter. She looked up. The ship from the Great Wrong Place was still a distant star. She still had time.

Painfully, bruised limbs aching, she crawled through the Secret Door for one last time.

The Moon People were still there, waiting for her. Tyche looked at them in the eye, one by one. Then she put her hands on her hips.

"I have a wish," she said. "I am going to go away. I'm going to make the Brain obey me, this time. I'm going to go and build a Right Place, all on my own. I'm never going to forget again. So I want you all to come with me." She looked up at the Magician. "Can you do that?"

Smiling, the man in the top hat nodded, spread his white-gloved fingers and whirled his cloak that had a bright red inner lining, like a ruby—

Tyche blinked. The Other Moon was gone. She looked around. She was standing on the other side of the Old One and the Troll, except that they looked just like rocks now. And the Moon People were inside her. *I should feel heavier, carrying so many people,* she thought. But instead she was empty and light.

Uncertainly at first, then with more confidence, she started walking back up Malapert Mountain, towards the Base. Her step was not a rabbit's, nor a panther's, nor a maiden's silky tiptoe, just her very own.

Michael Alexander (1950-2012) held advanced degrees in chemistry and pharmacology and read deeply in many other fields. He was an amateur astronomer and paleontologist with a keen interest in history and a love of science fiction. His stories, published in *Fantasy & Science Fiction* and *Analog*, reflect this range. In 2010 he achieved a long-held dream and attended the Clarion West Writer's Workshop where he met K.C. Ball. K.C. called him her brother from another mother. They were working on a sequel to "The Moon Belongs to Everyone" when Michael died. Those of a fanciful bent may imagine the two of them continuing that work now.

K.C. Ball fell in love with books at a very early age and credited an elderly librarian with feeding her habit. She learned how to turn writing into a profession by working as a newspaper reporter, Public Information Officer, and a Media Relations Coordinator. She moved to Seattle, Washington, in 2007 with her life partner, Rachael Buchanan, where they married in 2013.

In 2008, she began writing full time and the next year won the Writer's of the Future Award with her story, "Coward's Steel." She met Michael Alexander at the Clarion West Writers Workshop and the two formed an instant and lasting bond. K.C. had a quick wit and a wonderful sense of humor and always seemed to bring out the best in those around her. She passed suddenly on August 25, 2018, and is sorely missed by all who knew her.

THE MOON BELONGS TO EVERYONE
Michael Alexander and K.C. Ball

Mankind has always ventured into the unknown.

We take risks, accept surprises and adapt to new experiences. Such quests are worthwhile in and of themselves. They represent one way in which we express the human spirit. This country was built on that willingness to take risks. America is a great nation and a great nation must remain an exploring nation if it wishes to maintain its greatness.

I say today that the sky is no longer the limit.

I pledge that our nation will venture out into the unknown. We will take the risks, accept the surprises and eagerly await what lays beyond the bounds of our world. What we start today with my words will lead to an American walking on the surface of the Moon before the end of the next decade. And before twenty years have passed, I expect to see Americans venturing to Mars.

I want John Gillespie Magee's hopeful words to become America's reali-
ty. "With silent lifting mind, I have trod the untrespassed sanctity of space;
put out my hand to touched the face of God."
                    —**President Richard M. Nixon, State of the Union address,**
                                                      11 January 1962.

26 NOVEMBER 1979

I eased from the staging-shack airlock, just at the edge of the mammoth cylindrical melting tank. Beyond the open lip of the tank, a forty-feet-long hollow
tube of ice waited, gleaming in the raw sunlight. I couldn't shake the notion it
was a mammoth bullet ready to be loaded into the barrel of an enormous gun.

Sixty miles below *Odyssey's* selenocentric orbit, the Moon's sterile surface
looked pristine, crater walls and mountain peaks casting crisp black shadows
in the harsh sunlight.

I moved toward the ice. Maneuvering in a pressure suit still felt cumbersome
despite eight weeks' recent training. The resistance of the sandwiched layers of
the suit. A steady flow of chilled air. The constant hiss of communications gear.

All that hadn't become second nature. Not yet.

But I had all the practice I could ever want ahead of me, a twelve-month
work contract at Rockefeller Base, with an option to renew. In less than six
hours, I'd be on the Moon.

All through the weeks of training, I'd looked forward to being on a different world, doing different work. Beginning a new life. My past refused to let
me go, though.

"Laura Kerrigan," a man shouted, as I disembarked the cislunar tug at
Selene Station.

A big fellow arrowed toward me, swimming the station's zero-gee as if
he'd been born to it. He reminded me of Thomas Mitchell, the actor who
played Scarlett's father in *Gone with the Wind*.

Wide and solid, graying. Just a bit past sixty, maybe.

"How the hell's your old man?" he called, as he drew near.

I didn't know the man, but his face jarred loose memories of training-doc-
ument photos. I'd played job-related undercover games too long to flinch at
his approach. I let him wrap his arms around me in a friendly bear hug.

"I'm Tom Garver, Kerrigan," he whispered in my ear. "Call me Tom. Pretend I'm a friend of your father. Ask me for the tour I promised you." The
name produced more memories.

And so I called him Tom, we played our little scene and I gave up what sleep
I might have managed, in the little time I'd have on Selene Station, to ride pillion
with Garver on an open-cockpit work sled across the five-mile gap to *Odyssey*.

The Mars ship.

"I'm construction manager," Garver said, on the low-power suit-to-suit link, during the ride. "I got a situation that fits your old line of work. I'd be grateful for your point-of-view."

I heard: *You scratch my back, I'll scratch yours.*

It couldn't hurt to look. God knew I could use a friend in power. That was all I could ever do, though. *Look.* I no longer wore a badge, couldn't officially investigate anything.

That bastard, Liam Childs, had seen to that.

I reached the melting tank's shadow-line. A thin fiberglass cable stretched into the darkness of the tank from the big eye bolt melted into the near end of the ice tube. Sixteen tons of reaction mass for the voyage to Mars, waiting to be melted, and another chunk of ice would be on its way up from the surface in less than three days.

"*Odyssey,* I'm ready."

"Roger." Garver's baritone rumbled in my headphones.

A thin line ran from a tie-off on the shack bulkhead to an anchor point half-way along the ice. Two suited figures waited for me there. One of them held a heat-cutter.

I focused on memorized procedure. *Hook a suit safety line to the cable. Squeeze a quick burp from the maneuvering unit. Don't use your hands on the line to stop unless you have to.* I slid along the line, burped the other way at what I figured to be half-way, and stopped just short of the suited figures.

Just like I knew what I was doing.

The glare visors hid their faces from me.

"Who's in charge?" I asked.

"I am." A woman's voice. She lifted her arm, showed a red supervisor's band ringing the bicep of her white EVA suit.

Should have spotted that.

I turned to the second figure, the suit marked by a blue band. "You the one who found it?"

"Yeah." A man's voice. He tapped the frozen surface with a gloved finger. "Came to rig the lines to pull the ice inside. Saw that in there."

I moved close to examine the glittering surface, wiped my glove across the ice. "That looks like a—"

The woman interrupted, sounding insistent. "It's a foreign object in the ice."

"Yeah," the man said. "A foreign *object.*" He sounded as if he wanted to be somewhere else.

"How long will it take you to cut into that?" I asked.

"A few minutes. No more than five," the woman said. "It's warmed up quite a bit."

"Do it."

"I'm going back inside." The man tugged at the safety line and pulled himself around to face me.

I blocked his way. "I want that opened. You need to—"

"I don't *need* to do anything. This sort of stuff isn't in my contract."

The radio crackled. "Garver here. You two want to finish out your contract and get your bonus, do what you're told."

"No argument from me, Boss," the woman said.

Nothing from the man.

"You hear me, McAlvany?" Garver demanded.

"Copy," the man said, at last.

The woman pulled herself into position and helped the man brace the tip of the cutter against the glistening surface of the ice.

"Clear," the man called.

He keyed the unit. The resistance coil inside the thin shaft heated fast. The cutter eased into the ice. vapor streamed off into space. With the surety of a butcher opening a carcass, the man ran the cutter in a smooth circle two feet in diameter.

Finally, he backed away. He and the woman braced against their tethers, pushing at the disk with their booted feet. They muscled it into the cylinder.

I got no argument from either one when I waved them to the side. I pulled myself into place and peered into the hole.

The top of a suit helmet showed itself. Its side had been badly dented, but it remained intact. I reached through, still awkward in the suit, grabbed the locking ring and spun the suit.

"Well?" Garver demanded.

I studied the cold, dead face within the helmet. No sign of trauma. Then I rotated the helmet away, so I could examine the rest of the suited figure. A ragged gash ran along the left suit leg.

"It's not an empty suit," I said. "There is a body inside. Might be a suicide or unreported accident, but I wouldn't rule out murder."

A pause. "Copy that," Garver said.

I had time to consider what I'd seen outside on the lonely float along the ship's central corridor. With the minimum light and the quiet, the ship felt sterile, as if it were waiting to be used. As well it should, it was brand new.

We'd read all about *Odyssey* in orientation classes. A two-year build. Eighty men and women in orbit, sixty on the surface of the Moon. Twelve months of work, three months rotated back to Earth to rest and recover.

That's what the documentation said, anyway.

Construction had been completed three weeks ago, three days behind schedule. Garver and his finish crew were racing to catch up. Some of the orbital crew still waited on Selene Station for a berth back down to Earth.

Those who remained on-board were there to finish electrical tests, bring the NERVA reactors to full functionality and handle the last of the water uploads.

The schedule had no flex. The launch window for America's first manned interplanetary shot—on 1 January, 1980—drew near, and all Americans knew that if the ship didn't launch, the Russians would win the race to Mars.

The remaining workers bunked in the staging shack, back by the melting cylinder. Garver had set up quarters in the crew dormitory onboard *Odyssey* instead of staying in Selene Station. I wasn't sure I'd care to do that. Empty, the ship felt spooky, filled with strange echoes. It smelled funny, too, like the stink of long-used, over-loaded electrical equipment.

At least, I half-expected that.

"First time you go through an airlock, take off your suit," an instructor had told me, at the tavern down the road from the Florida training site. "You'll catch an acrid odor. The smell of ozone. We call it catching a whiff of vacuum."

He had plied me with drinks and stories most of the night, hoping for the same poke and tickle Childs had been after.

Neither had succeeded.

I grabbed the anchor bar mounted outside Garver's office, to brace against reaction, and knocked.

"Come on in," Garver called.

I pushed the door open, pulled myself inside. The room was good-sized, designed as quarters for six crew members. Military tidy, too, but full of Tom Garver. Books velcroed to every open surface. Engineering plans and photographs taped to bulkheads.

A framed photo of Garver in dress Naval uniform—a full commander—hung on the bulkhead above the built-in desk. A shot of Garver and President Reagan, shaking hands, shared the wall.

Scribbled notes stuck here and there. A floating ten-foot-long scale model of the ship, tethered at four points to a work table, took up the center of the room.

Sections of the scale model had been pulled away to show compartments. Two long cylinders in front of a shielded section containing the NERVA nuclear propulsion units, their heat exchangers looking like big ribbed wings. The ship's ancestry was evident. It had been birthed from modified upper-stage sections of the Saturn V rockets, as had Selene Station.

The place reeked of Captain Black tobacco. I wondered how Garver kept a pipe lit in weightlessness, not to mention how he got away with smoking in the first place.

The man had to have serious clout.

"Thanks for going out there, Kerrigan," Garver said.

"If I can call you Tom, you can call me Laura."

"All right, Laura." The construction manager straddled a saddle at the work desk. He wore his salt-and-pepper hair in a crew-cut, over a round, deeply seamed face that demanded trust. I hoped such trust would be deserved.

Garver waved for me to join him before a compact television monitor. "Come look at this," he said.

A color broadcast flickered on the screen. Garver tapped it. "Sent a crewman with a hard-wired camera out so I can tape everything while they pull the body out of the ice."

I watched over Garver's shoulder. Whoever handled the video camera knew enough to shoot with the Sun. The picture almost matched broadcast quality, caught all the details.

"Good camera work," I said.

"Good camera," Garver said. "A Betacam. Great for location shooting. Networks haven't seen one yet. I got six. They're for the mission, all mine until the ship leaves."

"I don't know that one."

"State-of-the-art from Sony."

"Japanese?"

"Yeah. The little bastards turn out good product."

The camera image zoomed in on the crushed helmet. The crew finished sliding the rigid body from the cylinder, a tight fit. They weren't being particularly careful.

"We've *got* to get that ice melted and in-tank," Garver said. "Sorry if they're screwing up your crime scene."

"*My* crime scene?"

"You're the only cop I've got."

I shook my head. "I went out there as a favor, Tom, gave you my professional opinion, but I'm not a marshal anymore."

"I know. I did my research," Garver said, taking up his pipe. "You got laid off fourteen months ago."

"I got fired."

Childs had done a real smear job, made sure my name was deeply buried in the mud. I hadn't even been able to get a private security job, at a time when companies were begging for former cops.

That was why I'd taken the moon job with LTC. They were so desperate they'd hire almost anyone.

"Want to get back at Childs?" Garver's hands seemed to move on their own accord, as he packed tobacco into the pipe.

"How could—"

"I know people who owe me favors," he said.

"But—"

He waved away my words. "I always do my research, I know what he did to you. You handle this for me, you'll be back on Earth. Full benefits, your jacket cleared. If that's what you want."

I felt as if I'd been pushed off safe footing into deep water. My father was a cop, his father before him, too. Working law enforcement had been the only thing I'd ever wanted, had ever done. Having to deal with the loss of my badge, not being able to land another law enforcement job, almost killed me.

"You okay?" Garver asked.

"Yeah."

Suck it up, kid, my father used to say.

"You want your job back?"

"Yeah."

Garver nodded. "Five deaths in two years in orbit. All verifiable accidents. The surface rate's been higher, but that's mining for you."

He tapped the screen with his pipe stem. "But this . . . this was no accident and the notion of murder pisses me off no end. I want to catch whoever did it. Even more I want to get my hands on whoever thinks he can mess with my schedule."

"Has there been other sabotage?"

Garver frowned. "Four times I'm sure of. Others, maybe. I don't run the show down there, so I don't see all the paperwork. There's been money lost, project down-time and injuries. Never murder, though."

"Could it have been the Russians?" I asked.

"Naw. The military types on Selene Station watch the Reds pretty close. Besides, they're way too busy with their own Mars ship down in low-earth orbit."

He glanced at me. "You see it?"

I knew what he wanted to hear. "Ugliest thing I ever saw."

Garver nodded. "It's different design philosophy. Brute-force but proven tech. They don't have nuclear thermal engines, so it's LOX-hydrogen for the trip out. Hypergolics for the ride home, dump everything and land in a couple of Soyuz capsules."

He paused to try to light the pipe. The match went out before it caught.

"Why did *we* go with nuclear engines?" I asked.

Garver shrugged. "Hell if I know, I'm not that kind of engineer. The way I hear it, nukes increase specific impulse, so you use less fuel."

He struck another match without success.

"And building the ship here in low lunar orbit cuts even more reaction mass, compared to LEO," he said. "No cryogenics means simpler tankage and so on. Mining metals and water on the moon's cheaper than fifty, sixty Saturn launches to LEO. It's all supposed to save time and money."

"How's that worked out so far?" I asked.

Garver grinned. "Who can say? Will American free enterprise beat the godless Communists? Not my department. My job's to make sure this crate's in shape to leave orbit New Year's Day."

He paused and drew a breath. "What were we talking about?"

"The miners," I said.

"Yeah. Old story. Work conditions suck. They don't get paid enough, don't get to go home enough. They want a union."

I remembered growing up in eastern Kentucky coal country, watching my friends' fathers come home from work too tired to scrub the blackness from their skin before they fell into bed. Seeing retired miners, old men before their time, slumped on dilapidated porches next to green bottles of oxygen.

Appalachian astronauts.

"Will they get a union?"

Garver fiddled with his pipe, not looking at me. "Someday," he said. "We can't afford one now."

I didn't say a word.

He spread his hands. "Laura, I sympathize with them. My old man was shop steward for his ship fitter's local at the Philly Navy Yard during the big war. He built the ships and I was a swabbie sailing on one of them."

This time he looked me in the eye. "Pop could sing The *Internationale* as well as Debs, but he knew there was a war to be won. Just like now, except the war's cold.

"I hate having to act like a company asshole, but I've got a fast ship to build and I'm sending it in harm's way. I've got to know if there's more trouble coming at me from the Moon."

"What do you want me to do?" I asked.

"Go down there. Poke around and stir the pot. Find out who's screwing with me. I don't care what you have to do. Just fix it. I've got thirty-six days until launch."

Garver glanced at his wristwatch.

"Speaking of time, let's get you back. Drop's three hours and . . . twenty-seven minutes.

"A scheduled truckload. Six engines, you and a guy named Anderson. I expect you know him from the training classes. They're expecting you, know you used to be a cop, but they know you've been through training, too."

"Understood."

He studied me for a moment. "Schedule's tight, but I can give you a little time to think it over."

I shook my head. "I don't need to think about it, Tom. I'm in."

Garver grinned. "I like a woman who knows her mind."

"So let's get going," I said.

He rubbed at his crew cut. "Just one thing—"

"Go on. I don't bite."

Garver shook his head. "I don't believe that for a second."

I raised my hand, palm out and fingers up. "You don't have to worry about me."

He shook his head. "Look, I'm old school. My pop taught me to take care of women, years ago before ERA became the law."

"I *said* I'd be all right."

"Don't get your Irish up," he said. "Just be careful."

I laid my hand on his shoulder. "You sound like my old man. It's sweet."

"Make fun of an old man all you like, but I mean it. I've read your jacket, Laura, know what you've done. I'll bet you're hell-on-wheels. But so was Leatherman, the other cop I sent."

He glanced at the monitor. The camera remained focused on the stove-in helmet. I tipped my chin toward the image. "That was Leatherman?"

"Yeah."

He struck another match and sucked on his pipe. It wouldn't catch. He tossed it at the desk, where it bounced back. He grabbed it without looking. "I don't know why I bother with that thing. Keeping it lit in zero gee's a bitch."

I checked my harness one more time. The soles of my feet tingled. My stomach fluttered.

Getting ready to take a no-frills ride.

Another suited figure stood opposite me, focusing on the harness, too. Around us, six recovered ascent engines had been strapped to the open platform of the landing truck, flaring expansion nozzles almost touching.

No pressurized cabin, no flight couches. No one who'd done the drop before to hold our hands and tell us not to worry. America's Lunar Technologies Consortium didn't spend a dollar when a penny was enough. I know Armstrong and Aldrin landed standing up, too. They had walls, though, but LTC had studies that said walls were unnecessary mass.

Someone with a nasty sense of humor had named the truck, marked it in big, red letters sprayed on its side. **Thumper**.

I closed my eyes and tried to think of other things.

The ride up to earth orbit came to mind. Six men and women crammed into a stripped Apollo capsule like stacked bodies in a morgue, going into space in a claustrophobic can. In Low Earth Orbit we had transferred to the cislunar tug for another two days to lunar orbit.

As I waited, I wondered if I'd signed up on the wrong side once again. When I did academy, it all looked black and white. You were either a good guy or a bad guy.

These days, it seemed the only thing I'd ever done, all those years as a cop, was keep the folks who didn't have a dime from taking one from those that did.

Got to pay the bills, kid, my father used to say. Maybe so, but I wasn't sure anymore if I cared for the cost.

I checked the telltale on my oxygen. Like the truck, the suits were simplified. No sophisticated adsorption canisters, no complex rebreathing circuit, just a six-hour tank of air.

Four, now.

"*Thumper*, Selene Station here."

Below, the lunar landscape slid by. I let the other rider respond. A thirty-ish fellow. Anderson. He'd proven during training he loved the sound of his own voice.

"Go ahead, Selene." Anderson again.

"You all ready for de-orbit burn?"

"Damned straight."

I answered in the affirmative, as well.

"Copy four, *Thumper*. Go for DOB. Ignition, thirty seconds."

I closed my fingers around one of the grab bars welded to the engine cowling and counted to myself. The truck's engine fired when I reach one-thousand-thirty-one.

Not bad.

My feet pressed against the grated floor. I set my jaw to keep my teeth from chattering in time to the vibrations. I felt the roar of the engine in my bones. My stomach fluttered again at the return of gravity. I counted down on the thirty-second burn. The engine cut off on the mark.

"*Thumper*, Selene. Burn nominal. Powered descent initiates in fifty-seven minutes at two-hundred-thirty nautical miles from Rockefeller Base."

"Copy, Selene." Anderson again.

I took in the view.

We had just under another hour of standing ahead of us, watching the moon roll beneath as we fell toward the surface in a long computer-planned arc following the terminator around the Moon. At the end, the truck would make its final powered descent into the darkness of the polar crater that sheltered America's Rockefeller Base.

I should be scared, I knew that. I stood on an open, free-falling platform sixty miles up, loaded with heavy equipment. The LTC preventable-accident record sucked vacuum, too.

It didn't matter.

I had gotten used to the view by now, and I loved amusement parks. The roller coasters and rail slides. The free-fall drops. I figured to enjoy every second on the greatest thrill ride any engineer had ever imagined.

I was facing in our direction of motion. As we came over the south pole I was watching the approaching horizon over the edge of the platform as the earth rose; bright, half full, distant, stunningly beautiful. I hummed the opening notes of *Thus Spake Zarathustra*.

"What's that?" Anderson asked over the suit link.

I didn't bother to explain. "Music from a movie," I said.

An hour later and fifty thousand feet above the surface, two hundred-thirty miles up-range from target, the engine flared to life again, slowing us.

At ten thousand feet, the landscape below barely crawling by, the truck pitched over to a near-vertical attitude. I saw our destination, a crater filled with darkness.

At three thousand feet, I caught sight of the lights outlining the bull's eye layout of the buried habitat. At seven hundred feet, I spotted scattered equipment and the base's junk pile in the lessening shadow near the east rim wall.

Suited figures moved about, here and there. A rover rolled toward the rim. Landing beacons flashed a rhythmic red, west of the habitat. All so familiar, so ingrained in my memory from training films and countless photographs it seemed as if I had come home.

But it felt as if we were coming in too fast.

My hands itched for a steering wheel, the old passenger's dilemma. There wasn't any. Either the computer did the job or it didn't. If it didn't, Anderson and I, the ascent engines, too, would become part of one more shattered monument to Mankind's reach for the planets.

The engines would be missed the most.

In the end, the truck slowed, hovered for a moment and sank to the lunar surface without incident, just as it had many times before. The engine shut down. Two suited figures skipped to the truck, began to check the cargo. They ignored us.

"This is Rockefeller Base." A woman's voice.

As opposed to, say, Detroit?

"We hear you," Anderson said.

"You two can come on inside any time you like," the woman said. "I'll meet you at the door."

I unhooked my harness, released the straps that held my duffel and the small equipment case Garver had provided me. I slid between the bells of two engines and stepped to the ladder.

Anderson arrived first. He began his climb down without even a glance at me. He paused at the last rung. "Watch this last step, Kerrigan," he said. "It's a lulu."

He dropped his duffel, let go the ladder and fell slowly the last few feet to the surface.

"Asshole," I whispered.

I forgot the common band was always on.

Anderson scooped up his duffel, turned away from the truck. And as he skip-stepped toward the habitat, he showed a gloved middle finger over his shoulder.

I hiked to the habitat, almost catching up with Anderson, taking care with the low-gravity gait they taught us in training. A skip-step that had looked strange in demonstration, in the films we'd seen. It worked well enough in practice. *Weight isn't mass,* they endlessly reminded us in training. *Take your time.*

The loose regolith in this area had been sucked up long ago as aggregate for the sulfur concrete used to build the habitat, so I didn't kick up any dust and left no footprints as I moved toward the rounded gray mounds that were the dormitories and common spaces of the base. Poured tubes half-buried in the floor of the crater. No windows, no exterior lights, except twenty-four-inch tall, green-neon script letters that blinked out **WEST ENTRANCE** above a rectangle of light. It was a nice touch.

Further to the west, I spotted the adit to one of the rim-wall mines, marked by a red neon arrow, pointing down. Someone had painted **ABANDON ALL HOPE, YE WHO ENTER HERE** in man-high red letters on the wall above the arrow.

As I closed on the entry lock, I passed collections of skeletal equipment. High chain-link fences, topped by razor-wire with access through a locked gate, surrounded some of them. Pharmaceutical plants. The fences kept the riff-raff out.

As we reached the habitat, the broad glass door beneath the sign swung open and a suited figure stepped out. The left leg and the right arm of the suit had been painted in an intricate, colorful pattern. A swirling band of red, blue and green crossed the torso at an angle, intertwining flowers, just like a complex tattoo inked upon a naked body.

Within the blossoms, I made out a name. **ZENDER**.

"Welcome to the Moon, folks." The same woman who had called them at the truck. "I'm Posey Zender, LTC personnel liaison. You can call me Posey. Wipe your feet before you come inside."

I returned the greeting. Anderson waved and moved inside.

Beyond the door, the airlock was a revolving drum, not too different from a darkroom safe door, except with gasketed edges, and made of plate glass, like the front door to some New York City office building. Anderson was already inside, moving like a man looking for the can.

"This lock made me nervous, when I first got here," Posey said. "But it's safe. Cheaper and easier than a pressure lock. Fool-proof, too, with fewer complex parts. Cuts down on repair time overhead. LTC figured if you have all the oxygen you need, conservation isn't a necessity. It just takes a long, hard push."

I kept my mouth shut and marked the lock as a place not to spend much time near. It might be fool-resistant, but I'd seen too often that nothing ever was completely fool-proof.

Beyond the lock, Anderson headed for a glass door to the habitats. He'd hung his plain-white suit in one of the twenty-five glass-faced lockers that filled the ten-feet-wide habitat section. About half the lockers contained vacuum suits. Most of them had been painted in some fashion.

Not all were as colorful as Posey's suit, but each carried some sort of statement from of its owner. A full-body skeleton. The alien from that Sigourney Weaver movie a couple years back. Flags of all sorts. Daffy Duck chased by Marvin the Martian.

"What's with the suits?" I asked.

"It's called freedom of expression," Posey said. "Everybody gets free rein to paint their suit anyway they like. There's always a couple extras at each lock."

"I'm not an artist."

Someone will help if you want. Any ideas?"

"I'll think of something."

"Whatever. Find a locker, stash your suit," Posey said. "This is only temporary. I'll get you a locker closer to your work assignment, once you're settled in."

I found a vacant locker, focused on removing my suit and wiping off its surfaces. Posey did the same. She turned out to be rail-thin, a forty-something, horse-faced woman with close-cut russet hair. She wore a green jumpsuit with a name patch over her heart.

Out of the suit, the tube felt chilly. It had a grungy look to it, too. Not overtly dirty but edge-worn, as if someone had been working on it with a dull file. Sounds bouncing from the concrete walls. The expanded metal floor had a hollow echo. The lights burned dimmer than in the trainer, half not even working. A glass door closed off the tube at the far end. A second airlock would have been nice. A scrolling, lighted sign above the door showed time and date. **1320 26 November 1979**.

Posey headed toward the door. "C'mon. Let's get you settled in. You go to work tomorrow."

"Do I get O.J.T?"

She laughed. "Yeah. Sure."

29 NOVEMBER 1979

The dark closed in as I stepped out of the airlock onto the surface of the Moon. Sunlight caught the tips of rim-wall peaks three thousand feet above me, but didn't touch the crater floor. The only real illumination where I stood came from a scatter of lights on the assembly line and my helmet lamps.

Edie DuPree, my shift partner, waited. She had worked with me patiently for the past three days, showing me the ropes. First day, I asked about days off. DuPree smirked and shook her head.

"Read your contract," she said. "Twelve hours on and twelve off. Seven days a week."

With DuPree's help, I learned to set up an ascent engine assembly while getting used to working on the lunar surface. To inspect a recycled RL-10 engine and attach it to the circular support structure. To test the pump tanks and fittings.

I felt confident I was ready to move on.

DuPree agreed. "You got your moon legs, Kerrigan. Let's build an icicle." She waved me on. I moved with her, the low-gravity gait now familiar.

"Remember. Think through every move," DuPree said, for the hundredth time. "If you don't know, don't pretend you do. You can kill yourself, if you have to, but for God's sake don't take me with you."

"Got it," I said. "Measure twice and cut once."

"Right. Training's over. We got to catch up for those three days. *Odyssey* burns at midnight on New Year's Eve and we've got to finish filling her reaction-mass tanks before she leaves."

"Why midnight?"

She looked at me as if I were a child. "The bad thing about leaving from Low Moon Orbit is that delta-V change in orbital planes creates a narrow window of opportunity. But it doesn't have to be midnight. That's pure show biz. They have to go at midnight because the President says they do, the People say they do, Corporate P.R. says they do. Paper puts up with anything."

Ahead were four large cylindrical tanks, two of them three times taller than the other two. Ladders ran up opposite sides of each tank.

Over them, a stringer crane ran on a track to the launch area. The engine assembly we had worked on last shift waited in a cradle there.

"Casting tanks," DuPree said, pointing to remind me. "The short ones for the LOX, tall ones for the liquid hydrogen. They poured one set yesterday after our shift and they're almost finished cooling. The two at the end are complete. They pulled the cope, froze the caps last shift. Time to build the stack."

"This whole thing still seems a bit nutty."

"Yeah, but it works. Since we have to lift the water to orbit anyway, why not save on raw materials and make the water the fuel tanks? It's fifty degrees absolute down here in the shadow. That ice is rock hard. We shoot it up to *Odyssey* where they melt it into the reaction tanks. Then they bring the engine assembly back down for another run."

I looked around. "Where are the winch controls?"

DuPree held up her gauntlets. "Right here. The motor they sent up cracked a bearing from the cold, first month. The second one lasted sixty days. They've been promising a redesigned one for eighteen months. Until they send one up, we use muscle."

"They didn't mention that in training."

"Lots of things they didn't mention, trust me."

Trust you? Maybe someday.

DuPree grabbed the chain dangling from the gang pulley and dragged the winch over to a short tank. I skipped to the tank. DuPree gestured toward a ladder. "Up you go."

I hopped up the rungs. As I came over the top I saw the circular disk of ice that would become the top of the tank, looking like a raw glass casting for a big telescope mirror.

"Heads up," DuPree said.

I grabbed the descending ring and guided it over the ice.

"Let me know when it's about four inches below the upper edge." I could hear the effort in DuPree's voice.

"Down. Down. Down. *Stop.*" I said.

I saw the chain swing, slap lightly against the tank, and I expected to hear a clang. None came.

Stay alert. No aural cues.

DuPree's helmet appeared over the opposite side. "Good job, good job. Ice looks good. You steady the ring while I lock it."

I leaned forward, stretched my arms to each side, trying to get the ring at as even a height as possible. I felt it snug up.

"Hands clear," DuPree said, grunting.

The ring settled into place.

"Sure it won't slip and break?" I asked.

"It—oh. Ice. Remember. That ice is fifty degrees above absolute zero. It's granite."

"Copy that," I said.

"Let's get this baby out of the cradle."

We both climbed back down.

I was surprised at how much effort something as simple as climbing a ladder at one sixth gee took. Something one of the Florida trainers had said popped into my head.

Half your work will be against the suit itself. Take your time. The biggest danger is overheating, even if it's cold outside. The Universe as Thermos bottle.

"Does the ice ever get stuck?" I asked.

"Once in a while. There's heating coils in the tank wall just in case. Most of the time, it's no problem. Let's give this a try.

We both pulled on the chain. The compound pulley above us rotated smoothly.

"The ice expands when the water freezes," DuPree said. "The tank's designed for that. It contracts some as it chills down, enough to give you windage."

Three more pulls. I looked up to see the ice peeking over the tank rim. "Looking good?" I asked.

"Lookin' sweet."

We continued pulling, a bit at a time, until the ice cylinder cleared the tank. "Okay, let's slide this down to the engine mount."

We took a step away and pulled. The winch resisted for a moment, then slid a few feet, ice dangling below.

"There's a clutch fitting that won't let it run free, not that you should trust it," DuPree said. "Last thing you want's for that sucker to take off on its own. Remember, weight isn't mass. How you doing?"

"Five by," I said. "Actually having fun."

"That's what the virgin said. By this time I'm a hooker."

I grinned. "In it for the money, huh?"

A pause. "No, I see it as my own small contribution to mankind's leap for the stars. Of course, I'm in it for the money. It's my job. Besides, I'm not going anywhere."

I remembered we were on an open circuit and made no reply. We slowly walked the ice down the hundred yards to the engine cradle, with not much more effort than pulling a child's wagon.

"Okay," DuPree said. "When we're done, that hunk's gotta be centered, true and flat. Let's take our time."

"Copy that."

We moved the cylinder slowly over the flat circle of ice on top of the engine platform.

"Okay," DuPree said. "I'm going to lower, you guide. Take your time. Get it right. Remember, that thing masses a lot more than it weighs."

The placement went uneventfully. I guided with one hand, the way I had steered sections of concrete sewer pipe, two summers on a job during college. "We're good, let it down."

DuPree lowered it the last quarter inch, walked over to inspect. "Good. I just got to go up top to check if it's level. Sometimes the casting can be off a bit."

"Can I try it?"

I felt DuPree give me the once over from behind her visor. Finally, she pulled a bubble level out of a suit leg pocket and handed it over.

"I'll hoist you up. Take cross measurements in the middle and at three points along the edge. Gotta be within a degree of vertical. The bubble's ethane, shouldn't freeze if you're quick about it."

DuPree hopped down past the cradle, grabbed a chain hanging from another pulley. Dragging it over, she handed a hook to me.

"Hold on tight," she said, and began hauling me up. A minute later I cleared the top of ice cylinder, let go of the chain and stepped onto the surface.

"Okay," I said. "Let's try this."

Bouncing to my knees, I put the level on the ice and studied the bubble. Less than half a degree. I inched sideways. Crosswise, dead center.

As I crawled toward the edge something hit me in the back. It wasn't much, a tap, but I wasn't expecting it. I fell forward. My chest hit the edge as I slid off the top, helmet down, toward the ground twenty feet below.

I opened my eyes and tried to sit up. "What the f—"

DuPree pushed me back onto the cot. "You're inside, safe."

The old line, *Must be a definition of the word 'safe' I'm not familiar with*, popped into my head.

"What happened?" I asked.

"Near as I can tell, when you let go the chain you must have given it a push. It came around and it caught you in the back."

"I must have hit my head in the fall. It knocked me out."

"First fall up here's scary. Maybe you fainted." DuPree offered a glass of something.

I accepted it, took a sip. It tasted like strawberry Kool-Aid. "The damned fall seemed to last forever."

DuPree's lips quirked. "Under three seconds, but no worse than falling four feet, back on Earth. Gives you a jolt, but it won't kill you. Just don't try it from the top of a fifty-foot hydrogen tank. That *will* kill you."

Was it an accident? Did you try to kill me, DuPree? Or try to scare me?

I took another sip, collecting my thoughts. I wasn't sure if I had pushed the hook and chain away or not. Either way, I'd have to be watch my step with even more care from now on.

"Just so you know," I said. "I don't faint from fear." I swirled the liquid in the glass. "This stuff's terrible. Got anything to dilute it with?"

"No alcohol allowed on the base."

I looked at her. "And you call yourself a miner?"

DuPree grinned. She walked to a desk and opened a drawer, pulled out a plastic container and another glass. "Got a vacuum still out behind the Ruzic cryostats," she said.

I held out my tumbler. DuPree cut the red liquid with the same amount of clear, then poured herself an equal dose. We touched glasses and drank. It was a surprise.

"I know it's an old line," I said, "But this is smooth hooch. Real grade-A moonshine, and I know my 'shine."

I polished off the drink in two gulps.

DuPree grinned. "If we ever get decent shipping costs, we could sell this stuff for good money, Earth side. Beats Stoli hollow." She collected my empty tumbler. "Regs say you rest for rest of shift."

"And let everyone think I'm a wuss *and* an incompetent?" I pushed up onto my elbows. "Get the medic to look at my pupils and let's get back to work."

"I'm all you get, so we go by regs. There's no medic, not since the last one did walkabout three months ago. Never did find her and they haven't shipped in a new one yet. Posey says it's *problematic* finding tech staff. I figure the real reason is the Company's too cheap to pay for one, this close to launch."

"Posey does seem harried, doesn't she?"

DuPree looked at her glass. She held the bottle out to me. I shook my head.

"Posey's like one of those thought experiments I read about in high school. A perfect, frictionless, rolling bitch." She knocked the drink back.

Later, I lay in my bunk, staring at the ceiling and sorting things out. Item: nobody would talk about Leatherman. Item: there was no evidence that what happened was anything but an accident. Item: It was remarkably easy to have an accident down here.

Posey could have done him in, or arranged it, if she had something to hide in her handling of the project and thought Leatherman was sniffing too hard. Her moonshadow-cold exterior might be cover for a deep insecurity. Or she might just be frozen to the core.

DuPree could have done it. She was hands-down the best roustabout on the surface; everyone I asked said so. Setting up an accident would be easy for her. The question was motive.

For that matter, any of a half-dozen miners could have done it. Bumping shoulders was easy here. The almost total lack of privacy, the grinding schedule, the seeming indifference of the Corporation to legitimate complaints. I'd arrested more than one man who had murdered because, "I didn't like the way he looked at me." When the moon was waiting to kill you just because you were here, nerves could get raw fast.

I had insufficient data. I had a long list of suspects with plenty of means, plenty of opportunity, even if motives were unclear. Shift change in four hours. The people I was getting to know would be all over me, razzing me for all they were worth.

Secretly glad it hadn't been them who'd taken the fall.

3 DECEMBER 1979

Sit-down meals were served every six hours. I wandered into the dining room just after the purely arbitrary 12:00 noon GMT chimed over the public address system. An hour until my shift began. I paused at the door, sniffed and wrinkled my nose. I knew that smell.

Chipped beef.

At the hot table I picked up a plate and spooned what looked like lumpy wheat paste onto toast. At least there was salad. I'd asked DuPree where the fresh greens came from.

"Little bootleg greenhouse, next to the still," she said. "I'll show you when we get the chance."

Last time the still had been in a side tunnel of the biggest mine. It seemed to move around.

I added instant mashed potatoes that looked like they'd been scavenged from old stores in a fallout shelter. There were empty chairs at a corner table with a fellow I had met a few days before.

He looked up as I approached. "Hey."

I cocked my head. "You mind, Jake?"

He gestured acceptance. "Help yourself."

I sat down.

"You ready to go home yet, Kerrigan?" he asked.

"You can call me Laura, Jake."

"You do what you like. I'll stick with Kerrigan. It's less personal." He turned his head to cough. "'Scuse me."

I heard home in Kadar's voice. Eastern Kentucky or maybe just over the Tug River in West Virginia.

I took a mouthful of chipped beef. It tasted the way it looked. "Jake, you're an old hand here. You've been up, what, two years now?"

"Twenty-three months, nine days and—" he looked at the clock on the wall. "—four hours." He coughed again.

"Excuse me again."

"You had a doctor listen to that?"

He shrugged. "The last medic told me I had sinus problems, just before she went walkabout. I figure I got Moon lung. The damned dust's everywhere. Funny thing. I came up here to get away from the dust in the coal mines back home."

Another thing they hadn't talked about in training.

"Can't the company do anything about it?" I asked.

"They could. They've talked electrostatic precipitators for years. That's all they do. Talk. How long you sign up for?"

I chewed, swallowed, decided maybe it was time to lose a couple of pounds. "Year, option for two."

"It'll be two, trust me. There's never enough return berths and the military up on Selene get priority. I've been on the wait list so long the ink's almost evaporated." He swallowed a mouthful of mashed potatoes and pushed his tray away.

"You know, you sound like Leatherman," he said.

"Who's Leatherman?" I asked.

"Who *was* Leatherman, you mean," Kadar said. "Short-termer. Asked lots of questions, just like you."

"What happened to him?"

"Up and disappeared ten days ago. We all marked it off to a walkabout. Sometimes it happens early like that. Scuttle now is they found him in an ice tank up in orbit. Hell of a way to go." Kadar coughed again. "At least he got off this rock."

I toyed with a forkful of lettuce. "Didn't anyone notice he was gone? I mean, there's procedures. Hell, I memorized a bunch of them."

Kadar waved his fork. "Sure, there's procedures. There's schedules, too. We ain't met one of those since this operation started. Supposed to be three teams out working on the same rocket, round the clock. That's what the rules say. We're lucky to get one full team every shift."

I sat silent, hoping he'd say more. He did.

"Leatherman probably slipped and fell in. It's dark out there. Whoever his partner was must've figured he went inside for something. Next shift put the cap on. Before you know it he's on his way to orbit."

"No one looked?"

"No one looked because no one thought to look," Kadar said. "There ain't no procedure seventy-eight, paragraph fourteen. *Look for a body inside the tank before sealing.*"

"Who was his partner that day?" I asked.

Kadar studied me. "You ask a lot of questions, for someone who says she *used* to be a cop."

I didn't blink. "A guy got killed. You know how old habits are."

Kadar leaned toward me. "Look, Kerrigan. This here's a small place. But all that means, you got no room and no right to stick your nose into other folk's business."

He coughed, long and hard, hacked up dirty phlegm into his closed fist. When he found his voice it sounded rusty. "We looked everywhere, didn't find him. Like I said, short-termers don't go walkabout that much, but it happens. And life goes on."

I wiped up the last of my gravy with a bit of toast. "How many have gone walkabout?"

"Ain't answering no more questions." Kadar pushed back his chair.

"You'd think that would free some return berths," I said.

Kadar laughed, a thick, angry snorting sound. He scooped up his tray. As he shuffled away, he hummed a tune I recognized.

Sixteen Tons.

5 DECEMBER 1979

Two days later, standing behind a berm under a makeshift roof, I watched as the countdown neared zero. It was the second launch I'd worked on, the first I'd had a chance to watch, and the first time I'd worn my painted pressure suit.

I'd found an image in the base Britannica that haunted me. An Ice Queen. A woman's face, pale-white skin glistening, icy blue eyes downcast, framed by a mass of silver hair. She wore a crown formed of ice-crystal shards. DuPree helped me copy the life-size image to the chest of my suit. We framed it in part with stark black lines.

"Suits you," DuPree said, when we were done. So far, no one else had said a word.

Three floodlights illuminated the glistening icicle in its cradle. More light on anything that I'd seen since I arrived. The ice rocket stood roughly the size of an old German V2. The larger hydrogen tank sat atop the LOX tank, both on top of the engine assembly.

Three thin spars ran up the sides with rings around the tanks, providing some additional integrity to the stack. Feed lines melted into the tanks connected them to the engine. The clever idea was to make the payload—the ice—double as the fuel tanks. No need for an expensive and time-consuming development of a metallurgical facility to make metal tanks.

"Does this whole thing really work out cheaper?" I asked.

DuPree made a verbal shrugging noise. "We haven't tried both ways, so I guess we'll never know, will we? I don't worry about it. It's just a job."

Under a minute.

"It gave America a moon colony," I said.

I heard the rancor in DuPree's voice. "No, it didn't. We got a mining operation and a supply base, with some corporate manufacturing. This isn't a restaurant. It's a fast-food joint."

Thirty seconds.

"And we got twenty-six days to serve up one-hundred-twelve tons of water." DuPree continued. "Seven more icicles. And LTC doesn't care squat about anything else. Neither does that prick Garver."

"Everything goes well, we'll be done by Christmas," I said.

The countdown hit zero. "Here we go," DuPree said.

There was no swirling water vapor around the rocket, but I saw ripples of refraction at the base as the engine caught. The rocket began to rise, slowly. Moving out of the floodlights it became hard to see, just the barely visible flame of the burning hydrogen.

"I expected it to take off faster," I said.

"These things are right on the edge in terms of performance envelope. It's got just enough oomph to make orbit and do the circularization burn on the other side."

The rocket was climbing faster, beginning to arc over. At two thousand feet it emerged into the sun, a tiny sliver of light. A second later the sliver seemed to blossom into a snow globe of twinkling points.

"God damn it!" DuPree said. "You jinxed that one, you and your *If everything goes well.*"

"Wha—"

"It shattered. Christ, couldn't you tell? God's pendulous nuts!"

I heard a click in my headset. "Selene Station! Zender here. You in line of sight yet?"

"Copy, Rockefeller Base."

"We just blew a load."

"Say again."

"Your ice delivery will shortly be scattered on the ground a few miles from here."

Garver joined the conversation. "When can you send up the next one? Schedule's getting tight." He sounded as if he'd stay calm through the Second Coming.

Posey took her time responding. "Will get back to you soonest on revised schedule."

"Copy. Selene Station out."

Posey's voice filled my headset. "Base meeting. In the mess hall. Now."

DuPree turned toward the lock. "Hope you're happy. Now you get to see Posey pissed."

"What do we do now?" I asked.

"We forget about celebrating Christmas."

7 DECEMBER 1979

"Kerrigan!"

I looked up from the book I'd been reading. Something by John Mac-Donald. Posey stood in the open door of my quarters.

"What?"

"Talk. My office. Now." She turned and hurried down the corridor.

I hesitated, then followed. As far as Rockefeller Base went, Posey *was* the Corporation. Management, personnel, records, everything. She was loud, overbearing, remote and twitchy enough make anyone uneasy. Since we lost the icicle two days ago, she had gotten worse.

Posey was already seated behind her desk by the time I got to her office/quarters. By moon standards, it was spacious.

"Close the door," she said, as I entered.

I did as told and took the chair opposite her. I didn't ask permission first.

"What's between you and Garver?" Zender asked without any preamble. She was still wound-up from the icicle loss.

"What do you mean?"

"You stopped in on him before coming down."

I saw no point in trying to deny it. "Garver and my father go back. I stopped by to pay respects."

"And I'm Marie of Romania. Everybody knows you were a cop. I think you're *still* a cop. What does Garver have you sniffing around for?"

I rubbed my forehead. The skin was getting dry and itchy from the canned air. "I *was* a cop. A federal marshal. Now I'm a LTC Operations Technician. A tinker in a space suit."

"Once a cop . . ."

"Bullshit. Some people hang on to the past. I don't."

"I tried to ship you out of here, after that icicle blew up. Garver blocked it."

"Like I said, he's a friend of my old man. They go way back to the Navy during the War."

Posey leaned forward. "Look. I know something and you know something, but you don't know everything."

"What's that supposed to mean?"

"I know what they found in that icicle that we delivered just before you came down."

"Scuttlebutt says it was a body."

She stared at me for a time, then sighed and gestured over her shoulder at a hand-drawn Gantt chart on the wall. "All right, play it that way. The right side of that chart is One January, Kerrigan. Two January doesn't exist. Got it?"

"Works for me."

Posey's eyes flicked from side to side. She looked over my shoulder. "Look, I'm sorry if I came down hard just now. I'm under the gun here."

I kept my face neutral. "I know that."

She nodded and leaned back in her chair.

"The Corporation promises me six drills. I get three. They promise four loaders, I get two. I have to melt that water before I can pour it. That takes power. A *lot* of power. And I have to crack some of that water for fuel and breathing air. That takes more power."

Posey was on a rant. I held on for the ride.

"They promised me five SNAP reactors. I got three. They promised a megawatt of solar arrays. I got two hundred kilowatts and I didn't want them. A reactor's easier, more reliable, but some senator's got a friend who makes photo-voltaics. That's why half the lights are never turned on."

She drew a ragged breath, close to the edge. "They promised a crew of sixty. I can barely hold on to thirty. They projected a launch failure rate of three percent. It turns out to be more like ten percent. I'm running low on engine assemblies and there's no time to get more. I have to have *Odyssey* fueled to go by January first. I have a crew on the edge of mutiny. I'm accused of sabotage—"

I interrupted. "You?"

"I'm in charge, I get the crap thrown in my face. Garver would just love to have a scapegoat to hang a failure on now, wouldn't he?"

"Why would he do that?"

Posey paused to cough. "Listen good, Kerrigan. A place like this, you don't keep secrets long. You snoop around anymore, I'll find out. I don't trust you, so don't get in my way."

"Or what?"

She stared at me, maybe realizing she'd said too much. She waved her hand in dismissal. "Get back to work."

I walked out and closed the door. Posey had been on the Moon since the base was completed. Three years plus. She coughed a lot, almost as much as Jake Kadar. It's was a wonder she hadn't gone walkabout.

15 DECEMBER 1979

"Fireworks?"

I stood outside the habitat, out of sight of others. I had the small transmitter Garver had given me jacked into my suit comm plug. It worked on a frequency only Garver would receive. When I spotted the point of light that was Selene Station rise in the south I called him. The signal was weak but clear.

"They're being loaded on the truck now," he said. "Be down in four hours with a support technician."

"Whose brilliant idea was this?"

"A certain fifteen-term Congressional bacterium," Garver said. "The Representative thought it would be wonderful to celebrate the New Year and *Odyssey*'s departure with a fireworks festival on the Moon."

If I could have slapped my forehead I would have. "Do the corporate big shots think it'll be visible from Earth? Will it even *work?*"

"They'll work; oxidizer is self-contained. The plan's to set them off just as *Odyssey* breaks orbit and to televise it from Selene Station. A royal sendoff."

Garver paused, continued. "Keep your eyes open, Laura."

"And my suit closed."

"Anything new?"

"Posey's calmed down, but some of the others are getting nervous. DuPree asked me yesterday why I keep walking off behind the habitat."

"And?"

"I told her I like to take a leak in private."

A static growl. "Keep an eye on her. The other newbie, too. I haven't been able to find out much about Mr. Anderson and when I don't know something it bothers me."

I saw an ellipse of light on the ground in front of the airlock and drew back a bit. "Tom, someone just came out, probably DuPree. We're scheduled to do the final checkout on the icicle before they tank it up."

"Anything on her?" Garver asked.

"Y'know, she seems all right. But they said that about Ted Bundy, didn't they? *He seemed like such a nice guy.*"

The station was moving across the sky. "Laura, I know I told you to get to the bottom of the Leatherman thing, but first priority is *Odyssey*. Check that; it's the *only* thing. The rest of that water has to get up here, period."

"We'll get it done, straw boss. There are some real beefs down here, but most of the crew know the score."

"You sound almost happy. Getting moonstruck?"

"The place grows on you. You know, like athlete's foot."

18 DECEMBER 1979

There are advantages to being in a small place, having good hearing and going through police training.

I was in the small galley adjacent to the mess hall on my turn at KP, scraping dishes and loading them in the industrial dishwasher.

All the comforts of home.

The mess room was empty save for two men sipping coffee at a corner table. Anderson and Kadar. Sound didn't carry well in the habitat's low pressure and they spoke in near-whispers.

But as I said, there are advantages. I heard most of what they said.

"Timing's everything."

". . . a statement. When you brace . . . before ship is overhead . . ."

". . . a dummy. Only one shot . . . go off with a . . ."

"For maximum effect make sure . . ."

". . . yeah, box is marked . . ."

I heard chairs slide, then footsteps.

"Later," Anderson said.

And they were gone.

One shot. Maximum effect. Box is marked.

Time to take a walk in the dark.

I suited up for my next shift two hours early and turned through the north lock, out on the surface nearest the supply dump for those materials that could stand the cold and vacuum.

Where are the fireworks?

If you wanted to smuggle up some sort of explosives, where better than in a shipment of explosives?

I skip-walked the hundred yards to the dump, regretting the need for my helmet lamp. Once there, I faced five hundred square feet of identical shipping containers with no discernible order.

I flicked off the lamp before I turned around, looking for any signs of movement or light behind me. Nothing. So I turned back to the scattered crates, flicking on the lamp and stood in the limp-armed stance I'd learned to minimize effort, as I began to examine the nearest crates.

Paranoid me. Thirty seconds later, I cut the lamp, turned to see if anyone was there. Still nothing, so I returned to my study of the crates.

A minute later, some sixth sense made me turn again, just in time to be hit hard in the shoulder. If I hadn't turned it would have been my helmet. I took two staggering steps back and fell, landing on my hip.

I raised my arms and hit the chin switch that turned my headlamp to full intensity. A suited figure loomed over me, some sort of bar grasped in a raised gauntlet.

What to do?

Lying on my back in the suit, I wasn't even sure I could stand up unassisted. The figure swung the bar down in a full arc.

Block it.

I let it land, taking the blow on one arm.

Grab the bar.

I grabbed the bar with my free hand. I pulled as hard as I could, rising a few inches as my attacker lost footing and toppled onto me.

My breath was coming hard and fast. I could feel the rush of adrenaline pushing me to act. I kept my grip on the bar and shoved my attacker up and to the side.

Roll over.

I pulled the bar free and jabbed it down, levering myself onto my chest. One deep breath and I pushed down as hard as I could, rose to a precarious angle and almost fell back again before I got the bar in place, using it like a cane.

The figure on the ground struggled to stand up. Whoever it was, they'd donned an unmarked suit, so I had no idea who had attacked me.

See how the bastard deals with a cracked faceplate.

I heard a thin whistling and suddenly felt cold and light-headed. I raised my arm and saw the cracked gauntlet ring, vapor streaming out.

Damn it! Get inside.

I reached down, increased my oxygen flow to maximum and turned, skip-walking as fast as I could to the airlock. My attacker would have to wait. Staying alive came first.

19 DECEMBER 1979

I blamed the suit failure on embrittlement from the cold. No one questioned me; metal can react strangely at those low temperatures. Only my attacker and I knew the truth, unless someone had given orders to the attacker. I tried to ignore that thought. I was getting as paranoid as Posey.

The bright point rose above the horizon. "Tom?"

"Here, Laura. Talk to me."

"Right. No questions until I'm finished."

I stood behind a boulder slightly taller than I was with my back to a wall of rock. Nobody would sneak up on me again. I laid out the events of the previous day quickly.

"The fireworks were in the pressurized storeroom. I chatted up the tech. Turns out it wouldn't be too good to keep them cold and in vacuum for very long."

"So."

"So this morning I snuck in to give the stuff a quick look-over."

"And?"

"I know a bit about weapons but I don't know zip about fireworks. Most of the stuff looks like stubby mortars. There's racks of them, some singles, what I guess are leveling gadgets."

"Maybe there's nothing there," Garver said.

"No. Nothing screams 'wrong' that I can tell, but there's something here. Whatever it is, I figure there was time to hide it somewhere else."

"Anything more?"

"Anderson and Kadar volunteered to assist the technician in the setup. Posey announced she's having an emergency bubble put up so the crew can watch from the surface. That was news to most of us. A bubble?"

"I heard about it," Garver said. "Another brilliant idea from the Corporate PR people. Show miners walking around in shirtsleeves on the surface. Arthur Clarke and all that. The Future."

"Right. Maybe helmet off, but no one here is stupid enough to actually shuck their suit and trust a plastic bag."

"Careful, Laura. You're going native."

I ignored him. "How high will fireworks go on the Moon?"

"Why do you—oh. I see where your headed. I'll find out."

"Okay. Anything new on Posey?" I asked.

"Just what I told you. She volunteered for the Moon. Before this, her career path was flat. She's got a hefty bonus coming once we launch."

"I suspect that you do, too."

Garver didn't answer right away. "You're right, I do. But then you've got a lot riding on it, too."

21 DECEMBER 1979

I walked into the mess hall just after midnight, hungry even though the main course smelled like microwaved cardboard. DuPree was already there, sitting at a table by herself. Kadar and Anderson were at a corner table, conversing quietly over coffee. They were now a work team, but they seemed to be every-where together recently.

I could feel the tension and excitement within the space, shared it without reserve. Another icicle was scheduled to go into orbit today, our fifth since the accident. Just three more to go.

Four weeks on the Moon had changed more than my attitude. My gait was steadier, more sure-footed. And the dark beyond the walls didn't bother me as much as when I first arrived. I ambled to the buffet and picked up a tray. Meatloaf, instant potatoes, what appeared to be green beans. They looked wilted.

SSDD.

I was even getting tired of DuPree's garden goods.

I loaded my tray, turned and nodded at Kadar, then settled in across from DuPree, who had her nose buried in a book. As I sat down, Kadar said something to Anderson I couldn't make out, then he got up and left, leaving his cup on the table.

Anderson stood, took both cups to the dirties tray and then drew a fresh cup of coffee. He walked to our table. "Hey, mind if I sit down?"

DuPree looked up long enough to grunt. I gestured at an empty chair. He sat and sipped his coffee.

I tipped my head to the door Kadar had just exited. "You two get off shift early?"

"Naw," Anderson said. "Posey moved us to your shift. I got to suit up in a few minutes. Icicle launch at 0630, you know, I'm helping with the final plumbing checkout."

It was the most he'd said to me in four weeks.

"You settled in okay?"

"Yeah. Amazing how quick being tired all the time takes away the wonder of walking on the Moon." He sipped his coffee. "Imagine how Jake feels."

DuPree set her book aside. "He counts the hours he's been here."

"Yeah," I said.

Anderson sat back and took another sip. "Poor guy don't talk about anything except getting off this rock. I'm amazed he hasn't gone walkabout by now."

"Kadar's tough," DuPree said.

I nodded. "I grew up around anthracite miners. They bitch and moan and talk the ear off their union rep, but there's a pride in those guys. They ride on their backs into a hole a mile inside a mountain and know damned few could take it."

I forced down another mouthful of string beans, waiting.

"Uh-huh," Anderson said. "He jabbers our shift away, going on about how we need to form a union, show solidarity."

I pushed at the potatoes with my fork, decided against it; there were limits.

"Yeah, we could just put down our tools and strike, but what good would that do?" DuPree said. "If we make the ship miss its tick we'd lose the goodwill of the whole damned country. You'd have to be really desperate to try something like that."

Anderson glanced at her. "What's the line in *Bobby McGee*? You know. *Freedom's just another word for nothing left to lose.*"

"Nuthin', not nothing."

He drained his cup and stood up. "Whatever. I got to take a leak and get out there or Posey will be down my throat so far she'll see daylight out my butt."

25 DECEMBER 1979

"Merry Christmas, Tom."

The bright dot rose over the rim wall, farther to the east after the final adjustment to the orbital plane.

"Copy that, Laura. Have any presents for me?"

Garver was in a good mood. Six more days to launch and only one more icicle to be sent up. He would make his schedule.

"Work on the final piece of ice is underway," I said. "And there's time to do another if there's a failure."

"Music to my ears," Garver said. "You've more than earned your prize. I'll have you up here the day after launch and on your way to Earth shortly after that."

"Uh huh."

"You don't sound excited," he said.

"I am. It's just—"

"You haven't caught your man."

"Yes. That's it."

"It doesn't matter, Laura," Garver said.

"Yes, it does!"

He changed the subject. "I've heard from Earth. Plans for the second Mars flight have been finalized. Construction will begin in ninety days. Launch in twenty-six months."

He was getting excited. "It's supposed to be faster, cut two months off the trip. The outbound leg will use hydrogen as a working fluid, bump engine efficiency to allow a bigger payload, including a lander this time. They're going to hold a contest to name it."

"As long as it isn't *Thumper*. Will you build it?"

Garver cleared his throat. "They want a younger man next time."

"What will you do?"

"I'm thinking about that." He cleared his throat again. "You see the pickup from the telephoto camera we mounted for the launch?"

"I did."

Selene Station was five miles from *Odyssey* in a following orbit. At a magnification of sixty the spacecraft appeared to be less than five hundred feet away. The orbital burn would be relayed live to Earth.

"It looks good," I said. "But I'll be with most of the crew in the bubble, watching naked-eye. Watching the crew as well."

"No need."

"The ship hasn't launched yet, Tom. What did you find out about a rocket launch from down here?"

"There's no danger."

"Are you sure?"

"Damn it, there's no danger! This conversation's over."

I stood, listening to static. He'd hung up on me.

31 DECEMBER 1979

Posey entered the west entrance locker room just as I lifted my helmet into place.

"Need some help?" she asked.

"Sure," I said. "They claimed in training the suits are designed so a single person can dress herself, but I always struggle. It's easier when you have a second pair of hands."

Posey shrugged. "Everything's easier if you don't have to do it by yourself. That's the manager's motto."

She stepped to a locker that held one of her four matching flower-power-painted suits. She kept one at each airlock, along with a few plain-white spares.

"Help me get into my suit first," she said.

For a time we worked in silence, checking each other's suit.

"Going out to watch the show?" I asked, as I slipped my head up into the helmet Zender held.

"Yes."

The big fireworks display laid out at North Rim would be set off in less than two hours to mark the midnight launch of *Odyssey*. The first second of the first day of a new decade, to be forever celebrated as the moment Americans took their next step to the stars. Except for those nerds who insisted the decade would begin at 1981.

At least, that was the corporate line all the network news services pushed.

For the men and women at Rockefeller Base it marked a day more personal and important. Twenty-four hours away from work and a chance to party. Posey made a big deal out of it when she made the announcement at a mandatory meeting three days before.

"This is happening because of us," she had said.

"Sure," DuPree had hissed in my ear. "And next day we'll all be back to work, good little drones pickin' that cotton."

"Did you hear me?" Posey asked. Her voice had taken on the hollow, mechanical sound of the suit radios.

"Sorry," I said. "Interference. What did you say?"

"I said, I wouldn't miss it. How about you? Why aren't you already out there? Miss the trolley?"

"No. I figured to watch it on the television in the lounge, but the reception's not very good."

It was a lie.

I had planned all along to be close to the fireworks site but wanted to stop by the spot where I had hidden the case Garver gave to me. If I had to stop a last-minute assault, I'd would need a weapon and there was a gun in the case.

"There's still plenty of time," Posey said.

"How's that?" I asked.

Posey tipped her helmet toward the glowing clock above the door. I looked, despite having a heads-up times display in her own helmet.

2240.

"We'll take one of the loaders. One of the perks of being boss, travelling in comfort."

"This can't be right?" I said. "My heads-up says I've only got a quarter-tank of oxygen. I know I topped the tank when I came back in last work shift."

Posey examined the gauges on the back of my life support pack. "I've got the same reading here. Everything looks okay. You must have forgotten."

"No. That's not possible. I've got to charge it."

"No time," Posey said. "Do it at the bubble. There's spare tanks there and it's only a fifteen-minute ride."

"I don't like doing that," I said.

She set her own helmet into place. "Up to you, but if you want a ride—"

"Can I catch a ride, too?"

I turned toward the corridor entrance. The noises of the suits, the sounds of our voices and the worry over the low oxygen, had masked DuPree's entrance.

"I don't think—" Posey said.

DuPree already stood at her locker. She pulled her suit out and held it out to me.

"Help me with this, will you?" she asked.

"There may not be room," Posey said.

I glanced at Posey. She looked like she had sucked on a lemon. "Come on, Posey," DuPree said, as she scrambled into her pressure suit. "Don't be a bitch. I won't take up that much room. We'll be fine."

At last, Posey nodded. She scooped up her gear bag. "All right," she said. "Hurry. I don't want to be late."

We rolled along the crater floor at six miles per hour, following the twin circles of light from the headlamps. Not exactly racing speeds, but twice as fast as they would have managed, walking in the bulky pressure suits and the rover's electric motors could keep up that speed for hours.

DuPree drove, at Posey's suggestion. I sat next to her and Posey stood behind us, gripping the seat backs. I couldn't hear so much as a whine from the vehicle, but felt the steady vibrations from the big electric motors that drove each of the six drive wheels.

"I need to make a stop," I said.

"For what?" Posey's voice sounded more authoritative on the suit's radio. Deeper and richer.

"Something for the party. It's around to the left."

"Hope it's something good." I heard the amusement and disdain in Posey's voice.

She probably thinks we're going to the still.

"Over at the far end," I said, pointing. "Back by the west corner. I'll tell you when we get close."

DuPree turned the vehicle and accelerated.

On foot, the cache lay eight minutes from the west lock. We covered the distance in just under four.

"Stop here," I said.

I clambered from the rover when it stopped. I'd done a good job on the cache, set it near a concrete piling, so it looked as if it were a piece of the superstructure.

The tricky part was kneeling in the pressure suit. I eased into place, went to one knee and tapped in the four-digit locking code. When I pulled the box open, the compressed-air pistol and the four flechette rounds it carried were gone.

I glanced toward the loader. Posey and DuPree were deep in conversation, not paying any attention to me or my empty junction box. I locked the lid and loped back to the rover.

I thought of growing up in Pikesville, running with my brother toward the family's Ford Country Squire station wagon, racing for the privilege of sitting up front with Dad.

"Shotgun," I muttered, sourly, as I climbed back in next to DuPree.

DuPree engaged the rover's six electric motors, the vehicle rolled away from the array.

Posey leaned close. "The pantry empty?"

"Yes."

"What happened?"

"I don't know," I said.

"If you hid a bottle there it would have frozen and exploded. I thought you knew better by now."

"Yeah, you nailed it," I lied.

I couldn't figure it. No one knew about the cache. Had I said something I shouldn't have? Had Jake Kadar or Mitchell Anderson twigged to my investigation in some other way?

Somehow, I'd miscalculated, revealed my intentions and led someone to my hiding place.

I thought I'd been so careful, though.

Time to change my plans. Whoever took the flechette gun had to be the one who planned to strike at *Odyssey* before the Mars ship moved out of range. And he would be waiting for me somewhere, with four plastic flechette shells filled with dozens of tiny steel darts.

The rover bounced across a rough stretch of floor, a set of rills. I glanced up, uncertain where we were, and saw none of the landmarks I'd learned over the last five weeks.

"I thought we were headed for the bubble," I said.

"I am," Posey said. "You're not."

I turned as much as the pressure suit would allow, trying to look behind me.

"Sit still," Posey snapped. "DuPree's doing what I told her to do. You need to do that, too. I've got the fancy gun of yours pressed against your friend's left shoulder."

"What's going on, Posey?" I asked.

There was a teasing tone to the other woman's voice I'd never heard before. "Maybe I'll tell you," she said. "Maybe I won't. Sit still for now and shut up."

When we stopped, my heads-up display read **2300**. An hour left until the fireworks display began. *Odyssey* was passing over the south pole, warming up the reactors for the engines. I worried more about the oxygen gauges. I had less than ten minutes worth of air left. Something had to be done soon.

"Get out, Kerrigan," Posey ordered.

"You can't—"

"I said, 'Get out!'"

I clambered from the Rover. I felt brief resistance and heard a short, brittle snap. Before I could turn back to the vehicle I heard a scrambling sound through the headphones that could only be two people struggling in pressure suits.

"Jesus!" DuPree sounded panicked. "Jesus! You can't do that!"

I turned in time to see Posey clawing at DuPree's life support pack. A cloud of white vapor steamed around DuPree's helmet, as if it were a cold day on Earth and she was breathing hard. She twisted and turned beneath Posey, at a disadvantage because of her position. I stepped toward the rover.

"God damn you," Posey screamed, waving the compressed-air gun toward me. "Stay where you are."

DuPree scrambled across the passenger seat on her belly, wallowing in the heavy suit. She kicked at Posey's hands, fell from the vehicle, catching herself with her gloved hands before her faceplate hit the regolith. She pushed, staggered onto her feet and stumbled toward me, went to her knees an arm's length away.

"She opened my tanks!" DuPree's voice sounded distant and hollow. "The bitch opened my tanks! Shut it down, Laura, shut it down!"

I reached to the controls, fumbled my first attempt, but them managed to return the valves to the proper position. I glanced at the gauges. DuPree had just a bit more than fifty minutes-worth of air.

"DuPree to Rockefeller control. We're low on oxygen, about an hour out to the northwest. Send help stat. We need help *now.*"

No response. I glanced at DuPree's suit. The radio antenna had been snapped in half. Posey's handiwork.

"They're not going to hear you."

Posey stood on the passenger seat, the pistol pointed at DuPree and me. "There's enough antenna left for up-close communication, but no one beyond a couple hundred yards can hear you."

"Did you kill Leatherman?" I asked.

"Back away," Posey said. "Back away or you die right now."

I helped lever DuPree to her feet.

"Did you kill him?"

"I said, 'back up.'"

The two of us shuffled backward until we were almost a hundred feet from the loader.

"Come on, Posey," I said. "Tell me. I want to know before I die."

Posey maneuvered into the driver's seat. "I didn't mean to. It was an accident, but no one will believe that now. Not after I stuffed him into the ice."

"Why did you do it?"

"The bastard was coming on to me. Christ, it had been over two years since I'd been with a man. And then he used me. I caught him snooping in my employee records. I thought he was a union rep. We argued and I lost it. I pushed him back and he hit his head on the wall. Freaking newbie couldn't handle the gravity. I got him into a suit and cut the leg to make it look like an accident."

"And now you're going to kill us."

She began to roll away. "No. The two of you just went walkabout. It happens a lot up here."

We watched her head off toward the observation bubble. DuPree turned to me before the vehicle disappeared.

"How much air to you have left?" she asked.

"Five, maybe six minutes. You?"

"Almost half an hour."

"Swell. You might be able to make it back to base."

"Not without you. You know how to do a two-person emergency air transfer?"

"Yeah. But even if we split what we've got, we don't have enough air to make it to the base in fifteen minutes. And if Posey's as smart as I know she is, we can't make it to the bubble in that time, either."

"Let's get started on the transfer," DuPree said. "We're pushing the time needed, as it is."

I turned to allow DuPree access to my life support pack. "But what good—"

DuPree interrupted. "You know that illegal still you're always asking me about?"

"Yeah?"

"It's no more than ten minutes' hike away and I've got oxygen tanks there."

DuPree had underestimated the distance to the still, either that or I was hyperventilating. My suit's oxygen level indicator had dropped into the red by the time DuPree pointed to a small rounded mound. A buried sulfur concrete dome.

"There it is," DuPree panted. "Told you we could make it.

There was no glass door, just the rotating lock. DuPree pointed that I should go first and it was no time to play Alfonse and Gaston. It still seemed to take forever before we were both inside.

We stood face to face, working each other's helmet rings. At last, my seal popped and I could breathe. I finished removing DuPree's helmet and leaned against a rough wall, sucking in breath after breath of oxygen.

The dome felt over-warm and the heady sour-mash scent of moonshine filled my nose. The dome wasn't much larger than my quarters at the base habitat. Eight feet in diameter and filled with DuPree's distillation equipment, it offered barely enough room for the two of us to stand, much less move. The dim light added to the sense of claustrophobia.

"Tight quarters," I said.

"Yeah," DuPree said. "But we're alive. Come on. There's more room below."

"Below?"

DuPree tipped her head. I spotted a hole in the floor near the far sloping wall. I jockeyed around, twisting so that DuPree could move past me toward it. When DuPree started down the ladder, I followed. "Where did you get this place, Edie?"

"Lunar scrimshaw. I got off-hours work in return for a share of the 'shine."

A small storage room lay below, down an obviously homemade ladder. Despite the metal shelves stacked full of supplies, the scavenged plastic barrels and the life-support equipment, there was enough space here to turn around without touching each other.

I pointed to the oxygen-charging port marked in vivid green. "Help me charge my suit, will you? I'm going after her."

DuPree didn't move. She studied me for a moment, her mouth set in a hard, straight line. "You're still law, aren't you?"

No more lies.

I shrugged. "I wasn't when I came down here five weeks ago. I lost my badge, back on Earth. This job was the best I could line up."

"And now?" DuPree asked.

"They offered me my badge back, just before I dropped from Selene Station, if I could find out who killed Leatherman."

"That's all?"

"I was supposed to stop the sabotage, too."

"And now?"

"Got the word this morning I had my badge back, if I wanted it. I'm going to use it to arrest Zender. Jake Kadar, too, if he's still alive. And I'm going to make sure there's a trial, so everybody back on Earth sees what's going on here."

"Okay."

DuPree fiddled with the oxygen fittings. I watched the dial as the marker began to move away from the big letter E.

The seconds ticked past. I watched the oxygen gauge climb toward full. The dome didn't feel so over-warm, anymore. I listened to the ticks and hisses of my suit, the creaking of the dome's equipment, and imagined what I might say to my father when this was over, if I still was alive, if I told him I wasn't going to take back the badge.

"I thought you killed him," I said, after a time.

"I figured as much," DuPree said. "My old man always said I had that sort of face."

"Your father?"

"Naw. My husband.

"You're still married?"

"Uh huh, but you couldn't prove it by that asshole. He went out for milk one night and didn't even send back the change."

I grunted once, almost a laugh. "It's better that everybody knows what's what here."

"If you say so. I don't figure it'll make any difference."

DuPree fiddled with the fittings again. I glanced at my heads-up display. My tanks were full.

"Help me with mine," DuPree said. She turned her back to me.

I began to set the lines. "When you get back to the base—"

DuPree interrupted. "Hell with that," she said. "I'm coming with you. Wouldn't miss this for a ride to Mars."

Down on Earth a billion people were looking up at the full moon. Gliding up its face from south to north *Odyssey* was visible only in the mind's eye, approaching the moment its nuclear engines would ignite over the moon's north pole.

The exhaust of the first fireworks rocket limned a fiery trail across the black void above North Rim. It exploded into an incandescent boll of rich green light that faded into nothingness.

"A waste of time and money," DuPree muttered. "No one on Earth will be able to see anything with the naked eye."

"There'll be a lot of people out with telescopes," I said. "And the cameras on Selene Station will pick it up. It's all part of the celebration."

"Part of the propaganda, don't you mean. Lot of good a trip to Mars is going to do us. That senator from Massachusetts, the guy who ran against Nixon, has it right."

"Kennedy?"

"Yeah, that's the guy. He says we ought to be spending the money to do some good at home."

"I suppose."

I hadn't ever really thought much about it while I wore a badge. I had left the politics to others and focused on my work. For all the good that did me.

It had taken us the better part of twenty minutes to hike from DuPree's hidden still to North Rim. The fireworks began on the dot at 2350, just as we crested a small ridge. The vantage offered a spectacular view of the display area, as well as the plain below where the techs bustled about, overseeing the detonations.

Jake Kadar was down there somewhere.

My inclination was to head down into the bustle, figure out which one was Kadar when I got there. Whether or not Garver thought much of the notion of a rocket launch aimed at *Odyssey*, I was convinced that was what Kadar planned.

Even so, Posey most likely waited in the portable bubble set up beyond the fireworks. She was an admitted murderer, premeditated or not. By all the rules, I had to go after her first.

DuPree had already started for the bubble. She stopped and turned, when she realized I wasn't with her.

"You okay?" she asked.

Even through the headset, I heard concern. DuPree didn't know about the planned rocket launch, though. Or maybe she did. Just because she wasn't responsible for Leatherman's death, didn't mean she wasn't involved in a conspiracy against the Mars ship.

"Yeah," I said. "Just fine."

DuPree waved a gloved hand. "Come on then. Let's get that bitch."

The fireworks show continued as we hiked across the plain, each shot more intense and colorful, more crowded with launches than the one before.

The finale launched just as we reached the bubble. The dome looked like half a giant soap bubble anchored to a flat expanse of regolith at the edge of the crater rim, fifty feet across and twenty feet high at center.

Two doubled sheets of sixty-gauge clear polyvinyl chloride formed the structure, one giant bubble within another and separated by a six-inch air space. The airlock was sealed within a plastic sleeve.

Its walls offered a clear view, as wave after wave of rockets climbed into the void, leaving dissolving lines of colored fire behind. Then they blossomed, a fast-fading bouquet of multi-colored globes of fiery light.

And as the sky turned charcoal black again, a brilliant star rose over the southeastern horizon as *Odyssey* reached for the zenith as it had so many times before.

About ten degrees above the rim the point of light appeared to grow much brighter. Five minutes from the pole *Odyssey's* engines fired, beginning the burn that would break it free from orbit and send it on its way to Mars.

Inside the clear bubble, the crowd of suited figures went wild. They might all be cynics, like DuPree, might think the *Odyssey* a work of hokum, but the sight of that star, that massive vehicle underway, a *thing* they helped make possible, stirred their souls.

The sounds of celebration filled my suit's headset; we were close enough now for reception. I felt a shiver tiptoe up my spine. Only five weeks on the job, but I felt the need to cheer.

"Go. Go. Go."

I helped make that happen.

"There!" DuPree breathed, pointing. "There she is."

Sure enough. I spotted Posey's distinctive pressure suit near the center of the clear plastic dome. Like the others, she had her back to us, to the pre-fab airlock, looking overhead.

DuPree grabbed at my arm, but before she took a single step toward the lock I glanced down into the maze of metal frames that had supported the launching tubes. The other workers were headed up the rim slope to the bubble, but a single suited figure remained below.

A skull-and-crossbones pattern. Jake Kadar.

As I watched, he raised a massive tube to his shoulder and pressed his helmet to a mechanism set at an angle atop the tube. It had to be the aiming sights. The tip of the tube traced ahead of the path of *Odyssey* across the heavens, then a gout of fire belched from the rear of the tube, and another rocket streaked into the sky.

"Jesus, what was that?" DuPree said.

There had been no cloud of dust, of course. The crew had cleared the floor of North Rim down to bare rock, but there still was reaction. Kadar rocked in place, buffeted by the blast, pulled off his feet but he didn't fall.

"He anchored himself in place," I said.

The man came prepared.

"Is that Kadar?" DuPree asked.

The rocket trail stretched toward where *Odyssey* would be in a few minutes.

"Looks that way," I said. "He's shooting at the ship. Let's hope his aim was wrong."

I wondered if Garver saw it, from his vantage point on Selene station, a dimmer star slowly separating from *Odyssey*. And I wondered if he still was unconcerned.

Finally, after what seemed eternity, though it couldn't have been more than a couple of seconds, the exhaust trail snuffed out. I began to count. As I reached forty-two a massive ball of white light appeared, more intense, more threatening than anything that had come before.

"Did he get his hands on an atom bomb?" I asked.

DuPree sounded excited. "That wasn't an a-bomb."

"You knew about it?"

"No. It wasn't nearly bright enough. You'd have been blind now if it was."

"Jake wanted to destroy *Odyssey*."

"I don't believe it. He helped build the damned thing, why would he want to blow it up? Besides, that bit of pyrotechnics went off at least thirty miles below the ship. Either someone miscalculated—"

"—or it was a scare tactic." I looked up again. *Odyssey* was almost directly overhead. Normally it would begin to move toward the northern horizon, blinking out as it moved into the moon's shadow. But it was falling slower, and yet slower, as it moved out of orbit, picking up steam.

There was a voice on the radio, the ship commander. "All systems nominal."

"Damn," I said. Too much was going on at once.

DuPree pointed. "Jake's on his way up here now. Bet he wants to turn himself in. Bet he wants to be arrested, get some attention. Somebody's got to talk about conditions here."

"I'm not worried about him," I said. "Watching Kadar, I forgot about Posey."

DuPree turned toward the dome. Most of the folks inside still watched *Odyssey*. Some were high-fiving and slapping each other on the back. A happy babble filled my headphones. But Posey Zender, her suit painting unmistakable, stood with her back to the others, her attention riveted on me and DuPree.

"Stay out here," I said. "She's got my gun."

"To hell with that. I want a piece of her."

And DuPree hurried after me toward the lock.

The crowd turned as I swept through the air lock. Thick interlocking rubber mats covered the floor. Electric heaters sat at the cardinal compass points. A head-high screen hid the sanitation units. Someone had stenciled a crescent half-moon upon the screen.

A portable air generator, identical to the unit in DuPree's distillery, sat near the airlock. Power for the lights and all the equipment fed from a cable leading back to a junction box below the solar arrays near the habitat. Nothing fancy. Still it was cozy and the four heaters, along with all the people in the bubble, kept it comfortable.

At first glance, the image of a herd of pregnant aliens popped into my head. The gathered technicians and miners still wore pressure suits, but had removed their helmets and clipped them to their suit fronts on quick-release rings.

Behind me, the air lock whooshed and the dome's plastic surface rippled, as DuPree came in. Posey took a step back and pulled the air pistol from a suit pouch at her hip.

"She's got a gun," someone shouted. "Posey's got a gun."

The crowd pushed back even more, those in the outer edges pressed against the flexible walls.

"Fancy seeing you two here," Posey said. "I didn't think you would be by."

"Put down the gun, Posey," someone suggested.

"Where did she get a gun?" someone else asked.

I eased toward Posey. "If you fire that in here and miss, you'll open up the bubble. A lot of people could die."

"Everyone put on your helmets," Posey said.

"She tried to kill us," DuPree said.

The crowd rumbled even louder. DuPree ignored them, moved forward, too, but eased away from me. I waved her on. If we made it difficult for Posey to see both of us at once, we might stand a chance of disarming her.

"Don't listen to her," Posey shouted. "They both want me dead."

Technicians and miners alike glanced back and forth between us. Some people had already slipped on and sealed their helmets, but most stood waiting, helmets in hand.

"Who are you going to believe?" DuPree demanded. "Me or Posey Zender?"

I shuffled to the left, adding distance between her and DuPree. Posey made a choice and turned with me. The crowd rotated with us, looking like a bunch of extras in some old Keystone comedy.

"What's going on?" someone asked.

"Posey killed Leatherman," I said.

"I thought that was an accident."

So everybody knew after all.

"It was Posey," DuPree said. "And an hour ago she tried to kill me and Kerrigan, drained our tanks and left us to die afoot."

"I have it all on tape," I said.

I didn't, but Posey didn't know that. Maybe it would stir the pot.

It worked. She pointed the pistol straight up.

"Get your helmets on," she shouted. "I'm going to fire on the dome in ten seconds."

"You'll die without a helmet, Posey."

"What's the difference? Dying here or rotting in some jail on Earth. I think I'll do it right now."

The airlock whooshed. The bubble quivered as it gulped the bit of vacuum brought in by the lock.

"All right, I did it," Kadar radioed. "I tried to shoot down the Mars ship. Chain me up and ship me back to Earth."

Everybody looked, even Posey, and DuPree jumped. She soared across the bubble, grabbed Posey's upstretched arm and pushed it toward the floor. I barely heard the chuff of the pistol discharging. The flechette dart bit into the rubber inches from my right boot. It remained intact.

Posey and DuPree were buried in a mound of squirming, pressure-suited people, wrestling for a chance to get at Posey and none of them very happy at the moment. I had never had so many impromptu enthusiastic deputies.

The point of light had passed to the north, but now instead of falling back down the sky it dropped more slowly. Soon it was almost stationary, receding on a line directly away from the viewers on the lunar surface.

The dot went dim as the first engine burn finished. *Odyssey* had embarked on its long ellipse to the fourth planet from the Sun.

Posey lay pinned to the floor. I ducked to pick up the gun, then turned and gave DuPree a thumbs-up.

"Hey!" Jake Kadar pulled off his helmet. "What about me? Who's going to arrest me?"

1 JANUARY 1980

I sat at the base radio when Selene Station rose over the horizon. It had been six hours since *Odyssey* pulled out of orbit. By now the crew would be busy mothballing the NERVA reactors, getting the craft into cruise mode. The Rockefeller staff was scattered about the base, in groups of one or two or more, celebrating the launch in the manner they preferred, including DuPree's excellent distillate.

Except for two burly miners.

They'd volunteered and I'd deputized them to ride with the shackled Anderson, Zender and Kadar on a truck ride up to Selene Station. Kadar had babbled before they left about how Anderson had convinced him that trying to shoot the ship down would get him charged and sent back to Earth for trial.

Jake would get his wish.

For the moment I was alone. I fidgeted, wishing I didn't have to wait to talk to Garver. I decided we'd need some sort of relay satellites. This waiting for line of sight stuff grew old.

There was a burp of static. "Rockefeller, Selene Station."

"Congratulations, Tom," I said into the mike.

"Good job to you, too, Laura," he replied.

"Yeah." I looked at the wall, thinking about the dark and the cold beyond. It didn't bother me so much, anymore.

"Thought you'd like to know," Garver said. "Anderson's spilling his guts. He's a fink for TLC. They sent him up here to stage an incident to make the base staff look bad, turn public opinion again the workers. Kadar's a patsy, a desperate man, no more than that."

I nodded. I hoped Jake got off lightly.

"That little scheme backfired," Garver said. "There are already calls for a Congressional investigation."

"You think it'll do any good?"

"I think so. Senator Goldwater from Arizona said something about not binding the mouths of the kine who tread the grain."

"That's good to hear," I said.

"Get things cleaned up down there soon as you can. I need some kind of report ASAP. I don't want to have today mucked up by a few pencil-pushers crying for their paperwork."

"Everything's under control. I'll scribble something and have it up to you by 1400."

I heard him sigh. He had to be as tired as I was, ready for an uninterrupted nap.

"Another truck will be down next time around," he said. "I can have you on a tug for LEO in twelve hours. You're priority, Laura, a small celebrity. The woman who saved the Mars mission and all that."

I closed my eyes. In my mind I saw the shining star pass overhead, rising up from the stark rim of this new world toward another one and not falling down again. I smelled the ever-present dust and hint of ozone, considered the place around me that would kill me in a moment if I made a mistake. I thought of radiation and vacuum and the cold, the cold the most.

And I recalled the way we all cheered *Odyssey*'s departure.

"Thanks," I said. "I won't need it."

"What's that?"

"I think I want to stay, be here when the ship gets back. There's a lot of work to be done in the meantime, lots of opportunity, getting ready for the second launch."

"Someone else can do it."

"I suppose."

"But—"

Earth was far away and long ago. "But the base staff voted to form a union. United Workers of Luna, Local 1. They invited me to be president."

I heard a grunt, then a soft chuckle. "What are your plans, Madam President?"

"Hey." DuPree stood at the open door, smiling and holding two glasses of red liquid.

I sat up straight. "Tom, I plan to have a taste of genuine moonshine. After that I'll play it out by ear."

"Save some for me, will you?" he said.

"Say again?"

"Save a glass for me. I'll see you in a couple of hours."

"Say again?"

This time the chuckle was full-out loud.

"If you're not coming up, I'm coming down. I can just catch that next truck If I hurry."

"Why?" I asked.

"You might need a backup, someone older with some sense."

"Are you *serious?*"

"I'm sixty-six years old, Laura. They've already told me I'll never ramrod another job, let alone one like this. I can go home to sit and rot. I'm not even sure I could get a *consulting* gig at some aerospace company. Like you said, there's opportunity down there. Besides, if I don't give it a shot my old man's ghost will never stop bugging me."

"Well, hell, come on down.

Garver spoke again. "How does the old song go? *You'll get pie in the sky when you die.* Bullshit. I'm in the sky and I'm not dead yet. This could be a lot of fun."

"You're crazier than I am," I said.

"Downright moonstruck. Need a shop steward?"

"No." I said. "We need a union president. If this is going to work we need someone with more clout than me. Someone just like you."

"What makes you think the crew would accept me?"

"Come on down and we'll make your case," I said.

"Okay, I'll give it a go. But then what about you?"

I smiled to myself. "Every town needs a sheriff."

In my mind's eye I saw Garver nodding.

"I like that notion," he said. "For now, Selene Station out."

I slipped off the headset, thinking of how another old tune my mother used to sing got the message wrong. The best things in life aren't always free, but if I had my way, the Moon *would* belong to everyone.

Ian McDonald is an SFF writer living in Northern Ireland, just outside Belfast. Always fascinated by the close, great light in the sky, he's been writing about the moon for six years now, beginning with this story. "The Fifth Dragon" is part of the Luna sequence, which concludes with the novel *Luna: Moon Rising* (Tor and Gollancz), published in early 2019.

THE FIFTH DRAGON
Ian McDonald

The scan was routine. Every moon worker has one every four lunes. Achi was called, she went into the scanner. The machine passed magnetic fields through her body and when she came out the medic said, you have four weeks left.

We met on the Vorontsov Trans-Orbital cycler but didn't have sex. We talked instead about names.

"Corta. That's not a Brazilian name," Achi said. I didn't know her well enough then, eight hours out from transfer orbit, to be my truculent self and insist that any name can be a Brazilian name, that we are a true rainbow nation. So I told her that my name had rolled through many peoples and languages like a bottle in a breaker until it was cast up sand-scoured and clouded on the beaches of Barra. And now I was taking it on again, up to the moon.

Achi Debasso. Another name rolled by tide of history. London born, London raised, M.I.T. educated but she never forgot—had never been let forget—that she was Syrian. Syria*c*. That one letter was a universe of difference. Her family had fled the civil war, she had been born in exile. Now she was headed into a deeper exile.

I didn't mean to be in the centrifuge pod with Achi. There was a guy; he'd looked and I looked back and nodded *yes, I will, yes* even as the OTV made its distancing burn from the cycler. I took it. I'm no prude. I've got the New Year Barra beach bangles. I'm up for a party and more, and everyone's heard about (here they move in close and mouth the words) *freefall sex*. I wanted to try it with this guy. And I couldn't stop throwing up. I was not up for zero gee. It turned everything inside me upside down. Puke poured out of me. That's not sexy. So I retreated to gravity and the only other person in the centrifuge arm was this caramel-eyed girl, slender hands and long fingers, her face flickering every few moments into an unconscious micro-frown. Inward-gazing, self-loathing, scattering geek references like anti-personnel mines. Up in the hub our co-workers fucked. Down in the centrifuge pod we talked and the stars and the moon arced across the window beneath our feet.

A Brazilian miner and a London-Syriac ecologist. The centrifuge filled as freefall sex palled but we kept talking. The next day the guy I had puked over caught my eye again but I sought out Achi, on her own in the same spot, looking out at the moon. And the whirling moon was a little bigger in the observation port and we knew each other a little better and by the end of the week the moon filled the whole of the window and we had moved from conversationalists into friends.

Achi: left Damascus as a cluster of cells tumbling in her mother's womb. And that informed her every breath and touch. She felt guilty for escaping. Father was a software engineer, mother was a physiotherapist. London welcomed them.

Adriana: seven of us: seven Cortas. Little cuts. I was in the middle, loved and adored but told solemnly I was plain and thick in the thighs and would have be thankful for whatever life granted me.

Achi: a water girl. Her family home was near the Olympic pool—her mother had dropped her into water days out of the hospital. She had sunk, then she swam. Swimmer and surfer: long British summer evenings on the western beaches. Cold British water. She was small and quiet but feared no wave.

Adriana: born with the sound of the sea in her room but never learned to swim. I splash, I paddle, I wade. I come from beach people, not ocean people.

Achi: the atoner. She could not change the place or order of her birth, but she could apologise for it by being useful. Useful Achi. Make things right!

Adriana: the plain. Mãe and papai thought they were doing me a favour; allowing me no illusions or false hopes that could blight my life. Marry as well as you can; be happy: that will have to do. Not this Corta. I was the kid who shot her hand up at school. The girl who wouldn't shut up when the boys were talking. Who never got picked for the futsal team—okay, I would find my own sport. I did Brasilian jujitsu. Sport for one. No one messed with plain Adriana.

Achi: grad at UCL, post-grad at M.I.T. Her need to be useful took her battling desertification, salinisation, eutrophication. She was an -ation warrior. In the end it took her to the moon. No way to be more useful than sheltering and feeding a whole world.

Adriana: university at São Paulo. And my salvation. Where I learned that plain didn't matter as much as available, and I was sweet for sex with boys and girls. Fuckfriends. Sweet girls don't have fuckfriends. And sweet girls don't study mining engineering. Like jujitsu, like hooking up, that was a thing for me, me alone. Then the economy gave one final, apocalyptic crash at the bottom of a series of drops and hit the ground and broke so badly no one could see how to fix it. And the seaside, be-happy Cortas were in ruins, jobless, investments in ashes. It was plain Adriana who said, I can save you. I'll go to the Moon.

All this we knew by the seventh day of the orbit out. On the eight day, we rendezvoused with the transfer tether and spun down to the new world.

The freefall sex? Grossly oversold. Everything moves in all the wrong ways. Things get away from you. You have to strap everything down to get purchase. It's more like mutual bondage.

I was sintering ten kilometres ahead of Crucible when Achi's call came. I had requested the transfer from Mackenzie Metals to Vorontsov Rail. The forewoman had been puzzled when I reported to Railhead. You're a dustbunny not a track-queen. Surface work is surface work, I said and that convinced her. The work was good, easy and physical and satisfying. And it was on the surface. At the end of every up-shift you saw six new lengths of gleaming rail among the boot and track prints, and on the edge of the horizon, the blinding spark of Crucible, brighter than any star, advancing over yesterday's rails, and you said, I made that. The work had real measure: the inexorable advance of Mackenzie Metals across the Mare Insularum, brighter than the brightest star. Brighter than sunrise, so bright it could burn a hole through your helmet sunscreen if you held it in your eye line too long. Thousands of concave mirrors focusing sunlight on the smelting crucibles. Three years from now the rail lines would circle the globe and the Crucible would follow the sun, bathed in perpetual noon. Me, building a railroad around the moon.

Then ting ching and it all came apart. Achi's voice blocking out my work-mix music, Achi's face superimposed on the dirty grey hills of Rimae Maestlin. Achi telling me her routine medical had given her four weeks.

I hitched a ride on the construction car back down the rails to Crucible. I waited two hours hunkered down in the hard-vacuum shadows, tons of molten metal and ten thousand Kelvin sunlight above my head, for an expensive ticket on a slow Mackenzie ore train to Meridian. Ten hours clinging onto a maintenance platform, not even room to turn around, let alone sit. Grey dust, black sky . . . I listened my way through my collection of historical bossanova, from the 1940s to the 1970s. I played Connecto on my helmet hud until every time I blinked I saw tumbling, spinning gold stars. I scanned my family's social space entries and threw my thoughts and comments and good wishes at the big blue Earth. By the time I got to Meridian I was two degrees off hypothermic. My surface activity suit was rated for a shift and some scramble time, not twelve hours in the open. Should have claimed compensation. But I didn't want my former employers paying too much attention to me. I couldn't afford the time it would take to re-pressurise for the train, so I went dirty and fast, on the BALTRAN.

I knew I would vomit. I held it until the third and final jump. BALTRAN: Ballistic Transport system. The moon has no atmosphere—well, it does, a very thin one, which is getting thicker as human settlements leak air into it. Maybe in a few centuries this will become a problem for vacuum industries, but to all intents and purposes, it's a vacuum. See what I did there? That's the engineer in me. No atmosphere means ballistic trajectories can be calculated with great precision. Which means, throw something up and you know exactly where it will fall to moon again. Bring in positionable electromagnetic launchers and you have a mechanism for schlepping material quick and dirty around the moon. Launch it, catch it in a receiver, boost it on again. It's like juggling. The BALTRAN is not always used for cargo. If you can take the gees it can as easily juggle people across the moon.

I held it until the final jump. You cannot imagine what it is like to throw up in your helmet. In free fall. People have died. The look on the BALTRAN attendant's face when I came out of the capsule at Queen of the South was a thing to be seen. So I am told. I couldn't see it. But if I could afford the capsule I could afford the shower to clean up. And there are people in Queen who will happily clean vomit out of a sasuit for the right number of bitsies. Say what you like about the Vorontsovs, they pay handsomely.

All this I did, the endless hours riding the train like a moon-hobo, the hypothermia and being sling-shotted in a can of my own barf, because I knew that if Achi had four weeks, I could not be far behind.

You don't think about the bones. As a Jo Moonbeam, everything is so new and demanding, from working out how to stand and walk, to those four little digits in the bottom right corner of your field of vision that tell you how much you owe the Lunar Development Corporation for air, water, space and web. The first time you see those numbers change because demand or supply or market price has shifted, your breath catches in your throat. Nothing tells you that you are not on Earth any more than exhaling at one price and inhaling at another. Everything—*everything*—was new and hard.

Everything other than your bones. After two years on the moon human bone structure atrophies to a point where return to Earth gravity is almost certainly fatal. The medics drop it almost incidentally into your initial assessment. It can take days—weeks—for its ripples to touch your life. Then you feel your bones crumbling away, flake by flake, inside your body. And there's not a thing you can do about it. What it means is that there is a calcium clock ticking inside your body, counting down to Moon Day. The day you decide: do I stay or do I go?

In those early days we were scared all the time, Achi and I. I looked after her—I don't know how we fell into those roles, protector and defended, but I protected and she nurtured and we won respect. There were three moon men for every moon woman. It was a man's world; a macho social meld of soldiers camped in enemy terrain and deep-diving submariners. The Jo Moonbeam barracks were exactly that; a grey, dusty warehouse of temporary accommodation cabins barely the safe legal minimum beneath the surface. We learned quickly the vertical hierarchy of moon society: the lower you live—the further from surface radiation and secondary cosmic rays—the higher your status. The air was chilly and stank of sewage, electricity, dust and unwashed bodies. The air still smells like that; I just got used to the funk in my lungs. Within hours the induction barracks self-sorted. The women gravitated together and affiliated with the astronomers on placement with the Farside observatory. Achi and I traded to get cabins beside each other. We visited, we decorated, we entertained, we opened our doors in solidarity and hospitality. We listened to the loud voices of the men, the real men, the worldbreakers, booming down the aisles of cabins, the over-loud laughter. We made cocktails from cheap industrial vodka.

Sexual violence, games of power were in the air we breathed, the water we drank, the narrow corridors through which we squeezed, pressing up against each other. The moon has never had criminal law, only contract law, and when Achi and I arrived the LDC was only beginning to set up the Court of Clavius to settle and enforce contracts. Queen of the South was a wild town. Fatalities among Jo Moonbeams ran at ten percent. In our first week, an extraction worker from Xinjiang was crushed in a pressure lock. The Moon knows a thousand ways to kill you. And I knew a thousand and one.

Cortas cut. That was our family legend. Hard sharp fast. I made the women's Brazilian jujitsu team at university. It's hard, sharp, fast: the perfect Corta fighting art. A couple of basic moves, together with lunar gravity, allowed me to put over the most intimidating of sex pests. But when Achi's stalker wouldn't take no, I reached for slower, subtler weapons. Stalkers don't go away. That's what makes them stalkers. I found which Surface Activity training squad he was on and made some adjustments to his suit thermostat. He didn't die. He wasn't meant to die. Death would have been easier than my revenge for Achi. He never suspected me; he never suspected anyone. I made it look like a perfect malfunction. I'm a good engineer. I count his frostbite thumb and three toes as my trophies. By the time he got out of the med centre, Achi and I were on our separate ways to our contracts.

That was another clock, ticking louder than the clock in our bones. I&A was four weeks. After that, we would go to work. Achi's work in ecological habitats would take her to the underground agraria the Asamoah family were digging under Amundsen. My contract was with Mackenzie Metals; working out on the open seas. Working with dust. Dustbunny. We clung to the I&A barracks, we clung to our cabins, our friends. We clung to each other. We were scared. Truth: we were scared all the time, with every breath. Everyone on the moon is scared, all the time.

There was a party; moon mojitos. Vodka and mint are easy up here. But before the music and the drinking: a special gift for Achi. Her work with Aka would keep her underground; digging and scooping and sowing. She need never go on the surface. She could go her whole career—her whole life—in the caverns and lava tubes and agraria. She need never see the raw sky.

The suit hire was cosmologically expensive, even after negotiation. It was a GP surface activity shell; an armoured hulk to my lithe sasuit spiderwoman. Her face was nervous behind the faceplate; her breathing shallow. We held hands in the outlock as the pressure door slid up. Then her faceplate polarised in the sun and I could not see her any more. We walked up the ramp amongst a hundred thousand boot prints. We walked up the ramp and few metres out on to the surface, still holding hands. There, beyond the coms towers and the power relays and the charging points for the buses and rovers; beyond the grey line of the crater rim that curved on the close horizon and the shadows the sun had never touched; there perched above the edge of our tiny world we saw the full earth. Full and blue and white, mottled with greens and ochres. Full and impossible and beautiful beyond any words of mine. It was winter and the southern hemisphere was offered to us; the ocean half of the planet. I saw great Africa. I saw dear Brazil.

Then the air contract advisory warned me that we were nearing the expiry of our oxygen contract and we turned our backs on the blue earth and walked back down into the moon.

That night we drank to our jobs, our friends, our loves and our bones. In the morning we parted.

We met in a café on the twelfth level of the new Chandra Quadra. We hugged, we kissed, we cried a little. I smelled sweet by then. Below us excavators dug and sculpted, a new level every ten days. We held each other at arms' length and looked at each other. Then we drank mint tea on the balcony.

I loathe mint tea.

Mint tea is a fistful of herbs jammed in a glass. Sloshed with boiling water. Served scalded yet still flavourless. Effete like herbal thés and tisanes. Held between thumb and forefinger: so. Mint leaves are coarse and hairy. Mint tea is medicinal. Add sugar and it becomes infantile. It is drinking for the sake of doing something with your fingers.

Coffee is a drink for grownups. No kid ever likes coffee. It's psychoactive. Coffee is the drug of memory. I can remember the great cups of coffee of my life; the places, the faces, the words spoken. It never quite tastes the way it smells. If it did, we would—drink it until our heads exploded with memory,

But coffee is not an efficient crop in our ecology. And imported coffee is more expensive than gold. Gold is easy. Gold I can sift from lunar regolith. Gold is so easy its only value is decorative. It isn't even worth the cost of shipment to Earth. Mint is rampant. Under lunar gravity, it forms plants up to three metres tall. So we are a nation of mint tea drinkers.

We didn't talk about the bones at once. It was eight lunes since we last saw each other: we talk on the network daily, we share our lives but it takes face to face contact to ground all that; make it real.

I made Achi laugh. She laughed like soft rain. I told her about King Dong and she clapped her hands to her mouth in naughty glee but laughed with her eyes. King Dong started as a joke but shift by shift was becoming reality. Footprints last forever on the moon, a bored surface worker had said on a slow shift rotation back to Crucible. What if we stamped out a giant spunking cock, a hundred kilometres long? With hairy balls. Visible from Earth. It's just a matter of co-ordination. Take a hundred male surface workers and an Australian extraction company and joke becomes temptation becomes reality. So wrong. So funny.

And Achi?

She was out of contract. The closer you are to your Moon Day, the shorter the contract, sometimes down to minutes of employment, but this was different. Aka did not want her ideas any more. They were recruiting direct from Accra and Kumasi. Ghanaians for a Ghanaian company. She was pitching ideas to the Lunar Development Corporation for their new port and capital at Meridian—quadras three kilometres deep; a sculpted city; like living in the walls of a titanic cathedral. The LDC was polite but it had been talking about development funding for two lunes now. Her savings were running low. She woke up looking at the tick of the Four Fundamentals on her lens. Oxygen water space coms: which do you cut down on first? She was considering moving to a smaller space.

"I can pay your per diems," I said. "I have lots of money."

And then the bones ... Achi could not decide until I got my report. I never knew anyone suffered from guilt as acutely as her. She could not have borne it if her decision had influenced my decision to stay with the moon or go back to Earth.

"I'll go now," I said. I didn't want to. I didn't want to be here on this balcony drinking piss-tea. I didn't want Achi to have forced a decision on me. I didn't want there to be a decision for me to make. "I'll get the tea."

Then the wonder. In the corner of my vision, a flash of gold. A lens malfunction—no, something marvellous. A woman flying. A flying woman. Her arms were outspread, she hung in the sky it like a crucifix. Our Lady of Flight. Then I saw wings shimmer and run with rainbow colours; wings transparent and strong as a dragonfly's. The woman hung a moment, then folded her gossamer wings around her, and fell. She tumbled, now diving heard-first, flicked her wrists, flexed her shoulders. A glimmer of wing slowed her; then she spread her full wing span and pulled up out of her dive into a soaring spiral, high into the artificial sky of Chandra Quadra.

"Oh," I said. I had been holding my breath. I was shaking with wonder. I was chewed by jealousy.

"We always could fly," Achi said. "We just haven't had the space. Until now."

Did I hear irritation in Achi's voice, that I was so bewitched by the flying woman? But if you could fly why would you ever do anything else?

I went to the Mackenzie Metals medical centre and the medic put me in the scanner. He passed magnetic fields through my body and the machine gave me my bone density analysis. I was eight days behind Achi. Five weeks, and then my residency on the moon would become citizenship.

Or I could fly back to Earth, to Brazil.

There are friends and there are friends you have sex with.

After I&A it was six lunes until I saw Achi again. Six lunes in the Sea of Fertility, sifting dust. The Mackenzie Metals Messier unit was old, cramped, creaking: cut-and-cover pods under bulldozed regolith berms. Too frequently I was evacuated to the new, lower levels by the radiation alarm. Cosmic rays kicked nasty secondary particles out of moon dust, energetic enough to penetrate the upper levels of the unit. Every time I saw the alarm flash its yellow trefoil in my lens I felt my ovaries tighten. Day and night the tunnels trembled to the vibration of the digging machines, deep beneath even those evacuation tunnels, eating rock. There were two hundred dustbunnies in Messier. After a month's gentle and wary persistence and charm from a 3D print designer, I joined the end of a small amory: my Chu-yu, his homamor in Queen, his hetamor in Meridian, her hetamor also in Meridian. What had taken him so long, Chu-yu confessed, was my rep. Word about the sex pest on I&A with the unexplained suit malfunction. *I wouldn't do that to a co-worker*, I said. *Not unless severely provoked*. Then I kissed him. The amory was warmth and sex, but it wasn't Achi. Lovers are not friends.

Sun Chu-yu understood that when I kissed him goodbye at Messier's bus lock. Achi and I chatted on the network all the way to the railhead at Hypatia, then all the way down the line to the South. Even then, only moments since I had last spoken to her image on my eyeball, it was a physical shock to see her at the meeting point in Queen of the South station: her, physical her. Shorter than I remembered. Absence makes the heart grow taller.

Such fun she had planned for me! I wanted to dump my stuff at her place but no; she whirled me off into excitement. After the reek and claustrophobia of Messier Queen of the South was intense, loud, colourful, too too fast. In only six lunes it had changed beyond recognition. Every street was longer, every tunnel wider, every chamber loftier. When she took me in a glass elevator down the side of the recently completed Thoth Quadra I reeled from vertigo. Down on the floor of the massive cavern was a small copse of dwarf trees—full-size trees would reach the ceiling, Achi explained. There was a café. In that café I first tasted and immediately hated mint tea.

I built this, Achi said. *These are my trees, this is my garden.*

I was too busy looking up at the lights, all the lights, going up and up.

Such fun! Tea, then shops. I had had to find a party dress. We were going to a special party, that night. Exclusive. We browsed the catalogues in five different print shops before I found something I could wear: very retro, 1950s inspired, full and layered, it hid what I wanted hidden. Then, the shoes.

The special party was exclusive to Achi's workgroup and their F&Fs. A security-locked rail capsule took us through a dark tunnel into a space so huge, so blinding with mirrored light, that once again I reeled on my feet and almost threw up over my Balenciaga. An agrarium, Achi's last project. I was at the bottom of a shaft a kilometre tall, fifty metres wide. The horizon is close at eye level on the moon; everything curves. Underground, a different geometry applies. The agrarium was the straightest thing I had seen in months. And brilliant: a central core of mirrors ran the full height of the shaft, bouncing raw sunlight one to another to another to walls terraced with hydroponic racks. The base of the shaft was a mosaic of fish tanks, criss-crossed by walkways. The air was warm and dank and rank. I was woozy with CO_2. In these conditions plants grew fast and tall; potato plants the size of bushes; tomato vines so tall I lost their heads in the tangle of leaves and fruit. Hyper-intensive agriculture: the agrarium was huge for a cave, small for an ecosystem. The tanks splashed with fish. Did I hear frogs? Were those ducks?

Achi's team had built a new pond from waterproof sheeting and construction frame. A pool. A swimming pool. A sound system played G-pop. There were cocktails. Blue was the fashion. They matched my dress. Achi's crew were friendly and expansive. They never failed to compliment me on my fashion. I shucked it and my shoes and everything else for the pool. I lolled, I luxuriated, I let the strange, chaotic eddies waft green, woozy air over me while over my head the mirrors moved. Achi swam up beside me and we trod water together, laughing and plashing. The agrarium crew had lowered a number of benches into the pool to make a shallow end. Achi and I wafted blood-warm water with our legs and drank Blue Moons.

I am always up for a party.

I woke up in bed beside her the next morning; shit-headed with moon vodka. I remembered mumbling, fumbling love. Shivering and stupid-whispering, skin to skin. Fingerworks. Achi lay curled on her right side, facing me. She had kicked the sheet off in the night. A tiny string of drool ran from the corner of her mouth to the pillow and trembled in time to her breathing.

I looked at her there, her breath rattling in the back of her throat in drunk sleep. We had made love. I had sex with my dearest friend. I had done a good thing, I had done a bad thing. I had done an irrevocable thing. Then I lay down and pressed myself in close to her and she mumble-grumbled and moved in close to me and her fingers found me and we began again.

I woke in the dark with the golden woman swooping through my head. Achi slept beside me. The same side, the same curl of the spine, the same light rattle-snore and open mouth as that first night. When I saw Achi's new cabin, I booked us into a hostel. The bed was wide, the air was as fresh as Queen of the South could make and the taste of the water did not set your teeth on edge.

Golden woman, flying loops through my certainties.

Queen of the South never went fully dark—lunar society is 24-hour society. I pulled Achi's unneeded sheet around me and went out on to the balcony. I leaned on the rail and looked out at the walls of lights. Apts, cabins, walkways and staircases. Lives and decisions behind every light. This was an ugly world. Hard and mean. It put a price on everything. It demanded a negotiation from everyone. Out at Railhead I had seen a new thing among some of the surface workers: a medallion, or a little votive tucked into a patch pocket. A woman in Virgin Mary robes, one half of her face a black angel, the other half a naked skull. Dona Luna: goddess of dust and radiation. Our

Lady Liberty, our Britannia, our Marianne, our Mother Russia. One half of her face dead, but the other alive. The moon was not a dead satellite, it was a living world. Hands and hearts and hopes like mine shaped it. There was no mother nature, no Gaia to set against human will. Everything that lived, we made. Dona Luna was hard and unforgiving, but she was beautiful. She could be a woman, with dragonfly wings, flying.

I stayed on the hotel balcony until the roof reddened with sun-up. Then I went back to Achi. I wanted to make love with her again. My motives were all selfish. Things that are difficult with friends are easier with lovers.

My grandmother used to say that love was the easiest thing in the world. Love is what you see every day.

I did not see Achi for several lunes after the party in Queen. Mackenzie Metals sent me out into the field, prospecting new terrain in the Sea of Vapours. Away from Messier, it was plain to me and Sun Chu-yu that the amory didn't work. You love what you see every day. All the amors were happy for me to leave. No blame, no claim. A simple automated contract, terminated.

I took a couple of weeks furlough back in Queen. I had called Achi about hooking up but she was at a new dig at Twe, where the Asamoahs were building a corporate headquarters. I was relieved. And then was guilty that I had felt relieved. Sex had made everything different. I drank, I partied, I had one night stands, I talked long hours of expensive bandwidth with my loved ones back on Earth. They thanked me for the money, especially the tiny kids. They said I looked different. Longer. Drawn out. My bones eroding, I said. There they were, happy and safe. The money I sent them bought their education. Health, weddings, babies. And here I was, on the moon. Plain Adriana, who would never get a man, but who got the education, who got the degree, who got the job, sending them the money from the moon.

They were right. I was different. I never felt the same about that blue pearl of Earth in the sky. I never again hired a sasuit to go look at it, just look at it. Out on the surface, I disregarded it.

The Mackenzies sent me out next to the Lansberg extraction zone and I saw the thing that made everything different.

Five extractors were working Lansberg. They were ugly towers of Archimedes screws and grids and transport belts and wheels three times my height, all topped out by a spread of solar panels that made them look like robot trees. Slow-moving, cumbersome, inelegant. Lunar design tends to the utilitarian, the practical. The bones on show. But to me they were beautiful. Marvellous trees. I saw them one day, out on the regolith, and I almost fell flat from the revelation. Not what they made—separating rare earth metals from lunar regolith—but what they threw away. Launched in high, arching ballistic jets on either side of the big, slow machines.

It was the thing I saw every day. One day you look at the boy on the bus and he sets your heart alight. One day you look at the jets of industrial waste and you see riches beyond measure.

I had to dissociate myself from anything that might link me to regolith waste and beautiful rainbows of dust.

I quit Mackenzie and became a Vorontsov track queen.

I want to make a game of it, Achi said. That's the only way I can bear it. We must clench our fists behind our backs, like Scissors Paper Stone, and we must count to three, and then we open our fists and in them there will be something, some small object, that will say beyond any doubt what we have decided. We must not speak, because if we say even a word, we will influence each other. That's the only way I can bear it if it is quick and clean and we don't speak. And a game.

We went back to the balcony table of the café to play the game. It was now on the 13th level. Two glasses of mint tea. No one was flying the great empty spaces of Chandra Quadra this day. The air smelled of rock dust over the usual electricity and sewage. Every fifth sky panel was blinking. An imperfect world.

Attempted small talk. Do you want some breakfast? No, but you have some. No I'm not hungry. I haven't seen that top before. The colour is really good for you. Oh it's just something I printed out of a catalogue ... Horrible awful little words to stop us saying what we really had to stay.

"I think we should do this kind of quickly," Achi said finally and in a breathtaking instant her right hand was behind her back. I slipped my small object out of my bag, clenched it in my hidden fist.

"One two three," Achi said. We opened our fists.

A *nazar*: an Arabic charm: concentric teardrops of blue, white and black plastic. An eye.

A tiny icon of Dona Luna: black and white, living and dead.

Then I saw Achi again. I was up in Meridian renting a data crypt and hunting for the leanest, freshest, hungriest law firm to protect the thing I had realised out on Lansberg. She had been called back from Twe to solve a problem with microbiota in the Obuasi agrarium that had left it a tower of stinking black slime.

One city; two friends and amors. We went out to party. And found we couldn't. The frocks were fabulous, the cocktails disgraceful, the company louche and the narcotics dazzling but in each bar, club, private party we ended up in a corner together, talking.

Partying was boring. Talk was lovely and bottomless and fascinating.

We ended up in bed again, of course. We couldn't wait. Glorious, impractical 1950s Dior frocks lay crumpled on the floor, ready for the recycler.

"What do you want?" Achi asked. She lay on her bed, inhaling THC from a vaper. "Dream and don't be afraid."

"Really?"

"Moon dreams."

"I want to be a dragon," I said and Achi laughed and punched me on the thigh: *get away*. "No, seriously."

In the year and a half we had been on the moon, our small world had changed. Things move fast on the moon. Energy and raw materials are cheap, human genius plentiful. Ambition boundless. Four companies had emerged as major economic forces: four families. The Australian Mackenzies were the longest established. They had been joined by the Asamoahs, whose company Aka monopolised food and living space. The Russian Vorontsovs finally moved their operations off Earth entirely and ran the cycler, the moonloop, the bus service and the emergent rail network. Most recent to amalgamate were the Suns, who had defied the representatives of the People's Republic on the LDC board and ran the information infrastructure. Four companies: Four Dragons. That was what they called themselves. The Four Dragons of the Moon.

"I want to be the Fifth Dragon," I said.

The last things were simple and swift. All farewells should be sudden, I think. I booked Achi on the cycler out. There was always space on the return orbit. She booked me into the LDC medical centre. A flash of light and the lens was bonded permanently to my eye. No hand shake, no congratulations, no welcome. All I had done was decide to continue doing what I was doing. The four counters ticked, charging me to live.

I cashed in the return part of the flight and invested the lump sum in convertible LDC bonds. Safe, solid. On this foundation would I build my dynasty.

The cycler would come round the Farside and rendezvous with the moonloop in three days. Good speed. Beautiful haste. It kept us busy, it kept us from crying too much.

I went with Achi on the train to Meridian. We had a whole row of seats to ourselves and we curled up like small burrowing animals.

I'm scared, she said. It's going to hurt. The cycler spins you up to Earth gravity and then there's the gees coming down. I could be months in a wheelchair. Swimming, they say that's the closest to being on the moon. The water supports you while you build up muscle and bone mass again. I can do that. I love swimming. And then you can't help thinking, what if they got it wrong? What if, I don't know, they mixed me up with someone else and it's already too late? Would they send me back here? I couldn't live like that. No one can live here. Not really live. Everyone says about the moon being rock and dust and vacuum and radiation and that it knows a thousand ways to kill you, but that's not the moon. The moon is other people. People all the way up, all the way down; everywhere, all the time. Nothing but people. Every breath, every drop of water, every atom of carbon has been passed through people. We eat each other. And that's all it would ever be, people. The same faces looking into your face, forever. Wanting something from you. Wanting and wanting and wanting. I hated it from the first day out on the cycler. If you hadn't talked to me, if we hadn't met . . .

And I said: *Do you remember, when we talked about what had brought us to the moon?* You said that you owed your family for not being born in Syria—and I said I wanted to be a dragon? I saw it. Out in Lansberg. It was so simple. I just looked at something I saw every day in a different way. Helium 3. The key to the post oil economy. Mackenzie Metals throws away tons of helium 3 every day. And I thought, how could the Mackenzies not see it? Surely they must . . . I couldn't be the only one . . . But family and companies, and family companies especially, they have strange fixations and blindnesses. Mackenzies mine metal. Metal mining is what they do. They can't imagine anything else and so they miss what's right under their noses. I can make it work, Achi. I know how to do it. But not with the Mackenzies. They'd take it off me. If I tried to fight them, they'd just bury me. Or kill me. It's cheaper. The Court of Clavius would make sure my family were compensated. That's why I moved to Vorontsov rail. To get away from them while I put a business plan together. I will make it work for me, and I'll build a dynasty. I'll be the Fifth Dragon. House Corta. I like the sound of that. And then I'll make an offer to my family—my final offer. Join me, or never get another cent from me. There's the opportunity—take it or leave it. But you have to come to the moon for it. I'm going to do this, Achi.

No windows in moon trains but the seat-back screen showed the surface. On a screen, outside your helmet, it is always the same. It is grey and soft and ugly and covered in footprints. Inside the train were workers and engineers; lovers and partners and even a couple of small children. There was noise and colour and drinking and laughing, swearing and sex. And us curled up in the back against the bulkhead. And I thought, *this is the moon.*

Achi gave me a gift at the moonloop gate. It was the last thing she owned. Everything else had been sold, the last few things while we were on the train.

Eight passengers at the departure gate, with friends, family, amors. No one left the moon alone and I was glad of that. The air smelled of coconut, so different from the vomit, sweat, unwashed bodies, fear of the arrival gate. Mint tea was available from a dispensing machine. No one was drinking it.

"Open this when I'm gone," Achi said. The gift was a document cylinder, crafted from bamboo. The departure was fast, the way I imagine executions must be. The VTO staff had everyone strapped into their seats and were sealing the capsule door before either I or Achi could respond. I saw her begin to mouth a goodbye, saw her wave fingers, then the locks sealed and the elevator took the capsule up to the tether platform.

The moonloop was virtually invisible: a spinning spoke of M5 fibre twenty centimetres wide and two hundred kilometres long. Up there the ascender was climbing towards the counterbalance mass, shifting the centre of gravity and sending the whole tether down into a surface-grazing orbit. Only in the final moments of approach would I see the white cable seeming to descend vertically from the star filled sky. The grapple connected and the capsule was lifted from the platform. Up there, one of those bright stars was the ascender, sliding down the tether, again shifting the centre of mass so that the whole ensemble moved into a higher orbit. At the top of the loop, the grapple would release and the cycler catch the capsule. I tried to put names on the stars: the cycler, the ascender, the counterweight; the capsule freighted with my amor, my love, my friend. The comfort of physics. I watched the images, the bamboo document tube slung over my back, until a new capsule was loaded into the gate. Already the next tether was wheeling up over the close horizon.

The price was outrageous. I dug into my bonds. For that sacrifice it had to be the real thing: imported, not spun up from an organic printer. I was sent from printer to dealer to private importer. She let me sniff it. Memories exploded like New Year fireworks and I cried. She sold me the paraphernalia as well. The equipment I needed simply didn't exist on the moon.

I took it all back to my hotel. I ground to the specified grain. I boiled the water. I let it cool to the correct temperature. I poured it from a height, for maximum aeration. I stirred it.

While it brewed I opened Achi's gift. Rolled paper: drawings. Concept art for the habitat the realities of the moon would never let her build. A lava tube, enlarged and sculpted with faces, like an inverted Mount Rushmore. The faces of the orixas, the Umbanda pantheon, each a hundred metres high, round and smooth and serene, overlooked terraces of gardens and pools. Waters cascaded from their eyes and open lips. Pavilions and belvederes were scattered across the floor of the vast cavern; vertical gardens ran from floor to artificial sky, like the hair of the gods. Balconies—she loved balconies—galleries and arcades, windows. Pools. You could swim from one end of this Orixa-world to the other. She had inscribed it: *a habitation for a dynasty*.

I thought of her, spinning away across the sky.

The grounds began to settle. I plunged, poured and savoured the aroma of the coffee. Santos Gold. Gold would have been cheaper. Gold was the dirt we threw away, together with the Helium 3.

When the importer had rubbed a pinch of ground coffee under my nose, memories of childhood, the sea, college, friends, family, celebrations flooded me.

When I smelled the coffee I had bought and ground and prepared, I experienced something different. I had a vision. I saw the sea, and I saw Achi, Achi-gone-back, on a board, in the sea. It was night and she was paddling the board out, through the waves and beyond the waves, sculling herself forward, along the silver track of the moon on the sea.

I drank my coffee.

It never tastes the way it smells.

My granddaughter adores that red dress. When it gets dirty and worn, we print her a new one. She wants never to wear anything else. Luna, running barefoot through the pools, splashing and scaring the fish, leaping from stepping stone, stepping in a complex pattern of stones that must be landed on left footed, right-footed, two footed or skipped over entirely. The Orixas watch her. The Orixas watch me, on my veranda, drinking tea.

I am old bones now. I haven't thought of you for years, Achi. The last time was when I finally turned those drawings into reality. But these last lunes I find my thoughts folding back, not just to you, but to all the ones from those dangerous, daring days. There were more loves than you, Achi. You always knew that. I treated most of them as badly as I treated you. It's the proper pursuit of elderly ladies, remembering and trying not to regret.

I never heard from you again. That was right, I think. You went back to your green and growing world, I stayed in the land in the sky. Hey! I built your palace and filled it with that dynasty I promised. Sons and daughters, amors, okos, madrinhas, retainers. Corta is not such a strange name to you now, or most of Earth's population. Mackenzie, Sun, Vorontsov, Asamoah. Corta. We are Dragons now.

Here comes little Luna, running to her grandmother. I sip my tea. It's mint. I still loathe mint tea. I always will. But there is only mint tea on the moon.

Berrien C. Henderson lives in the deepest, darkest wilds of southeast Georgia. He teaches high school Literature and Composition with a Southern accent. Berrien's writing has appeared in such diverse venues as *The Journal of Asian Martial Arts*, *The Doctor T.J. Eckleburg Review*, *The Dead Mule School of Southern Literature*, *Abyss & Apex*, *Kaleidotrope*, and *Bloody Knuckles: The MMAnthology*. His mini-collection of Southern magical realism, *Old Souls and the Grammar of Their Wanderings*, is available from Papaveria Press. In his not-so-copious free time, Berrien practices martial arts.

LET BASER THINGS DEVISE
Berrien C. Henderson

1: PIERRE

Before Clockwork Corp.'s space ape project heads managed to uplift the chimpanzee, he was simply known as No. 157. Some anonymous lab assistant nicknamed him Pierre, and the moniker stuck. After Pierre survived the rigors of testing and training, his world went dark for a time once the Neuroscience Division got their needles and scalpels and computer-brain interfaces onto and into him.

He was a child again. A sponge. Malleable. He had dreams and remembered them—the great ape facility from which he'd come, the jungle before that. A troop. He had flirted with moonlight and squinted against sunshine while his troop loped through the undergrowth and scampered up the trees and foraged amid the generous loam where he groomed and was groomed. Various *Shes* were there in limbo, too, between dream and memory. Pierre's mind reached out, clutching at phantoms from a blurry past and running into the long now—all of it oozing and *hrmmm*-ing like fluorescent lights with faulty ballasts. He weighed his new life amid antiseptic halls, an institution's sterility and scientists' data points and vagaries of conditioning against the harsher realities of death, quick in its smiting, in the tropics and faces framed with their own intelligence. He yearned for a place absent this new awareness—signals of higher and greater thoughts like thunder at the hem of distant mountains.

Inside a year, he learned to speak with his newly acquired vocal cords—3D bio-printed wonders of Clockwork Corp.'s NuFlesh(tm) proprietary systems—and, thus, No. 157 became the first uplifted articulate chimpanzee.

And he was going to the moon.

2: COMPED

Pierre received the ping of an incoming message on his way out the door. He had a mandatory conditioning session and made to ignore the message to queue up later, then fell short of his initial plans.

Bureau of Personhood.

He caught himself wanting to *oohoohooh* in anxiety and excitement but tamped down those impulses. Some quirks hadn't quite ironed out since uplift, and his human handlers and colleagues overlooked much, thank goodness.

"This is Pierre."

A woman's face greeted him with a sliver of a smile that bespoke scores of such practiced smiles daily and the beginnings of crow's feet at the edges of her eyes. Pierre wondered what kind of punishment the poor liaison had done to deserve shuffling files and contacting various hominids and none too few uplifted canines (a recent development) along with some advanced NuEmote(tm) Model Mark robots. Still, he was glad she had contacted him.

"Pierre, I have good news."

Finally.

"I've sent you a message with a printable, watermarked certificate of personhood."

"Thank you, Sarah, for all your help."

"Thank the lawyers at Clockwork Corp.," she said. "They saw the handwriting on the wall. You had the virtue of many legal precedents on your side."

"I"—the words sometimes wouldn't come—"appreciate your taking time to-*oohooh* face-contact me."

The practiced smile widened, and he saw the glimmers of a few teeth. "Why, thank you kindly, Pierre."

"At least I'm not working basic municipal services," he said. The majority of uplifted apes ended up employed in recycling facilities or treatment plants unless, of course, one was part of an R&D department for the largest corporation in the world and a handy PR football tossed around in the mining claims wars raging on the moon.

"Well, there's that," she said. "You realize how fortunate you are."

"Yes." And he felt immediately unlucky to be condescended to. Or complimented. He still had trouble navigating social mores. "Thank you."

"Have a good day, Pierre."

"You, too-*ooh*, Sarah."

As her image faded, Pierre stared at the screen and considered his newfound reality.

Personhood.

The company wanted a poster child for the new wave of lunar exploration. All he had to do was make a loathsome trip to Human Resources and request an addendum to his work contract for this upcoming expedition. The concept of money didn't escape him, but he had little use for it. He banked a pittance for little things like sodas. Sodas he loved.

The ideas grew. Humans talked with anticipation about taking vacations, and he wanted vacation time, which was not a component of his old contract. No more day passes into the city. No more permission requests for visits to museums or . . . or . . .

The possibilities unfurled in his mind, and Pierre smiled.

3: HUMAN RESOURCES

"Well, this is a first," said the HR rep. "Wonder if the company ought to consider changing the name of the department now?"

Pierre didn't laugh during the man's pregnant pause. "New territory."

"In more ways than one. First, congratulations on your official person-hood status. You've come a long way, Pierre."

"Hmmmm."

A flash of jungle memory stung him: sunlight lancing the canopy and the screams of another chimpanzee caught in a great cat's jaws. He could expect a headache—the single and sometimes debilitating side effect of the CBI gear in his head.

"You still have a week before launch. It takes three days to process a con-tract addendum request. I can message you."

"Do you see any reason it might be denied?"

"No more than any other request."

"*Ooh.*"

"What's that?"

"I mean, 'Oh.'"

They shuffled through several documents that required e-signatures, eye-stamps, and DNA proofs as Pierre did his best to maneuver the platitudes of small talk.

"Is this what they meant by signing in blood?"

The fat man chuckled. "I suppose so." He offered his hand to Pierre, who hesitated, then shook. A rarity. All of his physical reinforcement and inter-actions had consisted of claps on the shoulder and good-natured squeezes of the upper arm—even one high five. Very few handshakes. His hand met the clammy palmflesh of the fat man, who seemed quite appreciative.

When Pierre excused himself, he left with the distinct impression that the fat man was lonely despite dealing with other humans on a daily basis. Alone in a troop. Pierre was stung again as he walked the fluorescent-lit halls to the Fitness and Conditioning wing, signed out, and trained outside. A hard workout in the obstacle course would boost his endorphins and help him fight the headache. He hated the humans' pain relievers while understanding their necessity.

A bright yellow sun bathed him. A great eye whose warmth slithered down through a noisy canopy. Pierre allowed himself thoughts of trees and courting and earth and night-nesting, and the daydream became a nightmare Klaxon calling out his buried limbic fears of being hunted. Captured.

FLEE!

He scaled trunks and brachiated vines and limbs, missed one and plummeted to earth. He became a caged thing in a preserve; the trees were not the same—constructs for primates to climb and maintain their facade of health and activity. A group of handlers seized him and parleyed him to an alien, antiseptic landscape full of hooting and yowling.

The real nightmare, the waking one, happened when he fell asleep and woke to the reality of his uplifting and a flood of information, a cascade of new schema expanding exponentially—the synaptic flood churning and frothing in his mind from the cerebral implant. He understood the cries of the other animals the way an adult understands a child's cries—a mixture of sympathy tinged with the patina of intellectual distance.

The memory remained, still blunted by time and his uplifting—a photo fading from color to monochrome or perhaps spackled brightly, overexposed and portions blotted out.

He needed to get away.

4: TSUKI

The susurration of servos and hissing of actuators alerted Pierre as he finished his gymnastics and, planning to warm down with yoga, dropped to the ground.

The Model Mark II lunar-bot approached him in hexapod form, and Pierre couldn't help thinking of a gigantic arachnid, some mutant lurking and emerging from the shadows of the thick foliage of once-home, ready to snatch baby chimps from the troop. Still, Pierre's edginess softened when he saw Tsuki.

"Good afternoon, Pierre. News travels fast."

"Of?"

"Your having been granted personhood. How does that make you feel?"

Tendrils of the headache coiled around his brain. "I put in for a vacation after we revised the contract."

"A reward. I see." She skittered alongside him and used one of her four arms to retrieve his water bottle and hand it to him.

"Thank you, Tsuki. It still seems a mere formality."

"While conferring you wider latitude of rights and privileges."

"Today would have been the same regardless."

"A rather cynical view, if perhaps a valid observation."

His head echoed with the ghost-strains of the headache. A ripple from the back of his neck straight-lined from the CBI's scar and to his eyes.

"If you say so-*ooh*."

"Would you care to run through a mission simulation with me in the Augmentation Array?"

"Hold on a moment." Pierre retrieved his wafer tablet, which buzzed slightly, and he queued up his meager bank account. It had already been flagged for a deposit. "Huh. They actually did it."

"'They'?"

"The company. Given today's news, I've received dividends on shares retroactively for the duration of my employment. Good faith call on their part."

"That was charitable if manipulative."

"At least I have more money to put toward that vacation."

"And sodas."

Pierre smiled. "Good idea. Care to join me for a cafeteria pit stop?"

"Gladly."

5: "APOLLO'S DEATH (AND PERHAPS A RESURRECTION)"

REUTERS
OP-ED
Byron Pettigrew

The Apollo program ended in 1975 with the catastrophic failure of the Apollo 20 mission. Col. William "Memphis" Cato and geologist Dr. Angela Phelps had the unfortunate encounter with Mr. Murphy in the form of a cascade of failures. A dying retro-thruster. On the same side as the thruster—since the module came down harder—a leg collapsed. Other than the rough landing (and thankfully the LRV suffered no damage), Cato and Phelps had every reason to believe they could return to the orbiter. They could do what the stalwart trio of Apollo 13 did. Or the crew of Apollo 19.

Only, they couldn't, especially not when, after five hours of work, a baseball-sized meteor ripped through the top of the lunar module. The duo awaited the inevitable.

NASA held its memorial with the rest of the nation. The Cato and Phelps families held their respective memorials while Mission Control decided to close the Apollo program with this disaster and move on.

There is no better time to return to the moon than the fiftieth anniversary of the mission. Consider the time and tide of change: The joint venture featuring a Russian multistage rocket along with a United States orbiter and a Japanese lunar module that could only be capped with Clockwork Corp.'s lunar-bot, a Tsuki Model 2, and Pierre the Uplifted Chimp (so labeled by at least one children's book spinning out of the affair).

There have been the predictable protests about using uplifted animals, but because of a corporate law loophole along with legal precedents set in prior years for uplifted dogs and cats (and one gecko), Pierre would not be the first ape in space, but he would be the first uplifted ape to walk on the moon. Other such chimpanzees see this as quite a boon to their quest for equality.

That Pierre volunteered for the flight has been lost on some of the more vocal and otherwise well-intentioned anti-upli—.

::SKIP AD SURVEY? CONTINUE TO REMAINDER OF ARTICLE?::

6: FLY ME TO THE MOON

"Now that we are up here, I am farther removed from being a political football and poster child for a handful of advocacy groups," said Pierre. He swiveled his chair after he deleted a dozen invitations to speak from organizations.

"An interesting idiom," replied a section of the wall. Tsuki had slaved herself to the orbiter's computer system. The Clockwork Corp. lunar-bot had all-terrain capacity like her forebears, but the TLRV possessed additional mimetic qualities beta-tested in Earth's most inhospitable climates. Her maiden voyage was at hand with this mining mission. Even if something happened to the main computer, she could manage the rest. Designed for versatility, she was a good tool to have on board. "At least you are not configured into the hull's interior."

"But, Tsuki, you're saving space," said Pierre. "So very ergonomic. Efficient."

The pilot chuckled. "Never thought I'd be flying to the moon with a chimp and a robot, much less myself. Or hearing unintended puns."

"It was intended," said Pierre.

"Might I suggest some practice? It's a long enough ride."

"So, the UN and the North American Directorate finally opened up some lunar territory for mining," said the pilot. "And I get to ferry a robot and a sapient ape."

"More accurately, exploratory missions," said Tsuki.

"And furthering the accuracy, uplifted," said Pierre.

"Touché."

"Indeed," said Tsuki.

7: MARE SERENITATIS

Almost three full months into the rotation, and Pierre could taste his vacation amid the mapping and spectrography. He had to admit that the stillness and the gliding and jumping freedom of a low-gravity environment excited him, and farther out on their digs, he imagined Tsuki did her fair share of indulging his *ooh-ooh-ooh*'s of joy. If he played golf, he would've driven plenty of golf balls as far across the Sea of Serenity as possible.

But all such thoughts faded fast as he stared at a lunar lander.

"Tsuki, I need you at my location," said Pierre.

Her voice, tinny through his helmet's speakers, replied, "Are you all right, Pierre?"

"Yes. No. I've found something—*ooh-ooh*—some*things*, to be precise."

"ETA in seven minutes."

"Roger that."

He hop-drifted several more meters, and his concern grew.

Ooh-ooh-ooh.

Nearby lay an older model emergency habitat.

Pierre stared down from the ridge upon the swath of Mare Serenitatis, but closer were two bodies in spacesuits. He bounded down to them; they lay facing each other. Their desiccated faces grinned and yawned at each other from across the decades, and Pierre knew enough of history to realize that today's mining spectrometer experiments were rendered moot.

"Pierre?"

Tsuki had retracted her trundles into her back and skittered down to him on her hex-legs.

"We've found a fifty-years-dead pair of astronauts, Tsuki."

"Company protocol dictates immediate contact and securing of the site," said the 'bot.

"Already done that. Col. William Cato and Dr. Angela Phelps, it looks as if you two are finally going home," said Pierre.

All these years and frozen in such a tableau.

"We should follow our exact path in back out, Pierre, so as not to disturb further the site."

"You know they'll want to examine every millimeter and—Get a look."

He pointed at words written in the soil near Tsuki's legs.

"... let baser things devise / To die in dust, ..." Tsuki said. "Interesting final words."

Pierre figured there would be some closure for the descendants and the few aging members from that bygone era.

He had no inkling Tsuki possessed among a multitude of photos the one that would be voted Photo of the Year. It was here, now, etched in the lino-type of his uplifted mind: Pierre's crouching at the quote with one of Col. Cato's hands at the words in the lunar soil and another hand stretched back toward Dr. Phelps.

In his mind, only the curious tableau of a pair of bodies facing each other and space-gloved hands in a fifty-year clutch would remain.

8: INTERSTITIUM

Robot and Uplifted Chimp Discover Lost Apollo 20 Astronauts

—AP—A fifty-year mystery unfolded on the moon recently when a pair of Clockwork Corp. employees on a routine mining mission on the Sea of Serenity stumbled upon the remains of Col. Cato and Dr. Phelps. The families have prepared for a host of press conferences . . .

9: FROM CLOCKWORK CORP.

Pierre
Admin
RE: Recovery/Phelps-Cato
Cc: Tsuki
Pierre,

We have attached the link for the coffins' schematics. The Board decided to aid both the current space administration and the Phelps and Cato families. It is a powerful reminder of the human cost of lunar exploration—of space travel itself.

Once you have fabricated their coffins, transfer the bodies for transport to Camelot Base for pickup. Know that you and Tsuki have played a fundamental role in helping a pair of families find their lost loved ones.

Thank you for your professionalism in helping us handle the matter and for being a credit to the corporation.

With much appreciation,

The Board

10: LITTLE CUPIDS

"What do you extrapolate given the writing we found?" said Tsuki.

"The allusion sounds familiar," said Pierre.

She sent him the full text. He pored over it while the 3D printer whirred through its matrix.

"Based on biographical and scholarly cross-referencing, including its in-clusion in the *Amoretti* sequence, it may be less a note to us than simply a coda for themselves."

"A testament."

"Or testimony, if you will."

Whoever had considered Cato and Phelps being more than colleagues were, most of them, lost to time.

Pierre said, "I have to finish the coffins."

"Do you wish to be left alone, Pierre?"

"Yes. No. Sorry, Tsuki. I'm indecisive. Surely you have other tasks that would better suit you this evening."

The 'bot offered a wave of a four-fingered hand and trundled away. As the automatic door slid shut with a hiss, she looked at Pierre, who didn't notice her for his busyness.

Pierre's mind toiled while his hands engaged the mundanity of work. For a moment he looked at his hands as though they belonged to someone else, and his head became balloon-drifty as if he were in the midst of an out-of-body experience. He felt a pang for the trees and the games. *Her.* All of the *Shes.* A twinge of regret—no—*loss* insinuated itself through Pierre's heart like a tree viper.

Finishing the coffins was lonely work, he thought, glancing periodically at the door.

11: LXXV

After helping send the bodies back to Earth, Pierre couldn't bring himself to sleep it off, so he wandered the lonely halls of Camelot Base. He passed only a handful of humans—mere platitudes they offered each other—and a few 'bots and droids and found himself wanting to ping Tsuki for her company, but she had plenty of spectrography to analyze. And would she really need to indulge Pierre his melancholy at sending the corpses of Cato and Phelps on their way?

He entered the biosphere with its crisp temperate zone. Pierre inhaled the green and earthiness and moistness but resented the underlying counterfeit to it all. In his mind he was a mere hop, skip, and jump away from the awful steel and stone and polymer playrooms at the research facility. At just over a decade old, the trees could have stood more than limited growth, but at least it was a stand of trees, and trees he could enjoy. He fought the urge to snap off an armload of limbs and go ahead and nest for the night.

Sitting under one of the dwarf pines, Pierre queued up a reading list on his tablet. The screen cast its glow on Pierre's face as his eyelids drooped.

Words tunneled through his mind, then tried to string themselves along en-tangled metrical feet—looping in his alpha-state brain:

SONNET LXXV.

One day I wrote her name vpon the strand,
but came the waues and washèd it away:
agayne I wrote it with a second hand,
but came the tyde, and made my paynes his pray.
Vayne man, sayd she, that doest in vaine assay,
a mortall thing so to immortalize.
for I my selue shall lyke to this decay,
and eek my name bee wyped out lykewize.
Not so, (quod I) let baser things deuize,
to dy in dust, but you shall liue by fame:
my verse your vertues rare shall eternize,
and in the heuens wryte your glorious name.
Where whenas death shall all the world subdew,
our loue shall liue, and later life renew.

As he slept that night, Pierre cooed and reached up for elusive dream-limbs. When his arm tired and plopped down, his hand twitched, index finger dancing just above the floor and inscribing ghost words on the patterned tiles.

12: BANTER

Pierre woke and startled himself: arm outstretched and clutching the air and the dream receding fast. He jumped at the *whirr-buzz-shush* of Tsuki's servos and hissing actuators as she trundled into the room.

"You sounded . . . distressed."

He zipped into his worksuit and stifled a yawn. "Just talking in my sleep."

"More accurately, intoning with grunts and hoots," she said.

He put on his boots. "*Ooh.*"

"Would you like to be left alone?"

"Not really. Please join me while I eat?"

"Yes. We could play holo-chess."

"That would be nice."

A short trip down the hall brought them into the mess. A few humans ambled around—as always, congenial yet aloof. Everyone was here to do a job, and no one seemed interested in befriending a knuckle-walking novelty like Pierre.

He ate but didn't care. It was welcome stimulation to play chess and took his mind off work and dead astronauts.

"Based on our current timeline," said Tsuki, "we may return Earthside in a week. A day early, in fact."

"Has it already been so long?"

"Eleven weeks, approximately. The apropos idiom is, I believe, 'give or take.'"

"You're learning."

"Cross-referencing and extrapolating linguistic scenarios."

"Conversing, Tsuki."

"Pierre?"

"Yes?"

"Checkmate."

"Well—*ooh*—shit."

The 'bot said, "A crude if somewhat apropos remark."

"It fits. Come on. Let's go to work."

"I have been working while you slept."

"Infer, please."

"Ah. Your use of first-person plural indicates an implied continuance of company."

"Exactly, Tsuki. So long as it's not another game of chess."

Pierre could've sworn he heard hollow laughter from the 'bot. A most endearing trait on her part.

13: DEPARTURE

They went through their departure checklist and reached the Camelot Base launchpad. A sleek Clockwork Corp. courier hunkered on the pad. The pilot waved at them from behind his window, held up a wrist, and tapped it impatiently.

Pierre shook his head and glide-hopped ahead of Tsuki. They each kicked up plumes of lunar dust.

It was about time!

A goferit 'bot already waited on Pierre with his gear. He was so glad he'd pre-processed out.

"Well, Tsuki, it was good working with you."

"The sentiment is mutual, Pierre."

He sent the goferit 'bot aboard the ship.

"Don't work too hard."

"I have plenty of missions and data to continue analyzing."

"Stay in touch."

"Of course."

Pierre left Tsuki behind on the moon and shrinking amid Camelot Base in the wake of the courier's blast off. Out of his window, he thought he saw the 'bot waving good-bye.

After a while Pierre allowed himself the luxury of relaxing. Poring over spectrum analyses had left him fuzzy-headed and drained on top of the endemic mundanity and tedium.

Plus, Cato and Phelps.

Existing somewhere between a robot and a human left him even more drained—a murky middle state. The courier sped through the long emptiness between the moon and Earth. Pierre had his first dreamless sleep in a long time. He had no headache, especially when he received the ping from headquarters.

RE: LEAVE APPROVAL
noreply.confirmation
CLICK RECEIPT ACKNOWLEDGEMENT LINK.
INSERT CODE TH@SGR8 FOR FINALIZATION

14: CODA: *PAN TROGOLODYTES* OF GUINEA

Waves broke and hush-shushed ashore. Pierre listened to the waves' lulling susurration and found himself mesmerized even as the waves spoke louder for the incoming tide. Far behind him the jungle unspooled its teeming glossolalia of birdcalls and growls, grunts and hoots. Creatures dying. Mating. Hunger. Nature wanted propagation—its children's perpetuation.

Pierre wrote his name and another in the sand.

The moon crept out and blued the world as the tide reached Pierre, and he didn't begrudge its work upon the names in the sand. He massaged his neck and skull, then wished to have another hand to clutch.

Far down the beach a lioness and two cubs ventured out, and Pierre watched them with a twofold sense of flighty self-preservation and bemusement—the potential threat not lost on his old self nor the new one once the lioness probed the air and yawed her head in his direction. After a moment she and the cubs retreated to the luxuriant green treeline.

He needed to move, so he set his tablet to BUSY and shed his clothes, those faulty constructs that indulged society yet shamed Pierre himself.

He approached the shadow-swathed jungle.

With his toes he kneaded the loam. He sprang up to catch hold of and swing upon the nearest limb. As he clambered higher, thoughts of Tsuki and Cato and Phelps accompanied him—the need for troop and family and consortships.

Swinging, bounding, clambering now.

It had been too long since he had experienced the thrill of tempting Earth's gravity and cheating its constancy with each grab of a limb. Dark shapes bounded through the trees and brush, and Pierre kept both pace and distance. There was shame at his own scent they would no doubt catch if not already—too much blend of civilization and cleansing and humanity.

Paths opened before him. Night drew on while the moon cast her dapple-down light through the canopy. This was another kind of freefall, another kind of release. Before long, he was spent, so Pierre busied himself, snapping off branches and weaving them for his night's nesting, and his hands seemed for a moment—just a moment—to belong to some other chimpanzee.

Back on the beach the tide had long since taken the names even as night and exhaustion claimed Pierre and engrafted him among its humid folds. The sea shushed and grated its rhythms through the jungle.

He hugged himself amid a tangle of dreams and sought her name and whispered it as his arm lolled and hand twitched. Pierre clutched only the tropical night while the drift of moonlight played against his open palm and weaved itself through his fingers.

"*Ooh-ooh-ooh.*"

Indrapramit Das (aka Indra Das) is a writer and editor from Kolkata, India. He is a Lambda Literary Award-winner for his debut novel *The Devourers* (Penguin India/Del Rey), and has been a finalist for the Crawford, Tiptree, and Shirley Jackson awards. His short fiction has appeared in publications including *Tor.com, Clarkesworld,* and *Asimov's,* and has been widely anthologized. He is an Octavia E. Butler Scholar and a grateful graduate of Clarion West 2012. He has lived in India, the United States, and Canada, where he completed his MFA at the University of British Columbia.

THE MOON IS NOT A BATTLEFIELD
Indrapramit Das

e're recording.

I was born in the sky, for war. This is what we were told.

I think when people hear this, they think of ancient Earth stories. Of angels and superheroes and gods, leaving destruction between the stars. But I'm no superhero, no Kalel of America-Bygone with the flag of his dead planet flying behind him. I'm no angel Gabreel striking down Satan in the void or blowing the trumpet to end worlds. I'm no devi Durga bristling with arms and weapons, chasing down demons through the cosmos and vanquishing them, no Kali with a string of heads hanging over her breasts black as deep space, making even the other gods shake with terror at her righteous rampage.

I was born in the sky, for war. What does it mean?

I was actually born on Earth, not far above sea level, in the Greater Kolkata Megapolis. My parents gave me away to the Government of India when I was still a small child, in exchange for enough money for them to live off frugally for a year—an unimaginable amount of wealth for two Dalit street-dwellers who scraped shit out of sewers for a living, and scavenged garbage for recycling—sewers sagging with centuries worth of shit, garbage heaps like mountains. There was another child I played with the most in our slum. The government took her as well. Of the few memories I have left of those early days on Earth, the ones of us playing are clearest, more than the ones of my parents, because they weren't around much. But she was always there. She'd bring me hot jalebis snatched from the hands of hapless pedestrians, her hands covered in syrup, and we'd share them. We used to climb and run along the huge sea-wall that holds back the rising Bay of Bengal, and spit in the churning sea. I haven't seen the sea since, except from space—that roiling mass of water feels like a dream. So do those days, with the child who would become the soldier most often by my side. The government told our parents that they would cleanse us of our names, our untouchability, give us a chance to lead noble lives as astral defenders of the Republic of India. Of course they gave us away. I don't blame them. Aditi never blamed hers, either. That was the name my friend was given by the Army. You've met her. We were told our new names before training even began. Single-names, always. Usually from the Mahabharata or Ramayana, we realized later. I don't remember the name my parents gave me. I never asked Aditi if she remembered hers.

That, then, is when the life of asura Gita began.

I was raised by the state to be a soldier, and borne into the sky in the hands of the Republic to be its protector, before I even hit puberty.

The notion that there could be war on the Moon, or anywhere beyond Earth, was once a ridiculous dream.

So are many things, until they come to pass.

I've lived for thirty-six years as an infantry soldier stationed off-world. I was deployed and considered in active duty from eighteen in the Chandnipur Lunar Cantonment Area. I first arrived in Chandnipur at six, right after they took us off the streets. I grew up there. The Army raised us. Gave us a better education than we'd have ever gotten back on Earth. Right from childhood, me and my fellow asuras—Earth-bound Indian infantry soldiers were jawans, but we were always, always asuras, a mark of pride—we were told that we were stationed in Chandnipur to protect the intrasolar gateway of the Moon for the greatest country on that great blue planet in our black sky—India. India, which we could see below the clouds if we squinted during Earthrise on a surface patrol (if we were lucky, we could spot the white wrinkle of the Himalayas through telescopes). We learned the history of our home: after the United States of America and Russia, India was the third Earth nation to set foot on the Moon, and the first to settle a permanent base there. Chandnipur was open to scientists, astronauts, tourists and corporations of all countries, to do research, develop space travel, take expensive holidays and launch inter-system mining drones to asteroids. The generosity and benevolence of Bharat Mata, no? But we were to protect Chandnipur's sovereignty as Indian territory at all costs, because other countries were beginning to develop their own lunar expeditions to start bases. Chandnipur, we were told, was a part of India. The only part of India not on Earth. We were to make sure it remained that way. This was our mission. Even though, we were told, the rest of the world didn't officially recognize any land on the moon to belong to any country, back then. Especially because of that.

Do you remember Chandnipur well?

It was where I met you, asura Gita. Hard to forget that, even if it hadn't been my first trip to the Moon. I was very nervous. The ride up the elevator was peaceful. Like . . . being up in the mountains, in the Himalayas, you know? Oh—I'm so sorry. Of course not. Just, the feeling of being high up—the silence of it, in a way, despite all the people in the elevator cabins. But then you start floating under the seat belts, and there are the safety instructions on how to move around the platform once you get to the top, and all you feel like doing is pissing. That's when you feel untethered. The shuttle to the Moon from the top of the elevator wasn't so peaceful. Every blast of the craft felt so powerful out there. The gs just raining down on you as you're strapped in. I felt like a feather.

Like a feather. Yes. I imagine so. There are no birds in Chandnipur, but us asuras always feel like feathers. Felt. Now I feel heavy all the time, like a stone, like a—hah—a moon, crashing into its world, so possessed by gravity, though I'm only skin and bones. A feather on a moon, a stone on a planet.

You know, when our Havaldar, Chamling his name was, told me that asura Aditi and I were to greet and guide a reporter visiting the Cantonment Area, I can't tell you how shocked we were. We were so excited. We would be on the feeds! We never got reporters up there. Well, to be honest, I wanted to show off our bravery, tell you horror stories of what happens if you wear your suit wrong outside the Cantonment Area on a walk, or get caught in warning shots from Chinese artillery klicks away, or what happens if the micro-atmosphere over Chandnipur malfunctions and becomes too thin while you're out and about there (you burn or freeze or asphyxiate). Civilians like horror stories from soldiers. You see so many of them in the media feeds in the pods, all these war stories. I used to like seeing how different it is for soldiers on Earth, in the old wars, the recent ones. Sometimes it would get hard to watch, of course.

Anyway, asura Aditi said to me, "Gita, they aren't coming here to be excited by a war movie. We aren't even at war. We're in *territorial conflict*. You use the word war and it'll look like we're boasting. We need to make them feel at home, not scare the shit out of them. We need to show them the hospitality of asuras on our own turf."

Couldn't disagree with that. We wanted people on Earth to see how well we do our jobs, so that we'd be welcomed with open arms when it was time for the big trip back—the promised pension, retirement, and that big old heaven in the sky where we all came from, Earth. We wanted every Indian up there to know we were protecting their piece of the Moon. Your piece of the Moon.

I thought soldiers would be frustrated having to babysit a journalist following them around. But you and asura Aditi made me feel welcome.

I felt bad for you. We met civilians in Chandnipur proper, when we got time off, in the Underground Markets, the bars. But you were my first fresh one, Earth-fresh. Like the imported fish in the Markets. Earth-creatures, you know, always delicate, expensive, mouth open gawping, big eyes. Out of water, they say.

Did I look "expensive?" I was just wearing the standard issue jumpsuits they give visitors.

Arre, you know what I mean. In the Markets we soldiers couldn't buy Earth-fish or Earth-lamb or any Earth-meat, when they showed up every six months. We only ever tasted the printed stuff. Little packets; in the stalls they heat up the synthi for you in the machine. Nothing but salt and heat and protein. Imported Earth-meat was too expensive. Same for Earth-people, expensive. Fish out of water. Earth meant paradise. You came from heaven. No offense.

None taken. You and asura Aditi were very good to me. That's what I remember.

After Aditi reminded me that you were going to show every Indian on their feeds our lives, we were afraid of looking bad. You looked scared, at first. Did we scare you?

I wouldn't say scared. Intimidated. You know, everything you were saying earlier, about gods and superheroes from the old Earth stories. The stuff they let you watch and read in the pods. That's what I saw, when you welcomed us in full regalia, out on the surface, in your combat suits, at the parade. You gleamed like gods. Like devis, asuras, like your namesakes. Those weapon limbs, when they came out of the backs of your suit during the demonstration, they looked like the arms of the goddesses in the epics, or the wings of angels, reflecting the sunlight coming over the horizon—the light was so white, after Earth, not shifted yellow by atmosphere. It was blinding, looking at you all. I couldn't imagine having to face that, as a soldier, as your enemy. Having to face you. I couldn't imagine having to patrol for hours, and fight, in those suits—just my civilian surface suit was so hot inside, so claustrophobic. I was shaking in there, watching you all.

Do you remember, the Governor of Chandnipur Lunar Area came out to greet you, and shake the hands of all the COs. A surface parade like that, on airless ground, that never happened—it was all for you and the rest of the reporters, for the show back on Earth. We had never before even seen the Governor in real life, let alone in a surface suit. The rumours came back that he was trembling and sweating when he shook their hands—that he couldn't even pronounce the words to thank them for their service. So you weren't alone, at least.

Then when we went inside the Cantonment Area, and we were allowed to take off our helmets right out in the open—I waited for you and Aditi to do it first. I didn't believe I wouldn't die, that my face wouldn't freeze. We were on that rover, such a bumpy ride, but open air like those vehicles in the earliest pictures of people on the Moon—just bigger. We went through the Cantonment airlock gate, past the big yellow sign that reads "Chandnipur, Gateway to the Stars," and when we emerged from the other side Aditi told me to look up and see for myself, the different sky. From deep black to that deep, dusky blue, it was amazing, like crossing over into another world. The sunlight still felt different, blue-white instead of yellow, filtered by the nanobot haze, shimmering in that lunar dawn coming in over the hilly rim of Daedalus crater. The sun felt tingly, raw, like it burned even though the temperature was cool. The Earth was half in shadow—it looked fake, a rendered backdrop in a veeyar sim. And sometimes the micro-atmosphere would move just right and the bots would be visible for a few seconds in a wave across that low sky, the famous flocks of "lunar fireflies." The rover went down the suddenly smooth lunarcrete road, down the main road of the Cantonment—

New Delhi Avenue.

Yes, New Delhi Avenue, with the rows of wireframed flags extended high, all the state colours of India, the lines and lines of white barracks with those tiny windows on both sides. I wanted to stay in those, but they put us civilians underground, in a hotel. They didn't want us complaining about conditions. As we went down New Delhi Avenue and turned into the barracks for the tour, you and Aditi took off your helmets and breathed deep. Your faces were covered in black warpaint. Greasepaint. Full regalia, yes? You both looked like Kali, with or without the necklace of heads. Aditi helped me with the helmet, and I felt lunar air for the first time. The dry, cool air of Chandnipur. And you said "Welcome to chota duniya. You can take off the helmet." Chota duniya, the little world. Those Kali faces, running with sweat, the tattoos of your wetware. You wore a small beard, back then, and a crew-cut. Asura Aditi had a ponytail, I was surprised that was allowed.

You looked like warriors, in those blinding suits of armour.

Warriors. I don't anymore, do I. What do I look like now?

I see you have longer hair. You shaved off your beard.

Avoiding the question, clever. Did you know that jawan means "young man"? But we were asuras. We were proud of our hair, not because we were young men. We, the women and the hijras, the not-men, told the asuras who were men, why do you get to keep beards and moustaches and we don't? Some of them had those twirly moustaches like the asuras in the myths. So the boys said to us: we won't stop you. Show us your beards! From then it was a competition. Aditi could hardly grow a beard on her pretty face, so she gave up when it was just fuzz. I didn't. I was so proud when I first sprouted that hair on my chin, when I was a teenager. After I grew it out, Aditi called it a rat-tail. I never could grow the twirly moustaches, But I'm a decommissioned asura now, so I've shaved off the beard.

What do you think you look like now?

Like a beggar living in a slum stuck to the side of the space elevator that took me up to the sky so long ago, and brought me down again not so long ago.

Some of my neighbours don't see asuras as women or men. I'm fine with that. They ask me: do you still bleed? Did you menstruate on the Moon? They say, menstruation is tied to the Moon, so asuras must bleed all the time up there, or never at all down here. They think we used all that blood to paint ourselves red because we are warriors. To scare our enemies. I like that idea. Some of them don't believe it when I say that I bleed the same as any Earthling with a cunt. The young ones believe me, because they help me out, bring me rags, pads when they can find them, from down there in the city—can't afford the meds to stop bleeding altogether. Those young ones are a blessing. I can't exactly hitch a ride on top of the elevator up and down every day in my condition.

People in the slum all know you're an asura?

I ask again: what do I look like now?

A veteran. You have the scars. From the wetware that plugged you into the suits. The lines used to be black, raised—on your face, neck. Now they're pale, flat.

The mark of the decommissioned asura—everyone knows who you are. The government plucks out your wires. Like you're a broken machine. They don't want you selling the wetware on the black market. They're a part of the suits we wore, just a part we wore all the time inside us—and the suits are property of the Indian Army, Lunar Command.

I told you why the suits are so shiny, didn't I, all those years ago? Hyper-reflective surfaces so we didn't fry up in them like the printed meat in their heating packets when the sun comes up. The suits made us easy to spot on a lunar battlefield. It's why we always tried to stay in shadow, use infra-red to spot enemies. When we went on recon, surveillance missions, we'd use lighter stealth suits, non-metal, non-reflective, dark grey like the surface. We could only do that if we coordinated our movements to land during night-time.

When I met you and asura Aditi then you'd been in a few battles already. With Chinese and Russian troops. Small skirmishes.

All battles on the moon are small skirmishes. You can't afford anything bigger. Even the horizon is smaller, closer. But yes, our section had seen combat a few times. But even that was mostly waiting, and scoping with in-fra-red along the shadows of craters. When there was fighting, it was between long, long stretches of walking and sitting. But it was never boring. Nothing can be boring when you've got a portioned ration of air to breathe, and no sound to warn you of a surprise attack. Each second is measured out and marked in your mind. Each step is a success. When you do a lunar surface pa-trol outside Chandnipur, outside regulated atmosphere or Indian territory, as many times as we did, you do get used to it. But never, ever bored. If anything, it becomes hypnotic—you do everything you need to do without even think-ing, in that silence between breathing and the words of your fellow soldiers.

You couldn't talk too much about what combat was like on the Moon, on that visit.

They told us not to. Havaldar Chamling told us that order came all the way down from the Lieutenant General of Lunar Command. It was all con-sidered classified information, even training maneuvers. It was pretty silent when you were in Chandnipur. I'm sure the Russians and the Chinese had news of that press visit. They could have decided to put on a display of might, stage some shock and awe attacks, missile strikes, troop movements to draw us out of the Cantonment Area.

I won't lie—I was both relieved and disappointed. I've seen war, as a field reporter. Just not on the Moon. I wanted to see firsthand what the asuras were experiencing.

It would have been difficult. Lunar combat is not like Earth combat, though I don't know much about Earth combat other than theory and his-tory. I probably know less than you do, ultimately, because I've never experi-enced it. But I've read things, watched things about wars on Earth. Learned things, of course, in our lessons. It's different on the Moon. Harder to accom-modate an extra person when each battle is like a game of chess. No extra pieces allowed on the board. Every person needs their own air. No one can speak out of turn and clutter up comms. The visibility of each person needs to be accounted for, since it's so high.

The most frightening thing about lunar combat is that you often can't tell when it's happening until it's too late. On the battlefields beyond Chandni-pur, out on the magma seas, combat is silent. You can't hear anything but your own footsteps, the *thoom-thoom-thoom* of your suit's metal boots crunching dust, or the sounds of your own weapons through your suit, the rattle-kick of ballistics, the near-silent hum of lasers vibrating in the metal of the shell keeping you alive. You'll see the flash of a mine or grenade going off a few feet away but you won't hear it. You won't hear anything coming down from above unless you look up—be it ballistic missiles or a meteorite hurtling down after centuries flying through outer space. You'll feel the shockwave knock you back but you won't hear it. If you're lucky, of course.

Laser weapons are invisible out there, and that's what's we mostly used. There's no warning at all. No muzzle-flash, no noise. One minute you're sitting there thinking you're on the right side of the rocks giving you cover, and the next moment you see a glowing hole melting into the suit of the soldier next to you, like those time-lapse videos of something rotting. It takes less than a second if the soldier on the other side of the beam is aiming properly. Less than a second and there's the flash and pop, blood and gas and super-heated metal venting into the thin air like an aerosol spray, the scream like static in the mics. Aditi was a sniper, she could've told you how lethal the long-range lasers were. I carried a semi-auto, laser or ballistic; those lasers were as deadly, just lower range and zero warm-up. When we were in battles closer to settlements, we'd switch to the ballistic weaponry, because the buildings and bases are mostly better protected from that kind of damage, bullet-proof. There was kind of a silent agreement between all sides to keep from heavily damaging the actual bases. Those ballistic fights were almost a relief—our suits could withstand projectile damage better, and you could see the tracers coming from kilometers away, even if you couldn't hear them. Like fire on oil, across the jet sky. Bullets aren't that slow either, especially here on the Moon, but somehow it felt better to see it, like you could dodge the fire, especially if we were issued jet packs, though we rarely used them because of how difficult they were to control. Aditi was better at using hers.

She saved my life once.

I mean, she did that many times, we both did for each other, just by doing what we needed to do on a battlefield. But she directly saved my life once, like an Earth movie hero. Rocket-propelled grenade on a quiet battlefield. Right from up above and behind us. I didn't even see it. I just felt asura Aditi shove me straight off the ground from behind and blast us off into the air with her jetpack, propelling us both twenty feet above the surface in a second. We twirled in mid-air, and for a little moment, it felt like we were free of the Moon, hovering there between it and the blazing blue Earth, dancing together. As we sailed back down and braced our legs for landing without suit damage, Aditi never let me go, kept our path back down steady. Only then did I see the cloud of lunar dust and debris hanging where we'd been seconds earlier, the aftermath of an explosion I hadn't heard or seen, the streaks of light as the rest of the fireteam returned ballistic fire, spreading out in leaps with short bursts from their jetpacks. No one died in that encounter. I don't even remember whose troops we were fighting in that encounter, which lunar army. I just remember that I didn't die because of Aditi.

Mostly, we never saw the enemy close up. They were always just flecks of light on the horizon, or through our infrared overlay. Always ghosts, reflecting back the light of sun and Earth, like the Moon itself. It made it easier to kill them, if I'm being honest. They already seemed dead. When you're beyond Chandnipur, out on the mara under that merciless black sky with the Earth gleaming in the distance, the only colour you can see anywhere, it felt like *we* were already dead too. Like we were all just ghosts playing out the old wars of humanity, ghosts of soldiers who died far, far down on the ground. But then we'd return to the city, to the warm bustle of the Underground Markets on our days off, to our chota duniya, and the Earth would seem like heaven again, not a world left behind but one to be attained, one to earn, the unattainable paradise rather than a distant history of life that we'd only lived through media pods and lessons.

And now, here you are. On Earth.

Here I am. Paradise attained. I have died and gone to heaven.

It's why I'm here, isn't it? Why we're talking.

You could say that. Thank you for coming, again. You didn't have any trouble coming up the elevator shaft, did you? I know it's rough clinging to the top of the elevator.

I've been on rougher rides. There are plenty of touts down in the elevator base station who are more than willing to give someone with a few rupees a lending hand up the spindle. So. You were saying. About coming back to Earth. It must have been surprising, the news that you were coming back, last year.

FTL changed everything. That was, what, nine years ago?

At first it brought us to the edge of full-on lunar war, like never before, because the Moon became the greatest of all jewels in the night sky. It could become our first FTL port. Everyone wanted a stake in that. Every national territory on the Moon closed off its borders while the Earth governments negotiated. We were closed off in our bunkers, looking at the stars through the small windows, eating nothing but thin parathas from emergency flour rations. We made them on our personal heating coils with synthi butter— no food was coming through because of embargo, mess halls in the main barracks were empty. We lived on those parathas and caffeine infusion. Our stomachs were like balloons, full of air.

Things escalated like never before, in that time. I remember a direct Chinese attack on Chandnipur's outer defences, where we were stationed. One bunker window was taken out by laser. I saw a man stuck to the molten hole in the pane because of depressurization, wriggling like a dying insect. Asura Jatayu, a quiet, skinny soldier with a drinking problem. People always said he filled his suit's drinking water pods with diluted moonshine from the

Underground Markets, and sucked it down during patrols. I don't know if that's true, but people didn't trust him because of it, even though he never really did anything to fuck things up. He was stone cold sober that day. I know, because I was with him. Aditi, me and two other asuras ripped him off the broken window, activated the emergency shutter before we lost too much pressure. But he'd already hemorrhaged severely through the laser wound, which had blown blood out of him and into the thin air of the Moon. He was dead. The Chinese had already retreated by the time we recovered. It was a direct response to our own overtures before the embargo. We had destroyed some nanobot anchors of theirs in disputed territory, which had been laid down to expand the micro-atmosphere of Yueliang Lunar Area.

That same tech that keeps air over Chandnipur and other lunar territories, enables the micro-atmospheres, is what makes FTL work—the q-nanobots. On our final patrols across the mara, we saw some of the new FTL shipyards in the distance. The ships—half-built, they looked like the Earth ruins from historical pictures, of palaces and cities. We felt like we were looking at artifacts of a civilization from the future. They sparked like a far-off battle, bots building them tirelessly. They will sail out to outer space, wearing quenbots around them like cloaks. Like the superheroes! The quenbot cloud folds the space around the ship like a blanket, make a bubble that shoots through the universe. I don't really understand. Is it like a soda bubble or a blanket? We had no idea our time on the Moon was almost over on those patrols, looking at the early shipyards.

After one of the patrols near the shipyards, asura Aditi turned to me and said, "We'll be on one of those ships one day, sailing to other parts of the galaxy. They'll need us to defend Mother India when she sets her dainty feet on new worlds. Maybe we'll be able to see Jupiter and Saturn and Neptune zoom by like cricket balls, the Milky Way spinning far behind us like a chakra."

"I don't think that's quite how FTL works," I told her, but obviously she knew that. She looked at me, low dawn sunlight on her visor so I couldn't see her face. Even though this patrol was during a temporary ceasefire, she had painted her face like she so loved to, so all you could see anyway were the whites of her eyes and her teeth. Kali Ma through and through, just like you said. "Just imagine, maybe we'll end up on a world where we can breathe everywhere. Where there are forests and running water and deserts like Earth. Like in the old Bollywood movies, where the heroes and the heroines run around trees and splash in water like foolish children with those huge mountains behind them covered in ice."

"Arre, you can get all that on Earth. It's where those movies come from! Why would you want to go further away from Earth? You don't want to return home?"

"That's a nice idea, Gita," she said. "But the longer we're here, and the more news and movies and feeds I see of Earth, I get the idea it's not really waiting for us."

That made me angry, though I didn't show it. "We've waited all our lives to go back, and now you want to toss off to another world?" I asked, as if we had a choice in the matter. The two of us, since we were children in the juvenile barracks, had talked about moving to a little house in the Himalayas once we went back, somewhere in Sikkim or northern Bengal (we learned all the states as children, and saw their flags along New Delhi Avenue) where it's not as crowded as the rest of Earth still, and we could see those famously huge mountains that dwarfed the Moon's arid hills.

She said, "Hai Ram, I'm just dreaming like we always have. My dear, what you're not getting is that we have seen Earth on the feeds since we came to the Moon. From expectation, there is only disappointment."

So I told her, "When you talk about other worlds out there, you realize those are expectations too. You're forgetting we're soldiers. We go to Earth, it means our battle is over. We go to another world, you think they'd let us frolic like Bollywood stars in alien streams? Just you and me, Gita and Aditi, with the rest of our division doing backup dancing?" I couldn't stay angry when I thought of this, though I still felt a bit hurt that she was suggesting she didn't want to go back to Earth with me, like the sisters in arms we were.

"True enough," she said. "Such a literalist. If our mission is ever to play Bollywood on an exoplanet, you can play the man hero with your lovely rat-tail beard. Anyway, for now all we have is this grey rock where all the ice is underneath us instead of prettily on the mountains. Not Earth or any other tarty rival to it. *This* is home, Gita beta, don't forget it."

How right she was.

Then came peacetime.

We saw the protests on Earth feeds. People marching through the vast cities, more people than we'd ever see in a lifetime in Chandnipur, with signs and chants. No more military presence on the Moon. The Moon is not an army base. Bring back our soldiers. The Moon is not a battlefield.

But it was, that's the thing. We had seen our fellow asuras die on it.

With the creation of the Terran Union of Spacefaring Nations (T.U.S.N.) in anticipation of human expansion to extrasolar space, India finally gave up its sovereignty over Chandnipur, which became just one settlement in amalgamated T.U.S.N. Lunar territory. There were walled-off Nuclear Seclusion Zones up there on Earth still hot from the last World War, and somehow they'd figured out how to stop war on the Moon. With the signing of the

International Lunar Peace Treaty, every nation that had held its own patch of the Moon for a century of settlement on the satellite agreed to lay down their arms under Earth, Sol, the gods, the goddesses, and the God. The Moon was going to be free of military presence for the first time in decades.

When us asuras were first told officially of the decommissioning of Lunar Command in Chandnipur, we celebrated. We'd made it—we were going to Earth, earlier than we'd ever thought, long before retirement age. Even our COs got shitfaced in the mess halls. There were huge tubs of biryani, with hot chunks of printed lamb and gobs of synthi dalda. We ate so much, I thought we'd explode. Even Aditi, who'd been dreaming about other worlds, couldn't hold back her happiness. She asked me, "What's the first thing you're going to do on Earth?" her face covered in grease, making me think of her as a child with another name, grubby cheeks covered in syrup from stolen jalebis. "I'm going to catch a train to a riverside beach or a sea-wall, and watch the movement of water on a planet. Water, flowing and thrashing for kilometers and kilometers, stretching all the way to the horizon. I'm going to fall asleep to it. Then I'm going to go to all the restaurants, and eat all the real foods that the fake food in the Underground Markets is based on."

"Don't spend all your money in one day, okay? We need to save up for that house in the Himalayas."

"You're going to go straight to the mountains, aren't you," I said with a smile.

"Nah. I'll wait for you, first, beta. What do you think."

"Good girl."

After that meal, a handful of us went out with our suits for an unscheduled patrol for the first time—I guess you'd call it a moonwalk, at that point. We saluted the Earth together, on a lunar surface where we had no threat of being silently attacked from all sides. The century-long Lunar Cold War was over—it had cooled, frozen, bubbled, boiled at times, but now it had evaporated. We were all to go to our paradise in the black sky, as we'd wished every day on our dreary chota duniya.

We didn't stop to think what it all really meant for us asuras, of course. Because as Aditi had told me—the Moon was our home, the only one we'd ever known, really. It is a strange thing to live your life in a place that was never meant for human habitation. You grow to loathe such a life—the gritty dust in everything from your food to your teeth to your weapons, despite extensive air filters, the bitter aerosol meds to get rid of infections and nosebleeds from it. Spending half of your days exercising and drinking carefully rationed water so your body doesn't shrivel up in sub-Earth grav or dry out to a husk in the dry, scrubbed air of controlled atmospheres. The deadening beauty of grey horizons with not a hint of water or life or vegetation in sight except for the sharp lines and lights of human settlement, which we compared so unfavorably to the dazzling technicolour of images and video feeds from Earth, the richness of its life and variety. The constant, relentless company of the same people you grow to love with such ferocity that you hate them as well, because there is no one else for company but the occasional civilian who has the courage to talk to a soldier in Chandnipur's streets, tunnels and canteens.

Now the Moon is truly a gateway to the stars. It is pregnant with the vessels that will take humanity to them, with shipyards and ports rising up under the limbs of robots. I look up at our chota duniya, and its face is crusted in lights, a crown given to her by her lover. Like a goddess it'll birth humanity's new children. We were born in the sky, for war, but we weren't in truth. We were asuras. Now they will be devas, devis. They will truly be like gods, with FTL. In Chandnipur, they told us that we must put our faith in Bhagavan, in all the gods and goddesses of the pantheon. We were given a visiting room, where we sat in the veeyar pods and talked directly to their avatars, animated by the machines. That was the only veeyar we were allowed—no sims of Earth or anything like that, maybe because they didn't want us to get too distracted from our lives on the Moon. So we talked to the avatars, dutifully, in those pods with their smell of incense. Every week we asked them to keep us alive on chota duniya, this place where humanity should not be and yet is.

And now, we might take other worlds, large and small.

Does that frighten you?

I . . . don't know. You told us all those years ago, and you tell me now, that we asuras looked like gods and superheroes when you saw us. In our suits, which would nearly crush a human with their weight if anyone wore them on Earth, let alone walked or fought in them. And now, imagine the humans who will go out there into the star-lit darkness. The big ships won't be ready for a long time. But the small ones—they already want volunteers to take one-way test trips to exoplanets. I don't doubt some of those volunteers will come from the streets, like us asuras. They need people who don't have anything on Earth, so they can leave it behind and spend their lives in the sky. They will travel faster than light itself. Impossible made possible. Even the asuras of the Lunar Command were impossible once.

The Moon was a lifeless place. Nothing but rock and mineral and water. And we still found a way to bring war to it. We still found a way to fight there. Now, when the new humans set foot on other worlds, what if there is life there? What if there is god-given life that has learned to tell stories, make art, fight and love? Will we bring an Earth Army to that life, whatever form it takes? Will we send out this new humanity to discover and share, or will we take people like me and Aditi, born in the streets with nothing, and give them a suit of armour and a ship that sails across the cosmos faster than the light of stars, and send them out to conquer? In the myths, asuras can be both benevolent or evil. Like gods or demons. If we have the chariots of the gods at our disposal, what use is there for gods? What if the next soldiers who go forth into space become demons with the power of gods? What if envy strikes their hearts, and they take fertile worlds from other life forms by force? What if we bring war to a peaceful cosmos? At least we asuras only killed other humans.

One could argue that you didn't just fight on the Moon. You brought life there, for the first time. You, we, humans—we loved there, as well. We still do. There are still humans there.

Love.

I've never heard anyone tell me they love me, nor told anyone I love them. People on Earth, if you trust the stories, say it all the time. We asuras didn't really know what the word meant, in the end.

But. I did love, didn't I? I loved my fellow soldiers. I would have given my life for them. That must be what it means.

I loved Aditi.

That is the first time I've ever said that. I loved Aditi, my sister in arms. I wonder what she would have been, if she had stayed on Earth, never been adopted by the Indian government and given to the Army. A dancer? A Bollywood star? They don't like women with muscles like her, do they? She was bloody graceful with a jet-pack, I'll tell you that much. And then, when I actually stop to think, I realize, that she would have been a beggar, or a sweeper, or a sewer-scraper if the Army hadn't given us to the sky. Like me. Now I live among beggars, garbage-pickers, and sweepers, and sewer-scrapers, in this slum clinging to what they call the pillar to heaven. To heaven, can you believe that? Just like we called Earth heaven up there. These people here, they take care of me. In them I see a shared destiny.

What is that?

To remind us that we are not the gods. This is why I pray still to the gods, or the one God, whatever is out there beyond the heliosphere. I pray that the humans who will sail past light and into the rest of the universe find grace out there, find a way to bring us closer to godliness. To worlds where we might start anew, and have no need for soldiers to fight, only warriors to defend against dangers that they themselves are not the harbingers of. To worlds where our cities have no slums filled with people whose backs are bent with the bravery required to hold up the rest of humanity.

Can I ask something? How . . . how did asura Aditi die?

Hm. Asura Aditi of the 8th Lunar Division—Chandnipur, Indian Armed Forces, survived thirty-four years of life and active combat duty as a soldier on the Moon, to be decommissioned and allowed to return to planet Earth. And then she died right here in New Delhi Megapolis walking to the market. We asuras aren't used to this gravity, to these crowds. One shove from a passing impatient pedestrian is all it takes. She fell down on the street, shattered her Moon-brittled hip because, when we came here to paradise, we found that treatment and physio for our weakened bodies takes money that our government does not provide. We get a pension, but it's not much—we have to choose food and rent, or treatment. There is no cure. We might have been bred for war in the sky, but we were not bred for life on Earth. Why do you think there are so few volunteers for the asura program? They must depend on the children of those who have nothing.

Aditi fell to Earth from the Moon, and broke. She didn't have money for a fancy private hospital. She died of an infection in a government hospital.

She never did see the Himalayas. Nor have I.

I'm sorry.

I live here, in the slums around Akash Mahal Space Elevator-Shaft, because of Aditi. It's dangerous, living along the spindle. But it's cheaper than the subsidized rent of the Veterans Arcologies. And I like the danger. I was a soldier, after all. I like living by the stairway to the sky, where I once lived. I like being high up here, where the wind blows like it never did on the Moon's grey deserts, where the birds I never saw now fly past me every morning and warm my heart with their cries. I like the sound of the nano-tube ecosystem all around us, digesting all our shit and piss and garbage, turning it into the light in my one bulb, the heat in my one stove coil, the water from my pipes, piggybacking on the charge from the solar panels that power my little feed-terminal. The way the walls pulse, absorbing sound and kinetic energy, when the elevator passes back and forth, the rumble of Space Elevator Garuda-3 through the spindle all the way to the top of the atmosphere. I don't like the constant smell of human waste. I don't like wondering when the police will decide to cast off the blinders and destroy this entire slum because it's illegal. I don't like going with a half-empty stomach all the time, living off the kindness of the little ones here who go up and down all the time and get my flour and rice. But I'm used to such things—Chandnipur was not a place of plenty either. I like the way everyone takes care of each other here. We have to, or the entire slum will collapse like a rotten vine slipping off a tree-trunk. We depend on each other for survival. It reminds me of my past life.

And I save the money from my pension, little by little, by living frugally. To one day buy a basic black market exoskeleton to assist me, and get basic treatment, physio, to learn how to walk and move like a human on Earth.

Can . . . I help, in any way?

You have helped, by listening. Maybe you can help others listen as well, as you've said.

Maybe they'll heed the words of a veteran forced to live in a slum. If they send soldiers to the edge of the galaxy, I can only hope that they will give those soldiers a choice this time.

I beg the ones who prepare our great chariots: if you must take our soldiers with you, take them—their courage, their resilience, their loyalty will serve you well on a new frontier. But do not to take war to new worlds.

War belongs here on Earth. I should know. I've fought it on the Moon, and it didn't make her happy. In her cold anger, she turned our bodies to glass. Our chota duniya was not meant to carry life, but we thrust it into her anyway. Let us not make that mistake again. Let us not violate the more welcoming worlds we may find, seeing their beauty as acquiescence.

With FTL, there will be no end to humanity's journey. If we keep going far enough, perhaps we will find the gods themselves waiting behind the veil of the universe. And if we do not come in peace by then, I fear we will not survive the encounter.

I clamber down the side of the column of the space elevator, winding down through the biohomes of the slum towards one of the tunnels where I can reach the internal shaft and wait for the elevator on the way down. Once it's close to the surface of the planet, it slows down a lot—that's when people jump on to hitch a ride up or down. We're only about 1,000 feet up, so it's not too long a ride down, but the wait for it could be much longer. The insides of the shaft are always lined with slum-dwellers and elevator station hawkers, rigged with gas masks and cling clothes, hanging on to the nanocable chords and sinews of the great spindle. I might just catch a ride on the back of one of the gliders who offer their solar wings to travelers looking for a quick trip back to the ground. Bit more terrifying, but technically less dangerous, if their back harness and propulsion works.

The eight-year-old boy guiding me down through the steep slum, along the pipes and vines of the NGO-funded nano-ecosystem, occasionally looks up at me with a gap-toothed smile. "I want to be an asura like Gita," he says. "I want to go to the stars."

"Aren't you afraid of not being able to walk properly when you come back to Earth?"

"Who said I want to come back to Earth?"

I smile, and look up, past the fluttering prayer flags of drying clothes, the pulsing wall of the slum, at the dizzying stairway to heaven, an infinite line receding into the blue. At the edge of the spindle, I see asura Gita poised between the air and her home, leaning precariously out to wave goodbye to me. Her hair ripples out against the sky, a smudge of black. A pale, late evening moon hovers full and pale above her head, twinkling with lights.

I wave back, overcome with vertigo. She seems about to fall, but she doesn't. She is caught between the Earth and the sky in that moment, forever.

Nancy Kress is the author of thirty-four books, including twenty-six novels, four collections of short stories, and three books on writing. Her work has won six Nebulas, two Hugos, a Sturgeon, and the John W. Campbell Memorial Award. Her most recent work is *Terran Tomorrow* (Tor), the final book in her Yesterday's Kin trilogy. Kress's fiction has been translated into Swedish, Danish, French, Italian, German, Spanish, Polish, Croatian, Chinese, Lithuanian, Romanian, Japanese, Korean, Hebrew, Russian, and Klingon, none of which she can read. In addition to writing, Kress often teaches at various venues around the country and abroad, including a visiting lectureship at the University of Leipzig, a 2017 writing class in Beijing, and the annual intensive workshop Tao Toolbox. Kress lives in Seattle with her husband, writer Jack Skillingstead, and Cosette, the world's most spoiled toy poodle.

EVERY HOUR OF LIGHT AND DARK

Nancy Kress

1668

Delft, shrouded in rain, was uniformly gray. Hunched against the cold and wet, the artist walked from Oude Langendijk along the canal to his patron's house. Much as he hated this sort of occasion, inside the house would be warmth, food, wine. And quiet. His own house, crowded with children, was never quiet.

"You are welcome," said his patron's wife shyly as a servant took his cloak. "Pieter will be glad to see you."

Johannes doubted that. This celebration was not about him, nor one of his paintings, nor even the newly acquired Maes painting being shown for the first time. This celebration was about the patron: his wealth, his taste, his power. Johannes smiled at his pretty wife, another acquisition, and passed into the first of many lavishly furnished rooms, all warm from good fires.

In this room hung one of his own paintings. Johannes glanced at it in passing, then stopped abruptly. His eyes widened. He took a candle from a table and held it close to the picture. *Lady Sewing a Child's Bonnet*—he had painted it four years ago. Catharina had been the model. She sat, heavily pregnant, on a wooden chair, the light from an unseen window illuminating the top of her fair hair as she bent over her work. A broken toy lay at her feet, and what could be seen of her expression was somber. On the table beside her were her work basket, a glass of wine, and a pearl necklace, tossed carelessly as if she had thrown it off in discomfort, or despair. On the wall behind her was a painting-within-a-painting, van Honthorst's *Lute Player*. The painstaking detail in the smaller picture, the hint of underpainted blue in Catharina's burgundy-colored dress, the warm light on the whitewashed walls—how long it took to get that right!—all shone in the glow from Johannes's candle.

But he had not made this painting.

Inch by inch, he examined it, ignoring guests who passed him, spoke to him. *Lady Sewing a Child's Bonnet* was the most skillful forgery he had ever seen, but forgery it was. Did Pieter know? Presumably not, or the picture would not still be on the patron's walls. How had it come there? Who had painted it? And—

What should Johannes do about this?

The decision came swiftly—he should do nothing. He owed money all over the city. He had hopes of Pieter's commissioning another painting from him soon, perhaps tonight. The original could not have been switched with the forgery without Pieter's consent, not in this well-guarded house, and Pieter would not welcome attention drawn to whatever scheme he was participating in. Say nothing.

"Ah, Johannes!" said a booming voice behind him. "Admiring your own work, you vain man?"

Johannes turned to face the guest of honor, Nicolaes Maes. "No," he said. Maes waited, but Johannes said nothing more.

Not now, not ever.

2270

Cran is working on clearances at his console when Tulia bounces into the Project room. "Cran! They chose it! They really chose it!" She grabs his hands and twirls him in circles.

"Careful! You'll hit the Squares!"

She stops moving and drops Cran's hands. He hears his own tone: sour, disapproving, a cranky old man. He sees that Tulia understands immediately, but understanding isn't enough to erase the hurt. Torn between them, she chooses hurt.

"Aren't you happy for me?"

"Of course I am," he says, and forces a smile. And he is happy, in a way. How could he not be—Tulia is him, or at least 32 percent of her genes are. It's the other 68 percent that prompts this terrible, inexcusable jealousy.

She says softly, "Maybe next cycle the Gallery will choose one of your pictures."

It is the wrong thing to say; they both know that will never happen. Cran does not have Tulia's talent, has perhaps no talent at all. How does she do it, produce art that is somehow fresh and arresting, after working all day at the Project's forgeries? How? Sometimes he hates her for it. Does she know this?

Sometimes he loves her for it. She knows this.

Cran says, "I am happy for you. But I need to work."

Her eyes sharpen. She, after all, is also part of the Project. "Do you have something?"

"An ancient Egyptian vase, on Square Three. Go look."

She looks, frowning. "We cannot reproduce that."

"Doesn't matter. It's inside a tomb. We can Transfer a lump of rock and no one would ever know."

We could Transfer one of my sculptures, which are just as dreadful as my paintings.

"The tomb was never opened before—"

"No." No one ever names the Madness, if naming can be avoided. Even in a deliberately rational society—legally rational, culturally rational, genetically rational to whatever extent the geneticists can manage—superstitions seep in like moondust in airlocks. No one says the word aloud.

"Well, that's wonderful!" Tulia says. "Has the Director vetted it? Have you done the clearances?"

"Yes, he did, and I'm completing them now. When . . . when is your Gallery presentation?"

"Tuesday. I'll go now. I just wanted to tell you about . . . about my painting."

"I'm glad you did," Cran says, lying, hoping she doesn't realize that. Sixty-eight percent foreign genes.

Tulia leaves. Cran de-opaques the window wall and stares out. The Project is housed in its own dome, and sometimes the bleak lunar landscape calms him when he feels equally bleak. Not, however, this time.

On the horizon, the lights of Alpha Dome are just visible below stars in the black sky. Alpha was the first, the only dome to exist when the Madness happened on Earth. Six thousand lunar colonists, half of them scientists. They had the best equipment, the best scientific minds, the best planners. Earth had those who could not qualify; Earth had too many people and too many wars; Earth had the ability to create genetically boosted bioweapons so powerful that when the Madness began as just another war, it quickly escalated. In three months everyone on Earth was dead. How could they do that, those Terrans of two centuries ago? Those on Alpha watched in horror. There was nothing they could do except what they did: shoot down both incoming missiles and incoming, infected escapees.

He was not there, of course. He's old, but not that old. How long does it take for guilt to evaporate? Longer than two hundred years. Alpha Dome grew to sixteen more domes. If he squints hard, he might be able to see the robots constructing Sigma Dome on the western horizon, or the sprays of dirt thrown up from the borers digging the connecting tunnels. But through all the construction, all the genetic tinkering, all the amazing scientific progress, the guilt has not gone away. We humans murdered our own species. Thus, the Project.

Or perhaps, Cran thinks, that's wrong. There is, after all, a strong but polite political faction—all Luna's political factions are polite, or else they don't exist—that says the Project should be discontinued and its resources committed to the present and the future, not to rescuing the past. So far, this has not happened.

It takes Cran nearly an hour to finish the complicated clearance procedures for the Egyptian vase. He finds it hard to concentrate.

The clearances are approved almost immediately. They are, after all, only a formality; the Director, who is the Project's expert on art of the ancient world, has already inspected the image glowing in Square Three. Cran has worked a long day and it's late; he should go home. But he likes working alone at night, and he has the seniority to do so. He gazes at the vase, this exquisite thing that exists in dark beneath tons of rock in a buried tomb a quarter-million miles and three millennia away. A core-formed glass vessel, three inches high, its graceful, elaborately decorated curves once held perfumed ointment or scented oils. Perhaps it still does.

The Project room is lined with Squares, each a six-foot cube. Some of the Squares are solid real-time alloys; some are virtual simulations; some are not actually there at all—not in time or space. The Project is built on chaos theory, which says that the patterns of spacetime contain something called "strange attractors," a mathematical concept that Cran doesn't understand at all. He is, after all, a Project technician, not a physicist. A senior, trusted technician who will never be an artist.

Why Tulia? Why not me?

One of those questions that, like the Madness, has no answer.

2018

The guard at the National Gallery in Washington, D.C., made his early morning rounds. He unlocked each room, peered in, and moved on. He had worked there a long while and prided himself on knowing exactly what each exhibit held at any given time.

He unlocked a gallery, glanced in, and stopped cold.

Not possible.

This room held the Gallery's five Vermeers. At present, two were on loan. The other three should be on the off-white walls in their protected frames. They were.

But—

"Oh my God," the guard said under his breath, and then very loudly. His hands shook as he pressed the alarm on his pager.

2270

The Transfer happens, as always, blindingly fast. One moment Square Three holds a small stone. The next it holds a delicate purple vase trimmed in gold.

Cran doesn't touch it. He follows protocol and calls two members of the Handler Staff. Despite the hour, they both rush to the Project room. Marbet Hammerling's eyes water, an extravagance that Cran deplores even as he understands it.

Salvaging anything from the past is a slow, difficult, emotional triumph. Humanity's artistic heritage lay decaying on a deserted and contaminated Earth; nothing can be brought from the present without bringing contamination with it. But thanks to the genius of the Rahvoli Equations and the engineers who translated them to reality, some things can be saved from the past. Only things less than six cubic feet; only things deemed worthy of the huge expenditure of energy; only things non-living; only things replaced in Transfer by a rough equivalent in weight and size; only replacements that will not change the course of the timestream that has already unfolded. Otherwise, the Transfer simply did not happen. The past could only be disturbed so much.

Marbet whispers, "It is so beautiful." Reverently she lifts it from the faint shimmer of the Square.

Cran is permitted to touch it with one finger, briefly. Only that. The vase will go into the Gallery and thousands will come to view and glory in this rightful human inheritance.

The Handlers bear away the vase. Cran paces the Project room. It's well into the artificial lunar night; the lights of Alpha Dome have dimmed on the horizon. Cran can't sleep; it's been several nights since he slept. He's old, but it isn't that. Desire consumes him, the desire of a young man: not for sex, but for glory. Once, he thought he would be a great artist. Long ago reality killed the dream but not the gnawing disappointment, eating at his innards, his brain, his heart.

Tulia has a painting chosen for the Gallery.

His own work is shit, has always been shit, will always be shit.

Tulia, people are beginning to say, is the real thing. A genuine artist, the kind that comes along once in a generation.

Cran can't sit still, can't sleep, can't lift himself, yet again, from the black pit into which he falls so often. Only one thing helps, and he has long since gotten past any qualms about its legality.

He takes the pill and waits. Ten minutes later nothing matters so much, not even his inadequacy. His brain has been temporarily rewired. Nothing works optimally, either, including his hands and his brain, both of which tremble. Small price to pay. The gnawing grows less, the pit retreats.

A flash of color catches his eye. Square Two lights up. The endlessly scanning Project has found something.

2018

"*How?*" James Glenwood said. And then, "Is anything missing?"

Of the National's five Vermeers, *Girl with a Flute* and *Girl with the Red Hat* were on loan to the Frick in New York. *Woman Holding a Balance* and *Lady Writing* both hung on the walls. So did *Lady Sewing a Child's Bonnet*. Below that, propped against the wall in a room locked all night, sat its duplicate.

A fake, of course—but how the hell did it get there?

The guard looked guilty. But Henry had worked for the museum for twenty-five years. And naturally he looked upset—suspicion was bound to fall on him as the person who locked this room last night and opened it this morning. Glenwood, a curator for thirty years, remembered well the 1990 brazen theft of Vermeer's *The Concert* from the Isabella Stewart Gardner Museum in Boston. The picture had never been recovered.

Except this was not a theft. A prank? A warning of thefts to come—*Look how easily I can break into this place?*

Every other room in the National would now have to be meticulously checked, and every work of art. Security would have to be reviewed. The police must be called, and the Director. The curator pulled out his phone.

Only—

Phone in hand, he knelt in front of the painting that had so mysteriously appeared. Glenwood had studied seventeenth-century art his entire life. He had thousands and thousands of hours of experience, honed to an intuition that had often proved more correct than reason. He studied the picture propped against the wall, and then the one above it. His cell hung limply at his side, and a deep line crinkled his forehead.

Something here was not right.

2270

Cran has never seen anything like the picture whose image floats in Square Two.

The Squares seems to capture more three-dimensional objects than paintings, and only eleven have been Transferred since the Project began. Three Picassos, two medieval pictures that ignore perspective, two "abstracts" that seem to him nothing but blobs of paint, a Monet, a Renoir, a Takashi Murakami, and a faded triptych from some Italian church. None of them are like this.

The light! It falls on the figure, a woman bent over some sort of sewing. It glows on her burgundy gown, on the walls, on a pearl necklace lying on a table. Almost it outshines the soft glow of the Square itself. The woman seems sad, and so real that she makes Cran's heart ache.

He stares at the picture for a long time, his mind befuddled by the drug he's taken but his heart loud and clear. He must have this picture.

Not the Gallery. Him. For himself.

Not possible.

Unless . . .

He stumbles to his console and says, "Forgeries by Tulia Anson, complete catalogue, visual, at ten-second intervals."

The screen—not a Square, just a normal holoscreen—flashes the forgeries that Tulia has completed so far. Each awaits a Square's tracking the original somewhere in time. The catalogue is not random; curators and physicists have collaborated to estimate what periods and artworks have the greatest chance of appearing in the Squares. Cran does not, and has never tried to, understand the equations involved, those mysterious mathematical convolutions that make strange attractors out of chaos. He only knows that these are the pictures most likely to appear.

Several landscapes in various styles appear and disappear on the screen. Some portraits. More hideous abstracts. Tulia, the Project's best forger, works hard, and quickly. A bunch of still lifes, with and without fruit. And then—

"Stop catalogue!"

There it is. *Lady Sewing a Child's Bonnet*, by Johannes Reijniersz Vermeer, 1664. What a mundane name for such perfection. Cran *knows* this woman, knows her from the sad tilt of her head, the bonnet she sews for her unborn child, the broken toy at her feet, the pearl necklace she has flung off. He is sure that her unseen eyes are filled with tears. She is deeply unhappy; her life has not turned out as she hoped. Cran knows her. He is her.

How many pills did he take?

No matter. This is his painting, meant for him. And Tulia, who is 32 percent his genes, has completed a superb forgery. That, too, proves that what he is going to do was meant to be.

Yes.

He does not bother with clearances. Actually, he cannot. There must be no traces. Clean and quick. The universe, which has denied him so much, owes him this.

The Vermeer hangs on the silk-covered wall of what looks in the Square like a private house, although it's hard to be certain. Vermeer's house? A patron? It doesn't matter. Cran works quickly, calling for a 'bot to bring Tulia's painting from storage, erasing the 'bot's memory record, hoisting the forgery into the Square. Setting the controls. His hands fumble in their eagerness. It all must be done manually, to leave no record.

He makes the Transfer.

Tulia's forgery vanishes. Nothing appears in Square Two.

Nothing.

"No!"

Data flashes on the console below the Square. A mechanical voice says calmly, "Error. Error. Transfer malfunction."

And then, "Danger. Deactivate this Square."

"No!" Cran gasps, unable to breathe. The Square blinks on and off, as he has never seen a Square blink before. But he knows what this means; spacetime is being affected in what could be a permanent way if the Square is not deactivated immediately. Fingers trembling, he enters and speaks the commands.

The Square goes dark.

The console data still glows. Cran stares at it. He shakes his head.

TRANSFER 653
Transfer Date: Saturday, Decade 28, 2270
Transfer to Past:
    Planned Transfer: From present to March 16, 1668
    Achieved Transfer: From present to March 16, 1668
    Status: Transfer Successful
Transfer to Present:
    Planned Transfer: From March 16, 1668 to present
    Achieved Transfer: From March 16, 1668 to Unknown Time
    Status: Transfer failed
    Reason for Failure: Incomplete Data Entry (Clearances 60-75)

Cran wills the data holo to change, to say something else. It does not. Because he did not complete the clearances, which were not merely the stupid bureaucracy he had assumed, the Transfer has failed. Tulia's forgery has gone to 1668, replacing the original on some silk-covered wall. The real Vermeer has not come all the way forward in time. Where is it? Cran doesn't know. All he knows is that Transfers send forgeries to where there is a similar article, which always before has meant the original being brought forward to 2270. That's how the strange attractors formed by the mathematics of chaos theory work—they *attract*. Only, due to Cran's haste—or possibly his intoxicated fumbling—Tulia's forgery has gone to some other attractor of Vermeers. Are there now two of the paintings on that silk-covered wall in 1668? Or has the original stopped somewhere else in time, snagged on a strange attractor someplace/sometime?

He doesn't know. And it doesn't matter where the original has gone—he cannot retrieve it.

Cran slumps to the floor. But after a few minutes, he staggers again to his feet. Why did he panic so? No one knows what happened. No one knows why the Square malfunctioned. All he has to do is erase the record—a task well within his skills—and report a malfunction. The Squares are a machine; machines break. No one ever has to know. All he has to say is that it spontaneously broke before he made any Transfer. That way, no one will blame him for an anomaly loose somewhere in the past.

Unless someone discovers that Tulia's forgery is missing from storage.

But why would they look? The only reason to call up a forgery is if the original appears in a Square. Only—

He can't think. He is afraid of what he has set loose in the timestream. He needs to get out of here. But he can't, not yet. At his console, he carefully composes a report of spontaneous Square malfunction while not engaged in Transfer operations.

In his mind, he can still see the glowing light of his lost Vermeer.

2018

The two paintings sat on easels at the front of the room. Guards stood outside. All cell phones had been collected and stored in a lockbox. Everyone had been scanned for cameras and voice recorders, a procedure that at least half of those present found insulting. A few said so, loudly. But no one was protesting now. They were too enraptured.

Side by side, the two paintings of *Lady Sewing a Child's Bonnet* looked identical to anyone but a trained observer. Half the people in the room were trained observers, art historians. The other half were forensic scientists.

Glenwood listened to one of the scientists' summary of his long-winded analysis. He'd barely looked at the paintings, consulting only his notes. "This painting," he said, gesturing vaguely in the direction of the Vermeer that had hung in the National since being privately donated sixteen years ago, "shows aging commensurate with having come from the mid-1600's. As I explained, carbon dating is not particularly accurate when applied to time spans as short as a few hundred years. But the frame, canvas, and pigments in the paint are aged appropriately, and nearly all of them are ones that, you have told me, Vermeer habitually used. That has been verified by both Atomic Absorption Spectrophotometry and Pyrolysis-gas chromatography-mass spectrometry."

"Almost all?" Glenwood said. "Some of the pigments are not from Vermeer's historical period?"

"No," said the expert from New York's Met, "but they could have been added later during restoration attempts. After all, the provenance of this painting is clearly documented, and it includes several dealers throughout the centuries, some of whom might have tried to clean or repair the Vermeer for resale. And, of course, it *has* a provenance, which your newcomer does not."

The New York expert had already made her position clear. She thought the "newcomer" was a clear forgery and Painting #1 the real thing. Glenwood was not so sure. He thought scientists, and even art experts, oversimplified.

Really skillful forgeries were notoriously hard to detect, and Vermeer's art had been plagued by imitators. At one point, "experts" had attributed seventy paintings to him. Today the number was thirty-four, with more in dispute even under scientific analysis. Vermeer's *Young Woman Seated at the Virginals* was considered genuine until 1947, a fake from 1947 to 2004, and then genuine again, with some disagreement. Science could only go so far.

A craquelure expert spoke next, and scornfully. "I don't know, ladies and gentlemen, why we are even here. Painting #1 is clearly the real thing. Its pattern of surface cracking is completely in keeping with an age of 354 years, and with the Dutch template of connected networks of cracking. The 'newcomer' has almost no craquelure at all. Furthermore, look how bright and new its colors are—it might have been painted last year. Its total lack of aging tags it as a forgery to anyone actually *looking* at it. Dr. Glenwood, why *are* we here?"

Everyone looked at Glenwood. He pushed down the temper rising in response to the craquelure expert's tone.

"We are here because I, and not only I, am bothered by other differences between these two paintings—differences that were not obvious when we had only Painting #1 and could not compare them side by side. Now we can. Look at the pearl necklace in the second painting. Vermeer painted pearls often, and always they have the sparkle and luster of the second painting, which the first mostly lacks. The second also contains far more tiny detail in the painting-within-a-painting on the wall behind the woman sewing. That sort of painstaking detail is another Vermeer trademark. Look at the woman's gown. Both versions feature the underpainting in natural ultramarine that Vermeer did beneath his reds to get a purplish tinge—but in Painting #2, the result is crisper. And Painting #2—I regard this as significant—was revealed by the X-ray analysis to have underlying elements that the artist painted over. Vermeer was obsessive about getting his pictures exactly right, and so very often he painted out elements and replaced them with others. Painting #1 shows no overpainting. I think Painting #2 is the original, and the picture we have hung in the National for sixteen years is the forgery."

A babble of voices:

"You can't believe that!"

"Perhaps a young artist, not yet proficient in his craft—"

"We have a clear chain of ownership going all the way back to Pieter van Ruijven—"

"The scientific evidence—"

"The lack of aging—"

In the end, Glenwood's was the only dissenting voice. He was a Vermeer expert but not a forgery expert, and not the Director of the National Gallery. The painting that had mysteriously appeared would be banished to basement storage so that no one else would be fooled into paying some exorbitant sum for it. And the one that had hung in the museum for sixteen years would continue to hang there. It had been declared the real thing.

2270

The physicists spend six days trying to fix the Square. Finally they give up, because they can't find any indicator that it is actually broken. Cran, who knows that it is not, insists over and over that the Square simply went dark. For six days, he holds his breath, not knowing what might happen. There are now two versions of the Vermeer loose in the timestream—what if that turns out to be so significant that something terrible happens to the present?

Nothing does.

Scientists and engineers wait for something—anything—to appear in Square Two. On the sixth day, something does: a crude Paleolithic figurine. Everyone goes crazy: this is the oldest piece of art the Squares have ever found. The expert on Stone Age art is summoned. The Director is summoned. The stone figurine is replaced with a lump of rock. No Transfer this early will disturb the timestream, not even if it's witnessed; the Transfer will just be attributed to gods, or magic, or witchcraft. The fertility carving is reverently taken to the Gallery. Toasts are drunk. The past is being recovered; the Square works fine; all is well. Cran's chest expands as he finally breathes normally.

As he leaves, the chief physicist gives Cran a long, hard look.

A few days later Cran goes to the Gallery to attend the presentation of Tulia's painting. It is so beautiful that his heart aches. The picture is neither abstract nor mimetic but, rather, something of both. What moves Cran so much is the way she has painted light. It is always the use of light that he cares about, and Tulia has captured starlight on human figures in a way he has never seen done before. The light, and not their facial expressions, seems to indicate the mood of each of her three human subjects, although so subtly that it does not feel forced. The emotion feels real. Everything about the painting feels real.

A woman behind him says, "Pretty, yes—but actually, it's just an exercise in an archaic and irrelevant art. Flat painting in a holo age? I mean, who cares?"

Cran wants to slug her. He does not. He congratulates Tulia, forcing words past the tightening in his throat, and leaves.

At home, he can't sleep. He is agitated, dispirited, depressed. No—he is jealous, so jealous that his skin burns and his head feels as if it might explode. He hates himself for his jealousy, but he can't help it. It drives him to pace, to almost—but not quite—cry out in the silence of his room. He can't sit still. In the middle of the night he takes the underground tram to the Project dome.

No one is here. Constant attendance isn't required; when a Square glows, it keeps on glowing until someone makes a Transfer. One of the Squares is glowing now. Inside is the image of *Lady Sewing a Child's Bonnet*.

Cran is not really surprised. Previously, the Square had found, through the obscure mathematics of chaos, a strange attractor linked to this Vermeer. Once found, there was a strong chance it would find it again. But which picture is this—the original or Tulia's forgery?

It is the original. He *knows*. The judgment isn't reasoned; it doesn't have to be. Cran knows, and he is prepared.

From a closet he takes one of his own pictures. The same size and shape as the Vermeer, it's a portrait of Tulia, painted from memory and so bad that no one else has ever seen it. The Vermeer in the Square is surrounded by a wooden crate in darkness. Someone has, for whatever reason, boxed it up and stored it. Maybe it will be missed, maybe not. It no longer matters to him. All his movements are frenzied, almost spastic. Some small part of his mind thinks *I am not sane*. That doesn't matter either.

Only once before has he felt like this, when he was very young and in love for the first and only time. He thought then, *If I don't touch her, I will die*. He doesn't think that now, but he feels it deeper than thought, in his very viscera. This must be what Vermeer felt when he painted the picture, alone in his studio, consumed from the inside.

It is the link between them.

Cran makes the Transfer. His dreadful painting disappears. Cran lifts *Lady Sewing a Child's Bonnet*—not an image, the real thing—from the Square. For a long time he just holds it, drinking it in, until the painting grows too heavy and his eyes too dimmed with tears.

His plan is to box it into the same container in which he brought in his own painting. Cran has done research in the library database. He was careful to have a printer create four of Vermeer's signature pigments—natural ultramarine, verdigris, yellow ochre, lead white—and that is what the security scanner will identify and match with the package he brought in. He will have the Vermeer in his own room, where no one ever goes, not even Tulia.

He has done it.

The door opens and the Director comes in.

"Cran! You couldn't sleep either? Such a wonderful presentation of Tulia's *Life in Starlight*. It made me want to come over and see what else the Project might have—Good Lord, is that a Vermeer?"

The Director, whose specialty is Tang Dynasty pottery but of course has a broad knowledge of art history, squints at the painting. All the frenzy has left Cran. He is cold as the lunar surface.

The data screen behind him says:

TRANSFER 655
Transfer Date Tuesday, Decade 29, 2270
Transfer to Past:
    Planned Transfer: From present to March 31, 2018
    Achieved Transfer: From present to March 31, 2018
    Status: Transfer Successful
Transfer to Present:
    Planned Transfer: From March 31, 2018 to present
    Achieved Transfer: From March 31, 2018 to present
    Status: Transfer successfully completed

"Yes," he says, "a Vermeer. It just came through, from the twentieth century. I sent back a forgery. But I think this one is a forgery, too. Look—does it appear aged enough to you?"

A commission is assembled. They examine the painting, but not for very long. *Lady Sewing a Child's Bonnet* was painted, the database says, in 1664. If it had come naturally through time to 2018, it would be 354 years old. Scientific examination shows it to be less than ten years old.

Yes, Cran thinks. Four years from 1664 to 1668, plus a few weeks spent in 2018. Yes.

On the scientific evidence, the painting is declared a forgery. A skillful copy, but a copy nonetheless. It isn't the first time the Project scanners have targeted a forgery. Previously, however, that had only happened with sculptures, particularly Greek and Roman.

"We already tried once for the original," says the Director, "and got this. It would be too dangerous to the timestream to try again, I think, even if the original turns up in a Square. Given the math, that might happen."

The head physicist stares hard at Cran. Cran has already been removed from the Project for failing to file clearances, which he has explained with "the memory lapses of age—I'm getting them more frequently now." He will never be allowed near a Square again.

A handler says, "What shall I do with this forgery?"

The Director is bleak with disappointment. "It's useless to us now."

Cran says humbly, "May I have it?"

"Oh, why not. Take it, if you like fakery."

"Thank you," Cran says.

He hangs the Vermeer on the wall of his room. The sad lady sewing a bonnet, disappointed in her life—the broken toy, flung-aside pearls, drooping head, of course she is disappointed—glows in unearthly beauty. Cran spends an entire hour just gazing at the painting. When there is a knock on his door, he doesn't jump. The picture is legitimately his.

It is Tulia. "Cran, I heard that—"

She stops cold.

Cran turns slowly.

Tulia is staring at the picture, and she knows. Cran understands that. He understands—too late—that she is the one person who would know. Why didn't he think of this? He says, "Tulia . . ."

"That's not a forgery."

"Yes, it is. A skillful one, but . . . they did forensic tests, it's not even ten years old, not aged enough to—"

"I don't care. That's not a copy, not even one by a forger better than I am. That's the original Vermeer."

"No," Cran says desperately. But Tulia has stepped closer to the painting and is examining every detail. Seeing things he cannot, could never learn to see. She knows.

He debases himself to plead. "Tulia, you're an artist. The real thing. For centuries to come, people will be collecting and cherishing your work. I am nothing. Please—leave me this. Please."

She doesn't even look at him. Her eyes never leave the painting.

"I'm an old man. You can tell them the truth after I'm dead. But please, for now . . . let me have this. Please."

After an aeon, she nods, just once, still not looking at him. She leaves the room. Cran knows she will never speak to him again. But she won't tell.

He turns back to the Vermeer, drinking in the artistry, the emotion, the humanity.

1672

Johannes walked through the Square beside the Hague, toward the water. In a few minutes, he would go inside—they could wait for him a few minutes longer. He studied the reflection of the stone castle, over four hundred years old, in the still waters of the Hofvijer. The soft light of a May morning gives the reflected Hague a shimmer that the actual government building did not have.

He came here to judge twelve paintings. They originally belonged to a great collector, Gerrit Reynst, who'd died fourteen years ago by drowning in the canal in front of his own house. Johannes couldn't imagine how that had happened, but since then, the collection had known nothing but chaos. Parts of it had been sold, parts gifted to the king of England, parts bequeathed to various relatives. A noted art dealer offered twelve of the paintings to Friedrich Wilhelm, Grand Elector of Brandenburg, who at first accepted them. Then the Grand Elector's art advisor said the pictures were forgeries and should be sent back. The art dealer refused to accept them. Now they hung in the Hague while thirty-five painters—thirty-five!—gave learned opinions on the pictures' authenticity. One will be Vermeer.

He was curious to see the paintings. They were all attributed to great masters, including Michelangelo, Titian, Tintoretto, Holbein. Vermeer, who had never left the Netherlands, would not have another chance to see such works.

If they were genuine.

Opinions so far had been divided. It was sometimes difficult to distinguish copies from originals. Consider, for instance, his own *Lady Sewing a Child's Bonnet* . . .

He hadn't thought about that picture in years. Always, his intensity centered on what he was painting now. That, and on his growing, impossible debts. He was being paid for this opinion, or he could not have afforded the trip to give it.

A skillful forger could fool almost everyone. Johannes, who seldom left Delft and so had seen few Italian paintings, was not even sure that he would be able to tell the difference between a forged Titian and an original, unless the copy was very bad. And a good forgery often gave its owners the same pleasure as an original. Still, he would try. Deceivers should not be able to replace the real thing with imitations. Truth mattered.

But first he lingered by the Hofvijer, studying the shifting light on the water.

Rich Larson was born in Galmi, Niger, has studied in Rhode Island and worked in the south of Spain, and now lives in Ottawa, Canada. His work appears in numerous Year's Best anthologies and has been translated into Chinese, Vietnamese, Polish, Czech, French, and Italian. He was the most prolific author of short science fiction in 2015, 2016, and possibly 2017 as well. His debut novel, *Annex*, was published by Orbit Books in July 2018, and his debut collection, *Tomorrow Factory*, followed in October 2018 from Talos Press.

IN EVENT OF MOON DISASTER
Rich Larson

Sol is so intent on the fizzing comm channel that he doesn't notice Laurie is back until her gloved fist raps against the airlock window, sending shivery vibrations through the whole hopper.

"Sunnuvabitch."

He snaps out of his seat, pulling the headset down around his neck. Laurie is standing in front of the airlock, arms folded. She taps her foot for effect, but in the stiff suit and low gravity it looks more like she's keeping time to a slow-mo banjo. Sol gives her a few exaggerated claps as he dances over to the lever and heaves the exterior door open. Laurie gives him the finger and steps inside.

As soon as the atmosphere reader dings green, she hits the release on her helmet. It levers up off her face with a hiss, revealing her sharp chin, snub nose, dark eyes under knitted brows. She looks unnaturally pale in the airlock light, and her dirty blonde hair is matted with sweat.

Sol opens the interior door. "Well? You all right? I was about to suit up and go after you, Laurie, Christ." He jams his headset against one ear and buzzes Control, but gets silence again. "Still can't raise Control. Something's messing with the radio."

"I only lost transmitting functions," she says, stowing her helmet on the hook. "I could hear you just fine the whole time. What the hell were you chewing on?"

"Peanuts." Sol grabs the package off his seat's armrest and checks the label. "Honey-roasted. They're honey-roasted and pretty damn good. You want some?"

"No. Yeah. Give 'em." She clambers out of the suit and holds out her hand. Sol sees it shake a bit as he pours peanuts into her palm, but pretends not to notice. She scoops them into her mouth.

"So? You going to tell me what was down there, Laurie?"

She points to her full mouth.

"Oh, I get it. Revenge chewing. You're revenge chewing at me. I'm a nervous eater, Laurie, and you were in that crack with no radio contact for twenty-seven whole minutes."

Laurie swallows. "There was nothing," she says. "I took the readings. Big electromagnetic spike, like we saw from orbit, but no physical source that I could detect. No sign of the drone we sent down there. I don't know. It's fucking weird, is what it is." She runs her hands back along her hair. "I'm shot."

Sol makes a gun with two fingers. "Bang."

"As in I'm tired." Laurie pinches the bridge of her nose, then goes to her hanging helmet and pulls out the datastick. "Here, have a look. I start singing, at one point. To drown out the chewing. Ignore the song choice and the high notes."

Sol takes the stick. "All right. Hey, take a nap if you need it. Pickup window's in two-and-a-half hours."

"Thanks," Laurie mutters. She starts to slide past him, toward her chair, then stops. "There was nothing down there, Solly. But it was weird."

"Hey." He pats her on the shoulder. "We're on the fucking Moon."

"That is true," Laurie says, clambering past him into her chair. She unrolls a vacuum-packed blanket and pulls it over her head. Her voice comes muffled. "That is a fact."

Sol watches out of the corner of his eye, making sure she's breathing normally, as he verifies the pickup window and runs another engine diagnostic. Before long she's snoring, which seems like a good sign. He claps the headset on, plugs the datastick in, and reaches for the honey-roasted peanuts.

Sol has the feed from Laurie's helmet up on his screen, watching through her eyes as she makes her way along the bottom of the crevasse. She's right. There's no sign of whatever unidentified body struck the Moon's eastern hemisphere and plowed a half-kilometer crack through the dust and rock. No sign of the drone they sent to investigate. Just an empty, eerie tunnel.

Eerie, but he can't quite put his finger on why. Something about the juts and whorls of rock seems slightly off to him, something about their angles. He's leaning in for a closer look when someone knocks twice against the airlock window.

Sol bolts upright, heart hammering his ribs. Laurie shifts under her blanket. He claps both hands over his chest and exhales and tries to think of possible explanations. The best he comes up with is debris. Nothing more specific than that, just the word. Debris.

He goes to the airlock. Cold sweat drips from his armpits down his sides. Someone in a spacesuit is standing in the dust outside, shifting from foot to foot.

"You are not debris," Sol mutters.

The astronaut taps their helmet and signs a radio malfunction, then taps their padded wrist where a watch would be. Someone else is trying to investigate the impact. A rogue state, or some private corp, somehow got here first without anyone knowing. And somehow they are wearing Laurie's suit, with the distinctive smiley decal on the oxygen tank.

Sol suddenly gets chatter on his headset. He pulls it back up, dazed. Laurie's voice.

"Sol, don't fuck around, Sol, I blacked out down there," she says, sounding more panicked than he's ever heard her before. "I lost you on the radio, I blacked out and something happened. Let me in, Sol, god*damn* you."

The astronaut thunks their helmet up against the window and he can see Laurie's mouth through the faceplate, lips moving as she cusses him out.

Sol yanks his headset off. A convulsion runs up and down his body; for a second he thinks he's going to vomit. Then he strides back to the dash, to the chair where Laurie's snores are fluttering her blanket. He grips the corner with one sweaty hand, braces himself, and pulls.

Laurie's still there, splayed back in the chair. She raises an arm and drapes it over her face. "Go time?" she mutters.

"Uh." Sol shakes his head. "Don't know." He looks back at the airlock, where Laurie now has both gloved hands splayed against the window. He pulls his headset back up, but hears only hyperventilating, and he realizes Laurie can see herself in the chair.

A crackling sob comes through the radio. "Sol, who is that? Sol? Who's that in my . . . in the chair?"

In front of him, Laurie swings herself upright, rubbing her eyes. "You go through the footage?" she asks. "I did warn you, right? About the high notes."

"Oh, you were great," Sol says faintly. "Operatic, even. But. Laurie."

"That is not me, Sol," Laurie begs through the headset. "That is not fucking me! Let me in, Sol, something happened down there, and you have to let me in, please, please, please—"

Laurie in front of him sees the Laurie waiting at the airlock window. Her eyes widen. Sol remembers her taking off her suit in the airlock. How her face looked pale, almost waxy. When she goes to get up from the chair, he pushes her back down. Not hard, but hard enough.

"Who the hell's that?" she demands.

"Just. Stay seated, okay? Stay there for now. I'm calling Control." Sol keys his headset. "Control, we have a situation. We have, uh, a third party present."

"Sol, is that *me?* That sounded like me."

He waits the ten-second delay, clutching the headset hard to his ear. Still nothing. Nobody on the channel except Laurie, outside, begging to be let in.

"This is so fucked," Sol says. "I think her oxy's low. I have to at least let her into the airlock."

Laurie shakes her head side to side, side to side. Her eyes are glassy with shock. "Yeah," she finally says. "Yeah, you better."

"And then, you know, I have to figure out which of you is a shapeshifting alien parasite," Sol says, trying to wrench his mouth into a smile.

Laurie looks dead at him and flicks her tongue like a lizard.

"Don't do that, Laurie," Sol says. "Don't do stuff just to mess with me, okay? Please?"

He gives them numbers: Laurie One, who returned to the hopper at 0629 hours, and Laurie Two, who returned to the hopper at 0712 hours.

Laurie Two is significantly calmer now that she's in the airlock and has her helmet off. Her dirty blonde hair is sweat-starched into spikes, and her eyes have dark circles underneath them. She's taking deep gulps of the recycled air, pushing it out her nose. But she won't take her eyes off Laurie One, who is sitting on the other side of the inner airlock door.

"Just don't let her near the levers," Laurie Two reiterates, voice coming through tinny. "I don't want to get vented by my creepy alien doppelganger."

"Says the creepy alien doppelganger," Laurie One finishes. "I'm trying to keep an open mind about what's going on here. You could do the same."

"It's probably easier to be open-minded when you're on that side of the airlock, all wrapped up in my blanket," Laurie Two says.

"Laurie, maybe give her the blanket," Sol mutters. "As a peace offering."

"Sol, she doesn't want the . . ."

"I don't want the fucking blanket, Sol." Laurie Two sighs. "I want to know what's going on. I want to know who that is and how she beat me back to the hopper. I was only blacked out for a minute, tops." She holds up her helmet, then the helmet Laurie One shed earlier, comparing them. Shakes her head.

"She's been back for forty-five minutes already," Sol says. "If you blacked out, it was longer than a minute. Way longer."

Laurie Two digs the datastick out of her helmet. "See for yourself, Sol."

Sol goes to trigger the interior door, then pauses. "Just hand it to me, okay? Don't try to come in."

Laurie Two's face falls, and Sol feels it like a gut punch. "Solly, you really think . . . think I'm some kind of . . ." She blinks hard. "Oh, man. Okay. Yeah. I'll pass it through."

Laurie One looks away, grimacing.

"You get it, right?" Sol asks.

"I get it," Laurie Two says. "Wish I didn't."

"I'll wait over here," Laurie One says, pointing to the corner. "Away from the airlock controls."

"That's real considerate, alien Laurie," Laurie Two says.

Sol cracks the interior door. Laurie Two passes the datastick through, and he pretends not to notice how her hand is trembling. She tries to smile, but gives up halfway, leaving her mouth all stretched. Sol mouths the word *sorry* to her as he relocks the interior door, leaving her in limbo.

He slots the datastick into the dash and pulls up the video, playing it side-by-side with Laurie One's. The prep, the entry, the descent—all identical, down to the millisecond. Sol tries to concentrate on the footage, tries to ignore Laurie One biting her thumbnail in the corner and Laurie Two squatting in the airlock, head in her hands.

"Hallucination," Laurie One says. "We're all thinking that, right? Air filter's compromised. We're breathing carbon and talking to my empty spacesuit in the airlock."

"Or I'm still blacked out in the crevasse," Laurie Two says. "Contaminant in my oxygen tank."

"Under other circumstances, you know, I think you two would really hit it off," Sol says, but he runs a diagnostic on the air filter in a side window. Oxygen levels are green. He fumbles for the last of the peanuts and crunches them between his molars one at a time.

The footage is playing at triple time, a blur of identical motion, identical rock formations. Then, at the thirty-two minute mark, the computer detects divergence and slows it back down. Both helmets' owners are clambering back out of the crack, but taking slightly different routes. Sol rewinds, plays half-speed. Laurie Two never falters, never freezes. As far as he can tell, there's no blackout at all, but the timestamp has jumped forward forty minutes.

"You said you were only out for a minute," Laurie One says. "It jumps forty." "Impossible," Laurie Two says. "That's impossible. If I was down there an extra forty minutes I'd have run out of oxygen."

Sol shakes the empty peanut bag, desperately licks the salt and sugar off his palm. If he's the one hallucinating, maybe Laurie never came back at all. Maybe she's stuck down there while he argues with figments of his own imagination. He raps his knuckles against his temple and peers closer at the footage as it keeps playing, as both Lauries make their way out of the crevasse.

Then he sees it.

"That crag in the rock," he blurts. "It repeats. That whole stretch of tunnel, it repeats."

He restarts the video and claws the playback speed down to half, watching through Laurie's eyes as she descends. She's more focused on her footing than on the walls, but there's enough. The cracks and whorls in the tunnel hit an invisible marker and start to repeat themselves. Shifted, slightly condensed, but the same pattern. As Laurie goes deeper, it happens again.

"Let me see," Laurie Two says faintly.

Sol drags the footage onto his tablet and goes back to the airlock, Laurie One drifting along after him. She's chewing her lip the way she does when she's thinking of something unpleasant or complicated or both. The three of them huddle up around the interior door, Laurie Two on one side, Sol and Laurie One on the other, and they watch the video.

"So what are we saying?" Laurie One asks. "Whatever crashed into the rock was some kind of alien copy-print machine?"

A gloved fist raps against the airlock window.

Laurie Three has brought company in the form of Laurie Four, whose smashed faceplate is swathed in electrical tape. Her head is lolling inside her helmet, and her eyes are fluttered shut. Laurie Three is alert, if exhausted from having dragged Laurie Four from the crevasse to the hopper. She takes the presence of Laurie One and Laurie Two a little better for having already saved her own life.

"I found her facedown on my way out," Laurie Three says. "I thought I was having some kind of out-of-body experience, or something. You two must know all about that."

Laurie Two snorts. She and Laurie One nod. Everyone is inside the hopper now; the airlock is jammed with shed spacesuits and Sol is reasonably sure there are no shapeshifting alien parasites afoot. Laurie Four needs medical attention. She's lying on the chair now, still unconscious but with more color in her face and a blanket pulled over her. Laurie Three is hovering, feeling residually responsible. Laurie One and Laurie Two are on opposite sides of the cramped cockpit.

Sol is at the screen, checking the timestamps from Three and Four's helmets, or rather, Four and Three's.

"So first we had a forty minute jump, then a one-hour eighteen minute jump—except she slipped on her way out and cracked her faceplate—and then a one-hour forty-four minute jump," he says. "Which means for us, outside the crevasse, the arrivals are coming quicker and quicker."

"The copies," Laurie Two says glumly. "We're copies. You can say it."

"The electromag fluctuation," Laurie actually-Four says. "At the bottom of the crack. It's somehow spitting out clones of me?"

"Of her," Sol says, jabbing his thumb at Laurie One, who looks increasingly uncomfortable. "But yeah. Basically, that's the situation." He can feel panic blocking up his throat. He still can't raise Control, and the pickup window is approaching, and . . .

"Sol, I gotta talk to you for a second," Laurie One says abruptly, coming up off the wall. "Alone. Just for a second."

Sol shakes his head. "There's going to be another Laurie knocking any second. Do we really have time for—"

"Bathroom," Laurie One hisses. "Now."

"Yeah, okay," Sol says. He gives the other Lauries a pained look. "Be right back." "Original Laurie, asserting her authority," Laurie Two says dryly. "Why the need for privacy? I know you're going to be talking about—"

"Life support," Laurie Four says. "The hopper's not specced for this many people, neither's the ship. Weight restrictions, too, for launch."

Sol lets Laurie One drag him into the bathroom stall and shutter the door. "They're dead-on about the life support," he says. "Fuck."

"Solly, listen," Laurie One says with something rasping in her throat. "I'm not sure I'm the real Laurie."

"Oh, Christ, Laurie, don't say that," Sol groans. "Don't mess with me, remember?"

"I'm not."

Laurie One's breath is stale and hot and Sol desperately wants to get out of the bathroom, even though there's nowhere else to go but back to more Lauries.

"I blacked out, too, when I was down there," Laurie One says. "I didn't tell you about it earlier. Didn't want you stress-eating for the next two-and-a-half hours."

Sol grips his hair with both hands, weaving it through his fingers. "But you were the first one back. So it has to be you." His voice has a whiny edge to it he can't quite erase. "It has to be, Laurie. Come on."

Laurie One shakes her head. "Maybe I'm the first one back because I was the first copy," she says. "Maybe the real Laurie, like, the original Laurie, maybe she's wherever the drone is. And wherever the thing is. The unidentified body that made this trench in the first place."

"Does it matter?" Sol demands. "Jesus, look, you're Laurie to me, okay? You're Laurie to me. You'll be Laurie to everybody back on Earth. The pickup window is less than an hour away, and we can launch the hopper with three people aboard, max."

"But they're all me, too," Laurie One whispers. Her face is blotchy red and Sol can see tears pushed back under her eyes. His stomach rolls over like a dead fish.

"What can we do?" he asks.

"Number Four," Laurie One says. "She's been unconscious. She doesn't know any of this shit. Take her. Leave the rest of us."

"Technically, that's number Three," Sol says. "And are you fucking kidding me? Laurie, she could be brain-damaged. Or, or, barring that, what if she dissolves in twenty-four hours? Into some big puddle of alien goo?"

"I might do that, too."

"Or you might not, because you're the original Laurie, okay?" He grabs her by the shoulders and almost shouts it. "You're the original fucking Laurie!"

She glares at him and he glares back, neither of them moving. The bathroom light buzzes and flickers between their heads. Laurie One's breath smells even worse now, and Sol's about to say it, just to be a dick, but then she might take it as evidence of her mouth dissolving so he says nothing at all. Not until a gentle knock on the airlock window makes the wall tremble.

"I wonder who that could be," he says.

Laurie One does something between a laugh and a sob.

Laurie Five has her radio working; Sol listens to her voice pitching upward as she demands to be let in, demands to know why there are footprints all around the hopper, demands to know whose spacesuits are piled in the airlock. Finally he switches off his headset, and it becomes a silent film. Laurie Five pounding her gloved fists against the airlock window in slow motion, catching sight of a warped reflection behind her, turning to see Laurie Six struggling up from the crevasse.

"Don't watch," Laurie actually-Four says, from where she's checking on Laurie actually-Three's vitals. "That makes it worse for them. And us."

Sol drags his eyes away from the scene. Puts his back to the airlock and sits down. Laurie One and Laurie Two are already sitting cross-legged on the floor; Laurie Four is still tending to an unconscious Laurie Three.

"If we cleared the suits out, we could fit one more person in the airlock," Laurie One says miserably. "At least for a while."

Sol takes a deep breath. "No point," he says. "Max of three people to launch. So, we have to make a decision. Have to decide. On who, if anybody, comes with me and Laurie . . . One. Laurie One."

"Wait," Laurie Two interjects. "Why is she a sure thing? She doesn't even know if she's the real Laurie."

"We could hear you in the bathroom," Laurie Four says. "Sol gets loud when he's agitated."

Sol gives an irritable shrug.

"You really do, Solly," Laurie Two says.

"She's the most likely to be the original, okay?" he says. "If she doesn't come, and I take one of you guys instead, what if you dissolve into . . ."

"Why do you have this fucking fixation with alien goo?" Laurie Two sighs.

"And then no Laurie comes back at all," Sol finishes. "Her family has nobody at all, and Laurie's stuck asphyxiating on the surface of the goddamn Moon."

"If we don't dissolve, we'll be doing the same thing," Laurie Four says quietly.

Sol runs his hands through his hair again. "Can we agree that Laurie Three is out?" he asks. "She'll never know. She's unconscious."

Lauries One, Two, and Four all flinch.

"Goddamn it, Sol," Laurie Four snaps. "That's even worse, dumping someone out the airlock while they're asleep."

"How about we dump you, and take an all-Laurie crew back to the ship?" Laurie Two says, jutting out her chin.

Sol blinks. More than the words, the expression on her face punches a hole right through him. Then he remembers how panicked she was, begging him to let her into the cockpit, and how she deflated all at once when he told her to pass the datastick through the door. Guilt churns his stomach.

"Laurie, you don't mean that," Laurie One says. "He's the only one we know isn't a copy. He wasn't in the crevasse. He goes."

Laurie Four nods. Laurie Two gives a sour shrug.

"Look," Sol says shakily. "I know it sounds fucked up, but this whole situation, in case you haven't noticed, this whole situation is supremely fucked up."

Vibrations sing through the cockpit again, as if to punctuate his words. More fists banging on the airlock. Sol forces himself not to look.

"We'll put it to a vote," Laurie One says. "And if there's a tie, we rock-pa-per-scissors." She rubs hard at her face, kneading the skin. "Okay?"

Sol holds his breath. The other Lauries slowly nod.

"Good," he says hoarsely. "Who goes first?"

"You don't vote," Laurie One says. "And you don't watch, either."

Sol swallows. "But . . . Laurie."

"We're all Laurie," she says. "You don't get to know who stays."

Sol searches her face, trying to find some fleck of food, some distinct clump of hair that will let him differentiate her from the others. But she looks exactly like Laurie Two and exactly like Laurie Four, and maybe she's right. Maybe there is no original Laurie here, because they all are.

"Okay," he says.

Sol sits in the airlock while the Lauries decide. Outside, there's a crowd of new Lauries bounding around in their puffy white suits, crackling to each other on the radio or putting their helmets together to speak that way, gesticulating at the hopper, at the crevasse. He wonders what conclusions they're coming to. More and more of them are emerging from the crack, hauling themselves up the rock, and bouncing to their booted feet. Sol wipes the tears off his cheeks when he hears the interior door scrape open.

Two Lauries silently walk in and start suiting up. Sol looks between them, trying to guess, but there's no way of knowing. He looks back and sees Laurie Three, still unconscious in her chair, and the last Laurie sitting on the floor with her head in her hands.

"Just couldn't do it," one of the airlock Lauries says, stepping into her suit and working the zipper. "That dumbass caring instinct, I guess. Same reason we're always looking out for you, Solly."

"I'm sorry," Sol says. It's the only thing he can think to say.

"Yeah, yeah," the other Laurie says. "I know. It's. Uh. It's fucking tough." She blinks hard and reaches for her helmet. "We'll clear everyone away, if we can. So you have space to launch without frying a bunch of coworkers."

The other-other Laurie has a stuck zipper. Her chest is pumping sharp shallow breaths. "Fuck," she says. "This isn't right. It's not logical. She could be brain-damaged, you know?" She licks her dry lips. "And her, she went a little early with the scissors. I think. I think I want a rematch."

"Shut up, Laurie," Laurie says. "Come on. Let's just do this. You're brave. You better be, because if you're not, then I'm not." She reaches in and yanks the zipper free. "So. Am I?"

Laurie shakes herself, looks right at Sol, and for a second Sol's sure she's Laurie One, but then the feeling twists away. "We're brave," she says. "Sure. Or unlucky. Or both. Whatever."

"Have a safe trip home," Laurie says. "Bye, Solly."

They put their helmets on and seal them. Sol can see his grimacing reflection in their faceplates. He tries to smile; doesn't manage it. Salutes instead, and squeezes past them, back into the cockpit. Just how he did a lifetime ago at 0600 hours, he vents the airlock, waits for the thumbs up, and opens the outer door.

Laurie and Laurie step out into the gray dust, sending a ripple through the crowd of spacesuits, helmeted heads turning.

Sol staggers back to his chair. "Let's get prepped, Laurie," he says, not looking at her. "Yeah," she says, not looking at him. "Go time."

They secure Laurie Three between their chairs with insulation and electrical tape, making sure her head's as cushioned as possible. Then they strap in for launch. The hopper rumbles through its ignition sequence, testing each engine in turn. On the screen, Sol sees the pickup window flash green. The ship is directly above them, ready to retrieve them and their inconclusive data from the crevasse. He tries to raise Control one last time but gets nothing. So long as they're in position, the radio interference shouldn't matter.

Neither of them speaks as the countdown ticks away, and then the roar of the engines is too loud to speak anyway. It shakes them like pennies in a jar, and Sol reaches out an arm to brace Laurie Three. He sees Laurie's arm reaching from her end, too. Then the hopper shudders up into the sky, shedding gravity all at once. Not all of the Lauries cleared the area, and Sol tries not to imagine them bursting into flame.

They pull away from the Moon's surface, and on the screen Sol can see the crevasse blooming like a snow-white flower as more and more space-suited Lauries pour out of it, spilling in all directions across the gray rock. If it doesn't stop, the entire face of the Moon will be covered in asphyxiating astronauts.

Sol switches the screen to show the waiting ship, hanging in orbit. Are they observing the surface? Are they seeing the bloom? They must be. The thought of trying to explain what's happened makes Sol want to laugh and die at the same time. He checks their trajectory and sees it's a little off, but nothing serious.

"You're not going to tell me which one you are?" he finally asks.

"We figured that would be better for you," Laurie says dryly. "You don't have to know who you left behind."

"I left everyone behind," Sol says. "Christ, Laurie. I don't even know who I am now."

"Join the club." She leans forward in her seat. "Sol? What's that?"

Sol zooms the screen and his mouth goes dry. They're still on course for the ship, but so is someone else. He and Laurie watch speechlessly as a hopper, identical to their own, maneuvers into the dock on a gentle burn, cuts its engines, and slots perfectly into place.

ABOUT THE EDITOR

Neil Clarke is the editor of *Clarkesworld* and *Forever Magazine*; owner of Wyrm Publishing; and a six-time Hugo Award Finalist for Best Editor (short form). He currently lives in NJ with his wife and two sons. You can find him online at neil-clarke.com.